ARIS & PHILLIPS HISPANIC CLASSICS

EMILIA PARDO BAZÁN

La Tribuna

T0324033

Translation, introduction and notes by

Graham Whittaker

LIVERPOOL UNIVERSITY PRESS

First published 2017 by
Liverpool University Press
4 Cambridge Street
Liverpool
L69 7ZU

www.liverpooluniversitypress.co.uk

British Library Cataloguing-in-Publication data
A British Library CIP record is available

ISBN 978-1-78694-025-4 cased
ISBN 978-1-78694-026-1 paperback

Typeset by Tara Evans
Printed and bound in Poland by BooksFactory.co.uk

Cover image: *Cigarreiras*, a photograph from the private collection of Alonso Álvarez, Professor of History at the University of La Coruña.

CONTENTS

Photograph of Emilia Pardo Bazán from the Real Academia Galega archives.

ACKNOWLEDGEMENTS

This book took me much longer to write than I had hoped. All those people who contributed to its completion are acknowledged here.

I am greatly indebted to my wife Lynn who, with her inexhaustible support, created the necessary atmosphere for me to be able to devote myself to the task in hand.

I would like to thank Jonathan Thacker for his proofreading and invaluable advice throughout this project.

It gives me great pleasure acknowledging and thanking the staff of the outstanding institution RAG (Real Academia Galega), especially the enthusiasm and commitment with which Ricardo Axeitos Valiño and Mercedes Fernández-Couto Tella granted me permission to reproduce the pictures included in this volume. The photographs of Emilia Pardo Bazán and the Tobacco Factory are from the RAG archives. I must also thank Luís Alonso Álvarez, who is Professor of History at the University of La Coruña, for the photograph of the cigarette makers from his own private collection. My thanks also go to the photographer Xosé Castro for his photograph of the façade of the Tobacco Factory.

I accept full responsibility for any errors which have crept into the present volume.

INTRODUCTION

1. Foreword

Why *La Tribuna*? The idea came as I was contemplating a new bilingual text for the Aris and Philips Hispanic Classics series. I had already translated *Doña Perfecta* and another Galdós novel was a distinct possibility. I was also considering a collection of short stories by Leopoldo Alas, the acerbic and redoubtable literary critic who wrote under the pseudonym Clarín. The works of both writers invariably feature on university Spanish department reading lists: Galdós is generally considered not only the best novelist of the nineteenth century, but also, with Cervantes, the best of all time;[1] Alas, in addition to his acknowledged masterpiece *La Regenta*, is usually acclaimed as the greatest short story writer of nineteenth-century Spain. Both, however, remain relatively unknown in comparison with other European writers like Dickens, Zola, Flaubert, Tolstoy and Dostoyevsky. In fact, outside academic circles, much Spanish literature remains undiscovered or undervalued.[2]

With this in mind, I considered changing tack: rather than concentrating on the two most prominent nineteenth-century Spanish literary figures, maybe I should focus my endeavours elsewhere. My mind turned to Emilia Pardo Bazán, a major writer who nevertheless exemplifies the undeserved neglect of Spanish literature. I originally became acquainted with her work during a rainy summer in Galicia in the 1990s and had read a wide selection of her novels, short stories and essays over the next few years. Surely, I thought to myself, one of her novels would be an excellent addition to the Hispanic Classics series. At the same time my attention was drawn to the effusive review of the recent Penguin translation of *Los pazos de Ulloa* in *The Guardian*. I decided to embark on a Bazán reading bonanza and

---

1 '...no sólo el mejor novelista del siglo XIX sino, con Cervantes, el mejor de todos los tiempos'. Yolanda Arencibia, 'Benito Pérez Galdós': (http://www.academiacanarialengua.org/archipielago/benito-perez-galdos/obra/)

2 James Mandrell, 'Realism in Spain: Galdós, Pardo Bazán, Clarín and the European context', *Spanish Literature: A collection of Essays*, ed. D. W. Foster, D. Altamiranda, C. de Urioste (New York: Garland Publishing, 2001), p. 84: 'Apart from Cervantes – who is, as the author of *Don Quijote*, somewhat summarily invoked as the creator of the modern novel – and apart from the tradition of the picaresque novel, Spanish literature is dismissed as unimportant, uninteresting, or, worse yet, as lacking in quality comparable to the best of European, i.e. English, French, and German literature.'

my enthusiasm was rekindled. She is undeniably an extremely gifted and versatile writer, but the scale of her virtual anonymity can be gauged by the fact that a literary critic as eminent as Nicholas Lezard confesses, at the beginning of his aforementioned review, that he had not previously heard of either the book or its author.

It is better, according to Henry Gratton Doyle, to have read a great work of another culture in translation than never to have read it at all. Encouraged by this idea to compensate for the paucity of good, available translations of her fiction and to rise to the daunting challenge of her prose, all that remained was to decide which of her novels would be the best first choice for inclusion in the Aris and Phillips series. I hope my decision to translate *La Tribuna* will be vindicated and that it will play a part, however small that may be, in generating interest in a writer who, intent on dispelling the myth of 'dos literaturas, una femenina, que trasciende a *brisas de violetas*; otra masculina, que apesta a cigarro' (two types of literature, a feminine one that smells of *violet water*, and a masculine one that stinks of cigar),[3] should be considered not so much the greatest female author of her time as one of the greatest Spanish authors, irrespective of her sex, of all time.

There are various editions of *La Tribuna*, both in print and on the Internet. The Spanish text for this edition has been referenced against both the novel as it appears in La Biblioteca Virtual Miguel de Cervantes[4] and the one edited by Benito Varela Jácome (Madrid: Ediciones Cátedra, 1991). The footnotes in the Spanish text are my own and are the only time I have not provided a translation. The reason is simple: not only do I hope that students will read the original Spanish as much as possible, but also the meaning of the footnotes should be fairly obvious, especially in tandem with the translation of the novel on the opposite page.

I have consulted many primary and secondary sources in Spanish, Galician, French and English whilst writing this introduction; all the translations of quotations taken from these books and articles are my own. The purpose of this introduction is to help students to discover *La Tribuna*, its author and the context in which she produced her many works. I apologise in advance to those readers who are fazed by the number of footnotes, but I hope they may encourage some students to undertake further reading, or even engage in additional research, of the works and life of this fascinating writer.

---

3   'Carta Magna', *Obras completas, Tomo III* (Madrid: Aguilar, 1973), p. 657.
4   http://www.cervantesvirtual.com/obra/la-tribuna--0/.

*Photograph of the Tobacco Factory in La Coruña
from the Real Academia Galega archives.*

2. Emilia Pardo Bazán: her life

No serious evaluation of Spanish literature would be complete without
discussing important women novelists like Fernán Caballero (Cecilia Boehl
de Faber), Gertrudis Gómez de Avellaneda (a Cuban who lived in Spain) and
Carolina Coronado. However, the most controversial, prolific and influential
Spanish female writer of the nineteenth century is undoubtedly Emilia Pardo
Bazán.[5] She was born on September 16, 1851, the only child of well-to-do,
educated parents in Galicia. Her principal home was in the 'upper town' of
La Coruña and, like Amparo in *La Tribuna*, she was permitted to wander
about freely through the streets of el Barrio Abajo (the 'lower town') where
the fishermen and the struggling poor spent their lives.[6] She was an only

5   See, for example, the following books on Spanish literature:
    (i) M. Romera-Navarro, *Historia de la literatura española* (USA: D. C. Heath and
Company, 1926), p. 587: 'Doña Emilia Pardo Bazán [...] es la mujer más ilustre que han
tenido las letras españolas en el siglo XIX' ('Doña Emilia Pardo Bazán [...] is the most
illustrious woman that Spanish literature had in the nineteenth century).
    (ii) James Fitzmaurice-Kelly, *A New History of Spanish Literature* (London: Heinemann,
1898), p. 393: 'the best authoress that Spain has produced during the present century'.
6   See Carmen Bravo-Villasante, *Vida y obra de Emilia Pardo Bazán* (Madrid: Revista de
Occidente, 1962), p. 17: 'Las salidas y paseos al Barrio de Abajo se convierten en deseadas

child who received a formal education that went far beyond the training that was traditional for girls of her class at that time. When she was young the family spent winters in Madrid and she attended a French boarding school where, as pupils were forbidden to speak Spanish, the least slow-witted left jabbering away in French like little parrots.[7] This introduction to the French language also seems to have paved the way for her lifelong love of France and its cultural heritage.

Her mother, Amelia de la Rúa, dedicated her time to running the household. She also taught little Emilia to read, and her father, José Pardo Bazán y Mosquera, opened his considerable library to her. With her professed congenital love of learning she became a voracious reader, one of those children who spend the day quietly in a corner when they are given a book.[8] Allowed to read almost anything she wanted, her claim that, as a child, her favourite books were the Bible, *Don Quijote de la Mancha* and Homer provoked an accusation of pedantry from Marcelino Menéndez Pelayo and Pereda. She was banned only from reading the works of Dumas, Sue, George Sand, Victor Hugo and other leaders of French Romanticism, what she refers to as the apple of Paradise tempting her from the top shelf.[9] Young Emilia divided her time between her maternal and paternal influences, striving towards the highest academic, intellectual, artistic and literary standards, yet never disregarding the domestic role her mother instilled in her, that of a future mother and coordinator of all household responsibilities. Emilia filled the pages of her novels with the encyclopaedic knowledge she had acquired concerning philosophy, science,[10] literature, social and political thought and history,

---

aventuras llenas de inexplicable placer' (The outings and walks to the Barrio de Abajo became longed-for adventures full of inexplicable pleasure).

7 *Apuntes autobiográficos, Obras completas, Tomo III*, p. 703: '…como nos prohibían hablar español, las menos lerdas salimos de allí hechas unos loritos parlando francés a destajo.'

8 *Ibid.*, p. 702: 'Era yo […] de esos niños que se pasan el día quietecitos en un rincón cuando se les da un libro…'

9 *Ibid.*, p. 703. A few pages later in *Apuntes autobiográficos* (p. 706) she relates how, browsing through one of her friend's father's library she discovered Hugo's *Notre Dame de Paris*:
'No hubo lucha entre el deber y la pasión: ésta triunfó sin pelear […] Lo cogí a hurto, escondiéndolo entre el abrigo y trayéndolo a casa…' (There was no struggle between duty and passion: the latter triumphed without a fight […] I picked it up on the sly, hiding it under my coat and taking it home…).

10 See *Apuntes autobiográficos*, p. 716:
'…seguía los adelantos de la termodinámica; recibía la *Revue Philosophique*; me enfrascaba en libros como *El sol*, del padre Secchi, o la *Historia natural de la creación*, de Haeckel;' (…I was following progress in the field of thermodynamics; I subscribed to

while continuing to demonstrate a lively interest and expertise in the world of clothing and fashions, the culinary arts and other aspects of homemaking. Her father was for a time a Carlist representative in the National Assembly. After the September Revolution of 1868, which led to the abdication of the queen, he was elected Deputy to the *Cortes* as a member of Salustiano Olózaga's Progressive party, so the whole family moved to Madrid. He was recognised by Pope Pius IX for his vigorous defence of the Catholic faith as the state religion, and the pontifical title of 'conde de Pardo Bazán' was bestowed upon him in June 1870, which King Amadeo granted him permission to use in February 1872. At the age of sixteen Emilia married José Quiroga Pérez Pinal, an eighteen-year-old law student from the University of Santiago. The marriage was arranged by both sets of parents, but neither Emilia nor José objected to the match. Her first contact with Europe came in 1870 when the family moved to Vichy, an experience which proved useful for her second novel *Un viaje de novios*. In 1872 she visited the Universal Exhibition of Vienna and attended a performance of Wagner's *The Flying Dutchman*.[11] The following year, after Amadeo's abdication and the collapse of the Progressive party, her father judged it prudent to leave the country with his family, and so began a brief but enriching period of travel for Pardo Bazán, encompassing France, Italy, Austria and Switzerland.

When she was back in Spain she became intrigued by the ideas of the German philosopher Karl Christian Friedrich Krause. The curious phenomenon of Krausism was imported into Spain in 1844 when Julián Sanz de Río, sent to Germany by the Minister of the Interior as part of an initiative to reform the Spanish educational system, returned to Madrid. Overshadowed in his native Germany by philosophers like Fichte and Hegel, Krause attempted to reconcile faith and reason, religion and science, theology and philosophy in a rational and harmonious whole. With its aims of social progress and a universal brotherhood built on Christian morality, Krausism became the dominant intellectual force in Spain during the second half of the nineteenth century, especially between 1854 and 1874.

Revue Philosophique; I buried myself in books like *The Sun*, by Father Secchi, or Haeckel's *Natural History of Creation*).

11   For Pardo Bazán's love of Wagner, whom she describes in 'La vida contemporánea', *La Ilustración artística de Barcelona*, núm 897, March 6, 1899 as 'el último genio que ha producido Alemania' (the ultimate genius that Germany has produced), see Xosé-Carlos Ríos, 'Emilia Pardo Bazán ante el drama musical de Richard Wagner. Descubrimiento, admiración y pasión (1873–1921)', *La Tribuna. Cadernos de estudios da Casa museo Emilia Pardo Bazán* (A Coruña: RAG, 2012/3, Núm 9), pp. 155–212.

In 1880 she visited Victor Hugo and read Zola's *L'assommoir*. Later she stayed a while in Paris, met Zola, ate in Huysmans's house and frequented the Sunday meetings of the Goncourt brothers. In the Bibliothèque Nationale she read contemporary writers, becoming familiar with the ideas of Renan, Lemaitre, Revast and Bourget. Instrumental in promoting an awareness of French Naturalism in the Spanish reading public, she also discovered the works of Turgenev, Gogol, Tolstoy and Dostoyevsky. In 1891 she was invited to lecture at the Athenaeum of Madrid, and these lectures were later published under the title *La revolución y la novela en Rusia*.[12] Credited with introducing Russian literature to the Spanish public through these essays, Pardo Bazán approved of the spiritual element which for her was one of the most outstanding merits of Russian novels ('el elemento espiritualista de la novela rusa para mí es uno de sus méritos más singulares').[13]

The death in March 1890 of her beloved father, a feminist whom she defined in a letter to Menéndez Pelayo as one of those rare parents who for their children are friends, advisers and protectors during their whole life,[14]

---

12 Pardo Bazán sometimes lifts long passages directly from Melchor de Vogüé's *Le roman russe*. This apparent plagiarism generated a number of attacks from critics, especially Clarín who took delight in calling her Doña Emilia Pardo-Vogüé. However, she frequently acknowledges her debt to the French critic and his book, as shown in the following extract: '…voy a citar al pie de la letra dos párrafos, uno del mismo Gogol, otro de Melchor de Vogüé, el inteligentísimo crítico francés, cuya obra sobre la novela rusa me ha sido tan útil para estos estudios.' (I'm going to quote verbatim two paragraphs, one from Gogol himself, the other from Melchor de Vogüé, the very intelligent French critic whose work on the Russian novel has been so useful to me for these studies). *La revolución y la novela en Rusia, Obras completas, Tomo III*, p. 837.

Nevertheless, in his *Examen de críticos* (Madrid: Rivadeneyra, 1894), p. 91, Francisco de Icaza is highly critical of Pardo Bazán's reliance on secondary sources: '…cuando no cita a Vogüé lo copia, y cuando no lo copia lo cita. (…when she doesn't quote Vogüé she copies him, and when she doesn't copy him she quotes him).

13 *La revolución y la novela en Rusia*, p. 878. Cf. *La literatura francesa moderna, El naturalismo* (Madrid: Renacimiento, 1911) p. 112: 'Eran naturalistas tan crudos en lo formal, como podía serlo Zola […] sólo que se diferenciaban de él en una cosa sencillísima: para los novelistas eslavos, Cristo había venido al mundo' (They were Naturalists as coarse as Zola could be […] only they differed from him in one very simple thing: for the Slavic novelists Christ had come into the world).

14 '…para sus hijos son a la vez amigos, consejeros y protectores durante toda su vida' (*Epistolario*, vol. X, p. 321). In an interview carried out by 'El Caballero Audaz' for the series 'Nuestras visitas' in *La Esfera*, no. 7, (14 de febrero de 1914) she says her father gave her the following advice: '…si te dicen alguna vez que hay cosas que pueden hacer los hombres y las mujeres no, di que es mentira, porque no puede haber dos morales para los dos sexos' (…if they ever

and her disenchantment after her affair with Galdós renewed her commitment to some long-held causes which she now espoused with even greater fervour: feminism, opposition to capital punishment, and antimilitarism. In 1892 she participated in a pedagogical convention where she presented a paper entitled 'La educación del hombre y de la mujer; sus relaciones y diferencias'. Here she argued that education for men was based on the belief of the perfectibility of human beings, whereas the education of women was based on a negative view of female nature.[15]

The end of her life was characterised by recognition and disillusionment. In 1906 she became the first woman to be named Presidenta de la Sección de Literatura at the Ateneo. In 1908 King Alfonso XIII converted her papal title, inherited from her father, into the title of Countess and in 1910 she was named Consejera de Instrucción Pública. Her statue was erected in La Coruña in 1916 and she was appointed a professor of Romance literature at the Universidad Central in Madrid. However, she ceased giving lectures when attendance dropped to zero and a rupture of a previously amicable relationship with Clarín helped to thwart her lifelong desire to be accepted as a member of the Royal Academy. Later, in a period of greater enlightenment, her many supporters were prepared to nominate her for this honour again, but her death put an end to this hope. In fact, it was not until 1979 that the academy named a woman, Carmen Conde, to its ranks.

3. Feminism

…no queda a la mujer más salida que el matrimonio, y, en las clases pobres, el servicio doméstico, la mendicidad y la prostitución.

---

tell you that there are things which men can do but women can't, say it's a lie, because there cannot be two moral standards for the two sexes).

15   This did not always endear her to her male peers. Clarín's review of the pedagogical conference in *El Día*, 4513, 15 November 1892, concentrates on, and takes issue with, her tendency towards self-assertion, something he considers a masculine trait:

'…doña Emilia se presenta a defender *la enseñanza de la mujer*, causa por sí nobilísimo, con un radicalismo, con unos aires de fronda y con un *marimachismo*, permítaseme la palabra, que hacen antipática la pretensión de esa señora, ya de suyo vaga, inoportuna, prematura y precipitada.' (…Doña Emilia comes forth to defend *women's education*, a very noble cause in itself, with such a radicalism, with such revolutionary flourishes and with such a *marimachismo*, if I may be permitted the word, that the aspirations of that lady which are already vague, inopportune, premature and precipitate, become quite disagreeable).

Leopoldo Alas *Clarín, Obras completas IV Crítica (Segunda parte)*, (Oviedo: Nobel, 2003), p. 1853.

(...the only remaining path for women is marriage, and in the poorer classes, domestic service, begging and prostitution.)[16]

The Napoleonic invasion in the early nineteenth century was synonymous for conservatives in Spain with Republicanism, atheism and immorality, but persuaded many reformists that the liberal ideas of revolutionary French had the capacity to transform society, and even the potential to enhance the role of women. However, the defeat of the French by Spanish armies with the aid of British troops under the Duke of Wellington was followed by a repressive reaction and a return to even more traditional values after 1815. It also nurtured a deep-rooted hostility to the anti-patriotic, godless libertinism of what Menéndez Pelayo labelled 'aquella legión de traidores, de eterno vilipendio en los anales del mundo, que nuestros mayores llamaron *afrancesados*' (that legion of traitors, of eternal vilification in the annals of the world, which our elders called *pro-French*).[17]

Few inroads into long-established anti-feminism were made in nineteenth-century Spain. Low literacy rates – 'millones de mujeres españolas no saben leer ni escribir' (millions of Spanish women cannot read or write) declared Pardo Bazán[18] – were a tangible corollary of the general perception that females were intellectually inferior, and feminists like Concepción Arenal who argued that there was no basis for these misguided views were invariably ridiculed. Not even the most vehement anti-feminists could deny Emilia Pardo Bazán's impressive erudition,[19] a woman who corresponded in French with

---

16 'La España de ayer y la de hoy' (Madrid: Administración, 1899), p. 79. The lecture from April 18, 1899, can be accessed online at http://www.filosofia.org/aut/001/1899epb4.htm.

17 *Historia de los heterodoxos españoles*, *Libro séptimo*, *capítulo 1* (Alicante: Biblioteca Virtual Miguel de Cervantes, 2003), p. 673. An example of this hostility is given in Méndez Bejarano's *Historia política de los afrancesados (con algunas cartas y documentos inéditos)* (Madrid: Librería de los sucesores de Hernando, 1912), p. 195:
'–¿Es pecado matar a un francés?
–No, padre; por el contrario, se gana el cielo matando a uno de esos perros herejes'
(Is it a sin to kill a Frenchman?
No, Father; on the contrary, salvation is gained by killing one of those rotten heretics).

18 'La España de ayer y la de hoy', p. 79. The percentage of female illiteracy in 1870 is usually quoted as 91.

19 Nevertheless, in a letter to Juan Valera, the formidable scholar Menéndez Pelayo wrote the following:
'...es para mí muestra patente de la inferioridad intelectual de las mujeres – bien compensadas con otras excelencias – el que teniendo doña Emilia condiciones de estilo y tanta aptitud para estudiar y comprender las cosas, tenga al mismo tiempo un gusto tan rematado y una total ausencia de tacto y discernimiento' (...it is for me a patent example

Parisian Romantics and Naturalists alike, studied English because she was intent on reading Byron and Shakespeare in the original, and taught herself German to read Goethe, Schiller, Bürger and Heine. Her limitless capacity for intellectual inquiry and sheer stamina were equally irrefutable.[20] What was far easier to target, however, was the profound eclecticism which always kept her apart from any one system and allowed her to remain precisely in the middle, making extreme right conservatives think of her as 'advanced', the Carlists 'liberal' and the reds and Jacobins imagine her a devout, ferocious reactionary.[21] The contradictions, disparities and inconsistencies in her views are transparent: she was a polymath whose progressive, cosmopolitan outlook was juxtaposed with a combination of old-fashioned elitism and Galician provincialism, a 'modern', well-travelled woman who embraced new and foreign literature whilst voicing sympathies for 'old Spain' and for a while, in conjunction with her husband, the Carlist cause.[22] The product of a privileged background, she actively sought the title of countess and defended the strict maintenance of class hierarchy as if it were God-ordained. A firm patriot who

of the intellectual inferiority of women – well compensated with other talents – that Doña Emilia, having style and so much aptitude for studying and understanding things, should have at the same time such bad taste and a total lack of tact and discernment).

Quoted in Cristina Fernández Cubas, *Emilia Pardo Bazán* (Barcelona: Omega, 2000), pp. 43–44. For an analysis of Pardo Bazán's turbulent relationship with her male peers, see Cyrus DeCoster, 'Pardo Bazán and her Contemporaries,' *Anales Galdosianos* 19 (1984), pp. 123–31.

20   Miguel de Unamuno, 'Recuerdos personales de Doña Emilia', *Nuevo Mundo*, 27 de mayo de 1921:

'...mujer singular [que] nos ha dejado, entre otras lecciones, las de una laboriosidad admirable y la de una curiosidad inextinguible' (an exceptional woman [who] has left us, amongst other lessons, those of an admirable work ethic and an inextinguishable curiosity).

21   Clémessy, *Emilia Pardo Bazán como novelista* (Madrid: Fundación Universitaria Española, 1981), p. 111: '...su eclecticismo profundo la tuvo siempre alijada de todo sistema y le permitió quedarse en justa medida.'

Emilia Pardo Bazán, 'Crónicas de España', *La Nación*, Pardo Bazán, tómo 1, p. 452: '... los conservadores de la extrema derecha me creen "avanzada", los carlistas "liberal" [...] y los rojos y jacobinos me suponen una beatona reaccionaria feroz.'

22   Francisco Melgar, *Veinte años con don Carlos, Memorias de su secretario, el conde de Melgar* (Madrid: Espasa Calpe, 1940), p. 111:

'Ésta – doña Emilia – principió su carrera literaria muy joven, en el campo carlista, recorriendo toda España para dar conferencias de propaganda, yendo a visitar a doña Margarita y poniéndose a sus órdenes para ayudarla todo cuanto pudiera.' ('She – Doña Emilia – began her literary career very young, in the Carlist camp, going around the whole of Spain to give propaganda lectures, visiting Doña Margarita and putting herself at her command to help her as much as she could).

believed in 'la superioridad absoluta de la raza indoeuropea' (the absolute superiority of the Indo-European race),[23] she was not unknown to voice her antipathy towards Protestants or to express anti-Semitic sentiments.[24] On the other hand, though, she was far more egalitarian, and from today's perspective enlightened, when it came to the rights of men and women in educational, social and political matters. Indeed, she played a crucial role in bringing the discussion of feminism to the forefront of intellectual and popular debate, through her fiction as well as her essays.[25]

By the end of the 1880s 'la Pardo' began to focus more and more on the subservient role and position of the female. In 1889, writing from the Universal Exhibition of Paris, she contrasts the lack of opportunities for women in Western countries – 'le están cerrados todos los caminos' (all avenues are closed to her)[26] – with Russia, where, even though slavery had existed until a few years previously, 'la mujer se coloca al nivel del hombre' (women are equal to men).[27] In the same year she had already published 'La cuestión académica. A Gertrudis Gómez de Avellaneda'[28] as well as 'The Women of Spain'. The latter, her first major feminist article, came in

---

23   *La revolución y la novela en Rusia*, p. 768.

24   David Torres, 'Veinte cartas inéditas de Emilia Pardo Bazán a José Yxart (1883–1890)', *Boletín de la Biblioteca de Menéndez Pelayo* LIII, 1977, p. 426:

'…los protestantes me son antipáticos. Detesto la meticulosa y fría condición de esas gentes que no prefieren a todo el sol, la hermosura y el arte.' (…I don't like Protestants. I hate the cold, meticulous nature of those people who don't prefer the sun, beauty and art to everything).

See *Apuntes autobiográficos*, p. 720. Hugo's protestation that 'el tribunal de la Inquisición había achicharrado sin piedad escritores y sabios' (the Inquistion had burnt without pity writers and learned persons) elicits the nonchalant response that it had roasted only 'judaizantes, brujas e iluminados' (Jewish types, witches and illuminati).

25   María de los Ángeles Ayala, 'Emilia Pardo Bazán y la educación feminina', *Salina: revista de lletres*, 15, 2001, p. 183: 'La llamada *cuestión feminina* es una de las grandes batallas sociales a las que Emilia Pardo Bazán dedicó innumerables esfuerzos…' (The so-called *feminine question* is one of the great social battles to which Emilia Pardo Bazán dedicated innumerable efforts…).

26   *Al pie de la torre Eiffel, Obras completas, Tomo XIX* (Administración: Madrid), p. 166. Cf. Concepción Arenal: 'Tal es la situación de la mujer: abiertos todos los caminos del sentimiento, cerrados todos los de la inteligencia' (Such is the situation of women: all sentimental avenues are open, all intellectual ones are closed). Quoted in Carmen Bravo Villasante, *Vida y Obra de Emilia Pardo Bazán*, p. 183.

27   *Ibid.*

28   For a detailed explanation of what prompted Pardo Bazán to write this essay defending the rights of woman against any sexual discrimination, see Pilar Faus, *Emilia Pardo Bazán. Su época, su vida, su obra* (Fundación Pedro Barrié de la Maza, 2003), pp. 478–80.

response to a request for an essay on the Spanish woman from London's *The Fortnightly Review* as part of its series on European females. It was published in English in 1889 and opened with the disclaimer that the subject of the study 'would be a most embarrassing one if it were intended for a Spanish Review'.[29] Nevertheless, the essay appeared the following year in Spanish in the number XVII, May 1890, edition of Lázaro Galdiano's cultural magazine *La España moderna*.

Pardo Bazán's 'The Women of Spain' is a seminal study in itself, but also it is invaluable when examining the role and portrayal of the female in her fiction. Paradoxically, if the heroines of her first three novels, *Pascual López*, *Un viaje de novios* and *La Tribuna*, are rather one-dimensional and lacking in psychological depth, this unintentional weakness inadvertently corroborates the author's thesis that woman is 'as the man deliberately makes her',[30] and therefore vulnerable and ill-equipped to flourish in a male-dominated society. It is almost as if her statement in *Al pie de la torre Eiffel* – 'en nuestros países occidentales […] la mujer carece de personalidad' (in our Western countries […] women lack personality)[31] – were penned to validate the flat characterisation of the females in the aforementioned novels.

In chapter five of *Un viaje de novios* we discover that Lucía González is unaware that the sun is a star – '¿El sol … es una estrella? – interrogó asombrada la niña' – and does not know what the Milky Way is.[32] The impliction is that her inadequate education contributes to the tragic *dénouement* of the novel. We are told in the second chapter of *La Tribuna* that, when she became bedridden, Amparo's mother tried to force her into sedentary work; but, the girl's education being limited to 'la lectura […] y unos rudimentos de escritura' (reading […] and the rudiments of writing), the paralysed woman resigned herself to the hope of finding her daughter a

---

29 'The Women of Spain', *The Fortnightly Review*, no. 45, part 1 (1889), p. 877.

 Cf. *Cartas a Galdós* (Ediciones Turnes, 1978), p. 59: '…armaría un alboroto en España tal vez si se publicase en español' (…it would cause a commotion in Spain were it to be published in Spanish).

30 'The Women of Spain', p. 895.

31 *Obras completas, Tomo XIX* (Administración: Madrid), p. 166.

32 Cf. Emilia Pardo Bazán, *La mujer española y otros escritos*, ed. Guadalupe Gómez-Ferrer (Madrid: Cátedra, 1999), p. 88:

 '…muchos opinan lo mismo que el papá de una amiga mía, que, habiéndole preguntado su hija si Rusia está al norte, contestó muy enojado: A las mujeres de bien no les hace falta saber esto' (…many think like the dad of a friend of mine who, having been asked by his daughter if Russia is in the north, answered very angrily: good women don't need to know this).

place in the factory. Amparo's education may be minimal but she is proud
of her academic abilities:

> –Sé leer muy bien y escribir regular. Fui a la escuela, y decía el maestro
> que no había otra como yo. Le leo todos los días *La Soberanía Nacional* al
> barbero de enfrente.

> ('I can read really well and write quite well. I went to school and the teacher
> said there was no one like me. I read *The National Sovereignty* every day to
> the barber across the road.')

There are one or two readers in every workshop at the tobacco factory and
Amparo's talent is instrumental in making her one of the most valued, on
account of the feeling she imparted to the reading. Her ability to read aloud
the political debates set forth in the daily newspapers ignites her ideological
awakening and enables her to rise to a position of authority there.

At the same time, the rapid maturation which, according to the narrator,
is characteristic of the lower classes transforms her from a shapeless, pre-
pubescent 'boy in a skirt', who only spends six and a half minutes on
personal grooming, into a 'masterpiece' of femininity held in high esteem
even by Lola Sobrado: 'es hermosa y reúne mucha gracia' (she's pretty and
she possesses lots of charm). The young beauty, aware of her sexual identity,
starts to ask for toiletries as payment for reading progressive newspapers
to the barber and, putting together a trousseau worthy of a queen, blooms
into an object of male desire: Baltasar says 'dentro de dos años nos mareará
a todos' (within two years she'll be making us all dizzy), Borrén exclaims
'¡Olé y qué guapa se pone todos los días, hombre!' (Bravo, and she's getting
prettier every day!) and Chinto dotes on her with unconditional, unrequited
love. Furthermore, dressed in red, she becomes the personification of 'la niña
bonita', the name which 'sus fieles conspiradores' (its faithful conspirators)
affectionately gave the Republic during the whole of the nineteenth century.[33]
It is therefore quite fitting that Amparo is at her most stunning either as an
orator 'exclusivamente poseída del fervor político' (possessed exclusively by
political fervour), like the day she made a speech during the banquet at the
Red Circle, or as an agitator: she is 'bella en su indignación como irritada
leona' (as beautiful in her indignation as a lioness that has been provoked)
during her first exploit.

---

33   Salvador de Madariaga, *España: Ensayo de historia contemporánea* (Buenos Aires:
Editorial Sudamericana, 1944), p. 453.

However, not even the formidable combination of her intellectual and physical blossoming can compensate for the limitations of her background. As well as her deficient education, she has to contend with low parental aspirations and lack of guidance; the only advice we see her mother give is to accept Chinto's proposal, and her father threatens to break one of her ribs if she reads newspapers at the factory again. These shortcomings are instrumental in shaping her impressionable, combustible, changeable and superficial spirit, with their consequences plain to see in the political and sexual gullibility which allows a working-class girl, despite her innate intelligence and thirst for knowledge, to become a sacrificial victim of male values, authority and profligacy. Amparo, whose name means 'assistance' but who embodies 'lo difícil que es para una mujer adquirir cultura autodidáctica y llenar los claros de su educación' (how difficult it is for a woman to teach herself and fill the gaps in her education),[34] cannot help being swept along by the federal republican press which, with promises of equality that are never realised, describes the 1868 revolution as 'una hombrada' (a manly deed); at the same time she is taken in by the deceitful words and commitment invented by the seducer.

In a quasi reversal of sexuality, Amparo asssumes the phallic form of a cigar calling out 'Fumadme' (Smoke me) to Baltasar, whose face would have seemed effeminate were it not highlighted by a pointed, correctly outlined nose and a wide forehead, predestined for baldness. In the same way that her strong, powerful and intoxicating perfume acts as an aphrodisiac which causes a delightful dizziness and makes her irresistible to him, she loses her own head in flights of fantasy. Amparo, like her own mother before her, is a *cigarrera*, and Chinto, like the girl's late father, is a *barquillero*. However, Amparo's clamour for equality does not include Chinto, and, lacking her mother's pragmatism – 'Tú te quedarás pobre, y el señorito se irá riendo' (You'll remain poor and the rich young gentleman will go off laughing) – she lacks the necessary insight to see through Baltasar's plan of attack to conquer the orator's republican virtue, devised in cahoots with his Mephistophelian sidekick Borrén. Amparo craves social advancement and respectability through marriage whilst simultaneously demonstrating the supposed equality and opportunities of post-revolutionary society.

---

34 *Apuntes autobiográficos*, p. 711. In 'The Women of Spain', *The Fortnightly Review*, no. 45, part 1 (1889), p. 880, Pardo Bazán tells the story of her grandmother teaching herself to write, copying the letters from a printed book, with a pointed stick for a pen, and mulberry-juice for ink.

On a superficial level, the female protagonists in *La Tribuna* are strong figures of authority who are in control: Amparo manipulates her co-workers and bosses Chinto around; Doña Dolores is a matriarch whose materialistic designs resound in Baltasar's ears at the same time that the indignant voice of Señora Rosendo, the crippled woman who exercises 'tiranía doméstica' (domestic tyranny) from her bed, can be heard in her daughter's mind laying down the law:

> ¡Pin! En los oídos de Baltasar resonaba la voz de doña Dolores, exclamando: «Chico, ¿no sabes que las de García…, ¡pásmate!, ganan el pleito en el Supremo? Lo sé de fijo por el mismo abogado de aquí.» ¡Pin, pin! Y Amparo, a su vez, escuchaba frases coléricas: «Si te dieron palabras, que te las cumplan». ¡Pinnn!… Una hoja purpúrea descendía con lentitud… «Baltasarito, hijo, van a calzarse ciento y no sé cuántos miles de duros, si ganan».

> (Ping! Doña Dolores's voice resounded in Baltasar's ears as she exclaimed: 'My boy, don't you know that the Garcías … you'll be amazed! … have won their case in the Supreme Court? I know it for sure from the lawyer himself here.' Ping, ping! And Amparo, for her part, heard the irascible words: 'If he gave you his word, let him stick to it.' Ping!… A purple leaf was falling slowly… 'Baltasar, my dear son, if they win, they're going to get a hundred and who knows how many thousands of duros.')

However, these elements of ascendancy merely reinforce the overriding picture Pardo Bazán presents of women's subservience. In 'The Women of Spain' she contends that the social and political advances achieved in Spain during the nineteenth century actually had a negative impact on the status of women. The fact that men acquired new rights which women did not share exacerbated their position as 'un sexo verdaderamente esclavo, ya le aten grillos de hierro, ya cadenas de oro y diamantes' (a truly enslaved sex, one minute fastened with iron handcuffs, the next with chains made of gold and diamonds).[35]

Her portrayal of women of the differing social levels, especially the contrast she outlines between midddle class women's financial dependence on the male and lower class women's acceptance that they must earn a living, is developed in *La Tribuna*. Josefina García epitomises the 'bourgeoise' who has been inculcated with masculine ideas and prejudices, an elegant young girl, but frivolous and vacuous, groomed for a marriage where she

---

35   *Al pie de la torre Eiffel*, p. 167.

will be maintained by her husband.[36] As for Amparo, the expectation is that she will work – 'Que trabaje [...] como yo trabajé' (Let her work [...] like I worked) says her mother[37] – and her entry into the workforce is presented as a covenant, celebrated in the pastry cone seller's house with as much ceremony as if the girl were getting married.

La Tribuna depicts revolutionary politics as an inherently male activity. Although Josefina is capable of lively conversation, she claims ignorance and says she has no opinions as soon as discussions turn to politics. Despite her feminist stance, Pardo Bazán's profile of Amparo as the *tribunus plebis* who protects the interests and rights of her co-workers from the factory managers has a mocking undertone, and the girl's views are either derided or deemed irrelevant by virtually all the male characters in her life. In the city, men refer to her as 'la cigarrera guapa que amotina a las otras' (the good-looking cigar maker who stirs up the others) and in the district where she lives everyone, including the young man from the barber shop, teases her. For her father 'la insubordinación era [...] el más feo delito' (the ugliest crime was [...] insubordination), and as for Chinto, 'lejos de resolverse a aceptar los ideales políticos de Amparo [...] le parecía huero y vano todo el bullicio federal' (far from making any effort to accept Amparo's political ideals [...] this whole federal hubbub seemed empty and useless to him).

In response to Baltasar's amazement that males spend time on politics when God produces girls like Amparo, Borrén points at her and makes his feelings clear: 'esa chica aún politiquea más que los barbudos' (that girl is dabbling in politics even more than the bearded men). When Amparo and Baltasar are courting, the latter brings along novels to read out loud to her but, convinced that she is being silly when she cries as soon as the heroes die, puts an end to the books and forbids her from talking about politics. The once intrepid and loquacious 'Tribune of the people' becomes tongue-tied, as if a noose were knotted around her throat, when Baltasar breaks

---

36 In an article published in *La Unión* on July 15, 1879, Clarín argues that this lack of financial independence puts middle-class women in a worse position than their working-class counterparts:

'En la clase media, que hoy es la predominante en el mundo civilizado, la situación de la mujer es más triste en este aspecto que en las clases inferiores.' (In the middle class, which is the predominant one in the civilised world today, the situation of women is sadder in this aspect than in the lower classes).

37 Unlike Josefa García, work enables her to be financially independent: '...y como la labor era a destajo, en las yemas de los dedos tenía el medio de acrecentar sus rentas' (and as she was doing piecework, her fingertips had the means to increase her income).

his earlier promises, and this living symbol of youth, who encapsulates Liberty for the patriarch presiding over the banquet in Chapter 9, is duped, humiliated, abandonded and shackled with the 'traditional role' her seducer believes is incumbent upon women: 'las mujeres no tienen más oficio que uno' (woman have only got one job).[38]

In *Memorias de un solterón* (1894), the sequel to Amparo's story is related. After the birth which takes place at the end of *La Tribuna*, Amparo raises her son on her own, receiving neither money nor legal recognition from Baltasar. She manages to work her way to a top position in the factory, and her son, Ramón, is a handsome socialist typographer who swears revenge on his father and even sends him death threats. Baltasar finally marries Amparo and Ramón inherits his father's estate. Amparo, portrayed as 'intachable antes de que Baltasar la perdiese; y lo fue también después de ese desliz' (faultless before Baltasar led her astray, and equally so after that 'slip'),[39] is the victim of male exploitation who finally gets what she always wanted. In other words, poetic justice is seen to have taken place, but gender inequality remains unchanged.

4. The social and political background: revolution and republicanism

'España es una botella de cerveza y yo soy el tapón: en el momento en que éste salte, todo el líquido contenido se derramará, sabe Dios en qué derrotero'

(Spain is a bottle of beer and I am the cork: when that comes out, all the liquid will escape, God knows in what direction).[40]

Nineteenth-century Spain was a time of decline, unrest, political instability and short-lived governments, a battlefield where liberals and conservatives, failing to find a viable solution to their different outlooks, fought for supremacy.

38 Elsewhere Emilia Pardo Bazán makes the following similar comments:
    (i) *La España de ayer y la de hoy* (http://www.filosofia.org/aut/001/1899epb4.htm): 'Sólo para el hogar [...] ha nacido la mujer' (Women were born [...] only to be at home).
    (ii) 'La mujer española', *La mujer española y otros escritos,* ed. Guadalupe Gómez-Ferrer (Madrid: Cátedra, 1999), p. 100:
    'Hemos convenido que las señoritas no sirven para cosa alguna [...] la clase social a que pertenece la expulsaría de sus filas si supiese que cometía la incongruencia de hacer algo más que gobernar su casa' (We have agreed that women serve no purpose [...] the social class she belongs to would expel her from its ranks if it knew that she was committing the inconsistency of doing something more than managing her house).
39 Emilia Pardo Bazán, *Memorias de un solterón, Obras completas, Tomo II* (Madrid: Aguilar, 1947), p. 550.
40 Attributed to Fernando VII.

While progressive elements of society embraced the constitutional form of government brought to Spain by Napoleon, the more conservative elements objected to the foreign invaders' new ideas. This conflict led to the six-year War of Independence (1808–1814), which ended with the abdication of Joseph Bonaparte. The first Spanish constitution was put in place in 1812, but the great opposition to this liberal government from the nobility, the clergy and the peasants allowed Fernando VII to return to the throne in 1814. Apart from a brief liberal government after a successful uprising led by General Rafael del Riego, Spain was once again a traditional absolutist monarchy.

By 1830 Fernando VII had still not produced an heir. However, as his fourth wife was pregnant, he abrogated the semi-Salic law introduced by the Bourbon king Felipe V in 1713 forbidding the ascension of a woman to the throne unless there were no eligible male heirs. By declaring the earlier and more equitable law of succession in King Alfonso the Wise's Siete Partidas as the only legitimate mandate, he removed his brother as the next in the line of succession and ensured that, irrespective of its sex, the unborn child would succeed him as monarch. Isabel was born in October of that year and when her father died in 1833, she was duly proclaimed queen. As she was a minor, her widowed mother, María Cristina, ruled as regent. Unsurprisingly, opposition to the declaration came swiftly and a dynastic quarrel erupted as the 'two Spains' struggled for dominance: the conservative provincial upper class monarchists challenged the legitimacy of Isabel's succession and supported the deceased king's pious and reactionary brother, Don Carlos; those in favour of a liberal form of government supported Isabel. The first Carlist War, between Carlistas and Cristinos, broke out and lasted until 1839, when the Carlists were defeated. For three years, General Esparto, hero of the Carlist war, led a progressive government but Isabel was declared of age in 1843, when she was thirteen, and reigned for 25 years.

This was a period of political instability, conflict and military uprisings, at the end of which the 'Glorious Revolution' of September 1868, led by General Prim, toppled the queen from power. Six years of confusion ensued. Parliament, reassembled in 1869, decided in favour of a non-Bourbon monarch, but could not agree on a suitable candidate. At last General Prim chose Prince Amadeo of Savoy, second son of Vittorio Emanuele, king of Italy, as Spain's new monarch. However, Prim was assassinated on the very day of Amadeo's arrival in Spain and the foreign king's ephemeral reign never had any chance of success. He was opposed on the left by those who supported the Republic and on the right by the Carlists and

those who wanted the Bourbon dynasty restored. In 1872, the Carlists rose up again, sparking off the third Carlist War (1872–1876) and in February 1873 Amadeo I abdicated. The First Spanish Republic was declared but less than a year later it was ended by a military coup and Alonso XII, Isabel's son, was proclaimed king of Spain in December 1874. After just six years the Bourbons had been restored to the throne, thus marking the beginning of the historical period known as the Restoration which lasted until the proclamation of the Second Republic in 1931.

Whilst there are several references in *Pascual López* and *Un viaje de novios* to specific historical events, *La Tribuna* is Pardo Bazán's only novel to cover in any depth the period of social unrest and political upheaval between the advent of the 'Gloriosa' and the declaration of the First Republic. Although she was from a liberal family and initially welcomed the Revolution, Pardo Bazán soon became a fierce opponent because of 'los desplantes y excesos de la *gloriosa*' (the intemperance and excesses of the *Gloriosa*).[41] Her disillusionment with what she calls 'la guerra sistemática al catolicismo' (the systematic war on Catholicism),[42] combined with her aristocratic upbringing, may help to understand the general undertone of Pardo Bazán's presentation of the political and historical background. It is often possible to get a glimpse of her true feelings, fluctuating between indifference, dismissiveness, scepticism and cynicism, as much in the novel itself as in the expression of her avowed intentions in the prologue.

At the beginning of the prologue she plays down the political backdrop when she maintains that, whilst political events are woven into the plot, her novel is basically a study of local customs. This claim is closely followed, firstly by her denial of any satirical intent, and then her unequivocal statement that it is absurd for people to pin their hopes of redemption and happiness in forms of government that are unknown to them. The implication is that political idealism is not confined to the workers of a tobacco factory in La Coruña, and the reference in Chapter 9 to Pi y Margall's translation of Proudhon makes it clear that Pardo Bazán is targeting a federal brand of republicanism and that she is scornful of the idea that this form of government could ever be a panacea for contemporary Spain.

---

41   *Mi romería* (Madrid: Administración, 1909), p. 193.
42   *Apuntes autobiográficos*, p. 708. To counter this, Pardo Bazán stresses in *La Tribuna* that the *cigarreras'* religious devotion became even stronger as their revolutionary zeal increased. This, it is surmised in Chapter 13, is because the women believed the Republic would abolish conscription.

Although there is extensive coverage of a factual episode which took place in La Coruña in the summer of 1869 – the signing of the 'famoso Pacto' (famous Pact) she refers to in *Apuntes autobiográficos*[43] and what in *La Tribuna* is called 'La Unión del Norte' – the novel shows little or no analysis of the chain of events linking the September Revolution of 1868, aimed at removing Isabel II, to the rise of republicanism and the eventual birth of the First Republic in 1873. In fact, the time span is compressed and the narrator, rather than drawing any conclusions, presents the material in a rather disjointed, piecemeal way, as if to reflect the superficial grasp of cause and effect amongst the impressionable inhabitants of Marineda. The advent in Chapter 9 of 'la Gloriosa' seems to herald the awakening of Amparo's political awareness, but it becomes increasingly obvious that her commitment to social equality is inextricably linked with her personal goal of marrying Baltasar.

The novel provides an accurate picture of life in the tobacco factory: 'pode e debe considerarse a novela, polo seu carácter realista, como unha auténtica fonte para reconstruír a historia da fábrica nos anos setenta' (the novel can and should be considered, by virtue of its realistic character, as an authentic source to reconstruct the history of the factory in the 1870s).[44] The reality she describes is one which still retains the pre-capitalist merits of traditional working methods, the bustle and sense of fraternity Amparo's mother misses, and the pride in one's work displayed by the older women. However, the conflicting advice Amparo receives on her first day shows that the factory is in the process of becoming a soulless, mechanised, industrial organisation driven by productivity and profit:

> ...las viejas le recomendaban que cortase la capa más ancha, porque sale el cigarro mejor formado, y porque «así lo habían hecho ellas toda la vida»; y las jóvenes, que más estrecha, que se enrolla más pronto.

> (the old women recommended that she cut the wrapper wider, because the cigar emerges better shaped, and because 'that's the way they had done it all their lives'; and the young ones told her narrower because you could roll it faster.)

There is no doubt that Pardo Bazán also manages to capture the political climate of the epoch.[45] However, despite the claim made by Carlos Waternau,

---

43   *Op cit.*, p. 725.
44   Alonso Álvarez, Luis, 'A Palloza que viu dona Emilia', *As tecedeiras do fume. Historia da Fábrica de Tabacos da Coruña* (Vigo: A Nosa Terra, 1990), p. 105.
45   Victor Fuentes, 'La aparición del proletariado en la novelística española: Sobre "la

the French translator of *La Tribuna*, that 'le había interesado el libro como documento donde conocer la Revolución española, vista al través de la imparcialidad artística y sin exageraciones de partido' (the book had interested him as a document where one could find out about the Spanish revolution, seen with artistic impartiality and without party exaggeration),[46] Pardo Bazán's own political ideology pervades the novel. This is evident in the scepticism she voices in the prologue and, notwithstanding her protestations in *Apuntes autobiográficos*,[47] in the way she pokes fun at the disciples of federal republicanism and their extravagant prophecies. *La Tribuna* is undoubtedly a fine novel, but it does not provide the reader with a very objective or coherent picture of the sequence of events in this period of Spanish history.

5. The literary context: Realism, Naturalism and other -isms

Drama, poetry and the essay were the dominant forms of literary expression in Spain from the mid-seventeenth century until the early nineteenth century. Although, according to Rebecca Haidt, 'recent scholarship has developed a more nuanced picture of the novel during the eighteenth century in Spain',[48] the idea still prevails that this is a period characterised by a dearth in novelistic production and quality,[49] so much so that José Francisco de Isla's *Historia del*

Tribuna" de Emilia Pardo Bazán', *Grial*, no. 31, 1971, p. 93:

'...la novelista [...] presenta una fiel recreación del clima de expectación revolucionaria y de intenso activismo político republicano-federal que vive la ciudad, con creciente intensidad, desde la "Gloriosa" hasta la proclamación de la República en 1873' (...the novelist [...] presents a faithful recreation of the climate of revolutionary expectation and intense republican-federal political activism which the city lived through, with increasing intensity, from the 'Gloriosa' until the proclamation of the Republic in 1873).

46 *Apuntes autobiográficos*, p. 725.

47 Ibid: 'Ni el más leve conato de sátira encerraba el libro; lejos de recargar los efectos cómicos, hasta se me figura que los atenué' (Not even the slightest attempt at satire was contained in the book; far from stressing the humorous side, I even think I played it down).

48 'The Enlightenment and fictional form', *The Cambridge Companion to the Spanish Novel: From 1600 to the Present*, eds Harriet Turner and Adelaida López de Martínez (Cambridge: Cambridge University Press, 2003), p. 31.

49 See, for example, Joaquín Álvarez Barrientos, *La novela del siglo XVIII* (Alicante: Biblioteca Virtual Miguel de Cervantes, 2009), p. 11(http://www.cervantesvirtual.com/obra/la-novela-del-siglo-xviii--0/):

'La idea de que el XVIII es un siglo sin novelas es común todavía entre la mayoría de los que se dedican al estudio de dicho siglo' (The idea that the eighteenth century is a century without novels is still common among the majority of those who dedicate themselves to the study of that century).

famoso predicador fray Gerundio de Campazas, alias Zotes has sometimes been cited as the only eighteenth-century novel of any consequence. Only the introduction of Scott and the French novelists popular during the early 1800s ensured that fiction came back into vogue in Spain. The principal literary response to the influx of foreign novels was the prose sketches called *cuadros de costumbres* (paintings of local customs), which placed heavy emphasis on the observation and representation of typical scenes of Spanish life, often with a satirical or philosophical intent. In its delineation of traditional scenes, manners, and groups or individuals, *costumbrismo* was a conservative, reactionary type of literature which was primarily concerned with what was viewed as quintessentially Spanish.

The origins of *costumbrismo* can be traced back to the Golden Age of Spanish literature in the sixteenth and seventeenth centuries. However, it was a dominant feature of Spanish literature mainly from the 1830s to the 1850s, and it was still an important aspect of the work of writers like Fernán Caballero and Pedro Antonio de Alarcón, both of whom wrote novels set in Andalusia, and José María de Pereda, who wrote about the mountainous region of northern Castile. Although most of her fiction fits in the broad category of Realism, Pardo Bazán is a self-proclaimed eclectic whose work incorporates elements of various literary movements including *costumbrismo*.[50] However, she rejects the notion of the description of local customs for its own sake:

> Al escribir *La Tribuna*, me guiaban iguales propósitos que al trazar las páginas de *El Cisne*: estudiar y retratar en forma artística gentes y tierras que conozco, procurando huir del estrecho provincialismo, para que el libro sea algo más que pintura de usanzas regionales y aspire al honroso dictado de *novela*.

> (When I wrote *La Tribuna* I was guided by the same principles pursued in writing *El Cisne*: to study and portray in artistic form people and areas that I know, aiming to avoid narrow provincialism, so that the book be more than just a depiction of regional customs and achieve the honourable denomination of *novel*.)[51]

In *La Tribuna* there is the first notable example of *costumbrismo* in Pardo Bazán's work. There are entire chapters characterised by the *costumbrist* tradition of accumulating descriptions, such as the sketch of 'Donde vivía

---

50   Emilia Pardo Bazán, *Pedro Antonio de Alarcón, Obras completas, Tomo III*, p. 1389: '...ni soy idealista, ni realista, ni naturalista, sino ecléctica' (...I'm not an idealist, nor a realist, nor a naturalist, but an eclectic).
51   Emilia Pardo Bazán, 'Prólogo a *El cisne de Vilamorta', Obras completas, Tomo III*, p. 670.

la protagonista' in Chapter 30. These passages, however, are not what Pardo Bazán refers to as 'el pecado de pintar por pintar' (the sin of painting for painting's sake).[52] For example, the 'Carnaval de las cigarreras' is not just a description of the anarchic nature of the costumes or the jubilation and happy improvisation of youth; it is 'una afirmación enérgica de la femineidad de la fábrica' (a vigorous affirmation of the femininity of the factory) sandwiched between two eternities of monotonous labour, a brief ray of light which not only transforms the dark, sad rooms but also highlights, by way of contrast, the soul-destroying grind of the female workers' day-to-day existence in this 'verdadero infierno social' (real social hell).

Nevertheless, the elements of literary movements such as Romanticism and *costumbrismo* which are found in her work do not alter the essence of her novelistic production. This has usually been divided by critics into two halves: a Naturalistic period and a 'Spiritual' period in which, with an increasing focus on psychology, she directed her attention more on the middle classes and then the upper classes. Her move towards psychology echoed a resurgence of interest amongst French novelists in the inner selves of their characters as a backlash against Zola's reductive view of man and the working method he champions in the preface to *Thérèse Raquin*:

> J'ai simplement fait sur deux corps vivants le travail analytique que les chirurgiens font sur des cadavres.
>
> (I've simply done on two living bodies the analytical work that surgeons do on corpses.)[53]

It also reflected the works of Russian novelists like Turgenev, Gogol, Tolstoy and Dostoyevsky, whose translations into French she began to discover in March, 1885, when *Crime and Punishment* fell into her hands.[54]

The term 'Realist' began to be used in 1850, but it wasn't until a couple of decades later that it became a literary movement in Spain, the most influential writers being Galdós, Alas and Ibáñez. Realism was revolutionary and *épatant* at the time because it did not necessarily present a moral vision of society. Realist writers saw themselves as objective observers of everyday life and their literature endeavoured to portray people and society as they are rather than how we would like them to be.[55] The challenge for Pardo

---

52   *La cuestión palpitante, Obras completas, Tomo III*, p. 609.
53   'Préface de la deuxième édition', *Thérèse Raquin* (Paris: Livre de poche, 1971), p. 7.
54   *La revolución y la novela en Rusia*, p. 760.
55   In a lecture given at the Centro Gallego de Barcelona on March 30, 1953, Camilo José

Bazán was finding the right balance between idealising one's characters – what she refers in the prologue to *La Tribuna* as attributing to Caliban the seductive graces of Ariel – and debasing them into 'la pourriture humaine' (human rottenness) populating the works of Zola.

Unlike Mme de Staël, Chateaubriand and Lamartine, the Romantic writers she labelled 'los vencidos' (the vanquished) in the eighth essay of *La cuestión palpitante*, Stendhal and Balzac, 'los vencedores' (the victors) or leaders of the opposing school that followed, focused on the present, rather than a glorious past, and on average people, rather than heroes and exceptional individuals:

> Cuán preferible es retratar un ser humano, de carne y hueso, a fantasear maniquíes!
>
> (How preferable it is to portray a human being, made of flesh and blood, than to dream up puppets!)[56]

Realist novels include reams of detailed description, plots featuring everday issues, and dialogue where characters speak, with varying degrees of success, in a manner appropriate to their social class. Although Realist fiction is not necessarily didactic, there is often a strong moralising tone in these novels with authors attempting to raise awareness of the problems facing contemporary society. The Naturalists renounced any intention of direct teaching, an opinion with which Pardo Bazán consistently agreed,[57] but in

---

Cela praises Pardo Bazán for debunking the timeless, idealised region that Valle-Inclán depicts, 'esa Galicia paralela a la España de pandereta' (that Galicia parallel to the tourist Spain) in the same way that Cervantes 'killed' books of chivalry:

'La Pardo Bazán, Sras. y Sres., no tenía pelos en la lengua, llamaba a las cosas por sus nombres' (Pardo Bazán, Ladies and Gentlemen, didn't mince her words, she called things by their name). *La Tribuna. Cadernos de estudios da Casa museo Emilia Pardo Bazán* (A Coruña: RAG, 2004), p. 33.

56   *La cuestión palpitante*, p. 584.

57   'Prefacio a *Un viaje de novios*' (Barcelona: Editorial Labor, 1971), p. 61: '...aborrezco las píldoras de moral rebozadas en una capa de oro literario' (...I loathe moral pills hidden beneath a coat of literary gold).

'Prólogo de la autora', *Pascual López, Obras Completas II* (Madrid: Aguilar, 1947), p. 13: '...creo que toda obra bella eleva y enseña de por sí, sin que el autor pretenda añadir a la belleza la lección' (...I believe every work of beauty exalts and teaches in itself without the author's trying to add a lesson to the beauty).

'Carta Magna', *Obras completas, Tomo III*, p. 658: '...el objeto del arte no es defender ni ofender la moral, es realizar la belleza' (...the purpose of art is not to defend or offend morality, it is to achieve beauty).

the prologue she admits that she cannot hide the fact that finding its way into *La Tribuna*, almost in spite of herself, is a purpose that might be called *instructive*.

The terms Naturalism and Realism have often been used synonymously, occasionally by Pardo Bazán herself, but there is a clear-cut distinction between the two literary movements. While Naturalism shared the Realist objective of reproducing contemporary reality as it is lived and experienced, it differed in the emphasis it placed on applying the scientific method to the novel. Stylistically, Naturalism was influenced by the attempts of Auguste Comte to apply the methods of scientific observation to the social sciences, philosophy and religion. Extending that application to literature, the Naturalists attempted to recreate in their fiction the 'experimental method' elaborated by the physician Claude Bernard in his *Introduction à L'Étude de la médecine expérimentale*. It would usually be enough, Zola maintained, to replace the word 'médecin' (doctor) with the word 'romancier' (novelist) as he laid out the tenets of Naturalism, firstly in *Le roman experimental* (1880) and later in *Les romanciers naturalistes* (1881).

Naturalism was essentially a reponse to the mood of scientific confidence and optimism in nineteenth-century Europe. The Naturalist author saw human beings as products of nature (biology) and society (environment) and viewed the novel as a scientific experiment in which a hypothesis is tested and proved. Behind this experimental conception are Darwinism and Comte's positivist philosophy which rejected all theological and metaphysical speculation in favour of strict adherence to positive facts and observable phenomena. Equally influential were the theories of Hippolyte Taine, who posited in his *Histoire de la littérature anglaise* (1864) his famous doctrine of 'la race, le milieu, le moment': our lives are inescapably determined by a combination of heredity, surroundings and the historical moment in which we live.

In *Apuntes autobiográficos*[58] Pardo Bazán explains how, after the publication of the two volumes of *San Francisco de Asís*, in the winter of 1882 she was in Santiago intending to write a *Historia de la literatura mística española*. This project, however, was pushed aside for Naturalism and she sent twenty weekly articles to the Madrid newspaper *La Época* between November 1882 and April 1883. These essays, which shortly after were gathered together in the book *La cuestión palpitante* with a prologue by Clarín, sought to explain, defend and criticise the literary and philosophical movement of Naturalism as propounded by its founder, Emile Zola. The

58   *Op cit.*, pp. 720–21.

Spanish public was shocked that a woman should even be reading Zola, let alone commenting explicitly on him without unreservedly opposing this obscene and immoral movement.[59]

Although *La cuestión palpitante* is more the beginning of an attack than a statement in favour of the Naturalist doctrine,[60] Pardo Bazán's position was misunderstood and attacked because, as she explains in a letter to Menéndez Pelayo on October 10, 1883, when people talked about Naturalism they paid attention only to *L'assommoir*, *Nana* and *Pot-Bouille*.[61] The polemics engendered by this literary fashion were bitter and divisive, and prominent detractors included a host of traditionalists and conservatives like Pedro de Alarcón, Díaz Carmona, Cánovas del Castillo and Luis Alfonso.[62] In his article 'Crítica Dramática', *Revista de Madrid*, 1881, Cañete describes Naturalism as 'glorificador del adulterio y destructor de la familia' (glorifier of adultery and destroyer of the family). Valera believed his excellent friend Doña Emilia Pardo Bazán became a Naturalist without fully understanding what Naturalism meant,[63] a view shared by Menéndez Pelayo who, on September

---

59   Charles Bigot, 'Correspondancia de París', *Revista Contemporánea*, 30, April, 1876, pp. 238–39: 'No aconsejo a las mujeres delicadas que lean sus novelas, porque, tal, vez, les repugnarían y les ofendarían...' (I don't advise delicate women to read his novels, because they might be repulsed and offended by them...).

60   Carmen Bravo-Villasante, 'Introducción' in *La cuestión palpitante* (Madrid: Anaya, 1966), pp. 15–16:

'...*La cuestión palpitante* [...] es más un principio de ataque que un alegato en pro de la doctrina naturalista.'

61   '...la gente [...] al hablar de naturalismo sólo se fijan en el *Assommoir*, *Nana* y *Pot-Bouille*'. *Epistolario, vol. VI*, p. 21.

62   See *Apuntes autobiográficos*:

(i) p. 722: 'Sostuvo Alarcón una especie de polémica epistolar conmigo acerca del naturalismo, poco antes de su desapacible diatriba en la Academia, donde llamó a esta escuela literaria "mano sucia de la literatura"...' (Alarcón had a kind of epistolary discussion with me about Naturalism, a bit before his bitter diatribe in the Academy, where he called this literary school 'the dirty hand of literature'...).

(ii) p. 724: 'En *La Ciencia Cristiana* lo ha impugnado el instruido y elegante escritor Díaz Carmona, y en su libro sobre *El Solitario*, Cánovas del Castillo' (In *La Ciencia Cristiana* the well-educated and elegant writer Díaz Carmona refuted it, and Cánovas del Castillo in his book about *El Solitario*).

(iii) *Ibid.*: '...representa la opinión oficial del periódico de los salones' (represents the official opinion of the salon newspapers) in which 'la palabra *naturalismo* es de muy mal efecto y *shocking* en grado sumo' (the word *Naturalism* gives a very bad impression and is *shocking* in the extreme).

63   'Apuntes sobre el nuevo arte de escribir novelas', *Obras completas, Tomo II*, p. 696:

'...mi excelente amiga doña Emilia Pardo Bazán se hizo naturalista sin comprender bien

22 1886, sent him a letter with a dismissive and mysoginistic assessment of her stance: '…como toda mujer, tiene una naturaleza *receptiva* y se enamora de todo lo que hace ruido […]. Un dia se encapricha por San Francisco y otro día por Zola' (…like all women, she has a *receptive* nature and falls in love with everything that causes a stir […]. One day she takes a fancy to Saint Francis and another day to Zola).[64]

Eduardo Calcaño, the Venezuelan minister to Madrid, published his *Carta literaria*, an open letter to Victor Balaguer, poet and member of the Academy, bemoaning the shameful decadence of Spanish letters. He called on a long list of writers to act as a new Lepanto and save Hispanic culture, especially religious faith and the role of women, from 'las tinieblas espesas del materialismo envilecedor' (the dense gloom of vile materialism). In response to this letter, in which Naturalists are depicted as a band of pirates invading the Spanish mainland, Pardo Bazán published an article entitled 'Bandera negra' (*La Época*, 17/03/1984). Based on their absence from Calcaño's list of potential 'saviours', she deduced that the literary pirates must be Galdós, Pereda, Palacio Valdés, Ortega Munilla, Sellés, Cano, Ceferino Palencia, Clarín and herself. Luis Alfonso replied with 'Cartas son cartas' (*La Época*, 31/03/1984), berating her for the impudence of her uninvited intervention in an exchange between others. The scandal produced by a book, which the author herself described as 'un libro de guerrilla, de escaramuza' (a book of guerrilla warfare and skirmishes),[65] was such that her husband went on to insist she abandon her writing career. Fortunately for us, she refused to comply with his demands; unfortunately for them, this irreconcilable difference led to a separation which, whilst amicable, was permanent.

However, although she admired Zola – 'grande, eximio, extraordinario artista' (great, distinguished, extraordinary artist)[66] – and approved of the aim of uniting science and art,[67] she compared the enclosed nature of Naturalism

---

lo que el naturalismo significaba.'

64   http://www.larramendi.es/menendezpelayo/i18n/corpus/unidad.cmd?idCorpus =1002&idUnidad=152965&posicion=1

65   Quoted in Carmen Bravo-Villasante, *Vida y Obra de Emilia Pardo Bazán*, p. 92.

66   *La cuestión palpitante*, p. 625. Cf. *Epistolario*, vol. VII, p. 56: 'Sigo en mi herejía de atribuirle un talento prodigioso' (I continue in my heresy of attributing him with a prodigious talent).

67   'Lo que hay en el fondo de la cuestión es una idea admirable, con la cual soñé siempre: la unidad de método en la ciencia y el arte.' (What is at the heart of the matter is an admirable idea I have always dreamed of: the unity of method of science and art). Carmen Bravo-Villasante, *Vida y Obra de Emilia Pardo Bazán*, p. 91.

to very small rooms with low ceilings in which it is difficult to breathe.[68] Moreover, not only did she consider Zola's theories to be based on young and inexact sciences – 'el darwinismo es una hipótesis, o, mejor dicho, son tantas hipótesis' (Darwinism is a hypothesis, or, to put it better, so many hypotheses)[69] – but also she was highly critical of the cardinal vice of Naturalistic aesthetics: the extreme interpretation and application of the scientific method whereby thought and passion were subjected to the same laws which determine a stone falling down.[70]

For this reason, she would prefer to replace the word 'escuela' with the word 'método'.[71] She wrote several novels in a Naturalist style, but Zola's deterministic, fatalistic and pessimistic doctrines are contrary to the idea of achieving salvation through penitence and life transformation, and therefore diametrically opposed to her Catholic beliefs.[72] By choosing to write about people 'souverainement dominés par leurs nerfs et leur sang, dépourvus de libre arbitre, entraînés à chaque acte de leur vie par les fatalités de leur chair' (completely dominated by their nerves and blood, without free will, drawn into each action of their lives by the inexorable laws of their physical

---

68 *La cuestión palpitante*, p. 581: '…se parece a las habitaciones bajas de techo y muy chicas, en las cuales la respiración se dificulta.'

69 *Reflexiones científicas contra el darwinismo*, *Obras completas*, *Tomo III*, p. 538. In *La cuestión palpitante*, p. 624 she makes the same point:

'…el darwinismo no pertenece al número de aquellas verdades científicas demostradas con evidencia por el método positivo y experimental que Zola preconiza' (…Darwinism doesn't belong to the number of those scientific truths demonstrated with evidence by the positive and experimental method which Zola advocates).

70 'Someter el pensamiento y la pasión a las mismas leyes que determinan la caída de la piedra' (*La cuestión palpitante*, p. 580). In the same paragraph Pardo Bazán gives the example of Zola's *Une page d'amour* where the heroine 'manifiesta los grados de su enamoramiento por los de temperatura que alcanza la planta de sus pies' (shows the degrees of her love by the temperature the soles of her feet reach).

The fact that Pardo Bazán deals more harshly with Zola has not gone unnoticed. For example, E. Correa Calderón, *La Pardo Bazán en su época* (Madrid: Jura, 1952), p. 35:

'Es interesante que Emilia Pardo Bazán enjuicia a Emilio Zola con más dureza que y acritud que a ningún otro de los cultivadores del naturalismo' (It's interesting that Emilia Pardo Bazán passes judgement on Emile Zola with more severity and more pungency than on any other of those who cultivate Naturalism).

71 *Apuntes autobiográficos*, p. 723.

72 *La cuestión palpitante*, p. 631:

'Para mí no hay más moral que la moral católica, y sólo sus preceptos me parecen puros, íntegros, sanos e inmejorables' (For me there is no other morality than Catholic morals, and its precepts are the only ones which seem to be pure, whole, healthy and unbeatable).

nature),[73] Zola creates 'la *bestia humana*, o sea el hombre esclavo del instinto' (the *human beast*, that is to say man as a slave to instinct), an assortment of 'idiotas, histéricas, borrachos, fanáticos, dementes o personas tan desprovistas de sentido moral, como los ciegos de sensibilidad en la retina' (idiots, hysterics, drunkards, fanatics, lunatics or people as devoid of a moral sense as the blind are of sensitivity in their retina).[74] Conversely, Zola was baffled by Pardo Bazán's standpoint. When *La cuestión palpitante* was translated into French by Albert Savine, he praised it as one of 'los mejores trozos que se han escrito acerca del movimiento literario contemporáneo' (the best pieces that have been written about the contemporary literary movement).[75] However, unable to assimilate the apparent anomaly of a fervent, militant Catholic being a Naturalist, he concluded that her Naturalism is 'puramente formal, artístico y literario' (purely formal, artistic and literary), in other words free from scientific determinism.[76]

The titles of the second and third chapters of *La Tribuna* – 'Padre y madre' (Father and mother) and 'Pueblo de su nacimiento' (The town of her birth) – show an obvious debt to Naturalism, and send out a clear message that in order to understand Amparo we need to know about her parents and her social milieu. However, if it appears almost preordained that she should end up a *cigarrera* like her mother, she also transcends her destiny by becoming *la Tribuna*, and heredity and environment influence her fate only insofar as her ingenuousness and aspirations towards a better life make her easy prey for Baltasar Sobrado. Unlike Zola's protagonists, we never feel that she is the victim of inexorable and ineluctable forces beyond her control. If her ambitions to scale the social ladder through marriage end in disillusionment and disappointement, she is largely the author of her own fate.[77] Her life

---

73 'Préface de la deuxième édition', *Thérèse Raquin*, p. 6.

74 *La cuestión palpitante*, p. 624.

75 'Opiniones de Emilio Zola sobre *La cuestión palpitante*', *Obras completas, Tomo III*, p. 1033.

76 *Ibid.* Juan Valera shares this opinion. He says 'usted es idealista como yo, o más que yo, y no es naturalista como Zola' (you are an idealist like me, or more than me, and you're not a Naturalist like Zola), and goes on to refer to her as 'la inspirada, cristiana y fervorosa autora del libro sobre San Francisco de Asís' (the inspired Christian and fervent author of the book on Saint Francis of Assisi). 'Apuntes sobre el nuevo arte de escribir novelas', *Obras completas, Tomo II*, pp. 635 and 689.

77 This theme is explored in Pardo Bazán's *Las desnudas*. In this short story the narrator's stated purpose is to demonstrate that 'bajo la influencia de un mismo terrible suceso, cada espíritu conserva su espontaneidad y escoge, mediante su iniciativa propia, el camino, bueno o malo, que en esto precisamente estriba la libertad (under the influence of the same terrible

could have taken a completely different path if she had accepted Chinto's proposal, and her fate has none of the inevitability of either the hereditary determinism of Gervaise's descent into alcoholism in *L'assommoir* or the scientific explanation for the heroine's sexual and alcoholic appetites in the Goncourt Brothers' *Germinie Lacerteux.*

The many similarities between *La Tribuna* and Zola's masterpiece serve to underline the different overview of the two authors.[78] Gervaise's daughter Nana, with her 'quenottes blanches' (little white teeth), develops into an attractive teenager 'chatouillée de petits désirs' (with little tickling desires)[79] when men ogle her, and Amparo, with her 'dientes como gotas de leche' (teeth like drops of milk), becomes aware of her sexuality 'el día en que «unos señores» dijeron a Amparo que era bonita' (on the day when 'certain gentlemen' told Amparo that she was pretty). Both live in a sordid milieu which they relish – for Amparo 'la calle era su paraíso' (the street was her paradise) and for Nana and her companions 'la rue était à elles' (the street belonged to them)[80] – but from which they wish to escape. Both get carried away by the seductive allure of consumerism: just as nobody could stop Amparo believing that the luxurious shop windows, the temptations of the confectioners, the coloured phials of the chemist's and the picturesque leantos in the plaza were all hers, Nana imagines herself wearing the jewellery she sees in the shop window:

>...elle aurait bien voulu avoir une croix avec un velours au cou, ou encore de petites boucles d'oreille de corail, si petites, qu'on croirait des gouttes de sang.

>(...she would have loved to have a cross on a velvet ribbon round her neck, or some little coral earrings, so tiny that they looked like drops of blood.)[81]

Like Isidora Rufete in Galdós's *La desheredada*, a woman whose grasp of reality is transformed by idyllic *folletines* as much as Amparo's is by progressive newspapers, the desire for luxury goods seems to lead both Nana and Pardo Bazán's heroine to compromise their integrity. However, while

---

event, each spirit retains its spontaneity and chooses, by means of its own initiative, the path, good or bad, which is precisely what this freedom is based on). *Obras completas, Tomo I* (Madrid: Aguilar, 1947), p. 1619.

78   See Francisca González-Arias, 'Parallels and Parodies: Emilia Pardo Bazán's Response to Emile Zola (*La Tribuna* and *L'Assommoir*)', *Bulletin of Hispanic Studies*, Volume 67, Issue 4, 1990, p. 369.

79   Émile Zola, *L'assommoir* (Paris: Livre de poche, 1978), pp. 395 and 396.

80   *Ibid.*, p. 398.

81   *Ibid.*, p. 414.

Nana is 'gourmande [...] de galette' (fond [...] of money)[82] and her yearning for the coral earrings in the jeweller's shopwindow is the catalyst that leads to her descent into prostitution, Amparo's 'slip' in no way diminishes her widely applauded deed of relinquishing the earrings she bought from her own savings to help Rita who has just been dismissed from her job. It is as if Pardo Bazán is using this parallel to show human nature in a more positive light. Nana's downfall is the inescapable consequence of her milieu and her heredity; Amparo's laudable and disinterested gesture is a result of free choice and shows that, although there is a manipulative and calculating side to her character, her 'indómita generosidad popular' (indomitable working-class generosity) forms a sharp contrast with not only Zola's 'brutes humaines' but also, within the context of *La Tribuna*, the small-mindedness of Doña Dolores, whose matrimonial ambitions for her son are based entirely on pecuniary considerations.

The essays in *La cuestión palpitante* criticise the idealists,[83] argue that Naturalism is mistaken in its determinism, and draw a clear conclusion:

...el *realismo* en el arte nos ofrece una teoría más ancha, completa y perfecta que el *naturalismo*. Comprende y abarca lo natural y lo espiritual, el cuerpo y el alma, y concilia y reduce a unidad la oposición del naturalismo y del idealismo racional.

(...in art *Realism* offers us a broader, more complete, and more perfect theory than *Naturalism*. It includes and embraces both the natural and the spiritual aspects, the body and the soul, and it reconciles and brings into harmonious union the opposition between Naturalism and rational Idealism).[84]

Moreover, arguing that Spanish Realism has indigenous roots – '¡Nuestro realismo, el que ríe y llora en *La Celestina* y el *Quijote*' (Our realism, the one that laughs and cries in *La Celestina* and *Don Quijote*)[85] – Pardo

---

82 *Ibid.*, p. 413.
83 In 'Seguimos filosofando', the third essay, she makes the following statement, pp. 582–83:
   ' ...el idealismo está muy en olor de santidad, goza de excelente reputación y se cometen infinitos crímenes literarios al amparo de su nombre: es la teoría simpática por excelencia, la que invocan poetas de caramelo y escritores amerengados' (...idealism has the odour of sanctity, it enjoys an excellent reputation, and an infinite number of literary crimes have been committed in its name; it is the congenial theory *par excellence*, one evoked by candy-coated poets and meringue-covered writers).
84 *Op cit.*, p. 582.
85 'Prefacio a *Un viaje de novios*', p. 60.

Bazán puts forward the idea of a Catholic Naturalism based on the literary traditions of her homeland.

Although she maintains, in *La cuestión palpitante*, that Zola's descriptions constitute a considerable part of his merit of originality,[86] her praise in the preface to *Un viaje de novios* for 'la observación paciente, minuciosa, exacta, que distingue a la moderna escuela francesa' (the patient, meticulous, exact observation which distinguishes the modern French school)[87] is tempered by her disparagement of the long-winded, and at times tiresome, prolixity of the descriptions.[88] However, in this respect the Naturalists are no worse than Romantic authors like Scott, Dumas and Hugo, the main difference being what the authors choose to dwell on. Bazán believed that the novel should reflect reality 'sin escamotear la verdad para sustituirla con ficciones literarias más o menos bellas' (without hiding the truth to replace it with more or less beautiful literary fictions).[89] Accordingly, she pointed out that Cervantes 'hizo al lector trabar conocimiento con jiferos y rameras, arrieros, galeotes y pícaros de la hampa' (forced the reader to deal with thugs and harlots, muleteers, galley slaves and underworld types)[90] and that *Don Quijote de la Mancha* has passages which can deservedly be described as vulgar.[91] However, disapproving of Zola's 'mania de escoger lo más feo' (craze for choosing what is the ugliest),[92] she felt that our impression of life is different: it alternates between good and bad, between poetry and vulgarity, and this is what the Russian novelists bequeathed us, without leaving the solid ground of Naturalism.[93] Furthermore, she was insistent that literature should make life more beautiful, not uglier.

---

86 *Op cit.*, p. 629: 'Las descripciones de Zola [...] constituyen no escasa parte de su original mérito'.
87 Prefacio a *Un viaje de novios*, p. 59.
88 *Ibid.*: '...la prolijidad nimia, y a veces cansada, de las descripciones'.
89 *Apuntes autobiográficos*, p. 719.
90 *La cuestión palpitante*, p. 646.
91 *Ibid.*, p. 632: 'Es innegable que el *Quijote* encierra pasajes [...] con justicia se pueden calificar de groseros'.
92 *La revolución y la novela en Rusia*, p. 877.
93 *Ibid.*: 'La impresión de la vida es otra; alternativa de bueno y de malo, de poesía y vulgaridad; eso es lo que han sabido darnos los rusos, sin salir del terreno firme del arte naturalista.'
   One of the first serious studies of Naturalism was by Manuel de la Revilla. In his essay 'El naturalismo en el arte' (*Revista de España*, May 1879, vol. 68, pp. 164–84) he analyses the differences between Realism and Naturalism, highlighting the tendency in the latter to reproduce 'los más groseros y repugnantes aspectos de la realidad' (the filthiest and most repugnant aspects of reality).

Art and science, she maintains, have different aims: while the primary aim of science is truth, the supreme mission of art is the creation of beauty, the essence of which does not evolve and progress. When we observe the cave paintings of Altamira we must admit that, whilst style changes, beauty is already present and perfect in prehistoric times. This viewpoint shows that, although discussions of Pardo Bazán's work have tended to concentrate on the influence of Zola's Naturalism, her relationship with 'l'art pour l'art', a philosophy chiefly represented by Théophile Gautier, is also important. This is exemplified by her credo that every work of beauty exalts and teaches in itself and her declaration in *La cuestión palpitante*:

> ...el artista que se proponga fines distintos de la realización de la belleza, tarde o temprano, con seguridad infalible, verá desmoronarse el edificio que erija.

> (the artist who puts his mind to aims different from the realisation of beauty, will sooner or later, with unwavering certainty, see the building he is erecting come down.)[94]

Gautier and his associates were reacting against the use of literature as a weapon of propaganda. Without ever providing a precise definition of the *beauté* which was their object, they aimed at the elimination of moral judgement. Concentrating on perfection of form rather than content, 'le bon Théo' sees himself sculpting, filing and chiselling an unyielding block of language into a literary precious stone serving no purpose other than its own beauty. Pardo Bazán, equally attracted to words for their sensuous qualities, describes how she became enthralled by the gems and jewels of the Castilian language:

> ...descubriéndome sus arcanidades y tesoros, su relieve y numerosa armonía, y convirtiéndome en coleccionista infatigable de vocablos, en cuya sola hechura (aislada del valor que adquieren en el período) noto bellezas sin cuento, color, brillo y aroma propio, bien como el lapidario antes de engarzada la piedra preciosa admira su talla, sus luces y sus quilates.

> (...discovering its secrets and treasures, the complexity of its shapes and tones, and turning into a tireless collector of words, in whose shape alone (cut off from the value they acquire in a sentence) I notice countless beauties, the colour, the brilliance and their own aroma, just like a lapidary before a mounted precious stone admires its size, the way it reflects the light and its value.)[95]

---

94   *Op cit.*, p. 624.
95   *Apuntes autobiográficos*, p. 712.

This fascination with language is explored in the tenth essay which makes up *La cuestión palpitante*. Here Pardo Bazán looks at Flaubert and refers to the literary perfection of *Madame Bovary* where 'ni le falta ni le sobra requisito alguno' (no qualification is either lacking or redundant) and where 'cada cosa está en su lugar' (each thing is in its place). If he looks at the environment, she concludes, he does so not on a whim or to show off his knowledge but 'porque importa al asunto o a los caracteres' (because it is important to the subject or the characters) and this is why he is superior to Balzac, 'que usa tanto adorno superfluo' (who uses so much superfluous ornamentation).[96] If the detailed accounts of the back-breaking process of making *barquillos* in the opening pages of *La Tribuna* and the art of manufacturing cigarettes in Chapter 6 do not achieve the 'estilo cabal' (consummate style) of Flaubert, they reinforce the social aspects of the novel and, with their portrayal of commonplace realities and the psychology of the banal, are relevant to the development of her narrative.

La Tribuna incorporates many naturalistic features, including the historical framework (1868, Amadeo, the First Republic, the last Carlist war), the use of what Luis Alfonso called 'palabras de baja estofa' (second-rate words),[97] but especially the precise setting (every district, street, square, church and other building in Marineda, the author's fictional name for La Coruña, can be identified in its real life counterpart of 1872–73). In much the same way that Zola uses key buildings as focal points throughout his Rougon-Macquart series of novels, la Granera, the tobacco factory in la Coruña, becomes a kind of collective protagonist as well as a faithful pen picture of the Spanish nation. Also, in spite of Pardo Bazán's objections to Zola's fixation with the squalid,[98] the same criticism could easily be levelled at several sections of *La Tribuna*. Pardo Bazán takes us round the whole tobacco factory, from the Paradise of the cigarette workshop to the Purgatory of the section for cigars on the floor below and the Hell of the cutting rooms at the bottom, and does not balk at dwelling on the unpleasant aspects of factory life, especially the 'olor ingrato y herbáceo del Virginia humedecido y de la hoja medio verde, mezclado con las emanaciones de tanto cuerpo humano y con el fétido vaho de las letrinas próximas' (unpleasant, herbaceous smell of Virginia tobacco and the partly green leaves, mixed with the emissions from so many human bodies and the foul-smelling whiff of the nearby toilets).

---

96 *La cuestión palpitante*, p. 609.
97 Carmen Bravo-Villasante, *Vida y Obra de Emilia Pardo Bazán*, p. 88.
98 *La cuestión palpitante*, p. 630: '…creo que ve la humanidad aún más fea, cínica y vil de lo que es (…I believe that he sees humanity even uglier, more cynical and viler than what it is).

In the first two chapters we read about the wretched ground floor flat, the bedroom described as a cubbyhole, the greenish, filthy panes of the little window and the dark, narrow kitchen resembling a cave. However, this story of poverty and neglect, narrated in prose by a multitude of ugly objects ('la historia de la pobreza y de la incuria narrada en prosa por una multitud de objetos feos') serves a dual purpose. It leaves an indelible imprint of the dark, gloomy home environment from which Amparo loves to escape, whilst also giving an insight into her aspirations to transcend the barriers of her social class, especially by means of the striking contrast with the spacious, light environment of the Sobrado household. Here, surrounded by lavish furnishings and luxury items, Amparo, one of those who 'sin haber nacido entre sábanas y holandas, presume y adivina las comodidades y deleites que jamás gozó' (without having been born amidst sheets and fine linen instinctively guess and presume all those comforts and delights they never enjoyed), is described as being in her element.

Pardo Bazán's depiction of the sordid is particularly prevalent in the plethora of anatomical, pathological and physiological details with which she bombards the reader. The first description of Amparo's mother is 'una mujer de edad madura, agujereada como una espumadera por las viruelas, chata de frente, de ojos chicos' (a woman of mature years, pock-marked like a skimming ladle, with a flat face and small eyes). The two things we probably remember most about her father are his thumb, which had become 'una callosidad tostada, sin uña, sin yema y sin forma casi' (a toasted callus without nail or fingertip and almost without shape), and the sudden stroke which kills him. Amparo herself is undoubtedly blessed with natural beauty, but the imprint of poverty can be seen in her sallow complexion and tangled hair, and the author cannot resist informing us, with Naturalistic relish, that her teeth were served by 'un estómago que no conocía la gastralgia' (a stomach that did not suffer from gastralgia); Chinto 'tenía facciones abultadas e irregulares, piel de un moreno terroso, ojos pequeños y a flor de cara' (had exaggerated, irregular features, earthy, dark-coloured skin, small eyes flush with his face); Pepa the midwife, whose enormous face, 'circuida por colgante papada, tenía palidez serosa' (surrounded by a pendulous double chin, had a serous paleness about it). Not even minor characters are exempt from this relentless scrutiny: the group of carol singers in Chapter 5, with purple complexions whipped by the north wind, and the baby whose little face was wrinkled and withered like that of an old man 'por culpa de la mala alimentación y del desaseo' (because of his poor nourishment and grubbiness); the 'manos nudosas como

ramas de árbol seco' (hands gnarled like the branches of dried-up trees) of the women Amparo encounters when she starts working at the factory in Chapter 6; Guardiana's younger siblings described in Chapter 11 as 'todos marcados con la mano de hierro de la enfermedad hereditaria' (all marked by the iron hand of hereditary disease); the repugnant beggars in Chapter 25, including an elephantiac with a bilbous face, a man affected with herpes and a freak without arms or legs; the children where the protagonist lived (Chapter 30), 'horribles y encogidos como los fetos que se conservan en aguardiente' (as horrible and shrunken as foetuses preserved in liquor).

However, Pardo Bazán is resolute in her response to Luis Alfonso's repudiation of a scene at the end of the novel as 'un tratado de obstetricia' (a treatise on obstetrics).[99] The depiction of childbirth in *La Tribuna*, she states, is far less graphic than 'en conversaciones y diálogos de gente bien educada' (in the conversations and dialogues of well-educated people),[100] and there is nothing licentious or provocative about 'ese episodio tremendo de la vida femenina' (this tremendous event in a woman's life)[101] where the profound austerity of pain prevails. The birth of Amparo's son is, in fact, a good example of an attenuated Naturalism, what José Hesse refers to as 'un naturalismo asépitico, lo que antes se ha definido como "un naturalismo a la española"' (an aseptic Naturalism, what was previously defined as 'a Spanish-style Naturalism'),[102] and what Pardo Bazán says her colleagues on the other side of the Pyrenees would call '*du naturalisme à l'eau de rose*' (sentimental Naturalism).[103] The whole scene is described 'entre bastidores' (offstage), that is to say from the adjacent room where Amparo's mother lies in bed, the emphasis therefore being on what can be heard rather than seen. It would seem, then, that by reversing her usual tendency to pay far more attention to the visual than the auditory, Pardo Bazán was actually making a conscious effort to dilute the gruesome details and avoid 'la descripción clínica de Zola en *Pot-Bouille*' (the clinical description in Zola's *Pot-Bouille*).[104]

6. Emilia Pardo Bazán: her works

Emilia Pardo Bazán devoted most of her life to writing and, in a literary career which spanned more than forty years, she published volumes of

---

99   *Ibid.*
100 'Coletilla a *La cuestión palpitante*', *Obras completas, Tomo III*, p. 654.
101 *Ibid.*
102 Emilia Pardo Bazán, *La Tribuna* (Madrid: Taurus, 1981), p. 14.
103 *Epistolario*, vol VII, p. 271.
104 'Coletilla a *La cuestión palpitante*', p. 654.

poetry, plays, nineteen novels, twenty or so novellas and over five hundred short stories.[105] In addition, she was the author of books on subjects as diverse as travel, Spanish cookery[106] and St Francis of Assisi, as well as numerous volumes of literary essays, social commentaries, criticism, articles and reviews. In the late 1870s, she wrote a column called 'La ciencia amena' (popular science) for the *Revista compostelana*, contributing articles on heat, light, electricity, energy and other topics in physics. She had regular columns in other periodicals and edited several books for women under the heading *Biblioteca de la mujer*. Finally, from 1891 to 1893 she published a single-authored periodical called *Nuevo Teatro Crítico*, a title borrowed from the Enlightenment thinker Benito Feijóo's *El Teatro Crítico Universal*. Each edition contained a short story besides essays on topics of the day, ranging from fashion to submarines. However, in spite of this vast output, her work is comparatively little known, especially beyond the Iberian Peninsula.

Her literary vocation began at the age of nine when she threw 'ingenuas quintillas' (naive five-line stanzas) from the balcony of her house to the troops returning from the Spanish-Moroccan War.[107] When she was sixteen she published poems in *Almanaque de Galicia*, but her first serious publication was a critical monograph on the work of the eighteenth-century Benedictine monk Benito Jerónimo Feijóo, which won first prize in a literary contest. She admired him for his feminist ideas, epitomised by the conviction he expresses in his 'Defensa de las mujeres' that 'no es menos hábil el entendimiento de las mujeres, que el de los hombres, aun para las ciencias más difíciles' (women's understanding isn't less adept than that of men, even for the most difficult of sciences).[108] In the same essay he points out that, if we subscribe to the line of thought that the traditional role attributed to Eve

---

105   Acording to Juan Paredes Núñez, in *Los cuentos de Emilia Pardo Bazán* (Granada: Universidad de Granada, 1979), she wrote a total of 580 stories.

106   Pilar Faus attributes Pardo Bazán's corpulence in later life to her love of food and interest in gastronomy. Between 1905 and 1915 she published a series of articles about food, issues of cooking, and cuisine, as well as two cookbooks *La cocina española antigua* (1913) and *La cocina española moderna* (1914).

107   Carmen Bravo-Villasante, *Vida y Obra de Emilia Pardo Bazán*, p. 20:
    'Todo el mundo sabe que al regresar las tropas vencedoras de la guerra de Africa, al mando del conde de Lucena, y al desfilar por las calles de la Coruña, Emilia, en pleno ardor patriótico tira papeles con versos desde el balcón donde presencia el desfile.' (Everyone knows that when the victorious troops, led by the Count of Lucena, returned from the Spanish-Moroccan War and passed through the streets of La Coruña, Emilia, full of patriotic ardour, threw sheets of paper with verses on them from the balcony where she was present at the parade).

108   http://www.filosofia.org/bjf/bjft116.htm.

makes women worse than men, then by the same logic angels must be worse than women because 'como Adán fue inducido a pecar por una mujer, la mujer fue inducida por un Ángel' (just as Adam was induced to commit sin by a woman, that woman was induced by an angel).[109]

At the age of twenty-five she gave birth to her first child, Jaime, and published a collection of poetry inspired by her son. She wrote a semi-autobiographical novel of a medical student, *Pascual López, Autobiografía de un estudiante de medecina* in 1879, a biography of St. Francis and various literary essays. As Pardo Bazán's initial concept of the novel was that of a trivial form – 'libro de puro entretenimiento' (a book of pure entertainment)[110] – and a genre beyond the domain of her aspirations 'por requerer inventiva maravillosa' (because it required marvellous inventiveness),[111] she preferred to concentrate more on academic projects such as a refutation of Darwin's theories. However, the experimental method applied to literature appealed to her as a way of eradicating the subjectivism, idealism, sentimentalism and fantasy that had prevailed in the pre-Realist novel.[112] This, along with her discovery of certain key contemporary novelists brought about a change in her great desire.[113] Between 1879 and 1889 she published eight novels, two shorter works of fiction and a handful of short stories. Most of her early fiction is set in her native Galicia, a fact which has often caused her to be regarded as a regional novelist, but these works explore many ideas which transcend regional preoccupations. Especially prominent is the theme of ambition and aspirations developed against a background of tension or friction generated by the attitudes of one social class or group towards another. Other salient themes include the role of the female in contemporary Spanish society and political developments in Spain from the late 1860s to the mid-1880s.

Whilst Pardo Bazán uses a first-person narrator in her first novel, *Pascual*

---

109 *Ibid.*
110 *Apuntes autobiográficos*, p. 711.
111 *Ibid.*, p. 706.
112 'Prefacio a *Un viaje de novios*', p. 58:
    '…la novela ha dejado de ser obra de mero entretenimiento, modo de engañar gratamente unas cuantas horas, ascendiendo a estudio social, psicológico, histórico, pero al cabo estudio (…the novel has ceased being a work of mere entertainment, a way of pleasantly killing a few hours, elevated to a social, psychological and historical study, but at the end of the day a study).
113 In a letter from August 2, 1885, she wrote:
    'Sólo empecé a pensar en novelar después de leer a Flaubert, Pereda, Galdós y Valera' (I only thought about writing novels after reading Flaubert, Pereda, Galdós and Valera). *Epistolario*, vol. VII, pp. 271–72.

López, the rest of her early novels, excluding *Bucólica* and *Insolación*, resort to third-person narrators. However, in spite of this difference in perspective, many of these novels explore a common theme: that of a woman who, either against her better judgement or with Quixotic idealism, gives everything up for a man who is not worthy of her. In *El cisne de Villamorta*, Leocadia Otera is driven to suicide, having acquired a crippling debt and sacrificed her son and home for Segundo García, a mediocre poet who loves another woman. In *Los pazos de Ulloa*, the gentle Nucha is the victim of an abusive, socially-imposed marriage to her idle, cruel cousin Pedro Moscoso. Manuela, her daughter in the sequel *La madre naturaleza*, is incapable of resolving the dilemma of her love for Perucho, her illegitimate half-brother, and finally seeks refuge in a convent. Francisca de Asís Taboada, a 32-year-old widow of noble status in *Insolación*, falls in love with Diego Pacheco, a lazy, quarrelsome womaniser whom her friend Gabriel Pardo describes as 'célula ociosa en el organismo social' (an idle cell in the social body) and whom Clarín dismisses as 'un imbécil de Sevilla' (an imbecile from Seville).[114] Unable to banish him from her mind, she allows him to sleep with her and ends up marrying him, fully cognizant of the reality of the situation. Like Don Quijote, who explains in chapter 25 of Cervantes's novel that Dulcinea de Toboso is as much an invention as the ladies praised by most poets, and 'hermosa y honesta' (lovely and virtuous) because that is how he wishes her to be, Asís knows that what she sees in Diego Pacheco's dashing appearance is 'algo sublime, que realmente no existía' (something sublime, which did not actually exist).[115]

Esclavitud, the protagonist of *Morriña*, is a particularly tragic figure. The name not only encapsulates Pardo Bazán's view of female servitude (her translation of John Stuart Mill's *The Subjection of Women* is entitled *La esclavitud femenina*) but also suggests, as we read the novel, that the working-class girl is a slave to forces beyond her control. Telling herself 'estarás eternamente en pecado mortal' (you will eternally be in mortal sin) because she is a priest's illegitimate daughter, and suffering from *morriña* (homesickness) for her native Galicia, she goes to work as a maid for Doña Aurora in Madrid. She falls in love with her employer's son, Rogelio, but, despite the innocence of their relationship, one of Aurora's acquaintances

---

114   *Insolación* (Madrid: Espasa, 2002), p. 166.

Leopoldo Alas, *Emilia Pardo Bazán y sus últimas obras*, *Folletos literarios VII*, *Obras completas IV Crítica (Segunda parte)* (Oviedo: Nobel, 2003), p. 1469.

115   *Insolación*, p. 168.

implies that something is going on between the young couple. Aurora decides to find Esclavitud a job elsewhere and take her son to Galicia for the summer, but, the night before they leave, Rogelio seduces Esclavitud. Like her mother before her, she has become a fallen woman and, realising that her lowly status and shameful origins stand in the the way of her Quixotic dream of being united with Rogelio, she sees suicide as her only option. All of these stories, as we shall see, have certain similarities with the main storyline in Pardo Bazán's third novel.

7. *La Tribuna*

The plot of *La Tribuna* is straightforward. Amparo, the daughter of a bed-ridden ex-*cigarrera*, gets work in the tobacco factory, and her father, who made and sold *barquillos*, dies. Her ability to read out loud the political news makes her a leader at the factory, and her enthusiasm for the republic inspires her to speak at political meetings. At the same time she is admired by two men: Chinto, a rustic lad who has taken on her father's duties, and a middle-class army captain, Baltasar Sobrado. She rejects the former and is seduced and abandoned by the latter. As the novel ends Amparo gives birth to a son and, crying out for justice for the common people, she hears shouts announcing the arrival of a federal republic which, in theory, will bring justice to all.

It is worth reiterating that *La Tribuna*, appearing two or three years after translations of *L'assommoir*, *Nana*, *Une page d'amour* and various editions of *Thérèse Raquin* had burst onto the Spanish literary scene, was published in 1883 more or less simultaneously with *La cuestión palpitante*.[116] Firstly, it underlines the extent to which these two key works in her *œuvre* are different sides of the same coin, a twin response to Naturalism, one intellectual and the other creative. Although *La cuestión palpitante* was critical of what she saw as a perspective which highlighted the negative traits of human character, she implemented many Naturalistic practices in *La Tribuna*, partly because she admired Zola but also as a way of establishing herself in a literary scene dominated by men who would tend to regard a young woman with artistic designs as an amateur or dilettante.

---

116   Pilar Faus, *Emilia Pardo Bazán. Su época, su vida, su obra*, p. 199:
'Aunque la novela se publicó después de *La cuestión palpitante*, a juzgar por la fecha del prólogo ya estaba escrita cuando se inicia la aparición del estudio en las páginas de *La Época*' (Although the novel was published after *La cuestión palpitante*, judging from the date of the prologue it was already written when the study began to appear in the pages of *La Época*).

Secondly, the fact that the articles which later became *La cuestión palpitante* were published in *La Época* shows how conscious the author was of the power of newspapers to reach out to the public, a theme she develops in *La Tribuna* with the education and politicisation of the *cigarreras* in general, and Amparo in particular, via the revolutionary press. In the ninth chapter of *La Tribuna*, Pardo Bazán explains that the factory was sympathetic to the federalist cause and that the republican horizon was opened up to the cigar makers by means of oral propaganda, but mainly by 'los periódicos que pululaban' (the newspapers that were proliferating) in the various workshops.[117] It doesn't take long for the factory bosses, realising the subversive nature of these newspapers read out loud with great passion by Amparo, to ban them.

We should not overlook the fact that *La Tribuna* is a novel written by a woman about a woman. In spite of the vast social and economic gulf between the author and her protagonist, there are also certain noteworthy similarities. They were both born in the early 1850s and in *Apuntes autobiográficos* reference is made to three events, following in quick succession, which symbolise Emilia's initiation into adulthood: 'me vestí de largo, me casé y estalló la revolución de septiembre' (I put on a long skirt, got married and the Revolution of 1868 broke out).[118] These three events are equally significant in Amparo's adolescence: she reaches 'la edad en que invenciblemente desea agradar la mujer' (the age in which a woman invincibly desires to please), she dreams of getting married to Baltasar, and the 'Gloriosa' is the catalyst for her baptism into political matters. They are also united in their connection to tobacco: whilst Amparo rolls cigars for other people to appreciate, Emilia was quite open about her enjoyment of smoking. Finally, although there is a huge difference in their background and cultural knowledge, they share common interests in newspapers and the theatre, what were probably at the time the two most effective means of divulging ideas and swaying opinion. *La Tribuna* underlines the key role played in the *cigarreras*' ideological

---

117   During the 'sexenio revolucionario' (the revolutionary period of six years following the Gloriosa), partly as a result of the provisional government's Decreto de Libertad de Imprenta of October 23, 1868, there was a huge increase in the number of newspaper publications. In Galicia alone 118 new newspapers appeared between the constitution of the provisional government and the arrival of Amadeo. In Chapter 10 of *La Tribuna* the narrator mentions *El Vigilante Federal*, *El Representante de la Juventud Democrática* and *El Faro Salvador del Pueblo Libre*. Although none these publications appear in Enrique Santos Gayoso's *Historia de la prensa gallega 1800–1986* (Coruña: Ediciós do Castro, 1990), there is ample evidence of many newspapers with similar titles.

118   *Obras completas, Tomo III*, p. 706.

evolution by revolutionary newspapers actively promoting the arrival of a federal republic. Equally, the penultimate chapter of the novel shows, by means of the performance of a play which Amparo attends, the emotional power of a medium which does not require a literate public.

It is worth considering this particular episode because the theatre plays a vital role in at least two other great novels of the period. In *Madame Bovary*, the dissatisfied eponymous heroine attends a provincial performance of the opera *Lucia di Lammermoor*, and Ana Ozores, the female protagonist of *La Regenta*, goes to see the play *Don Juan Tenorio*. Although the première of Francisco Palanca y Roca's *¡Valencianos con honra!* was a great success in Valencia on January 8, 1870, this three-act play dedicated 'A la honradez del Gran Partido Republicano' (to the honour of the Great Republican Party) differs from Donizetti's opera or Zorilla's play because it is a minor work, and Pardo Bazán's acquaintance with it was probably only as a result of her busy social life at this time: 'todas las noches, a teatros o saraos' (every night, to theatres or *soirées*).[119] The similarity lies more in the fact that in all three novels the spectacle functions as a *mise en abîme*[120] with each heroine relating to a character, theme or concept that duplicates or illuminates her particular predicament. Ana Ozores, feeling herself transported to the times of Don Juan, compares herself with 'la hija del Comendador' (the novice), and the adulterous Emma Bovary, giving herself up to the flow of Donizetti's melodies, constructs an elaborate fantasy in which, like Lucia, she flees away from life, locked in a passionate embrace. Amparo identifies with the republican and revolutionary ideology, but in the same way that her involvement with Baltasar diverts her attention from political matters, the presence of her rival, Josefina García, in the theatre temporarily distracts her from the play. However, although she is angry and momentarily regrets not having posted the anonymous letter, the honourable conduct of the protagonists of Francisco Palanca y Roca's play reflects Amparo's refusal to commit such an ignoble deed.

Several nineteenth-century novels like *La Regenta*, *La aldea perdida* and *El Intruso* deal with certain aspects of proletarian life in Spain, but they were

---

119 *Ibid.*
120 André Gide, *Journal 1889–1939 Tome I* (Gallimard, Bibliothèque de la Pléiade), p. 41: 'J'aime assez qu'en une œuvre d'art on retrouve ainsi transposé, à l'échelle des personnages, le sujet même de cette œuvre. Rien ne l'éclaire mieux et n'établit plus sûrement toutes les proportions de l'ensemble.' (In a work of art, I rather like to find thus transposed, at the level of the characters, the subject of the work itself. Nothing sheds more light on the work or displays the proportions of the whole work more accurately).

published after *La Tribuna* and the main themes and protagonists are not predominantly working-class. *La desheredada* examines the slums of Madrid and preceded *La Tribuna*, but Pardo Bazán's third novel is 'la primera novela española de protagonismo obrero' (the first Spanish novel of working-class prominence),[121] the first to look in depth at females working in a factory. In Spain the incorporation of women into the industrial workforce was behind other developed western nations, but in the textile and tobacco industries female presence was felt as early as the eighteenth century. In 1755 a new tobacco factory was opened in Seville and it proved so profitable that factories appeared throughout the Spanish peninsula, including La Coruña. Initially, when the production was predominantly 'el tobaco de rapé' (snuff), most of the workers were men because the job was very physically demanding. However, sales of snuff were in decline towards the end of the eighteenth century whilst those of 'el tobaco de humo' (smoking tobacco or cigars) increased. The fact that cigar production required dexterity rather than strength, combined with the notorious lack of discipline amongst male workers, led to women, who carried out the same work more skilfully and for less pay, achieving a virtual monopoly of jobs in tobacco factories. This phenomenon lent them a status which gave rise to a sense of solidarity Pardo Bazán is keen to explore in *La Tribuna*. In contrast with the self-seeking malice exhibited by most of the co-workers and companions in Zola's novels, Pardo Bazán's *cigarreras*, even though their political differences are illustrated by the fact that the women from rural areas were sceptical and less federalistic, are united in their opposition to conscription and demonstrate a sense of community spirit and mutual co-operation, which is present in the poor Marinedan neighbourhoods, but lacking in the individualism of the bourgeois society epitomised by the Sobrados.

Set in a tobacco factory in La Coruña in the revolutionary years prior to the birth of the First Republic in 1873, a possible real life model for Amparo has been detected: 'una cigarrera conocida como «La Republicana» por su entusiasta defensa de tal ideología' (a cigar maker known as 'The Republican' on account of her enthusiastic defence of this ideology).[122] For

121 *La Tribuna*, ed Benito Varela Jácome (Madrid: Cátedra, 1991), p. 48.

Cf. Asunción Doménech Montagut, *Medecina y enfermedad en las novelas de Pardo Bazán* (Valencia: Centro Francisco Tomás y Valiente, 2000), p. 39:

'*La Tribuna* es la única entre las novelas de Pardo Bazán donde el protagonismo corresponde exclusivamente al mundo obrero' (*La Tribuna* is the only one of Pardo Bazán's novels where the leading roles are exclusively from the world of work).

122   J.M. González Herrán, '*La Tribuna* de E Pardo Bazán y un posible modelo real de su

the setting, Pardo Bazán used two main methods to prepare the material: as well as reading and consulting contemporary pamphlets and newspapers like *El Anunciador* and *El Diario de la Unión Republicana de la Coruña y de Galicia*, she employed 'un sistema muy poco usual entonces en España' (a system not at all customary then in Spain)[123] but common in English writers like Dickens and already frequently adopted in France by the masters of Realism,[124] which enabled her, 'cunha precisión de detalles que se lles escaparon a tan finos observadores da realidade como o cónsul francés Leclercq ou o mesmo Pascual Madoz' (with a precision of details that escaped such fine observers of reality like the French consul Leclerq or even Pascual Madoz),[125] to describe the tobacco factory:

Dos meses concurrí a la Fábrica mañana y tarde, oyendo conversaciones, delineando tipos, cazando al vuelo frases y modos de sentir. Me procuré periódicos locales de la época federal (que ya escaseaban); evoqué recuerdos, describí La Coruña según era en mi niñez...

(During two months I went to the factory morning and afternoon, listening to conversations, sketching types, catching on the fly phrases and attitudes. I got local newspapers of the federal period (which were already scarce); I evoked memories, I described La Coruña as it was in my childhood...)[126]

---

protagonista', *Ínsula*, 1975, núm 346, p. 6.

In his 'Recuerdos personales de doña Emilia' Miguel de Unamuno remembers the long after-dinner talks during which Pardo Bazán talked about her practice of modelling characters on real people she knew. This aspect of her approach to fiction is confirmed in a letter she sent to Oller in January 1884:

'Borrén es en efecto un tipo raro; yo, sin embargo, le conocí y le conozco; no es oficial, es un hombre inteligente, de buena facha y aficionadísimo a andar entre faldas [...] He desfigurado el tipo en algunos rasgos para que no se conozca...' (Borrén is indeed a strange guy; however, I met him and I know him; he's not an officer, he's an intelligent man, good looking and very fond of ladies [...] I've disguised some of his characteristics so that he won't be recognised...) N. Oller, *Memòries literàries* (Barcelona, 1962), p. 70.

123 'Intimidades madrileñas, una visita a Doña Emilia Pardo Bazán', *Madrid Cómico*, April 23, 1898, no. 792, p. 318.

124 *La cuestión palpitante*, p. 590: 'Dickens [...] se paseaba por las calles de Londres días enteros anotando en su cartera lo que oía, lo que veía, las menudencias y trivialidades de la vida cotidiana' (Dickens [...] walked around the streets of London for whole days noting down in his diary what he heard and saw, the minutiae and trivia of everyday life).

'Intimidades madrileñas, una visita a Doña Emilia Pardo Bazán', *Madrid Cómico*, April 23, 1898, no. 792, p. 318: '...ya en Francia adoptado con frecuencia por los maestros del realismo'.

125 Alonso Álvarez, Luis, 'A Palloza que viu dona Emilia', *As tecedeiras do fume. Historia da Fábrica de Tabacos da Coruña* (Vigo: A Nosa Terra, 1990), p. 85.

126 *Apuntes autobiográficos*, p. 725. She was justifiably proud of her investigations. In

Pardo Bazán seems to have an ambivalent attitude towards her protagonist. On the one hand, she represents the hopes and frustrations of a working girl who believes not only that the Revolution of 1868 will usher in times of equality, but also that she can make a substantial contribution to the building of a better society. In this respect, she is portrayed by the feminist author as incarnating the qualities extolled in the Prologue as being abundant among her people: warmth of heart, lively generosity, inexhaustible and ready charitableness, sincere piety and righteous judgement.

Nevertheless, her aspirations and motives are consistently punctured by the sceptical, politically conservative author.[127] Although the narrator's compassion in her depiction of working-class conditions is apparent in the notion that it is perfectly normal for Amparo to want a more exciting life, the protagonist's limited understanding of the political events taking place is exposed, especially in her conversation with Carmela the lace-maker in Chapter 16. At the same time, and shown to be equally misguided, is Amparo's conviction, even in the face of Baltasar's reluctance to be seen in public with her, that traditional class boundaries are a thing of the past, that 'se acabaron esas tiranías' (that old tyranny is over). In much the same way that her earlier claim to be able to write quite well is ultimately contradicted by the anonymous, error-strewn epistle she goes on to compose with *the Weasel*, the ingenuousness of her assertion that education makes all social classes equal is underlined, and her own credibility undermined, by the lower-class speech pattern she employs: 'la istrucción iguala las clases'. She backs up her faith in this newfangled equality, when warned by her peers about her liaison, with an apocryphal story which, set against the widespread hostility surrounding his arrival in January 1871, paints Amadeo in a good light by illustrating his common touch:

> ...ese rey que trajeron dice que da la mano a todo el mundo, y la mujer abrazó
> en Madrid a una lavandera;

a letter to Galdós she states that she would consider the two months in the tobacco factory inhaling nicotine well spent even if all it had brought was his three sheets (i.e. letter of praise):

'Aunque mi *Tribuna* no me hubiese reportado sino el placer de recibir sus tres pliegos de usted, daría yo por muy bien empleado los dos meses que pasé en la fábrica de tabacos respirando nicotina...' (Quoted in Pilar Faus, *Emilia Pardo Bazán su época. Su vida, su obra*, p. 207).

127   Emilia Pardo Bazán (28/06/14) 'Cartas de la Condesa', *Diario de la Marina*, Pardo Bazán, 2003, p. 265: 'Yo soy, en materias políticas, una espectadora que lleva en las venas dosis de escepticismo...' (I am, in political matters, a spectator who carries a dose of scepticism in her veins).

(that king they brought in, they say he shakes hands with everybody, and his wife embraced a washerwoman in Madrid…)

When Amparo becomes involved with Baltasar, her concern for working conditions at the factory and wider political matters is supplanted by self-centred interests: a preoccupation with personal appearance; the two-fold vanity of enticing others to envy her for the largesse she doesn't actually receive and wanting Baltasar not to consider her mercenary; and a desire to better herself by becoming 'señora de Sobrado'. Primo Cova's words to the narrator in *Memorias de un solterón* (1894) pinpoint the lack of true conviction we feel about Amparo's commitment to change:

¿Ve V. los socialistas, los anarquistas, los dinamiteros? Deles V. ropa decentita y guantes ingleses … y verá qué pronto cuelgan las armas.

(Do you see the socialists, anarchists, dynamiters? Give them decent clothes and English gloves … and you'll see how quickly they hang up their weapons.)[128]

Indeed, in *Memorias de un solterón* when Amparo does finally become Baltasar's wife, her son exchanges his socialist ideals for 'corbatas de seda y guantes de piel británica' (silk ties and gloves made of English leather).[129]

The shallowness of Amparo's republicanism is echoed in her love life. It is never suggested that either she or her suitor has very deep feelings towards the other:

'Baltasar y Amparo se hallaron como dos cuerpos unidos un instante por la afinidad amorosa, separados después por repulsiones invencibles'

(Baltasar and Amparo were like two bodies joined together for an instant by some amorous affinity, separated afterwards by invincible repulsions).

Baltasar has only one goal and Amparo appears to allow herself to be seduced as a way of hammering down the nail with which she imagines she will secure him for all time. If the brief union that culminates in her surrendering her virginity represents the disappearance of class divisions, her subsequent pregnancy – the condition of being more than one person – reflects the duality of the 'two Spains', and her abandonment is the price she pays for transforming her belief in egalitarianism into the pursuit of social advancement through marriage into the bourgeoisie. Born on the same day that news of the declaration of the First Republic reaches Marineda, her

---

128 Emilia Pardo Bazán, *Memorias de un solterón, Obras completas, Tomo II*, p. 600.
129 *Ibid.*, p. 599.

bastard son symbolises Pardo Bazán's view of the lineage and legitimacy that emerged from the Revolution of 1868, as well as the reality, rather than what Pardo Bazán referred to as 'vacías idealizaciones' (empty idealisation), that will finally disabuse Amparo of her false hopes and provide her with a more indispensable role than that of 'la Tribuna del pueblo', even if it is the very one her duplicitous nemesis proclaims is what women were made for.

Another way Pardo Bazán debunks Amparo is by revealing the underlying streak of insincerity and arrogance in her character. Baltasar's ulterior motives strike the reader as being no more morally reprehensible than the probable rationale for the working girl's capitulation. If it is hinted, as she imagines herself with Baltasar sharing a house like the one the Sobrado family had, that her grandiose principles might not extend to inviting round her erstwhile friends, her unmitigated aversion towards Chinto is indicative of an egalitarian who only desires equality with her superiors:

> Enfadábale todo en él: la necia abertura de su boca, la pequeñez de sus ojos, lo sinuoso y desgarbado de su andar, su glotona manera de comer el caldo.

> (Everything about him made her angry: the stupid way he opened his mouth, the smallness of his eyes, his tortuous, ungainly gait and the gluttonous manner with which he ate his broth.)

This hypocrisy is accentuated by the similarity between her attitude and the uncharitable comments Josefina García, who lacks the natural beauty of Amparo's big eyes and thick eyelashes, makes about lower-class women: 'esas mujeres ordinarias me parecen todas iguales, cortadas por el mismo patrón' (those common women look the same to me, all cut from the same pattern). Amparo's antipathy also spotlights the extent to which Chinto and Baltasar are as much polar opposites as the two characters from *The Tempest*, Caliban and Ariel, mentioned in the prologue. Whilst Baltasar is a false-hearted, smooth-tongued, unfaithful egotist whose principal characteristic is hedonism – 'la ley y norte de su vida era el placer, siempre que no riñese con el bienestar' (the law and aim of his life was pleasure, as long as it didn't conflict with his well-being) – Amparo fails to see beyond his presentable appearance and good prospects. Chinto, on the other hand, is a kind-hearted, hard-working peasant whose selfless faithfulness (he is even willing to bring up Baltasar's son as his own) is so imperceptible to Amparo beneath his uncouth dialect and coarse exterior that, in common with everyone except Carmela, she deals with him in an inhumane, un-Christian way.

Chinto is treated like a packhorse and portrayed as a subhuman brute with

bovine strength who sweats like a bull. Amparo refers to him as 'aquel animal' (that animal) or 'un mulo' (a mule), throws him the mixed-up leftovers on a plate 'como para un perro' (as if for a dog), bumps into him at the factory gates, 'triste como can apaleado por su amo' (as sad as a dog that had been beaten by its master), and considers him her social inferior – 'como generosa yegua de pura sangre a la cual pretendiesen enganchar haciendo tronco con un individuo de la raza asinina' (like a noble, thoroughbred mare, which they try to harness to a member of the donkey tribe in order to make a team) – in the same way the urban tobacco-factory workers look down on their rural counterparts:

> Alguna duquesa confinada en oscuro pueblo, después de adornar los saraos de la corte, debe de sentir por los señoritos del poblachón lo que la pitillera por Chinto.
>
> (Any duchess, confined to an obscure little town after she'd graced the court *soirées*, must feel for the rich kids of this one-horse town what the cigar maker felt for Chinto.)

La Tribuna is the first of Pardo Bazán's novels to give due consideration to the question of the influence of the physical environment on individual behaviour. Amparo's affection for the streets, the city and its people is presented in the early chapters of the novel as the expression of her desire to escape, with the speed of a bird, the 'cage' of overwhelming poverty of her milieu. Her fortuitous arrival, with her carol-singing friends, at the wealthy Sobrado family home brings together two distinct levels of society, and Baltasar's suggestion that Enrique Borrén recommend Amparo for a job at the factory initiates the sequence of events which constitutes much of the dramatic and thematic development of the novel.

When she begins to work in the tobacco factory she misses the freedom and excitement of the streets, and feels oppressed by the restrictions and conditions of the workplace. Yet she soon adjusts and exchanges her individual freedom for 'ese orgullo y apego inexplicables que infunde la colectividad y la asociación: la fraternidad del trabajo' (that inexplicable pride and attachment which community and association instil: the brotherhood of labour). With the advent of the Revolution of 1868, the author shows how impressionable and vulnerable Amparo is. The choice of the word 'antiliteraria' to describe the press Amparo devours is of interest, especially in tandem with the fact that she believes every word with a 'fe virgen' (virgin faith), making up in 'crédulo asentimiento' (gullible consent) for what the

newspapers lacked in sincerity. It intimates that a female who consumes literature uncritically, be it newspapers or the fiction Baltasar brings along, also lacks the skills to 'read' real life.

In Cervantes's masterpiece, which he himself describes on several occasions as 'una invectiva contra los libros de caballerías' (an invective against books of chivalry), Alonso Quijano fills his head with impossible nonsense from all the chivalric romances he reads and, watched disapprovingly by his friend the barber, loses his mind and transmutes into the knight errant Don Quijote. Likewise, Amparo, a street child permeated 'hasta los tuétanos' (down to the marrow) by the progressive newspapers she reads to the barber and the transcendental, enraged articles she reads out loud in the factory in Chapter 9, metamorphosises first of all into the persuasive speech-maker *la Tribuna*, and subsequently the agitator whose first exploit is to incite her companions, who have already shunned *la Píntiga* because of her rumoured conversion, to lash out against the Protestants they run into. The incident is memorable because the missionaries are vilified as tricksters like the Benedictine monks whom Don Quijote demonises as enchanters and at whom he charges with his lance lowered. The vehemence of Amparo and her colleagues' response, which is similar to an episode in *La Regenta* when some women from the working-class district try to stone to death a Protestant pastor, spells out their reaction to the granting of religious toleration in the Constitution of 1869.

Don Quijote dreams of 'deshaciendo todo género de agravio' (undoing all kind of wrong).[130] Similarly, Amparo's febrile imagination, in the midst of all the banality and dullness of her daily life and the monotony of her work, fabricates dangers, struggles and dark plots conspired to stifle liberty – 'el Gobierno de Madrid sabía ya a tal hora que una heroica pitillera marinedina realizaba inauditos esfuerzos para apresurar el triunfo de la federal' (the government in Madrid already knew that at such-and-such a time a heroic cigar maker from Marineda was making exhaustive efforts to hasten the triumph of the federalistic cause) – and imagines her portrait appearing next to that of Mariana Pineda, among the pictures representing the martyrs to Liberty. While Don Quijote dies in bed, having recovered his sanity, Amparo gives birth to a new life in bed, fully cognizant of her maternal duties.

Despite what is said in *Apuntes autobiográficas*, heredity and physical environment are not really presented as decisive influences on Amparo's behaviour. The sedentary work, foul atmosphere and poor diet which ensure

---

130 Miguel de Cervantes, *Don Quijote de la Mancha*, *volumen 1*, edición de Juan Alcina Franch (Barcelona: Brugera, 1979), p. 110.

that anaemia and chlorosis are rife in the factory do not impact on her health and, whilst she has inherited her father's good looks and ruddy complexion, she is a demagogue who has none of his unyielding laconism, the principal voice of the federal republican cause who does not share his resignation or conviction of the idleness of words. Although Pardo Bazán puts into practice a number of tenets of Naturalism, the novel is certainly not an affirmation of what George Becker described as 'pessimistic materialistic determinism'.[131] Far from subscribing to a deterministic interpretation of man's actions, she shares Saint Augustine's view of our ability to redeem ourselves by fighting immoral instincts with reason: 'aun bajo el influjo de pasiones fuertes – ira, celos, amor –, la voluntad puede acudir en nuestro auxilio' (even under the influence of strong passions – anger, jealousy, love – will-power can come to our aid).[132] Nevertheless, she readily acknowledges that her orthodox Catholic view is tempered with a mixed conception of human will, something she credits with opening up vast horizons in literature:

> Si en principio se admite la libertad, hay que suponerla relativa, e incesantemente contrastada y limitada por todos los obstáculos que en el mundo encuentra.
>
> (If in principle we accept freedom, we have to think of it as relative, and incessantly checked and limited by all the obstacles that it encounters in the world.)[133]

These obstacles include our educational and spiritual formation. And with females, they are often the product of deficiencies in upbringing and education, exploited by and the victims of males.

Pardo Bazán's 1880 article 'Estudios de literatura contemporánea: Pérez Galdós' gives psychology equal status with the description of the external world. However, in *La cuestión palpitante*, which began to appear in *La Época* just after *La Tribuna* was completed in October 1882, she singles out psychology as the most rewarding territory for the novelist to explore.[134] Unfortunately, this priority is not always evident in her work, especially her early novels, where the emphasis often seems to be more on outer style and

---

131 *Documents of Modern Literary Realism* (Princeton: Princeton University Press, 1963), p. 35.
132 *La cuestión palpitante*, p. 579.
133 *Ibid.*
134 '…de todos los territorios que puede explorar el novelista realista y reflexivo, el más rico, el más variado e interesante es sin duda el psicológico' (…of all the areas which the thoughtful realist novelist can explore, the richest, the most varied and interesting is undoubtedly the psychological one). *Ibid.*, p. 645.

literary form rather than inner substance.[135] *La Tribuna* undoubtedly builds up a vivid picture of the living and working conditions of lower-class Marineda. However, it is essentially a series of episodes and descriptions which neither develop nor explore Pardo Bazán's claims that the manufacturing environment, the nervous tension, blood deficiencies and unhealthy urban surroundings 'crean una mujer nueva, mucho más complicada y más desdichada, por siguiente, que la campesina' (are creating a new woman, much more complicated and therefore unhappier than the countrywoman).[136]

Amparo does not strike the reader as being a complicated woman and her attitudes and inner feelings are never probed in any depth. Not only is her seduction glossed over – perhaps the only place in the novel where the author does not state clearly what is happening – but also the reasons for it are never scrutinised beyond Amparo's desire for social advancement. Leopoldo Alas, a former supporter of Pardo Bazán's ideas who turned into one of her most relentless critics,[137] is complimentary in his article '*La Tribuna* novela original de Doña Emilia Pardo Bazán' and advises her to persevere with the same style. He does, however, reproduce various negative viewpoints of the novel, comparing the abundance of physical details about the protagonist with the absence of psychological analysis: 'lo principal en este libro no son las personas por dentro, sino su apariencia y las cosas que las rodean' (the main thing in this book isn't people's inner being, but their appearance and the things which surround them).[138] Another comment is to the effect that there is no psychology in the novel 'amén de una escena de celos mezclados de orgullo, y de varios arranques patrióticos, que no se puede asegurar que sean

---

135   See Leopoldo Alas, *Nueva campaña (1885–86)* (Madrid: E. Rubiños, 1887), p. 225: 'Mira con cierto desdén *los intereses del alma*, prefiriendo siempre la luz de fuera, las formas plásticas, y en el ineludible *argumento*, someras relaciones sociales, y, cuando más, estudios de caracteres sencillos y aun vulgares' (She looks with a certain disdain at *matters of the soul*, always prefering the light from outside, plastic forms, and in the inescapable *storyline*, shallow social relations, and, at most, simple and even vulgar character studies).
136   *Apuntes autobiográficos*, p. 726.
137   In a letter to D. Emilio Ferrari on July 26, 1901, shortly after Clarín's death, Pardo Bazán wrote: '…yo pasé cuatro o seis años de mi vida sin que un solo instante dejasen de resonar en mis oídos los ladridos furiosos del can.' (…I spent four or six years of my life where the sound of the furious barking of the dog didn't stop resonating in my ears for a single moment). José María Martínez Cachero, 'La Condesa de Pardo Bazán escribe a su tocayo, el poeta Ferrari (ocho cartas inéditas de doña Emilia)'. http://www.cervantesvirtual.com/obra-visor-din/la-condesa-de-pardo-bazn-escribe-a-su-tocayo-el-poeta-ferrari-ocho-cartas-inditas-de-doa-emilia-0/html/ffc09cb0-82b1-11df-acc7-002185ce6064_1.html#I_1_
138   *Sermón perdido, Obras completas IV* (Madrid: Ediciones Nobel, 2003), p. 543.

cosa del alma' (except for a scene of jealousy mixed with pride, and various patriotic outbursts, which it cannot be sure are things from the heart).[139]

Most of the characters in the novel are flat and lacking psychological penetration. Amparo's inner being is largely unexplored territory and on the few occasions when we are privy to her thoughts, it is via the third-person narrator. Although Baltasar is aware of the military threat of Carlism and echoes the author's outrage when he condemns 'esos salvajes que quieren entrar en burro en las iglesias y fusilan por chiste las imágenes' (those savages who want to ride their donkeys into church and shoot at the holy images for fun), he is little more than a *nouveau riche*, moustachioed seducer like Alex D'Urberville in Thomas Hardy's *Tess of the d'Urbervilles* (another novel where the seduction is glossed over). In fact, there seems to have been no attempt on the author's part to make the Garcías and the Sobrados, with the possible exception of Lola, anything other than a collective stereotype of the smug, materialistic and unsympathetic bourgeoisie.

However, some of the secondary characters like *la Guardiana* and *the Weasel* are more compelling. Chinto is a stereotypical yokel, but his character is developed in a number of interesting ways. In Chapter 7 we learn that, although he took a long time to acclimatise to his new environment, watching a knifegrinder at work and contemplating the sea helped to appease his homesickness. Pointing out that the sea and the turning of a wheel are appropriate images of the infinite, the author, who admired Flaubert's 'impassibilité' (impersonality) but does not adhere to his principle that the artist should be invisible like God,[140] cannot resist intervening with the aside that Chinto didn't know anything about metaphysics. His taste for 'una chiquita' (a little glass of wine) has nothing in common with the alcoholism, determined by heredity and poor living conditions, we encounter in *L'assommoir*. In fact, Pardo Bazán presents Chinto's penchant for wine in a much more light-hearted and comical way, something which helps him to endure the harsh conditions of his working life, and she uses it to highlight the hypocritical attitude towards drinking displayed by Amparo's mother.

The fact that Chinto's mother was a *lavandera* is a meaningful detail

---

139   *Ibid.*
140   'Lettre à Mademoiselle Leroyer de Chantepie, Paris, 18 March, 1857', *Correspondance de Flaubert II* (Paris: Gallimard, 1980), p. 691: C'est un de mes principes qu'il ne faut pas *s'écrire*. L'artiste doit être dans son oeuvre comme Dieu dans la création, invisible et tout-puissant; (It is one of my principles that he must not *describe himself*. The artist must be in his work like God in His creation, invisible and all-powerful).

because it establishes a link with two important influences on Pardo Bazán's work: Zola and Golden Age realism. In both *L'assommoir* and *Lazarillo de Tormes* Nana's mother, Gervaise, and Lazarillo's mother respectively are washer women. In conjunction with her prologue to *La Tribuna*, Pardo Bazán explains in *Apuntes autobiográficos* the genesis of *La Tribuna*:

> Un día recordé que aquellas mujeres, morenas, fuertes, de aire resuelto, habían sido las más ardientes sectarias de la idea federal en los años revolucionarios, y parecióme curioso estudiar el desarrollo de una creencia política en un cerebro de hembra.

> (One day I remembered that those swarthy, strong, resolute women had been the most ardent disciples of the federal idea in the revolutionary years, and I thought it would be interesting to study the development of poltical awareness in a female brain.)[141]

Her various statements also set the novel in the context of a masculine literary tradition represented by works such as Galdós's *La desheredada* and the Goncourt brothers' *Germinie Lacerteux*. Although she does not refer to any other models and influences, a probable real life model for Amparo has been discovered and there are also two literary precedents, the more well-known one being Mérimée's novella *Carmen* (and Bizet's opera) with its story of a *cigarrera* and a cavalryman.[142]

However, *La Tribuna* has far more in common with a lesser-known novel. We can safely assume that Pardo Bazán was familiar with Faustina Sáez de Melgar's *Rosa, la cigarrera de Madrid* because she contributed two articles, 'La cigarrera' and 'La gallega', to *Las mujeres españolas, americanas y lusitanas pintadas por sí mismas*. This was a collection of *costumbrista* portraits by female authors describing women from different regions and social classes, published under the direction of Faustina Sáez de Melgar. *La Tribuna* and *Rosa, la cigarrera de Madrid* have much in common, including

---

141   *Obras completas, Tomo III*, p. 725.
142   See Diego Pardo Amado, 'As cigarreiras na literatura: *La Tribuna* (1883) de Emilia Pardo Bazán' (http://ruc.udc.es/bitstream/2183/13232/1/CC-128_art_20.pdf): 'Na literatura decimonónica e no imaxinario popular, as cigarreiras son concibidas como mulleres amantes da liberdade e da independencia, obxecto de inspiración para innúmeros artistas.' (In nineteenth century literature and popular imagination, *cigarreras* are conceived as women who loved freedom and independance, the object inspiration for numerous artists).
       As well as Mérimée's *Carmen* and Pardo Bazán's *La Tribuna*, he gives the examples of the zarzuela *Las cigarreras*, by Ángel Munilla and Luis Ferreiro, and *La salida de las cigarreras de la Fábrica de Tabacos de Sevilla* by the painter Gonzalo Bilbao Martínez.

the portrayal of working-class urban environments and the way elements of the protagonists' lives coincide with key events in nineteenth-century Spain (for example, the birth of Amparo's son coincides with the proclamation of the First Republic). Even more striking, though, is the similarity of the plots. Faustina Sáez de Melgar's novel tells the story of Rosa, from her initial seduction by Jaime when a teenager, to her becoming captain of a troop of rebels following the abandonment of her lover, moving to Madrid where she works in a tobacco factory, her active participation in the revolutionary riots of 1854 and her marriage with a repentant Jaime.

8. Language

There have not been any changes in the Spanish language over the last one hundred and fifty years which in themselves impede comprehension. It is, however, worth pointing out one specific feature of word order that is frequently encountered in *La Tribuna*. Up to the early twentieth century it was common practice in literary Spanish to place an object pronoun on the end of a conjugated verb. An example of this can be found in the the very first paragraph of Chapter 1:

Terminadas estas operaciones preliminares, estremecióse de frío ...

(When these preliminary operations were finished, he trembled with cold ...)

In modern Spanish, of course, 'estremecióse' would be written as 'se estremeció'.

In the prologue to *La dama joven*, Pardo Bazán states that, even though it incurs the risk of critical censure, she deems it an unforgivable artifice for writers to alter or correct popular speech forms.[143] This is why she praises Cervantes – 'el genio realista [...] le impulsó a hacer que Sancho, por ejemplo, hablase muy mal' (the realist nature [...] drove him to make Sancho, for example, speak very badly) – and criticises Valera, in whose novels 'no hay Sanchos, todos son Valeras' (there are no Sanchos, they are all Valeras),[144] alluding to the fact that all his characters speak in the same way. *La Tribuna* is set in Pardo Bazán's native region and in the prologue she promises that her characters will speak 'como realmente se habla en la región en donde los saqué' (as people really do speak in the region whence I took them).

---

143   *Obras completas, Tomo III*, p. 666: 'Juzgo imperdonable artificio en los escritores alterar o corregir las formas de la oración popular'.
144   *La cuestión palpitante*, p. 640.

From her meticulous observation in the factory Pardo Bazán picked up a quantity of popular modes of speech and used them to make her characters talk with the authentic speech of the common people. She maintained, several years later in *Apuntes autobiográficos*, that she would like to write a novel in which all the characters were countrymen, but the enormous problem of dialogue is essentially insoluble and even the maestro Zola, the most daring of novelists, makes his peasants in *La Terre* speak French rather than *patois*. The predicament facing Pardo Bazán was a direct consequence of the linguistic dichotomy in Galicia: whilst the urban bourgeoisie and gentry spoke *castellano,* the sharp, pertinent and mischievous things said by the country folk and disadvantaged socio-economic groups were, in her opinion, inseparable from *gallego*, their everyday language of communication. Nevertheless, being adamant that 'un libro arlequín, mitad gallego y mitad castellano, sería feísimo engendro' (a harlequin book, half Galician and half Castilian, would be a real monstrosity),[145] she makes all her characters, even the rural *cigarreras*, speak Spanish.

Although the novel contains a sprinkling of words, frequently italicised, given colloquial pronunciations, the indicated pronunciations would be common to many, and sometimes most, regions of Spain. Such words include *libertá* (libertad), *verdá* (verdad), *salú* (salud) *to* (todo), *Madrí* (Madrid), *revolusión* (revolución). Other colloquialisms include the misplacing of object pronouns – *para te llevar a la cárcel* (para llevarte a la cárcel) or the confusing of verb pairs (e.g. *aprender* used as 'to teach' instead of 'to learn', a common 'mistake' in Galicia). A number of distinctive lexical, syntactical and phonological features illustrate the pervasive influence of Galician throughout *La Tribuna*. This is particularly evident in items of vocabulary like *achinados* (rich), *amohado* (a type of batter made with flour and sugar or honey), *boh* (interjection indicating disgust or indifference), *can* (dog), *dengue* (shawl), *gaita* (bagpipes), *indina* (unworthy) and *rapaz* (boy).

Other *galleguismos* relate to verbs, especially endings such as *hacedes*, *sabedes* and *tenedes* as well as a tendency to replace the pluperfect (*había dejado*) with the imperfect subjunctive *dejara*. Pardo Bazán also includes a couple of examples of *gheada*, a phonetic trait of some Galician dialects which, although held up by many intellectuals as a unique and innovative phonemic and sociolinguistic phenomenon among the Romance languages, is frequently stigmatised as being synonymous with rustic and uneducated speech.[146]

---

145   *Apuntes autobiográficos*, p. 728.
146   For a phonetic and historical explanation of this linguistic characteristic, see Juan Antonio Thomas, 'The Use of *gheada* in Three Generations of Women from Carballo, A

9. Translation

> The difficulty in translation just lies in the fact that both the content and the
> style are already existent in the original and as a result, you will have to do
> your best to reproduce them as they are in quite a different language.[147]

Translations, according to Edmond Jaloux, are like women: when they
are beautiful, they are not faithful; and when they are faithful, they are
not beautiful.[148] This well-known analogy, however flippant it may appear,
highlights the elusive 'Holy Grail' of translation: creating something that is
faithful to the original as well as being aesthetically pleasing.

Although it is essential when translating a text to keep close to the original,
too literal a translation can sound stilted or even nonsensical. A less faithful
approach which attempts to penetrate the real meaning by interpreting the
global sense rather than individual words will often come across as far more
natural. This, however, runs the risk of introducing what Anton Popovič
called shifts of intellectual and aesthetic values which reflect the translator's
idiolect, style and values as much as, if not more than, the exact meaning
the writer wished to convey.

As the etymology of the name suggests, the role of a translator is essentially
to 'carry across' the author's work from one language to another. In practice,
of course, this is not as easy as it sounds, because even where words seem to
have an unproblematic match between two languages, the imprecision and
precariousness of equivalent concepts cannot be overlooked. Susan Bassnett
illustrates the Sapir-Whorf hypothesis that no two languages represent the
same social reality with a simple example: even though the English word
butter and the Italian word *burro* refer to an edible dairy product sold in the
form of a block of fat, there are significant differences which prevent us from
saying that they mean the same thing in both cultural contexts.[149] Normally,
burro has a light colour, has a sweet taste, is used mainly for cooking and is
devoid of social connotations; *butter*, on the other hand, is often deep yellow,
salted, spread on bread and toast, and carries with it associations of a certain
social status or class. Similar instances of different cultural frameworks can

---

Coruña'. (http://www.lingref.com/cpp/wss/3/paper1527.pdf)

147   Liu Zhongde, *Ten Lectures on Literary Translation* (Beijing: China Translation &
Publishing Corporation, 1991), p. 7.

148   'Les traductions sont comme les femmes: quand elles sont belles, elles ne sont pas
fidèles; et quand elles sont fidèles, elles ne sont pas belles.'

149   *Translation Studies* (London: Routledge, 2002), pp. 27–28.

be found throughout *La Tribuna*. The word *ceceo* has to be translated by *lisp* but the two things are not quite the same, and entail a different set of associations; *el paseo* can be rendered as *promenade* or *esplanade*, but they probably conjure up different mental pictures; *la cascarilla* is the basis of a similar drink to cocoa but the connotative meanings are not necessarily interchangeable.[150] If relatively straightforward words like these, along with many others, can cause such anguish, it is easy to imagine the amount of soul-searching presented by some of the trickier aspects of the novel. That is why I've probably spent longer producing this English translation than Emilia Pardo Bazán, whom Clarín denigrated for writing too quickly, spent composing *La Tribuna*. I hope I have managed to do some justice to the original and that any shortcomings of this edition will be offset by the help it provides Hispanists to access the novel.

There is no doubt that *La Tribuna* is not an easy read, if only because of its vast lexicon. This hurdle is compounded by structurally ambiguous phrases, semantic ambiguity and items of vocabulary which do not appear in dictionaries, or for which there is no English equivalent. In addition, there are archaic usages and metaphorical words and phrases, some beyond the understanding of even highly educated native speakers. Of course, complications of translation generally depend on the nature of the text as well as the two languages involved. Contrary to what we might erroneously deduce after struggling with instructions that have been rendered into English, the utilitarian and precise language of technical manuals is much easier to translate than creative writing steeped in literary traditions, allusions, and figurative language. Poetry, as Robert Frost famously said, is what gets lost in translation. By this he meant that the nuances and aesthetic qualities of language are essential to poetry, and that those features are what do not translate. If Pardo Bazán is not remembered primarily as a poet, her literary style is, with its comprehensive lexical range, a hybrid which blends the prosaic detail and data of Zola's Naturalism with the poeticism of Catholic spirituality.

La Tribuna is set in Pardo Bazán's native Galicia and she has made a concerted effort to reproduce local and regional colloquial speech.

---

150 Interestingly, in *Apuntes sobre el nuevo arte de escribir novelas* (*Obras completas, Tomo II*, p. 631), Juan Valera touches upon the inevitable failure of semantic transference. He argues that the audience at the first performance of Vigny's translation of *Othello* in 1829 was not misguided to whistle and hiss at the inclusion of a 'low' word they deemed had no place in a tragedy, because '*mouchoir* no es lo mismo que *handkerchief* o que *pañuelo*: *mouchoir* implica, evoca y contiene en sí la idea de *mocos*' (*mouchoir* is not the same as *handkerchief* or *pañuelo*: *mouchoir* implies, evokes and contains the idea of *mucus*).

This is certainly one of the many strengths of the novel, but it is often troublesome replicating 'faltas de lenguaje, barbarismos y provincialismos' (errors, barbarisms and local expressions)[151] in another language. In fact, the considerable challenges posed by translating everyday dialogue are particularly acute with substandard communication, dialect or speech defects. The most obvious examples in *La Tribuna* are found in the cigar makers' vernacularisms, the idiosyncratic speech patterns of the Protestant missionary in Chapter 25, and the little girl Nisita in Chapters 3, 4 and 5. On one occasion, in order to indicate a 'violation' of the ear ('la istrucción' for 'la instrucción'), I have resorted to nonstandard spelling or 'violation' of the eye ('educashun' for 'education'). This example of what George P. Krapp termed 'eye dialect' is an attempt to convey the discrepancy between Amparo's idealism (education makes all social classes equal) and reality (the girl's own lack of formal education). Elsewhere, such as when señora *Porreta* murmurs «Salú y liquidasión sosial» ('To health and social liquidation'), conventional spelling has been retained because, in my opinion, the imitation of demotic speech patterns introduces no discernible trace of authorial irony. I make no claim that this inconsistency is an ideal solution; I am merely explaining the rationale behind the decision.

Another issue for a translator is when characters play with language, as in Chapter 34 with the similar sounding words 'barricada' (barricade) and 'borricada' (silly thing):

–Hacen barricadas– exclamó una cigarrera que recordaba los tiempos de la Milicia Nacional.

–¡Borricadas, borricadas– exclamaba una maestra –nos va a dar por cara todo este barullo!

It is rarely easy to translate a pun like this into another language without sacrificing the ludic element. However, by substituting the obvious cognate 'barricade' with a slightly less accurate alternative, it is possible on this occasion to get across the meaning without having to rely on an explanatory footnote:

'They're setting up blockades,' exclaimed one of the cigar makers who remembered the days of the National Guard.

'Block'eads, block'eads,' exclaimed one of the maestras, 'that's what all this racket will make us look like!'

---

151 'Prologo a *La dama joven', Obras completas, Tomo III*, p. 666.

Dialogue, however, only accounts for a small percentage of the novel and the author's style is a veritable minefield of snares and pitfalls.

Realistic fiction is often opposed to romantic fiction in its endeavour to present an accurate imitation of life as it is. Any writer who wants to achieve the illusion of everyday existence as we perceive it will inevitably explore the semantic field of proximal and distal stimuli. However, whilst perceptual organs are, in most cases, similar from one person to another, there is substantial variation in how different languages describe and capture sensory experiences. Attempts to evoke sensations that transcend language require a subtlety of terminology and style which will enable us to apprehend our surroundings with a new and fresh intensity. This is one of the reasons why a writer like Pardo Bazán, who is constantly expanding the repertoire of words related to the five senses with intersensory metaphors and synaesthetic phrases, can be difficult to translate. In spite of her 'fama de sorda' (reputation for being deaf),[152] she explores auditory impressions to great effect on a number of key occasions. As well as the childbirth scene, other notable examples involve Baltasar's two female rivals. The first is when Baltasar is strolling along the Paseo de las Filas with Josefina and places a small piece of paper in her hand:

> Susurraban las acacias, llenaba el aire el misterioso silabeo de las conversaciones de última hora y el amoroso gemido del mar, besando el parapeto, completaba la sinfonía.

> (The acacias were whispering, the mysterious syllabication of the last-minute conversations filled the air, and the amorous moaning of the sea, as it kissed the parapet, completed the symphony.)

Even more memorable, however, is the soundscape Pardo Bazán evokes for the only part of the novel where she refuses to speak plainly, the moment when Baltasar seduces Amparo: 'sólo se escuchó el delgado silbo del aire cruzando las copas de los olmos del camino y el lejano quejar del mar' (the slight whistling of the air crossing through the tops of the elm trees and the distant moaning of the sea).

Her awareness of the olfactory system is equally evident throughout the novel. Whereas Chinto suffers the consequences of the acute sense

---

152 'La vida contemporánea', *La Ilustración artística de Barcelona*, no. 1.293, October 8, 1906, p. 650. In this article she explains this reputation in the following way:

'Es posible que, según la teoría de Wagner, mi oído necesite, para penetrarse de la belleza de la música, el auxilio de mi vista' (It is possible that, according to Wagner's theory, my hearing needs the help of my sight in order to become fully aware of the beauty of the music).

of smell for which cigar makers are renowned when Amparo berates him for smoking or drinking, Baltasar is helpless prey to the mysterious and emotional power of scent. Amparo's satin-like skin, combining the spheres of different senses, seems to him 'un puro aromático y exquisito' (an exquisite, aromatic cigar) and her strong, powerful and intoxicating perfume causes a delightful dizziness in him, especially 'el balsámico olor de tabaco' (the balsamic aroma of tobacco) which impregnates her.

Whilst Pardo Bazán's attempts to make articulate what is essentialy ineffable can be problematic for the translator, the main challenges in *La Tribuna* are probably more a consequence of what she calls her 'temperamento de colorista' (colourist nature). In chapter eleven of *La cuestión palpitante* she describes the Goncourt brothers as 'mis autores predilectos' (my favourite authors).[153] Amazed that anyone should classify them as 'meros *fotógrafos*' (mere *photographers*), she prefers to see them as '*pintores*' (painters), admiring the way they harness language so that words produce vivid chromatic sensations.[154] Several years later, in her essay 'Edmundo de Goncourt y su hermano' from 1891, she reiterates her appreciation of their desire to convey through words 'la intensidad de la sensación y la visión lúcida de las cosas exteriores' (the intensity of the sensation and the clear vision of external things).[155] They will go to almost any length in their quest to mirror observable reality, especially richness of colour, without the introduction of any falsifying distortion. Instead of exclaiming, as third-rate writers are wont to do, that they cannot find the words to express this or that, 'se propusieron *hallar palabras* siempre, aunque tuviesen que inventarlas' (they were intent on always *finding words*, even if they had to invent them). In fact, she goes on to claim, they were 'los más osados neologistas del mundo' (the most daring neologists in the world),[156] extending, enriching and dislocating the French language in order to create the desired effect:

> Los Goncourt se valen de todos los medios imaginables para lograr sus fines: repiten una misma palabra con objeto de que la excitación reiterada acreciente la intensidad de la sensación; emplean dos o tres sinónimos para nombrar un objeto; cometen tautologías y pleonasmos; inventan vocablos; sustantivan los adjetivos; incurren a cada paso en defectos que horrorizarían a Flaubert.

---

153   *Obras completas, Tomo III*, p. 611.
154   *Ibid.*, p. 614: '...escriben de suerte que las palabras produzcan vivas sensaciones cromáticas'.
155   'Edmundo de Goncourt y su hermano', *Obras completas, Tomo III*, p. 962.
156   *La cuestión palpitante*, p. 613.

(The Goncourts make use of all imaginable means to achieve their ends: they repeat the same word with the aim that the reiterated excitement will increase the intensity of the sensation; they employ two or three synonyms to name an object; they commit tautology and pleonasms; they invent words; they nominalise adjectives; at every step they commit faults which would horrify Flaubert.)[157]

Leopoldo Alas recognises, in Pardo Bazán's work, the same painter-like traits she discusses and praises in the work of the Goncourt brothers:

De todos los novelistas del naturalismo, son los Goncourt los que más pintan y los que más enamorados están del color. La señora Pardo Bazán es de todos los novelistas de España el que más pinta: en sus novelas se ve que está enamorada del color y que sabe echar sobre el lienzo haces de claridad como Claudio Loreno.

(Of all the Naturalist novelists, the Goncourts are those who paint the most and those who are most in love with colour. Señora Pardo Bazán is, of all the novelists in Spain, the one who paints the most: in her novels it can be seen that she is in love with colour and that she can put on the canvas beams of light like Claudio Loreno).[158]

Pardo Bazán did not consider the rendering of the external world to be the only aim of the novelist and the concern in her work goes beyond a simple search for brilliance of visual effect for its own sake. However, the long sentences with contortions of syntax, complex phraseology and other deviations from normal usage are an integral part of her desire to revitalise and modernise Spanish literature. They are what make her prose always rewarding to read, but frequently difficult to translate.

---

157   *Ibid.*, pp. 613–14.
158   'La Tribuna, novela original de doña Emilia Pardo Bazán', *Sermón perdido, Obras completas IV*, p. 542.

BIBLIOGRAPHY

Pardo Bazán, E. 1892. 'Una opinión sobre la mujer', *Nuevo Teatro Crítico 2* (March).
Pardo Bazán, E. 1947. *Obras completas, Tomo II* (Madrid: Aguilar).
Pardo Bazán, E. 1973. *Obras completas, Tomo III* (Madrid: Aguilar).
Pardo Bazán, E. 1991. *La Tribuna*, ed. Benito Varela Jácome (Madrid: Cátedra).

Brown, D. F. 1957. *The Catholic Naturalism of Emilia Pardo Bazán* (Chapel Hill, NC).
Clémessy, N. 1973. *Emilia Pardo Bazán, romancière (la critique, la théorie, la pratique)* (Paris: Centre de Recherches Hispaniques).
Faus, P. 2005. *Emilia Pardo Bazán: su época, su vida, su obra* (La Coruña: Fundación Pedro Barrié de la Maza).
Giles, M. E. 1980. Feminism and the Feminine in Emilia Pardo Bazán's Novels, *Hispania* 63 (2) (May).
Hemingway, M. 1983. *Emilia Pardo Bazán: The Making of a Novelist* (Cambridge: Cambridge University Press).
Henn, D. 1988. *The Early Pardo Bazán* (Liverpool: Francis Cairns).
Kirkpatrick, S. 1989. *Las Románticas: Women Writers and Subjectivity in Spain, 1835–1850* (Berkeley: University of California Press).
Laffitte, M. 1964. *La mujer en España* (Madrid: Aguilar).
Osborne, R. E. 1964. *Emilia Pardo Bazán su vida y sus obras* (Mexico: Ediciones de Andrea).
Pattison, W. 1971. *El naturalismo español* (1965) *Emilia Pardo Bazán* (New York: Twayne Publishers).
Pérez, J. 1988. *Contemporary Women Writers of Spain* (Boston: Twayne Publishers).
Tolliver, J. 1998. *Cigar Smoke and Violet Water: Gendered Discourse in the Stories of Emilia Pardo Bazán* (Lewisburgh: Bucknell University Press).
Villasante, C.-B. 1962. *Vida y obra de Emilia Pardo Bazán* (Madrid: Revista de Occidente).

Photograph of the façade of the Tobacco Factory taken by Xosé Castro.

LA TRIBUNA

THE TRIBUNE

PRÓLOGO DE LA AUTORA
A LA PRIMERA EDICIÓN

Lector indulgente: No quiero perder la buena costumbre de empezar mis novelas hablando contigo breves palabras. Más que nunca debo mantenerla hoy, porque acerca de *La Tribuna* tengo varias advertencias que hacerte, y así caminarán juntos en este prólogo el gusto y la necesidad.

Si bien *La Tribuna* es en el fondo un estudio de costumbres locales, el andar entretejidos en su trama sucesos políticos tan recientes como la Revolución de Setiembre de 1868, me impulsó a situarla en lugares que pertenecen a aquella geografía moral de que habla el autor de las *Escenas montañesas*, y que todo novelista, chico o grande, tiene el indiscutible derecho de forjarse para su uso particular. Quien desee conocer el plano de *Marineda*, búsquelo en el atlas de mapas y planos privados, donde se colecciona, no sólo el de Orbajosa, Villabermeja y Coteruco, sino el de las ciudades de R***, de L*** y de X***, que abundan en las novelas románticas. Este privilegio concedido al novelista de crearse un mundo suyo propio, permite más libre inventiva y no se opone a que los elementos todos del *microcosmos* estén tomados, como es debido, de la realidad. Tal fue el procedimiento que empleé en *La Tribuna*, y lo considero suficiente – si el ingenio me ayudase – para alcanzar la verosimilitud artística, el vigor analítico que infunde vida a una obra.

Al escribir *La Tribuna* no quise hacer sátira política; la sátira es género que admito sin poderlo cultivar; sirvo poco o nada para el caso. Pero así como niego la intención satírica, no sé encubrir que en este libro, casi a pesar mío, entra un propósito que puede llamarse *docente*. Baste a disculparlo el declarar que nació del espectáculo mismo de las cosas, y vino a mí, sin ser llamado, por su propio impulso. Al artista que sólo aspiraba retratar el aspecto pintoresco y característico de una *capa social*, se le presentó por añadidura la moraleja, y sería tan sistemático rechazarla como haberla buscado.

Porque no necesité agrupar sucesos, ni violentar sus consecuencias, ni desviarme de la realidad concreta y positiva, para tropezar con pruebas de que es absurdo el que un pueblo cifre sus esperanzas de redención y ventura

THE AUTHOR'S PROLOGUE
TO THE FIRST EDITION

Indulgent reader: I do not wish to get out of the good habit of beginning my novels by speaking a few brief words with you. Today, more than ever, must I uphold it, because I have various observations to make to you concerning *The Tribune*, and in this way pleasure and necessity will go together in this prologue.

Although *The Tribune* is fundamentally a study of local customs, the introduction into its plot of political events as recent as the Revolution of September 1868 impelled me to locate its action in places which belong to that moral geography that the author of *Mountain Scenes*[i] talks about, and which all novelists, minor or major, have the unquestionable right to forge for their personal use. Whoever wishes to know the street plan of Marineda,[ii] look for it in the atlas of private maps and charts, where not only those of Orbajosa, Villabermeja and Coteruco[iii] are collected, but also the ones for the cities of R***, L*** and X***, that abound in romantic novels. This privilege, granted to novelists to create their own private world, allows greater freedom of invention and isn't at odds with all the elements of the microcosm being taken, as is right and proper, from reality. This is the procedure I use in *The Tribune*, and I consider it sufficient – with the help of my wits – to achieve artistic verisimilitude, the analytical vigour which infuses life into a work.

When I wrote *The Tribune*, political satire was not what I wanted to achieve. Satire is a genre which I accept but cannot cultivate; I have little or no ability in that area. But just as I deny any satirical intention, I cannot hide the fact that finding its way into this book, almost in spite of myself, is a purpose that might be called *instructive*. Let it suffice for me to excuse it by declaring that it was born from the actual sight of things, and that it came to me, without being summoned, through its own impulse. The artist who only aspired to portray the picturesque and characteristic aspect of a *social stratum* was presented with the added element of a moral, and it would be just as dogmatic to reject it as to have sought it.

Because I did not find it necessary to group together events, nor distort their consequences, nor deviate from concrete and positive reality in order to encounter the evidence that it is absurd for a people to place their hopes

en formas de gobierno que desconoce, y a las cuales por lo mismo atribuye prodigiosas virtudes y maravillosos efectos. Como la raza latina practica mucho este género de culto fetichista e idolátrico, opino que si escritores de más talento que yo lo combatiesen, prestarían señalado servicio a la patria.

Y vamos a otra cosa. Tal vez no falte quien me acuse de haber pintado al pueblo con crudeza naturalista. Responderé que si nuestro pueblo fuese igual al que describiesen Goncourt y Zola, yo podría meditar profundamente en la conveniencia o inconveniencia de retratarlo; pero resuelta a ello, nunca seguiría la escuela idealista de Trueba y de la insigne *Fernán*, que riñe con mis principios artísticos. Lícito es callar, pero no fingir. Afortunadamente, el pueblo que copiamos los que vivimos del lado acá del Pirineo no se parece todavía, en buen hora lo digamos, al del lado allá. Sin dar en optimista, puedo afirmar que la parte del pueblo que vi de cerca cuando tracé estos estudios, me sorprendió gratamente con las cualidades y virtudes que, a manera de agrestes renuevos de inculta planta, brotaban de él ante mis ojos. El método de análisis implacable que nos impone el arte moderno me ayudó a comprobar el calor de corazón, la generosidad viva, la caridad inagotable y fácil, la religiosidad sincera, el recto sentir que abunda en nuestro pueblo, mezclado con mil flaquezas, miserias y preocupaciones que a primera vista lo oscurecen. Ojalá pudiese yo, sin caer en falso idealismo, patentizar esta belleza recóndita.

No; los tipos del pueblo español en general, y de la costa cantábrica en particular, no son aún – salvas *fenomenales excepciones* – los que se describen con terrible verdad en *L'assommoir, Germinie Lacerteux* y otras obras, donde parece que el novelista nos descubre las abominaciones monstruosas de la Roma pagana, que, unidas a la barbarie más grosera, retoñan en el corazón de la Europa cristiana y civilizada. Y ya que por dicha nuestra las faltas del pueblo que conocemos no rebasan de aquel límite a que raras veces deja de llegar la flaca decaída condición del hombre, pintémosle, si podemos, tal cual es, huyendo del *patriarcalismo* de Trueba como del socialismo humanitario de Sue, y del método de cuantos, trocando los frenos, atribuyen a Calibán las seductoras gracias de Ariel.

of redemption and happiness in forms of government that are unknown to them, and to which for that reason they attribute prodigious virtues and marvellous effects. As the Latin race practises this kind of fetishistic and idolatrous worship a lot, I am of the opinion that if writers of greater talent than me fought against this, they would lend distinguished service to our native land.

Let us move on to something else. There may be no shortage of those who accuse me of having depicted our people with naturalistic crudeness. I will respond by saying that if our people were like those that the Goncourts and Zola describe, I would be able to meditate profoundly on the appropriateness or inappropriateness of depicting them; but set on doing it, I would never follow the idealistic school of Trueba and the renowned *Fernán*,[iv] which clashes with my artistic principles. It is legitimate to keep quiet, but not to pretend. Fortunately, the people that those of us who live on this side of the Pyrenees copy are not yet similar, I'm happy to say, to those on the other side. At the risk of being taken for an optimist, I can confirm that the section of people I observed at close hand when I planned these studies surprised me pleasantly with the qualities and virtues which, like rustic shoots from an uncultivated plant, sprouted from them right before my eyes. The implacable method of analysis which modern art imposes on us helped me to verify the warmth of heart, the lively generosity, the inexhaustible and ready charitableness, the sincere piety, the righteous judgement which is abundant among our people, mixed with a thousand weaknesses, miseries and preoccupations which at first sight obscure it. If only I could show this hidden beauty without falling into false idealism.

No, the types that make up the Spanish people in general, and the Cantabrian coast in particular are – with certain *phenomenal exceptions* – not yet those described with terrible truth in *L'assommoir*, *Germinie Lacerteux* and other works,[v] where it seems that the novelist reveals to us the monstrous abominations of pagan Rome, which, along with the crudest barbarism, germinate in the heart of Christian and civilised Europe. And since, fortunately for us, the faults of the people we know do not exceed that limit which the weakened, decadent condition of man rarely fails to reach, let us paint it, if we can, as it is, avoiding Trueba'a *patriarchalism* as well as Sue's[vi] humane socialism and the methodology of all those who, manipulating everything, attribute the seductive charms of Ariel to Caliban.[1]

---

1 Ariel and Caliban, two sharply contrasted characters, are both servants of Prospero in Shakespeare's *The Tempest*.

En abono de *La Tribuna* quiero añadir que los maestros Galdós y Pereda abrieron camino a la licencia que me tomo de hacer hablar a mis personajes como realmente se habla en la región de donde los saqué. Pérez Galdós, admitiendo en su *Desheredada* el lenguaje de los barrios bajos; Pereda, sentenciando a muerte a las zagalejas de porcelana y a los pastorcillos de égloga, señalaron rumbos de los cuales no es permitido apartarse ya. Y si yo debiese a Dios las facultades de alguno de los ilustres narradores cuyo ejemplo invoco, ¡cuánto gozarías, oh lector discreto, al dejar los trillados caminos de la retórica novelesca diaria para beber en el vivo manantial de las expresiones populares, incorrectas y desaliñadas, pero frescas, enérgicas y donosas!

Queda adiós, lector, y ojalá te merezca este libro la misma acogida que *Un viaje de novios*. Tu aplauso me sostendrá en la difícil vía de la observación, donde no todo son flores para un alma compasiva.

EMILIA PARDO BAZÁN
Granja de Meirás, octubre de 1882

In defence of *The Tribune* I want to add that the masters Galdós and Pereda[vii] opened the way for the liberty I take of making my characters speak as people really do speak in the region whence I took them. Pérez Galdós, accepting the language of the lower-class districts in his *The Disinherited Lady*; Pereda, sentencing the porcelain shepherdesses and shepherds of the eclogues to death, blazed a trail from which it is no longer possible to stray. And if I should owe God the faculties of some of the illustrious story-tellers whose example I invoke, how much you would enjoy, discreet reader, abandoning the well-trodden paths of everyday novelistic rhetoric to drink from the living spring of popular expressions, incorrect and careless, but fresh, energetic and witty!

All that remains is to say farewell, reader, and I hope this book deserves the same reception from you as *A Wedding Trip*.[2] Your applause will sustain me on the difficult road of observation, where it's not all flowers for a compassionate soul.

EMILIA PARDO BAZÁN
Granja de Meirás, October 1882

---

2   Emilia Pardo Bazán's novel *Un viaje de novios* was published in 1881.

I

BARQUILLOS

Comenzaba a amanecer, pero las primeras y vagas luces del alba a duras penas lograban colarse por las tortuosas curvas de la calle de los Gastros, cuando el señor Rosendo, el barquillero que disfrutaba de más parroquia y popularidad en Marineda, se asomó, abriendo a bostezos, a la puerta de su mezquino cuarto bajo. Vestía el madrugador un desteñido pantalón grancé,[1] reliquia bélica, y estaba en mangas de camisa. Miró al poco cielo que blanqueaba por entre los tejados, y se volvió a su cocinilla, encendiendo un candil y colgándolo del estribadero de la chimenea. Trajo del portal un brazado de astillas de pino, y sobre la piedra del fogón las dispuso artísticamente en pirámide, cebada por su base con virutas, a fin de conseguir una hoguera intensa y llameante. Tornó del vasar un tarterón, en el cual vació cucuruchos de harina y azúcar, derramó agua, cascó huevos y espolvoreó canela. Terminadas estas operaciones preliminares, estremecióse de frío – porque la puerta había quedado de par en par, sin que en cerrarla pensase y descargó en el tabique dos formidables puñadas.

Al punto salió rápidamente del dormitorio o cuchitril contiguo una mozuela de hasta trece años, desgreñada, con el incierto andar de quien acaba de despertarse bruscamente, sin más atavíos que una enagua de lienzo y un justillo de dril, que adhería a su busto, anguloso aún, la camisa de estopa. Ni miró la muchacha al señor Rosendo, ni le dio los buenos días; atontada con el sueño y herida por el fresco matinal que le mordía la epidermis, fue a dejarse caer en una silleta, y mientras el barquillero encendía estrepitosamente fósforos y los aplicaba a las virutas, la chiquilla se puso a frotar con una piel de gamuza el enorme cañuto de hojalata donde se almacenaban los barquillos.

Instalóse el señor Rosendo en su alto trípode de madera ante la llama chisporroteadora y crepitante ya, y metiendo en el fuego las magnas tenazas, dio principio a la operación. Tenía a su derecha el barreño del amohado,[2] en el cual mojaba el cargador, especie de palillo grueso; y extendiendo una leve capa de líquido sobre la cara interior de los candentes hierros, apresurábase a envolverla en el molde con su dedo pulgar, que a fuerza de repetir este acto se había convertido en una callosidad tostada, sin uña, sin

---

1 El color rojo que resulta al teñir los paños con la raíz de la rubia granza (*rubia tinctorum*).
2 Pasta líquida, a base de harina y azúcar o miel, para hacer los barquillos. Palabra gallega cuya ortografía correcta es *amoado*.

1
PASTRY CONES

Day was beginning to break, but the first faint light of dawn was barely managing to filter through the winding curves of the Calle de los Rastros, when Señor Rosendo, the pastry cone maker who enjoyed the most business and popularity in Marineda, looked out and yawned as he opened the door of his wretched ground floor flat. This early riser was wearing faded, red trousers, a leftover from the war, and was in shirt sleeves. He looked out at the little patch of sky that appeared white between the tiled roofs, and went back into his small kitchen, lighting an oil lamp and hanging it from the hook in the fireplace. He brought in an armload of pine chips from the hallway and arranged them artistically in a pyramid on the stone base of the hearth, fed from beneath with wood shavings, to produce an intense, blazing fire. He took down from the shelf a large cake tin, into which he emptied paper cones of flour and sugar, poured water, cracked eggs and sprinkled cinnamon. When these preliminary operations were finished, he trembled with cold – because the door had been left wide open, without his thinking to close it – and he pounded twice on the thin partition wall.

Immediately a young girl, no more than thirteen years old, appeared rapidly out of the adjoining bedroom, or little cubbyhole, dishevelled and with the unsteady gait of someone who has just woken up suddenly, wearing nothing more than a linen petticoat and a bodice made of drill which clung to her still undeveloped bust, and a hessian shirt. The girl neither looked at Señor Rosendo nor greeted him; dulled with sleep and wounded by the morning cold which bit into her skin, she flopped into a small chair, and whilst the pastry cone maker noisily lit matches and applied them to the wood shavings, the young girl began to rub with a chamois cloth the enormous tin tube where the pastry cones were stored.

Señor Rosendo perched himself on his high, wooden three-legged stool in front of the flames which were already sparkling and crackling, and putting the great tongs into the fire, he started off the procedure. To his right he had the bowl of batter into which he dipped the spreader, a kind of thick stick; and applying a thin layer of the liquid over the inside of the red-hot iron, he quickly covered the mould with it, using his thumb which, with

yema y sin forma casi. Los barquillos, dorados y tibios, caían en el regazo de la muchacha, que los iba introduciendo unos en otros a guisa de tubos de catalejo, y colocándolos simétricamente en el fondo del cañuto; labor que se ejecutaba en silencio, sin que se oyese más rumor que el crujir de la leña, el rítmico chirrido de las tenazas al abrir y cerrar sus fauces de hierro, el seco choque de los crocantes barquillos al tropezarse, y el silbo del amohado al evaporar su humedad sobre la ardiente placa. La luz del candil y los reflejos de la lumbre arrancaban destellos a la hojalata limpia, al barro vidriado de las cazuelas del vasar, y la temperatura se suavizaba, se elevaba, hasta el extremo de que el señor Rosendo se quitase la gorra con visera de hule, descubriendo la calva sudorosa, y la niña echase atrás con el dorso de la mano sus indómitas guedejas que la sofocaban.

Entre tanto, el sol, campante ya en los cielos, se empeñaba en cernir alguna claridad al través de los vidrios verdosos y puercos del ventanillo que tenía obligación de alumbrar la cocina. Sacudía el sueño la calle de los Castros, y mujeres en trenza y en cabello, cuando no en refajo y chancletas, pasaban apresuradas, cuál en busca de agua, cuál a comprar provisiones a los vecinos mercados; oíanse llantos de chiquillos, ladridos de perros; una gallina cloqueó; el canario de la barbería de enfrente redobló trinando como un loco. De tiempo en tiempo la niña del barquillero lanzaba codiciosas ojeadas a la calle. ¡Cuándo sería Dios servido de disponer que ella abandonase la dura silla, y pudiese asomarse a la puerta, que no es mucho pedir! Pronto darían las nueve, y de los seis mil barquillos que admitía la caja sólo estaban hechos cuatro mil y pico. Y la muchacha se desperezó maquinalmente. Es que desde algunos meses acá bien poco le lucía el trabajo a su padre. Antes despachaba más.

El que viese aquellos cañutos dorados, ligeros y deleznables como las ilusiones de la niñez, no podía figurarse el trabajo ímprobo que representaba su elaboración. Mejor fuera manejar la azada o el pico que abrir y cerrar sin tregua las tenazas abrasadoras, que además de quemar los dedos, la mano y el brazo, cansaban dolorosamente los músculos del hombro y del cuello. La mirada, siempre fija en la llama, se fatigaba; la vista disminuía; el espinazo, encorvado de continuo, llevaba, a puros esguinces, la cuenta de los barquillos que salían del molde. ¡Y ningún día de descanso! No pueden los barquillos hacerse de víspera; si han de gustar a la gente menuda y golosa, conviene que sean fresquitos. Un nada de humedad los reblandece. Es preciso pasarse la

constant repetition of this action, had become a toasted callus without nail or fingertip and almost without shape. The warm, golden cones fell into the lap of the girl, who inserted one inside the other like the tubes of a spyglass, and placed them symmetrically at the bottom of the tubular container; a task she undertook in silence without any sound being heard other than the crackling of the wood in the fire, the rhythmic squeaking of the tongs opening and closing their iron jaws, the crisp impact of the brittle cones as they came into contact with each other, and the hiss of the batter as its moistness evaporated on the burning-hot metal surface. The light of the oil lamp and the reflections of the fire drew glints from the clean tinplate and the glazed earthenware of the pots on the kitchen shelf, and the temperature moderated and rose to such a degree that Señor Rosendo removed his cap with the oilskin visor, revealing his sweaty bald patch, and with the back of her hand the young girl pushed back the long, unruly locks that were smothering her.

In the meantime, the sun, now proudly ensconced in the sky, was set about getting some light to sift through the greenish, filthy panes of the little window whose duty it was to illuminate the kitchen. The Calle de los Castros was shaking off sleep, and women with their hair down, even in underskirts and flip-flops, hurried by, some after water, some to buy provisions from neighbouring markets; you could hear small children crying, dogs barking; a hen clucked and the canary in the barber's shop opposite warbled away like a lunatic. From time to time the pastry maker's daughter glanced longingly towards the street. When would it suit God's purpose to allow her to abandon the hard chair and look out of the door? It wasn't much to ask! It would soon be nine o'clock and of the six thousand pastry cones the box held only just over four thousand were done. The girl stretched herself spontaneously. The fact is that for a few months now her work had not impressed her father very much. She used to turn out more.

No one who saw those golden, light and crumbly pastry tubes like childhood dreams could imagine the enormous effort that went into their production. It would be better to wield a hoe or a pickaxe than to be relentlessly opening and shutting the scorching-hot tongs which, as well as burning your fingers, hand and arm, painfully fatigued the shoulder and neck muscles. Your eyes, forever staring into the flames, grew weary; your sight deteriorated; your spine, constantly bent over, kept count, just by the number of sprains, of the pastry cones as they came out of the mould. And not a single day of rest! The pastry cones cannot be made the night before; if they are to please little ones with a sweet tooth, they have to be very fresh. The slightest hint

mañana, y a veces la noche, en fabricarlos, la tarde en vocearlos y venderlos. En verano, si la estación es buena y se despacha mucho y se saca pingüe jornal, también hay que estarse las horas caniculares, las horas perezosas, derritiendo el alma sobre aquel fuego, sudando el quilo, preparando provisión doble de barquillos para la venta pública y para los cafés. Y no era que el señor Rosendo estuviese mal con su oficio; nada de eso; artistas habría orgullosos de su destreza, pero tanto como él, ninguno. Por más que los años le iban venciendo, aún se jactaba de llenar en menos tiempo que nadie el tubo de hojalata. No ignoraba primor alguno de los concernientes a su profesión; barquillos anchos y finos como seda para rellenar de huevos hilados, barquillos recios y estrechos para el agua de limón y el sorbete, hostias para las confiterías – y no las hacía para las iglesias por falta de molde que tuviese una cruz –, flores, hojuelas y *orejas de fraile* en Carnaval, buñuelos en todo tiempo… Pero nunca lo tenía de lucir estas habilidades accesorias, porque los barquillos de diario eran absorbentes. ¡Bah! En consiguiendo vivir y mantener la familia…

A las nueve muy largas, cuando cerca de cinco mil barquillos reposaban en el tubo, todavía el padre y la hija no habían cruzado palabra. Montones de brasa y ceniza rodeaban la hoguera, renovada dos o tres veces. La niña suspiraba de calor, el viejo sacudía frecuentemente la mano derecha, medio asada ya. Por fin, la muchacha profirió:

–Tengo hambre.

Volvió el padre la cabeza, y con expresivo arqueamiento de cejas indicó un anaquel del vasar. Encaramóse la chiquilla trepando sobre la artesa, y bajó un mediano trozo de pan de mixtura,[3] en el cual hincó el diente con buen ánimo. Aún rebuscaba en su falda las migajas sobrantes para aprovecharlas, cuando se oyeron crujidos de catre, carraspeos, los ruidos característicos del despertar de una persona, y una voz entre quejumbrosa y despótica llamó desde la alcoba cercana al portal:

–¡Amparo!

Se levantó la niña y acudió al llamamiento, resonando de allí a poco rato su hablar.

–Afiáncese, señora…, así…, cárguese más…, aguarde, que le voy a batir este jergón…– y aquí se escuchó una gran sinfonía de hojas de maíz, un *sirrisssch* … prolongado y armonioso.

---

3 Pan de varias semillas.

of dampness softens them. You have to spend the morning, and sometimes the night, making them, the afternoon peddling them and selling them. In summer, if the weather is good and they get rid of a lot and a bumper day's wage comes in, you also have to spend the hottest hours, the hours for taking it easy, melting your soul over that fire, slaving away, preparing a double supply of pastry cones for public sale and the cafés. And it wasn't that Señor Rosendo was bad at his trade – nothing of the sort – there were probably artists proud of their skill, but none of them as much as him. However much the years were taking their toll on him, he still would boast about filling the tin tube in less time than anyone else. Not a single detail of the skills relating to his profession by-passed him: wide pastry cones as fine as silk for a filling of egg and sugar sweetmeat; tough, narrow cones for lemon ice and sorbet, wafers consecrated in the Eucharist for the confectioner's – and he didn't make them for the churches because he didn't have a mould with a cross in it – cakes shaped like flowers, small leaves and *orejas de fraile*[3] during Carnival, fritters at any time of year… But he never had to show off these accessory skills because the everyday pastry cones were so demanding of his time. Nonsense! As long as one managed to live and support the family…

Even well after nine o'clock, when nearly five thousand pastry cones were resting in the tube, father and daughter had still not exchanged a single word. Piles of embers and ash surrounded the fire, which had been revived two or three times. The girl sighed because of the heat, the old man frequently shook his right hand, half-toasted by now. Finally the girl declared:

'I'm hungry.'

The father turned his head, and with an expressive arching of the eyebrows indicated one of the kitchen shelves. The young girl climbed up on the trough, and brought down a medium-sized chunk of mixed rye and corn bread into which she vigorously sank her teeth. She was still carefully searching her skirt for any leftover crumbs to put to good use when the creaking of a bed, the clearing of a throat and the characteristic noises of a person waking up could be heard, and a voice half-plaintive, half-despotic called out from the bedroom next to the hallway:

'Amparo!'

The girl stood up and answered the call, her voice soon resounding through there.

'Hold on tight … that's it … move over a little more… I'm going to beat this mattress for you…' (And here you could hear a great symphony of corn

---

3   Fritters prepared with flour dough, eggs and milk

La voz quejumbrosa dijo opacamente algo, y la infantil contestó:

—Ya la voy a poner a la lumbre ahora mismo... ¿Tendrá por ahí el azúcar? Y respondiendo a una interpelación altamente ofensiva para su dignidad, gritó la chiquilla:

—Piensa que... ¡Aunque fuera oro puro! Lo escondería usted misma... Ahí está, detrás de la funda... ¿Lo ve?

Salió con una escudilla desportillada en la mano, llena de morena melaza, y arrimando al fuego un pucherito donde estaba ya la cascarilla,[4] le añadió en debidas proporciones azúcar y leche, y volvióse al cuarto del portal con una taza humeante y colmada a reverter. En el fondo del cacharro quedaba como cosa de otra taza. El barquillero se enderezó llevándose las manos a la región lumbar, y sobriamente, sin concupiscencia, se desayunó bebiendo las sobras por el puchero mismo. Enjugó después su frente regada de sudor con la manga de la camisa, entró a su vez en el cuarto próximo; y al volver a presentarse, vestido con pantalón y chaqueta de paño pardo, se terció a las espaldas la caja de hoja de lata y se echó a la calle. Amparo, cubriendo la brasa con ceniza, juntaba en una cazuela berzas, patatas, una corteza de tocino, un hueso rancio de cerdo, cumpliendo el deber de condimentar el caldo del humilde menaje. Así que todo estuvo arreglado, metióse en el cuchitril, donde consagró a su aliño personal seis minutos y medio, repartidos como sigue: un minuto para calzarse los zapatos de becerro, pues todavía estaba descalza; dos para echarse un refajo de bayeta y un vestido de tartán; un minuto para pasarse la punta de un paño húmedo por ojos y boca (más allá no alcanzó el aseo); dos minutos para escardar con un peine desdentado la revuelta y rizosa crencha, y medio para tocarse al cuello un pañolito de indiana... Hecho lo cual, se presentó, más oronda que una princesa, a la persona encamada a quien había llevado el desayuno. Era ésta una mujer de edad madura, agujereada como una espumadera por las viruelas, chata de frente, de ojos chicos. Viendo a la chiquilla vestida, se escandalizó:

—¿Adónde iría ahora semejante vagabunda?

—A misa, señora, que es domingo... ¿Qué volver con noche ni con coche? Siempre vine con día, siempre... ¡Una vez de cada mil! Queda el caldo preparadito al fuego... Vaya, abur.

Y se lanzó a la calle con la impetuosidad y brío de un cohete bien disparado.

---

4 Las cáscaras de las almendras tostadas de cacao.

husks, a prolonged and harmonious *swiisssh...*).

The plaintive voice said something gloomily, and the youthful one replied:

'I'm going to put it on the fire right now... You wouldn't have any sugar round here?'

And answering a plea that was highly offensive to her dignity, the young girl shouted:

'You think that... Even if it were pure gold! You've probably hidden it yourself... Here it is, behind the pillow... you see?'

She came out with a chipped bowl full of dark molasses in her hand, and moving a small cooking pot already containing cocoa onto the fire, she added sugar and milk in the right proportions, and returned to the bedroom off the hallway with a steaming cup filled to overflowing. At the bottom of the earthen pot there remained roughly another cup. The pastry cone maker straightened up, put his hands against his lower back and in a restrained, ungreedy way had his breakfast, drinking the remains straight from the pot. Then he wiped his sweat-covered brow with his shirt sleeve, at the same time as he went into the adjoining room; and when he appeared again, wearing trousers and a brown woollen jacket, he threw the tin box over his shoulder and made his way out onto the street. Amparo covered the burning embers with ash, put some cabbages, potatoes, a rind of bacon and a rancid hog bone all together in a casserole dish, thereby fulfilling her duty to prepare the broth for the humble household. As soon as everything was arranged, she returned to her squalid little room, where she spent six and a half minutes on her personal grooming, distributed as follows: one minute to put on her calfskin shoes, because she was still barefoot; two minutes to throw on a flannel underskirt and a tartan dress; a minute to pass the tip of a damp cloth over her eyes and mouth (her ablutions went no further); two minutes to untangle the unkempt, curly parting in her hair with a toothless comb, and half a minute to tie a small, printed calico scarf around her neck... When this had been done, she appeared, more puffed up than a princess, before the bedridden person to whom she had taken breakfast. This was a woman of mature years, pock-marked like a skimming ladle, with a flat face and small eyes. She was scandalised to see the young girl dressed:

'Where would a gadabout like you be going now?'

'To Mass, it's Sunday ... come back at night without a car? I've always come home when it's still light, always! Maybe once in a thousand times! The broth is ready on the fire... All right, so long.'

And she shot out into the street with the impetuousness and determination

II
PADRE Y MADRE

Tres años antes, la imposibilitada estaba sana y robusta y ganaba su vida en la fábrica de tabacos. Una noche de invierno fue a jabonar ropa blanca al lavadero público, sudó, volvió desabrigada y despertó tullida de las caderas. –Un aire,[5] señor– decía ella al médico.

Quedóse reducida la familia a lo que trabajase el señor Rosendo: el real diario que del *fondo de hermandad* de la fábrica recibía la enferma no llegaba a medio diente. Y la chiquilla crecía, y comía pan y rompía zapatos, y no había quien la sujetase a coser ni a otro género de tareas. Mientras su padre no se marchaba, el miedo a un pasagonzalo sacudido con el cargador la tenía quieta ensartando y colocando barquillos; pero apenas el viejo se terciaba la correa del tubo, sentía Amparo en las piernas un hormigueo, un bullir de la sangre, una impaciencia como si le naciesen alas a miles en los talones. La calle era su paraíso. El gentío la enamoraba, los codazos y enviones la halagaban cual si fuesen caricias, la música militar penetraba en todo su ser produciéndole escalofríos de entusiasmo. Pasábase horas y horas correteando sin objeto al través de la ciudad, y volvía a casa con los pies descalzos y manchados de lodo, la saya en jirones, hecha una sopa, mocosa, despeinada, perdida, y rebosando dicha y salud por los poros de su cuerpo. A fuerza de filípicas maternales corría una escoba por el piso, sazonaba el caldo, traía una herrada de agua; en seguida, con rapidez de ave, se evadía de la jaula y tornaba a su libre vagancia por calles y callejones.

De estos instintos nómadas tendría bastante culpa la vida que forzosamente hizo la chiquilla mientras su madre asistió a la fábrica. Sola en casa con su padre, apenas éste salía, ella le imitaba, por no quedarse metida entre cuatro paredes; ¡vaya!, y que no eran tan alegres para que nadie se embelesase mirándolas. La cocina, oscura y angosta, parecía una espelunca,[6] y encima del fogón relucían siniestramente las últimas brasas de la moribunda hoguera. En el patín, si es verdad que se veía claro, no consolaba mucho los ojos el aspecto de un montón de cal y residuos de albañilería, mezclados con

---

5   Un aire: un ataque de parálisis.
6   Cueva, gruta, caverna oscura tenebrosa.

of a rocket fired at full force.

2

FATHER AND MOTHER

Three years before, the disabled woman was healthy and robust and earning her living in the tobacco factory. One winter night she went to clean some whites at the public washing place, worked up a sweat, came back without a coat and woke up paralysed in the hips.

'A paralytic attack,' she said to the doctor.

The family was reduced to living on what Señor Rosendo earned: the one *real*[viii] per day the invalid woman received from the *Association Fund* at the factory was barely enough to make ends meet. And the young girl was growing, and she ate bread and she wore out shoes, and there was no one to make her do the sewing or any other kind of tasks. As long as her father had not left the house, the fear of an unpleasant rap from his spreader kept her quiet, lining up and arranging pastry cones; but no sooner had the old man slung the leather strap of the tubular container across his shoulder than Amparo felt a tingling in her legs, a boiling in her blood, an impatience as if thousands of wings were coming to life in her heels. The street was her paradise. She just loved the throng, the elbowing and shoving gave her the same pleasure as if they were caresses; the military music penetrated her innermost being, producing shivers of enthusiasm in her. She spent hours and hours running about aimlessly across the city, and came home barefoot and splattered with mud, her skirt in tatters, soaked to the skin, her nose running and her hair unkempt, lost, exuding happiness and health through the very pores of her body. As a result of her mother's haranguing she ran a broom over the floor, seasoned the broth, brought in a bucketful of water; straight away, with the speed of a bird, she escaped the cage and went back to freely wandering the streets and alleys.

Such nomadic instincts could be blamed in no small measure on the life the child was forced to lead whilst her mother was at the factory. Alone in the house with her father, no sooner did he leave than she followed his example so as not to stay cooped up in those four walls; well, they weren't so cheerful that anyone would be enraptured looking at them. The dark, narrow kitchen looked like a cave, and the last embers of the dying fire shone ominously on top of the hearth. In the courtyard, even if you could see things clearly, there was little consolation for your eyes among the pile of quicklime and

cascos de loza, tarteras rotas, un molinillo inservible, dos o tres guiñapos viejos y un innoble zapato que se reía a carcajadas. Casi más lastimoso era el espectáculo de la alcoba matrimonial: la cama en desorden, porque la salida precipitada a la fábrica no permitía hacerla; los cobertores color hospital, que no bastaban a encubrir una colcha rabicorta; la vela de sebo, goteando tristemente a lo largo de la palmatoria de latón veteada de cardenillo; la palangana puesta en una silla y henchida de agua jabonosa y grasienta; en resumen: la historia de la pobreza y de la incuria narrada en prosa por una multitud de objetos feos; historia que la chiquilla comprendía intuitivamente, pues hay quien, sin haber nacido entre sábanas y holandas, presume y adivina todas aquellas comodidades y deleites que jamás gozó. Así es que Amparo huía, huía de sus lares camino de la fábrica, llevando a su madre, en una fiambrera, el bazuqueante caldo; pero soltando a lo mejor la carga, poníase a jugar al corro, a *San Severín*, a la viudita, a cualquier cosa con las damiselas de su edad y pelaje.

Cuando la madre se vio encamada quiso imponer a la hija el trabajo sedentario; era tarde. El rústico arbusto ya no se sujetaba al espalder. Amparo había ido a la escuela en sus primeros años, años de relativa prosperidad para la familia, sucediéndole lo que a la mayor parte de las niñas pobres, que al poco tiempo se cansan sus padres de enviarlas y ellas de asistir, y se quedan sin más aprendizaje que la lectura, cuando son listas, y unos rudimentos de escritura. De aguja, apenas sabía nada Amparo. La madre se resignó con la esperanza de colocarla en la fábrica. «Que trabaje –decía–, como yo trabajé.» Y al murmurar esta sentencia, suspiraba recordando treinta años de incesante afán. Ahora, su carne y sus molidos huesos se tendían gustosamente en la cama, donde reposaba tumbada panza arriba, ínterin sudaban otros para mantenerla. ¡Que sudasen! Donada por el terrible egoísmo que suele atacar a los viejos cuya mocedad fue laboriosa, la impedida hizo del lecho de dolor quinta de recreo. Lo que es allí, ya podían venir penas; lo que es allí, a buen seguro que la molestasen el calor ni el frío. ¿Que era preciso lavar la ropa? Bueno; ella no tenía que levantarse a jabonarla; le había costado bien caro una vez. ¿Que estaba sucio el piso? Ya lo barrerían, y si no, por ella, aunque en todo el año no se barriese… ¿De qué le había servido tanto romper el cuerpo cuando era joven? De verse ahora tullida «¡Ay, no se sabe lo que es la salud

bricklaying remains, mixed together with fragments of crockery, broken cake tins, a useless hand mill, two or three old rags and an ignoble shoe torn open as if roaring with laughter. Almost more pitiful was the sight of the couple's bedroom: the bed in a mess because the hurried departure for the factory left no time to make it; the hospital-coloured bedspreads that didn't manage to cover a short-cropped counterpane; the tallow candle dripping sadly all along the brass candlestick streaked with verdigris; the washbowl placed on a chair and filled with soapy, greasy water; to sum up, a story of poverty and neglect, narrated in prose by a multitude of ugly objects, and which the young girl understood intuitively; because there are those who without having been born amidst sheets and fine linen instinctively guess at and visualise all those comforts and delights they never enjoyed. So it is that Amparo fled, fled from her home on the way to the factory, bringing her mother some broth slopping about in a dinner pail; but, once she had rid herself of her burden as best she could, she started to play ring-a-ring-a-roses, *San Severín, la viudita*,[ix] or anything else with the damsels of her age and kind.

When the mother became bedridden she tried to force her daughter into sedentary work; it was too late. The rustic shrub could no longer be attached to the trellis. Amparo had gone to school in her earlier years, years of relative prosperity for the family, the same thing happening to her as to the majority of poor young girls, that their parents soon tire of sending them and they of going, so they are left with no learning other than the ability to read, if they are quick, and the rudiments of writing. About needlework Amparo knew next to nothing. Her mother resigned herself to the hope of finding her a place in the factory. 'Let her work,' she would say, 'like I worked.' And as she murmured this sentence she sighed, remembering thirty years of incessant commitment. Now her flesh and her aching bones were gladly stretched out in bed, where she could rest with her belly facing up, while others were sweating to support her. Let them sweat! Endowed with the terrible selfishness that usually attacks old people who worked hard in their youth, the disabled woman made the bed that was her rack of pain into a recreation house. As for what's round the corner, let hardships come as they may; as for the near future, it was certain that neither heat nor cold would bother her. If clothes needed to be washed? All right; she didn't have to get up to clean them – that had once cost her very dearly. The floor was dirty? They would sweep it, and if they didn't, as for her, even if it weren't swept all year… What good had it done to wear out her body so much when she was young? To find herself disabled now. 'Oh, you

hasta después de que se pierde!», exclamaba sentenciosamente, sobre todo los días en que el dolor artrítico le atarazaba las junturas. Otras veces, jactanciosa, como todo inválido, decía a su hija: «Sácateme de delante, que irrita el verte; de tu edad era yo una loba que daba en un cuarto de hora vuelta a una casa.»

Sólo echaba de menos la animación de su fábrica, las compañeras. A bien que las vecinas de la calle solían acercarse a ofrecerle un rato de palique: una sobre todo, Pepa la comadrona, por mal nombre señora *Porreta*.[7] Era esta mujer colosal, a lo ancho más aún que a lo alto; parecíase a tosca estatua labrada para ser vista de lejos. Su cara enorme, circuida por colgante papada, tenía palidez serosa. Calzaba zapatillas de hombre y usaba una sortija, de tamaño masculino también, en el dedo meñique. Acercábase a la cama de la impedida, sometía las ropas, abofeteaba la almohada para que «quedase a gusto» y después se sentaba, apoyando fuertemente ambas manos en los muslos, a fin de sostener la mole del vientre, y, con voz sorda y apagada, empezaba a referir chismes del barrio, escabrosos pormenores de su profesión, o las maravillosas curas que pueden obtenerse con un cocimiento de ruda, huevo y aceite; con la hoja de la malva bien machacadita, con romero hervido en vino, con unturas de enjundia de gallina. Susurraban los maldicientes que entre parleta y parleta solía la matrona entreabrir el pañuelo que le cubría los hombros y sacar una botellica que fácilmente se ocultaba en cualquier rincón de su corpiño gigantesco; y ya corroboraba con un trago de anís el exhausto gaznate, ya ofrecía la botella a su interlocutora «para ir pasando las penas de este mundo». A oídos del señor Rosendo llegó un día esta especie, y se alarmó; porque mientras estuvo en la fábrica no bebía nunca su mujer más que agua pura; pero por mucho que entró impensadamente algunas tardes, no cogió *in fraganti* a las delincuentes. Sólo vio que estaban muy amigotas y compinches. Para la ex cigarrera valía un Perú[8] la comadrona; al menos esa hablaba, porque lo que es su marido… Cuando éste regresaba de la diaria correría por paseos y sitios públicos, y bajando el hombro soltaba con estrépito el tubo en la esquina de la habitación, el diálogo del matrimonio era siempre el mismo:

–¿Qué tal? –preguntaba la tullida.

Y el señor Rosendo pronunciaba una de estas tres frases: «Menos mal», «Un regular», «Condenadamente».

---

7 (En) porreta o porretas: desnudo, en cueros.
8 Según la Real Academia Española, 'valer un Perú' equivale a 'ser de mucho precio o estimación'. El origen de la frase se remonta a la época de la conquista del Perú cuando los cronistas españoles tomaron nota de las inmensas riquezas de los Incas.

don't know what health is until after it's lost!' she exclaimed sententiously, especially on the days when arthritic pain gnawed at her joints. At other times, boastful like all invalids, she would say to her daughter: 'Get away from me, just seeing you irritates me; when I was your age I was a fiend who could clean a house in a quarter of an hour.'

The only thing she missed was the bustle of the factory: her companions. It's true that the neighbours on the street used to come over for a bit of a natter; one in particular was Pepa the midwife, impolitely called Señora *Starkers*.[4] She was a huge woman, even more so in width than in height; she looked like a rough statue that had been carved to be seen from a distance. Her enormous face, surrounded by a pendulous double chin, had a serous pallor about it. She wore a man's slippers and a man-sized ring on her little finger. She would come over to the crippled woman's bed, arrange the bed linen, slap the pillow so that it 'felt just right', and then sit down, leaning both hands heavily on her thighs in order to support the bulk of her stomach; and in her muffled, quiet voice she would begin recounting the neighbourhood gossip, salacious details about her profession, or the marvellous cures that can be obtained with a brew of rue, egg and oil, or with finely crushed mallow leaves, with rosemary boiled in wine, or with ointments made from hen's fat. Slanderous tongues whispered that, in between one bit of idle chitchat and another, the midwife would half-open the shawl that covered her shoulders and take out a small bottle easily hidden in some corner of her enormous bodice, and firstly re-invigorate her exhausted gullet with a swig of anisette, then offer the bottle to the woman with whom she was talking 'to wear off the sorrows of this world'. One day this piece of news reached Señor Rosendo's ears, and he was alarmed, because while she was at the factory his wife only drank pure water; but no matter how many afternoons he went in unexpectedly, he never caught the criminals redhanded. All he could see was that they were real cronies and partners in crime. For the ex-cigar maker the midwife was worth her weight in gold; at least she talked, because as for her husband… When he returned from his daily rounds of the esplanades and public places, and lowered his shoulder to release the tubular container noisily in a corner of the room, the dialogue between husband and wife was always the same:

'How did it go?' the paralysed woman would ask.

And Señor Rosendo uttered one of these three phrases: 'It could be

---

4   The interjection 'porreta' is constantly used by the midwife, Pepa. 'En porreta' is a colloquial expression that means 'starkers'.

Aludía a la venta, y jamás se dio caso de que agregase género alguno de amplificación o escolio a sus oraciones clásicas. Poseía el inquebrantable laconismo popular, que vence al dolor, al hambre, a la muerte y hasta a la dicha. Soldado reenganchado, uncido en sus mejores años al férreo yugo de la disciplina militar, se convenció de la ociosidad de la palabra y necesidad del silencio. Calló primero por obediencia, luego por fatalismo, después por costumbre. En silencio elaboraba los barquillos, en silencio los vendía, y casi puede decirse que los voceaba en silencio, pues nada tenía de análogo a la afectuosa comunicación que establece el lenguaje entre seres racionales y humanos, aquel grito gutural en que, tal vez para ahorrar un fragmento de palabra, el viejo suprimía la última sílaba, reemplazándola por doliente prolongación de la vocal penúltima:

–Barquilleeeeé...

worse', 'So-so', 'Damnedly'.

He was referring to his sales, and never gave any thought to adding any kind of amplification or scholium to his classical remarks. He possessed that unyielding, working-class laconism that overcomes pain, hunger, death and even happiness. As a reenlisted soldier, subjected throughout his best years to the iron yoke of military discipline, he became convinced of the idleness of words and the necessity of silence. At first he kept silent out of obedience, later through fatalism, afterwards out of habit. He made the pastry cones in silence, he sold them in silence, and one could almost say that he hawked them in silence, because there was no similarity between the expression of affective communication that language establishes between rational human beings and that guttural shout in which, perhaps to save using a fragment of a word, the old man suppressed the last syllable, replacing it with a mournful prolongation of the penultimate vowel:

'Pastreeeee…'

III

PUEBLO DE SU NACIMIENTO

Al sentar el pie en la calle, Amparo respiró anchamente. El sol, llegado al zenit, lo alegraba todo. En los umbrales de las puertas los gatos, acurrucados, presentaban el lomo al benéfico calorcillo, guiñando sus pupilas de tigre y roncando de gusto. Las gallinas iban y venían escarbando. La bacía del barbero, colgada sobre la muestra y rodeada de una sarta de muelas rancias ya, brillaba como plata. Reinaba la soledad; los vecinos se habían ido a misa o de bureo, y media docena de párvulos, confiados al Ángel de la Guarda, se solazaban entre el polvo y las inmundicias del arroyo, con la chola descubierta y expuestos a un tabardillo. Amparo se arrimó a una de las ventanas bajas, y tocó en los cristales con el puño cerrado. Abriéronse las vidrieras, y se vio la cara de una muchacha pelinegra y descolorida, que tenía en la mano una almohadilla de labrar donde había clavados infinidad de menudos alfileres.

–¡Hola!

–¡Hola, Carmela! ¿Andas con la labor a vueltas? Pues es día de misa.

–Por eso me da rabia … contestó la muchacha pálida, que hablaba con cierto ceceo, propio de los puertecitos de mar en la provincia de Marineda.

–Sal un poco, mujer … vente conmigo.

–Hoy… ¡quién puede! Hay un encargo … diez y seis varas de puntilla para una señora del barrio de Arriba… El martes se han de entregar sin falta.

Carmela se sentó otra vez con su almohadilla en el regazo, mientras los hombros de Amparo se alzaban entre compasivos e indiferentes, como si murmurasen: «¡Lo de costumbre!» Apartóse de allí, y sus pies descendieron con suma agilidad la escalinata de la plaza de Abastos, llena a la sazón de cocineras y vendedoras, y enhebrándose por entre cestas de gallinas, de huevos, de quesos, salió a la calle de San Efrén, y luego al atrio de la iglesia, donde se detuvo deslumbrada.

Cuanto lujo ostenta un domingo en una capital de provincia se veía reunido ante el pórtico, que las gentes cruzaban con el paso majestuoso de personas bien trajeadas y compuestas, gustosas en ser vistas y mutuamente resueltas a respetarse y a no promover empujones. Hacían cola las señoras aguardando su turno, empavesadas y solemnes, con mucha mantilla de blonda, mucho

3
THE TOWN OF HER BIRTH

When she set foot in the street, Amparo breathed deeply. The sun, having reached its zenith, made everything cheerful. Cats, curled up on the thresholds of the doorways, offered their backs to the nice beneficial warmth, winking their tiger-like pupils and purring with pleasure. The hens were coming and going, scratching the ground. The barber's bowl, hanging from the sign and surrounded by a string of now rotting teeth, was shining like silver. Solitude reigned; the neighbours had gone to Mass or out on the town, and half a dozen children, entrusted to the Guardian Angel, enjoyed themselves amidst the dust and rubbish of the gutter, their heads uncovered and exposed to sunstroke. Amparo flattened herself against one of the ground floor windows, and rapped on the panes with her closed fist. The window opened and revealed the face of a pale, black-haired girl holding a pincushion studded with countless small pins.

'Hello!'

'Hello, Carmela! Are you on with that needlework again? It's a day for going to Mass.'

'That's what makes me angry,' the pale girl answered, speaking with a certain lisp, typical of the small seaports in the province of Marineda.

'Come on out a bit ... come with me.'

'Today ... if only! There's a job ... sixteen yards of lace for a lady in the Arriba district... It has to be delivered on Tuesday without fail.'

Carmela sat down again with the cushion in her lap, whilst Amparo's shoulders rose up, half compassionate and half indifferent, as if they were murmuring: 'The same old story!' She moved away, and with consummate agility her feet descended the steps of the Plaza de Abastos, which at that time was filled with female cooks and sellers, and threading her way through baskets of hens, eggs and cheeses, she came out on the Calle de San Efrén, and then the church atrium where she stopped in a daze.

Whatever luxury a provincial capital might flaunt on a Sunday could be seen gathered in front of the portico, which the people passed through with the majestic step of smart, well-dressed persons, keen to be noticed and with the mutual resolve to respect one another and not engage in pushing and shoving. The ladies were waiting their turn in a queue, dressed up and

devocionario de canto dorado, mucho rosario de oro y nácar, las madres vestidas de seda negra, las niñas casaderas, de colorines vistosos. Al llegar a los postigos que más allá del pórtico daban entrada a la nave, había crujidos de enaguas almidonadas, blandos empellones, codazos suaves, respiración agitada de damas obesas, cruces de rosarios que se enganchaban en un encaje o en un fleco, frases de miel con su poco de vinagre, como «¡Ay! Usted dispense…», «A mí me empujan, señora; por eso yo…», «No tire usted así, que se romperá el adorno…», «Perdone usted…»

Deslizóse Amparo entre el grupo de la buena sociedad marinedina, y se introdujo en el templo. Hacia el presbiterio se colocaban las señoritas, arrodilladas con estudio, a fin de no arrugarse los trapos de cristianar, y como tenían la cabeza baja, veíanse blanquear sus nucas, y alguna estrecha suela de elegante botita remangaba los pliegues de las faldas de seda. El centro de la nave lo ocupaba el piquete y la banda de música militar, en correcta formación. A ambos lados, filas de hombres, que miraban al techo o a las capillas laterales, como si no supiesen qué hacer de los ojos. De pronto lució en el altar mayor la vislumbre de oro y colores de una casulla de tisú; quedó el concurso en mayor silencio; las damas alzaron sus libros en las enguantadas manos, y a un tiempo murmuró el sacerdote: *Introibo*, y rompió en sonoro acorde la charanga, haciendo oír las profanas notas de *Traviata*, cabalmente los compases ardientes y febriles del dúo erótico del primer acto. El son vibrante de los metales añadía intensidad al canto, que, elevándose amplio y nutrido hasta la bóveda, bajaba después a extenderse, contenido, pero brioso, por la nave y el crucero, para cesar, de repente, al alzarse la Hostia; cuando esto sucedió, la Marcha Real, poderosa y magnífica, brotó de los marciales instrumentos, sin que a intervalos dejase de escucharse en el altar el misterioso repiqueteo de la campanilla del acólito.

A la salida, repetición del desfile; junto a la pila se situaron tres o cuatro de los que ya no se llamaban dandis ni todavía gomosos, sino *pollos*[9] y *gallos*, haciendo ademán de humedecer los dedos en agua bendita, y tendiéndolos bien enjutos a las damiselas para conseguir un fugaz contacto de guantes vigilado por el ojo avizor de las mamás. Una vez en el pórtico, era lícito

---

9 El término 'pollo', según Galdós, fue aplicado a los jóvenes de buena sociedad desde 1846:

El llamar pollos a los muchachos es uso moderno, y data del 46 […] nombre de pollos tuvieron ya para in aeternum todos los jovencitos bien vestidos y arrogantes que buscan dotes o pretenden los favores de mujeres hechas, más o menos casadas, bien o mal avenidas con sus esposos. *Narváez* (Madrid: Est. Tip. de la Viuda e Hijos de Tello, 1902), capítulo XV, pp. 152–53.

solemn, with lots of lace mantillas, lots of gilt-edged prayer books, lots of rosaries of gold and mother-of-pearl, mothers dressed in black silk, the nubile girls in bright colours. When they reached the wickets, which opened into the nave at the far end of the portico, there was the crackling of starched petticoats, gentle shoving, polite elbowing, the agitated breathing of obese ladies, rosary crosses which got caught on a bit of lace or a fringe, honeyed words sprinkled with vinegar, like, 'Oh, excuse me...', 'They're pushing me, madam, that's why I...', 'Don't pull like that, or the decoration will break...', 'Forgive me...'

Amparo slipped through the group of Marinedan high society, and made her way into the temple. The young ladies stood near the presbytery, carefully kneeling so as not to wrinkle their Sunday finery, and since their heads were bowed, you could see the whiteness of the backs of their necks and occasionally the narrow sole of an elegant high-topped shoe as it hitched up the folds of their silk skirts. The centre of the nave was occupied by the picket guard and the military music band in correct formation. On both sides, rows of men looking at the ceiling or the side chapels, as if they didn't know what to do with their eyes. Suddenly the glimmer of gold and colours of a lamé chasuble shone on the high altar; the congregation became even more silent; the ladies raised their books in gloved hands, and at the same time the priest murmured: *Introibo*, and the brass band broke out into loud strains, with everyone hearing the profane notes from *La Traviata*, precisely the ardent and feverish measures of the erotic duet in the first act. The vibrant sound of the brass added intensity to the song, which, rising up fully and loudly to the vault, descended then and spread out, restrained yet spirited, through the nave and transept, suddenly stopping when the Host was raised; when this happened, the national anthem burst forth powerfully and magnificently from the martial instruments, without it stopping the mysterious tinkle of the acolyte's handbell being heard every now and then on the altar.

On the way out the same parade was repeated; next to the font were three or four of the sort no longer called dandies, and not yet fops, but *popinjays* and *peacocks*, pretending to wet in holy water and then extend their slender fingers to the damsels in order to achieve brief contact with their gloves, all

levantar la cabeza, mirar a todos lados, sonreír, componerse furtivamente la mantilla, buscar un rostro conocido y devolver un saludo. Tras el deber, el placer; ahora, la selecta multitud se dirigía al paseo, convidada de la música y de la alegría de un benigno domingo de marzo, en que el sol sembraba la regocijada atmósfera de átomos de oro y tibios efluvios primaverales. Amparo se dejó llevar por la corriente y presto vino a encontrarse en el paseo.

No tenía entonces Marineda el parque inglés que, andando el tiempo, hermoseó su recinto; y las Filas, donde se daban vueltas durante las mañanas de invierno y las tardes de verano, eran una estrecha avenida, pavimentada de piedra, de una parte guarnecida por alta hilera de casas, de otra por una serie de bancos que coronaban toscas estatuas alegóricas de las estaciones, de las virtudes, mutiladas y privadas de manos y narices por la travesura de los muchachos. Sombreaban los asientos acacias de tronco enteco, de clorótico follaje (cuando Dios se lo daba), sepultadas entre piedras por todos lados, como prisioneros en torre feudal. A la sazón carecían de hojas, pero la caricia abrasadora del sol impelía a la savia a subir, a las yemas a hincharse. Las desnudas ramas se recortaban sobre el limpio matiz del firmamento, y a lo lejos, el mar, de un azul metálico, como empavonado, reposaba, viéndose inmóviles las jarcias y arboladura de los buques surtos en la bahía, y quietos hasta los impacientes gallardetes de los mástiles. Ni un soplo de brisa, ni nada que desdijese de la apacibilidad profunda y soñolienta del ambiente.

Caído el pañuelo y recibiendo a plomo el sol en la mollera, miraba Amparo con gran interés el espectáculo que el paseo presentaba. Señoras y caballeros giraban en el corto trecho de las Filas, a paso lento y acompasado, guardando escrupulosamente la derecha. La implacable claridad solar azuleaba el paño negro de las relucientes levitas, suavizaba los fuertes colores de las sedas, descubría las menores imperfecciones de los cutis, el salseo de los guantes, el sitio de las antiguas puntadas en la ropa reformada ya. No era difícil conocer al primer golpe de vista a las notabilidades de la ciudad; una fila de altos sombreros de felpa, de bastones de roten o concha con puño de oro, de gabanes de castor, todo puesto en caballeros provectos y seriotes, revelaba claramente a las autoridades, regente, magistrados, segundo cabo, gobernador civil; seis o siete pantalones gris perla, pares de guantes claros y flamantes corbatas denunciaban a la dorada juventud; unas cuantas sombrillas de raso, un ramillete de vestidos que trascendían de mil

under the vigilant eyes of the mothers. Once in the portico, it was permitted to raise one's head, look around in all directions, smile, rearrange your mantilla furtively, search for a familiar face and return a greeting. After duty, pleasure; now the select multitude headed for the esplanade, invited by the music and the joy of a mild Sunday in March, when the sun was spreading its cheerful atmosphere of golden atoms and warm spring vapours. Amparo let herself be carried along by the current and soon came to find herself on the esplanade.

At that time Marineda did not have the English park which later on embellished this area; and Las Filas, where people would stroll during winter mornings and summer afternoons, was a narrow avenue paved with stone, garnished by a high row of houses on one side, and on the other by a series of benches crowned with crude allegorical statues of the seasons and the virtues, mutilated and deprived of hands and noses by youngsters' pranks. The seats were shaded by acacia trees with frail trunks and chlorotic leaves (when God granted them any), buried amidst stones on all sides, like prisoners in a feudal tower. At that time of year they had no leaves, but the scorching caress of the sun caused the sap to rise and the buds to swell. The naked branches stood out against the limpid shade of the sky, and in the distance the sea, a metallic azure, like bluing glaze, lay calm, and you could see the motionless rigging and the masts of the boats anchored in the bay, and even the impatient pennants on the masts were still. Not a breath of breeze, nor anything that might clash with the profound, sleepy calmness of the atmosphere.

With her scarf off and the sun beating straight down on the crown of her head, Amparo watched with great interest the spectacle offered on the esplanade. Ladies and gentlemen were circulating along the short length of Las Filas at a slow, measured pace, scrupulously keeping to the right. The relentless brightness of the sun made the black fabric of the shiny frock coats look blue, softened the intense colours of the silks, and revealed the slightest imperfections of the complexion, the stains on the gloves and the marks of the old stitches on altered clothes. It wasn't difficult to recognise the notable persons of the city at first glance; a row of high plush hats, rattan or inlaid tortoiseshell walking sticks with gold handles, beaver skin coats, all worn by elderly, solemn gentlemen, clearly pointed out the authorities, the Regent, the magistrates, the second in command and the civil governor; six or seven pairs of pearl-grey trousers, light-coloured gloves and garish ties betrayed the gilded youth; several satin parasols and a select assortment of dresses,

leguas a importación madrileña, indicaban a las dueñas del cetro de la moda. Las gentes pasaban, y volvían a pasar, y estaban pasando continuamente, y a cada vuelta se renovaba la misma procesión, por el mismo orden.

Un grupo de oficiales de Infantería y Caballería ocupaba un banco entero, y el sol parecía concentrarse allí, atraído por el resplandor de los galones y estrellas de oro, por los pantalones rojo vivo, por el relampagueo de las vainas de sable y el hule reluciente del casco de los roses. Los oficiales, gente de buen humor y jóvenes casi todos, reían, charlaban y hasta jugaban con un enjambre de elegantes niñas, que ni la mayor sumaría doce años, ni la menor bajaba de tres. Tenían a las más pequeñas sentadas en las rodillas, mientras las otras, de pie y con unos atisbos de pudor femenil, no osaban acercarse mucho al banco, haciendo como que platicaban entre sí, cuando realmente sólo atendían a la conversación de los militares. Al otro extremo del paseo se oyó entonces un grito conocidísimo de la chiquillería.

–Barquilleeeeé...

–Batilos ... a mí batilos, chilló al oírlo una rubilla carrilluda, que cabalgaba en la pierna izquierda de un capitán de infantería portador de formidables mostachos.

–Nisita, no seas fastidiosa; te llevo a mamá –amonestó una de las mayores, con gravedad imponente.

–Pué teo batilos, batiiilos –berreó descompasadamente la rubia, colorada como un pavo y apretando sus puñitos.

–Tiene usted razón, señorita, díjole risueño un alférez de linda y adamada figura, al ver que el angelito pateaba y hacía pucheros para romper a llorar. Espérese usted, que habrá barquillos. Llamaremos a ese digno funcionario... Ya viene hacia acá. Usted, Borrén –añadió dirigiéndose al capitán...–, ¿quiere usted darle una voz?

–¡Eh..., chis! ¡Barquilleeeeró! –gritó el capitán mostachudo, sin notar que el círculo de las grandecitas se reía de su ronquera crónica.

No obstante la cual, el señor Rosendo le oyó, y se acercaba, derrengado con el peso de la caja, que depositó en el suelo delante del grupo. Se oyeron como píos y aleteos, el ruido de una canariera cuando le ponen alpiste, y las chiquillas corrieron a rodear el tubo, mientras las grandes se hacían las desdeñosas, cual si las humillase la idea de que a su edad las convidaran a barquillos. Inclinada la rubia pedigüeña sobre la especie de ruleta que coronaba la caja de hojalata, impulsaba con su dedito la aguja, chillando

that reeked even from a thousand miles away of having been imported from Madrid, pointed out the owners as the pinnacle of fashion. People passed, and passed again, and kept passing continually, and with each turn the same procession would renew itself, in the same order.

A group of infantry and cavalry officers were occupying an entire bench, and the sun seemed to be concentrated there, attracted by the brilliance of the braid and gold stars, the bright red trousers, the flashing of the scabbards of the sabre and the shiny oilskin surface of the shakos. The officers, almost all good-humoured young men, were laughing, chatting and even playing with a swarm of elegant little girls, the oldest no more than twelve and the youngest no less than three. They had the smallest ones seated on their knees, while the others, on their feet showing signs of feminine modesty, did not dare to get very close to the bench, making out as if they were talking amongst themselves, when in reality they were listening only to the officers' conversation. At the other end of the esplanade a cry that was very familiar to the little children could then be heard:

'Pastreee…'

'Pastwies … me wants pastwies,' screeched a little, chubby-cheeked blonde girl when she heard him, riding horsey on the left leg of an infantry captain with a formidable moustache.

'Nisita, don't be a pest; I'll take you back to mama,' warned one of the older girls with imposing gravity.

'But me want pastwies, pastweees,' the blonde girl bawled rudely, as red as a turkey and clenching her fists.

'You're right, young lady,' said a smiling second lieutenant with a nice, effeminate face when he saw that the little angel was stamping her feet, screwing up her face and about to start crying. 'Just you wait, there will be pastry cones. We'll call over that worthy …. … he's coming over here. Borrén,' he added, addressing the captain, 'would you give him a call?'

'Hey … psst! Mr Pastry man!' shouted the moustachioed captain, without realising that the circle of older girls were laughing at his chronic hoarseness.

In spite of this, Señor Rosendo heard him, and came over, bent over by the weight of the box, which he deposited on the ground in front of the group. The sound of chirping and fluttering could be heard, like the noise of a canary cage when birdseed is put in, and the small girls ran over to surround the tubular container, whilst the older ones acted with disdain, as if the idea that at their age they be invited to have pastry cones was humiliating. The persistent blonde girl leaning over the kind of roulette wheel that crowned

de regocijo cuando se detenía en un número, ya ganase, ya perdiese. Su júbilo rayó en paroxismo al punto que, tendiendo la mano abierta, encima de cada dedo fue el señor Rosendo calzándole una torre de barquillos; quedóse extasiada mirándolos, sin atreverse a abrir la boca para comérselos.

Estando en esto, el alférez volvió casualmente la cabeza y divisó del otro lado de los bancos un rostro de niña pobre que devoraba con los ojos la reunión. Figuróse que sería por apetito de barquillos, y le hizo una seña, con ánimo de regalarle algunos. La muchacha se acercó, fascinada por el brillo de la sociedad alegre y juvenil; pero al entender que la brindaban con tomar parte en el banquete, encogióse de hombros y movió negativamente la cabeza.

–Bien harta estoy de ellos –pronunció con desdén.

–Es *la hija* –explicó sin manifestar sorpresa el barquillero, que embolsaba la calderilla y bajaba el hombro para ceñirse otra vez la correa.

–Por lo visto, eres la señorita de Roséndez –murmuró el alférez en son de broma–. Vamos, Borrén, usted que es animado, dígale algo a esta pollita.

El de los mostachos consideraba a la recién venida atentamente, como un arqueólogo miraría un ánfora acabada de encontrar en una excavación. A las palabras del alférez contestó con ronco acento:

–Pues vaya si le diré, hombre. Si estoy reparando en esta chica, y es de lo mejorcito que pasea por Marineda. Es decir, por ahora está sin formar, ¿eh? –y el capitán abría y cerraba las dos manos como dibujando en el aire unos contornos mujeriles–. Pero yo no necesito verlas cuando se completan, hombre; yo las huelo antes, amigo Baltasar. Soy perro viejo, ¿eh? Dentro de un par de años... –y Borrén hizo otro gesto expresivo cual si se relamiese.

Miraba el alférez a la muchacha, y admirábase de las predicciones de Borrén; es verdad que había ojos grandes, pobladas pestañas, dientes como gotas de leche; pero la tez era cetrina, el pelo embrollado semejaba un felpudo, y el cuerpo y traje competían en desaliño y poca gracia. Con todo, por seguir la broma, hizo el alférez que asentía a la opinión del capitán, y pronunció:

–Digo lo que el amigo Borrén: esta pollita nos va a dar muchos disgustos...

Los oficiales se echaron a reír, y Amparo a su vez se fijó en el que hablaba, sin comprender al pronto sus frases.

the tin box, propelled the needle with her little finger, screaming with delight whenever it stopped on a number, whether she won or lost. Her joy was verging on paroxysm at the moment when, holding her hand open, Señor Rosendo piled a tower of pastry cones on each of her fingers; she stood there in ecstasy looking at them, not daring to open her mouth to eat them up.

While this was going on, the second lieutenant casually turned his head and made out the face of a poor young girl on the other side of the benches, devouring the gathering with her eyes. He imagined that she would have an appetite for some pastry cones, and he made a sign to her with the intention of buying her some. The girl approached, fascinated by the splendour of the cheerful children, but when she realised that she was being invited to partake in the banquet, she shrugged her shoulders and shook her head.

'I've had my fill of them,' she proclaimed disdainfully.

'She's my daughter,' the pastry cone seller explained without showing any surprise, as he pocketed the small change and lowered his shoulder to fit on the leather strap again.

'Apparently you're Señorita Roséndez,' murmured the second lieutenant in a jesting manner. 'Come on, Borrén, you're the lively one, say something to this little chick.'

The one with the moustache examined the recent arrival attentively, like an archaeologist would look at an amphora he had just found in an excavation. He replied to the second lieutenant's words in a hoarse voice:

'I'm going to tell her. I've been paying attention to this girl, and she's the best thing walking around Marineda. That is to say, she's not fully developed yet, eh?' and the captain opened and closed his two hands as if sketching womanly curves in the air. 'But I don't need to see them when they're completely finished; I can sniff them out beforehand, my dear friend Baltasar. I'm an old hand, eh? Within a couple of years ...' and Borrén made another gesture as if he were licking his chops.

The second lieutenant was looking at the girl, and was amazed at Borrén's predictions; it's true that she had big eyes, thick eyelashes, teeth like drops of milk; but her complexion was sallow, her tangled hair looked like a doormat, and her body and her dress were equally slovenly and graceless. Nevertheless, to carry on the joke, the second lieutenant acted as if he agreed with the captain's opinion, and proclaimed:

'I agree with our friend Borrén: this little thing is going to give us lots of grief ...'

The officers started laughing, and in turn Amparo stared at the one who was talking, without at first understanding his meaning.

–Cosas de Borrén… Ese Borrén es célebre –exclamaron con algazara los militares, a quienes no parecía ningún prodigio la chiquilla.

–Reparen ustedes, señores –siguió el alférez–; la chica es una perla; dentro de dos años nos mareará a todos. ¿Qué dices tú a eso, señorita de Roséndez? Por de pronto, a mí me ha desairado no aceptando mis barquillos… Mira, te convido a lo que quieras, a dulces, a jerez … pero con una condición.

Amparo enrollaba las puntas del pañuelo sin dejar de mirar de reojo a su interlocutor. No era lerda, y recelaba que se estuviesen burlando; sin embargo, le agradaba oír aquella voz y mirar aquel uniforme refulgente.

–¿Aceptas la condición? Lo dicho, te convido … pero tienes que darme algo tú también: me darás un beso.

Soltaron la carcajada los oficiales, ni más ni menos que si el alférez hubiese proferido alguna notable agudeza; las niñas grandecitas se volvieron haciendo que no oían, y Amparo, que tenía sus pupilas oscuras clavadas en el rostro del mancebo, las bajó de pronto, quiso disparar una callejera fresca, sintió que la voz se le atascaba en la laringe, se encendió en rubor desde la frente hasta la barba, y echó a correr como alma que lleva el diablo.

'That's Borrén all over ... That Borrén is famous,' exclaimed uproariously the soldiers, to whom the young girl did not seem anything special.

'Just take heed, gentlemen,' the second lieutenant continued, 'the girl is a pearl; within two years she'll be making us all dizzy. What do you say to that, Señorita Roséndez? For the moment, you've snubbed me by refusing my pastry cones ... Look, I'll invite you to whatever you want, sweets, sherry ... but with one condition.'

Amparo rolled up the ends of her scarf, still looking out of the corner of her eye at the man who was talking to her. She wasn't slow-witted, and she feared that they were laughing at her; however, she enjoyed hearing that voice and looking at that shining uniform.

'Do you accept the condition? All right then, I invite you ... but you also have to give me something: you'll give me a kiss.'

The officers burst out laughing, just as if the second lieutenant had uttered some notable witticism; the older girls turned away, acting as if they hadn't heard, and Amparo, who had her dark pupils fixed on the young man's face, suddenly lowered them, tried to fire off some fresh streetwise remark, felt that her voice was drying up in her throat, started to blush from her forehead to her chin, and started running like a bat out of hell.

IV
QUE LOS TENGA MUY FELICES

Se ha mudado la decoración; ha pasado casi un año; corre el mes de enero. No llueve; el cielo está aborregado de nubes lívidas que presagian tormenta, y el viento costeño, redondo, giratorio como los ciclones, arremolina el polvo, los fragmentos de papel, los residuos de toda especie que deja la vida diaria en las calles de una ciudad. Parece como si se hubiesen asociado vendaval y cierzo: aquél para aullar, soplar, mugir; éste para herir los semblantes con finísimos picotazos de aguja, colgar gotitas de fluxión en las fosas nasales, azulear las mejillas y enrojecer los párpados. En verdad que con semejante tiempo los Santos Reyes, que caballeros en sus dromedarios venían desde el misterioso país de la luz, atravesando la Palestina, a saludar al Niño, debieron notar que se les helaban las manos, llenas de incienso y mirra, y subir más que a paso la esclavina de aquellas dulletas de armiño y púrpura con que los representan los pintores. A falta de esclavina, los marinedinos alzaban cuanto podían el cuello del gabán o el embozo de la capa. Es que el viento era frío de veras, y sobre todo, incómodo; costaba un triunfo pelear con él. Entrábase por las bocacalles, impetuoso y arrollador, bufando y barriendo a las gentes, a manera de fuelle gigantesco. En el páramo de Solares, que separa el barrio de Arriba del de Abajo, pasaban lances cómicos: capas que se enrollaban en las piernas y no dejaban andar a sus dueños; enaguas almidonadas que se volvían hacia arriba con fieros estallidos; aguadores que no podían con la cuba, curiales a quienes una ráfaga arrebataba y dispersaba el protocolo, señoritos que corrían diez minutos tras de una chistera fugitiva, que, al fin, franqueando de un brinco el parapeto del muelle, desaparecía entre las agitadas olas… Hasta los edificios tomaban parte en la batalla: aullaban los canalones, las fallebas de las ventanas temblequeaban, retemblaban los cristales de las galerías, coreando el dúo de bajos, profundo, amenazador y temeroso, entonado por los dos mares, el de la bahía y el del Varadero. Tampoco estaban ellos para bromas.

En cambio, celebrábase gran fiesta en una casa de ricos comerciantes del barrio de Abajo, la de Sobrado Hermanos. Era el santo de Baltasar, único vástago masculino del tronco de los Sobrados, y cuando más diabluras hacía fuera el viento, circulaban en el comedor los postres de una pesada comida de provincia, en que el gusto no había enmendado la abundancia.

4
MANY HAPPY RETURNS

The scenery has changed; almost a year has passed; it is currently the month of January. It isn't raining; the sky is covered with pale clouds presaging a storm, and the coastal wind, spinning round like a cyclone, swirls the dust, the fragments of paper, the refuse of all kinds left by daily life in the streets of a city. It seems as if the strong sea wind had joined forces with the north wind; the former to howl, blow, roar; the latter to sting faces with very fine needle pricks, to leave small drops of discharge hanging from nostrils, to turn cheeks blue and eyelids red. To tell the truth, in such weather the holy Wise Men, riding camels through Palestine from the mysterious country of light to hail the Christ-child, must have noted that their hands, full of incense and myrrh, were freezing, and they must have hastily pulled up the short capes of those quilted ermine and purple coats in which the painters represent them. Lacking such a cape, the people of Marineda raised the collar of their overcoats or the flaps of their cloaks as high as they could. The fact is the wind was really cold and above all uncomfortable; it was a huge effort struggling against it. Along the side streets it blew, violent and overwhelming, gusting and sweeping people along like a gigantic bellows. In the Páramo de Solares, which separates the Barrio de Arriba from the Barrio de Abajo,[x] comic incidents occurred: capes twisting around legs, preventing their owners from walking, starched petticoats blown up in the air with wild, cracking sounds, water sellers unable to manage their casks, court clerks whose legal records were snatched away and dispersed by a gust of wind, young gentlemen who spent ten minutes running after their top hats which finally, bounding over the parapet wall of the wharf, disappeared in the agitated waves … Even the buildings took part in the battle; the gutters were howling, the door and window catches were shaking violently, the glass along the galleries was shaking, the duet of basses singing in chorus, in a deep, threatening and fearsome way, intoned by the two seas, those of the bay and the Varadero. And nor were they in a mood for joking.

On the other hand, a grand fiesta was being celebrated at the house of some rich merchants in the Barrio de Abajo, that of the Sobrado brothers. It was Baltasar's saint's day,[xi] the only male descendant of the Sobrado line, and as the wind was making more mischief outside, in the dining room they were circulating the desserts of a heavy provincial style meal, in which good

Sucediéranse, plato tras plato, los cebados capones, manidos y con amarilla grasa; el pavo relleno; el jamón en dulce con costra de azúcar tostado; las natillas, con arabescos de canela, y la tarta, el indispensable ramillete de los días de días, con sus cimientos de almendra, sus torres de piñonate, sus cresterías de caramelo y su angelote de almidón ejecutando una pirueta con las alas tendidas. Ya se aburrían los grandes de estar en la mesa; no así los niños. Ni a tres tirones se levantarían ellos, cabalmente en el feliz instante en que era lícito tirarse confites, comer con los dedos, hacer, de puro ahítos, mil porquerías y comistrajos con su ración. Todo el mundo les dejaba alborotar; era el momento de la desbandada; se habían pronunciado brindis y contado anécdotas con mayor o menor donaire; pero ya nadie tenía ánimos para sostener la conversación, y el Sobrado tío, que era grueso y abotargado, se abanicaba con la servilleta. Levantó la sesión el ama de casa, doña Dolores, diciendo que el café estaba prevenido en la sala de recibir.

En ésta se habían prodigado las luces: dos bujías a los lados del piano vertical; sobre la consola, en los candelabros de cinc, otras cuatro de estearina rosa, acanaladas; en el velador central, entre los álbumes y estereóscopos, un gran quinqué con pantalla de papel picado. Iluminación completa. ¡Es que por Baltasar echaban gustosos los Sobrados la casa por la ventana, y más ahora que lo veían de uniforme, tan lindo y galán mozo! A la fiesta habían sido convidados todos los íntimos: Borrén, otro alférez llamado Palacios, la viuda de García y sus niñas, de las cuales la menor era Nisita, la rubia de los barquillos, y por último, la maestra de piano de las hermanas de Baltasar. La velada se organizó, mejor dicho, se desordenó gratamente en la sala: cada cual tomó el café donde mejor le plugo: doña Dolores y su cuñado, que resoplaba como una foca, se apoderaron del sofá para entablar una conferencia sobre negocios. Sobrado el padre fumaba un puro del estanco, obsequio de Borrén, y saboreaba su café, aprovechando hasta el del platillo. La niña mayor de García, Josefina, se sentó al piano, después de muy rogada, y entre cien remilgos dio principio a una fantasía sobre motivos de Bellini; Baltasar se colocó a su lado para volver las hojas, mientras sus hermanas gozaban con las gracias de Nisita, que roía un trozo de piñonate; manos, hocico y narices, todo lo tenía empeguntado de almíbar moreno.

taste had not been the equal to abundance. The dishes followed one after another: capons fattened for eating, gamey and yellow with grease; stuffed turkey; boiled, sugar-crusted ham; custard, cinnamon arabesques, and the cake, the indispensable centrepiece of this day of days, with its foundations of almonds, its towers of candied pine nuts, its caramel cresting and its large corn starch angel performing a pirouette with its wings extended. The adults were already bored with sitting at the table; not so the children. Wild horses wouldn't drag them away, exactly at that fortuitous moment when they were allowed to throw sweets at each other, to eat with their fingers, and, because they were so stuffed, to make a pig's ear or a dog's dinner of their portions. Everyone let them run amok; it was time for an exodus; toasts had been offered and anecdotes recounted with more or less wit; but nobody was now in the mood for carrying on the conversation, and Uncle Sobrado, who was thickset and bloated, was fanning himself with his napkin. The mistress of the house, Doña Dolores, adjourned the session, saying coffee was ready in the parlour.

In this room they had been lavish with lights: two candles on the console tables on either side of the upright piano; another four fluted, pink stearin candles in the zinc candelabra; a large oil lamp with a pinked paper shade standing on the round pedestal table in the middle, among the albums and the stereoscopes. Total illumination. The fact is that the Sobrado family was perfectly happy to go to any expense for Baltasar, and especially now when they could admire him in his uniform, so handsome and gallant a young man! All their close friends had been invited to the party: Borrén, another second lieutenant named Palacios, the widow García and her daughters, of whom the youngest was Nisita, the blonde girl with the pastry cones, and finally Baltasar's sisters' piano teacher. The evening gathering was organised, or rather it broke up pleasantly, in the parlour; they all took coffee where it best pleased them. Doña Dolores and her brother-in-law, who was snorting like a seal, claimed the sofa in order to start up a discussion about business; Sobrado, the father, was smoking a cigar from the government-licensed tobacconist's, a gift from Borrén, and savouring his coffee, making the most of even what had spilled into the saucer. The eldest García girl, Josefina, sat down at the piano after much begging and pleading, and very primly and demurely started playing a fantasia based on motifs from Bellini. Baltasar sat down beside her to turn over the pages, while her sisters enjoyed Nisita's antics, as she chewed away on a piece of candied pine nuts; hands, mouth and nostrils, the whole lot was smeared with dark syrup.

–¡Estás bonita! –exclamaba Lola, la mayor de Sobrado–. ¡Puerca, babada, te quedarás sin dientes!

–No me impies –chillaba el angelito–; no me impies ... voy a chucharme ota ves. –Y sacaba de la faltriquera un adarve del castillo de la tarta.

–¿Ha visto usted qué día? –preguntaba Borrén a la viuda de García, que bien quisiera dejar de serlo–. Una garita ha derribado el viento; por más señas que cayó sobre el centinela, ¿eh?, y a poco le mata. Y usted, ¿cómo se vino desde su casa?

–¡Jesús ... puede usted figurarse! Con mil apuros... Yo no sé cómo me arreglé para sujetar la ropa ... y así todo...

–¡Quién estuviera allí! Ya conozco yo alguno...

–¡Jesús ... no sé para qué!

–Para admirar un pie tan lindo ... y para darle el brazo, ¡hombre!, a fin de que el viento no se la llevase.

Juzgó la viuda que aquí convenía fingirse distraída, y cogió el estereóscopo, mirando por él la fachada de las Tullerías. Del piano saltó entonces un *allegro vivace*, con muchas octavas, y el tecleo cubrió las voces ... sólo se oyeron fragmentos del diálogo que sostenían la agria voz de doña Dolores y la voz becerril de su cuñado.

–La fábrica, bien ... de capa caída ... las hipotecas ... al ocho... Liquidaron con el socio ... la competencia...

–Josefina –gritó la viuda a la pianista– ¿qué haces, niña? ¿No te encargó doña Hermitas que pusieses el pedal en ese pasaje?

–Y lo pone –intervino la maestra de piano–; pero debía ser desde el compás anterior... A ver, quiere usted repetir desde ahí ... *sol, la, do, la, do...*?

–¡Lo hace hoy... Jesús, qué mal! ¡Por lo mismo que hay gente! –murmuró la madre–. Cuando está sola, aunque embrolle...

–Pues yo bien vuelvo las hojas; en mí no consiste –dijo risueño Baltasar–. Y debe usted esmerarse, pollita, que estoy de días, y Palacios la oye a usted boquiabierto y entusiasmado.

–¡Bueno! –gritó la mujercita de trece años, suspendiendo de golpe su fantasía–. Me están ustedes cortando ... ea, ya no sé poner los dedos. Como no aprendí la pieza de memoria, y este papel no es el mío... Voy a tocar otra cosa.

'Just look at you!' exclaimed Lola, the eldest Sobrado. 'Filthy, slobbering pig, you'll end up with no teeth!'

'No cwean me,' the little angel screeched; 'no cwean me ... I gonna eat more.'

And she pulled out of her pocket a piece of the parapet walk from the castle of the cake.

'Have you ever seen such a day?' Borrén asked the widow García, who would willingly have given up being that. 'The wind blew down a sentry box; to be precise, it fell on top of the guard and almost killed him. And how about you, how did you get here from your house?'

'Good heavens... you can imagine! With a massive struggle ... I don't know how I managed to hold down my clothes ... and in spite of everything...'

'I wish I'd been there! I know of one...'

'Good heavens ... I don't know what for...'

'To admire such a pretty foot ... and to give you my arm, so that the wind wouldn't carry you away.'

The widow concluded that it would be more appropriate at this point for her to appear interested in something else, and she picked up a stereoscope and looked through it at the facade of the Tuileries. At that moment an *allegro vivace* burst forth from the piano, with many octaves, and the playing drowned out the voices ... all that could be heard were fragments of the dialogue which the tart voice of Doña Dolores and the calf-like voice of her brother-in-law were holding.

'The factory, well ... on the decline ... the mortgages ... at eight percent ... Liquidation with the partner ...the competition...

'Josefina,' the widow shouted at the pianist, 'what are you doing, child? Didn't Doña Hermitas ask you to press the pedal down during that passage?'

'And she is pressing it down,' the piano teacher intervened, 'but it should have been down starting from the previous measure... All right, will you repeat it from there ... *so, la, do, la, do...?*'

'Now she does it... Lord, what's the use! Just when there are people!' her mother muttered. 'When she's on her own, even if she gets into a mess...'

'Well, I'm fine turning the pages; it's not my fault,' said Baltasar with a smile. 'And you'd better do your best, chick, because it's my saint's day, and Palacios is listening to you open-mouthed and fired with enthusiasm.'

'All right,' shouted the little thirteen-year-old lady, suddenly stopping her fantasia. 'You're making it hard for me ... I don't know where to put my fingers any more. As I didn't learn this piece by memory and this score isn't mine ... I'm going to play something else.'

Y echando atrás la cabeza y a Baltasar una mirada fugaz, arrancó del teclado los primeros compases de mimosa habanera. La melodía comenzaba soñolienta, perezosa, yámbica; después, de pronto, tenía un impulso de pasión, un nervioso salto; luego tornaba a desmayarse, a caer en la languidez criolla de su ritmo desigual. Y volvía monótona, repitiendo el tema, y la mujercita, que no sabía interpretar la página clásica del maestro italiano, traducía en cambio a maravilla la enervante molicie amorosa, los poemas incendiarios que en la habanera se encerraban. Josefina, al tocar, se cimbreaba levemente, cual si bailase, y Baltasar estudiaba con curiosidad aquellos tempranos coqueteos, inconscientes casi, todavía candorosos, mientras tarareaba a media voz la letra:

Cuando en la noche la blanca luna…

Diríase que fuera había aplacado la ventolina, pues los goznes de las ventanas ya no gemían, ni temblaban los vidrios. Mas de improviso se escuchó un derrumbamiento, un fragor como si el cielo se desfondase y sus cataratas se abriesen de golpe. Lluvia torrencial, que azotó las paredes, que inundó las tejas, que se precipitó por los canalones abajo, estrellándose en las losas de la calle. En la sala hubo un instante de sorpresa; Josefina interrumpió su habanera; Baltasar se aproximó a la ventana; la viuda soltó el estereóscopo, y a Nisita se le cayó de las manos el piñonate. Casi al mismo tiempo otro ruido, que subía del portal, vino a dominar el ya formidable del aguacero; una algarabía, un *chascarrás*[10] desapacible, unas voces cantando destempladamente con acompañamiento de panderos y castañuelas. Saltaron alborotadas las chiquillas, con Nisita a la cabeza.

–Ya están ahí esas holgazanas –dijo ásperamente doña Dolores–. Anda, Lola –añadió dirigiéndose a su hija mayor–: dile a Juana que las eche del portal, que lo ensuciarán.

–Mamá… ¡lloviendo tanto! –suplicó Lola–. ¡Parece no sé qué decirles que se vayan! ¡Se pondrán como sopas! ¿No oye usted que el cielo se hunde?

–¡Es que eres tonta! –pronunció con rabia la madre–. Si las dejas tocar ahí, después no hay remedio sino darles algo a esas perdidas…

–¿Qué importa, mamá? –intervino Baltasar–. Hoy es mi santo.

---

10   Onomatopeya que imita el sonido de las conchas o de las castañuelas al tañerlas.

And throwing back her head and casting a fleeting glance at Baltasar, she plucked the first measures of an affectionate habanera from the piano keyboard. The melody started up, drowsy, lazy, with iambic stress; then, suddenly, it had passionate drive, a nervous leap; then it grew faint again, descending into the Creole languor of its uneven rhythm. And it turned monotonous, repeating the theme, and the little lady, who didn't know how to interpret the classical page of the Italian maestro, was nevertheless marvellous at conveying the enervating and amorous voluptuousness, the incendiary poems locked up in the habanera. As she played, Josefina gently swayed, as if she were dancing, and Baltasar studied with curiosity those early signs of flirtatiousness, almost unconscious and still innocent, as she softly hummed the words:

When at night the white moon …

It would seem that the light wind outside had abated, because the hinges on the windows were no longer moaning, nor were the panes rattling. But suddenly a great downpour could be heard, a clamour, as if the bottom had fallen out of the heavens and its waterfalls had suddenly opened. Torrential rain that lashed the walls, flooded the roof tiles, and poured down the gutters, crashing onto the flagstones in the street. There was a moment of surprise in the parlour; Josefina interrupted her habanera, Baltasar went over to the window; the widow let go of the stereoscope, and the candied pine nuts fell from Nisita's hands. Almost at the same time, another sound coming up from the hallway overpowered the already awesome noise of the downpour; a hullabaloo, a harsh clicking and rattling, and voices singing out of tune to the accompaniment of tambourines and castanets. The little girls jumped up and down jubilantly, Nisita in front.

'Those layabouts are here again,' Doña Dolores said harshly. 'Come on, Lola,' she added, addressing her eldest daughter, 'get Juana to clear them from the front door, or they'll get it all dirty.'

'Mum … with all that rain!' pleaded Lola. 'I don't think I can tell them to go away! They'll be soaking wet! Can't you hear that the sky is tumbling down?'

'You're so silly!' her mother proclaimed angrily. 'If you let them perform up here, then I'll have no choice but to give something to those down and outs …'

'What does it matter, mum?' interceded Baltasar. 'Today is my saint's day.'

–Que suban, que suban a cantar los Reyes –gritó unánime la concurrencia menor de tres lustros.

–Te uban… Batasal, te uban, te uban –berreó Nisita cruzando sus manos pringosas.

–Que suban, hombre, veremos si son guapas –confirmó Borrén.

Lola de esta vez no necesitó que le reiterasen la orden. Ya estaba bajando las escaleras dos a dos.

'Let them come up, let them come up to sing their carols!' shouted unanimously the gathering of those under three lustra.[5]

'Get dem gum up …, Batasal, get dem gum up, get dem gum up,' bawled Nisita as she crossed her sticky hands.

'Let them come up, and we'll see if they're pretty,' Borrén agreed.

This time Lola didn't need the order to be repeated. She was already going down the stairs two at a time.

---

5 Aged fifteen (lustrum is a period of five years).

V

VILLANCICO DE REYES

No tardaron en resonar pisadas en el corredor; pisadas tímidas y brutales a la vez, de pies descalzos o calzados con zapatos rudos. Al mismo tiempo las panderetas repicaban débilmente y las castañuelas se entrechocaban bajito como los dientes del que tiene miedo... Doña Dolores se incorporó con el entrecejo desapaciblemente fruncido.

–Esa Lola... ¡Pues no las trae aquí mismo! ¿Por qué no las habrá dejado en la antesala? ¡Bonita me van a poner la alfombra! ¡A ver si os limpiáis las suelas antes de entrar!

Hizo irrupción en la sala la orquesta callejera; pero al ver las niñas pobres la claridad del alumbrado, se detuvieron azoradas sin osar adelantarse. Lola, cogiendo de la mano a la que parecía capitanear el grupo, la trajo casi a la fuerza al centro de la estancia.

–Entra, mujer ... que pasen las otras... A ver si nos cantáis los mejores villancicos que sepáis.

Lo cierto es que la viva luz de las bujías, tan propicia a la hermosura, patentizaba y descubría cruelmente las fealdades de aquella tropa, mostrando los cutis cárdenos, fustigados por el cierzo; las ropas ajadas y humildes, de colores desteñidos; la descalcez y flacura de pies y piernas, todo el mísero pergeño de las cantoras. Entre estas las había de muy diversas edades, desde la directora, una ágil morenilla de catorce, hasta un rapaz de dos años y medio, todo muerto de vergüenza y temor, y un mamón de cinco meses, que por supuesto venía en brazos.

–¡Hombre! –exclamó Borrén al ver a la morena.

–¡Pues si es la chiquilla del barquillero! Somos conocidos antiguos, ¿eh?

–Sí, señor... –contestó ella intrépidamente–. La misma. Y yo le conocí a usted también. Es usted el que estaba en las Filas el año pasado un día de fiesta.

Como para los pobres suele no haber estaciones, Amparo tenía el mismo traje de tartán, pero muy deteriorado, y una toquilla de estambre rojo era la única prenda que indicaba el tránsito de la primavera al invierno. A despecho de tan mezquino atavío, no sé qué flor de adolescencia empezaba a lucir en su persona; el moreno de su piel era más claro y fino, sus ojos negros resplandecían.

–¿Qué tal, eh? –murmuró Borrén volviéndose hacía Baltasar y Palacios–. Esto empieza a picar como las guindillas... Miren ustedes para aquí.

5

CHRISTMAS CAROLS

It wasn't long before footsteps were resounding in the corridor, steps that were timid and brutish at the same time, made by feet that were either bare or wearing clodhoppers. At the same time, the tambourines were jangling softly and the castanets were clicking like the teeth of someone who is frightened … Doña Dolores joined in with a bad-tempered frown.

'That Lola … Well, she's not bringing them all here! Why didn't she leave them in the antechamber? They'll make a fine mess of my rug! Let's see if you wipe your feet before coming in!'

The street orchestra burst into the room, but when the poor young girls saw the brightness of the lighting, they stopped, embarrassed, without daring to step forward. Lola, taking hold of the hand of the girl who seemed to be in charge of the group, half-pulled her into the centre of the room.

'Come in, dear … let the others in too … Let's see if you can sing us the best carols you know.'

The truth of the matter is that the bright light of the candles, so favourable to beauty, brought out and cruelly exposed the ugliness of that troupe, showing the purple complexions whipped by the north wind, the crumpled and humble clothes, faded in colour, the skinniness of the legs and bare feet; the whole wretched appearance of the street singers. Among them were children of every age, from the leader, a dark-haired, agile girl of fourteen, to a toddler of two and a half, absolutely mortified with shame and fear, and a five-month-old baby who was of course being carried.

'Well!' exclaimed Borrén when he saw the dark-haired girl. 'If it isn't the pastry cone seller's little girl! We're old friends, aren't we?'

'Yes, sir …' she answered boldly. 'The very same. And I recognised you too. You're the one who was on Las Filas last year during a holiday.'

As all the seasons are usually the same for the poor, Amparo was wearing the same tartan dress, now very worn, and a red worsted shawl was the only article of clothing that indicated the passage from spring to winter. In spite of such wretched attire, a certain adolescent bloom was beginning to radiate from her person; the dark shade of her skin was lighter and more delicate, her black eyes were shining.

'What do you think, eh?' murmured Borrén, turning towards Baltasar and Palacios. 'This is beginning to get hot like chillies… Take a look here.'

Y tomando un candelero lo acercó al rostro de la muchacha. Como Baltasar se había aproximado, sus pupilas se encontraron con las de Amparo, y ésta vio una fisonomía delicada, casi femenil, un bigotillo blondo incipiente, unos ojos entre verdosos y garzos que la registraban con indiferencia. Acordóse, y sintió que se le arrebataba la sangre a las mejillas.

–El señorito del paseo –balbució–. También me acuerdo de usted.

–Y yo de ti, niña bonita –respondió él, por decir algo.

–¿Quiere usted poner el candelero en su sitio, Borrén? –interpeló Josefina con voz aguda–. Me ha manchado usted todo el traje.

–¡Mire usted qué graciosilla es esta, hombre! –advirtió Borrén señalando a Carmela la encajera, que tenía los ojos bajos–. Algo descolorida ... pero graciosa.

–¡Calle! –dijo la viuda de García...–. ¿Tú por aquí? Me llevarás mañana un pañuelo imitando Cluny...

–¡La de las puntillas! –exclamó doña Dolores–. ¡Buena pieza! Ahora las hacéis muy mal, tú y tu tía... Ponéis hilo muy gordo.

–¡Se ve tan poco!... ¡Los días son tan cortos! Y tiene una las manos frías; en hacer una cuarta de puntilla se va una mañana. Casi, descontando lo que nos cuesta el hilo, no sacamos para arrimar el puchero a la lumbre...

Entre tanto Nisita se iba abriendo camino al través de piernas y sillas, hasta acercarse a la niña de ocho años que llevaba en brazos al rorro.

–Un tiquito ... un tiquito –gritaba la rubilla mirándole compadecida y embelesada–. Ámelo.

–No podrás con él –respondía desdeñosamente la niñera.

–Le oy teta –argüía Nisita haciendo el ademán correspondiente al ofrecimiento.

–¿Quién os enseñó a cantar? –preguntó a la encajera la viuda de García.

–Enseñar, nadie... Nos reunimos nosotras. Tenemos un libro de versos.

–¿Y andáis por ahí divirtiéndoos?

–Divertir, no nos divertimos ... hace frío –contestó Carmela con su voz cansada y dulce–. Es por llevar unos cuantos reales a la casa.

–¡Mamá, Osepina, Loló! –vociferaba la rubilla–. Un tiquito, un nino Quetús. Mía, mía.

Todos se volvieron y divisaron a la infeliz oruga humana, envuelta en un mantón viejísimo, con una gorra de lana morada, que aumentaba el tono de cera de su menuda faz, arrugada y marchita como la de un anciano por culpa

And taking hold of a candlestick, he brought it closer to the girl's face. As Baltasar had approached, his eyes met Amparo's and she was able to make out the delicate, almost effeminate features of his face, the beginnings of a little blond moustache, and greenish-blue eyes examining her indifferently. She suddenly became self-conscious and felt the blood rushing to her cheeks.

'The young gentleman from the esplanade,' she stammered. 'I remember you too.'

'And I you, my pretty girl,' he replied, just to say something.

'Would you put the candlestick in its place, Borrén,' implored Josefina in a sharp voice. 'You've stained my whole dress.'

'Just look what a little charmer she is,' Borrén observed as he pointed to Carmela, the lace maker, who was looking down . 'A bit pale ... but cute.'

'Quiet!' said the widow García. 'What are you doing here? Aren't you supposed to be bringing me a handkerchief of imitation Cluny lace by tomorrow ...'

'The girl who does the lace edging!' exclaimed Doña Dolores. 'She's a fine one! You and your aunt do it very badly now ... You use heavy thread.'

'It's so hard to see ... the days are so short! And your hands are cold; it takes a morning to make a quarter of lace edging. Taking off what the thread costs us, we barely make enough to put some stew on the fire ...'

In the meantime, Nisita was pushing her way through the legs and the chairs, until she reached the eight-year-old girl holding the baby in her arms.

'A wickle baby ... a wickle baby,' the little blonde girl shouted as she looked at it with tenderness and fascination. 'Me 'ave it.'

'You won't know what to do with him,' the girl caring for him responded disdainfully.

'Me if him titty,' Nisita argued as she made the gesture that went with her offer.

'Who taught you to sing?' the García widow asked the lacemaker.

'Nobody taught us ...We meet up. We have a book with words.'

'And you go around having fun?'

'Fun, no, we don't have fun. ... it's cold,' answered Carmela in her sweet, tired voice. 'It's just so we can bring home a few coppers.'

'Mummy, Osepina, Loló!' the little blonde girl shouted. 'A wickle baby, a baby Yeezus. Mine, mine.'

Everyone turned round and made out the wretched human caterpillar, wrapped in a very old shawl with a purple woollen cap that emphasised the waxen pallor of his tiny face, wrinkled and withered like that of an

de la mala alimentación y del desaseo. Sus ojuelos negros, muy abiertos, miraban en derredor con vago asombro, y de sus labios fluía un hilo de baba. La viuda de García, que era bonachona, lanzó una exclamación que corearon las niñas de Sobrado.

—¡Jesús!... Angelito de Dios..., tan pequeño, por esas calles y con este día! Pero ¿qué hace su madre?

—Mi madre tiene tienda en la calle del Castillo... Somos siete con este, y yo soy la mayor... —alegó a guisa de disculpa la que llevaba la criatura.

—¡Jesús!... ¿Pero cómo hacéis para que no llore? ¿Y si tiene hambre?

—Le meto la punta del pañuelo en la boca para que chupe... Es muy listito, ya se entretiene mucho.

Riéronse las niñas, y Lola tomó al nene en brazos.

—¡Qué ligero! –pronunció–. ¡Si pesa más la muñeca grande de Nisita!

Pasó de mano en mano el leve fardo, hasta llegar a Josefina, que lo devolvió a la portadora muy deprisa, declarando que olía mal.

—No ven el agua ni una vez en el año –decía confidencialmente a su cuñado doña Dolores– y salen más fuertes que los nuestros. Yo, matándome, y sin poder conseguir que esa Lola se robustezca.

Amparo observaba la sala, el piano de reluciente barniz, el menguado espejo, las conchas de Filipinas y aves disecadas que adornaban la consola, el juego de café con filete dorado, los trajes de las de García, el grupo imponente del sofá, y todo le parecía bello, ostentoso y distinguido, y sentíase como en su elemento, sin pizca ya de cortedad ni extrañeza.

—¿Y tú, qué haces, señorita de Rosendez? –interrogó Baltasar–. ¿Andar de calle en calle canturreando? Bonito oficio, chica; me parece a mí que tú...

—¿Y qué quiere que haga? –replicó ella.

—Encajes, como tu amiguita.

—¡Ay!, no me *aprendieron*.[11]

—¿Pues qué te *aprendieron*, hija? ¿Coser?

—¡Bah! Tampoco. Así, unas puntaditas...

—¿Pues qué sabes tú? ¿Robar los corazones?

—Sé leer muy bien y escribir regular. Fui a la escuela, y decía el maestro

---

11 Por 'enseñaron'.

old man because of his poor nourishment and grubbiness. His small black eyes looked all round with vague astonishment and a thin stream of dribble flowed from his lips. The widow García, who was good-natured, let out an exclamation echoed by the Sobrado girls.

'My lord ... sweet angel of God ... so small to be on these streets and on a day like this! What does his mother do?'

'My mother has a shop on the Calle del Castillo ... There are seven of us including this one, and I'm the eldest ...' pleaded the girl carrying the child by way of an apology.

'Good lord! What do you do to stop him crying? And what if he gets hungry?'

'I put the end of my handkerchief in his mouth for him to suck on ... He's very bright and has such a good time.'

The girls all laughed and Lola took the baby in her arms.

'He's so light!' she proclaimed. 'Even Nisita's big doll weighs more!'

The light bundle passed from hand to hand until it reached Josefina, who returned it very quickly to the girl who had been carrying it, declaring that he smelt bad.

'They don't see a drop of water even once a year,' Doña Dolores said to her brother-in-law in confidence, 'and they come out stronger than our children. Here I am, killing myself and without managing to get that Lola to grow stronger.'

Amparo looked around the drawing room: the piano with its shiny varnish finish, the small-sized mirror, the Philippine shells and stuffed birds decorating the console table, the coffee set with the gilded fillet, the García girls' dresses, and the imposing group on the sofa. It all seemed beautiful, ostentatious and distinguished to her, and she felt like she was in her own element, without so much as a trace of shyness or strangeness.

'And what do you do, Señorita de Roséndez?' asked Baltasar. 'Go from street to street humming? That's a nice job, dear; it seems to me that you ...'

'And what do you want me to do?' she replied.

'Make lace, like your little friend.'

'Oh, they didn't *learn* me.'

'Well what did they *learn* you, child? To sew?'

'Bah! Nor that. A few little stitches ...'

'Well, what can you do? Steal hearts?'

'I can read read really well and write quite well. I went to school and the

que no había otra como yo. Le leo todos los días *La Soberanía Nacional* al barbero de enfrente.

–Pusiste una pica en Flandes. ¿No sabes más?

–Liar puros.

–¡Hola! ¿Eres cigarrera?

–Fue mi madre.

–Y tú, ¿por qué no?

–No tengo quien me meta en la fábrica... Hacen falta empeños y recomendaciones...

–Pues mira, casualmente este señor puede recomendarte... Oiga usted, Borrén, ¿no es usted primo del contador de la fábrica? Diga usted.

–¡Hombre! Es cierto. Del contador, no; pero de su señora... Es murciana; somos hijos de primos hermanos.

–¡Magnífico! Dile tu nombre y tus señas, chica.

–Sí, hija..., se hará lo posible, ¿eh? Por servir a una morena tan sandunguera... Vas a valer más pesetas con el tiempo... Hombre, ¿no repara usted, Baltasar, lo que ganó desde el año pasado?

–Mucho más guapa está –declaró Baltasar.

–¿Pero estas chiquillas no cantan? –interrumpió con dureza Josefina García–. ¿Han venido aquí a hacernos tertulia? Para eso, que se larguen. No se ganan los cuartos charlando.

–¡A cantar! –contestaron resignadamente todas; y al punto redoblaron las castañuelas, repiquetearon los panderos, rechinaron las conchas, exhaló su estridente nota el triángulo de hierro, y diez voces mal concertadas entonaron un villancico:

> Los pastores en Belén
> todos a juntar en leña
> para calentar al Niño
> que nació en la Nochebuena...

Y al llegar al estribillo:

> Toquen, toquen rabeles y gaitas,
> panderetas, tambores y flautas...

se armó un estrépito de dos mil diablos: chillaban y tocaban a la vez, con ambas manos, y aun hiriendo con los pies el suelo. Hasta el rorro, asustado

teacher said there was no one like me. I read *The National Sovereignty* every day to the barber across the road.'[6]

'That was no mean feat. Can you do anything else?'

'Roll cigars.'

'So, you're a cigar maker?'

'My mother was one.'

'And why aren't you?'

'I don't have anyone to get me in the factory .... You need backers and recommendations ...'

'Well, look. This gentleman happens to be able to recommend you ... Hey, Borrén, aren't you the factory bookkeeper's cousin?'

'Yes. It's true. Not the bookkeeper's, but his wife's ... She's from Murcia; we're the children of first cousins.'

'Wonderful! Tell him your name and address, my dear.'

'Yes, my dear ... we'll do our best, eh? Doing a favour for such a charming brunette ... You're going to be priceless eventually ... Hey, Baltasar, haven't you noticed how much she's improved since last year?'

'She's much prettier,' Baltasar declared.

'But aren't these little girls going to sing?' Josefina García interrupted brusquely. 'Have they come here just to sit around and talk? If that's the case, then they can clear off. You don't earn money by chatting.'

'Let the singing commence!' they all replied with resignation; and at once the castanets were clicking, the tambourines jingling, the conches scraping, the iron triangle giving off its strident note, and ten discordant voices singing a carol:

The shepherds in Bethleham
all gathering firewood
to warm the Child
born on Christmas Eve ...

And when they came to the refrain:

Play, play the rebecks and bagpipes,
tambourines, drums and flutes ...

the devil of a racket rent the air: they were screaming and playing at the same time, with both hands, and even stamping on the floor with their feet.

---

6   Founded and edited by Ángel Fernández de los Ríos, this 'diario progresista' (progressive newspaper) first appeared on the 16th December 1864.

por la bulla o desentumecido por el calor y vuelto a la conciencia de su hambre, se resolvió a tomar parte en el concierto. Las niñas de Sobrado y García, locas de regocijo, se asieron de las manos, y empezaron a bailar en rueda, con las trenzas flotantes y volanderas las enaguas. Nisita, igualitaria como nadie, cogió el parvulillo de dos años y lo metió en el corro, donde la pobre criatura hubo de danzar mal de su grado, soltando a cada paso sus holgadas babuchas. Borrén, por hacer algo, jaleó a las bailadoras. Aprovechando un momento de confusión, Lola se escurrió y volvió trayendo en la falda del vestido una mescolanza de naranjas, trozos de piñonate, almendras, bizcochos, pasas, galletas, relieves de la mesa amontonados a escape, que comenzó a distribuir con largueza y garbo. Doña Dolores saltó hecha una furia.

–Esta chiquilla está loca…, me desperdicia todo … cosas finas… ¡y para quién! Vean ustedes!… ¡Con una taza de caldo que les diesen!… ¡Y el vestido…, el vestido azul estropeado!…

Diciendo lo cual, se aproximó disimuladamente a Lola y le apretó con ira el brazo. Baltasar intercedió una vez más: era su santo, un día en el año. Sobrado padre tartamudeó también disculpas de su hija, a quien quería entrañablemente; y Borrén, siempre obsequioso, acabó de repartir las golosinas. Carmela, la encajera, y Amparo rehusaron con dignidad su parte; pero la chiquillería despachó su ración atragantándose en las mismas barbas de doña Dolores, que consumó la venganza dando por terminados los villancicos y poniendo en la escalera a músicos y danzantes.

Even the baby, frightened by the row or roused by the heat and conscious once again of his hunger, resolved to take part in the concert. The Sobrado and García girls, wild with joy, took hold of each other's hands and began to dance in a ring, their plaits floating and their skirts flying outward. Nisita, as egalitarian as anyone, grabbed the little two-year-old child and put him in the circle, where the poor creature had to dance, much against his will, losing his floppy, heelless slippers at every step. Borrén, just to do something, cheered on the dancers. Taking advantage of a moment of confusion, Lola slipped away and returned carrying in the skirt of her dress a hotchpotch of oranges, pieces of candied pine nut, almonds, sponge cakes, raisins, biscuits, leftovers from the table, hurriedly piled up, which she began to distribute with generosity and grace. Doña Dolores leaped up furiously.

'This girl's crazy ... she's wasting everything ... exquisite things ... and for whom! Just look! ...They'd have been happy with a cup of broth! ... And her dress ... her blue dress is ruined!'

As she said this, she furtively approached Lola and angrily squeezed her arm. Baltasar interceded once again: it was his saint's day, one day in the whole year. Old man Sobrado also stuttered excuses for his daughter, whom he loved dearly; and Borrén, forever obsequious, ended up sharing out the titbits. Carmela, the lacemaker, and Amparo refused their share with dignity; but the kids disposed of their portions wolfing it down right under the very nose of Doña Dolores, who completed her vengeance by terminating the carol singing and showing the musicians and dancers the staircase.

VI

CIGARROS PUROS

Hizo Borrén, en efecto, la recomendación a su prima, que se la hizo al contador, que se la hizo al jefe, y Amparo fue admitida en la fábrica de cigarros. El día en que recogió el nombramiento, hubo en casa del barquillero la fiesta acostumbrada en casos semejantes, fiesta no inferior a la que celebrarían si se casase la muchacha. Hizo la madre decir una misa a Nuestra Señora del Amparo, patrona de las cigarreras, y por la tarde fueron convidados a un asiático festín el barbero de enfrente, Carmela, su tía, y la señora *Porreta*, la comadrona; hubo empanada de sardina, bacalao, vino de Castilla, anís y caña a discreción, rosoli,[12] una enorme fuente de papas de arroz con leche.

Privado de la ayuda de Amparo, el barquillero había tomado un aprendiz, hijo de una lavandera de las cercanías. Jacinto, o *Chinto*, tenía facciones abultadas e irregulares, piel de un moreno terroso, ojos pequeños y a flor de cara; en resumen, la fealdad tosca de un villano feudal. Sirvió a la mesa, escanció, y fue la diversión de los comensales, por sus largas melenas, semejantes a un ruedo, que le comían la frente; por su faja de lana, que le embastecía la ya no muy quebrada cintura; por su andar torpe y desmañado, análogo al de un moscardón cuando tiene las patas untadas de almíbar; por su puro dialecto de las Rías Saladas, que provocaba la hilaridad de aquella urbana reunión. El barbero, que era *leído, escribido* y muy redicho; la encajera, que la daba de fina, y la comadrona, que gastaba unos chistes del tamaño de su panza, compitieron en donaire burlándose de la rusticidad del mozo. Amparo ni lo miró, tan ridículo le había parecido la víspera cuando entró llorando, trayéndolo medio a rastras su madre. Carmela fue la única que le habló humanamente, y le dijo el nombre de dos o tres cosas, que él preguntaba sin lograr más respuesta que bromas y embustes. Así que todos manducaron a su sabor, echaron las sobras revueltas en un plato, como para un perro, y se las dieron al paisanillo, que se acostó ahíto, roncando formidablemente hasta el otro día.

Amparo madrugó para asistir a la fábrica. Caminaba a buen paso, ligera

---

12 Licor compuesto de aguardiente, anís seco, azúcar, canela, agua y otros ingredientes olorosos.

6
CIGARS

Borrén did indeed make the recommendation to his cousin, who made it to the bookkeeper, who made it to the manager, and Amparo was admitted into the cigar factory. The day she went to pick up her appointment, there was a celebration in the pastry cone seller's house, as was customary on such occasions, a celebration just as important as if the girl were getting married. Her mother had a Mass said to Nuestra Señora del Amparo, the patron saint of cigar makers, and in the afternoon the barber from across the way, Carmela, her aunt and Señora *Starkers*, the midwife, were invited to a sumptuous feast; there were sardine pies, cod, and as much Castilian wine,[xii] anisette or rum as you liked, rossolis liqueur and an enormous dish of rice and milk porridge.

Now that he was deprived of Amparo's help, the pastry cone seller had taken on an apprentice, the son of a washerwoman in the neighbourhood. Jacinto, or *Chinto*, had exaggerated, irregular features, earthy, dark-coloured skin, small eyes flush with his face; in short, the coarse ugliness of a feudal peasant. He was serving at the table, pouring the drinks, and was a constant source of amusement for the dinner guests, because of his long mop of hair, like a round mat that ate away his forehead; because of his woollen sash, which increased his already not very constrained waist; because of his ungainly, clumsy gait, akin to that of a bluebottle when its legs are smeared with syrup; because of his dialect,[xiii] typical of the northern salt-filled estuaries, which provoked hilarity among the urban gathering. The barber, who was *well-read, knowledgeable* and very affected, the lacemaker, who always put on airs, and the midwife, who joked about the size of her belly, competed with witticisms, making fun of the lad's uncouthness. Amparo didn't even look at him, so ridiculous had he seemed the night before when his mother half dragged him in crying. Carmela was the only one who spoke to him in a humane manner, and she told him the names of two or three things which he had asked without getting any response other than jokes and untruths. So they all gobbled down their food in their own way, threw the mixed-up leftovers on a plate, as if for a dog, and gave them to the pitiful country bumpkin, who then went to bed stuffed, snoring loudly until the following day.

Amparo got up early to go to the factory. She walked at a good pace,

y contenta como el que va a tomar posesión del solar paterno. Al subir la cuesta de San Hilario, sus ojos se fijaban en el mar, sereno y franjeado de tintas de ópalo, mientras pensaba en que iba a ganar bastante desde el primer día; en que casi no tendría aprendizaje, porque al fin los puros la conocían, su madre le había enseñado a envolverlos, poseía los heredados chismes del oficio, y no le arredraba la tarea. Discurriendo así, cruzó la calzada y se halló en el patio de la fábrica, la vieja Granera. Embargó a la muchacha un sentimiento de respeto. La magnitud del edificio compensaba su vetustez y lo poco airoso de su traza, y para Amparo, acostumbrada a venerar la fábrica desde sus tiernos años, poseían aquellas murallas una aureola de majestad, y habitaba en su recinto un poder misterioso, el Estado, con el cual sin duda era ocioso luchar, un poder que exigía obediencia ciega, que a todas partes alcanzaba y dominaba a todos. El adolescente que por vez primera huella las aulas experimenta algo parecido a lo que sentía Amparo.

Pudo tanto en ella este temor religioso, que apenas vio quién la recibía, ni quién la llevaba a su puesto en el taller. Casi temblaba al sentarse en la silla que le adjudicaron. En derredor suyo, las operarias alzaban la cabeza: ojos curiosos y benévolos se fijaban en la novicia. La maestra del partido estaba ya a su lado, entregándole con solicitud el tabaco, acomodando los chismes, explicándole detenidamente cómo había de arreglarse para empezar. Y Amparo, en un arranque de orgullo, atajaba a las explicaciones con un «ya sé cómo», que la hizo blanco de miradas. Sonrióse la maestra y le dejó liar un puro, lo cual ejecutó con bastante soltura; pero al presentarlo acabado, la maestra lo tomó y oprimió entre el pulgar y el índice, desfigurándose el cigarro al punto.

—Lo que es saber, como lo material de saber, sabrás... —dijo alzando las cejas–. Pero si no despabilas más los dedos ... y si no les das más hechurita... Que así parece un espantapájaros.

—Bueno —murmuró la novicia confusa–: nadie nace aprendido.

—Con la práctica... —declaró la maestra sentenciosamente, mientras se preparaba a unir el ejemplo a la enseñanza–. Mira, así ... a modito...

No valía apresurarse. Primero era preciso extender con sumo cuidado,

nimble and happy like someone going to take possession of an ancestral home. As she made her way her up the Cuesta de San Hilario, her eyes were fixed on the sea, serene and fringed with opal tints, while she thought about the fact that she was going to earn a sufficient amount from the very first day; and that she would have almost no apprenticeship, because after all she was familiar with cigars, her mother had taught her how to wrap them, she possessed all the tools she had inherited for the job, and the task didn't frighten her. As she ruminated in this way, she crossed the road and found herself in the courtyard of the factory, the old Granary. A feeling of respect overwhelmed the girl. The magnitude of the building compensated for its antiquity and its inelegant appearance, and for Amparo, accustomed to venerating the factory since her tender years, those walls possessed an aureole of majesty, and within its grounds there resided a mysterious power, the State, against which it was undoubtedly pointless to fight, a power that demanded blind obedience, that reached out everywhere and dominated everyone. The adolescent who steps into the classroom for the first time experiences something akin to what Amparo felt.

So powerful in her was this religious fear that she hardly noticed who welcomed her or who took her to her place in the workshop. She was almost trembling when she sat down in the chair they had assigned her. All around her the women workers raised their heads: curious, benevolent eyes were fixed on the novice. The forewoman was soon at her side, solicitously handing her the tobacco, arranging the work tools, explaining at great length how you had to get yourself ready in order to start. And Amparo, with a sudden burst of pride, interrupted the explanations saying, 'I already know', which made her the target of everyone's stares. The forewoman smiled and let her roll a cigar, which she executed fairly easily; but when she presented the finished product, the forewoman took it and squeezed it between her thumb and index finger and the cigar immediately lost its shape.

'When it comes to knowing, like the physical act of knowing, you probably know,' she said, raising her eyebrows. 'But if you don't liven up those fingers more … and if you don't give them more craftmanship… This one looks like a scarecrow.'

'All right,' murmured the confused novice, 'nobody is born knowing how.'

'With practice…' the forewoman declared sententiously, whilst she prepared to add her example to the lesson. 'Look, like this … like I do it…'

It was no good hurrying. First of all it was necessary to stretch out with

encima de la tabla de liar, la envoltura exterior, la epidermis del cigarro, y cortarla con el cuchillo semicircular trazando una curva de quince milímetros de inclinación sobre el centro de la hoja para que ciñese exactamente el cigarro, y esta capa requería una hoja seca, ancha y fina, de lo más selecto, así como la dermis del cigarro, el *capillo*, ya la admitía de inferior calidad, lo propio que la tripa o *cañizo*. Pero lo más esencial y difícil era rematar el puro, hacerle la punta con un hábil giro de la yema del pulgar y una espátula mojada en líquida goma, cercenándole después el rabo de un tijeretazo veloz. La punta aguda, el cuerpo algo oblongo, la capa liada en elegante espiral, la tripa no tan apretada que no deje respirar el humo ni tan floja que el cigarro se arrugue al secarse, tales son las condiciones de una buena tagarnina. Amparo se obstinó todo el día en fabricarla, tardando muchísimo en elaborar algunas, cada vez más contrahechas, y estropeando malamente la hoja. Sus vecinas de mesa le daban consejos oficiosos; había diversidad de pareceres; las viejas le recomendaban que cortase la capa más ancha, porque sale el cigarro mejor formado, y porque «así lo habían hecho ellas toda la vida»; y las jóvenes, que más estrecha, que se enrolla más pronto. Al salir de la fábrica, le dolían a Amparo la nuca, el espinazo, el pulpejo de los dedos.[13]

Poco a poco fue habituándose y adquiriendo destreza. Lo peor era que la afligía la nostalgia de la calle, no acertando a hacerse a la prolija jornada de trabajo sedentario. Para Amparo la calle era la patria…, el paraíso terrenal. La calle le brindaba mil distracciones, de balde todas. Nadie le vedaba creer que eran suyos los lujosos escaparates de las tiendas, los tentadores de las confiterías, las redomas de color de las boticas, los pintorescos tinglados de la plaza; que para ella tocaban las murgas, los organillos, la música militar en los paseos, misas y serenatas; que por ella se revistaba la tropa y salía precedido de sus maceros con blancas pelucas el excelentísimo Ayuntamiento. ¿Quién mejor que ella gozaba del aparato de las procesiones, del suelo sembrado de espadaña, del palio majestuoso, de los santos que se tambalean en las andas, de la custodia cubierta de flores, de la hermosa Virgen con manto azul sembrado de lentejuelas? ¿Quién lograba ver más de cerca al capitán general portador del estandarte, a los señores que alumbraban, a los oficiales que marcaban el paso en cadencia? Pues ¿y en Carnaval? Las mascaradas caprichosas, los confites arrojados de la calle a los balcones y viceversa, el *entierro de la sardina*, los cucuruchos de dulce de

---

13   Emilia Pardo Bazán pasó dos meses en la Fábrica de Tabacos observando el ambiente y la actividad de las cigarreras para recrear el clima laboral de *La Tribuna*.

the utmost care the outer wrapping, the skin of the cigar, on top of the rolling board, and cut it with a semicircular knife tracing a curve with an inclination of fifteen millimeters over the centre of the leaf so that it would fit exactly around the cigar; and this wrapper required a wide, dry, fine leaf, the most select, just as the dermis of the cigar, the *binder*, allowed for a leaf of inferior quality, the same as the insides or *filler*. But the most essential and difficult thing was finishing off the cigar, forming the tip with a skilful twist of the tip of the thumb and a spatula dipped in liquid gum, and then cutting off the end with a quick snip. The sharp tip, the somewhat oblong body, the wrapper rolled into an elegant spiral, the insides not so tightly pressed as to prevent the smoke from drawing, or so loosely packed that the cigar became wrinkled when it got dry: these are the conditions of a good cigar. Amparo persisted all day in manufacturing it, taking a very long time to put some together, more and more misshapen, and badly spoiling the leaves. Her table companions gave her helpful advice; there was a range of opinions: the old women recommended that she cut the wrapper wider, because the cigar emerges better shaped, and because 'that's the way they had done it all their lives'; and the young ones told her narrower because you could roll it faster. When she left the factory, the back of Amparo's neck, her spine and the fleshy parts of her fingers were aching.

Little by little she was becoming accustomed to it and acquiring dexterity. The worst thing was that she was afflicted by a great longing for the life of the street, not managing to get used to the tedious day of sedentary work. For Amparo, the street was her homeland … her paradise on earth. The street offered her thousands of distractions, all for nothing. Nobody could stop her believing that the luxurious shop windows, the temptations of the confectioners, the coloured phials of the chemist's and the picturesque lean-tos in the plaza were all hers; that the street musicians, barrel organs and military bands on the esplanades, at the Masses and serenades were playing for her; that the local garrison dressed in all its finery was because of her, that the most excellent town council came out, preceded by its mace bearers in their white wigs, because of her. Who enjoyed the pomp and ceremony of the processions more than she, the cattails scattered all over the ground, the majestic canopy, the saints swaying on the portable platforms, the monstrance covered with flowers, the beautiful Virgin with her blue mantle covered in sequins? Who managed to get a closer look at the field marshal bearing the standard, the gentlemen who lit the way, the officers marking time in cadence? And what of Shrovetide? The whimsical masquerades, the sweets thrown from the street to the balconies and vice versa, the *burial of*

la Piñata, todo lo disfrutaba la hija de la calle. Si un personaje ilustre pasaba por Marineda, a Amparo pertenecía durante el tiempo de su residencia; a fuerza de empellones, la chiquilla se colocaba al lado del rey, del ministro, del hombre célebre; se arrimaba al estribo de su coche, respiraba su aliento, inventariaba sus dichos y hechos.

¡La calle! ¡Espectáculo siempre variado y nuevo, siempre concurrido, siempre abierto y franco! No había cosa más adecuada al temperamento de Amparo, tan amiga del ruido, de la concurrencia, tan bullanguera, meridional y extremosa, tan amante de lo que relumbra. Además, como sus pulmones estaban educados en la gimnasia del aire libre, se deja entender la opresión que experimentarían en los primeros tiempos de cautiverio en los talleres, donde la atmósfera estaba saturada del olor ingrato y herbáceo del Virginia humedecido y de la hoja medio verde, mezclado con las emanaciones de tanto cuerpo humano y con el fétido vaho de las letrinas próximas. Por otra parte, el aspecto de aquellas grandes salas de cigarros comunes era para entristecer el ánimo. Vastas estanterías de madera ennegrecida por el uso, colocadas en el centro de la estancia, parecían hileras de nichos. Entre las operarias, alineadas a un lado y a otro, había sin duda algunos rostros jóvenes y lindos; pero así como en una menestra se destaca la legumbre que más abunda, en tan enorme ensalada femenina no se distinguían al pronto sino greñas incultas, rostros arados por la vejez o curtidos por el trabajo, manos nudosas como ramas de árbol seco.

El colorido de los semblantes, el de las ropas y el de la decoración se armonizaba y fundía en un tono general de madera y tierra, tono a la vez crudo y apagado, combinación del castaño mate de la hoja, del amarillo sucio de la vena, del dudoso matiz de los serones de esparto, de la problemática blancura de las enyesadas paredes, y de los tintes sordos, mortecinos al par que discordantes, de los pañuelos de cotonía, las sayas de percal, los casacos de paño, los mantones de lana y los paraguas de algodón. Amparo se perecía por los colores vivos y fuertes, hasta el extremo de pasarse a veces una hora delante de algún escaparate contemplando una pieza de seda roja; así es que los primeros días el taller, con su colorido bajo, le infundía ganas de morirse.

Pero no tardó en encariñarse con la fábrica, en sentir ese orgullo y apego inexplicables que infunde la colectividad y la asociación: la fraternidad del trabajo. Fue conociendo los semblantes que la rodeaban, tomándose interés por algunas operarias, señaladamente por una madre y una hija que se

the sardine, the paper cones of sweets for the piñata, the child of the streets enjoyed it all.[xiv] If an illustrious personage passed through Marineda, he belonged to Amparo during the time of his residence there; by pushing and shoving the young girl ended up standing next to the king, the minister, or the famous man; she leant against the footboard of his coach, took in his breath, made a mental note of what he said and did.

The street! A forever varying and new spectacle, always well-attended, always open and free. There was nothing more suited to Amparo's temperament, so fond was she of noise and crowds, so rowdy, meridional and effusive was she, so much in love with everything that shines brightly. In addition, as her lungs were brought up on outdoor exercise, it is easy to understand the oppressive feeling she experienced on those early days of captivity in the workshops, where the atmosphere was saturated with the unpleasant, herbaceous smell of Virginia tobacco and the partly green leaves, mixed with the emissions from so many human bodies and the foul-smelling whiff of the nearby toilets. In addition, the appearance of those big communal rooms of cigars was enough to sadden the spirits. Huge wooden shelves blackened with use, placed in the centre of the room, looked like rows of niches. Amongst the working women lined up on either side there were undoubtedly a number of young, pretty faces; but just as the most abundant vegetable stands out in a stew, at first all that could be distinguished in such an enormous hotchpotch of women was unkempt tangles of hair, faces wrinkled by old age or hardened by work, and hands gnarled like the branches of dried-up trees.

The colouring of the faces, the clothes and the decor harmonised and merged into a general tone of wood and earth, a tone that was both coarse and dull, a combination of the matt chestnut colour of the leaves, the dirty yellow of their veins, the uncertain shade of the large, esparto grass panniers, the problematic whiteness of the plastered walls, and the muted, dull, even discordant tints of the dimity scarves, the percale skirts, the cloth coats, the woollen shawls and the cotton umbrellas. Amparo longed for bright, lively colours, to the point of sometimes spending an hour in front of a shop window contemplating a piece of red silk; so it was that during her first days, the workshop with its dull colouring filled her with a desire to die.

But she didn't take long to grow fond of the factory, to feel that inexplicable pride and attachment which community and association instil: the brotherhood of labour. She began to recognise the faces surrounding her, taking interest in some of the workers, especially a mother and daughter

sentaban a su lado. Medio ciega ya y muy temblona de manos, la madre no podía hacer más que *niños*, o sea la envoltura del cigarro; la hija se encargaba de las puntas y del corte, y entre las dos mujeres despachaban bastante, siendo muy de notar la solicitud de la hija y el afecto que se manifestaban las dos, sin hablarse, en mil pormenores: en el modo de pasarse la goma, de enseñarse el mazo terminado y sujeto ya con su faja de papel, de partir la moza la comida con su navaja, y de acercarla a los labios de la vieja.

Otra causa para que Amparo se reconciliase del todo con la fábrica fue el hallarse en cierto modo emancipada y fuera de la patria potestad desde su ingreso. Es verdad que daba a sus padres algo de las ganancias, pero reservándose buena parte; y como la labor era a destajo, en las yemas de los dedos tenía el medio de acrecentar sus rentas, sin que nadie pudiese averiguar si cobraba ocho o cobraba diez. Desde el día de su entrada vestía el traje clásico de las cigarreras; el mantón, el pañuelo de seda para las solemnidades, la falda de percal planchada y de cola.

who sat beside her. Half-blind and with hands that trembled badly, the mother could only make the *niños*, that is the outer wrappings of the cigars; the daughter took care of the tips and the cutting, and, between the two women, they produced a fair amount; very noticeable were the daughter's solicitude and the affection the two women showed each other, without saying anything, in myriad details: in the way they passed each other the gum, how they showed one another the bundle finished and wrapped in its paper band, how the younger woman cut the food with a knife and brought it up to the old lady's lips.

Another reason for Amparo to become completely reconciled with the factory was that she found herself emancipated to some degree and beyond paternal authority from the moment she joined. It's true she gave her parents some of her earnings, but she kept a good part of it for herself; and as she was doing piecework, her fingertips had the means to increase her income, without anybody being able to find out if she was getting eight or ten. From the day of her entry, she wore the classical dress of cigar makers: the shawl, the silk scarf for religious occasions and the ironed percale skirt with a train behind.

VII

PRELUDIOS

Tardó Chinto en aclimatarse; mucho tiempo pasó echando de menos la aldea. Dos cosas ayudaron a distraer su morriña; un amolador, que se situaba bajo los soportales de la calle de Embarcaderos, y el mar. Cuantos momentos tenía libres el paisanillo, dedicábalos a la contemplación de alguno de sus dos amores. No se cansaba jamás de ver los altibajos de la pierna del amolador, el girar sin fin de la rueda, el rápido saltar de las chispas y arenitas al contacto del metal, ni de oír el *¡rssss!* del hierro cuando el asperón lo mordía. Tampoco se hartaba de mirar al mar, encontrándolo siempre distinto: unas veces ataviado con traje azul claro; otras, al amanecer, semejante a estaño en fusión; por la tarde, al ocaso, parecido a oro líquido, y de noche, envuelto en túnica verde oscura listada de plata. ¡Y cuando entraban y salían las embarcaciones! Ya era un gallardo bergantín, alzando sus dos palos y su cuadrado velamen; ya una graciosa goleta, con su cangreja desplegada, rozando las olas como una gaviota; ya un paquete, con sus alas de espuma en los talones y su corona de humo en la frente; ya un fino laúd; ya un elegante esquife; sin nombrar las lanchas pescadoras, los pesados lanchones, los galeones panzudos, los botes que volaban al golpe acompasado de los remos... Si Chinto no fuese un animal, podría alegar en su abono que el Océano y el voltear de una rueda son imágenes apropiadas de lo infinito; pero Chinto no entendía de metafísicas.

Más adelante, al reparar en Amparo, se halló mejor en el pueblo. Si algo se burlaba de él la despabilada chiquilla, al fin era una muchacha, un rostro juvenil, una voz fresca y sonora. Entre el señor Rosendo y su triste laconismo; la tullida y su tiranía doméstica; Pepa la comadrona, que lo asustaba de puro gorda, y lo crucificaba a chistes, o Amparo, desde luego se declararon por ésta sus simpatías. Todas las tardes, con el cilindro de hojalata terciado al hombro, iba a buscarla a la salida de la fábrica. Esperaba rodeado de madres que aguardaban a sus hijas, de niños que llevaban la comida a sus madres, de gente pobre, que rara vez hacía gasto de barquillos, como no fuese por la exorbitante cantidad de un ochavo o un cuarto. No obstante, Chinto no faltaba un solo día a su puesto.

Algo variado en su exterior estaba el aprendiz. Patizambo como siempre,

7
PRELUDES

Chinto took a long time to acclimatise; he spent a lot of time missing his village. Two things helped to distract his homesickness: a knifegrinder, who was located under the colonnades of the Calle de Embajadores, and the sea. Whatever moments the country bumpkin had free he would spend contemplating one or the other of his two loves. He never tired of watching the up and down movement of the knife grinder's leg, the endless spinning of the wheel, the rapid flying of the sparks and small grindings as they made contact with the metal, or of hearing the *rsss!* of the iron as the sandstone bit into it. Nor did he get fed up with looking at the sea, always finding it different: sometimes dressed up in a light blue garb, at other times, at dawn, similar to melting tin; in the evening, towards sunset, like liquid gold, and at night, wrapped in a silver-striped, dark green tunic. And when the boats came in and went out! One minute a graceful brig, hoisting its two masts and square sails; next an elegant schooner with its fore-and-aft sail unfurled, skimming over the waves like a seagull; then a packet boat with wings of spume at its heels and its crown of smoke at the front; now a slender catboat, or an elegant skiff; without counting the fishing boats, the hefty barges, the potbellied galleons and the boats whizzing by to the rhythmic beat of their oars ... If Chinto weren't such an oaf, he might assert, to his credit, that the Ocean and the turning of a wheel are appropriate images of the infinite, but Chinto didn't know anything about metaphysics.

Later, when he noticed Amparo, he felt better living in town. If the quick-witted girl made fun of him somewhat, at least she was a girl, a youthful face, a fresh, resonant voice. Between Señor Rosendo and his sad, laconic manner, the crippled woman and her domestic tyranny, Pepa the midwife, who frightened him just because she was so fat and crucified him with her jokes, or Amparo, his feelings of course were for the latter. Every afternoon, with his tin tubular container slung over his shoulder, he went to meet her as she left the factory. He waited, surrounded by mothers waiting for their daughters, children bringing food for their mothers, poor people who rarely went to the expense of a pastry cone, if only because of its exorbitant cost of a farthing or halfpenny. Nevertheless, Chinto didn't miss a single day at his post.

The apprentice was outwardly somewhat changed. As knock-kneed as

era en sus movimientos menos brutal. La vida ciudadana le había enseñado que un cuerpo humano no puede tomarse toda la calle por suya, y está obligada a permitir que otros cuerpos transiten por donde él transita. Chinto dejaba, pues, más lugar; se recogía; no se balanceaba tanto. La blusa de cutí azul dibujaba sus recias espaldas, descubriendo cuello y manos morenas; ancho sombrerón de detestable fieltro gris honraba su cabeza, monda y lironda ya por obra y gracia del barbero.

Una hermosa tarde estival aguardaba a Amparo muy ufano, porque en los bolsillos de la blusa le traía melocotones, adquiridos en la plaza con sus ahorros. Como un cuarto de hora llevaban de ir saliendo las operarias ya, y la hija del barquillero sin aparecer. Gran animación a la puerta, donde se había establecido un mercadillo; no faltaba el puesto de cintas, dedales, hilos, alfileres y agujas; pero lo dominante era el marisco: cestas llenas de mejillones cocidos ya, esmaltados de negro y naranja; de erizos verdosos y cubiertos de púas; de percebes arracimados ya correosos; de argentadas sardinas, y de mil menudos frutos de mar –bocinas, lapas, almejas, calamares –que dejaban pender sus esparcidos tentáculos, como patas de arañas muertas. Semejante cuadro, cuyo fondo era un trozo de mar sereno, un muelle de piedras desiguales, una ribera peñascosa, tenía mucho de paisaje napolitano, completando la analogía los trajes y actitudes de los pescadores que no muy lejos tendían al sol redes para secarlas. En pie, en el umbral del patio, un ciego se mantenía inmóvil, muerta la cara, mal afeitadas las barbas que le azuleaban las mejillas, lacio y en trova el grasiento pelo, tendiendo un sombrero abollado, donde llovían cuartos y mendrugos en abundancia.

Miraba Chinto a la bahía con la boca abierta, y cuando al fin salió Amparo, no pudo verla: ella en cambio le divisó desde lejos, y veloz como una saeta, varió de rumbo, tomando por la insigne calle del Sol, que componen media docena de casas gibosas y dos tapias coronadas de hierba y alhelíes silvestres. Corrió hasta alcanzar el camino del Crucero, y dejándolo a un lado, atravesó a la carretera y a la cuesta de San Hilario, donde refrenó el paso creyéndose en salvo ya. ¡También era manía la del zopenco aquel, de no dejarla a sol ni a sombra, y darle escolta todas las tardes! ¡Y como su compañía era tan divertida, y como él hablaba tan graciosamente, que no parece sino que tenía la boca llena de engrudo, según se le pegaban las palabras a la lengua!... Así discurría Amparo, mientras bajaba hacia la

ever, he was less brutish in his movements. Life in the city had taught him that a human body can't take up the whole street for itself, and that one is obliged to allow other bodies to pass along in the same places where one is passing by. So Chinto left more room; he drew back and didn't sway to and fro so much. His smock, made of blue ticking, outlined his strong shoulders, revealing his neck and dark hands; a big wide hat, made of loathsome grey felt, graced his head, now plain and ordinary, thanks to the barber.

On a beautiful summer afternoon, he waited for Amparo, full of pride, because in the pockets of his smock he had brought peaches for her, which he had acquired in the plaza with his savings. The women workers had been coming out for about a quarter of an hour, and the pastry cone seller's daughter was nowhere to be seen. There was a lot of activity at the gate where a small market-place had been set up; a stall with ribbons, thimbles, thread, pins and needles was there, but what stood out was the seafood: baskets full of boiled mussels, adorned with black and orange; greenish sea urchins covered with spines; clusters of leathery barnacles; silvery sardines, and endless small shellfish – whelks, limpets, clams, squid, with the tentacles all spread out and hanging down like dead spiders' legs. Such a picture, with a bit of serene sea as a background, a wharf with uneven stones and a rocky shore, had much of a Neapolitan landscape about it, with the similarity being completed by the dress and postures of the not too distant fishermen spreading out their nets to dry in the sun. Standing motionless at the threshold to the courtyard, with no expression on his face, was a blind man, his badly shaven beard giving his cheeks a bluish tinge, his greasy hair lank and scraggy, holding out a dented hat into which small coins and crusts of bread were pouring in.

Chinto was looking out at the bay with his mouth open, and when Amparo finally came out, he didn't see her; she, on the other hand, spied him from afar and changed direction as quick as a dart, making her way along the well-known Calle del Sol, which is made up of half a dozen hunchbacked houses and two garden walls topped with wild grass and wallflowers. She ran until she reached the Camino del Crucero, and leaving it on one side, she crossed the road and the Cuesta de San Hilario, where she slowed down, thinking she was now safe. It was an obsession of that clot to give her not a moment's peace, to be her escort every afternoon! And since he was such delightful company, and since he spoke so elegantly, just like he had a mouthful of paste from the way words stuck to his tongue! … Amparo was reasoning in this way as she made her way down towards the Puerto del

puerta del Castillo, defendida todavía, como *in illo tempore*, por su puente levadizo y sus cadenas rechinantes.

Al propio tiempo subían unas señoras, con las cuales se cruzó la cigarrera. Iban casi en orden hierático; delante las niñas de corto, entre quienes descollaba Nisita, ya espigada, provista de una gran pelota; luego el grupo de las casaderas, Josefina García, Lola Sobrado, luciendo sus mantillas y sus colas recientes; los flancos de este pelotón los reforzaban Baltasar y Borrén, y como Baltasar no se había de poner al ladito de su hermana, tocábale ir cerca de Josefina. Cerraban la marcha la viuda de García y doña Dolores, ésta carilarga y erisipelatosa de cutis, la viuda sin tocas ni lutos, antes muy empavesada de colores alegres.

Los destellos del sol poniente, muriendo en las aguas de la bahía, alumbraron a un tiempo a Baltasar y a Amparo, haciendo que mutuamente se viesen y se mirasen. El mancebo, con su bigote blondo, su pelo rubio, su tez delicada y sanguínea, el brillo de sus galones que detenían los últimos fulgores del astro, parecía de oro; y la muchacha, morena, de rojos labios, con su pañuelo de seda carmesí, y las olas encendidas que servían de marco a su figura, semejaba hecha de fuego. Ambos se contemplaron un instante, instante muy largo, durante el cual se creyeron envueltos en la irradiación de una atmósfera de luz, calor y vida. Al dejar de contemplarse, fuese que el esplendor del ocaso es breve y se extingue luego, fuese por otras causas íntimas y psicológicas, imaginaron que sentían un hálito frío y que empezaba a anochecer. Oyóse la palabra ronca de Borrén el inaguantable.

–¿La has visto?

–¿A quién? –balbució el teniente Baltasar, que fingía considerar con suma atención la punta de sus botas, por no encontrarse con la ojeada investigadora de Josefina.

–¿A la chiquilla del barquillero … a la cigarrera?

–¿Cuál? ¿Era esa que pasaba? –contestó al fin, aceptando la situación.

–Sí, hombre, ésa… ¿Qué tal? ¿Tengo buen ojo?

Castillo, which was still protected as *in illo tempore*,[7] by its drawbridge and its clanking chains.

At the same time making their way up were a number of ladies whom the cigar maker passed. They were walking along almost in hieratical order; in front the littlest girls, standing out amongst whom was Nisita, now tall and slim, with a big ball; then the group of marriageable girls, Josefina García and Lola Sobrado, sporting their mantillas and the recently acquired trains of their dresses; the flanks of this group were reinforced by Baltasar and Borrén, and since Baltasar wasn't about to walk by his sister's side, it fell upon him to walk next to Josefina. The widow García and Doña Dolores brought up the rear, the latter looking very long-faced and with erysipelatous redness in her skin;[8] the widow, without a black veil or mourning clothes, was rather decked out in cheerful colours.

The sparkles of light from the setting sun, dying in the waters of the bay, bathed Baltasar and Amparo in light at the same time, causing them to see and look at each other. The young man, with his blond moustache, his fair hair, his delicate, sanguine complexion, and the gleaming chevrons which caught the dying splendour of the heavenly body, seemed like gold; and the dark girl with her red lips, her crimson silk scarf and the glowing waves which served to frame her face, looked to be made of fire. They both contemplated each other for a moment, a very long moment, during which they believed themselves wrapped in the irridation of an atmosphere of light, warmth and life. When they stopped contemplating each other, either because the splendour of the setting sun is brief and then fades away, or because of other intimate psychological causes, they imagined that they could feel a cold breeze and that night was beginning to fall. The unbearable Borrén's hoarse voice could be heard:

'Did you see her?'

'Who?' stammered Lieutenant Baltasar, pretending to contemplate with the utmost attention the toes of his boots, in order not to meet Josefina's questioning glance.

'The pastry cone seller's daughter … the cigar maker.'

'Which one? Was she the one who passed by?' he finally responded, resigned to the situation.

'Yes indeed, that's her… What do you reckon? Do I have a good eye?'

---

7   In that time.
8   Affected with erysipelas, a disease caused by a bacterial infection and characterised by inflammation of the skin, producing a deep red colour.

–Yo también la conocí –pronunció Josefina, cuya voz de tiple ascendía al tono sobreagudo.

– A mí no me ha saludado… –añadió Borrén–. No me conoció tal vez … y eso que yo la metí en la Granera … yo la recomendé. ¡Bien dije siempre que había de ser una chica preciosa! Lo que es de otra cosa no entenderé, hombre; pero de ese género… ¿Qué les pareció a ustedes?

–¿A mí? –murmuró Josefina entre dientes y con agresivo silbido de vocales–. No me pregunte usted, Borrén… Esas mujeres ordinarias me parecen todas iguales, cortadas por el mismo patrón. Morena…, muy basta.

–¡Ave María, Josefina! –dijo escandalizada Lola Sobrado–. No tuviste tiempo de verla; es hermosa y reúne mucha gracia. Fíjate otra vez en ella…; si vuelve a pasar, te daré al codo.

–No te molestes … no merece la pena; es el tipo de una cocinera, como todas las de su especie.

Baltasar hallaba incómoda la conversación y buscaba un pretexto para cambiarla. Atravesaban por delante de un campo cubierto de hierba marchita, especie de landa estéril cercada por lienzos de muralla de las fortificaciones. Había allí una parada de borricos de alquiler, que aguardaban pacíficamente, con las orejas gachas, a sus acostumbrados parroquianos, mientras los burreros y espoliques, sentados en el malecón, jugaban con sus varas, departían amigablemente, y picando con la uña un cigarro de a cuarto, abrumaban a ofrecimientos a los transeúntes.

–¿Un burro, señorito? ¿Un burro precioso? ¿Un burro mejor que los caballos? ¿Vamos a Aldeaparda? ¿Vamos a la Erbeda?

Acercóse Baltasar a las niñas de corto, y dijo a Nisita:

–¿Una vuelta por el campo?

A la chiquilla se la encandilaron los ojos, y soltando la pelota, echó los brazos al teniente con sonrisa zalamera. Baltasar la aupó, colocándola sobre los lomos de un asnillo, que aún tenía puestas jamugas de dorados clavos. Y tomando la vara de manos del alquilador, comenzó a arrear… «¡Arre, burro! ¡Arre! ¡Arre! ¡Arre!».

Amparo, al llegar a la entrada de las Filas, sintió detrás de sí una respiración anhelosa y como el trotar de una acosada alimaña montés, y casi al mismo tiempo emparejó con ella Chinto, sudoroso y jadeante. La perseguida se volvió desdeñosamente, fulminando al perseguidor una mirada de despidehuéspedes.

–¿Para qué corres así, majadero? –díjole en desabrido tono–. ¿Si creerás que me escapo? Cuidado que…

'I recognised her too,' declared Josefina, whose soprano voice became super high-pitched.

'She didn't greet me …' added Borrén. 'Perhaps she didn't recognise me … and I was the one who found her a job in the Granary … I recommended her. I always said she was bound to be a lovely girl. I may not know about other things, but stuff like that … How did she seem to you?'

'To me?' Josefina muttered with an agressive whistle in her vowels. 'Don't ask me, Borrén … Those common women look the same to me, all cut from the same pattern. Dark … very coarse.'

'Hail Mary, Josefina!' Lola Sobrado said, scandalised. 'You didn't have time to look at her; she's pretty and she possesses lots of charm. Take another look at her … if she passes by again, I'll nudge you with my elbow.'

'Don't bother … it's not worth it; she's the sort who looks like a cook, like all the others of her kind.'

Baltasar was finding the conversation unsettling and was looking for a pretext to change it. They were crossing in front of a field covered with withered grass, a kind of barren moor surrounded by the walls of the fortified ramparts. There was a stand there with donkeys for hire, waiting calmly with their ears drooping down for their usual customers, while the drivers and grooms, seated on the jetty, were playing with their rods, conversing amicably, picking away on cheap cigars with their nails, and inundating the passers-by with their offers.

'A donkey, young master? A beautiful donkey? A donkey better than any horse? Shall we go to Aldeaparda? Shall we go to La Erbeda?'

Baltasar went up to the young girls and said to Nisita:

'Do you fancy a ride through the countryside?'

The little girl's eyes lit up and, letting go of the ball, she threw her arms around the lieutenant with a flattering smile. Baltasar lifted her up and put her on the back of a small donkey, which still had a sidesaddle with golden studs. And taking the rod from the man renting the animals, he began to gee up the donkey … 'Gee up, donkey! Gee up! Gee up! Gee up!'

When Amparo reached the entrance to Las Filas, she sensed heavy breathing behind her like that of a small, wild verminous creature being chased, and almost at the same time Chinto caught up with her, sweating and panting. The pursued girl turned around disdainfully, giving her pursuer a withering, dismissive look!

'Why are you running like that, you idiot?' she said in a harsh tone of voice. 'If you're thinking that I'm running away? Watch out that…'

–Allí... –contestó él echando los bofes, tal era su sobrealiento...– allí...,
porque no te vinieses sin compañía..., allí..., ¡yo me entretuve con el vapor
de la Habana, que salía... más bonito, conchas! ¡Humo que echaba! ¿Por
dónde viniste que no te vi?

–Por donde me dio la gana, ¡repelo! Y ya te aviso que no me vuelvas a
pudrir la sangre con tus compañías... ¿Soy yo aquí alguna niña pequeña?
Anda a vender barquillos, que ahí en el paseo hay quien compre, y en la
fábrica maldito si sacas un real en toda la tarde...

'There...' he answered with great effort, such was his difficulty breathing, 'there ... so that you didn't come back on your own ... there ... I amused myself with the steamer heading out for Havana ... gosh, so pretty! The smoke pouring out! Which way did you come out that I didn't see you?'

'I came out where I felt like it, hang it! And I'm warning you not to make my blood boil again with your company ... Do I look like some little girl? Go and sell pastry cones because there on the promenade there are people to buy them, whilst in the damn factory if you get a single *real* all afternoon ...'

VIII

LA CHICA VALE UN PERÚ

Mal que le pese a Josefina y a todas las señoritas de Marineda, las profecías de Borrén se han cumplido. No se equivoca un inteligente como él al calificar una obra maestra.

Sucede con la mujer lo que con las plantas. Mientras dura el invierno, todas nos parecen iguales; son troncos inertes; viene la savia de la primavera, las cubre de botones, de hojas, de flores, y entonces las admiramos. Pocos meses bastan para trasformar al arbusto y a la mujer. Hay un instante crítico en que la belleza femenina toma consistencia, adquiere su carácter, cristaliza por decirlo así. La metamorfosis es más impensada y pronta en el pueblo que en las demás clases sociales. Cuando llega la edad en que invenciblemente desea agradar la mujer, rompe su feo capullo, arroja la librea de la miseria y del trabajo, y se adorna y aliña por instinto.

El día en que «unos señores» dijeron a Amparo que era bonita, tuvo la andariega chiquilla conciencia de su sexo: hasta entonces había sido un muchacho con sayas. Ni nadie la consideraba de otro modo: si algún granuja de la calle le recordó que formaba parte de la mitad más bella del género humano, hízolo medio a cachetes, y ella rechazó a puñadas, cuando no a coces y mordiscos, el bárbaro requiebro. Cosas todas que no le quitaban el sueño ni el apetito. Hacía su tocado en la forma sumaria que conocemos ya; correteaba por plazas, caminos y callejuelas; se metía con las señoritas que llevaban alguna moda desusada, remiraba escaparates, curioseaba ventaneros amoríos, y se acostaba rendida y sin un pensamiento malo.

Ahora… ¿quién le dijo a ella que el aseo y compostura que gastaba no eran suficientes? ¡Vaya usted a saber! El espejo no, porque ninguno tenían en su casa. Sería un espejo interior, clarísimo, en que ven las mujeres su imagen propia y que jamás las engaña. Lo cierto es que Amparo, que seguía leyéndole al barbero periódicos progresistas, pidió el sueldo de la lectura en objetos de tocador. Y reunió un ajuar digno de la reina, a saber: un escarpidor de cuerno y una lendrera de boj; dos paquetes de horquillas, tomadas de orín; un bote de pomada de rosa; medio jabón *aux amandes amères*, con

8
THE GIRL IS WORTH HER WEIGHT IN GOLD

Whether Josefina and all the young ladies of Marineda like it or not, Borrén's prophecies have come to pass. An intelligent person like him doesn't make a mistake when he assesses a masterpiece.

The same happens with women as with plants. While winter lasts, they all seem the same to us; they are inert stems; the sap of spring arrives, covers them with buds, leaves and flowers, and then we admire them. A few months are enough to transform shrubs and women. There is a critical moment in which feminine beauty takes on consistency, acquires its character, crystallises, so to speak. The metamorphosis is more unexpected and rapid among the lower orders than in other social classes. When a woman reaches the age in which she invincibly desires to please, she breaks out of her ugly cocoon, throws away the livery of poverty and work, and adorns and beautifies herself by instinct.

On the day when 'certain gentlemen' told Amparo that she was pretty, the footloose young girl became aware of her sexual identity: until that time she had been a boy with skirts. Nor did anyone consider her in any other way: if some street urchin reminded her that she belonged to the more beautiful half of the human species, he did it partly with a slap in the face, and she rejected the barbaric compliment with punches, if not kicks and bites. All of these were things which troubled neither her sleep nor her appetite. She arranged her hair in the summary fashion we already know; she ran about the squares, roads and back streets; she teased young ladies who wore out-of-date fashions, stared and stared at shop windows, snooped around open windows to spy on romances, and went to bed exhausted and without a single bad thought in her head.

Now ... who told her that the attention with which she made her toilet was insufficient? Who knows! Not the mirror because they didn't have one in their house. It must be an inner mirror, a very clear one, in which women see their own image and which never deceives them. What is certain is that Amparo, who carried on reading progressive newspapers to the barber, asked for toiletries as payment for her reading. And she put together a trousseau worthy of a queen, namely: a wide-toothed comb made of horn and a fine-tooth comb made of boxwood; two packets of rusty hairpins; a jar of rose ointment; half a bar of soap *aux amandes amères*,[9] with little hairs cut from

---
9   Bitter almond.

pelitos de la barba de los parroquianos, cortados y adheridos todavía; un frasco, casi vacío, de esencia de heno, y otras baratijas del mismo jaez. Amalgamando tales elementos logró Amparo desbastar su figura y sacarla a luz, descubriendo su verdadero color y forma, como se descubre la de la legumbre enterrada al arrancarla y lavarla. Su piel trabó amistosas relaciones con el agua, y libre de la capa del polvo que atascaba sus poros finos, fue el cutis moreno más suave, sano y terso que imaginarse pueda. No era tostado, ni descolorido, ni encendido tampoco; de todo tenía, pero con su cuenta y razón, y allí donde convenía que lo tuviese. La mocedad, la sangre rica, el aire libre, las amorosas caricias del sol, habíanse dado la mano para crear la coloración magnífica de aquella tez plebeya. La lisura de ágata de la frente; el bermellón de los carnosos labios; el ámbar de la nuca, el rosa trasparente del tabique de la nariz; el terciopelo castaño del lunar que travesea en la comisura de la boca; el vello áureo que desciende entre la mejilla y la oreja y vuelve a aparecer, más apretado y oscuro, en el labio superior, como leve sombra al esfumino,[14] cosas eran para tentar a un colorista a que cogiese el pincel e intentase copiarlas. Gracias sin duda a la pomada, el pelo no se quedó atrás y también se mostró cual Dios lo hizo, negro, crespo, brillante. Sólo dos accesorios del rostro no mejoraron, tal vez porque eran inmejorables: ojos y dientes, el complemento indispensable de lo que se llama un *tipo moreno*. Tenía Amparo por ojos dos globos, en que el azulado de la córnea, bañado siempre en un líquido puro, hacía resaltar el negror de la ancha pupila, mal velada por cortas y espesas pestañas. En cuanto a los dientes, servidos por un estómago que no conocía la gastralgia,[15] parecían treinta y dos grumos de cuajada leche, graciosísimamente desiguales y algo puntiagudos, como los de un perro cachorro.

Observábanse, no obstante, en tan gallardo ejemplar femenino rasgos reveladores de su extracción: la frente era corta, un tanto arremangada la nariz, largos los colmillos, el cabello recio al tacto, la mirada directa, los tobillos y muñecas no muy delicados. Su mismo hermoso cutis estaba predestinado a inyectarse, como el del señor Rosendo, que allá en la fuerza de la edad había sido, al decir de las vecinas y de su mujer, guapo mozo. Pero, ¿quién piensa en el invierno al ver el arbusto florido?

Si Baltasar no rondó desde luego las inmediaciones de la fábrica, fue que destinaron a Borrén por algún tiempo a Ciudad Real, y temió aburrirse yendo solo.

---

14 Alusión al procedimiento de empastar las sombras del dibujo.
15 El ácido estomacal ataca el esmalte de los dientes.

customers' beards still sticking to it; an almost empty bottle of velvet grass perfume, and other trifles of the same sort. By amalgamating such elements, Amparo managed to remove the rough edges from her face and highlight it, revealing its true colour and form, just as the true appearance of a buried tuber is revealed when it's torn out of the ground and washed. Her skin struck up a friendly relationship with water, and once it was free of the layer of dust clogging its fine pores, her dark complexion was smoother, healthier and softer than one could imagine. It was neither tanned, nor faded, nor glowing; it had everything, but within reasonable limits, and had it just where it was most needed. Youth, rich blood, fresh air and the loving caresses of the sun had joined together to create the magnificent colouring of that plebeian complexion. The agated smoothness of her forehead; the vermilion of her fleshy lips; the amber of the nape of her neck; the pink transparency of her nasal septum; the chestnut-coloured velvet of the mole cavorting at the corner of her mouth; the golden down descending between her cheek and her ear and reappearing denser and darker on her upper lip, like the fine shading on a stump drawing: these were things to tempt a colourist to pick up a brush and try to copy. Thanks no doubt to pomade, her hair was not left behind and also showed itself as God had made it, black, curly and shiny. Only two accessories of her face showed no improvement, perhaps because they were unimprovable: her eyes and her teeth, the indispensable complement of what is called a *brunette type*. Amparo had two spheres for eyes, in which the blue of her cornea, always bathed in a pure liquid, made the blackness of the wide pupil stand out in the poor protective shade of the short, thick lashes. As for her teeth, served by a stomach that did not suffer from gastralgia, they were like thirty-two curds of coagulated milk, uneven in a very pleasing way and somewhat pointed like those of a puppy dog.

One could, nevertheless, detect in such a fine feminine specimen telltale traits of her origins: her forehead was low, her nose a bit turned up, her eyeteeth long, her hair coarse to the touch, her glance very direct, and her ankles and wrists not very slender. Even her beautiful skin was predestined to turn ruddy, as it was with Señor Rosendo, who in his heyday, according to what his neighbours and wife said, had been a handsome fellow. But who thinks about winter on seeing a flowering shrub?

If Baltasar didn't prowl around the vicinity of the factory, it was because Borrén had been posted to Ciudad Real for a period of time, and he was afraid of being bored if he went out alone.

IX

LA GLORIOSA

Ocurrió poco después en España un suceso que entretuvo a la nación siete años cabales, y aún la está entreteniendo de rechazo y en sus consecuencias, a saber: que en vez de los pronunciamientos chicos acostumbrados, se realizó otro muy grande, llamado Revolución de septiembre de 1868. Quedóse España al pronto sin saber lo que le pasaba y como quien ve visiones. No era para menos. ¡Un pronunciamiento de veras, que derrocaba la dinastía! Por fin el país había hecho una hombrada, o se la daban hecha: mejor que mejor para un pueblo meridional. De todo se encargaban Marina, Ejército, progresistas y unionistas. González Bravo y la reina estaban ya en Francia cuando aún ignoraba la inmensa mayoría de los españoles si era el Ministerio o los Borbones quienes caían «para siempre», según rezaban los famosos letreros de Madrid. No obstante, en breve se persuadió la nación de que el caso era serio, de que no sólo la raza real, sino la monarquía misma, iban a andar en tela de juicio, y entonces cada quisque se dio a alborotar por su lado. Sólo guardaron reserva y silencio relativo aquellos que al cabo de los siete años habían de llevarse el gato al agua.

Durante la deshecha borrasca de ideas políticas que se alzó de pronto, observóse que el campo y las ciudades situadas tierra adentro se inclinaron a la tradición monárquica, mientras las poblaciones fabriles y comerciales, y los puertos de mar, aclamaron la república. En la costa cantábrica, el Malecón y Marineda se distinguieron por la abundancia de comités, juntas, *clubs*, proclamas, periódicos y manifestaciones. Y es de notar que desde el primer instante la forma republicana invocada fue la federal. Nada, la unitaria no servía: tan sólo la federal brindaba al pueblo la beatitud perfecta. ¿Y por qué así? ¡Vaya a saber! Un escritor ingenioso dijo más adelante que la república federal no se le hubiera ocurrido a nadie para España si Proudhon no escribe un libro sobre el principio federativo y si Pi no lo traduce y lo comenta. Sea como sea, y valga la explicación lo que valiere, es evidente que el federalismo se improvisó allí y doquiera en menos que canta un gallo.

La fábrica de tabacos de Marineda fue centro simpatizador (como ahora se dice) para *la federal*.[16] De la colectividad fabril nació la confraternidad política; a las cigarreras se les abrió el horizonte republicano de varias maneras: por medio de la propaganda oral, a la sazón tan activa, y también,

---

16   Apelativo con que se denomina a la futura República española.

9
THE GLORIOUS REVOLUTION

Not long afterwards there ocurred in Spain an event that engaged the nation for seven full years, and is still engaging it indirectly and in its consequences: that is to say, instead of the customary minor insurrections, another far greater one called the Revolution of September 1868 was carried out.[xv]

At first Spain didn't know what was happening, like someone having visions. Quite right too. A real uprising, which overthrew the dynasty! At last, the nation had performed a brave act, or one had been handed over already done; so much the better for southern Europeans. The navy, the army, Progressives and Unionists were taking charge of everything. González Bravo and the Queen were already in France at a time when the vast majority of Spaniards still didn't know if it was the Ministry or the Bourbons who had fallen 'for ever', as the famous notices in Madrid were saying. Nevertheless, the nation was soon persuaded that the matter was serious, that not only the royal lineage, but the monarchy itself, was going to be called into question, and at that point, absolutely everyone took to stirring things up as he saw fit. The only ones who maintained their reserve and relative silence were those who, at the end of those seven years, would have to win the day.

During the violent storm of political ideas that suddenly rose up, it could be seen that the countryside and cities in the interior were inclined to favour monarchic tradition, while the manufacturing and commercial towns and seaports acclaimed the Republic. On the Cantabrian coast, El Malecón and Marineda were characterised by the abundance of committees, meetings, clubs, proclamations, newspapers and demonstrations. And it should be noted that the form of republicanism invoked from the first moment was federal. A centralised, unitary form was of no use; a federal form of government and nothing else could offer the people perfect happiness. And why was it so? You'll find out! An ingenious writer later said that a federal republic for Spain would never have occurred to anyone if Proudhon had not written a book on the federative principle, and if Pi had not translated it and written a commentary. [xvi] Be that as it may, and for whatever worth the explanation may have, it is evident that federalism was improvised there and everywhere in a flash.

The tobacco factory in Marineda was a centre that was sympathetic (as they say nowadays) to the *federalist cause*. Political brotherhood was born out of the collectivity of the factory; the republican horizon was opened up to the cigar makers in various ways: by means of oral propaganda, so active

muy principalmente, de los periódicos que pululaban. Hubo en cada taller una o dos lectoras; les abonaban sus compañeras el tiempo perdido, y adelante. Amparo fue de las más apreciadas, por el sentido que daba a la lectura; tenía ya adquirido hábito de leer, habiéndolo practicado en la barbería tantas veces. Su lengua era suelta, incansable su laringe, robusto su acento. Declamaba, más bien que leía, con fuego y expresión, subrayando los pasajes que merecían subrayarse, realzando las palabras de letra bastardilla, añadiendo la mímica necesaria cuando lo requería el caso, y comenzando con lentitud y misterio, y en voz contenida, los párrafos importantes, para subir la ansiedad al grado eminente y arrancar involuntarios estremecimientos de entusiasmo al auditorio, cuando adoptaba entonación más rápida y vibrante a cada paso. Su alma impresionable, combustible, móvil y superficial, se teñía fácilmente del color del periódico que andaba en sus manos, y lo reflejaba con viveza y fidelidad extraordinarias. Nadie más a propósito para un oficio que requiere gran fogosidad, pero externa; caudal de energía incesantemente renovado y disponible para gastarlo en exclamaciones, en escenas de indignación y de fanática esperanza. La figura de la muchacha, el brillo de sus ojos, las inflexiones cálidas y pastosas de su timbrada voz de contralto, contribuían al sorprendente efecto de la lectura.

Al comunicar la chispa eléctrica, Amparo se electrizaba también. Era a la vez sujeto agente y paciente. A fuerza de leer todos los días unos mismos periódicos, de seguir el flujo y reflujo de la controversia política, iba penetrando en la lectora la convicción hasta los tuétanos. La fe virgen con que creía en la Prensa era inquebrantable, porque le sucedía con el periódico lo que a los aldeanos con los aparatos telegráficos: jamás intentó saber cómo sería por de dentro; sufría sus efectos, sin analizar sus causas. ¡Y cuánto se sorprendería la fogosa lectora si pudiese entrar en una redacción de diario político, ver de qué modo un artículo trascendental y furibundo se escribe cabeceando de sueño, en la esquina de la mugrienta mesa, despachando una chuleta o una ración de merluza frita! ¡La lectora, que tomaba al pie de la letra aquello de «Cogemos la pluma trémulos de indignación», y lo otro de «La emoción ahoga nuestra voz, la vergüenza enrojece nuestra faz», y hasta lo de «Y si no bastan las palabras, ¡corramos a las armas y derramemos la última gota de nuestra sangre!».

Lo que en el periódico faltaba de sinceridad sobraba en Amparo de

at that time, and also mainly by the newspapers that were proliferating. There were one or two readers in every workshop; their companions would guarantee them the time they lost, and so things moved ahead. Amparo was one of the most valued, on account of the feeling she imparted to the reading; she had already acquired the habit of reading aloud, having practised it so many times in the barbershop. Her tongue was smooth, her larynx untiring, her accent robust. She declaimed rather than read, full of fire and expression, stressing the passages that were worthy of stress, emphasising words in italics, adding the necessary mimicry when the occasion required it, and beginning the important paragraphs slowly and mysteriously, in a restrained voice, to raise anxiety to an elevated level and wrench involuntary shivers of enthusiasm from her audience when she adopted a more rapid and vibrant intonation as she went along. Her impressionable, combustible, changeable and superficial spirit easily adapted itself to the tone of the newspaper that was in her hands, and she reflected it with extraordinary vividness and fidelity. There was nobody more suitable for a job which requires great mettle, if only on the outside; a wealth of energy, constantly renewed and available for use in exclamations, in scenes of indignation and fanatical hope. The girl's face, the gleam in her eyes, the warm, rich inflections of her well-toned contralto voice all contributed to the surprising effect of her reading.

As she spread this electric spark, Amparo electrified herself too. She was agent and recipient at the same time. By dint of reading some of the same newspapers every day, of following the ebb and flow of political controversy, conviction was gradually penetrating down to the reader's very marrow. The virgin faith with which she believed in the press was unshakeable, because what was happening to her with newspapers was the same as among small-town people with telegraph equipment: she never tried to find out what it was like inside; she experienced its effects without analysing its causes. And how the spirited reader would be surprised if he could enter a political daily newspaper office and see the way in which a transcendental, enraged article is written by someone nodding sleepily on the corner of a filthy desk while disposing of a cutlet or a portion of fried hake! The reader followed to the letter all that about 'we take up our pen trembling with indignation', and other phrases like 'emotion stifles our voice, shame turns our face red' and even 'and if words do not suffice, let's resort to arms and spill the last drop of our blood!'

What the newspaper lacked in sincerity, Amparo made up for in gullible

crédulo asentimiento. Acostumbrábase a pensar en estilo de artículo de fondo y a hablar lo mismo: acudían a sus labios los giros trillados, los lugares comunes de la prensa diaria, y con ellos aderezaba y componía su lenguaje. Iba adquiriendo gran soltura en el hablar; es verdad que empleaba a veces palabras y hasta frases enteras cuyo sentido exacto no le era patente, y otras las trabucaba; pero hasta en eso se parecía a la desaliñada y antiliteraria prensa de entonces. ¡Daba tanto que hacer la revuelta y absorbente política, que no había tiempo para escribir en castellano! Ello es que Amparo iba teniendo un pico de oro; se la estaría uno oyendo sin sentir cuando trataba de ciertas cuestiones. El taller entero se embelesaba escuchándola, y compartía sus afectos y sus odios. De común acuerdo, las operarias detestaban a Olózaga, llamándole *el viejo del borrego*, porque andaba el muy indino buscando un rey que no nos hacía maldita la falta … sólo por cogerse él para sí embajadas y otras prebendas; hablar de González Bravo era promover un motín; con Prim estaban a mal, porque se inclinaba a la forma monárquica; a Serrano había que darle de codo; era un ambicioso hipócrita, muy capaz, si pudiese, de hacerse rey o emperador, cuando menos.

Creció la efervescencia republicana mientras que trascurría el primer invierno revolucionario; al acercarse el verano subió más grados aún el termómetro político en la fábrica. En el curso de horas de sol, sin embargo, decaía la conversación, y entre tanto la atmósfera se cargaba de asfixiantes vapores y espesaba hasta parecer que podía cortarse con cuchillo. Penetrantes efluvios de nicotina subían de los serones llenos de seca y prensada hoja. Las manos se movían a impulsos de la necesidad, liando tagarninas; pero los cerebros rehuían el trabajo abrumador del pensamiento; a veces una cabeza caía inerte sobre la tabla de liar, y una mujer, rendida de calor, se quedaba sepultada en sueño profundo. Más felices que las demás, las que espurriaban la hoja, sentadas a la turca en el suelo, con un montón de tabaco delante, tenían el puchero de agua en la diestra, y al rociar, muy hinchadas de carrillos, el Virginia, las consolaba un aura de frescura. Tendidas las barrenderas al lado del montón de polvo que acababan de reunir, roncaban con la boca abierta y se estremecían de gusto cuando la suave llovizna les salpicaba el rostro. Revoloteaban las moscas con porfiado zumbido, y ya se unían en el aire y caían rápidamente sobre la labor o las manos de las

consent. She was growing accustomed to thinking in the style of an editorial and speaking the same: the hackneyed turns of phrase and clichés of the daily press came to her lips, and she embellished and composed her language with them. She gradually acquired great fluency of speech; it's true that she sometimes used words and even whole phrases whose exact meaning was not clear to her, and she even mixed up some others, but even there she was like the careless and anti-literary press of the time. This complicated and absorbing political life meant there was so much to do that there wasn't time to write in Castilian. The fact is that Amparo was gradually getting the gift of the gab; you could be listening to her without hearing when she dealt with certain questions. The entire workshop was enraptured listening to her, and shared her affections and hatreds. By common consent the women working in the factory detested Olózaga,[xvii] calling him *the old goat* because the cheeky rascal was running around looking for a king which was the last damn thing we needed ... just to grab ambassadorships and other perks for himself. Talk of González Bravo was enough to start a riot; they were on bad terms with Prim because he tended to prefer a monarchic form of government; Serrano[xviii] had to be kept at arm's distance; he was an ambitious hypocrite, quite capable, given the opportunity, of making himself at least king or emperor.

Republican effervescence grew as the first revolutionary winter went by; as summer approached, the political thermometer in the factory rose several degrees. During the course of sunlight hours, however, conversation waned and in the meantime the atmosphere became filled with asphyxiating vapours and it grew thick until it seemed it could be cut with a knife. The penetrating odour of nicotine rose up from the large baskets filled with dried and pressed leaves. Their hands kept moving, driven by necessity, rolling cigars, but their brains avoided the burdensome effort of thinking; at times a head fell lifelessly onto the rolling board and one of the women, exhausted by heat, lay buried in deep sleep. More fortunate than the others were those who were watering the leaves, squatting on the floor with a pile of tobacco in front of them, holding a pot of water in their right hand and, as they sprayed the Virginia tobacco with water from their swollen cheeks, a cool gentle breeze comforted them. Stretched out beside the pile of dust they had just gathered, the sweepers were snoring away with mouths open and quivering with pleasure whenever the gentle drizzle sprinkled their faces. The flies buzzed around persistently, first joining forces in the air and dropping swiftly onto the materials or the hands of the workers, then getting

operarias, ya se prendían las patas en la goma del tarrillo, pugnando en balde por alzar el vuelo. Andaban esparcidos por las mesas, y mezclados con el tabaco, pedazos de borona, tajadas de bacalao crudo, cebollas, sardinas arenques. Con semejante temperatura, ¿quién había de tener ganas de comerse la pitanza?

Por fin, a eso de las cuatro de la tarde, la refrigerante brisa marina comenzaba a correr: dilatábanse los oprimidos pechos, los dientes funcionaban despachando los humildes manjares, y le tocaba su turno a la lectura política.

Leíanse publicaciones de Madrid y periódicos locales. En la prensa de la Corte se llevaban la palma los discursos de Castelar, por entonces muy distante de haberse *gastado*. ¡Cuánta palabra linda, y qué bien que enganchaban unas en otras! Parecían versos. Es verdad que la mayor parte no se entendían, y que danzaban por allí nombres tan raros, que sólo el demonio de Amparo podía leerlos de corrido; mas no le hace: lo que es bonito, era muy bonito aquello. Y bien se colegía que la sustancia del discurso era a favor del pueblo y contra los tiranos, de suerte que lo demás se tomaba por adorno y floreo delicado.

Cuando en vez de discursos cuadraba leer artículos de fondo, de esos kilométricos y soporíferos, que hablan de justicia social, redención de las clases obreras, instrucción difundida, generalizada y gratis, fraternidad universal, todo en estilo de homilía y con oraciones largas y enmarañadas como fideos cocidos, alterábase la voz de Amparo y se humedecían los ojos de sus oyentes. Leve escalofrío recorría las filas de mujeres, las cuales se miraban como diciéndose: «¿Eh? ¿Qué tal? ¡Este sí que lo parla!» Y leído el último párrafo, que terminaba anunciando el próximo advenimiento de una era de perfecta libertad y bienestar absoluto, solían cruzar las manos, sonriendo y sintiéndose tan relajadas en sus fibras, tan blandas y dulces como un plato de huevos moles. Trabajo les costaba reprimir los impulsos de abrazarse que se les iban y venían.

En cambio, si el escrito pertenecía al género bélico y tocaba a somatén, parecía que les daban a beber una mixtura de pólvora y alcohol. Montaban en cólera tan aína como se encrespan las olas del mar. Sordas exclamaciones acompañaban y cubrían a veces la voz de la lectora. Era contagiosa la ira, y mujer había allí de corazón más suave que la seda, incapaz de matar una mosca, y capaz a la sazón de pedir cien mil cabezas de los pícaros que viven chupando la sangre del pueblo.

their legs caught in the gum in the small jars and struggling in vain to fly off. Pieces of corn bread, slices of raw cod, onions and herrings were scattered over the tables and mixed with the tobacco. With the temperatures like this, who could feel like eating up their daily ration?

Finally, at about four in the afternoon, the cooling sea breeze began to blow; oppressed bosoms expanded, teeth set to work, disposing of the humble foodstuffs, and it was time for the political reading.

Publications from Madrid and local papers were read. In the press from the capital, Castelar's speeches carried the day, for at that time he was still a long way from *having seen better days*. So many pretty words and how nicely they connected with each other![xix] They were like poetry. It's true that the majority of them were incomprehensible and that such strange names kept bobbing up and down there that only that little devil Amparo could read them fluently, but it made no difference: because as for being really pretty, all that was very pretty. And everyone readily concluded that the substance of the speech was in favour of the people and against the tyrants, in such a way that the rest was taken for adornment and delicate flourish.

When it was deemed suitable to read editorials instead of speeches, those interminable, soporific articles about social justice, the redemption of the working class, free education for everyone and universal brotherhood, all in a homiletic style and with long sentences tangled up like cooked noodles, Amparo's voice changed and her listeners' eyes filled with tears. A slight shiver went through the rows of women who were looking at each other as if to say, 'So, what do you reckon? This one sure can talk!' And when the final paragraph had been read, which ended up announcing the imminent arrival of an era of perfect freedom and absolute well-being, they usually crossed their hands, smiling and feeling relaxed to their very core, as tender and sweet as a dish of egg yolk dessert. It took a great effort to suppress their desire to embrace each other as the feeling came over them again and again.

On the other hand, if the document belonged to a bellicose genre and sounded the alarm, it seemed like they were being given a mixture of gunpowder and alcohol to drink. They flew into a rage as quickly as the waves in the sea get choppy. Suppressed exclamations accompanied and sometimes drowned out the reader's voice. The anger was contagious and there were women there with hearts as soft as silk, incapable of killing a fly, yet capable at that moment of demanding a hundred thousand heads of those scoundrels who lived by bleeding the people dry.

X

ESTUDIOS HISTÓRICOS Y POLÍTICOS

Más partido tenían en la fábrica los periódicos locales que los de la Corte. Naturalmente, los locales exageraban la nota, recargaban el cuadro; sus títulos acostumbraban ser por este estilo: *El Vigilante Federal,* órgano de la democracia republicana federal-unionista; *El Representante de la Juventud Democrática; El Faro Salvador del Pueblo Libre.* Y como, aparte de algunas huecas generalidades del artículo de fondo, discurrían acerca de asuntos conocidos, era mucho mayor el interés que despertaban. No es fácil imaginar cuán honda sensación producía en el concurso alguna gacetilla rotulada, por ejemplo: «Acontecimiento incalificable.»

–A ver, a ver. Oír. Callar. Silencio, charlatanas.

Y reinaba un mutismo palpitante, escuchándose tan sólo el retintín de los tijeretazos que cercenaban el rabo de las tagarninas.

–«Acontecimiento incalificable –repetía Amparo–. Se nos asegura que hará dos días entraron tres guardias civiles francos de servicio en el café de la Aurora, y un oficial que allí había los arrestó...»

–Arrestaría, arrestaría...

–Callad, bocas...

–«...los arrestó por tan enorme delito...»

–¿Por entrar en un café?

–¡Y dicen que hay *libertá*!

–¡Qué ha de haberla, mujer!

–«Y preguntándoles la causa de su entrada en el local, le respondieron que su objeto era tomar café. No obstante tan naturales explicaciones, fueron arrestados por tres días, y hasta no faltan personas bien informadas que aseguren se ha dado orden para que los individuos del benemérito cuerpo no puedan entrar en los cafés de la Aurora ni del Norte. De ser esto cierto, sobre constituir un ataque infundado a los sagrados derechos individuales, lo es también a la industria libre y honrosa de los cafeteros, y...»

–¡Y le resobra la razón, así Dios me salve! ¿Y de qué come el pobre del cafetero si le espantan la parroquia?

–El pillo del oficial, como tiene su paga...

–¡Eso, eso!

–¡De ahí, de ahí!

10
HISTORICAL AND POLITICAL STUDIES

The local newspapers had more support in the factory than those from Madrid. Naturally, the local papers had an exaggerated style and overdid their depictions; their titles were generally something along these lines: *The Federal Guardian*, organ of the republican Federal-Unionist democracy, or *The Representative of Democratic Youth*, or *The Redemptive Beacon of the Free People*. And since, apart from some hollow generalisations in the editorials, they talked about well-known matters, they aroused far greater interest. It isn't easy to imagine how profound a sensation was produced among that gathering by a section of local news items with a title like, 'An Unspeakable Happening.'

'Let's see, let's see. Listen. Quiet. Silence, you chatterboxes.'

And a palpitant silence reigned, the only noise being the snip of scissors as they cut off the ends of the cigars.

'"An Unspeakable Happening,"' repeated Amparo. '"We are assured it must be two days ago that three off-duty civil guards went into the Café de la Aurora and an officer who was there arrested them ..."'

'Reportedly arrested them, reportedly arrested them ...'

'Quiet, loudmouths...'

'"... arrested them for such an enormous crime ..."'

'For going into a café?'

'And they say there's *freedom*!'

'There ought to be, that's for sure!'

'"And on being asked the reason for their entry into the premises, they responded that their intention was to have a coffee. In spite of such reasonable explanations, they were detained for three days, and there are even well-informed persons who maintain that orders have been given forbidding members of this worthy body from entering the Café de la Aurora or the Café del Norte. If this is true, as well as constituting an unwarranted attack on the sacred rights of individuals, it is also one on the free and honourable trade of café owners, and ..."'

'And they're only too right, as God is my witness! And what does the poor café owner live off if they scare away his customers?'

'That rogue of an officer, as long as he gets his pay ...'

'That's right, that's right!'

'That's why, that's why!'

–Habiendo *libertá* no hay injusticias. ¡Olé por ella!

–«¿Qué piensan los que así resucitan arranques del agonizante despotismo militar, propios de épocas terroríficas que pasaron a la Historia? ¿Se les ha figurado que estamos en aquellos siglos, cuando un señor tenía poder para abrir el vientre a sus vasallos?...»

Aquí se salió de madre el río. Exclamaciones, interjecciones, gritos y risas se cruzaron de un lado a otro; pero las risueñas estaban en minoría: dominaban las espantadas. Una vieja medio sorda se hizo una trompetilla con ambas manos, creyendo que sus oídos la engañaban.

–¡Ave María de gracia!

–¡En mi vida tal oí!

–¡Abrir la barriga!

–No sería en tierra de cristianos, mujer.

–¿Y eso fue a los pobrecitos civiles? –interrogó la sorda.

–¡Chis! –gritó Amparo–. Aquí viene lo bueno, señores: «...abrir el vientre a sus vasallos para calentarse los pies con su sangre...»

–¡Señor y Dios de los cielos!

–Parece que todo el estómago me da una vuelta.

–¡Pobre del pobre!

–¡Cuándo vendrá la federal para que se acaben esas infamias!

Otra cuerda que siempre resonaba en aquel centro político femenino era la del misterio. Cualquier periodiquillo, el más atrasado de noticias, contenía un suelto que, hábilmente leído, despertaba temores y esperanzas en el taller. Amparo empezaba por hacer señas al concurso para que estuviese prevenido a importantes revelaciones. Después comenzaba, con reposada voz:

–«Atravesamos momentos solemnes. De un día a otro deben cambiar de rumbo los acontecimientos...»

–Lo que yo digo. Esta situación, de por fuerza se la tienen que llevar los demonios.

–Hasta que llegue la nuestra...

–No, pues cuando éste lo huele... Por Madrid andará buena la cosa.

–Así los parta a todos un rayo, comilones, tiránicos, chupadores.

–A ver si calláis.

–«La situación está próxima a entrar en el camino que desde el primer día de la revolución debió emprender. Hay que vencer grandes obstáculos...» (Movimiento general.) «Los enemigos encubiertos de la revolución...»

'With *freedom*, there's no injustice. Hooray for that!'

'"What do they think, those who in this way resurrect the impetus of a dying military despotism, worthy of terrifying epochs which have passed into history? Do they imagine we are back in those centuries when a lord had the power to rip open the bellies of his vassals?..."'

At this point the river burst its banks. Exclamations, interjections, shouts and laughter crossed from one side of the audience to the other, but laughter was in the minority; horrified expressions were predominant. A half-deaf old woman, thinking her ears were deceiving her, made an ear trumpet with both hands.

'Hail Mary, full of grace!'

'I never heard the like in my life!'

'Opening up someone's belly!'

'It wouldn't happen in a Christian land.'

'And that's what happened to those poor civil guards?' asked the deaf woman.

'Shhh!' shouted Amparo. 'Here comes the good bit, everybody: "...to open up the bellies of his vassals to warm his feet with their blood..."'

'Holy Father in heaven!'

'I feel like my whole stomach's turning over.'

'The poor thing.'

'When will there be a federal system to put an end to these outrages!'

Another chord that was always struck in that feminine political centre was one of mystery. Any third-rate newspaper lacking up-to-date news might contain an item which, if skilfully read, would awaken fears and hopes in the workshop. Amparo would begin by making signs to the gathering to get ready for some important revelations. Then she would start in a calm voice:

'"We are going through solemn times. From one day to the next events must change course..."'

'That's what I say. To hell with this situation.'

'Until our own comes about...'

'No, because when this one smells it ... maybe things are going well in Madrid.'

'So damn them all, those gluttons, tyrants and drunkards.'

'Can you quieten down.'

'"The situation is close to going down the path it should have taken from the first day of the revolution. Great obstacles have to be overcome..." (General movement.) "The hidden enemies of the revolution..."'

–¿Quién será? ¿Lo dirá por el alcalde?

–No, mujer… Por ese maldito de cuñado de la reina…

–Y por el Napoleón de allá de Francia, boba, que no nos puede ver.

–¡Chis! «…de la revolución, están acechando el instante en que poder descargar sobre la situación un golpe decisivo y liberticida. No desmayemos, sin embargo. La revolución pasará triunfante por cima de tanto reaccionario como aparenta servirla con fines siniestros. En donde menos se piensa se esconde la reacción fijando su ojo de tigre…»

–Tiene razón, tiene razón. Está muy bien comparado.

–«…ojo de tigre … en la libertad, para estrangularla. Los más temibles son los que, llegados a la cima del poder, hacen traición a sus antiguos ideales que les sirvieron de pedestal para escalar las grandezas…»

–Si es lo que yo os predico siempre –exclamaba al llegar aquí la lectora, tomando la ampolleta–. Los peorcitos están arriba, arriba. Quien no lo ve, ciego es. Ínterin no agarre el pueblo soberano una escoba de silbarda, como esa que tenemos ahí … (y señaló a la que manejaba la barrendera del taller) y barra sin misericordia las altas esferas… ¡ya me entendéis! El mismo día en que se proclamó la libertad y se le dio el puntapié a los Borbones, había yo de publicar un decreto… ¿sabéis cómo? (la oradora abrió la mano izquierda, haciendo ademán de escribir en ella con una tagarnina:) «Decreto yo, el Pueblo soberano, en uso de mis derechos individuales, que todos los generales, gobernadores, ministros y gente gorda salga del sitio que ocupan, y se lo dejen a otros que nombraré yo del modo que me dé la realísima gana. He dicho».

–¡Bien, bien!

–¡Venga de ahí!

–¡Esa es la fija! Y a mí que no me digan…

–¿Pues no estamos viendo, mujer, que hay empleados de los tiempos del *espotismo*? ¿Se mudó, por si acaso, la *oficialidá* de los regimientos? Si a hablar fuésemos…

Y la arenga bajó de tono y se hizo cuchicheo.

–¡Si a hablar va uno…, aquí mismo…, repelo! ¡Mudaron al jefe, por plataforma!… ¡Sólo faltaba! Pero los subalternos…

Aquí la maestra del partido, mujer alta y morena, de pocas y dificultosas palabras, que solía oír a las operarias con seria indiferencia, intervino.

'Who can it be? Is he talking about the mayor?'

'No … about the queen's accursed brother-in-law…'

'And about that Napoleon over there in France, you fool, who can't bear us.'

'Shhh! "…of the revolution are lying in wait for the moment when they can inflict a decisive and and liberticidal blow to the situation. Let us not, however, be faint of heart. The revolution will go on triumphantly over and above the interests of any reactionary who pretends to serve it with sinister designs. Reaction lies hidden where you least expect it, fixing its tiger's eye…"'

'He's right, he's right. It's a very good comparison.'

'"…tiger's eye, in freedom, to strangle it. The ones to be feared most are those who, having reached the height of power, betray their former ideals which served them as a pedestal to scale the heights…"'

'That's what I always preach to you,' exclaimed the reader when she reached this point, taking control. 'The worst are at the top, right at the top. Those who can't see that are blind. As long as the sovereign people don't grab a broom made with the dried branches of Jew's myrtle, like the one we've got over there…' (and she pointed to the one the workshop sweeper was handling) 'and mercilessly sweep away the upper echelons … you understand me now! On the same day that liberty was proclaimed and the Bourbons were given the boot, I would have published a decree … you know what it would have been?' (the orator opened her left hand and made as if she were writing on it with a cigar). '"I, the sovereign people, do decree, in accordance with my individual rights, that all the generals, governors, ministers and fat cats leave the place they occupy, and that those places be given to others whom I shall name in the manner it damn well suits me. That's what I have to say."'

'Well said! Well said!'

'Hear, hear!'

'That's for sure! And they don't need to tell me…'

'But aren't we seeing that there are civil servants left over from the days of *despotism*? Did, by any chance, the *officers* of the regiments change? If we were going to talk…'

And the harangue toned down and whispering began.

'If anyone is going to talk … do it right here … hang it! They moved the boss, for show … the last straw. But the subordinates…'

Here, the group maestra, a tall, dark woman, of few albeit unpleasant words, who usually listened to the workers with earnest indifference, intervened.

–A tratar cada uno de lo que importa ... y a liar cigarritos...

–No decimos cosa mala... –alegó Amparo.

–Decir no dirás, pero hablar hablas sin saber lo que hablas... Pensáis que no hay más que mudar y mudar y meter pillos... Aquí se requiere honradez.

–Eso ya se sabe.

–Por de contado que sí... Demasiado.

–Pues el que os oiga... Y vamos acá. Si vierais, como yo vi, el último del mes que se hace el arqueo, la caja abierta, con sacos de lienzo a barullo, a barullo, así de oro y plata... –y la maestra adelantó los brazos en arco, indicando un vientre hidrópico–. ¿Pues se os figura que si el contador y el depositario–pagador, y los oficiales, y los ayudantes, digo yo, fuesen, quiero decir...?

–¿Fuesen ... de la uña?

–¡Pues! Ya veis que aquí no puede venir cualesquiera. Hay *responsabilidá*.

'Let everyone deal with what's important … and rolling cigars…'

'We're not saying anything bad…' Amparo asserted.

'You might not actually say anything, but you'll be speaking without knowing what you're talking about… You all think you just have to make changes and more changes… What's needed here is honesty.'

'We already know that.'

'Of course we do… Only too well.'

'But anyone hearing you … let's get to the point. If you were to see, as I saw, the last day of the month when they check all the money, with the safe wide open, with stacks of linen bags, stacks of them, like this with gold and silver…' and the forewoman moved her hands forward in an arc, indicating an hydropic belly. 'Well, can you imagine if the bookkeeper and the cashier-paymaster, and the company officials and their assistants, let's say, they were, I mean…?'

'They were … light-fingered?'

'Well! You can see that not just anybody can come here. There's a certain *responsibility*.'

XI

PITILLOS

Quiso Amparo mudarse de taller, y solicitó pasar al de cigarrillos, donde le agradaba más el trabajo y la compañía.

Entre el taller de cigarros comunes y el de cigarrillos, que estaba un piso más arriba, mediaba gran diferencia: podía decirse que éste era a aquél lo que el Paraíso de Dante al Purgatorio. Desde las ventanas del taller de cigarrillos se registraba hermosa vista de mar y país montañoso, y entraba sin tasa por ellas luz y aire. A pesar de su abuhardillado techo, las estancias eran desahogadas y capaces, y la infinidad de pontones y vigas de oscura madera que soportan la armazón del tejado le daban cierto misterioso recogimiento de iglesia, formando como columnatas y rincones sombríos en que puede descansar la fatigada vista. Si bien en los desvanes se siente mucho el calor, la cantidad relativamente escasa de operarias reunidas allí evitaba que la atmósfera se viciase, como en las salas de abajo. Asimismo la labor es más delicada y limpia, los colores más gratos, y hasta parece que la claridad del sol entra más alegre a bañar los muros. La limpia blancura de los librillos, el amarillo bajo de las fajas, el gris de estraza de las cajetillas, componían una escala de tonos simpáticos a la pupila. Y los personajes armonizaban con la decoración.

Preponderaban en el taller de pitillos las muchachas de Marineda: apenas se veían aldeanas; así es que abundaban los lindos palmitos, los rostros juveniles. Abajo, la mayor parte de las operarias eran madres de familia, que acuden a ganar el pan de sus hijos, agobiadas de trabajo, arrebujadas en un mantón, indiferentes a la compostura, pensando en las criaturitas que quedaron confiadas al cuidado de una vecina; en el recién, que llorará por mamar, mientras a la madre la revientan los pechos de leche... Arriba florecen todavía las ilusiones de los primeros años y las inocentes coqueterías que cuestan poco dinero y revelan la sangre moza y la natural pretensión de hermosearse. La que tiene buen pelo lo peina con esmero y gracia, que para eso se lo dio Dios; la que presume de talle airoso se pone chaqueta ajustada; la que sabe que es blanca se adorna con una toquilla celeste.

11

CIGARETTES

Amparo wanted to change workshop, and she asked to move to the cigarette section where the work and the company were more pleasing to her.

Between the cigar workshop and the one where cigarettes were made, which was on the floor above, there was a great difference: it could be said that the latter was to the former what Dante's Paradise was to his Purgatory. From the windows of the cigarette workshop there was a beautiful view of the sea and the mountainous countryside, and unlimited light and air came through them. In spite of its garret-shaped ceiling, the rooms were clear and spacious, and the innumerable boards and rafters made of dark wood, that supported the framework of the roof, endowed it with a certain mysterious, church-like seclusion, forming something like colonnades and shaded corners, where one's weary gaze can rest. Although heat is felt a lot in lofts, the relatively scant number of working women gathered there prevented the atmosphere from becoming polluted, as in the workrooms down below. Also, the work is more delicate and clean, the colours more pleasing, and it even seems that the sun's brightness enters more cheerfully to bathe the walls in light. The clean whiteness of the packets of cigarette papers, the pale yellow of the bands and the grey rag paper used for the cigarette packets made up a scale of shades pleasing to the eye. And the characters there were in keeping with the decor.

The girls from Marineda predominated in the cigarette workshop; girls from the rural towns were scarcely seen; so it was that there was an abundance of pretty bodies and youthful countenances. Down below, the majority of the women workers were mothers of families, coming in to earn bread for their children, up to their eyes in work, wrapped up in a shawl, indifferent to their appearance, thinking of their poor little things entrusted to the care of a neighbour; of their new-born baby, who must be crying for food, whilst its mother's breasts were overflowing with milk ... Still blooming upstairs were the hopes of early years and the innocent coquettishness which costs little money and yet reveals the fire of youth and the natural aim to make oneself beautiful. The one with nice hair combs it carefully and gracefully, for that is why God gave it her; the one who likes to show off an elegant figure puts on a tight jacket; the one who knows she is fair-skinned adorns herself with a sky blue headscarf.

Por derecho propio, Amparo pertenecía a aquel taller privilegiado. Encontró en él muy buena acogida y dos amigas: a la una se aficionó de suyo, movida de un instinto protector; llamábanle *Guardiana*; era nacida al pie del santuario de Nuestra Señora de Guardia, tan caro a Marineda, y según ella misma decía, la Virgen le había de dar la gloria en el otro mundo, porque en éste no le mandaba más que penitas y trabajos. *Guardiana* era huérfana; su padre y madre murieron del pecho,[17] con diferencia de días, quedando a cargo de una muchacha de dos lustros de edad, cuatro hermanitos, todos marcados con la mano de hierro de la enfermedad hereditaria: epiléptico el uno, escrofulosos y raquíticos dos, y la última, niña de tres años, sordomuda. *Guardiana* mendigó, esperó a los devotos que iban al santuario, rondó a los que llevaban merienda, pidiéndoles las sobras, y tanto hizo, que nunca les faltó a sus chiquillos de comer, aunque ella ayunase a pan y agua. Al raquítico dio en abultársele la cabeza, poniéndosele como un odre: fue preciso traerle médico y medicinas, todo para salir al cabo con que era una bolsa de agua, y que la bolsa se lo llevaba al otro mundo. A bien que el médico no sólo se negó a cobrar nada, sino que, compadecido de *la Guardiana*, tuvo la caridad de meterla en la fábrica, que fue como abrirle el cielo, decía ella. Después de la Virgen de la Guardia, la fábrica era su madre. Nunca les había faltado nada a sus pequeños desde que era cigarrera, y aún le sobraban siempre golosinas que llevarles; fruta en verano, castañas y dulces en invierno. Amparo saqueaba la caja de los barquillos de Chinto con objeto de enviar finezas a la sordomudita. El taller entero tenía entrañas maternales para aquellos niños y su valerosa hermana, afirmando que sólo la Virgen era capaz de infundirle los ánimos con que trabajaba, sostenía las criaturas, y vivía alegre y contenta como un cuco.

Del casco mismo de Marineda procedía la otra amiga de Amparo; aunque frisaba en los treinta, lo menudo de su cuerpo la hacía parecer mucho más joven. Pelirroja y pecosa, descarnada y puntiaguda de hocico, llamábanla en el taller *la Comadreja*, mote felicísimo que da exacta idea de su figura y ademanes. Bien sabía ella lo del apodo; pero ya se guardarían de repetírselo en su cara, o si no... Ana tenía por verdadero nombre, y a pesar de su delgadez y pequeñez, era una fierecilla a quien nadie osaba irritar.

---

17   Se trata de tisis o tuberculosis.

In her own right, Amparo belonged in that privileged workshop.

She was made very welcome and found two new friends in it: she became intrinsically fond of one of the girls, moved by a protective instinct. They called her *Guardiana* because she was born at the foot of the shrine of Our Lady of the Guard, so dear to Marineda, and according to what she herself said, the Virgin was going to have to offer her bliss in the next world, because in this one she sent her nothing but sorrow and toil. *Guardiana* was an orphan; her father and mother had died of consumption within days of each other, leaving a ten-year-old girl in charge of four little brothers and sisters, all marked by the iron hand of hereditary disease; one was epileptic, two suffered from scrofula and rickets, and the last one, a little girl of three, was deaf and dumb. *Guardiana* went out begging, waited for pious souls who were going to the shrine, hovered around those who had brought a snack, asking them for the leftovers, and she did so well that her charges never wanted for food, even if she fasted on bread and water. The ricketish child's head started to swell, making it look like a wineskin; they had to bring him a doctor and medicine, the end result of it all being that it was a sac full of fluid, and that the sac was going to carry him into the next world. Fortunately the doctor not only refused to charge anything, but also, feeling sorry for *la Guardiana*, was kind enough to have her placed in the factory, which, according to her, was like opening the gates of heaven. After the Virgin of the Guard, the factory was her mother. Ever since she had become a cigar maker, her little ones hadn't wanted for anything, and there was even enough to bring them titbits; fruit in summer, chestnuts and sweets in winter. Amparo used to plunder Chinto's box of pastry cones, with the intention of sending small gifts to the little deaf-mute girl. The whole workshop had a mother's heart towards those children and their courageous sister, affirming that only the Virgin was capable of instilling in her the spirit with which she worked, supported those poor little things, and lived as cheerfully and contentedly as a cuckoo.

Amparo's other friend came from the central part of the city of Marineda itself; although she was getting on for thirty, her diminutive body made her look a lot younger. With her red hair, freckles, gauntness and sharp-pointed nose, they called her *the Weasel* in the workshop, a very apt nickname which gives an accurate idea of her shape and posture. She was well aware of her nickname, but they took care not to repeat it to her face, because if they did... Her real name was Ana, and in spite of her thinness and small size, she was a wildcat whom nobody dared irritate. Her hands, so skinny that

Sus manos, tan flacas que se veía en ellas patente el juego de los huesos del metacarpo, llenaban el tablero de pitillos en un decir Jesús; así es que el día le salía por mucho, y alcanzábale su jornal para vivir y vestirse, y – añadía ella – para lo que le daba la gana. Conversaba con causticidad y cinismo; estaba muy desasnada, cogíanla de susto pocas cosas, y tenía no sé qué singular y picante atractivo en medio de su fealdad indudable. Presumía de bien emparentada y relacionada; un primo suyo desempeñaba la secretaría del Casino de Industriales; una tía ricachona vendía percales, franelas y pañolería en la calle estrecha de San Efrén; la mayor parte de sus amigas *cosían por las casas* o eran oficialas de la mejor modista. Además, conocía mucho *señorío*, del cual hablaba con desenfado. ¡Buenas cosas sabía ella de personas principales!

Sentábanse las tres amigas juntas, no lejos de la ventana que daba al puerto. Al través de los sucios vidrios, barnizados de polvo de rapé, que se había ido depositando lentamente, y en cuyos ángulos trabajaban muy a su sabor las arañas, se divisaban la concha de la bahía, el cielo y la lejana costa. La zona luminosa de un rayo de sol, bullendo en átomos dorados, cortaba el ambiente, y el molino de la picadura acompañaba las conversaciones del taller con su acompasado y continuo *tacatá, tacatá*. Agitábanse las manos de las muchachas con vertiginosa rapidez; se veía un segundo revolotear el papel como blanca mariposa, luego aparecía enrollado y cilíndrico, brillaba la *uña* de hojalata rematando el bonete, y caía el pitillo en el tablero, sobre la pirámide de los hechos ya, como otro copo de nieve encima de una nevada. No se sabía ciertamente cuál de las amigas despachaba más; en cambio, a su lado, encaramada sobre un almohadón, había una aprendiza, niña de ocho años, que con sus deditos amorcillados y torpes apenas lograba en una hora liar media docena de papeles. *Guardiana* le enseñaba y daba consejos (porque la chiquilla, silenciosa y triste, le recordaba su sordomudita, inspirándole lástima), mientras Ana contaba noticias de la ciudad, que sabían al dedillo. Un día que hablaron de lo que suelen hablar las muchachas cuando se reúnen, *la Comadreja* confesó que ella «tenía» un capitán mercante, que le traía de sus viajes mil monadas y regalos, y proyectaba casarse con ella, andando el tiempo, cuando pudiese. En cuanto a *la Guardiana*, declaró que no soñaba con tener novio, pues era imposible; ¿qué marido había de cargar

any movement of the metacarpal bones was plain to see, filled the table top with cigarettes in no time at all; so it is that each day worked out productive for her, and her wages were enough for food and clothes, and – she would add – for what took her fancy. Her conversation was caustic and cynical; she was very civilised; few things filled her with fear and she had a certain odd, piquant appeal in the midst of her undeniable ugliness. She considered herself as having many prominent relatives and being well connected; a cousin of hers held the secretaryship of the Casino de Industriales; a well-heeled aunt sold percale, flannel and all sorts of handkerchiefs and scarfs in the narrow Calle de San Efrén; the majority of her girlfriends *sewed for the best houses* or were assistants to the finest dressmaker. Besides, she knew a lot of *distinguished people*, of whom she spoke in a free-and-easy manner. She knew many a thing about illustrious people!

The three friends would sit together, not far from the window that overlooked the port. Through the dirty windowpanes, varnished with tobacco powder that had slowly been deposited there, and in whose corners spiders worked at their leisure, you could make out the horseshoe bay, the sky and the distant coast. The luminous area of a sunbeam, bubbling with golden atoms, cut through the atmosphere, and the mill for shredding the tobacco accompanied the conversations in the workshop with its rhythmic and continuous *tacata, tacata*. The girls' hands moved with vertiginous speed; for a second you could see the paper fluttering like a white butterfly, and then it would appear rolled up in the shape of a cylinder; the tin gripper gleamed as it finished off the tip and the cigarette fell on the table top onto the pyramid of those that had already been done, just like another snowflake on top of a snowfall. You couldn't know for sure which one of the friends was turning out the most; on the other hand, next to them was an apprentice, an eight-year-old girl, sitting up on a large pillow, who scarcely managed to roll half a dozen papers in an hour with her sausage-like, clumsy little fingers. *Guardiana* showed her how to do it and gave her advice (because the silent, sad little girl reminded her of her own little deaf-mute, and made her feel sorry for her), while Ana recounted news of the city, which she had at her fingertips. One day, while they were talking about what girls generally talk about when they get together, *the Weasel* confessed that she 'was involved' with a merchant marine captain, who brought her back loads of treats and presents from his voyages, and was planning to marry her eventually, when it was possible. As for *la Guardiana*, she declared that she had no dreams of having a sweetheart, because it was impossible; which husband would

con sus pequeños? ¡Y ella no los dejaba ni por el mismo general Serrano que la pretendiese! Muchos le decían cosas; pero si se trataba de boda, ¡quién los vería echando a sus niños al Hospicio! ¡Ángeles de Dios! Y pensar que ella se metiese en malos tratos, era excusado; así es que nada, nada; la Virgen es mejor compañera que los hombrones. Animada por las confidencias, Amparo insinuó que a ella un señorito, un militar, la seguía alguna vez por las calles.

–Ya sé quién es –chilló *la Comadreja*–. Es el de Sobrado.

–¿Quién te lo dijo, mujer? –exclamó Amparo maravillada.

–Todo se sabe –afirmó magistralmente Ana–.

Pero estás fresca, hija. Ese lo que quiere es pasar el tiempo, y a vivir. ¡Buena gente son los Sobrados! Los conozco lo mismo que si viviese con ellos, porque justamente la que les cose es hermana de una amiga mía íntima. Avaros, miserables como la sarna. La madre y el tío son capaces de llorarle a uno el agua que bebe; el padre no es tan *cutre*, pero es un infeliz; le tienen dominado y pide permiso a su mujer cuando corta pan del mollete. Para hacerles a las hijas un vestido echan cuentas seis meses, y a la chica que llaman a coserlo la hacen ir tempranísimo para sacarle bien el jugo. Un día de convite parece que echan la casa por la ventana; pero todo se recoge y no va a la cocina ni tanto así. Y están achinados de dinero.[18]

Amparo oía atónita. Nada más ajeno a su carácter rumboso, imprevisor, que la estrechez voluntaria.

–La madre…, ¿ves aquella risita falsa?, pues es terrible. No puede entrar en su casa una muchacha regular; en seguida abrasa al marido a celos. Esta chica que les cosía no pudo aguantar… Allí no hay nadie bueno sino la chiquilla mayor.

–Nos dio dulces una vez … es bien natural –respondió Amparo, que sintió cruzar por su espíritu la visión de la noche de Reyes.

–¿Esa? Una santa … y no le hacen caso ninguno. La segunda, idéntica a su madre; le preguntaron un día con quién se había de casar, y dijo: «Con el tío Isidoro, que es rico.» ¡El hermano de su padre, aquel viejo gordo, que parece una tinaja!

Guardiana soltó el trapo a reír con la mejor voluntad del mundo; Amparo, acordándose de una frase leída en un periódico, exclamó:

–¡Pero ha de poder tanto el vil interés! –y meneando la cabeza, añadió–: Lo diría de broma, mujer.

---

18 *Achinado*: adjetivo gallego que significa rico.

burden himself with her little ones? And she wouldn't abandon them even if General Serrano himself were to court her. Many fellows said things to her, but if it came to a wedding, who would see their little ones put in the Orphanage! God's little angels! And as for getting into an abusive relationship, that was out of the question; so there was nothing for her, nothing; the Virgin is a better companion than big, lusty men. Encouraged by these confidences, Amparo insinuated that a young gentleman, a military man, sometimes followed her through the streets.

'I know who it is,' shrieked *the Weasel* . 'It's that Sobrado.'

'Who told you?' exclaimed Amparo in astonishment.

'Everybody knows everything,' Ana stated pompously.

'But you're wrong about him. What that one wants is to pass the time, and to live. Nice people those Sobrados! I know them the same as if I lived with them, because it happens the girl who sews for them is a very close friend of mine's sister. Miserly, as mean as mange. The mother and uncle are capable of taking away the water you drink with their sob stories; the father isn't so *stingy*, but he's a poor wretch; they've got him under their thumb, and he asks his wife permission when he cuts a muffin. To have a dress made for their daughters they take six months to pay it off, and the girl they call in to do the sewing is made to come really early to squeeze every last drop out of her. It seems they really go to town when they have a party, but they collect all the left-overs, and not even that much ever goes out to the kitchen. And they're rolling in it.'

Amparo listened in astonishment. Nothing was more alien to her generous, improvident character than self-imposed austerity.

'The mother ... have you seen that false snigger? Well, she's awful. A normal girl can't come in the house; she abashes her husband straight away with her jealousy. This girl who sewed for them couldn't stand it... Nobody there is kind except the oldest girl.'

'She gave us some sweets once ... she's really genuine,' Amparo replied, as she felt the vision of that Twelfth Night pass through her spirit.

'That one? A saint ... and they don't pay her any attention. The second one is exactly the same as her mother; they asked her one day who she was going to marry, and she said, "Uncle Isidoro, because he's rich." Her father's brother, that fat old man who looks like a barrel.'

Guardiana burst out laughing with the best of intentions; Amparo, recalling a phrase she had read in a newspaper, exclaimed:

'But can vile self-interest have so much power!' and shaking her head, she added: 'She'd be saying it as a joke.'

–¡Sí, sí … buena broma te dé Dios! En esa familia todos son iguales, mujer; cortados por una tijera. Pues no digo nada del señorito, de tu adorador. Hace la rosca a la chiquilla de García, una empalagosa que no piensa más que en componerse y no sabe dar una puntada; pero el asunto es que se la hace por lunas, porque esas de García… ¿No te gusta el cuento?

–Sí, mujer –gritó la oradora amostazada–. ¿Piensas tú que estoy muerta por semejante muñeco? Vaya, que me das gana de reír. Cuenta, mujer, que también se pasa el tiempo.

–Digo que le hace la rosca por lunas, porque esas de García tienen allá un pleito en Madrid, de no sé qué intereses del marido, que era corredor y se metió en una sociedad por acciones … en fin, no será así, pero es lo mismo. Si ganan, quedarán millonarias o poco menos, y cuando hay esperanzas de eso, la madre del de Sobrado le manda que se arrime a la doña Melindritos, y cuando viene de Madrid una mala noticia, que se desaparte… ¡Huy, qué tipos!

Amparo, con la cabeza baja, enrollaba a más y mejor, febrilmente. *Guardiana* se hacía cruces.

–Es una pobre… –murmuraba–. Es una pobre, y no será capaz de acciones así…

–¿Y el otro? –siguió la implacable *Comadreja*, que estaba ya resuelta a vaciar el saco– ¿Y el amigote, el de los bigotazos, que parece que habla dentro de una olla?

–¿El que le llaman Borrén?

–Ese, ése… Un baboso con todas: a todas nos dice algo, y el caso es que con ninguna, chicas. Podéis creerme: ni esto. Tan aficionado a jarabe de pico, y tiene más miedo a una mujer que a los truenos.

Detúvose *la Comadreja*, y mirando fijamente a Amparo, añadió:

–Tú aún tienes otro obsequiante; pero te callas.

–¿Quién, mujer?

–El barquillero. ¡Sí, que no está derretido por ti!

–¡Aquel animal! –exclamó Amparo–. Parece una patata cruda… Mujer, hazme más favor.

'Yes, yes ... a good joke that! They're all alike in that family, all cut from the same cloth. I'm not saying anything about the young gentleman, about your admirer. He sucks up to the García girl, a sickly-sweet bore who thinks only about dressing up and can't do anything; the thing is he's doing it for selfish reasons, because those García women... Don't you like my story?'

'Yes I do,' shouted the orator, somewhat provoked. 'Do you really think I'm just fainting away over a stuck-up sissy like that? Come on, you make me want to laugh. Tell your story, because time keeps moving.'

'I was saying that he sucks up to her for selfish reasons, because those García women are involved in a lawsuit there in Madrid, to do with certain business interests of the husband, who was a broker and got involved with a stock company... Anyway, it's probably not like that, but it's the same thing. If they win, they'll be millionaires or very nearly, and as long as there are hopes of that, the Sobrado fellow's mother tells him to stick close to Little Miss Fusspot, and if bad news should come from Madrid, he can drop her on the spot... Ugh, what people!'

Amparo, with her head down, was frantically rolling lots of cigarettes. *Guardiana* kept crossing herself.

'She's a poor thing...,' she murmured. 'She's a poor thing, and she won't be capable of actions like that...'

'And the other fellow?' the implacable *Weasel* continued, now that she was set on letting it all out. 'That sidekick of his, the one with the big moustache, who speaks as if he were inside a big pot?'

'The one called Borrén?'

'That's him, that's him ... fawning over us all: he says something to all of us, and yet he has nothing to do with any particular one of us. You can take my word: not even this. He's got the gift of the gab, but he's more afraid of women than of thunder.'

The Weasel stopped and, staring at Amparo, added:

'You also have another attentive fellow, but you're keeping quiet.'

'Who's that?'

'The pastry cone boy. Yes, he's just crazy about you!'

'That oaf!' Amparo exclaimed. 'He looks like a raw potato... Please, do me a favour.'

XII

AQUEL ANIMAL

Aquel animal trabajaba entre tanto a más y mejor. Si faltase él, ¿quién había de encargarse de toda la labor casera? Muy cascado iba estando el señor Rosendo, y la tullida a cada paso se hallaba mejor en su cama, y se extendía entre sábanas más voluptuosamente al ver el ademán de fatiga con que soltaba su marido el cilindro por las noches. Y cuenta que de algún tiempo acá, el señor Rosendo no fabricaba barquillos sino en casos de gran necesidad, porque el fuego le inyectaba la tez, le arrebataba y sofocaba todo. Pero allí estaba Chinto para dar vueltas a la noria, y ser panacea universal de los males domésticos y comodín servible y aplicable a cuanto se ofreciese. No sólo se levantaba con estrellas, a fin de emprender la labor de Sísifo de llenar el tubo –labor que desempeñaba con mecánica destreza y rapidez–, sino que antes de salir a la venta, quedábale tiempo de barrer el portal y la cocina, de limpiar los chismes del oficio, de ir por agua a la fuente, por sardinas al muelle o al mercado, y freírlas luego; de arrimar el caldo a la lumbre, de partir leña; de cumplir, en suma, todas las tareas de la casa, incluso las propiamente femeniles, porque traía en la faltriquera un dedal perforado y un ovillo de hilo, y en la solapa, clavada, una aguja gorda; y así pegaba un botón en los calzones de su principal como echaba un remiendo de estopa en su propia morena camisa. Y si no se ofrecía a coser las sayas de Amparo y no le hacía la cama, era por unos asomos de natural y rústico pudor que no faltan al más zafio aldeano. A la tullida le daba vueltas, le sacudía los jergones y la sacaba en vilo del lecho, tendiéndola en un mal sofá comprado de lance, mientras se arreglaba su cuarto.

Lo gracioso del caso está en que, siendo el paisanillo tan útil, por mejor decir, tan indispensable, no hubo criatura más maltratada, insultada y reñida que él. Sus más leves faltas se volvían horribles crímenes, y por ellos se le formaba una especie de consejo de guerra. Llovían sobre él a todas horas improperios, burlas y vejaciones.

La explotación del hombre por el hombre tomaba carácter despiadado y feroz, según suele acontecer cuando se ejerce de pobre a pobre, y Chinto

12

THAT OAF

In the meantime that oaf was working flat out. If he weren't there, who would take charge of all the household chores? Señor Rosendo was getting more and more worn out, and at every step the crippled woman felt better in her bed, where she stretched out even more voluptuously between the sheets when she saw the expression of fatigue with which her husband freed himself of the cylindrical box at night. And remember that Señor Rosendo had not been baking pastry cones for some time now, except for in cases of great need, because the fire turned his face red, scorched and suffocated him completely. But Chinto was there to keep the wheels turning, and be a universal panacea for all domestic troubles, a serviceable Jack-of-all-trades to be used for whatever came up. Not only did he rise with the stars still shining, so he could undertake the Sisyphean[xx] task of filling the tube – a task he carried out with mechanical dexterity and speed – but before he went out to sell them, he had time to sweep the entryway and kitchen, clean the bits and pieces he used for his trade, go to the fountain for water, to the wharf or the market for sardines, and then to fry them; to put the broth by the fire and cut firewood; in short, to carry out all the household chores, including the more strictly feminine ones, because he carried an open thimble and a ball of thread in his pockets, and kept a thick needle stuck in his lapel, so he could attach a button to his boss's trousers like he put a soft burlap patch on his own dark shirt. And if he didn't offer to sew Amparo's skirts and didn't make her bed, it was because of some vestiges of natural, rustic modesty still present in the most uncouth of country boys. He would turn the crippled woman around, beat the straw mattresses and lift her out of her bed and stretch her out on a lousy sofa purchased second-hand, while straightening out her room.

The amusing thing about it is that whilst this wretched country boy was so useful, or to put it better, so indispenasable, there was no living creature more mistreated, insulted and scolded than he. His slightest mistakes turned into horrible crimes and a kind of Council of War was set up for them. Raining down on him at every moment were insults, gibes and humiliation.

The exploitation of one man by another man took on a heartless and fierce character, as usually happens when it is practised by one poor person against another, and Chinto found himself squeezed, pressed, jostled and trampled

se veía estrujado, prensado, zarandeado y pisoteado al mismo tiempo. Le habían calificado y definido ya: era un mulo, y nada más que un mulo.

Acertó un día Chinto a volver unas miajas más tarde de lo acostumbrado, y acercóse a la cama de la tullida para vaciar sus faltriqueras, donde danzaban los cuartos de la colecta diaria. Encontrábase allí Amparo, y le dio al punto en la nariz un desusado tufillo. Por sorprendente que parezca la noticia, la acuidad del sentido del olfato es notable en las cigarreras: diríase que la nicotina, lejos de embotar la pituitaria, aguza los nervios olfativos, hasta el extremo de que si entra alguien en la fábrica fumando, se digan unas a otras con repugnancia: «¡Puf, huele a hombre!». Así es que Amparo solía apartarse de Chinto –aunque sea inverosímil–, repelida por el olor de las malas colillas que chupaba en secreto; pero lo que a la sazón percibía era peor que el tabaco; así es que pegó un brinco.

–¡Vete de ahí –le gritó–; vete, maldito, que nos apestas! Anda, pellejo, despabílate.

Chinto la consideraba atónito, con los brazos colgantes, abriendo cuanto podía los ojos, cual si por ellos oyese.

–Que te largues, ¡repelo contigo!, que no se aguanta ese olor: confundes a la gente.

–¿A qué apestas, demontre? –preguntó la tullida–. Serán esos puros del estanquillo.

–¡No, señora, que es a vino! –exclamó Amparo.

–¡A vino! –clamó la impedida alzando los brazos tan escandalizada como si ella sólo catase el agua, porque en el pueblo los viejos, con sinceridad completa, se otorgan a sí propios el derecho de «echar un trago» que niegan a los mozos–. ¡A vino! ¡Tú quiéreste perder, condenado!

–Yo … pero yo … quiérese decir que yo… –balbució Chinto abrumado por el peso de su culpa.

–¡Aún tendrás valor para contar mentira! –chilló la enferma–. ¡Llégate acá, bruto! – Chinto se llegó compungido–. Echa el aliento –Chinto lo echó–. Más fuerte, más fuerte… –y la tullida asió de los indómitos pelos al paisano y le obligó, mal de su grado, a carearse con ella–. ¡Puf! ¡Pues es verdá y muy verdá! ¿Dónde te metiste? ¿Andas ya arrastrado por las tabernas, bribón?

–Yo…, no; no fue cosa mala ninguna…, no fue perrita, ni licor… Fue…

–Cuenta la verdad, borrachón de los infiernos, como si estuvieses difunto en el tribunal del divino Señor…

at the same time. They had already characterised and defined him: he was a mule, and nothing more than a mule.

One day Chinto happened to return a tiny bit later than usual, and went over to the crippled woman's bed to empty his pockets, where the coins from his daily collection were dancing. Amparo was there and an unusual slight malodour suddenly struck her nose. However surprising this news may seem, cigar makers are renowned for their acute sense of smell; far from dulling the pituary gland, nicotine seems to sharpen the olfactory nerves to the extent that if someone comes into the factory smoking, some women say to each other with repugnance, 'Phew, it smells like a man!' So it is that Amparo usually moved away from Chinto – even if it seems unlikely – repelled by the smell of the cheap cigar butts he secretly puffed on; but what she was noticing at that moment was worse than tobacco, and so she gave a start.

'Get out of here!' she shouted at him. 'Get out, you wretch, you're stinking us out. Come on, drunkard, hurry up.'

Chinto looked at her in astonishment, his arms hanging down, opening his eyes as much as he could, as if he could hear through them.

'Clear out of here, hang you! That smell is unbearable. You're upsetting people.'

'What the devil do you stink of?' asked the crippled woman. 'It must be those cigars from the tobacco store.'

'No, it's wine!' Amparo exclaimed.

'Wine!' the disabled woman cried out raising her hands, as scandalised as if she herself only tasted water, because in small towns old people grant themselves the right, with complete sincerity, to 'have a swig', a right they deny the young. 'Wine! Do you want to ruin yourself, you damned fool!'

'I ... but I ... I mean that I ...' stammered Chinto, overwhelmed by the weight of his guilt.

'You still have the gall to lie,' the invalid screamed. 'Come here, you beast!' Chinto went over full of remorse. 'Breathe out.' Chinto did so. 'Harder, harder ...,' and the crippled woman grabbed the country boy's unruly hair and forced him, against his will, to come face to face with her. 'Phew! It's true, completely true! Where did you go? Do you now hang around the taverns, you loafer?'

'I ... no. It wasn't anything bad ... it wasn't a binge, nor was there any liquor ... It was ...'

'Tell the truth, you damned drunkard, as if you were dead and standing in judgement before the Lord ...'

–No fue nada más sino que encontré un amigo de allí…, de la Erbeda, que cayó soldado…, allí…, me convidó, me dijo así: –«¿Quieres una chiquita?» Y yo…, allí, le dije: «Bueno.» Y él me llevó allí…, a casa de…

–¡Calla, calla y recalla ya, que siquiera sabes lo que dices, con la mona que traes a cuestas!… ¡Como otra vez te vea yo así perdido de vino, he de decirle a Rosendo que te arree una tunda con la correa de la caja, que te has de chupar los dedos; chiquilicuatro, mocoso, viciosón! Convidarte, ¿eh? Me convides. ¡Quien te da vino, no te da pan, mulo! ¡Anda afuera, que me mareas la cabeza toda!

Amparo ejecutó el decreto materno empujando a Chinto por los hombros a las tinieblas exteriores del portal, y Chinto resignado optó por acostarse. Lo único que sentía confusamente era no poder ver a la muchacha un rato. Ahora le entretenía casi tanto mirar a Amparo, como antes contemplar la rueda del amolador y la bahía. Admirábale a él, rudo y tardío de eloquio como suele serlo el aldeano, la facilidad y rapidez con que la pitillera se expresaba, la copia de palabras que sin esfuerzo salían de su boca. Si lo que experimentaba Chinto era enamoramiento, podía llamarse el enamoramiento por pasmo. Ello es que se le venían con frecuencia suma impulsos de tratar a Amparo como a las chiquillas de su aldea, las tardes de gaita; de pellizcarla, de soltarle un pescozón cariñoso, de echarle la zancadilla, de darle un varazo suave con la recién cortada vara de mimbre. Pero tan osados pensamientos no llegaban a realizarse nunca. Amparo sí que solía empujar a Chinto, y no por vía de halago, bien lo sabe Dios, sino de pura rabia que le tuvo siempre. Si pudiese leer en el alma del paisano, adivinar cómo le hervía la sangre al acercarse a ella, le hubiera cobrado asco, amén del odio inveterado ya.

Para Amparo, hija de las calles de Marineda, ciudadana hasta la médula de los huesos, Chinto era un idiota. Alguna duquesa confinada en oscuro pueblo, después de adornar los saraos de la corte, debe de sentir por los señoritos del poblachón lo que la pitillera por Chinto. Enfadábale todo en él: la necia abertura de su boca, la pequeñez de sus ojos, lo sinuoso y desgarbado de su andar, su glotona manera de comer el caldo. Le entraban irritaciones sordas a la vista de objetos dejados por él; un par de zapatos viejos y torcidos, una faja de lana roja pendiente de una percha, una colilla negra y pegajosa caída en el suelo. Y fortificaba su antipatía el que Chinto, con

'It was just that I met a friend from there … from la Erbeda, who was taken to be a soldier … so … he invited me, he said: "Do you want a little glass of wine?" And I … so, I said to him: "All right." And he took me there … to…'

'Shut up, shut up and shut up for good, because you don't even know what you're saying with that monkey on your back! The next time I see you drunk on wine, I'll have to tell Señor Rosendo to give you a thrashing with the leather strap from his box, and you'll have that pleasure to remember; you snotty-nosed nonentity, you big debauchee! Invited, eh? You'd do better to invite me. Whoever gives you wine isn't giving you your daily bread, you ass! Get out, you're making me feel sick!'

Amparo carried out the maternal decree by pushing Chinto by his shoulders into the darkness of the entryway, and Chinto resigned himself to lie down and sleep. The only thing he was vaguely sorry about was that he wouldn't be able to see the girl for a while. He now enjoyed watching Amparo almost as much as he had before gazing at the grinder's wheel and the bay. Rough and slow of speech as a country boy usually is, he admired the ease and speed with which the cigar maker expressed herself, the multitude of words that came effortlessly from her mouth. If what Chinto felt was falling in love, it could be called falling in love out of sheer amazement. The thing is that he frequently had an urge to treat Amparo like the young girls from his village on festive occasions; to pinch her, to give her an affectionate slap on the back of her neck, to trip her up and flick her with a willow twig he had just cut. But such daring thoughts were never caried out. It was Amparo who usually pushed Chinto around, and not as a form of flattery, God knows only too well, but rather out of the sheer anger she always felt towards him. If she were able to read into the rustic lad's soul, to guess at how his blood boiled whenever he approached her, she would have been filled with disgust, in addition to the inveterate hatred she already had for him.

For Amparo, a child of the streets of Marineda, a city girl to the very marrow of her bones, Chinto was an idiot. Any duchess, confined to an obscure little town after she'd graced the court *soirées*, must feel for the rich kids of this one-horse town what the cigar maker felt for Chinto. Everything about him made her angry: the stupid way he opened his mouth, the smallness of his eyes, his tortuous, ungainly gait and the gluttonous manner with which he ate his broth. She started to feel suppressed irritation when she saw the objects he left around: a pair of old, misshapen shoes, a red, woollen sash hanging from a clothes rack, a sticky, black cigar butt dropped on the floor. And her antipathy towards Chinto was strengthened even more by the fact

la desconfianza socarrona propia del labriego, lejos de resolverse a aceptar los ideales políticos de Amparo, daba a entender, a su modo, que le parecía huero y vano todo el bullicio federal. Con risa entre idiota y maliciosa, solía decir a veces a la muchacha:

–Andas metiéndote en cuentos… Aún han de venir a buscarte los civiles, para te *llevar* a la cárcel…

that he, with the sly mistrust typical of farm labourers, far from making any effort to accept Amparo's political ideals, gave her to understand, in his own way, that this whole federal hubbub seemed empty and useless to him. With a half-stupid, half-malicious smile, he would sometimes say to the girl:

'You're getting involved with nonsense... Some day the police will *come for to take you off* to jail...'

XIII

TIRIAS Y TROYANAS

También en la fábrica observaba Amparo que las paisanas eran las menos federales, las menos calientes. Llenas de escepticismo y de picardía, decían, meneando la cabeza, que a ellas la república «no las había de sacar de pobres». Alguna tenía sus puntas y ribetes de reaccionaria; y en conjunto, todas profesaban el pesimismo fatalista del labrador, agobiado siempre por la suerte, persuadido de que si las cosas se mudan, será para empeorarse. No se arrancaba de ellas la más leve chispa de fuego patriótico; empeñábanse en no exaltarse sino cuando viesen que iban a menos las contribuciones y a más los frutos de la tierra. Así es que en la Fábrica gozaban de detestable reputación, y eran tachadas de ávidas, tacañas y apegadas al dinero, y acusadas de cebarse en la ganancia, abandonando su casa por un ochavo, al par que las de Marineda se jactaban de rumbosas, y se preciaban de mejores madres. No obstante, pronunció la revolución tres palabras áureas que a todas sacaron de quicio: «¡No más quintas!». Hasta las mismas aldeanas abrieron ansiosamente el corazón y el alma para beberse la dulce promesa.

¡Si la república fuese, como decían diariamente los periódicos favoritos del taller, la supresión del impuesto de sangre, vamos, merecía bien que una mujer se dejase hacer pedazos por ella! En el taller de cigarrillos, aunque dominaban las mocitas solteras, bastaba hablar de quintas para que se moviese una tempestad de federalismo.

–Miren ustedes –decía Amparo– que eso de que arranquen a una de sus brazos al hijo de sus entrañas y lo lleven a que los cañones lo despedacen por un rey, ¡clama al cielo, señores! Por lo mismo queremos la república republicana, la santa república democrática federativa. Con ella Marineda será capital, y Vilamorta también, y hasta Aldeaparda será capital hecha y derecha. Sólo *Madrí*, que a ése se le acaba la ganga; ya no nos chupará la sustancia; se va a hacer una cosa *manífica*, que se llama *descentraizar*; y veremos cómo después se le baja el orgullo a la corte. ¡Si es inicuo y absolutista lo que está pasando! Aquí no nos mandan, voy a poner por caso, sino tabaco de segunda, filipino, y para eso espérelo usted un mes o dos.

13

TYRIANS AND TROJANS[xxi]

Amparo noticed in the factory as well that the women from rural areas were the least federalistic, the least spirited. Filled with scepticism and guile, they would shake their heads and say that the republic 'wasn't going to take them out of poverty'. Some had a reactionary streak in them; and as a whole they professed the fatalistic pessimism of the farmworker, always overwhelmed by fate, persuaded that if things do change, it will be for the worse. You couldn't get the slightest spark of patriotic fire out of them; they insisted on not getting excited, except when they saw that their taxes were decreasing and the fruits of the earth were increasing. So it is that they enjoyed a hateful reputation in the factory and were branded as greedy, stingy and devoted to money, accused of feeding on personal gain, of abandoning their homes for a few pennies, while the women from Marineda boasted about their generosity and prided themselves on being the best mothers. Nevertheless, the revolution did pronounce three golden words which touched everybody: 'No more conscription!' Even the rural women anxiously opened their hearts and souls to drink up the sweet promise.

If there were a republic, as the favourite newspapers in the workshop proclaimed every day, the suppression of this blood tax, let it be said, was well worth a woman being torn to shreds for! In the workshop where cigarettes were made, even though young unmarried girls were predominant, to talk about military conscription was enough to stir up a storm of federalism.[xxii]

'Look here,' Amparo would say, 'this business of them dragging your precious son from your arms and taking him to be blown to pieces by cannons in the name of a king, cries out to heaven! For this reason we want the republican republic, the holy, democratic, federative republic. With that, Marineda will be a capital, and Vilamorta[10] too, and even Aldeaparda will be a fully-fledged capital. Except for Madrid, whose cushy number is over; it won't be sucking the life out of us any more; they're going to set up something *manificent*, something called *decentrise*, and then we'll see how the court in Madrid isn't so high and mighty. Why, what's happening is wicked and absolutist! Here, I'll give as an example, all they send us is second-rate Philippine tobacco, and you'll wait a month or two for that. The

---

10 Literary name for Carballiño, a municipality in the province of Ourense. It is the setting of Pardo Bazán's *El cisne de Vilamorta*.

Las regalías y las conchas se hacen en *Madrí*... ¡Como si nuestros dedos no fuesen de carne humana! ¿Somos aquí esclavas o algunas torponas que no sabemos *perficionar* la labor? Y luego allí, paguita siempre corriente, consignas a barullo... ¡Ciudadanas, es preciso sacudir el yugo tiránico con nobleza y energía cuando venga lo que se aguarda! ¿Eh, chicas?

A las dos formas de gobierno que por entonces contendían en España, se las representaba el auditorio de Amparo tal como las veía en las caricaturas de los periódicos satíricos; la monarquía era una vieja carrancuda, arrugada como una pasa, con nariz de pico de loro, manto de púrpura muy estropeado, cetro teñido en sangre, y rodeada de bayonetas, cadenas, mordazas e instrumentos de suplicio; la república, una moza sana y fornida, con túnica blanca, flamante gorro frigio, y al brazo izquierdo el clásico cuerno de la abundancia, del cual se escapaba una cascada de ferrocarriles, vapores, atributos de las artes y las ciencias, todo gratamente revuelto con monedas y flores. Cuando la fogosa oradora soltaba la sin hueso, pronunciando una de sus improvisaciones, terciándose el mantón y echando atrás su pañuelo de seda roja, parecíase a la república misma, la bella república de las grandes láminas cromolitográficas; cualquier dibujante, al verla así, la tomaría por modelo.

Y la muchacha iba ascendiendo a personaje político. En la ciudad comenzaban a conocerla, y hasta oyó una vez, al pasar por la calle Mayor, que murmuraban en un corrillo de hombres: «Esa es la cigarrera guapa que amotina a las otras». En su barrio todos la embromaban: el mancebo de la barbería pronunciaba un festivo «¡Viva la república!» siempre que Amparo cruzaba ante su puerta; y la señora *Porreta* murmuraba con voz cascajosa y opaca: «Salú y liquidasión sosial.» Si alguien cree que fue rápida la metamorfosis de la niña callejera en agitadora y oradora demagógica, tenga en cuenta que más prontamente aún que la fábrica de tabacos de Marineda, se *gaseó* la nación hispana. Ni visto ni oído. Contaba la gloriosa menos de un año, y ya nadie sabía a qué santo encomendarse, ni a dónde íbamos a parar, ni dónde dar de cabeza. Abundaban las manifestaciones pacíficas, acabando siempre como el rosario de la aurora. En la frontera, agitación carlista; el Gobierno interna que te internarás, y los internados acá, volviendo a meterse en España media legua más allá, mientras en Madrid se fabricaban activamente, y sin gran reserva, fornituras, arneses y mantillas,

higher quality cigars, the regalías and the conchas, are made in Madrid ...
As if our fingers weren't made of human flesh! Are we slaves here or some
bunglers who don't know how to *perfick* the work? And besides that, there
they always get standard pay and consignments galore ... Citizen workers,
we must shake off the yoke of tyranny with nobility and energy when what
we're waiting for comes! Eh, girls?'

Amparo's audience represented the two forms of government in contention
at that time in Spain, just as you could see them in the satirical newspapers'
caricatures; the monarchy was a stuck-up old woman, as wrinkled as a raisin,
with a nose like a parrot's beak, a very tatty purple cloak, a sceptre stained
with blood, and surrounded by bayonets, chains, gags and instruments of
torture; the republic, a healthy, robust girl, with a white tunic, a resplendent
revolutionary cap, and on her left arm the classic horn of plenty, out of which
leaked a cascade of railroads, steamers and symbols of the arts and sciences,
all pleasingly mixed up with coins and flowers. When the fiery orator was
shouting her mouth off, making one of her improvised pronouncements,
throwing her shawl diagonally across her chest and pushing back her red,
silk scarf, she looked very much like the Republic herself, the beautiful
Republic in the large chromolithographic engravings; any illustrator seeing
her like this would take her for the model.

And the girl was working her way up to be a political figure. They were
beginning to get to know her in the city, and once as she was walking along
the Calle Mayor she even heard a small group of men murmur: 'That's the
good-looking cigar maker who stirs up the others.' In the district where
she lived, they all teased her: the young man from the barber shop said a
cheerful 'Long live the Republic!' whenever Amparo walked past his door;
and Señora *Starkers* would murmur in her dull, gravelly voice: 'To health
and social liquidation.' If anyone thinks that the metamorphosis of this street
child into an agitator and demagogic orator was rapid, bear in mind that
the Hispanic nation *erupted* even more promptly than the tobacco factory
in Marineda. Like lightning. The Glorious Revolution was less than one
year old, and already nobody knew which way to turn, nor where we would
end up, nor when it would fall on hard times. There were lots of peaceful
demonstrations that always ended up in confusion and disorder. There was
Carlist agitation at the border;[xxiii] the government was interning and exiling
people right and left, and those who had been interned in one place would
make their way back into Spain half a league further down, whilst people
in Madrid were quite unreservedly busy manufacturing cartridge belts,

que en los ángulos lucían una corona y las iniciales «C. VII», y en Vitoria recorrían las calles grupos de jóvenes con boina blanca y garrote en mano, vitoreando a las mismas iniciales. A bien que en Puerto Rico la guarnición aclamaba otras cosas, y en Écija mil republicanos protestaban contra «la presencia en España del intruso Antonio de Borbón», y en las cercanías de Barcelona los payeses, armados de azadas y bieldos, perseguían a un alcalde y le obligaban a encastillarse en las casas consistoriales. A todo esto, el poder, representado por el regente Serrano, al cual se tributaban honores casi regios, estaba realmente en las vigorosas manos de Prim, que olfateando la ruina de la Gloriosa, como el marino vislumbra en el remoto horizonte el huracán, sin entretenerse en fruslerías demagógicas, sólo pensaba en traer un monarca, llamado a sosegar el país. España estaba próxima a la gran lucha de la tradición contra el liberalismo, del campo contra las ciudades; lid magna que tenía en la fábrica de Marineda su representación en pequeño.

Todas las mañanas, en efecto, al entrar las operarias en los talleres, al encontrarse en el camino, solían, urbanas y rurales, invectivarse ásperamente y dirigirse homéricos insultos, ni más ni menos que si fuesen las avanzadillas de los dos partidos enemigos que presto iban a encender la guerra civil. El pretexto de las riñas era que las de Marineda mostraban asombrarse de que las campesinas, viniendo quizá de tres leguas de distancia, estuviesen ya allí cuando apenas asomaba el día, y hacían rechifla de tal diligencia.

—¡Vaya, que es buen madrugar de Dios, hijas!

—¿Venidas a caballo del Sol?

—¡Andar, lamponas![19] ¡Dejáis la cama por hacer y el chiquillo por mamar! ¡Madrastras!

—¡Ni os peinades tan siquiera!... ¡Andáis arañando en el pelo con los dedos por llegar seis minutos antes, ansiosas de Judas!

—¡Tú dormiste en el camino, avariciosa! Imposible que a tu casa llegases. Tanto madrugar, y tanto madrugar, y luego no hacedes[20] ni medio cigarro, en to el día, que mismo no sabedes menear los dedos, que mismo los tenedes que parecen chorizos, que mismo Dios os hizo torponas, que mismo...

Aquí ya la sorna y flema de las interpeladas tocaba a su fin, y respondían coléricas, pero entre dientes:

—¿Y luego? Cada uno se vale como puede, y vusté tendrá otras rentas,

---

19 Bribonas, desvergonzadas.
20 Hacéis. La forma gallega es *facedes*, lo mismo que el *sabedes* (sabéis) que viene a continuación.

harnesses and caparisons, which displayed a crown and the initials 'C.VII' in the corners; and in Vitoria groups of young men, with white berets and clubs in their hands, were running through the streets cheering the very same initials. Fortunately, the garrison in Puerto Rico was cheering other things, and a thousand republicans in Ecija were protesting against 'the presence in Spain of the intruder Antonio de Borbón', and in the the outskirts of Barcelona, peasants, armed with hoes and pitchforks, pursued a mayor and forced him to take refuge in the town hall.[xxiv] What's more, power, represented by the regent Serrano, upon whom almost royal honours were being bestowed, was really in the vigorous hands of Prim, who, sniffing the ruin of the Glorious Revolution, like the sailor who dimly glimpses the hurricane on the distant horizon without entertaining demagogic trifles, thought only of bringing in a monarch destined to calm down the country. Spain was close to the great struggle between traditionalism and liberalism, of the countryside against the cities; a great fight that was represented in miniature in the factory in Marineda.

Indeed, every morning when the women workers entered the workshops or met en route, the city dwellers and rural women would bitterly hurl abuse and direct Homeric insults at each other, neither more nor less than if they were the vanguard of the two enemy parties who were soon to spark off civil war. The pretext for these conflicts was the fact that those from Marineda were amazed that the rural women, who came maybe three leagues distance to get to work, were already there when day had barely dawned, and they mocked such diligence.

'Well, you must get up at a God early hour, girls.'

'Did you come on the sun's chariot?'

'Come now, you shameless things! You leave your beds unmade and don't suckle your babies! Like stepmothers!'

'You don't even comb your hair...! You run your fingers through your hair to get here six minutes early, you money-grabbers!'

'You must have fallen asleep on the way, you greedy thing! No way did you make it home. All that getting up early, and so much getting up early, and then you don't make even half a cigar all day long, and you don't even know how to lift your fingers, and they look just like sausages, and God made you all clumsy, and even...'

Here the slow and phlegmatic nature of the insulted women reached an end, and they replied angrily, muttering:

'And what about it? Each does as she can, and you all probably have

y más otros señoríos…, y ganarálo de otra manera diferente, y Dios sabe cómo será…, que yo no lo sé ganar sino trabajando, *higa*.[21]

–Yo lo gano con tanta honra como usté…, y no injuriar a nadie.

–Calle usté, que empezó. Yo no le dije cosa mala.

–¡Avarientas, rañas, ahorcádevos por un ochavo!

–¡Sinvergüenzas! –replicaban, furiosas, las campesinas.

–¡Servilonas, carlistas! –contestaban las ciudadanas, ya en actitud agresiva.

–¡Malvadas, que echades contra Dios! –rugían las insultadas.

Y en medio del tumulto se oía el agudísimo ¡ay! de una mujer, a la cual manos furibundas intentaban arrancar de un solo tirón la trenza entera de sus cabellos. Por espacio de diez segundos imperaban la confusión y el desorden, y había empujones, pellizcos convulsivos, arañazos, violentos repelones; pero apenas iban aproximándose a las cercanías de la fábrica, donde el severo reglamento prohibía los escándalos, cesaba el griterío, comenzaba el torrente femenil a precipitarse dentro del patio y restablecíase la paz, ya que no la serenidad interior, en la fiel imagen abreviada de la nación española.

---

21   Hija; ejemplo de *geada* (una variante dialectal del gallego).

other incomes and other property … and you probably earn it in other ways, and God knows how … but I only know how to earn a living by working.'

'I earn my living just as honestly as you do … and don't insult anyone.'

'You shut up, because you started it. I didn't say anything bad to you.'

'You greedy, tightfisted things, you'd hang yourselves for a few pennies!'

'You have no shame!' the country women answered furiously.

'Bootlickers, Carlists!' the city women replied with a very aggressive attitude.

'You wicked sinners, you're going against God!' roared the women who had been insulted.

In the midst of this tumult, a very piercing 'Ay!' from a woman could be heard as frenzied hands attempted to pull out an entire braid of her hair with one tug. Confusion and disorder prevailed for ten seconds, and there was shoving, convulsive pinching, scratching and violent tugging of hair; but no sooner had they reached the vicinity of the factory, where stringent regulations prohibited scandalous behaviour, than the uproar ceased, the flood of women started to rush inside the courtyard, and peace was established once more, perhaps without inner serenity, in this faithful pen picture of the Spanish nation.

XIV

SORBETE

Josefina García estaba aquella noche muy compuesta y emperejilada en el paseo de las Filas, y la acompañaban las de Sobrado. Cuanto se ponía Josefina ajustábase siempre a los últimos decretos de la moda, no sin cierta exageración y nimiedad, que olía a figurín casero. Era la condición del cuerpo de la señorita semejante a la de la gelatina que los escultores usan para vaciar sus estatuas, que recibe toda forma que se le quiera imprimir. Josefina entraba dócil en los moldes impuestos por la moda, sin rebelarse ni protestar jamás. Tenía su físico algo de impersonal, una neutralidad que le permitía variar de peinado y de adorno sin mudar de tipo. Mediana de estatura, su rostro prolongado y sus agradables facciones no ofrecían rasgos característicos. Sus ojos, ni chicos ni grandes, ni eran feos, pero sí dominantes y escudriñadores más de lo que a su edad y doncellez convenía; su sonrisa, entre reservada y cándida, demasiado permanente en los labios, para que no tuviese visos de fingida y afectada; su talle, modelado por el corsé, sería pobre de formas si hábiles artificios del traje, como un volante sobre los hombros, o en la cadera, no reforzasen sus diámetros. Sin aliño y despeinada, Josefina debía parecer poca cosa; ayudada por el tocado, adquiría cierta postiza morbidez. En realidad, era un fruto prematuramente caído del árbol, una doncella núbil antes de tiempo; a los trece, cuando tocaba habaneras, tenía ya las coqueterías, los celos, los caprichos de la mujer, y ahora aquella flor rápida y precoz se había deshojado, y en vez de la lozanía seductora de la juventud, notábase en Josefina la tiesura y empaque de una señora formal y los remilgos de una lugareña. Figurábase que la distinción, el buen tono, consistían en contrahacer los menores movimientos, ajustándolos a una pauta preestablecida; que había un modo elegante y otro cursi de reír, de estornudar, de abanicarse; que hasta existían opiniones distinguidas y bien vistas, y opiniones que ya no se llevaban; y que en todo, lo más selecto y fino eran las medias tintas, la insustancialidad, lo insípido, inodoro e incoloro. Hablando de cosas superficiales, no le faltaba cierta charla vivaz, semejante al trinar del jilguero; pero apenas se tocaban asuntos serios, creíase obligada, por su papel de niña elegante y casadera,

14

SHERBET

That night Josefina García was very smart and all dressed up as she strolled along the Paseo de las Filas, accompanied by the mother and daughters of the Sobrado family. Everything Josefina put on always complied with the latest dictates of fashion, but not without a certain exaggeration and excess suggesting a homemade clothes model. The quality of the young lady's body was similar to that of the gelatin sculptors use to cast their statues, which takes on any form you might wish to impress on it. Josefina meekly fitted into the moulds imposed by fashion, without ever rebelling or protesting. Her physique had something impersonal about it, a neutral quality that allowed her to change hairstyle and adornment without altering her figure. She was of medium height and her long face and pleasant features offered no characteristic traits. Her eyes, neither small nor large, weren't ugly, but they were more authoritative and probing than was becoming for a maiden of her age; her half-reserved, half-innocent smile was too permanent on her lips for it not to have an element of falseness and affectation; her figure, moulded by a corset, would be lacking shape without skilful artifices, like a ruffle at the shoulders or around the hips, to reinforce her lines. If she were without ornamentation and unkempt, Josefina would not look anything special; with the help of a proper hair-do, she acquired a certain artificial softness. She was, in fact, a fruit that had fallen prematurely from the tree, a nubile maiden before her time; at the age of thirteen, when she played a habanera, she already possessed the coquetry, jealousy and caprices of a woman, and now that rapid, precocious bloom had lost its leaves, and instead of the seductive freshness of youth, you could see in Josefina the stiffness and presence of a mature and formal woman and the fussiness of a local girl. She imagined that distinction and class consisted of imitating the slightest movements, adapting them to a pre-established model; that there was an elegant way and another affected way to laugh, sneeze and fan herself; that there even existed distinguished, highly-regarded opinions, as well as opinions no longer in fashion; and that in all things those that were most select and refined were half-measures, insubstantiality, anything insipid, odourless and colourless. When she talked of superficial things, she didn't lack a certain lively conversation, like the trill of a goldfinch; but no sooner were more serious matters touched on than she felt obliged, because

a encogerse de hombros, hacer cuatro dengues y mudar de conversación. Tal cual era Josefina, muchas señoritas la imitaban, porque, según se decía, «sacaba las novedades»; y aunque tachándola de exagerada y rara, a veces, con el rabillo del ojo observaban las innovaciones de indumentaria que lucía, para reproducirlas al punto.

Aquel año comenzaba a imperar el traje corto, revolución tan importante para el atavío femenino, como la de Setiembre para España; las avanzadas en ideas se habían apresurado a cercenar sus faldas, mientras las conservadoras no se resolvían a suprimir la cuarta de tela con que barrían las inmundicias del piso. Josefina, que en materia de vestir era radical, llevaba la moda nueva en todo su rigor, con túnica de seda negra adornada de bellotas de pasamanería, cayendo sobre redonda falda de glasé azul. Un velo de rejilla formaba a su rostro la misteriosa aureola de un confesionario, y los *cuernos* de su peinado bajaban con gracia y simetría hacia la nariz. Por la espalda y en la cintura, un lazo negro muy pronunciado servía para abultar lo que entonces quería la *voluble diosa* que abultase. Echaba la señorita los codos atrás con objeto de destacar el busto, actitud que escrupulosamente copiaba la segunda de Sobrado, Clara. Lola, que iba en medio, era la única a poner el cuerpo como Dios se lo dio. La luz de la luna, que se alzaba iluminando el paseo de las Filas y el mar, la hora y la temperatura envidiable de una noche de verano, incitaban a amantes efusiones, o siquiera a galanteos, y hasta el ruido de la concurrencia se brindaba a ser cómplice de tiernas palabras pronunciadas a media voz; así lo comprendía Baltasar, que acompañaba a las muchachas, inamovible al lado de Josefina, y haciendo, sin escrúpulo, que sus hermanas llevasen la cesta. A lo lejos, el blando murmullo de las olas, que parecían un lago de plata, decía cosas embriagadoras y poéticas; cantaba un idilio intraducible al humano lenguaje. La conversación del grupo era, no obstante, por todo extremo, vulgar.

–Está desanimado el paseo, ¿verdad, Sobrado?

–Sí, animadísimo lo encuentro yo. ¿Por qué dice usted eso?...

Y los ojos de Baltasar buscaron los de Josefina, y una mirada se cruzó entre ambos.

–¡Qué cosas tiene usted! Vaya, falta gente: usted no lo notará, pero sí falta.

–Yo –intervino Lola– me aburro con tanto dar y dar vueltas... En cualquier

of her role as an elegant, marriageable young girl, to shrug her shoulders, make a show of affected modesty and change the topic of conversation. Whatever Josefina was like, many young ladies imitated her, because, as everyone said, 'she brought out new styles'; and although they might accuse her of being exaggerated and extravavagant, they sometimes observed out of the corners of their eyes the innovations in clothes she was displaying, in order to reproduce them at once.

That year short dresses were beginning to prevail and it was as important a revolution for feminine attire as the September one was for Spain; the women with advanced ideas had hastened to shorten their skirts, while the more conservative ones couldn't decide whether to remove the span of cloth with which they swept the dirt on the ground. Josefina, who was radical in matters of dress, wore the new fashions to the last detail, with a black silk tunic adorned with acorn-shaped trimmings, which came down over a circle skirt of blue taffeta silk. A lattice-like veil made the mysterious aureole of a confessional on her face, and the *horns* of her coiffure dropped gracefully and symmetrically towards her nose. In the back and at the waist, a very pronounced black bow served to exaggerate what at that time the *fickle goddess* wanted to be exaggerated. The young lady thrust her elbows back with the aim of highlighting her bust, a posture which Clara, the second of the Sobrado sisters, scrupulously copied. Lola, who was in the middle, was the only one who maintained her body as God had given it to her. The light of the moon, which was rising up to illuminate the Paseo de las Filas and the sea, the time of day and the enviable temperature of a summer night, encouraged outpourings of love, or at least flirting, and even the noise made by those present offered themselves as accomplices to softly spoken tender words; Baltasar understood it this way as he accompanied the girls, immovable at Josefina's side, and, without any scruples, making his sisters play gooseberry. In the distance, the soft murmur of the waves, which looked like a lake of silver, was saying intoxicating and poetic things, singing an idyll which could not be translated into human language. The group's conversation, however, was extremely banal.

'The promenade isn't very lively, is it, Sobrado?'

'Yes, I find it very lively. Why do you say that?'

And Baltasar's eyes sought out Josefina's and they exchanged a glance.

'The things you come out with! Come on, there aren't many people; you won't notice it, but there aren't.'

'I get bored,' intervened Lola, 'with all this walking round and round...

sitio me divertiría más. No hubiera salido hoy, si no fuese por la octava de San Hilario... Pero ni aun la octava estuvo a mi gusto; faltó muchísima gente de la que acostumbra alumbrar... ¿Sabéis por qué?

–No –dijo maquinalmente Josefina.

–Sí –declaró Baltasar–, porque fueron a esperar al muelle a los delegados de Cantabria.

–Los delegados... ¿de qué? –preguntó Josefina, jugando con el abanico.

–De Cantabria... Vienen a firmar la Unión del Norte... –explicó Lola–. ¡A mí me gustaría ver el desembarco! Si hubiese tenido con quién ir...

–Yo fui... ¡Qué lástima! –dijo Baltasar.

–Chica... ¡Vaya una idea! –exclamó Josefina soltando menudas carcajaditas–. Yo huyo de esas confusiones... Me aterra pensar que pueden gentes sin educación apachucarme,[22] pisarme... ¡Qué fastidio! Y al fin poco tendrá que ver... Diga usted, Sobrado, ¿se ha divertido usted mucho?

–No, por cierto... ¡Diversión! ¿Qué diversión ha de ser? Pero es curioso... ¡Hubo vivas, y mueras, y un silbido vergonzante, y abrazos, y apretones de manos!

–¡Bien por el que silbó! –dijo Lola batiendo palmas–. ¡A eso, a eso quería yo ir: a silbar con la llave de la puerta!

–Dice el tío Isidoro –intervino Clara– que si esto sigue así, van a tener que cerrarse los comercios y se concluirá la industria.

–¡Y también se cerrarán las iglesias! –recalcó Lola con más calor aún–. ¡Malditos revoltosos! ¡A silbar, a silbar debió ir todo el mundo!

–¡Chis! ¡Por Dios! –suplicó Josefina–. Estamos llamando la atención... Luego dirán que nos metemos en política.

–Pues yo me meto... ¿y qué? Ahora todo el mundo se mete –afirmó Lola.

–¡Ay!... ¡Yo no! Qué ridiculez, ¿eh, Sobrado? Yo no entiendo de eso.

–¿No tiene usted opiniones, polla?

–No ... es decir, no me gustan los alborotos. ¡Cuando hay trifulca el teatro está tan soso!... Ni queda humor para vestirse y salir.

–Vamos, usted debe tener sus preferencias... ¿Será usted carlista?

–¡Ay, no! ¡La Inquisición me da un miedo!... –dijo riendo.

---

22 Apretarme.

I'd enjoy myself more anywhere else. I wouldn't have gone out today, if it weren't the octave of Saint Hilary... But not even the octave was to my taste; a lot of the people who usually carry a candle were missing... Do you know why?'

'No,' Josefina said perfunctorily.

'Yes,' Baltasar declared, 'because they went to the pier to wait for the arrival of the delegates from Cantabria.'

'The delegates ... from what?' asked Josefina as she played with her fan.

'From Cantabria... They're coming to sign the agreement for the Northern Union...' Lola explained. 'I'd love to see them disembark! If I'd had someone to go with ...'

'I went... What a pity!' said Baltasar.

'Really ... what an idea!' Josefina exclaimed, bursting out into little titters. 'I avoid those disorderly affairs. I'm terrified at the thought that people without manners could squeeze me and trample on me... How tiresome! And at the end of it all, there'll be little to see... Tell me, Sobrado, did you enjoy yourself very much?'

'No, of course not... As for amusement, what kind of amusement could you expect? But it's curious... There was cheering, hooting, a disgraceful hissing, and hugging and shaking of hands!'

'Good for those who did the hissing!' said Lola, clapping her hands. 'That's why, that's what I wanted to go for: to whistle and hiss with the door key!'

'Uncle Isidoro says,' Clara interrupted, 'that if things go on like this, shops will have to close and industry will come to a halt.'

'And the churches will be closed too!' Lola stressed with even more ardour. 'These accursed rebels! To hiss, everyone should have gone there to hiss!'

'Shhh! For heaven's sake!' Josefina pleaded. 'We're drawing attention... Then they'll say we're involved in politics!'

'Well, I am involved ... and what about it? Nowadays, everybody's involved,' stated Lola.

'Oh!... I'm not! How ridiculous, eh, Sobrado? I don't understand anything about it.'

'Don't you have any opinions, my sweet?'

'No ... what I mean is I don't like commotions. It's such poor taste when there's a row in the theatre! You're in no mood to dress up and go out.'

'Come on now. You must have your preferences... Perhaps you're a Carlist?'

'No way! The Inquisition mortifies me...!' she said with a laugh.

–¿Republicana?

–¡Qué horror! ¡Cosa más cursi!…

–Moderada, ea. Es usted moderada, de fijo.

–Tal vez, tal vez, algo moderada… La pobre reina me da mucha lástima.

–Bueno, ahora ya sé que es usted moderada y lo voy a divulgar por ahí para que la prendan a usted por conspiradora.

–No, por Dios, que no sueñen que hablamos de estas cosas… Se reirían de mí y dirían que parecemos un club. ¿No sabe usted alguna noticia? ¿Qué me cuenta usted del prestidigitador que trabaja en el teatro?

–¿El húngaro? ¡Bah! Como todas esas funciones… Muy pesado, mucho cubilete y los pistoletazos de cajón…

–¡Pistoletazos! Los odio; me asustan atrozmente. En viendo que preparan la pistola, ya estoy tapándome los oídos; las chicas se ríen y mamá me dice siempre: «Niña, que te miran…» Pero yo no puedo…

–¡Mejor! Si la miran a usted, ¿qué más quieren los espectadores? –declaró Baltasar, cediendo a la destreza con que Josefina traía el diálogo al terreno personal.

Mientras pasaba este coloquio, las madres, que venían detrás, se sentaron en un banco, sin que su plática, por versar sobre asuntos de muy otra especie, cediese en animación a la de la gente joven. Un momento, al pasar por delante de ellas, Lola se volvió a preguntarles no sé qué; al mismo tiempo Josefina tocó levemente en el codo a Baltasar, el cual se inclinó, y por un movimiento simultáneo cayeron los brazos de ambos y sus manos se unieron el espacio de un segundo, depositando la mano varonil en la femenina un papelito blanco, tamaño como una mariposa. Susurraban las acacias, llenaba el aire el misterioso silabeo de las conversaciones de última hora y el amoroso gemido del mar, besando el parapeto, completaba la sinfonía.

Ni se escapó el detalle del papel al ojo avizor de la viuda ni a la vigilante atención de doña Dolores, quien puso torcido y avinagrado gesto, levantándose al punto y anunciando que era hora de retirarse. Al tiempo que regresaban las dos familias, desde las Filas a la calle Mayor, la señora de Sobrado meditaba una épica pequeñez, una tontería trascendental y feroz que le sirviese para dar despachaderas a las de García y quedarse sola con sus hijas. Y como llegasen cerca de las puertas del café de la Aurora, que dejaban pasar la luz amarilla y cruda del gas, ocurriósele, por fin, la liliputiense estratagema, y con felina amabilidad dijo la viuda:

'A republican?'

'How dreadful! There's nothing in poorer taste!'

'Well then, a moderate. You're a moderate for sure.'

'Perhaps, perhaps, something like a moderate... I feel very sorry for the poor Queen.'

'All right, now I know you're a moderate and I'm going to spread it around so they arrest you as a conspirator.'

'For heaven's sake, no, don't let them even dream we're talking about these things... They'd laugh at me and say we're like a club. Don't you know any news? What can you tell me about the prestidigitator who's performing at the theatre?'

'The Hungarian? Bah! Like all those performances... Very boring, mainly goblets and obvious pistol shots...'

'Pistol shots! I hate them; they frighten me terribly. The moment I see them preparing the pistol, I cover my ears. The girls laugh and mama always says to me, "My dear child, they're looking at you..." But I can't...'

'All the better! If they look at you, what more could the spectators want?' Baltasar declared, giving in to the skill with which Josefina was bringing the dialogue towards her own affairs.

While this dialogue was going on, their mothers, who were walking behind them, sat down on a bench, without their conversation, which dealt with matters of an entirely different nature, being in any way less animated than that of the younger people. For a moment, as they passed in front of them, Lola turned to ask them something or other; at the same time, Josefina tapped lightly on Baltasar's elbow; he leaned over, and with a simultaneous movement they both dropped their arms and their hands joined together for a second, the male hand placing a white scrap of paper, the size of a butterfly, in the female hand. The acacias were whispering, the mysterious syllabication of the last-minute conversations filled the air, and the amorous moaning of the sea, as it kissed the parapet, completed the symphony.

The detail of the scrap of paper escaped neither the widow's watchful eye, nor the vigilant attention of Doña Dolores, who made a twisted, sour grimace, and stood up immediately, announcing it was time to leave. All the time the two families were returning from Las Filas to the Calle Mayor, Señora de Sobrado pondered some epic triviality, some fierce, transcendental nonsense which would serve to snipe at the Garcías and leave her alone with her children. And as they approached the doorway to the Café de la Aurora, which let the harsh, yellow gaslight through, a Lilliputian strategy finally occurred to her and she said to the widow with feline amiability:

–Y ahora, ¿qué se hacen ustedes? Nosotros pensábamos entrar a tomar un refresco... ¿Nos acompañarán ustedes? Un sorbetito, cualquier cosa...

–¡Jesús..., pues no faltaba más! –contestó la viuda, abochornada como persona a quien ofrecen de mala gana y por fórmula un obsequio que cuesta dinero–. Nosotras tenemos que hacer, y nos retiramos.

–¡Baltasar! –gritó doña Dolores a su hijo, que iba delante con las muchachas–. ¡Baltasarito, entra aquí, que vamos a tomar sorbete!...

–Vengan ustedes, señoritas –murmuró el teniente, creyendo que se trataba de convidar a la familia García.

–No, estas señoras no quieren nada –se apresuró a advertir la madre, clavando a su hijo a la puerta del café con una mirada elocuentísima.

A pesar del aplomo de buen género que creía Josefinita poseer, se vieron a la claridad del gas sus ojos preñados de lágrimas de orgullo y su tez encendida, como si la abofeteasen. Dijo un seco «adiós» a Clara y Lola; a Baltasar y a doña Dolores ni palabra. Cogióse del brazo de la viuda y pronto se confundieron en la oscuridad del fin de la calle sus espaldas, erguidas con dignidad propia de espaldas de destronadas reinas. Baltasar se volvió hacia su madre.

–Pero, mamá... –pronunció.

–¡Chis! –murmuró ella en voz baja, casi al oído del mancebo...–. Eres un bolo,[23] que te comprometes en público con ellas, y tienen medio perdido su asunto. Van a quedar en la calle, chiquillo... He confesado a la infeliz de la madre y no pudo negármelo... Yo ya lo sabía por un abogado. Va muy mal todo eso... Niñas, sentaos –añadió dirigiéndose a Lola y Clara–. Mozo, cuatro medios de leche y barquillos.

–Yo no tomo... –dijo Baltasar.

–Mozo, tres medios no más... Pues mira cómo andas, porque esa mocosa, con su gesto de todo me fastidia, te va a envolver... La tendrás que mantener, y a las cuñaditas, y a la viuda...

–Pero si no pienso... Usted todo lo abulta. Sólo que las cosas hechas así de este modo se comentan y dan que hablar... ¿No se empeñó usted misma en que las acompañase?

–Con permiso de ustedes –dijo el mozo, colocando en la mesa tres vasos de leche amerengada coronados de canela, y un cestito de paja lleno de barquillos. Clara y Lola se pusieron a absorber su refresco, comprendiendo que no debían oír el diálogo de su madre y su hermano.

---

23 Ignorante, torpe, de escasa habilidad.

'What would you like to do now? We were thinking of going inside for some refreshment... Will you accompany us? A little sherbet, anything...'

'Good heavens ... certainly not!' the widow replied, embarrassed as anyone would be who, reluctantly and as a matter of form, is offered a treat which costs money. 'We have things to do and we're off.'

'Baltasar!' Doña Dolores shouted to her son, who was walking ahead with the girls. 'Baltasarito, come in with me, because we're going to have some sherbet!'

'Come in, ladies,' murmured the lieutenant, thinking the García family had been invited.

'No, these ladies don't want anything,' his mother hastily warned him, fixing her son at the café door with an extremely eloquent glance.

In spite of the considerable aplomb that Josefinita thought she possessed, you could see by the gaslight her eyes full of tears of pride and her face flushed, as if she had been slapped. She said a curt 'goodbye' to Clara and Lola; not a single word to Baltasar and Doña Dolores. She took hold of the widow's arm and their backs were soon lost in the darkness at the end of the street, walking erect and proud, with the dignity of the backs of dethroned queens. Baltasar turned towards his mother:

'But mama...' he asserted.

'Shhh!' she muttered in a low voice, almost in the young man's ear. 'You're a fool to compromise yourself with them in public, and they've all but lost their case. They're going to end up in the street, my dear boy... I've confessed to that unhappy mother and she couldn't deny it... I already knew about it from a lawyer. It's all going very badly... Sit down, girls,' she added, addressing Lola and Clara. 'Waiter, four small milks and some pastry cones.'

'I'm not having any...' said Baltasar.

'Waiter, just three... But you watch out where you're going, because that little brat, with her look of being annoyed by everything, is going to ensnare you... You'll have to support her, and the little sisters-in-law and the widow...'

'But I'm not even thinking of ... you exaggerate everything. It's just that when you do things like that, people comment and gossip... Didn't you yourself insist that I should accompany them?'

'If I may,' said the waiter as he placed on the table three glasses of meringue milk crowned with cinnamon, along with a small straw basket full of pastry cones. Clara and Lola started to suck up their refreshments, realising that they shouldn't be hearing the dialogue between their mother and brother.

–Que las acompañases, sí…, porque no me figuraba yo que iba a resultar tal compromiso… Si pierde el pleito, ni sé cómo pagarán las costas… Han de acudir al bolsillo del prójimo…, acuérdate de lo que te digo; como si todo el mundo tuviese ahí el dinero a disposición.

–Pues yo –declaró Baltasar– no vuelvo a meterme en otra… Mire usted bien las cosas antes, porque esto de andar así, hoy tomo y mañana dejo, es ridículo y le pone a uno en evidencia. Dirá la gente que cazamos…, que cazo un dote… ¡Ya ve usted!

–¡Dios quiera que los cazados no seamos nosotros! –tartamudeó doña Dolores con las mejillas horriblemente sumidas por los esfuerzos de absorción que practicaba, a fin de convertir su barquillo en bomba ascendente de la leche garapiñada.

'Accompanying them, yes ... because I didn't imagine it would result in such a commitment... If the lawsuit is lost, I don't even know how they'll pay the costs... They'll have to turn to someone else's pocket ... remember what I'm telling you; as if everyone had money readily available.'

'As for me,' Baltasar declared, 'I'm not getting involved again with any other... Look properly at things beforehand, because this business of going about like this, taking up today and dropping tomorrow, is ridiculous and shows you up. People will say we're hunting ... that I'm hunting for a dowry... You see!'

'May God grant that we're not the ones who are hunted!' Doña Dolores stammered, with her cheeks horribly sunken by the efforts she was making to convert her pastry cone into a suction pump for the frozen milk.

XV
HIMNO DE RIEGO, DE GARIBALDI. MARSELLESA

Era Baltasar un hijo, no de este siglo, sino de su último tercio, lo cual es más característico y peculiar. Calificábanle las señoras de atento; sus compañeros, de muchacho corriente y agradable; su tío, de chico listo y con el cual se podía departir acerca de asuntos de comercio. Su temperatura moral no subía ni bajaba a dos por tres; no se le conocía ardor ni entusiasmo por ninguna cosa; la fiebre de la mocedad no le había causado una hora de franca y declarada calentura. Ni juego, ni bebida, ni mujeres le sacaban de quicio. En política era naturalmente doctrinario. Su madre le juzgaba mozo de gran porvenir y altos destinos, porque dejándole la paga para gastos menudos y diversiones, Baltasar ahorraba y nunca se halló sin blanca en el bolsillo del chaleco. Destinado a la carrera militar, más por vanidad de su familia que por vocación, no era, sin embargo, cobarde, pero sí yerto; prefería los ascensos a la gloria, y a la gloria y a los ascensos reunidos anteponía una buena renta que disfrutar sin moverse de su casa ni estar a merced del ministro de la Guerra. Secretamente, con cautela suma (porque Baltasar respetaba la opinión pública y todo lo que hay que respetar para vivir con sosiego), la ley y norte de su vida era el placer, siempre que no riñese con el bienestar. Tenía vanidad, pero vanidad encubierta y en cierto modo solitaria. A sus creencias, vacilantes y endebles, no quería tocar, como si fuesen un diente próximo a caerse y con el cual evitase morder cortezas duras. Vivía a su gusto y talante, sin meterse en más libros de caballerías. Físicamente tenía Baltasar mediana estatura, la tez fina y blanca, y de un rubio apagado el ralo cabello; pero la parte inferior de su fisonomía era corta y poco noble; la barbilla chica y sin energía, la boca delgada de labios, como la de doña Dolores. En conjunto, su rostro pareciera afeminado a no acentuarlo la aguda nariz, diseñada correctamente, y la frente espaciosa, predestinada a la calvicie.

Al huir del café, como si huyese de sí mismo, dejando a su madre y a sus hermanas ocupadas en agotar los sorbetes, sintió que le daban una palmadica en la espalda, y volviéndose conoció a Borrén, que ya hacía días estaba de retorno de Ciudad Real, contando que allí había unas chicas … hombre, ¡cosa notable! Se cogieron del brazo y se dieron a vagar por las

15

RIEGO'S HYMN. GARIBALDI'S. THE MARSEILLAISE^{xxv}

Baltasar was a son not of this century, but of only the last third, which is more characteristic and peculiar. The ladies described him as attentive; his companions as an ordinary, pleasant fellow; his uncle as a clever boy with whom you could converse about business matters. His moral temperature neither rose nor dropped all of a sudden; he didn't have either ardour or enthusiasm for anything; youthful fever had never caused him a single hour of frank, open heat. Neither gambling, nor drink, nor women unhinged him. In politics he was doctrinaire by nature. His mother considered him a young man with a great future and destined for high places, because with the money he kept from his pay for various small expenses, Baltasar was able to save and was never without change in his waistcoat pocket. Destined for a military career, more out of family vanity than vocation, he was not, however, a coward, but he was rigid; he preferred promotions to glory and, before promotions and glory joined together, he placed a good income to be enjoyed without moving house or being at the mercy of the minister of war. Secretly, and with the utmost caution – because Baltasar respected public opinion and everything that has to be respected in order to live peacefully – the law and aim of his life was pleasure, as long as it didn't conflict with his well-being. He had a certain vanity, but a vanity that was hidden and to some extent solitary. He didn't want to touch his own indecisive, weak beliefs, as if they were a tooth about to fall out and with which he should avoid biting into hard crusts. He lived according to his own tastes and moods, without interfering in other people's business. Physically, Baltasar was of average height, had a fine, white complexion, and thin, dull blond hair; but the lower part of his physiognomy was compressed and lacked nobility: a small, weak chin and a mouth with thin lips, like Doña Dolores's. As a whole, his face would have seemed effeminate, were it not highlighted by a pointed, correctly outlined nose and a wide forehead, predestined for baldness.

When he fled from the café, as if he were fleeing from himself, leaving behind his mother and sisters, who were busy finishing off their sherbets, he felt a gentle tap on his back, and, turning around, he recognised Borrén, who had been back from Ciudad Real for some days already, telling him there were some girls over there … well, who were something else! They took one another by the arm and started wandering about the streets, for

calles, que no aconsejaba otra cosa la serenidad y hermosura de la noche de estío. Baltasar desahogó sus cuitas en aquel amigo pecho. Él no estaba ciego por Josefina, ni cosa que lo valga; pero ahora recelaba que sería mal visto plantarla de golpe y porrazo.

–Entreténgala usted –aconsejó maquiavélicamente Borrén–y distráigase por otro lado. ¿Va usted a vivir así a su edad? ¡Pues no faltaba más, hombre!

–Es una diablura; en este pueblo todo se sabe, y después, líos, historias, lances que molestan... Se me figura que voy a pedir que me destinen a Andalucía o a Cataluña... Si me quedo aquí, hay una muchacha que me da a veces en qué pensar..., ¿y para qué se ha de meter uno en un atolladero?

–Una muchacha... No es la de García, ¿eh?

–No, hombre... Esos son lances a la alta escuela y por todo lo fino, que no le quitan a uno el sueño... Es ... una cigarrera.

–¡Hola..., picarón! ¿Esas tenemos, y tan callandito?

–Usted mismo me la enseñó y me habló de ella... La chica del barquillero.

Borrén chasqueó la lengua contra el paladar.

–¡Ya lo creo! ¡Toma, toma! ¡Pues si es una joyita, hombre! ¡Caramba con usted y cómo las gasta! ¿No se lo decía yo a usted?, ¿eh?

–Debo advertir que por ahora no hay nada... No se eche usted a maliciar ya.

–Principio quieren las cosas, hombre.

Hablaban así al atravesar una calle principal, cuando de pronto les llamó la atención el corro de gente parada a la puerta de una sociedad de recreo. Dentro del marco de las iluminadas ventanas se veían agitarse figuras negras que gesticulaban animadamente, y detrás de ellas medio se columbraba una mesa servida con copas, botellas y dulces. A veces se dibujaba sobre el fondo de luz la silueta de una mano que alzaba una copa, y el clamor que seguía al brindis era delatado por el retemblido de los cristales.

–El Círculo Rojo –dijo Borrén–. Están obsequiando a los delegados de Cantabria.

–¡Llegar por mar ahora mismo y tener humor para correrla! –exclamó el teniente–. ¡Lástima de naufragio!

–¿A usted qué le parece de estas algaradas, Sobrado?

the serenity and beauty of the summer night recommended nothing better. Baltasar unburdened his troubles to his bosom friend. He wasn't crazy about Josefina, nor anything like it, but then again, he feared that it would look bad if he suddenly dropped her.

'Entertain her,' Borrén advised in a Machiavellian way, 'but, on the other hand, keep yourself amused. Are you going to live this way at your age? Well, that's all we need, eh!'

'It'd be a miracle; in this town everybody knows everything, and afterwards, entanglements, gossip, affairs that cause trouble... I think I'll ask to be transferred to Andalusia or Catalonia... If I do stay here, there's one girl who sometimes gives me something to think about ... but why get oneself in a fix?'

'A girl... It isn't the García girl, eh?'

'No, indeed... Those are affairs on a higher level, and very refined, that you don't lose sleep over... It's ... a cigar maker.'

'Hello ... you rogue! Is that what we're up to on the quiet?'

'You yourself pointed her out to me and spoke to me about her... The pastry cone seller's daughter.'

Borrén clicked his tongue against the roof of his mouth.

'I believe it! Well well! She really is a little gem! Good for you; you know how to pick them! Didn't I tell you? Eh?'

'I must warn you that for the time being there's nothing going on... Don't start having your suspicions.'

'Things have to start somewhere.'

They were talking in this way as they crossed a main street, when their attention was suddenly attracted by a circle of people gathered at the doorway of the meeting hall of a social club. Framed by the lighted windows, you could see dark figures moving about and gesticulating in a lively way, and behind them, you could make out a table set with glasses, bottles and sweets. At times, the silhouette of a hand raising a glass was outlined against the background of light, and the uproar that followed the toast was exposed by the rattling of the windows.

'The Red Circle,' said Borrén. 'They're having a reception for the delegates from Cantabria.'

'To have just arrived here by sea and be in a mood to live it up!' the lieutenant exclaimed. 'A pity they weren't shipwrecked!'

'What do you make of this racket, Sobrado?'

–¿Qué me ha de parecer? Que antes de dos meses nos embromarán allá por Navarra los del Terso...

–¡Quia! Eso nunca, hombre. Eso murió, y los muertos no resucitan.

–Usted entiende más de chicas guapas que de política, amigo Borrén. Nos van a divertir, créame usted. Ya anda en danza Elío, un militar si los hay... Eso se va a organizar; verá usted cómo salen de la tierra igual que los hongos cuando llueve, pero equipaditos y con armamento. Y estos otros también van a sacar las uñas por Barcelona y donde haya blusas y fábricas. Lo peor de todo es que harán de España mangas y capirotes...

Un golpe de gente que desembocaba en la calle cortó la réplica de Borrén. A la luz del astro nocturno se veía blanquear los instrumentos de metal y los papeles de música. Al llegar ante el Círculo Rojo instaló la banda sus atriles en el centro del corro que aumentaba, y previas algunas palabras en voz baja y un golpe de batuta, rasgó los aires el bullanguero himno que todo español conoce y ama o detesta. Del concurso partieron gritos.

–¡Himno de Garibaldi!

–¡Marsellesa, Marsellesa! –contestó un grupo más compacto.

Y enmudecieron los metales y, presto, volvió a alzarse su formidable acento, entonando la trágica Marsellesa. Impensadamente se abrieron las ventanas del Círculo, y fue como si la sala llena de claridad, de gente y de tumulto se viniese a meter entre los espectadores.

En primer término asomaron las cabezas los recién venidos, y al punto calló la música y se oyeron vivas a los delegados, a Cantabria, dominando el clamoreo una voz aguardentosa que desde la esquina repetía incansable: «¡Viva la honradez!» Una mujer se adelantó, y entrando en el círculo de luces, gritó con voz fresca y potente:

–¡Que brinden a la salud del pueblo!... ¡Que brinden!...

Volvióse uno de los delegados, y al punto le trajeron una copa rebosando champaña, que elevó a los cielos al pronunciar el brindis. Las luces de los atriles alumbraron su barba de nieve, sus mejillas sonrosadas como las de los viejos santos bizantinos. Baltasar sacudió el brazo de su confidente, señalando a la mujer:

–¿La ve usted?

–La veo. ¡Olé y qué guapa se pone todos los días, hombre!

–Pero se me hace muy cargante con estas cosas políticas. Las mujeres no tienen más oficio que uno.

'What should I think? That within two months El Terso's followers will be making fools of us up there in Navarre...'[xxvi]

'Never! That'll never happen. All that died and the dead don't come back to life.'

'You understand more about pretty girls than politics, my dear Borrén. They're going to give us a merry time, believe me. Elío, a real soldier if there ever was one, is already making a move...[xxvii] It's going to get organised; you'll see how they sprout from the ground like mushrooms when it rains, but fully equipped and armed. And these others are also going to show their claws around Barcelona and wherever there are workers' smocks and factories. The worst part of it all is that they'll ignore what's best for Spain...'

A crowd of people pouring out onto the street cut off Borrén's reply. By the light of the nocturnal heavenly body you could see the brass instruments and the sheets of music gleaming white. As they arrived in front of the Red Circle, the band members set up their music stands in the middle of the gathering crowd, and after a few words in a hushed voice and a rap of the baton, the air was rent by the rowdy hymn, which the whole of Spain knows and either loves or hates. Shouts erupted from the throng of people.

'Garibaldi's hymn!'

'The Marseillaise! The Marseillaise!' a more compact group replied.

And the brass instruments grew silent; quickly, their formidable sound rose up again, intoning the tragic Marseillaise. The windows of the Circle opened unexpectedly, and it was as if the room full of light, people and tumult had come out to merge with the spectators.

In the foreground, those who had just arrived leaned their heads out and the music immediately stopped; cheering for the delegates, and for Cantabria, could be heard, the clamour dominated by a husky voice from the corner which was tirelessly repeating: 'Hurrah for honesty!' A woman came forward and, entering the circle of lights, shouted in a calm, powerful voice:

'Let them drink to the welfare of the people...! Let them drink...!'

One of the delegates turned round, and they immediately brought him a glass overflowing with champagne, which he raised up high as he proposed the toast. The lights from the music stands illuminated his snowy white beard and his pink cheeks, like those of the old Byzantine saints. Baltasar shook his confidant's arm and pointed at the woman.

'Can you see her?'

'I see her. Bravo, and she's getting prettier every day!'

'But she's becoming very tiresome with these political matters. Woman have only got one job.'

–¡Sí, hombre…; quién la mete a ella…; tiene chiste!

–Es una epidemia. Almorzamos política y comemos ídem. Se va volviendo España un manicomio. ¡Bah! Si no estuviese aquí, donde todo el mundo me conoce, las extravagancias de esa muchacha no dejarían de divertirme… ¿La ve usted aplaudiendo a rabiar al del brindis? ¿Cómo se llamará ese ciudadano? Parece el Oroveso de *Norma*.

–¡Pcsh!… Mañana lo sabremos.

'Yes, indeed...; whoever gets to have her...; it's funny!'

'It's an epidemic. We lunch on politics and ditto for the evening meal. Spain is turning into a madhouse. Bah! If I weren't here, where everybody knows me, that girl's absurd ideas wouldn't stop amusing me. ...Can you see her applauding like crazy the man who made the toast? What must that citizen's name be? He looks like Oroveso in *Norma*.'[11]

'Pshaw...! We'll find out tomorrow.'

---

11 *Norma* is an opera in two acts by Bellini with a libretto by Felice Romani, after *Norma, ossia L'Infanticidio* by Alexandre Soumet. Norma is the daughter of the Druid leader Oroveso.

XVI
REVOLUCIÓN Y REACCIÓN MANO A MANO

En la calle de los Castros estaba Carmela, la encajerita, descolorida como siempre y ocupada en oír de boca de Amparo los sucesos de la víspera. Asomada Carmela al tablero, disimulaba su talle encorvado ya por la habitual labor; pero no sus ojos ribeteados y cansados de fijarse en la blancura del hilo. No obstante su atareado vivir, la encajera gastaba humor apacible e inalterable y poseía la dulzura de las personas melancólicas, una benevolencia claustral. Amparo narraba animadamente; los delegados de Cantabria habían desembarcado entre inmenso gentío que llenaba el muelle y la ribera; ella pensó por la mañana alumbrar en la octava de San Hilario; pero ¡qué octava ni octava!, en cuanto supo la venida del buque, allá se plantó, en el desembarcadero, abriéndose calle a codazos... Los delegados son unos señores..., ¡vaya!, de mucho trato y de mucho mundo; ¡saludan a todos y se ríen para todos! ¡Republicanos de corazón, ea! Y aquí Amparo se descargó una puñalada en el pecho. A la señora María, la *Ricachona*, mira tú, porque dijo que les quería dar la mano, la abrazaron a vista de todo Dios... Luego los había acompañado al Círculo Rojo, y oído la serenata y el discurso que echó uno de ellos... ¡un viejo que parece un santo!, y otro..., un señor serio, de mal color...

–Y ¿qué tal? ¿ Predican bien?

–¡Dicen cosas... que se le hace a uno agua la boca de oírlas! Quisiera yo que estuviesen allí los que creen que la federal trae desgracias y belenes... El viejo no habló sino de que ya no había tiranía..., de que todo se iba a arreglar con moralidad y atención..., de que nos quisiéramos mucho los republicanos, porque ya todo ha de ser concordia entre los hombres.

–Tú tienes un memorión... A mí se me iría el santo al cielo. Mi memoria es de gallo. Y el otro, ¿qué dijo?

–El otro, el otro ... el otro habla despacio, pero echa unos términos, que a veces cuesta caro entenderlo... Predicó mucho de nuestros derechos y

16

REVOLUTION AND REACTION, HAND IN HAND

Carmela, the young lacemaker, was on the Calle de las Castros, as pale as ever and busy listening to the events of the previous night from Amparo's mouth. Poking her head over the door panel, Carmela could conceal her figure, already stooped from her customary needlework; but not her eyes, which were red-rimmed and tired from staring at the whiteness of the thread. In spite of her busy existence, the lacemaker displayed a gentle, inalterable mood and she possessed the sweetness of melancholy people, a cloistral benevolence. Amparo was recounting it animatedly; the delegates from Cantabria had disembarked amidst a crowd that filled the quay and the shore; that morning she had intended to carry a lighted candle for the celebration of the octave of Saint Hilary, but what chance did the octave have?[12] As soon as she found out about the arrival of the ship, she planted herself there, on the landing stage, elbowing her way to the front... The delegates are gentlemen ... well, with a lot of experience, men of the world. They have a greeting and a laugh for everyone! True republicans, be sure! And thereupon, Amparo punched herself on the chest. Señora María, that's *Mrs Filthy Rich*, look here, just because she said she wanted to shake hands with them, they hugged her in full view of everyone... After that, I accompanied them to the Red Circle, and heard the serenade and speech one of them gave ... an old man who's like a saint, and another man ... a serious gentleman, who looked off colour...

'And, how was it? Do they preach well?'

'They say things ... that make your mouth water when you hear them! I'd like those people who think a federal system brings misfortune and bedlam to have been there... All the old man spoke of was that there was no longer any tyranny ...that everything was going to be sorted out with morality and courtesy ... that we republicans would love one another, because soon there will be harmony between all men.'

'You've got an amazing memory... I'd have completely forgotten. My memory is like a sieve. And what did the other one say?'

'The other one, the other one ... the other one speaks slowly, but he throws out some terms which are sometimes difficult to understand...

---

12   In the traditional calendar, January 14 is the feast of Saint Hilary, Bishop of Poitiers (13 January in the new calendar, which was originally the Octave of Epiphany).

del trabajo, y de lo que representa esta Unión del Norte…, y de que las clases trabajadoras, si se unen, pueden con las demás… Habían de venir allí arrastrados de las orejas los que piensan que los republicanos dicen cosas malas. No señor; allí se cantaba clarito lo que somos: paz, libertad, trabajo, honradez y la cara y las manos muy limpias.

–Dime una cosa, mujer.

–Mas que sean dos.

–Y ¿qué significa eso de República federal?

–Significa…, ¿qué ha de significar, repelo? Lo que predicaron ésos.

–Pero no me hice bien de cargo… ¿Qué más tiene eso que el Gobierno que hay ahora?

–Tiene, tiene, tiene … tiene que Madrí no se nos monte encima, y que haya honradez, paz, libertá, trabajo…

–Pero … vamos, una pregunta, por preguntar, mujer. ¿No decían cuando vino el barullo de la revolución el año pasado, que nos iban a dar todo eso? Conforme aquellos no lo dieron también podrá cuadrar que no lo den estotros.

–No puede ser, y no, y no, porque estos son otros hombres de otra manera, que miran por el bien del pueblo… No digas tontadas.

La encajerita se rió con su risa tenue.

–No, si lo que vienen a dar es trabajo, por acá no falta… Y digo yo y preguntando otra vez, si es verdá que quitan la estancación del tabaco, vamos a ver, ¿cómo os valéis las cigarreras? Pidiendo limosna.

–¡Esa es una burrada de las gordas! –exclamó Amparo, fuerte ya en la controversia del punto concreto–. Oye y atiende, mujer, te lo voy a poner claro como el sol. Ahora el Gobierno nos tiene allí sujetas, ¿no es eso? Ganamos lo que a él se le antoja; si vienen, un suponer, buenas consignas, porque vienen, y si no, fastidiarse. Él chupa y engorda y se hace de oro, y nosotras, infelices, lo sudamos. Que se desestanca, que se desestancó; ¡hala con ella! Las reinas somos nosotras, las que tenemos nuestra habilidad en los dedos; con nosotras han de venir a batir el consumidor y el estanquero, y si a mano viene, el ministro del ramo… ¿Aún no entendiste, tercona?

Meneaba suavemente la cabeza la encajerita, mientras los hilos de la

He preached a lot about our rights and about labour, and about what this Northern Union represents … and that if the working classes unite, they'll be able to handle the others… Those who think the republicans say evil things ought to be dragged there by their ears. No, indeed; they sang out there loudly and clearly what we are: peace, liberty, work, honesty and a clean face and hands.'

'Tell me one thing, though.'

'I'll maybe tell you two.'

'What does all this about a federal republic mean?'

'It means … what do you think it means, hang it? What those men preached.'

'But I didn't really understand… What does it have better than the government we've got now?'

'It has, it has, it has … it has that Madrid might get off our backs, and that there could be honesty, peace, liberty, work…'

'But … well, one question, if I may ask. Didn't they say, when the uproar of the revolution happened last year, that they were going to give us all that? If we agree those people didn't give us it, we can also agree that these others won't give it either.'

'That can't be, no, no way; because these are different men, with different ways, who look out for the good of the people… So don't say stupid things.'

The young lacemaker laughed with her faint laughter.

'No, if what they've come to give us is work, there's no end of need around here… And I say and I ask again, if it's true they're going to take away the state monopoly of tobacco, let's see, how are you cigar makers going to manage? Going out begging?'

'That's a big load of nonsense!' Amparo exclaimed, firmly ensconced in a controversy over a concrete point. 'Listen and pay attention, my dear, I'm going to set it out for you as clear as day. Right now the government has us tied down, isn't that so? We earn whatever it fancies giving us. Let's suppose some good consignments arrive, that's all right, and if not, then we have to put up with it. They milk us dry and get fat and make a fortune, and we miserable women, we sweat it out. If they want to remove the state monopoly, let them remove it; get on with it! We're the real queens, the ones with the skill in our fingers; the consumer and the tobacconist should come with us to fight, and if it comes to that, the appropriate minister… Did you still not understand, you pig-head?'

The little lacemaker gently shook her head while the threads slipped,

labor se deslizaban, se cruzaban, se entretejían al través de sus dedos y los palillos de boj, chocando unos con otros, hacían una musiquilla flauteada.

–Es que … tú pintas las cosas… Pero dime…

–¡Qué porfiosa del dianche!

–Dime con verdad… ¿Falta ahora gente que pretenda entrar en la fábrica?

–¡Faltar! ¡Más empeños andan danzando!

–Pues, catá… El día que quiten la estancación se echa medio mundo a trabajar en cigarros, y habiendo mucho quien trabaje, el trabajo anda por los suelos de barato. ¿Qué me está pasando a mí? Empezó la tía a hacer encajes, y le salieron dos o tres de Portomar a poner la competencia … porque ahora son mucha moda estas puntillas, hasta para pañuelos; lo que estoy rematando es un pañuelo.

Descubrió ufana su almohadilla, alzando un pañizuelo que velaba parte de labor terminada ya y viose una afiligranada crestería, un alicatado de hilo, donde el menudo dibujo se desplegaba en estrellitas microscópicas, en finos rombos, en exquisitos rectángulos, todo ello unido con arte y gracia formando primorosa orla. Amparo aprobó.

–Está muy bonito –dijo.

–Pues con todo y que se lleva tanto, como ya somos muchas a menear los palitroques, hay que arreglar los precios… Yo –murmuró suspirando levemente–no puedo hacer más; a veces trabajo con luz, pero no me lo resisten los ojos, y así me arrimo cuanto más puedo al tablero hasta que no se ve el día… La tía también se quedó medio ciega; ya ni puntillas gordas hace; sólo sirve para ir por las casas a vender lo que yo trabajo…

Batida en el terreno crematístico, Amparo tocó otra cuerda para seguir hablando de sus entusiasmos; que no se la cocía el pan en el cuerpo hasta desembuchar cuanto había visto y esperaba ver.

–¡El día que lleguen por tierra los delegados de Cantabrialta…, se prepara una buena! ¿No sabes?

–¿Mucha fiesta?

–Los han de esperar con coches… Y… –Amparo se detuvo, bajando la voz para acrecentar el efecto de la estupenda noticia–los iremos a alumbrar con hachas.

crossed and interwove through her fingers, and the boxwood bobbins, colliding one against the other, made a sweet, flute-like tune.

'It's just that … you paint things… But, tell me…'

'What a persistent devil you are!'

'Tell me truthfully … is there a shortage of people who hope to work in the factory?'

'A shortage! There are more than ever out there looking!'

'Well, then… The day they take away the state monopoly, almost everybody will start working on cigars, and as there are so many who'll be working, wages will be rock bottom. What do you think is happening to me? My aunt started making lace, and two or three women came from Portomar to compete … because this lace edging is very much in fashion now, even for handkerchiefs; what I'm finishing off is a handkerchief.'

She proudly revealed her pin cushion, raising a small piece of material that concealed a part of the lacework already finished, and you could see a filigreed crenellation, a woven arabesque in which the small pattern opened out in microscopic stars, delicate rhombuses and exquisite rectangles, all artfully and gracefully joined together, forming a magnificent border. Amparo approved.

'It's very pretty,' she said.

'Well, in spite of all that and even if it's so much in fashion now, as there are lots of us moving these little sticks, we have to keep adjusting the prices… As for me,' she murmured, sighing lightly, 'I can do no more; sometimes I work with plenty of light, but my eyes can't hold out, and so I move as close as I can to the open door panel until there's no daylight… My aunt also ended up half-blind; she can't even make coarse edging now; all she's good for now is to go around to all the houses selling what I make…'

As she had been dragged into the sphere of chrematistics,[13] Amparo touched on another keynote so she could continue speaking about what enthused her; she wouldn't settle until she'd come out with everything she had seen and hoped to see.

'The day the delegates from Cantabrialta set foot here … they're preparing something good! Didn't you know?'

'A big celebration?'

'They're going to wait for them in coaches… And,' Amparo stopped, lowering her voice to increase the effect of the stupendous news, 'we're going to light their way with large candles.'

---

13 The science of the wealth of nations; political economy.

—¡Ave María de Gracia! ¿Qué me dices, mujer? ¿Alumbrarlos como a los santos?

—Andando.

—¿Y quién? ¿Las de la fábrica?

—Ajá. Una ristra de ellas. Ya estamos habladas.

—¿Van tus amigas?... ¿Aquellas dos?...

—¡Espera por ellas! No, mujer, no. Ana, como se trata con un capitán mercante, no se quiere rebajar a que la vean alumbrando; dice que cuando llegue la *Bella Luisa* la avergonzaría su marino... ¡Y aquella tonta de *Guardiana* tuvo valor a decirme que ella sólo cogería un hacha para ir en la procesión de Nuestra Señora de la Guardia!

—Pues yo digo otro tanto..., *mas* que te enfades, mujer. ¡Vaya unos dioses y unas imágenes que vais a llevar en procesión! Eso parece cosa de idólatras. Alumbrar solamente a las cosas de la Iglesia, el *veático*, las octavas...

—Calla, que eres más nea que los neos.

—¡Y para el favor que me están haciendo a mí esos señorones que predican la libertá! ¡Dicen que van a echar a todas las monjas a la calle y a no dejar convento con convento!

Amparo retrocedió tres pasos, se puso en jarras, enarcó las cejas y después se persignó media docena de veces, con extraña prontitud.

—Me valga San... Pero ¿tú hablas formal, mujer? ¿Te quieres meter en aquella prisión por toda, toda, toda la vida? Arreniégote.

—Querer, quiero... ¡Ay! Quise desde que fui así, pequeñita... Pero ¡bah!, ¡no puedo! ¿Dónde te van a recibir ahora sin el dote? ¡Buenas están las monjas para meterse en despilfarros! Y yo, ¿cómo he de juntar el dote, dime tú? Si pido, nadie me dará... A no ser que Dios me mande una sorpresa...

—Mujer, rica no soy; pero un par de duros aún no me hacen falta para comer mañana —dijo espontáneamente Amparo.

La pálida sonrisa de la encajerita alumbró su rostro.

—Se estima la voluntá... Necesito una atrocidá de dinero para el caso, y ya sé que juntar, no lo he de juntar nunca... En fin, paciencia nos dé Dios.

—Y ¿tú estarías a gusto presa entre cuatro paredes?

—Bien presa vivo yo desde que acuerdo... Siquiera los conventos tienen huerta, y vería una árboles y verduras que le alegrasen el corazón.

'Holy Mother of Mary! What are you telling me? Light their way like they do for saints?'

'Going on foot.'

'And who? The women from the factory?'

'Precisely. A string of them. We're already spoken for.'

'Are your friends going...? Those two...?'

'I wouldn't wait for them! No, my dear, no. Since Ana is involved with a merchant ship captain, she doesn't want to stoop to being seen lighting their way; she says when the *Bella Luisa* comes in, her sailor would embarrass her... And that fool of a *Guardiana* had the nerve to tell me she would only pick up a candle to walk in the procession of Our Lady of the Guard!'

'Well, I say the same ... no matter how angry you may get. Those really are some gods and holy images you're going to carry in the procession! It looks like some kind of idolatry. You're only supposed to light the way for things to do with the Church, the *viaticum*, the octaves...'

'Be quiet, because you're more Catholic than the pope.'

'And as for the favours those big shots who preach liberty are doing me! They say they're going to throw all the nuns out into the street, and they're not going to leave a single convent standing!'

Amparo drew back three steps, her arms akimbo, raised her eyebrows and promptly crossed herself half a dozen times.

'Give me strength, Saint... But are you speaking seriously? Do you want to shut yourself away in that prison for your whole, whole, whole life? I give up.'

'Want, what I want... Oh! I've wanted it ever since I was this big, just a little girl... But, bah! I can't! Where would they ever take you in nowadays without required payment? Don't expect those nuns to get into squandering money! And as for me, how am I ever going to raise that dowry, you tell me? If I ask, nobody will give it me... Unless God should send me a surprise...'

'Listen, I'm not rich, but I have a few coins I don't need just to be able to eat tomorrow,' Amparo replied spontaneously.

The lacemaker's pale smile lit up her face.

'Your good will is appreciated... I need a silly amount of money for this matter and I already know that as for raising it, I'll never be able to raise it... Oh well, may God grant us patience.'

'And you think you'd be happy as a prisoner inside four walls?'

'I've been a living prisoner since I can remember... At least the convents have a garden and you'd see trees and greenery to warm your heart.'

XVII

ALTOS IMPULSOS DE LA HEROÍNA

Eran las horas meridianas, las horas de calor, cuando salieron desempedrando las calles de Marineda carruajes en que iban las comisiones del partido a esperar a los delegados de Cantabrialta. Las dos leguas de camino real que van de la ciudad al ex portazgo (como se decía entonces) hallábanse cuajadas de gente en expectativa, asaz empolvada y sudorosa. Poca levita, mucha tuína y chaqueta; de higos a brevas, un uniforme; buen número de mujeres, roncas ya, con los labios secos, los ojos inyectados, arrebatadas las mejillas, más o menos descompuesto el peinado y el traje. Engalanadas con colgaduras ostentaba sus casas el pobre suburbio de la Riberilla; quién había destinado a manifestar su civismo la colcha de la cama, quién las cortinas de la humilde alcoba, quién una sábana o mantel. Al ingreso de la barriada se alzaban arcos de triunfo, entretejidos con ramaje.

Cuando regresaron los coches, trayendo ya a los esperados viajeros, el contraste que ofrecía el espectáculo convidaba a parar la consideración en él. Acercábase el sol a su ocaso, y las colinas que limitaban el horizonte pasaban del suave azul ceniciento al lila más delicado. Las playas de la Barquera y el mar alternaban en zonas de nítida blancura y de limpio color de zafiro; a los últimos destellos del poniente, el arenal brillaba como si estuviese salpicado de plata, y vaporosas franjas de espuma, tan pronto formadas como deshechas, corrían un instante por el borde de las olas. Soberana y majestuosa paz, unida al recogimiento de la hora vespertina, se elevaba de aquellas diáfanas lejanías al cielo puro, donde apenas de trecho en trecho leves nubecillas, semejantes a copos de algodón, se esparcían tiñéndose de oro. Así se preparaba al sueño la Naturaleza, mientras en la carretera, una multitud abigarrada y polvorosa se desojaba mirando al punto por donde asomaría muy luego la comitiva, y recreaba la vista en contemplar los guiñapos y telas de colorines pendientes de los balcones, y el marchito verdor de los arcos de triunfo; y se recibían y daban pisotones recios, y *metidos* feroces, y algún furtivo pellizco, y se tragaba y se mascaba el árido polvo del camino, oyendo a poca distancia, como irónica burla, el blando gemir de las ondas de la ría.

De tiempo en tiempo, las bombas de palenque[24] trataban de armar un escándalo en la atmósfera, pero en balde; diríase que era la detonación

---

24 Cohetes de un solo estallido.

17

THE HEROINE'S LOFTY IMPULSES

It was during the midday hours, the very hottest time, when down the streets of Marineda dashed carriages carrying the party committee members who were on their way to await the arrival of the delegates from Cantabrialta. The two leagues of main road that run from the city to the former tollhouse (as it was then called) were filled with waiting people, exceedingly dusty and sweaty. Few frock coats, but many long full jackets and sack coats; once in a blue moon, a uniform; a good number of women, already hoarse, with dry lips and bloodshot eyes, their cheeks flushed and their hair and attire somewhat dishevelled. The poor suburb of La Riberilla was parading its houses, all festooned with hangings; one person had used a bedspread to declare his public-spiritedness, another, the curtains of his humble bedroom, another, a sheet or a tablecloth. At the entryway to the district, they had raised up arches of triumph, interwoven with branches.

When the coaches returned, bringing back the long-awaited travellers, the contrast offered by the spectacle was an invitation to stop and consider it. The sun was near to setting and the hills that delimited the horizon were changing from a soft blue to a most delicate shade of lilac. The beaches of La Barquera and the sea alternated in areas of clear whiteness and the pure colour of sapphire; by the dying flashes of the setting sun, the sandy parts were shining, as if they were flecked with silver, and vaporous bands of foam, constantly forming and breaking apart, ran for an instant along the edge of the waves. Sovereign, majestic peace, combined with the religious recollection of the vespertine hour, rose up from that diaphanous remoteness into the pure sky, where light clouds, like cotton balls, were scattered sparsely here and there, tinged with gold. In this way Nature prepared for sleep, whilst on the main road, a motley, dusty crowd strained their eyes, watching the spot where the retinue would very soon make its appearance; they entertained their eyes by contemplating the brightly-coloured tatters and pieces of cloth hanging from the balconies, and the withered greenery of the triumphal arches. People were treading on each other's feet and ferociously *shoving* one another, with some furtive pinching, and they were swallowing and chewing the arid dust of the road, hearing nearby, like ironic ridicule, the gentle moaning of the waves of the estuary.

From time to time, the single-fire skyrockets tried to cause a commotion in the atmosphere, but in vain; it could be said it was the detonation of

de algún vergonzante petardo, que así alteraba la amplia serenidad del ambiente, como el zumbido de un mosquito turbaría el reposo de un gigante. Las tocatas de la banda de música, hecha pedazos de puro soplar himnos y más himnos patrióticos, se empequeñecían en el libre y anchuroso espacio, hasta asemejarse al estallido de una docena de buñuelos al caer en el aceite hirviendo donde se fríen. Y visto desde la playa, el mismo numeroso gentío podía compararse a un avispero, y la bandera roja, a un trapo de los que los chicos cuelgan de una caña a fin de pescar ranas en las ciénagas.

Para que la comitiva adquiriese unos asomos de solemnidad, fue preciso que entrase en los mezquinos arrabales del pueblo. Con la frescura de la noche que caía todo el mundo se halló más a gusto, los de los coches respiraron, sin dejar de saludar a diestro y siniestro, y comenzaron a abrir en las tinieblas sus pupilas de fuego los reverberos de la ciudad, las farolas y las hachas de cera que encendían algunas mujeres para alumbrar a los carruajes. Así que brilló el cordón de luces, las portadoras de las hachas se alinearon en buen orden, bajando los ojos modestamente porque aquello olía a procesión. Entonces, algunos curiosos de Marineda que no habían querido molestarse en ir más lejos para ver la función, se abrieron paso y situaron convenientemente, con propósito de estudiar los semblantes de las que en otra ocasión se llamarían devotas. Si las encontraban mozas y lindas, decíanles cosas almibaradas; si viejas y feas, barbaridades capaces de enojar y abochornar a un santo de leño. Cuando pasaba Amparo, que iba una de las primeras, al lado del rojo estandarte, era un fuego graneado de piropos, una descarga cerrada de ternezas a quema ropa. Es que la muchacha se lo merecía todo; la luz del blandón descubría su rostro animado, encendía sus ojos rechispeantes y mostraba la crespa melena, desanudada por la agitación de la caminata y flotando en caprichosas roscas por su frente, hombros y cuello. Baltasar y Borrén, de americana y hongo, se colaron entre la apiñada muchedumbre y quizá le murmuraron al oído cien mil dislates; pero no estaba el alcacer para gaitas, es decir, no estaba Amparo de humor de requiebros, hallándose exclusivamente poseída del fervor político.

Sentíase sobreexcitada, febril, en días tan memorables. Por todas partes fingía su calenturienta imaginación peligros, luchas, negras tramas urdidas para ahogar la libertad. De fijo, de fijo, el Gobierno de Madrid sabía ya a tal hora que una heroica pitillera marinedina realizaba inauditos esfuerzos

some shamefaced firecracker which spoilt the extensive serenity of the surroundings like the buzzing of a mosquito would disturb the repose of a giant. The toccatas played by the band, worn out after blowing one patriotic anthem after another, were diminished in the wide, free spaces, to the point of sounding like the crackle of a dozen fritters when they drop into the boiling oil in which they are being fried. And seen from the beach, even the enormous throng could be compared to a swarm of wasps, and the red flag to a rag that children hang from a rod to catch frogs in the marshes.

In order for the retinue to acquire a hint of solemnity, they had to enter the wretched outskirts of the town. As the coolness of night fell, everyone was more comfortable and those inside the coaches breathed more easily, continuing to wave left, right and centre, and the reflections of the city, the street lamps and the big candles some women had kindled to light the way for the carriages all began to open their fiery pupils in the darkness. As soon as the string of lights began to shine, the women carrying the candles lined up in orderly fashion, lowering their eyes modestly because it smelt of a religious procession. At this point, a number of onlookers from Marineda, who hadn't wanted to take the trouble to go any further to see the performance, made their way through and found a convenenient place to stand, so as to study the face of those women who in other circumstances would be called devotees. If they found them young and pretty, they would say sweet things to them; if they were old and ugly, insulting comments capable of annoying and embarrassing a wooden saint. When Amparo, who was one of the first, passed by, alongside the red standard, it was a sustained fire of flirtatious compliments, a volley of sweet nothings at point-blank range. The fact is the girl deserved every bit of it; the light of her wax taper revealed her animated expression, lit up her sparkling eyes and displayed her long, curly hair, which had come undone from all the commotion of the long walk, and was floating down in capricious spirals over her forehead, her shoulders and her neck. Baltasar and Borrén, wearing jackets and bowler hats, slipped through the packed crowd and perhaps murmured endless nonsensical bits of flattery in her ear; but this lovely flower didn't want any bother; that is to say, Amparo was not not in a mood for flattery because she was possessed exclusively by political fervour.

She felt overexcited and feverish on such memorable days. On every side, her febrile imagination fabricated dangers, struggles and dark plots conspired to stifle liberty. For sure, for certain, the government in Madrid already knew that at such-and-such a time a heroic cigar maker from Marineda was

para apresurar el triunfo de la federal; y con estos pensamientos latíale a Amparo su corazoncillo y se le hinchaba el seno agitado. En medio de la vulgaridad e insulsez de su vida diaria y de la monotonía del trabajo siempre idéntico a sí mismo, tales azares revolucionarios eran poesía, novela, aventura, espacio azul por donde volar con alas de oro. Su fantasía inculta y briosa se apacentaba en ellos. Las enfáticas frases de los artículos de fondo, los redundantes períodos de los discursos resonaban en sus oídos como el *ritornello* del vals en los de la niña bailadora. Aquella llegada de los individuos de la Asamblea de la Unión fue para Amparo lo que sería la de los Apóstoles para un pueblo que oyese hablar del Evangelio y de pronto viese arribar a sus costas a los encargados de anunciarlo.

Tenía Amparo por cosa cierta que se acercaba la hora de señalarse con algún hecho digno de memoria; ansiaba, sin declarárselo a sí misma, emplear las fuerzas de abnegación y sacrificio que existen latentes en el alma de la mujer del pueblo. ¡Sacrificarse por cualquiera de aquellos hombres, venidos de Cantabria a vaticinar la redención; inmolarse por el más viejo, por el más feo, prestándole algún extraordinario y capital servicio! Llamar a su puerta a las altas horas de la noche; decirle con voz entrecortada que «ahí viene la Policía» y que se oculte; acompañarlo por recónditas callejuelas a un escondrijo seguro; meterle en la mano unos cuantos pesos ahorrados a fuerza de liar pitillos; recibir, en cambio, un haz de proclamas para repartir al día siguiente, con la advertencia de que «si se las cogen, puede contarse ánima del Purgatorio»; distribuirlas con sigilo y celo, y por recompensa de tantas fatigas, de riesgos semejantes, ganar un expresivo apretón de manos, una mirada de gratitud del proscrito... Si el heroísmo es cuestión de temperatura moral, Amparo, que se hallaba a cien grados, tal vez se dejara fusilar por *la causa* sin decir esta boca es mía, y quién sabe si andando los tiempos no figuraría su retrato al lado de Mariana Pineda, en los cuadros que representan a los mártires de la Libertad... Feliz o desgraciadamente, lo que ustedes quieran, que por eso no reñiremos, los tiempos eran más cómicos que trágicos, y los loables esfuerzos de Amparo no le conquistaron otra corona de martirio sino el que en la fábrica se prohibiese la lectura de diarios, manifiestos, proclamas y hojas sueltas, y que a ella y a otras cuantas que pronunciaron vivas subversivos y cantaron canciones alusivas a la Unión del Norte las suspendiesen, como suele decirse, de empleo y sueldo.

making exhaustive efforts to hasten the triumph of the federalistic cause; and with these thoughts Amparo's tender heart beat fast and her agitated breast heaved. In the midst of all the banality and dullness of her daily life and the monotony of her work, always the same, such revolutionary hazards were poetry, fiction and adventure, a blue space through which to fly on wings of gold. Her uncultivated, spirited fantasy fed on them. The emphatic remarks of the editorials, the redundant sentences of the speeches resounded in her ears like the *ritornello* of a waltz in those of a girl dancer. That arrival of the individual members of the Assembly of the Union was for Amparo what the arrival of the apostles would be for a people who had heard speak of the gospel and suddenly saw those charged with its announcement arriving at their shores.

Amparo was absolutely certain that the hour was approaching when she must distinguish herself by some memorable deed; without admitting it to herself, she yearned to make use of the forces of abnegation and sacrifice that lie dormant in the soul of a woman of the people. To sacrifice oneself for any of those men who had come from Cantabria to predict the redemption; to immolate oneself for the oldest of them, for the ugliest, rendering him some exraordinary and capital service in this way! To knock at his door in the early hours of night, to tell him in a voice choked with emotion that 'the police are coming' and that he should go into hiding; to accompany him through obscure alleys to a safe hiding place; to put in his hand a few pesos saved up by rolling cigarettes; to receive, in exchange, a bundle of proclamations to distribute on the following day, along with a warning that 'if they catch you, you can consider yourself a soul in purgatory'; to distribute them secretly and zealously, and, as a reward for so much hardship and risks of this kind, receive an expressive handshake, a look of gratitude from the exile … If heroism is a question of moral temperature, Amparo, who was at one hundred degrees centigrade, might let herself be shot for the *cause* without saying a word to anyone, and who knows if, in time, her portrait might not appear next to that of Mariana Pineda,[xxviii] among the pictures representing the martyrs to Liberty … Happily or unhappily, whichever you should want, for we won't quarrel over that, the times were more comic than tragic, and Amparo's laudable efforts did not conquer another crown of martyrdom for her; but rather the fact that in the factory reading from newspapers, manifestos, proclamations and handbills be forbidden, and that she and any others who had shouted subversive cheers and sung songs alluding to the Northern Union be suspended, as they usually say, from employment and wages.

XVIII
TRIBUNA DEL PUEBLO

El Círculo Rojo echa el resto; no se habla en Marineda sino del banquete que ofrece a los delegados de Cantrabria y Cantabrialta. No tiene el Círculo Rojo socios tan opulentos como el Casino de Industriales y la Sociedad de Amigos; pero sóbrale alma y desprendimiento, cuando la ocasión lo requiere, para sangrarse los bolsillos, empeñarse, si es preciso, hasta los ojos y salir con color y presentar una mesa que no le avergüence.

Llamada a conferenciar con el presidente del Círculo la «persona de buen gusto», que nunca falta en los pueblos para dirigir las solemnidades, entró al punto en el desempeño de sus funciones, y se dio tal maña, que en breve pudo negociar un empréstito de candeleros de plata, centros de mesa, vajilla fina, mantelería adamascada y nueva, palilleros caprichosos y pureras sorprendentes. Obtenido lo cual, el correveidile se frotó las manos, asegurando al presidente que la mesa estaría regiamente exornada.

–Regiamente, no señor –contestó el presidente algo fosco–. Republicanamente, dirá usted.

No quiso el organizador de la fiesta discutir el adverbio, y satisfecho de haber encontrado los accesorios, se dio a buscar lo principal, o sea, la comida. Bregando con fondistas y cafeteros, consiguió combinar platos, vinos y helados del modo que le pareció más ortodoxo y elegante; pero quiso su desdicha que, a última hora, el entusiasmo político lo echase todo a perder, instigando a un bodegonero federal a enviar «la prueba» de sus vinos, y a un hornero, a remitir media docena de robustas empanadas, que cayeron en el banquete como barbarismos en selecto trozo de latinidad clásica. Menudencias que la Historia no registrará seguramente.

De propósito, se empezó tarde la comida, y circulaban aún las dos sopas de hierbas y de puré, cuando los camareros cerraron las maderas de las ventanas y encendieron las bujías de los candelabros y los aparatos de gas. Viose entonces salir de las vaguedades del crepúsculo la mesa, la larga mesa de sesenta cubiertos, con sus brillantes objetos de plata, sus ramos de flores simétricamente colocados, sus altos ramilletes de dulce, sus temblorosas gelatinas, donde la luz rielaba como en un lago. El presidente del Círculo tendió en derredor una mirada de orgullo. En verdad que el aspecto del

18

TRIBUNE OF THE PEOPLE

The Red Circle is going all out; they talk about nothing in Marineda except the banquet being offered for the delegates from Cantabria and Cantabrialta. The Red Circle doesn't have members as opulent as those of the Industrialists' Club and the Friends' Society, but it has more than enough spirit and generosity, when the occasion demands it, to dig deep into its pockets, even get up to its neck in debt if necessary, and come out with flying colours, and present a table of which there was nothing to be ashamed.

Called upon to confer with the president of the Circle, the 'person of good taste' who is there in every town to direct such formal occasions immediately began to carry out his duties, and managed so well that before long he was able to negotiate the loan of silver candlesticks, centrepieces, fine china, new damask table linen, whimsical toothpick holders and surprising humidors. When this had been obtained, the go-between rubbed his hands together, assuring the president that the table would be regally embellished.

'Not regally,' answered the president, somewhat sullenly. 'Republicanly, you might say.'

The organiser of the festivities refused to discuss the adverb, and satisfied at having found the accessories, set about fetching what was most important, that is, the food. After quarrelling with restaurant and café owners, he managed to combine dishes, wines and frozen desserts in a way that seemed most orthodox and elegant to him; but misfortune would have it that, at the very last minute, political enthusiasm ruined everything for him, by inciting a federal wine dealer to send out 'samples' of his wines, and a baker, to deliver half a dozen robust meat pies, which went down in the banquet like linguistic barbarisms in a select passage of classical Latinity. Odds and ends which History will surely not record.

The dinner began late deliberately, and the two types of soup – julienne and purée – were still being served when the waiters closed the window shutters and lit the candles in the candelabra and the gaslights. Then, emerging from the vague shadows of twilight, you could see the table, the long table with sixty place settings, with its shining silver objects, its symmetrically placed bouquets of flowers, its collection of sweetmeats piled high, its quivering jellies, where the light shimmered as if upon a lake. The Circle president glanced around proudly. Truthfully the appearance of the banquet was

banquete era majestuoso. Imperaba en él todavía la reserva de los primeros momentos; la gente comía con moderación y delicadeza; los camareros y mozos de servicio andaban discretamente, sin taconear; las cucharas producían leve música al tropezar con los platos; la virginidad del mantel alegraba los ojos, y el vaho aperitivo de la sopa no desterraba del todo las fragantes emanaciones de las rosas y claveles de los floreros. No obstante, al servirse la primer entrada, comenzaron a dialogar los vecinos de mesa y el rumor creciente de las conversaciones envalentonó a los mozos, que pisaron ya más recio.

Presidía la mesa el viejo de blanca barba, y la teatral nobleza de su figura completaba la decoración. A su derecha tenía al presidente del Círculo, y a su izquierda, al orador de tenebrosa faz, el que, según Amparo, «echaba términos» difíciles de entender. Seguían los demás delegados por orden de respetabilidad, alternando con individuos de la Junta, de la Prensa, del partido.

Fue poco a poco acrecentándose el ruido de la charla y desatándose las lenguas, por donde rebosaba ya la abundancia del corazón. El que, merced a su ancianidad venerable, podía ser llamado patriarca, sonreía, aprobaba, estaba de acuerdo con todo el mundo, mientras el delegado tétrico y ceñudo se las componía lo mejor posible para disputar. Al tercer plato disparó con bala rasa contra la propiedad, el capital y la clase media, y el presidente del Círculo, patrón y dueño de establecimiento, hubo de amoscarse; poco después fue el patriarca mismo el enojado, a causa de no sé qué frases sobre el derecho de insurrección y el empleo de medios violentos y coercitivos. Ninguno le parecía al patriarca lícito; en su concepto, el amor, la paz, la fraternidad eran las mejores bases para fundar la unión federativa, no sólo de Cantabria y de España, sino del mundo. Cada cual alegaba sus razones, tratando de quimera el ajeno parecer; la discusión se hacía general; intervenían en ella periodistas y delegados, desde los más remotos extremos de la mesa; alguien brindaba sin ser oído; personas de voz escasa exclamaban, en tono suplicante: «Pero oigan ustedes, señores...; si ustedes oyesen una palabra...». Era en balde. El grupo central se lo hablaba todo; de su confuso vocerío sólo se destacaban frases sueltas, airadas, empeñadas en descollar: «Eso son utopías, utopías fatales... No, es que le convenzo a usted con la Historia en la mano... Sí, sí, hagámonos de miel... La Revolución francesa... Era en otro régimen,

majestic. The reserve of the first moments still dominated, the people were eating with moderation and delicacy; the waiters and commis boys walked about discreetly, without clicking their heels; the spoons produced soft music as they scraped the plates, the pristine white table cloth was a joy to behold, and the appetising aroma of the soup in no way excluded the fragrant smell of the roses and carnations in the flower vases. Nevertheless, as they served the first entrée, people began to communicate with their neighbours, and the rising murmur of the conversations emboldened the waiters, who now trod more loudly.

Presiding over the table was the old man with the white beard, and the theatrical nobility of his face rounded off the décor. To his right was the president of the Circle, and to his left, the orator with the gloomy expression, who, according to Amparo, 'bandied about terms' which were difficult to understand. The rest of the delegates followed in order of respectability, with members of the committee, the press and the political party alternating between them.

Little by little, the noise of the talking was increasing and tongues grew looser, so the abundance of the heart was already overflowing. The one who, thanks to his venerable old age, could be called a patriarch, was smiling, approving, agreeing with everyone, while the sullen, scowling delegate was managing his best to be contentious. During the third course, he fired away full blast against property, capital and the middle-class, and the Circle president, a landlord and owner of a business establishment, had to get cross. Shortly after, it was the patriarch himself who was angry, on account of certain remarks concerning the right to insurrection and the use of violent, coercive means. None of these seemed legitimate to the patriarch; in his view, love, peace and fraternity were the finest bases upon which to found the federative union, not only in Cantabria and Spain, but throughout the whole world. Everyone put forward their reasons, treating others' opinion as a pipe dream; the discussion became general; journalists and delegates were taking part in it from the farthest ends of the table; someone made a toast without being heard; people with weak voices exclaimed, almost in supplication, 'But listen, gentlemen … if you would just listen to one word …' It was in vain. The central group did all the talking; out of the confused shouting, all that was discernible were isolated phrases, angry and determined to stand out: 'Those are utopias, fatal utopias … No, because I'm going to convince you with History in my hand … Yes, yes, let's be kind … the French Revolution … That was during another regime, gentlemen …

señores... No confundamos los tiempos... Está usted en un error... Un hecho no es ley general... Eso lo ha dicho Pi... Cantú es un reaccionario... El bautismo de la sangre... Horrores infecundos...» Mientras duraba la polémica, los mozos no se entendían para pasar las fuentes del asado y para escanciar el champaña... Uno de ellos se inclinó hacia el presidente y le dijo al oído no sé qué... El presidente se levantó al punto y salió de la sala, volviendo a entrar presto, seguido de un grupo de mujeres.

Amparo lo capitaneaba. Penetró airosa, vestida con bata de percal claro y pañolón de Manila de un rojo vivo que atraía la luz del gas, el rojo del *trapo* de los toreros. Su pañuelito de seda era del mismo color, y en la diestra sostenía un enorme ramo de flores artificiales: rosas de Bengala, de sangriento matiz, sujetas con largas cintas lacre, donde se leía, en letras de oro, la dedicatoria. Diríase que era el genio protector de aquel lugar, el duende del Círculo Rojo; las notas del mantón, del pañuelo, de las flores y cintas se reunían en un vibrante acorde escarlata, a manera de sinfonía de fuego.

Adelantóse intrépida la muchacha, levantando en alto el ramo y recogiendo con el brazo libre el pañolón, cuyos flecos le llovían sobre las caderas. Y como el conspicuo disputador, dejando su asiento, mostrase querer tomar el exvoto que la muchacha ofrecía en aras de la diosa Libertad, Amparo se desvió y fuese derecha al patriarca. El corro se abrió para dejarle paso.

La muchacha, sin soltar el ramo, miraba al viejo. Éste, en pie, con su barba plateada y levemente ondulada, como la de los ermitaños de tragedia, con su calva central guarnecida de abundantes mechones canos, con su alta estatura, un tanto encorvada ya, se le figuraba la ancianidad clásica, adornada de sus atributos, coronando la cima de los tiempos. Y el patriarca, a su vez, creía ver en aquella buena moza el viviente símbolo del pueblo joven. Ambos formularon en sus adentros el pensamiento de simpatía que los dominaba.

«Este señor mete respeto lo mismo que un obispo», se dijo Amparo.

«Esta chica parece la Libertad», murmuró el patriarca.

Entre tanto, la muchacha comenzaba su peroración. Temblábale la voz al principio; dos o tres veces tuvo que pasarse la mano, yerta, por la frente húmeda, y sin saber lo que hacía, accionó con el ramo, cuyas cintas culebrearon como serpientes de llama, y carraspeó para deshacer un nudo que le apretaba el galillo. Poco a poco, el rumor de la mesa, el cuchicheo de

Let's not confuse the times … You're wrong … A fact is not a general law … Pi has already said that … Cantú[xxix] is a reactionary … the baptism of blood … sterile horrors …' While the polemic was going on, the waiters couldn't agree with each other about passing around the platters of roast meat and pouring the champagne … One of them leaned over the president and said something or other in his ear … The president stood up immediately and left the room, returning shortly, followed by a group of women.

Amparo was the leader. She entered gracefully, dressed in a robe of light percale and a bright red Manila shawl, the red of a bullfighter's cape, that attracted the gaslight. Her silk scarf was of the same colour, and in her right hand she held an enormous bouquet of artificial flowers: imitation roses of a blood-red shade, fastened with long, bright red ribbons, on which a dedication in golden letters could be read. You might say she was the protecting spirit of that place, the sprite of the Red Circle; the colours of her shawl, the scarf, the flowers and ribbons united in a vibrant scarlet chord, like a symphony of fire.

The girl moved forward intrepidly, lifting up the bouquet and using her free arm to gather up her shawl, the fringes of which rained down over her hips. As our eminent disputant left his seat, anxious to accept the votive offering extended by the girl in honour of the goddess Liberty, Amparo turned away and went straight up to the patriarch. The circle of women opened out to let her pass.

The girl, without letting go of the bouquet, looked at the old man. Standing there, with his silvery, slightly wavy beard, like those of hermits in tragic theatre, his mid frontal baldness garnished with abundant grey tufts, with his tall stature, rather stooped now, she imagined him as the classic figure of old age, adorned by his attributes, the top of his head crowned by the seasons. And the patriarch, for his part, thought he saw in that fine girl the living symbol of youth. Both formed in their innermost being the thought of affection that dominated them.

'This man commands respect just like a bishop,' Amparo said to herself.

'This young girl looks like Liberty,' murmured the patriarch.

In the meantime, the girl was starting her peroration. At first her voice trembled; two or three times she had to run her rigid hand over her damp forehead, and without realising what she was doing, she gesticulated with the bouquet, the ribbons of which were wriggling like flaming serpents, and she cleared her throat in order to remove a knot that was pressing her uvula. Little by little, the murmur at the table, the whispering of the more

los convidados más distantes, la luz de los mecheros de gas que le calentaba los sesos, el aroma de los vinos y la espuma del champaña, que aún parecía bullir en la iluminada atmósfera, la embriagaron, y sintió fluir de sus labios las palabras y habló con afluencia, con desparpajo, sin cortarse ni tropezar. Los convidados se daban al codo sonriendo, pronunciando entre dientes algún «¡bravo!, ¡muy bien!», al oír que las operarias republicanas de la fábrica ofrecían aquel ramo a la Asamblea de la Unión del Norte y al Círculo Rojo en prueba de que..., y para manifestar cuanto..., y como testimonio de que los corazones que latían..., etc. El patriarca se colocaba la mano sobre el pecho, se la llevaba a la boca con sincerísima complacencia, mientras el disputador, tieso y serio, inclinaba de cuando en cuando, lentamente, la cabeza en señal de aprobación. Por fin, la oradora acabó su discurso, entregando el ramo al patriarca y gritando: «¡Ciudadanos delegados, salud y fraternidad!».

Tomó el viejo la ofrenda y la pasó al presidente, que se quedó con ella muy empuñada y sin saber qué hacer. Confusas las compañeras de Amparo por el silencio repentino, miraban de reojo hacia todas partes, maravillándose del esplendor de la mesa y algo sorprendidas de que el banquete republicano fuese cosa de tanto orden y de que los delegados comiesen, en vez de salvar la patria. El patriarca se acercó a Amparo; sus mejillas arrugadas y marchitas tenían a la sazón sonrosados los pómulos.

–Gracias, hijas... –tartamudeó, cabeceando senilmente–. Gracias, ciudadanas... Acércate, Tribuna del pueblo ... que nos una un santo abrazo de fraternidad... ¡Viva la Tribuna del pueblo! ¡Viva la Unión del Norte!

–¡Viva! –balbució Amparo, toda enternecida, ahogándose–. ¡Viva usted ... muchos años!

Y el viejo y la niña no estaban a dos dedos de romper a llorar, y algunos de los convidados se reían a socapa viendo aquel brazo paternal que rodeaba aquel cuello juvenil.

distant guests, the light of the gaslamps warming her very brain, the aroma of the wines and the froth of the champagne that still seemed to bubble in the luminous atmosphere, intoxicated her, and she felt the words flow from her lips and she spoke with eloquence and self-confidence, without getting embarrassed or tripping over words. The guests elbowed one another and smiled, mumbling an occasional 'bravo! very good!' as they heard that the female republican workers at the factory were offering that bouquet to the Assembly of the Northern Union and the Red Circle as a token of ... and to show how much ... and as testimony to the fact that hearts that beat ... etc. The patriarch placed his hand over his chest, raised it to his mouth with most sincere pleasure, while the disputant, stiff and grave, slowly tilted his head from time to time as a sign of approbation. The orator finally finished her speech, handing over the bouquet to the patriarch and shouting: 'Citizen delegates, to prosperity and brotherhood!'

The old man took the offering and passed it to the president, who was left clutching it and not knowing what to do. Amparo's companions, confused by the sudden silence, looked out of the corners of their eyes in every direction, marvelling at the splendour of the table and somewhat surprised that the republican banquet should be such an orderly affair, and that the delegates should be eating instead of saving their country. The patriarch approached Amparo; his wrinkled and withered cheeks were rosy at that moment.

'Thank you, my daughters...' he stammered, nodding his head in a senile manner. 'Thank you, citizen ladies... Come closer, Tribune of the people ... and let us be united by a holy fraternal embrace... Long live the Tribune of the people! Long live the Northern Union!'

'Long live!' Amparo stuttered, completely touched, choking. 'May you live ... many years!'

And the old man and the young girl came within an inch of bursting into tears, and some of the guests surreptitiously laughed at the sight of that paternal arm around that youthful neck.

XIX
LA UNIÓN DEL NORTE

¡Cuidado si hace calor! Sobre el duro azul de un celaje no empañado por la más leve bruma ondean las flámulas, colocadas en mástiles a la veneciana alrededor del baluarte de la Puerta del Castillo, y sus gayos colores no desdicen del júbilo radiante del cielo y de la estrepitosa y alegre multitud. Arcos y ondas de follaje verde corren de mástil a mástil, disonando y contrastando con el tono cerúleo del firmamento. En mitad del anfiteatro se alza el palco destinado a la Asamblea de la Unión, con su tribuna al centro, y flanqueado de otros dos más bajos, pero mayores, destinados a las comisiones del partido. Bien podía la Asamblea constitutiva de la Unión del Norte de la Costa Ibérica –que así se nombraba en sus documentos oficiales–ocupar oronda y satisfecha el palco presidencial: pocas sesiones y breves horas le habían bastado para sentar las bases del gran contrato unionista federativo; actividad gloriosa, sobre todo comparándola con la flema y machaconería de aquellas holgazanas de Cortes Constituyentes, que tardaban meses en redactar un código fundamental y definitivo para la nación.

Caminaba impetuosa hacia el anfiteatro la comitiva, compuesta del partido y *juventud* republicana, de mucha chiquillería, de los comités rurales, de los delegados y de todo fiel cristiano que, movido de curiosidad, quiso injerirse en la procesión. Apresuradamente, como si fuese un ser único animado por un solo soplo vital, y tuviese por voz la banda de música que aturdía el ambiente con himnos y más himnos, adelantábase la palpitante masa humana; y empujadas por la compacta muchedumbre, las banderas, coronadas de flores, vacilaban cual si estuviesen ebrias, y tan pronto daban traspiés y se inclinaban acá o acullá como tornaban a erguirse rectas y altivas. Y las casas del tránsito parecían contemplar el cuadro y entender su asunto, y de unas llovían flores, ramos, coronas, y otras, en menor número, cerradas a piedra y lodo, dijérase que fruncían el ceño y se ponían hurañas y serias al sentir el roce de la ola revolucionaria.

Cuando éstas llegaron a estrellarse en el baluarte, se esparcieron y derramaron por doquiera. El gentío trepó a las escaleras, cabalgó en el

19
THE NORTHERN UNION

Watch out, it's hot!

Pennants placed on flagpoles around the bastion of the Puerta del Castillo are fluttering against the harsh blue of a sky dappled with clouds, untarnished by even the slightest haze, and their bright colours do not clash with the radiant jubilation of the heavens and the noisy, cheerful multitude. Arches and waves of green foliage run from pole to pole, out of harmony and contrasting with the cerulean tone of the firmament. In the middle of the ampitheatre, the stand intended for the Assembly of the Union rises up with its rostrum in the centre, flanked by two others, lower down but larger, destined for the delegations of the party. The Constituent Assembly of the Northern Union of the Iberian Coast – for that is what it was called in its official documents – could well afford to occupy the presidential stand with smug satisfaction; just a few sessions and brief hours had sufficed for it to establish the bases of the great unionist, federative contract; a glorious activity, especially compared with the apathy and tediousness of those loafers who made up the Constituent Assembly, who took months to draw up a fundamental, definitive code for the nation.

Walking impetuously towards the ampitheatre was the retinue, composed of party members and republican *youth*, lots of kids, rural committees, delegates and any other faithful Christian soul who, out of sheer curiosity, wanted to break into the procession. Hurriedly, as if it were a single being animated by a single vital breath, and as if it had for its voice the musical band which made the atmosphere dizzy with anthem after anthem, the palpitating human mass of humanity pressed forward; and pushed on by the compact crowd, the flags, crowned with flowers, hesitated as if they were inebriated, and no sooner did they stumble and lean here and there, than they would straighten up again, erect and haughty. And the houses along the route seemed to contemplate the scene and undestand its business; from some of them flowers, bouquets and garlands rained down, while others, fewer in number, were shut tight, and you might say they were knitting their brows and appearing diffident and grave as they felt the graze of the revolutionary wave.

When they all came up against the bastion, they scattered and spread out everywhere. The throng climbed the stairs, sat astride the ridge of

caballete de los bastiones, invadió los palcos de los comisionados y se extendió coronando las alturas vecinas; por los troncos de los mástiles se encaramó más de un granuja, resuelto a dominar la situación. Penetró majestuosamente en el palco de la Asamblea, y así que los delegados ocuparon sus asientos, el tumulto se apaciguó como por magia, y cerca de veinte mil personas guardaron silencio religioso. Sólo se oyó salir, de algún rincón del anchuroso escenario, el melancólico grito que pregonaba: «¡Agua de limón fría, barquillos, agua, azucarillos, agua!». Dos fotógrafos, situados en el lugar oportuno para tomar la vista, enfocaban cubriéndose la cabeza con el paño de bayeta verde, y sus máquinas parecían los ojos de la Historia contemplando la escena. Casi se oiría el volar de una mosca, sobre todo en las cercanías del palco presidencial.

Procedióse a la firma y lectura del contrato de unión. Desde lejos se veía en el palco una agrupación de cabezas, entre las cuales se destacaba la negra cabellera melodramática del disputador y sus quevedos de oro, y la barba nívea del patriarca, resplandeciente al sol, como la de Jehová en los cuadros bíblicos. Estaban Baltasar y Borrén apoyados en un lienzo de parapeto, en pie sobre un sillar de piedra, lo cual les permitía ver cuanto ocurría. Ambos prestaban atención suma, comprendiendo que presenciaban un episodio interesante del drama político español.

–Aquí se cuece algo, hombre –exclamó Borrén inclinándose hacia su amigo.

–¡Claro que se cuece! ¡El desbarajuste universal ... y el picadillo que van a hacer de España esos señores!

–Hombre, dice que no... Dice que lo que desean es confederarnos, para que estemos más uniditos que antes... ¿No ve usted que esto se llama Unión?

–¡Sí, sí, corte usted un dedo y péguelo después con saliva!

–A bien que una nación no es ninguna naranja para hacer cuarterones tan fácilmente... ¿Sabe usted lo que me contaron de ese viejecito..., del patriarca? Mire usted: yo me explico que sea republicano... ¡Había cosas en aquellos tiempos antiguos! ¡Era el segundo de una casa rica..., poderosa, hombre! El mayorazgo arrampló con todo, ¿eh?, mimos y hacienda, y a él le quedó un palomar viejo y la memoria de las azotainas... Otro se hubiera hecho misántropo... Él se hizo filántropo, y luego progresista, y

the bastion, invaded the stands for the delegates, and stretched out and crowned the nearby heights; more than one ragamuffin climbed the length of the poles, determined to have the optimum view of the situation. The assembly majestically made its way onto the stand, and as soon as the delegates occupied their seats, the tumult abated as if by magic and about twenty thousand people maintained a religious silence. The only sound you could hear, emanating from some corner of that spacious setting, was the melancholy shout that was hawking 'cold lemonade, pastry cones, water, lemon candy flavouring, water!' Two photographers, in just the right place to view it all, were focusing their cameras and covering their heads with the green baize cloth, and their equipment resembled the eyes of History contemplating the scene. You could almost have heard a pin drop, especially around the area of the presidential stand.

They proceeded to the signing and the reading of the contract for the Union. From a distance, a cluster of heads could be seen in the presidential stand, amongst which the melodramatic black head of hair of the disputatious delegate stood out, and his golden pince-nez, and the patriarch's snowy-white beard, resplendent in the sunlight, just like Jehova in biblical pictures. Baltasar and Borrén were leaning against the wall of a parapet, standing on top of a stone ashlar, which allowed them to see what was happening. Both were paying careful attention, realising they were witnessing an interesting episode in the Spanish political drama.

'There's something cooking up here,' exclaimed Borrén, leaning towards his friend.

'Of course something is cooking! Universal chaos ... and the mincemeat those men are going to make of Spain!'

'It's not saying... It's saying what they want is to form us into a confederation, so we're more united than before... Don't you see that this is called a Union?'

'Yes, yes, cut off a finger and stick it back on with saliva!'

'Of course, a nation isn't an orange that can be cut into quarters so easily ... Do you know what they told me about that little old man ... the patriarch? Look: I can understand him being a republican... There were things going on in those days of old! He was the second son of a rich family ... a powerful one! The eldest son made off with everything, eh? All the attention and the whole estate, and the second son was left an old dovecote and the memory of all the hidings he had. ...Any other man would have become a misanthropist ... He became a philanthropist, and then a progressive and finally a federalist

luego federal..., y es un bienaventurado que abraza a todo el mundo, y oye misa, y es incapaz de hacer daño a nadie... Acá, *inter nos*, lo tengo por algo chocho...

–¿Y aquel moreno..., el de los quevedos?

–¡Ah! Ése ... ése dicen que es de los que quieren perder las colonias y salvar los principios: hombre de línea recta, de geometría... Según Palacios, que lo conoce, la ecuación entre la lógica y el absurdo; no en balde es ingeniero. Si para lograr sus ideales tuviese que desollarnos... ¡pobre pellejo!

–¿Y si tuviese que desollarse a sí mismo?

–¡Cáspita!, de la epidermis ajena a la propia... Con todo, no seamos escépticos, hombre. Allí tiene usted a aquel otro..., al del bigote negro..., el que está a la izquierda del patriarca. Pues mire usted, hombre, que le ha costado ya dinero y disgustos esta mojiganga política..., emigrado, encausado, maltratado..., y se libró de ir a las Marianas... no sé cómo... Hay humor para todo en este mundo sublunar... ¡Y decir que cuando Dios produce chicas como ésa se ocupen en politiquear los muchachos!

Al pronunciar estas palabras, señalaba Borrén a Amparo, cuyos rojos atavíos la distinguían del círculo femenino que la rodeaba.

–Pues esa chica aún politiquea más que los barbudos... ¿No sabe usted...?

Y el incidente del banquete fue comentado, desmenuzado, acribillado por las dos bocas masculinas, que lo adornaron con festones satíricos. Entre tanto se leía el contrato de la Unión, y a pesar de que el sol no estaba en el cenit, ni mucho menos, la gente arracimada y prensada producía una temperatura insufrible, y se oían exclamaciones de este jaez:

–Nos morimos.

–Nos asfixiamos.

–¡Cuándo vendrá un poco de fresco!

–Pero, hombre, no nos estruje usté.

–Ave María, qué bárbaro.

–Estése usté quieto.

–Pues si no ve, fastidiarse; ¿s'a figurao que vemos los demás?

–¡Tan siquiera puede uno meter la mano en el bolsillo para sacar un triste pañuelo!

… and he's a happy soul who embraces the whole world, and goes to Mass, and is incapable of doing anyone any harm… Now, *inter nos*, I consider him somewhat doited…'

'And that dark-haired fellow … the one with the pince-nez?'

'Oh! That one … they say he's one of those who would like to lose our colonies and save our principles: a man of straight lines and geometry… According to Palacios, who knows him, he's the equation between the logical and the absurd; he's not an engineer for nothing. If he had to skin us alive to achieve his ideals … pity our poor skins!'

'And if he had to skin himself?'

'My goodness! From someone else's epidermis to your own … Still, let's not be sceptical. You've got that other one there … the one with the black moustache … the one who's to the left of the patriarch. Well, look, because this political farce has already cost him money and troubles … emigration, prosecution, maltreatment … and he escaped going to the Marianas… I don't know how… There's a mood for everything in this sublunary world… And to think that when God produces girls like that, boys spend their time dabbling in politics!'

As he uttered these words, Borrén pointed at Amparo, whose red ensemble distinguished her from the circle of females surrounding her.

'Well, that girl is dabbling in politics even more than the bearded men… Don't you know…?'

And the incident of the banquet was discussed, scrutinised and riddled with holes by the two men's mouths, which adorned it with satirical festoons. Meanwhile, the contract for the Union was being read, and even though the sun was not at its zenith, far from it, the people clustered and pressed together produced an unbearable temperature and exclamations of this sort could be heard:

'We're dying.'

'We're suffocating.'

'When are we going to get a bit of cool air!'

'Just stop pressing into us.'

'For God's sake, how rude.'

'You keep quiet.'

'Well, if you can't see, just put up with it; didya think we can see any better?'

'You can hardly put your hand in your pocket to take out a miserable handkerchief!'

–Cuidado con el reloj; palpa si lo tienes.

Y la voz del lector del Pacto volaba por cima del mar de cabezas, y las palabras «garantías sacrosantas..., dogmas de libertad..., derechos invulnerables..., ideales benditos..., pueblo honrado y libre...» se dilataban en el cálido y sereno ambiente. Una lluvia de flores vino, de improviso, a oscurecerlo, y multitud de blancas palomas fueron lanzadas a él, abatiendo al punto el vuelo con aletear trabajoso, y cayendo sobre la muchedumbre, entorpecidas de tener tanto tiempo ligadas las patas. Un estruendoso cubo de cohetes de lucería salió bufando en todas direcciones; retumbó la música; hubo un minuto de gritos, vivas, estruendo y confusión, y nadie reparó en que un pobre viejo, un barquillero, salía del recinto mitad arrastrado y mitad en brazos de dos hombres.

–Le dio un accidente –decían al verlo pasar, sin añadir otro comentario.

'Mind your watch; feel if it's still there.'

And the voice of the reader of the pact flew high above the sea of heads, and the words 'sacrosanct guarantees ... dogmas of liberty ... invulnerable rights ... blessed ideals ... free and honourable people...' spread out in the warm, serene atmosphere. A shower of flowers suddenly came down to obscure him, and a host of white doves, numb from having their legs tied together for such a long time, were let loose upon him, immediately swooping down in flight with a laborious flapping of wings, falling onto the crowd of people. A thunderous series of sparkling skyrockets sputtered out from a whirling wheel in all directions; the music boomed out; there was a spell of shouts, hurrahs, turmoil and confusion, and nobody noticed that a poor old man, a pastry cone seller, was being taken out of the place, half dragged and half carried in the arms of two men.

'He fainted,' they were saying as they saw him pass by, without adding further comment.

XX

ZAGAL Y ZAGALA

Y del accidente se murió aquella noche misma, sin confesión, sin recobrar los sentidos. ¿Fue el sol abrasador? Mil veces le cayó verticalmente sobre el cráneo al señor Rosendo en sus épocas de vida militar, y vamos, que el de la isla de Cuba pica en regla... ¿Fue el haber vuelto a manejar las tenazas y a elaborar barquillos para el extraordinario consumo de aquellos días solemnes? ¿Fue, como dijeron algunas comadres, el orgullo de ver a su hija tan elocuente y bizarra, y tan agasajada por los señores de la Asamblea? Quédese para la posteridad el arduo fallo, si bien parece infundada la última suposición, por cuanto el señor Rosendo, lejos de manifestar complacencia cuando la chica se metía en semejantes trifulcas, había roto pocos días antes su mutismo para decirle cosas muy al alma sobre eso de buscar tres pies al gato y perder su colocación por locuras. El servicio militar había formado de tal suerte el carácter del viejo, que la insubordinación era para él el más feo delito, y su divisa, obediencia automática, pasiva; así es que amenazó a Amparo, poniendo los ojos fieros y la voz tartajosa, con romperle una costilla si volvía a leer periódicos en la fábrica. Algunos años antes no hubiera amenazado, sino ejecutado; pero la cigarrera, desde que lo es, sale en cierto modo de la patria potestad, y por eso se creyó el señor Rosendo en el caso de guardar consideraciones a su progenitura. Sabiendo cuánto influyen en los sacudimientos cerebrales y en las hemorragias internas los accesos de furor, puede creerse que tal vez la rabia, y no el orgullo, de ver a su hija elevada a la categoría de *Tribuna del pueblo* determinaron en la pletórica constitución del viejo la apoplejía fulminante.

En fin, a él lo enterraron, y quedáronse las dos mujeres cual es de suponer en los primeros momentos: aturdidas, maravilladas de ver cómo «se va uno al otro mundo». Desequilibrio económico no lo hubo, porque Amparo, indultada, había vuelto a la fábrica, y Chinto, trabajando como un mulo porfiado que era, ganaba lo mismo que antes y traía fielmente la colecta todas las noches, según costumbre, con la diferencia de que ni recogía ni reclamaba su mezquino sueldo. Pareció el nuevo sistema muy ventajoso y cómodo a la tullida, que venía a estar como si tuviese dos hijos y ambos ganasen para sustentarla. Pero Amparo vivía inquieta, habiendo advertido cierto peregrino cambio en la actitud y modales de Chinto. Mostrábase éste mandón y muy interesado por las cosas de la humilde casa, que indicaba

20

A LAD AND A LASS

And that very same night he died from the attack, without confession, without recovering his senses. Was it from the scorching sun? It had fallen vertically on Señor Rosendo's skull a thousand times during the period of his military service, and come on, the sun on the island of Cuba really burns... Was it that he had gone back to using the tongs and producing pastry cones for the extraordinary demand of those solemn days? Was it, as some neighbourhood gossips said, the pride at seeing his daughter so eloquent and brave, and so cherished by the men of the Assembly? Let this arduous judgement remain for posterity, since this last supposition seems groundless, inasmuch as Señor Rosendo, far from showing pleasure when the girl became involved with rows of this sort, had broken his silence a few days before to tell her things very close to his heart about this business of complicating matters and perhaps even losing her job over such madness. Military service had formed the character of the old man in such a way that for him the ugliest crime was insubordination, and his motto was automatic, passive obedience; thus it was that, his eyes wild and his voice stammering, he threatened Amparo with breaking one of her ribs if she read newspapers at the factory again. A few years before, he would not have threatened to do that, but carried it out; however, a cigar maker, as soon as she is one, abandons paternal authority to some extent, and for that reason Señor Rosendo believed in showing consideration to his offspring. Knowing how much outbursts of anger contribute to strokes and internal haemorrhages, it is conceivable that perhaps his rage, and not his pride, at seeing his daughter elevated to the category of *Tribune of the People*, was the cause in the old man's plethoric constitution of the sudden stroke.

In short, they buried him, and the two women were left like one would suppose in those first moments: bewildered and amazed on seeing how 'one goes off to the next world'. There was no economic imbalance because Amparo, having been pardoned, had gone back to work at the factory, and Chinto, working like the persistent mule he was, earned the same as before and brought back his takings every night, as was his custom, with the difference that he neither collected nor claimed his paltry wages for himself. This new system seemed very advantageous and convenient for the crippled woman, who was as if she had two children with both earning

considerar como suya; se tomaba otra vez la libertad de esperar a la muchacha a la salida de la fábrica, y aun de acompañarla a la ida, si lo consentía la labor de los barquillos; gastaba con ella chanzas finas como tafetán de albarda, y, en suma, desde la muerte del viejo, se las daba de protector y cabeza de casa, sin que en modo alguno procediese como criado, único papel que Amparo le señalaba siempre, mortificada de ver que el tosco labriego le prestaba servicios. Indignada y ofendida, tratólo con más despego que nunca, y para colmo de disgusto, vio que Chinto correspondía a sus desaires con rústicas ternezas, y a sus pruebas de desvío, con pruebas de confianza y afición. Una vez le trajo un pliego de aleluyas, y otra, como la oyese alabar ciertos pendientes de cristal negro, fue y se los presentó a la noche muy orondo.

Ella se negó a estrenarlos.

Hallábase una mañana Amparo en su cuarto vistiéndose para salir a la fábrica, cuando sintió que una mano indiscreta alzaba el pestillo, y con gran sorpresa encontró delante de sí a Chinto, de un talante como nunca lo había visto la muchacha, pues traía el sombrero ladeado sobre la oreja, los carrillos sofocados, el aire resuelto y un cigarro de a cuarto en la boca, preparativos todos que había juzgado indispensables el aldeanillo para realizar la proeza de *cantar claro*. La muchacha cruzó prestamente su bata, que aún tenía sin abrochar, y arrojó al osado una mirada olímpica; pero Chinto venía tal, que ni las ojeadas de un basilisco le hicieran mella.

—¿A qué entras aquí, a ver? —gritó la cigarrera—. ¿Qué se te ofrece?

—Se me ofrecía… dos palabritas.

—¿Palabritas? Tengo que hacer más que oír tus tontadas.

—No, pues yo te quería decir de que … allí…, como ya tengo aprendido el oficio…, es decir, vamos, que quedándome las herramientas por lo que me debía tu padre de soldada…, allí, yo, como ya en la quinta del mes pasado libré … y como, vamos…

—¿Acabarás hoy o mañana? Habla expedito, que parece que estás comiendo sopas.

enough money to support her. But Amparo, having noticed an odd change in Chinto's attitude and manners, was anxious. He was bossy and showed a great interest in the affairs of the humble household, which he gave every indication of considering his own; once again he was taking the liberty of waiting for the girl at the factory exit, and even accompanying her there if his work with the pastry cones permitted. He would play jokes as refined as coarse packsaddle material on her, and, in short, ever since the old man's death, he made himself out to be the protector and head of the household, without ever behaving as a servant in any way, the only role Amparo always designated for him, mortified as she was to see this uncouth farm boy offering his services. She was indignant and offended and treated him more coolly than ever, and to make her disgust even worse, she saw that Chinto repaid her snubs with rustic acts of tenderness, and her demonstrations of indifference with tokens of trust and fondness. Once he brought her a sheet with doggerels on it, and another time, as he had heard her praise a certain pair of black, crystal earrings, he went out and presented them to her that night with considerable pride.

She refused to put them on.

One morning Amparo was in her room, getting dressed to go to the factory, when she sensed an indiscreet hand raising the latch on her door; and to her great surprise she found Chinto standing before her with a manner such as she had never seen before, because he was wearing his hat tilted over his ear, his cheeks were hot and bothered, he had an air of resolve, and a cheap cigar in his mouth, all preparations this country bumpkin deemed indispensable for carrying out the heroic deed of *speaking his mind*. The girl quickly closed her robe, which she hadn't yet done up, and cast a look of contempt at the impudent fellow; but Chinto was in such a state that not even a glance from a basilisk would have made an impression on him.

'Tell me, why have you have come in here?' shouted the cigar maker. 'What do you want?'

'What I would like … one or two little words.'

'Little words? I have other things to do than listen to your foolishness.'

'No, I just wanted to tell you that … well … since I've now learned the trade … that's to say, all right, since the set of tools left me for what your father owed me in wages… well, I, since I escaped conscription for last month … and since, let's say…'

'Are you going to finish today or tomorrow? Hurry up, because you look as if you're eating sops.'

–Mujer, quiérese decir... que si tú admites el arriendo del trato, puedes, es decir, podemos ... casarnos los dos.

La risa homérica que soltó la insigne *Tribuna* al verse requerida de amores por aquella montés alimaña se cambió presto en cólera al advertir que Chinto continuaba brindándole su mano y corazón con las discretas razones ya referidas.

–Porque yo, lo que es tenerte voluntá..., te tengo muchísima, ya desde mismo que te vi..., y me gustas que no sé, que parece que mismo no pienso sino en tus quereres..., así me veo yo tan destruido, que cuasimente no como y propiamente no me quiere dormir el cuerpo..., Por trabajar, ya sabes que trabajaré hasta que me reviente el alma ... y por mantenerte...

–¡Mira..., si no te quitas de delante, te repelo, hago contigo una desgracia! –gritó, ya furiosa, Amparo, dando al mozo, que estaba próximo a la puerta, un soberano empellón para arrojarle del aposento.

Pero el movimiento brusco y familiar despertó la sangre aldeana de Chinto, y con los brazos abiertos se fue hacia Amparo. Ésta, a su vez, sintió que renacía la chiquilla callejera de antaño, y bajándose prontamente, alzó del suelo una botita y estampó el tacón de plano en la inflamada mejilla que vio próxima a las suyas; y con tanto brío menudeó los golpes, que, a uno que le alcanzó entre los ojos, el bárbaro galán hubo de exhalar imprecaciones sofocadas, retrocediendo y dejando el campo libre. Mal segura aún la muchacha, agarró una silla; mas sobraban ya los aprestos bélicos, porque el mozo, restituido a la razón por el vapuleo, se había arrojado de bruces sobre la cama, y escondiendo y revolcando el rostro en la ropa tibia aún del cuerpo de Amparo, lloraba como un becerro, alzando en su dialecto el grito primitivo, el grito de los grandes dolores de la infancia que reaparece en las siguientes crisis de la existencia:

–¡Madre mía, madre mía!

Encogióse Amparo de hombros, y fuese a su fábrica, que urgía el tiempo y era preciso ganar el pan, porque el entierro del viejo había consumido sus menguados ahorros. Al regresar, contó a su madre lo ocurrido, y con no pequeña admiración oyó que la impedida la reprendía por no haber aceptado la propuesta matrimonial; y es el caso que la lógica de la tullida parecía contundente.

–Tú, ¿qué eres, mujer? –le decía–. Cigarrera, como yo. Y él, ¿ qué es, mujer? Barquillero, como tu padre, que en paz descanse. Que te dicen por

'Well, what I mean ... that if you accept my renting the business, you could, that is to say, we could ... the two of us get married.'

The Homeric laughter unleashed by the distinguished *Tribuna* on seeing herself wooed by that wild vermin quickly changed to anger when she noticed that Chinto continued to offer his hand and heart with the aforementioned discreet explanations.

'Because with me, as for being fond of you ... very much so, ever since I first saw you ... I like you so much I can't say, that it seems I think of nothing but what you want ... and I see myself so ravaged that I almost can't eat and my body really won't let me sleep... As for working, you already know I'll work till I burst ... and as for supporting you ... '

'Look here ... if you don't get out of the way, I'll drive you back, do something terrible to you!' Amparo shouted, furious by now, giving a powerful shove to the young fellow near the door in order to hurl him out of her room.

But her brusque, familiar movement aroused Chinto's rustic blood, and he moved towards Amparo with his arms open. She, in turn, felt the young street girl of long ago come to life again, and bending over suddenly, she picked up a small boot from the floor and stamped the heel directly on the inflamed cheek she saw next to hers; and she repeated the blows with such vigour that, after one caught him between the eyes, the uncouth suitor was forced to utter stifled imprecations as he retreated and left the field. The girl, still insecure, grabbed a chair, but these bellicose preparations were already superfluous, because the young fellow, his reason restored by the beating, had thrown himself face down on the bed, and hiding and rolling his face about in the clothes that were still warm from Amparo's body, he sobbed like a young calf, raising up a primitive shout in his native dialect, the shout of great pain in childhood, which reappears in the successive crises of our existence:

'Good heavens, good heavens!'

Amparo shrugged her shoulders and went off to the factory, for time was pressing and she had to earn her bread, because the old man's burial had used up her depleted savings. When she returned, she told her mother what had happened, and it was with no small degree of amazement that she heard the disabled woman reprimand her for not having accepted the proposal of marriage; and the fact of the matter is that the crippled woman's logic seemed convincing.

'You, what are you?' she said to her. 'A cigar maker like me. And he, what is he? A pastry cone seller like your father, may he rest in peace. They

ahí si eres graciosa, si eres tal y cual... Conversación y más conversación. Él trabaja, ¿eh? Pues a eso vamos, que lo otro..., patarata.

Sin querer oír más, la muchacha declaró que no sólo repugnaba casarse con semejante bestia, sino que iba a echarlo de casa volando; no era cosa de tener que atrancar la puerta cada vez que se vistiese. No, y no; antes prefería que la espasen viva que sufrirlo allí a todas horas. Lamentóse la tullida, recordó que el jornal de Chinto las ayudaba a vivir: todo se estrelló contra la firmeza de la *Tribuna*. Y cuando volvió de fuera Chinto a soltar el tubo vacío y a entregar, cabizbajo y humilde como un borrego, sus ganancias del día, Amparo le intimó la orden de no dormir ya aquella noche en casa. El mozo la oyó con rostro entre abatido y atónito; y así que se convenció de que se le condenaba al ostracismo, salió de la estancia a paso redoblado. La tullida se inclinó hacia su hija cuanto pudo para decirle:

–Mira que le debemos cuartos.

–Se los restregaré por la cara –respondió Amparo, con magnífico desdén.

A los dos minutos se presentó otra vez Chinto, cargado con los chismes de la barquillería: tenazas, cargador, lebrillo y hasta un haz de leña. Amparo se puso en actitud defensiva cuando le vio blandir en el aire los hierros; mas no fue sino para desunirlos con fuerza bovina y tirarlos a un rincón desdeñosamente; y en seguida, juntando las tarteras, la leña y el cañuto de hojalata, lo pateó todo hasta reducir a añicos los cacharros y a un bollo informe el reluciente tubo. Ejecutada la hazaña, a puntapiés mandó los tristes restos a la esquina de la habitación, de la cual se retiró sin volver atrás el rostro.

may tell you over there that you're cute, and all that … it's all talk, nothing but talk. He's working, right? Well, that's what counts, because the rest … nonsense.'

Not wanting to hear any more, the girl declared that not only was it revolting to marry such a brute, but that she was going to send him flying from the house; there was no reason for having to bolt the door every time she got dressed. No, no; she would rather be crucified alive than put up with him at all hours of the day. The crippled woman complained, reminding her that Chinto's daily wages helped them to live; but it was all thwarted by *Tribuna*'s firm resolve. And when Chinto returned home from the outside to unfasten the empty container and hand over his earnings for the day, dejected and as meek as a lamb, Amparo notified him that he could not sleep in the house that night. The young fellow heard her, his face somewhere between crestfallen and astounded; and as soon as he was convinced he was being condemned to ostracism, he left the room double quick. The bedridden woman leaned over towards her daughter as far as she could and said to her:

'Look, we owe him money.'

'I'll rub it in his face,' Amparo replied with magnificent disdain.

Within two minutes, Chinto appeared again, loaded down with the things to make pastry cones: tongs, applicator, the earthenware bowl and even a bundle of firewood. Amparo assumed a defensive attitude when she saw him brandish the iron instruments in the air; but it was only to separate them with bovine strength and throw them disdainfully into a corner; and straight away, putting the baking pans, the wood and the tin tubular container together, he stamped on all of it until the crockery was reduced to smithereens and the shiny tube into a shapeless lump. Once the deed had been executed, he kicked the sad remains into the corner of the room and withdrew without looking back.

XXI

TABACO PICADO

A los pocos días supo Amparo en la Granera, convento laico donde nada se ignora, que Chinto andaba pretendiendo ingresar en el taller de la picadura. Empezó a correr y comentarse en la fábrica la leyenda del mozo transido de amor, que por estar cerca de su adorado tormento se metía en los infiernos del picado, en el lugar doliente a cuya puerta hay que dejar toda esperanza. De qué manera se las compuso Chinto para lograr su deseo no hace al caso: lo cierto es que obtuvo la plaza y que Amparo se lo encontró frecuentemente a la entrada y a la salida, triste como can apaleado por su amo, y sin que le dijese nunca más palabras que «Adiós, mujer…; vayas muy dichosa». No cabía que Amparo, generosa de suyo, dejase de ser la primera en trabar otra vez conversación con él; hablaron de cosas indiferentes, de sus respectivas labores, y Amparo prometió visitar el taller de Chinto, que con venir diariamente a la Granera no lo conocía aún.

La Comadreja la acompañó en la visita. Descendieron juntas al piso inferior, con propósito de aprovechar la ocasión y verlo todo. Si los pitillos eran el Paraíso y los cigarros comunes el Purgatorio, la analogía continuaba en los talleres bajos, que merecían el nombre de Infierno. Es verdad que abajo estaban las largas salas del oreo, y sus simétricos y pulcros estantes; el despacho del jefe y el cuadro de las armas de España, trabajadas con cigarros, orgullo de la fábrica; los almacenes, las oficinas; pero también el lóbrego taller del desvenado y el espantoso taller de la picadura.

En el taller del desvenado daba frío ver, agazapadas sobre las negras baldosas y bajo sombría bóveda, sostenida por arcos de mampostería, y algo semejante a una cripta sepulcral, muchas mujeres, viejas la mayor parte, hundidas hasta la cintura en montones de hoja de tabaco, que revolvían con sus manos trémulas, separando la vena de la hoja. Otras empujaban enormes panes de prensado, del tamaño y forma de una rueda de molino, arrimándolos a la pared para que esperasen el turno de ser escogidos y desvenados. La

21

CUT TOBACCO

Several days later in the Granary, a kind of lay convent where nothing remained secret, Amparo found out that Chinto was going around trying to get a job in the workshop where the tobacco was cut. In the factory there started to circulate, and be commented on, the legend about the young fellow, overwrought with love, who, to be near the adored cause of his torment, put himself in the hell where they did the cutting, in the sorrowful place at whose doors one leaves all hope behind.[14] In what way Chinto managed to fulfil his desire is irrelevant: what is certain is that he got the job and that as she was coming in or leaving Amparo ran into him frequently, as sad as a dog that had been beaten by its master, and the only words he would say to her were 'Hello … I hope you're happy'. It wasn't fitting that Amparo, generous by nature, should stop being the first to strike up a conversation with him again; they spoke of trivialities, of their respective jobs, and Amparo promised to visit Chinto's workshop, which with going to the old Granary every day she still didn't know.

The Weasel accompanied her on her visit. Together they went down to the lower floor, with the intention of taking advantage of the opportunity to see everything. If the section for cigarettes was Paradise, and cigars Purgatory, the analogy continued for the workshops below, which deserved the name of Hell. It is true that down below, with their tidy, symmetrical shelves, there were long rooms for airing the goods; the manager's office and the representation of the Spanish coat-of-arms, fashioned with cigars, which was the pride of the factory; the stores, the offices, but also the gloomy workshop where the veins were removed from the leaves, and the frightful workshop where the cutting was done.

In the workshop where the veins were removed from the leaves, it was chilling to see, crouching on the black floor tiles and under a sombre vault held up by masonry arches, a bit like a burial crypt, a good number of women, most of them old, buried to the waist in piles of tobacco leaves, which they turned round and round with trembling hands, separating the veins from the leaves. Other women were pushing enormous bales of pressed leaves, the size and shape of a mill wheel, moving them closer to the wall to wait for

---

14   The gate of Hell in Dante's *Inferno* bears the inscription 'Lasciate ogne speranza, voi ch'intrate' (Abandon all hope, ye who enter here).

atmósfera era a la vez espesa y glacial. *La Comadreja* andaba a saltos, por no pisar el tabaco, y a veces llamaba por su nombre a una de las desvenadoras.

–¡Hola…, señora Porcona!²⁵ –exclamó, dirigiéndose a una que parecía tener los párpados en carne viva y los labios blancos y colgantes, con lo cual hacía la más extraña y espantable figura del mundo–. ¡Hola!… ¿Cómo le va? ¿Cómo están esos parientes? Tú no sabes –añadió, volviéndose a Amparo–que la señora Porcona es parienta, muy parienta, del señor de las Guinderas, aquel tan rico que tiene dos hijas y vive en el Malecón, y viene aquí a veces; y él se empeña en negarlo y en no darle un ochavo; pero ella se lo ha de ir a contar a las hijas el día que vayan más majas por el paseo. ¿Verdá, señora Porcona?

–Yyyy…, y es como el Evangelio, hiiigas… –contestó una voz temblosa como el balido de la cabra, y aguardentosa además.

–Explíquenos el parentesco, ande –sugirió Amparo, prestándose a la broma de su amiga.

La vieja alzó sus manos sarmentosas, se las pasó por los sangrientos ojos, y con muchas oscilaciones del labio inferior:

–Aunque… Diiios en persona estuviese allí –pronunció, señalando a uno de los gigantescos panes de tabaco–, yo no he de contar mentira. Oíd, espectadores del caso. Es de saber que el padre del padre de mi madre, o quiérese decir mi bisabuelo, digo, el abuelo de mis padres, era cuñado carnal, o quiérese decir, medio hermano, de la abuela de la madre política del señor de las Guinderas… De modo y manera es que yo vengo a ser parienta de muy cerquita, por la infinidá de la sangre…

–Y es mucha picardía que no le den siquiera un realito diario para aguardiente –sugirió malignamente *la Comadreja*.

–¡Aaaa… guardiente! –clamó la vieja acentuando el trémolo–. ¡Diera Diiios pan!

–Vamos, que un sorbito ya entró.

–Ni maldito olor dél me llegó tan siquiera; y eso que a mis añitos, hiiigas, ya os gustará calentar el estómago, que se pone como la pura nieve.

–¿Qué años tendrá, señora Porcona? Sin mentir.

–¡Busssss! –pronunció la desvenadora–. Así Dios me salve, ni sé de verdad el año que nací. Pero… –y bajó la temblona voz–sepades que cuando se

---

25   Apodo que significa mujer sucia.

their turn to be chosen and deveined. The atmosphere was squalid and icy cold at the same time. *The Weasel* was hopping about so as not to step on the tobacco leaves, and she sometimes called one of the women removing the veins by her name.

'Hello ... Señora Slattern!' she exclaimed, addressing one who seemed to have eyelids of raw flesh and white, dangling lips, which gave her the strangest, most frightening appearance in the world. 'Hello...! How's it going? How are those relatives of yours? You don't know it,' she added, turning to Amparo, 'but Señora Slattern is a relative, a very close relation to Señor de las Guinderas, that man who's so rich and has two daughters and lives in El Malecón, and who comes here sometimes; and he insists on denying it and not giving her a penny, but she ought to go up and tell his daughters any time they go, looking so nice, along the promenade. True, Señora Slattern?'

'Aaaand ... and it's the Gospel truth...,' replied a voice that trembled like the bleating of a goat, and husky too.

'Explain the relationship to us, go on,' suggested Amparo, lending herself to her friend's joke.

The old lady raised her gnarled hands, passed them over her bloodshot eyes, and with considerable oscillation of her bottom lip:

'Even if ... Go-oh-od were here in person,' pointing at one of the gigantic bales of tobacco, 'I'm not going to tell you a lie. Listen here, all you spectators, to this case. I want you to know that my mother's father's father, that is to say, my great-grandfather, I mean, my parents' grandfather, was a full brother-in-law, that is to say, a half-brother, of the grandmother of Señor de las Guinderas' mother-in-law... One way or another, that's how I come to be a very close relative, by blood infinity...'

'And it's a downright insult that they don't give you even a measly *real* a day for brandy,' *the Weasel* suggested maliciously.

'Braaaan ... dy!' the old lady exclaimed, accenting the tremolo: 'May Go-oh-od grant me bread!'

'Come on, a little sip has already gone down.'

'Not even a cursed sniff did I get of it; and even though when you're as old as I am ... you too will enjoy warming up your insides, which get to be like pure snow.'

'How old will that be, Señora Slattern? Without lying.'

'Pooh!' remarked the woman who deveined the leaves. 'May God help me, I don't really know the year I was born. But...' and she lowered her

puso aquí la fábrica, de las dieciséis primeritas fui yo que aquí trabajaron...

–¡Dónde irá la fecha! –murmuró *la Comadreja*.

Amparo le tiró del brazo, horrorizada de aquella imagen de la decrepitud que se le aparecía como vaga visión del porvenir. Recorrieron la sala de oreos, donde miles de mazos de cigarros se hallaban colocados en fila, y los almacenes, henchidos de bocoyes, que, amontonados en la sombra, parecen sillares de algún ciclópeo edificio, y de altas maniguetas de tabaco filipino envueltas en sus finos miriñaques de tela vegetal; atravesaron los corredores, atestados de cajones de blanco pino, dispuestos para el envase, y el patio interior, lleno de duelas y aros sueltos de destrozadas pipas; y por último, pararon en los talleres de la picadura.

Dentro de una habitación caleada, pero negruzca ya por todas partes, y donde apenas se filtraba luz al través de los vidrios sucios de alta ventana, vieron las dos muchachas hasta veinte hombres vestidos con zaragüelles de lienzo muy arremangados y camisa de estopa muy abierta, y saltando sin cesar. El tabaco los rodeaba; habíalos metidos en él hasta media pierna; a todos les volaba por hombros, cuello y manos, y en la atmósfera flotaban remolinos de él. Los trabajadores estribaban en la punta de los pies, y lo que se movía para brincar era el resto del cuerpo, merced a repetido y automático esfuerzo de los músculos; el punto de apoyo permanecía fijo. Cada dos hombres tenían ante sí una mesa o tablero, y mientras el uno, saltando con rapidez, subía y bajaba la cuchilla picando la hoja, el otro, con los brazos enterrados en el tabaco, lo revolvía para que el ya picado fuese deslizándose y quedase sólo en la mesa el entero, operación que requería gran agilidad y tino, porque era fácil que, al caer la cuchilla, segase los dedos o la mano que encontrara a su alcance. Como se trabajaba a destajo, los picadores no se daban punto de reposo: corría el sudor de todos los poros de su miserable cuerpo, y la ligereza del traje y violencia de las actitudes patentizaba la delgadez de sus miembros, el hundimiento del jadeante esternón, la pobreza de las garrosas canillas, el térreo color de las consumidas carnes. Desde la puerta, el primer golpe de vista era singular: aquellos hombres, medio desnudos, color de tabaco y rebotando como pelotas, semejaban indios cumpliendo alguna ceremonia o rito de sus extraños cultos. A Amparo no se le ocurrió este símil, pero gritó:

–Jesús... Parecen monos.

trembling voice, 'I'll have you know that when the factory was put here, I was one of the first sixteen who worked here ...'

'Where does it go!' murmured *the Weasel*.

Amparo pulled her by the arm, horrified by that image of decrepitude appearing before her like a vague vision of the future. They made their way through the airing room where thousands of bundles of cigars were lined up in rows, and the storerooms, stuffed with large casks, which, piled up in the background, look so much like the ashlars of some Cyclopean edifice; with tall bundles of Philippine tobacco wrapped in their fine-looking crinoline of vegetable fabric; they crossed through the corridors, crammed with white pine boxes ready for packing, and the inner patio, full of staves and loose metal hoops from broken barrels; and finally stopped in the workshops where the cutting was done.

Inside a whitewashed room, which was now black in every place and where the light was barely able to filter through the dirty panes of a high window, the two girls saw up to twenty men, wearing baggy linen breeches, rolled up very high, and wide open burlap shirts, jumping up and down nonstop. They were surrounded by tobacco; some were standing in it halfway up their legs; it flew all round their shoulders, necks and hands, and clouds of it were floating in the air. The workers would stand on the tips of their toes, and it was the rest of their bodies that they moved to jump up and down, thanks to repeated, automatic efforts of the muscles; the point of support remained fixed. Each pair of men had a table or a board in front of them, and while one of them, jumping up and down rapidly, was raising and lowering the large knife and cutting the leaves, the other one, his arms buried in tobacco, was turning it round and round, so that the pieces already cut slid off and only the whole leaves would remain on the table, an operation that required great agility and skill, because when the blade fell it was easy to slice off fingers or a hand that might be within reach. As they were doing piecework, the cutters didn't take time out to rest: the sweat ran from every pore of their wretched bodies, and the lightness of their clothes and the violence of their postures displayed their slender limbs, their sunken, panting chests, their feeble, twisted armbones, and the earthy colour of their emaciated flesh. From the doorway, the first glance gave an odd impression: those half-naked, tobacco-coloured men, bouncing around like balls, looked like Indians performing some ceremony or rite from their strange cults. This simile didn't occur to Amparo, but she shouted:

'My God... They look like monkeys.'

Chinto, al ver a las muchachas, se paró de pronto, y soltando el mango de la cuchilla, y sacudiéndose el tabaco, como un perro cuando sale de bañarse sacude el agua, se les acercó todo sudoroso, y con un sobrealiento terrible:

–Aquí se trabaja firme... –dijo, con ronca voz y aire de taco–. Se trabaja... –prosiguió jactanciosamente– y se gana el pan con los puños... ¡Se trabaja de Dios, conchas!

–Estás bonito; parece que te chuparon –exclamó *la Comadreja*, mientras Amparo lo miraba entre compadecida y asquillosa, admirándose de los estragos que en tan poco tiempo había hecho en él su perruno oficio. Le sobresalía la nuez, y bajo la grosera camisa se pronunciaban los omóplatos y el cúbito. Su tez tenía matices de cera, y a trechos manchas hepáticas; sus ojos parecían pálidos y grandes con relación a su cara enflaquecida.

–Pero, bruto –exclamó *la Tribuna*, con bondadoso acento–, estás sudando como un toro, y te plantas aquí, entre puertas, en este pasillo tan ventilado..., para coger la muerte.

–Bah... –y el mozo se encogió de hombros–. Si reparásemos a eso... Todo el día de Dios estamos aquí saliendo y entrando, y las puertas abiertas, y frío de aquí y frío de allí... Mira dónde afilamos la cuchilla.

Y señaló una rueda de amolar colocada en el mismo patio.

–La calor y el abrigo, por dentro... Ya se sabe que no teniendo aquí una gota... –y se dio una palmada en el diafragma.

–Así apestas, maldito –observó Ana–. Anda, que no sé qué sustancia le sacáis al condenado vinazo.

–Antes –pronunció sentenciosamente Amparo– sólo probabas vino algún día de fiesta que otro... Pues aquí no tienes por qué tomar vicios, que, gracias a Dios, la borrachera, a las cigarreras, poco daño nos hace...

–Las de arriba bien habláis, bien habláis... Si os metieran en estos trabajitos... Para lo que hacéis, que es labor de señoritas, con agua basta... Quiérese decir, vamos..., que un hombre no ha de ponerse chispo; pero un rifigelio..., un tentacá... ¿Queréis ver cómo bailo?

Volvió a manejar la cuchilla, mostrando su agilidad y fuerza en el duro ejercicio. De esta entrevista quedaron reconciliados la pitillera y el picador, que la acompañó algunas veces por la cuesta de San Hilario abajo, sin renovar sus pretensiones amorosas.

Chinto stopped suddenly when he saw the girls, and letting go of the knife handle and shaking off the tobacco like a dog shakes off water after a bath, went up to them, full of sweat and panting badly:

'You work hard here...' he said in a husky voice and in an easygoing manner. 'You work...' he continued boastfully, 'and you earn your crust by sheer hard work... You slave away, by God!'

'Just look at you; it looks like they've sucked the life out of you,' exclaimed *the Weasel*, while Amparo looked at him, half in pity and half in disgust, astonished at the ravages this dog's life had wrought on him in such a short time. His Adam's apple protruded and his shoulder blades and forearm bones were well defined under his coarse shirt. His complexion was the colour of wax, with hepatic spots here and there; his eyes seemed pale and large in contrast to his thin face.

'But you idiot,' exclaimed *la Tribuna* in a kindly tone, 'you're sweating like a bull, and you stand here, with doors on either side, in this drafty passageway ... you'll catch your death.'

'Bah...,' and the young man shrugged his shoulders. 'If we paid any attention to that... We're here the whole God-given day, going out and coming in, and the doors are open, and the cold comes from here and it comes from there... Look where we sharpen our knives.'

And he pointed to a grindstone set up right in the patio.

'Warmth and shelter, here inside you... Everyone knows that if you don't have a drop of something...' and he patted himself on the diaphragm.

'That's what makes you stink, you damn fool,' Ana observed. 'Come now, because I don't know what benefit you lot get from that confounded strong wine.

'Before,' Amparo pronounced sententiously, 'you only drank wine on one or two public holidays... So there's no reason to pick up new vices here, because, thank God, drunkenness isn't really a problem for us cigar makers...'

'All very well for you girls from upstairs, all very well. ...If you had to do these little jobs... For what you all do, which is work for young women, water is fine... What I mean, well ... a man shouldn't get tipsy; but refreshment ... a little something... Would you like to see how I dance?'

He started handling the cutting knife again, showing his agility and strength in this difficult exercise. This interview reconciled the cigar maker and the tobacco cutter, and he sometimes accompanied her along the Cuesta de San Hilario, without however resuming his amorous overtures.

XXII

EL CARNAVAL DE LAS CIGARRERAS

Unos días antes de carnavales se anuncia en la fábrica la llegada del *tiempo loco*, por bromas de buen género que se dan entre sí las operarias. Infeliz de la que, fiada en un engañoso recado, se aparta de su taller un minuto; a la vuelta le falta su silla, y vaya usted a encontrarla en aquel vasto océano de sillas y de mujeres que gritan a coro: «Atrás te queda. Delante te queda». A las víctimas de estos alegres deportes les resta el recurso de llevar bien escondido debajo del mantón un puntiagudo cuerno, y enseñarlo, por vía de desquite, a quien se divierte con ellas. También se puede, por medio de una tira estrecha de papel y un alfiler doblado a manera de gancho, aplicar una *lárgala* en la cintura, o estampar, con cartón recortado y untado de tiza, la figura de un borrico en la espalda. Otro chasco favorito de la fábrica es, averiguado el número del billete de lotería que tomó alguna bobalicona, hacerle creer que está premiado. Todos los años se repiten las mismas gracias, con igual éxito y causando idéntica algazara y regocijo.

Pero el jueves de Comadres es el día señalado entre todos para divertirse y echar abajo los talleres. Desde por la mañana llegan las cestas con los disfraces, y obtenido el permiso para bailar y formar comparsas, las oscuras y tristes salas se trasforman. El Carnaval que siguió al verano en que ocurrieron los sucesos de la Unión del Norte se distinguió por su animación y bullicio; hubo nada menos que cinco comparsas, todas extremadas y lucidas. Dos eran de mozas y mozos del país, vestidos con ricos trajes que traían prestados de las aldeas cercanas; otra, de grumetes; otra, de *señoritos* y *señoras*, y la última comparsa era una estudiantina. Las dos de labradores se diferenciaban mucho. En la primera se había buscado, ante todo, el lujo del atavío y la gallardía del cuerpo; las cigarreras más altas y bien formadas vestían con suma gracia el calzón de rizo, la chaqueta de paño, las polainas pespunteadas y la montera ornada con su refulgente pluma de pavo real, y para las mozas se habían elegido las muchachas más frescas y lindas, que lo parecían doblemente con el dengue de escarlata y la cofia ceñida con cinta de seda. La segunda comparsa aspiraba, más que

22

THE CARNIVAL OF THE CIGAR MAKERS

A few days before the period of carnival, the arrival of the *crazy time* is announced in the factory by the good-humoured jokes the women workers play on each other. Unfortunate is she who, trusting in a deceptive message, leaves her workplace for even a minute; upon her return, her chair is missing, and just try to find it in that vast ocean of chairs and women who are shouting in a chorus: 'It's behind you. It's in front of you.' For the victims of these lively jests there remains the recourse of carrying a sharp-pointed horn, carefully hidden beneath their shawls, and showing it as a form of retaliation to anyone enjoying herself at their expense. You can also use a narrow strip of paper and a pin bent like a hook, and attach it with the words *smack me* to someone's waist, or, with a piece of cardboard that had been cut out and smeared with chalk, imprint the shape of a donkey on someone's back. Another favourite trick in the factory is, having discovered the number of the lottery ticket some nitwit has purchased, to make her believe she's won a prize. The same jokes are repeated every year with equal success and causing exactly the same uproar and delight.

But the penultimate Thursday before Lent is the special day amongst all of them to enjoy oneself and throw the workshops into disorder. From the morning onwards, baskets arrive with the fancy dress, and once permission has been obtained to dance and form groups, the dark, sad rooms are transformed. The Carnival celebration which followed the summer of the events of the Northern Union was distinguished by its liveliness and its bustle; there were no less than five costumed groups, all supremely and splendidly turned out. Two consisted of country lasses and lads dressed in lovely costumes borrowed from nearby villages; another was made up of ship's boys; another of *young gentlemen and ladies*, and the last one was a student music group. The two groups of farm labourers were very different from each other. In the first group they had sought, above all, luxurious costumes and graceful bodies; the tallest and most nicely-shaped cigar makers were dressed with supreme grace in terry velvet breeches, woollen jackets, backstitched leggings and cloth caps adorned with a bright peacock feather; for the lasses those selected had been the prettiest and most fresh-looking girls, who seemed doubly so in their scarlet shawls and their caps surrounded by silk ribbons. What the second group aspired to, more than splendour of costume, was

a la bizarría del traje, a representar fielmente ciertos tipos de la comarca. Enrollada la saya en torno de la cintura; tocada la cabeza con un pañuelo de lana, cuyos flecos le formaban caprichosa aureola; asido el ramo de tejo, de cuyas ramas pendían rosquillas, ved a la peregrina que va a la romería famosa, a que no se eximen de concurrir, según el dicho popular, ni los muertos; a su lado, con largo redingote negro, gruesa cadena de similor, barba corrida y hongo de anchas alas, el *indiano*; acompáñanlo dos mozos de las rías saladas, luciendo su traje híbrido, pantalón azul con cuchillos castaños, chaleco de paño con enorme *sacramento* de bayeta en la espalda, faja morada, sombrero de paja con cinta de lana roja. Los estudiantes habían improvisado manteos con sayas negras y tricornios de cartón; con cuchara y tenedor de palo cruzados completaban el avío; los grumetes tenían sencillos trajes de lienzo blanco y cuellos azules; en cuanto a la comparsa de *señores*, había en ella un poco de todo, guantes sucios, sombreros ajados, vestidos de baile ya marchitos, mucho abanico y antifaces de terciopelo.

En mitad del taller de cigarros comunes se formó un corro y se alzó gran vocerío alrededor de la *Mincha*,[26] barrendera vieja, pequeña, redonda como una tinaja, que bailaba vestida de moharracho, con dos enormes jorobas postizas, un serón por corona, una escoba por cetro, un ruedo por manto real, la cara tiznada de hollín y un letrero en la espalda que decía, en letras gordas: «Viva la broma.» Incansable, pegaba brincos y más brincos, llevando el compás con el cuento de la escoba sobre las carcomidas tablas del piso. Pero bien pronto le robó la atención de sus admiradoras la estudiantina, que estaba toda encaramada en una mesa de metro y medio de largo por un metro escaso de ancho. Cómo danzaban allí unas doce chicas es difícil decirlo; ellas danzaban, acompañándose con panderetas y castañuelas y coreando al mismo tiempo habaneras y polcas. En aquella comparsa, la más alborotadora y risueña, figuraba *Guardiana*. Nunca el júbilo y la feliz improvisación de los pocos años brillaron como en el rostro de la pobre chica, que a tan poca costa y con tan poca cosa divertía sus penas. Era la valerosa pitillera chiquita y delgada; tenía a la sazón el rostro encendido, ladeado el tricornio, y con picaresco ademán repicaba un pandero roto ya, y muy engalanado de cintas.

Ana y Amparo figuraban entre los grumetes. *La Comadreja* hacía un grumete chusco, travieso y cínico; Amparo, el más hermoso muchacho que imaginarse pueda. Todo lo que su figura tenía de plebeyo lo disimulaba

---

26 Apodo que significa pequeña de cuerpo como el caracol marino llamado *mincha* en gallego.

a faithful representation of certain types from the region. See the pilgrim girl – her skirt wrapped round her waist; wearing a woollen headscarf, the fringes of which formed a capricious aureole; a yew branch held tightly, with caterpillars hanging from its boughs – on her way to the famous holy site at which, according to the poular saying, not even the dead are exempt from gathering. By her side, the well-off emigrant back from the New World,[xxx] with a long, black redingote, heavy pinchbeck chain, bushy beard and wide-brimmed bowler hat; two lads from the saline estuaries accompany him, sporting their hybrid costume of blue trousers with chestnut-coloured gores, woollen waistcoats with enormous religious symbols made from flannel on the back, purple sashes and straw hats with ribbons of red wool. The students had improvised long cloaks with black skirts and three-cornered hats made of cardboard; crossed wooden spoons and forks completed the gear; the ship's boys had simple white linen suits with blue collars. As for the group of *ladies and gentlemen*, there was a little bit of everything in it: dirty gloves, crumpled hats, faded dance dresses, lots of fans and velvet masks.

A ring was formed in the middle of the cigar workshop and they raised a hullabalo around *Periwinkle*, an old sweeper, short and rotund like an earthenware jar, who was dancing there, dressed as a clown with two enormous artificial humps, a large basket for a crown, a broom for a sceptre, a round mat for a royal mantle, her face blackened with soot, and a notice on her back in heavy letters which said 'Hurray for fun and jokes'. She seemed tireless as she kept jumping and jumping, keeping time with the tip of her broomstick against the rotten floorboards. But before very long, her admirers' attention was stolen by the student music group, who had climbed up onto a table that was a metre and a half long and barely a metre in width. How twelve or so girls could dance there is difficult to say; but they did dance, accompanying themselves with tambourines and castanets, and singing habaneras and polkas in chorus at the same time. The most boisterous and cheerful one appearing in that group was *Guardiana*. Never had the jubilation and happy improvisation of youth shone as they now did in the face of that poor girl who, with so little cost and effort, diverted her mind from sorrows. The valient cigar maker was so small and slender; at this moment her face was glowing, her three-cornered hat tilted to one side, and with an impish pose she was beating a broken tambourine all adorned with ribbons.

Ana and Amparo figured amongst the ship's boys. *The Weasel* made a droll, mischievous and cynical ship's boy; Amparo, the most attractive boy one could imagine. Everything that was common about her figure was

el traje masculino; ni las gruesas muñecas ni el recio pelo dañaban a su gentileza, que era de cierto notable y extraordinaria. La comparsa recorrió los talleres bailando y cantando, recibiendo bromas de las *señoras*, y alegrando la oscuridad de las salas con la nota blanca y azul de sus trajes. Sin embargo, no se podía dudar que la victoria quedaba por los labradores. A la cabeza de éstos estaba una mujer, casada ya, celebrada por buena moza, Rosa, la que llenaba con mayor presteza los *faroles* de picadura. Con el traje propio de su sexo, Rosa era un tanto corpulenta en demasía; con el del labrador no había que pedirle. La camisa de lienzo labrado dibujaba su ancho pecho; el calzón se ajustaba a maravilla a sus bien proporcionadas caderas; pendiente del cuello llevaba un ancho escapulario de raso, bordado de lentejuelas y sedas de colores. Debajo de la montera, un pañuelo de fular azul, atado a la usanza de los labriegos, le cubría el pelo. Apoyábase en la *moca* o porra claveteada de clavos de plata, y con acento melancólico y prolongado cantaba una copla del país, y contestábale desde enfrente una morenita vestida de ribereño, con su chaleco muy guarnecido de botones de filigrana y su faja recamada de pájaros y flores extravagantes, *echando la firma*, consistente en tres versos irregulares, improvisados siempre, con sujeción al asunto de la copla; al concluir la *firma*, salían del corro de espectadores varios ¡ju..., jurujú! agudísimos. Lo que hacía maravilloso efecto era oír, en los intervalos en que callaban las cantoras, unas malagueñas resonando en el otro extremo de la sala, mientras, por su parte la estudiantina se consagraba a las habaneras, cual si la anarquía de los trajes se comunicase a las canciones. En la comparsa de las *señoras* había una chica poseedora de bien timbrada voz y de muchísimo donaire para las coplas propias de la ciudad, tan distintas de las rurales, que, al paso que en éstas las vocales se alargan como un gemido, en las otras se pronuncian brevemente, produciendo al final de algunos versos una inflexión burlesca:

En el medio de la mar
Suspiraba una ballenaú,
y entre suspiros deciaú,
«Muchachas de Cartaenaú».

Y ¿quién tenía valor para trabajar en medio de la bulliciosa carnavalada? Algunas operarias hubo que al principio se encarnizaron en la labor, bajando la cabeza por no ver las máscaras; pero a eso de las tres de la tarde, cuando

concealed by the masculine costume; neither her thick wrists nor her coarse hair in any way spoilt her gracefulness, which was truly considerable and extraordinary. The group went round the workshops dancing and singing, subjected to the *señoras'* jesting remarks, brightening up the darkness of the rooms with the white and blue tones of their costumes. There was no doubt, however, that the victory belonged to those dressed as farmhands. At the head of these was a married woman, Rosa, admired for her good looks, who filled the paper wrappers with shredded tobacco very quickly. With clothes befitting her sex, Rosa was a bit too heavily-built; with a farmer's clothes, you couldn't ask for more. Her embroidered linen shirt outlined her full bosom; her breeches fitted marvellously over her well-proportioned hips; she wore a wide satin scapular hanging from her neck, embroidered with coloured sequins and bits of silk. Under her cloth cap, a blue foulard, tied according to the style of farmers, covered her hair. She was leaning on a *moca* or heavy club studded with silver nails, and singing a country ballad with a melancholy, prolonged tone; and opposite was a little brunette dressed as a riverside dweller, her waistcoat all garnished with filigree buttons and her sash embroidered with birds and extravagant flowers, *delivering the refrain*, consisting of three irregular lines, always improvised and subject to the same theme as the ballad; when she finished *the refrain*, several very piercing 'ju … jurujus' came from the circle of spectators. What produced a marvellous effect, during the intervals when the women were quiet, was hearing malagueñas resounding at the other end of the room, while, for its part, the student music group devoted itself to habaneras, as if the anarchic nature of the costumes had been communicated to their songs. In the group of *señoras* there was a girl who possessed a voice with excellent timbre and lots of the wit needed for ballads typical of the city, so different from those of the country; while in the latter, the vowels are dragged out like a sigh, in the others they are pronounced briefly, producing a burlesque inflection at the end of some lines:

In the middle of the sea
A whale did sigh-uh
And between sighs it did say-uh
'Maidens of Cartagena-uh.'

And who had the courage to work in the midst of that tumultuous carnival spirit? There were a number of workers in the shop who at first tried to devote themeselves wholeheartedly to their work, lowering their heads

la inocente saturnal llegaba a su apogeo, las manos cruzadas descansaban sobre la tabla de liar, y los ojos no sabían apartarse de los corros de baile y canto. Ocurrió un incidente cómico. El taller del desvenado quiso echar su cuarto a espadas, y organizó una comparsa numerosa; empeñáronse en formar parte de ella las más ancianas, las más felices, y la mascarada se improvisó de la manera siguiente: envolviéndose todas por la cabeza los mantones, sin dejar asomar más que la nariz, o una horrible careta de cartón, y colocándose en doble fila, haciendo de batidores cuatro que llevaban cogida por las esquinas una estera, en la cual reposaba, con los ojos cerrados, muy propia en su papel de difunta, la decana del taller, la respetable señora Porcona. Así colocadas y con extraño silencio recorrieron los talleres, dando no sé qué aspecto de aquelarre a la bulliciosa fiesta. Al punto recibió título aquella nueva y lúgubre comparsa: llamáronla la *Estadea*,[27] nombre que da la superstición popular a una procesión de espectros.

Diríase que el mago Carnaval, con poderoso conjuro, había desencantado la fábrica, y vuelto a sus habitantes la verdadera figura en aquel día. Muchachas en las cuales a diario nadie hubiera reparado quizá, confundidas como estaban entre las restantes, resplandecían, alumbradas por una ráfaga de hermosura, y un traje caprichoso, una flor en el pelo, revelaban gracias hasta entonces recónditas. Y no porque la coquetería desplegada en los disfraces llegase al grado que alcanza entre la gente de alto coturno que asiste a bailes de trajes y suele reflexionar y discurrir días y días antes de adoptar un disfraz –habiendo señorita que se viste de *Africana* por lucir una buena mata de pelo, o de *Pierrette* por mostrar un piececito menudo–; no, por cierto. Semejantes refinamientos se ignoraban en la fábrica. Ni a las viejas se les daba un comino de enseñar en la fuga del baile la seca anatomía de sus huesos, ni a las mozas un rábano de desfigurarse, verbigracia, pintándose bigotes con carbón. El caso era representar bien y fielmente tipos dados; un mozo, un quinto, un estudiante, un grumete. Habíalas con tan rara propiedad vestidas, que cualquiera las tomaría por varones; las feas y hombrunas se brindaban sin repulgos a encajarse el traje masculino, y lo llevaban con singular desenfado. Y de un extremo a otro de los talleres, entre el calor creciente y la broma y bullicio que aumentaban, corría una oleada de regocijo, de franca risa, de diversión natural, de juego libre y

---

27 Cortejo fúnebre que, según se dice, recorría de noche los caminos de la aldea.

in order not to see the masked figures, but by about three that afternoon, when the innocent Saturnalia had reached its peak, their crossed hands were resting on the rolling boards, and their eyes were unable to turn away from the clusters of women dancing and singing. A comic incident took place. The workshop where they deveined the leaves wanted to stick its oar in, and organised a large group; the oldest, happiest women in the section insisted on being a part of it, and a masquerade was improvised in the following manner: all of them covering their heads with a shawl, with only their noses poking out, or a horrible cardboard mask, and standing in a double line, making advance marchers of four women who were holding a straw mat by the corners, on which the senior member of the section, the respectable Señora Slattern, was resting with her eyes closed, very fitting in her role as a dead woman. Arranged in this fashion, they made their way through the workshops with a strange silence, giving a certain look of a witches' coven to the bustling festivities. That new and lugubrious carnival group was immediately given a title: they called it the *Funeral Cortège*, a name that popular superstition gives to a procession of ghosts.

One might almost say that the carnival wizard, with powerful magic, had freed the factory from a spell and returned its inhabitants to their natural appearance that day. Girls whom perhaps nobody would have noticed any other day, blending in as they did with the rest, were radiant, illuminated by a flash of beauty, and a capricious costume or a flower in the hair revealed charms hidden away until then. And not because the coquetry displayed in the disguises reached the level it attains amongst people in high society who attend fancy-dress balls and often spend days on end reflecting and pondering before adopting a costume – take the young lady who dresses as *Africana* in order to show off a fine head of hair, or *Pierrette* to display a dainty little foot; no, of course not. Such refinements were unheard of at the factory. Neither did the old ladies care less about revealing their dried up, bony anatomy in the flight of the dance, nor the young girls give a hoot when they disfigured themselves, for example, by painting on moustaches with coal. The point was to represent certain types faithfully and well; a young man, a conscript, a student, a ship's boy. There were some dressed with such total likeness that anyone would take them for men; the ugly, mannish ones offered to put on male clothing without any compunction and wore it with an extraordinary lack of inhibition. And from one end of the workshops to the other, amidst the rising heat and the jesting and tumult that kept on growing, ran a wave of rejoicing, frank laughter, natural fun, and

sano; una afirmación enérgica de la femineidad de la fábrica. No cohibidas por la presencia del hombre, gozaban cuatro mil mujeres aquel breve rayo de luz, aquel minuto de júbilo expansivo situado entre dos eternidades de monótona labor.

Hacia las cuatro de la tarde no cabía ya la algazara y bulla en las salas; todo el mundo perecía de calor; a las disfrazadas de aldeanos las ahogaba su traje de paño, y se apoyaban, descoyuntadas de tanto reír, molidas de tanto bailar, roncas de tanto canticio, en los estantes, abanicándose con la montera. *La Comadreja*, que ya no sabía cómo procurarse un poco de fresco, tuvo una idea.

–Si nos dejasen armar un corro en el patio, chicas, ¿eh?

Pareció de perlas la ocurrencia, y salieron al patio de entrada, y de allí al árido campillo colindante, perteneciente también a la fábrica. Estaba el día sereno y apacible; el sol doraba las hierbas quemadas por la escarcha, y se colaba en tibios rayos oblicuos al través de los desnudos árboles. El ambiente era más templado que otra cosa, como suele suceder en el clima de Marineda durante los meses de febrero y marzo. Al desembocar en el campo la alegre multitud, huyeron espantadas unas cuantas gallinas y algunos borregos sucios y torpes patos, que correteaban por allí y eran los únicos pobladores del mezquino oasis, limitado de una parte por la vetusta tapia, de otra, por cobertizos atestados de fardos de vena, y de otra, por el taller de cigarros peninsulares, aislado del edificio de la Granera. Al punto se formaron dos corros con más espacio que arriba, y la frescura de la tardecita restituyó las ganas de bailar a las exhaustas máscaras.

¡Oh, si ellas hubiesen sabido que, desde las próximas alturas de Colinar, las miraban dos pares de ojos curiosos, indiscretos y osados! De la cima de un cerrillo que permitía otear todo el patio de la fábrica, dos hombres apacentaban la vista en aquel curioso cuanto inesperado espectáculo. Uno de ellos rondaba muchas veces las cercanías de la Granera, pero nunca en aquel predio había visto más seres vivientes que canteros picando sillares de granito y aves de corral escarbando la tierra. Baltasar ignoraba los detalles del Carnaval de las cigarreras, y apenas entendería lo que estaba viendo, si Borrén, mejor informado, no se tomase el trabajo de explicárselo.

–Generalmente, estas mascaradas son de puertas adentro; pero hoy, como

free, wholesome playfulness; a vigorous affirmation of the femininity of the factory. Uninhibited by the presence of men, four thousand women enjoyed that brief ray of light, that moment of expansive jubilation situated between two eternities of monotonous labour.

By four that afternoon, the uproar and racket was no longer limited to the rooms inside; everyone was dying of heat; women dressed up as country boys and girls were feeling stifled in their heavy woollen clothes and were leaning against the shelves, their sides splitting from so much laughter, exhausted from so much dancing, hoarse from so much singing, fanning themselves with their cloth caps. *The Weasel*, who could no longer come up with some way to cool off a bit, had an idea.

'What if they let us form a group in the courtyard, eh girls?'

It seemed a splendid idea, and they went out into the courtyard at the entrance, and from there into a small, arid field adjoining it, which also belonged to the factory. The day was serene and mild; the sun gilt the frost-damaged grass and filtered through the naked trees with its warm, oblique rays. The atmosphere was more temperate than anything else, as often happens with the weather in Marineda during the months of February and March. As the joyful multitude flowed out into the field, a few hens ran away in fright, as well as some dirty lambs and some awkward ducks that were running around there and were the only occupants of that wretched little oasis, bordered on one side by the very old wall, on another by sheds crammed with bundles of tobacco leaf veins, and on another by the workshop where they made cigars from Spanish tobacco, isolated from the main building of the Granary itself. They immediately formed two groups with more space than upstairs, and the cool air of the late afternoon rekindled the desire to dance in these exhausted, masked women.

But if they had only known that from the nearby heights of Colinar two pairs of curious, indiscreet and bold eyes were watching them! From the top of a small hill, which allowed you to survey the entire factory courtyard, two men were feasting their eyes on that curious, entirely unexpected spectacle. One of them was often prowling around the area near the Granary, but he had never seen any living things on that property other than stonecutters breaking up granite ashlars and chickens scratching at the ground. Baltasar had no knowledge of the details of the Carnival of the cigar makers, and probably wouldn't understand what he was seeing if Borrén, who was better informed, didn't take the trouble to explain it to him.

'These masquerades are generally held indoors; but today, as it's hot

hace calor y el día está bueno, salen al fresco a bailar... ¡Qué casualidad, hombre!

–Casualidad es, tiene usted razón. En todas partes he de encontrármela.

Y al decir así, señalaba el teniente al corro de los grumetes. Mientras los paisanos punteaban y repicaban un paso de baile regional, los grumetillos habían elegido el zapateado, donde la viveza del meridional bolero se une al vigor muscular que requieren las danzas del Norte. Bien ajena que la viese ningún profano, puesta la mano en la cadera, echada atrás la cabeza, alzando de tiempo en tiempo el brazo para retirar la gorrilla que se le venía a la frente, Amparo bailaba. Bailaba con la ingenuidad, con el desinterés, con la casta desenvoltura que distingue a las mujeres cuando saben que no las ve varón alguno, ni hay quien pueda interpretar malignamente sus pasos y movimientos. Ninguna valla de pudor verdadero o falso se oponía a que se balancease su cuerpo siguiendo el ritmo de la danza dibujando una línea serpentina desde el talón hasta el cuello. Su boca, abierta para respirar ansiosamente, dejaba ver la limpia y firme dentadura, la rosada sombra del paladar y de la lengua; su impaciente y rebelde cabello se salía a mechones de la gorra, como revelación traidora del sexo a que pertenecía el lindo grumete –si ya la suave comba del alto seno y las fugitivas curvas del elegante torso no lo denunciasen asaz–. Tan pronto, describiendo un círculo, hería con el pie la tierra, como, sin moverse de un sitio, zapateaba de plano, mientras sus brazos, armados de castañuelas, se agitaban en el aire, y bajaban y subían a modo de alas de ave cautiva que prueba a levantar el vuelo.

and such a fine day, they've come out in the open air to dance... What a coincidence!'

'It's a coincidence, you're right. I seem to be running into her everywhere.'

And as he said this, the lieutenant pointed to the group of ship's boys. While the country boys and girls plucked and beat out the step of a regional dance, the little ship's boys had chosen the zapateado, a tap dance which combines the lively character of the meridional bolero with the muscular vigour required for the dances of the North. Totally oblivious that some profane eye might be watching her, Amparo was dancing with her hand on her hip, her head thrown back, raising her arm from time to time to pull back the small cap that kept coming down over her forehead. She was dancing with the ingenuousness, selflessness and chaste naturalness that is characteristic of women when they know that no male can see them, and when there is nobody to interpret their steps and movements in a malicious way. No barrier of true or false modesty stood in the way of her body swaying to the rhythm of the dance, tracing a serpentine line from her heels to her neck. Her mouth, open so she could breathe eagerly, revealed her strong, clean teeth, the pink shadow of her palate and her tongue; locks of her impatient, rebellious hair kept falling out from her cap, as a treacherous revelation of the sex to which the pretty ship's boy belonged – if the soft sweep of her full bosom and the fleeting curves of her elegant torso didn't betray her enough. No sooner did she describe a circle and stamp on the ground than she tapped her foot directly upon it, without moving place, while her arms waved in the air with the castanets she was holding, moving up and down like the wings of a captive bird trying to rise up in flight.

XXIII

EL TENTADOR

Al descender de su observatorio, echados por las sombras de la noche, que envolvían el patio de la fábrica y cubrían la estruendosa retirada de las cigarreras vestidas ya con sus trajes usuales, Baltasar iba silencioso y concentrado, Borrén muy locuaz. El bueno del capitán no cabía en sí de gozo, ni más ni menos que si la aventura de ver bailar a *la Tribuna* le importase a él directamente. Hay en el mundo aficiones y gustos muy diversos: éste chochea por monedas roñosas; aquél, por libracos viejos; el de más acá, por caballos, y el de más allá, por sellos y cajas de fósforos... Borrén había chocheado, chocheaba y chochearía toda su arrastrada vida por la hermosura, encantos y perfecciones de la mujer. Había adquirido para conocer la belleza, y sobre todo el atractivo, ese golpe de vista, ese tino especial que permite a los expertos, sin ejercer ni dominar las artes, apreciar con exactitud el mérito de un cuadro, el estilo de un mueble, la época de un monumento. Nadie como Borrén para descubrir beldades inéditas, para predecir si una muchacha valdría o no «muchas pesetas» andando el tiempo y decidir si poseía la quisicosa llamada gracia, salero, gancho, ángel, *chic*, buena sombra y de otros mil modos, lo cual prueba que es indefinible.

La originalidad del caso está en que con toda su afición a las faldas y sus profundos conocimientos de estética aplicada, no se refería de Borrén la más insignificante historieta. Viviendo siempre en una atmósfera fuertemente cargada de electricidad amorosa, nunca le hirió la chispa. Practicaba, en materia de amoríos, el más puro y desinteresado altruismo. Si no podía andar entre las muchachas asegurándoles que Fulanito se alampaba[28] por ellas, o que Zutanito se moría por sus pedazos, se arrimaba a los jóvenes, calentándoles los cascos, encendiéndoles la sangre, hablándoles del pie de tal chica: «Hombre, un pie que me cabe en la palma de la mano»; o del color de cuál otra: «Hombre, si parece que se da agua de Barcelona, y no me consta que aquello es natural.» Borrén sabía de las criadas que llevan y traen cartitas, de los paseos retirados donde es fácil tropezarse cuando hay buena voluntad, de los peladeros de pava, de las butacas que en el teatro ofrecen más comodidad para hacer el oso; era el primero a olfatear los trapicheos,

---

28 Se apasionaba.

23

THE TEMPTER

Baltasar was silent and absorbed and Borrén very talkative when they descended from their observatory, driven away by the shadows of night shrouding the factory courtyard and covering the noisy departure of the cigar makers, now dressed in their everyday clothes. The good captain couldn't contain his great pleasure, no more or less than if the adventures of watching *la Tribuna* dance were of direct importance to him. There are all sorts of interests and tastes in the world: this one dotes on rusty old coins; that one on tedious old books; yet another on horses, and still another on stamps and match boxes … Borrén had doted, was still doting and would dote for his whole miserable life on the beauty, charms and perfections of women. In order to recognise beauty, and above all appeal, he had acquired that glance, that special skill which allows experts, without even practising or mastering the arts, to appraise the merits of a painting, the style of a piece of furniture or the period of a monument with great precision. There was no one like Borrén for discovering unknown beauties, for predicting whether a certain girl would or wouldn't be worth 'her weight in gold' with the passage of time, and deciding if she possessed that enigmatic quality called grace, allure, sex appeal, charm, chic, wit and countless other things, which goes to prove that it can't be defined.

The remarkable aspect of the matter lies in the fact that, with all his fondness for skirt and his profound knowledge of applied aesthetics, there was no mention of Borrén in even the most trivial anecdote. Living constantly in an atmosphere strongly charged with amorous electricity, the spark never struck him. In matters regarding love affairs, he always practised the purest and most selfless altruism. If he was unable to go around among the girls assuring them that Tom was longing for them, or that Dick was madly in love with them, he would get close to the young men, egging them on, heating up their blood, speaking to them about a certain girl's foot: 'Indeed, a foot that fits in the palm of my hand'; or about another's complexion: 'Why, it looks like she uses water from Barcelona, and that doesn't seem natural to me.' Borrén knew about which servants would deliver and bring back love notes, about the remote public walks where it is easy to run into someone with a bit of good will, about the places to go wooing, or the most comfortable seats at the theatre for courting; he was the first to sniff out any shady dealing,

las bodas, los escandalillos y los truenos incipientes. No era Borrén un casamentero, porque, generalmente hablando, el casamentero se propone un fin moral, y a Borrén la moral –hombre, con franqueza– le tenía sin cuidado. Si el cuento acababa en boda, bien, y si no, lo propio; Borrén hacía arte por el arte; el amor le parecía objeto suficiente de sí mismo.

Para todo enamorado de Marineda, especialmente si pertenecía a la guarnición, el complemento de la dicha era esta idea: «Voy a contárselo a Borrén.» Y Borrén, como un espejo complaciente, de los que hacen favor, le devolvía la imagen de su felicidad, no exacta, sino aumentada, embellecida, multiplicada, radiante. «Vamos a pasearle la calle a la novia», le decían sus amigos, cogiéndole del brazo. Y Borrén giraba tardes enteras delante de una manzana de casas, parafraseando las observaciones de algún amador novel que exclamaba: «Ya alzó el visillo…, se asoma…, no; es la hermana… Ahora sí… ¡Cómo me mira…! ¡Hola!, tiene la mantilla puesta…» Jamás mostró Borrén cansarse de su papel de reflector y comentador; y cuentan que las chicas, guiadas por infalible instinto, le trataban como se trata a los inofensivos y a los mandrias; aunque él se derretía, acaramelaba y amerengaba todo, jamás le tomaron por lo serio.

Baltasar no le había buscado para confidente; Borrén se ofreció, y es más, atizó el incendio, echó leña a la hoguera con sus frases de pólvora y dinamita. Aquella tarde, cuando juntos bajaban hacia la ciudad, el más animado, el más exaltado era Mefistófeles; Fausto callaba, meditando en lo comprometidos y engorrosos que son ciertos enredos en poblaciones de provincia, donde uno tiene madre y hermanas. Mefistófeles, ¡pobre diablo!, no se cansaba, entre tanto, de ponderar los primores del grumete. Cada vez que el confidente y el enamorado pasaban cerca de un farol, la luz se proyectaba en la fisonomía de Borrén, siempre movida, agitada y descompuesta, cómica a pesar del exagerado carácter viril que a primera vista le imprimían los cerdosos mostachos, las pobladas cejas y la prominente nuez. En su aspecto, Borrén era semejante a los guardias civiles de madera que suelen colocarse en el frontispicio de los hórreos y molinos del país: a despecho de sus bigotazos formidables, bien se les conoce que son muñecos.

–Dígole a usted, Borrén –exclamó Baltasar, resolviéndose por fin a formular en voz alta su pensamiento–, que no comprende usted lo que es Marineda … ni lo que es mi madre. Me resultarían mil disgustos, mil complicaciones… Aborrezco los escándalos.

weddings, little scandals and bombshells about to burst. Borrén was not a matchmaker, because, generally speaking, a matchmaker has a moral purpose in mind, and Borrén, well frankly, he didn't care about morality. If the affair ended in a wedding, great, and if not, it was all the same. Borrén practised art for art's sake; love seemed a sufficient justification in itself to him.

For anyone in Marineda who was in love, especially if he belonged to the local garrison, the ultimate in good fortune was this idea: 'I'm going to tell Borrén about it.' And Borrén, like an obliging mirror, one of those that do you a favour, would return his image of happiness, not exactly the same, but enlarged, embellished, multiplied and radiant. 'Let's take a stroll down the street where my sweetheart lives,' his friends would say to him, taking hold of his arm. And Borrén would spend entire afternoons in front of a block of houses, paraphrasing the observations of some inexperienced lover as he exclaimed, 'She's just raised the lace curtain … she's looking out … no; it's her sister… Now it's her… See how she's looking at me…! Hello, she's got her mantilla on…' Borrén never showed any sign of tiring of his role as a reflector and a commentator; and they say the young girls, guided by an infallible instinct, treated him as you would treat inoffensive and useless people; even though he came over all sentimental, making everything sweet and sugary, they never took him seriously.

Baltasar had not sought him out as a confidant; Borrén had offered himself, and even more he fanned the flames, added fuel to the fire with the gunpowder and dynamite of his remarks. That afternoon, while they were going down towards the city together, Mephistopheles was the more animated, the more excited; Faust was quiet, meditating on the compromising and awkward thing about certain love affairs in provincial towns where one has a mother and sisters. In the meantime, Mephistopheles – the poor devil! – didn't tire of weighing up the delights of the ship's boy. Every time the confidant and the enamoured young man passed near a streetlamp, the light was cast on Borrén's face, forever restless, agitated and distorted, comic in spite of the exaggerated virility imprinted upon it at first glance by the bristly moustache, the bushy eyebrows and the prominent Adam's apple. In appearance, Borrén was similar to the wooden figures of rural policemen that are usually placed on the front part of country granaries and mills: in spite of their formidable moustaches, you can plainly see that they are just puppets.

'I'm telling you, Borrén,' Baltasar exclaimed when he decided at last to express his thoughts aloud, 'you don't understand what Marineda is like … nor what my mother is like. I would end up with a thousand vexations, endless complications … I loathe scandals.'

–¡Hombre, qué juventud tan sosa son ustedes! Parece mentira que habiendo visto lo que vimos...

–No me conviene, lo dicho; me alegraré de que me destinen a cualquiera parte. Si me quedo aquí, es fácil... Y después, ¿sabe usted lo que es esa fábrica? Una masonería de mujeres, que, aunque hoy se arranquen el moño, mañana se ayudan todas como una legión de diablos. Me desacreditarían; me crearían un conflicto.

–No le hacía a usted tan medroso.

–La verdad, Borrén; tengo más miedo a las hablillas, si cuadra, que a un balazo. Será una tontería, pero me fastidia infinito ser el héroe de la temporada.

–Vamos, hombre, franqueza. Usted también recela verse envuelto en las redes de esa chica, y tener que casarse...

Baltasar sonrió sin afectación, pero con tal señorío de sí mismo, que Borrén se encogió de hombros.

–Pues entonces...

–Por un lado, sí, lo acierta usted; soy un majadero en abrigar tales escrúpulos. Pasa uno así los mejores años de su vida, y ¿qué? Llega uno a viejo sin haber vivido...

Aquí el teniente se detuvo; una idea burlesca le impulsaba a sonreírse otra vez, pensando que el capitán se hallase justamente en el caso de declinar hacia la edad madura sin tener qué ofrecer a Dios ni qué contar al diablo. Borrén, entre tanto, aprobaba calurosamente las últimas palabras de Baltasar, las desenvolvía, las consideraba desde nuevos aspectos; en suma, soplaba a fin de que la llama prendiese mejor. Tan bien desempeñó su oficio mefistofélico, que Baltasar convino en reunirse al día siguiente con él para meditar un plan de ataque que debelase la republicana virtud de la oradora. Pero al acudir a la entrevista, que era, por más señas, en el terreno neutral del café, Borrén conoció que Baltasar traía alguna extraordinaria nueva.

–Ya no hay necesidad de concertar planes –declaró el teniente con forzada risa–. ¿No se lo decía yo a usted? Me destinan allá..., a Navarra. La cosa anda mal.

–¡Bah!... Cuatro bandidos que salen de aquí y de acullá; hombre, partidillas sueltas.

–Partidillas sueltas... Ya, ya me lo contará usted dentro de unos meses. El cariz del asunto se pone cada vez más feo. Entre esos salvajes que quieren

'Truly, you young people are so silly! It's unbelievable that after what we've seen...'

'It doesn't suit me, you can't deny it; I'll be happy for them to post me anywhere. If I stay here, it's easy. ...And afterwards, do you have any idea what the factory is like? A Masonic lodge for women who, even if they pull each other's hair out today, will all help each other like a legion of demons tomorrow. They would bring disgrace on me; they would create all kinds of discord.'

'I didn't consider you so fearful.'

'To tell the truth, Borrén, I'm more afraid of gossip, if there's some truth in it, than a bullet wound. It may be foolish, but it annoys me no end being the romantic hero of the season.'

'Come on, let's be frank. You're also wary of finding yourself enmeshed in that girl's nets, and having to get married...'

Baltasar smiled without affectation, but with such self-mastery that Borrén shrugged his shoulders.

'Well, then...'

'On the one hand, yes, you're right; I'm a fool to harbour such scruples. You spend the best years of your life in this way, and what's left? You end up old without having really lived...'

At this point the lieutenant stopped; a funny idea was causing him to smile again, thinking that the captain might find himself in that exact situation of declining into his mellow years without having anything to offer God or anything to recount to the Devil. Borrén, in the meantime, enthusiastically approved of Baltasar's last words, unravelling and considering them from new perspectives; in short, he was blowing on them so that the flame might burn better. So well did he carry out his Mephistophelian duty that Baltasar agreed to meet up with him the following day to work out a plan of attack to conquer the orator's republican virtue. But when he turned up at the interview, which, to be precise, took place in the neutral terrain of a café, Borrén realised that Baltasar had some extraordinary news for him.

'There's no longer any need to make plans,' the lieutenant declared with forced laughter. Didn't I tell you so? They're posting me over there ... in Navarre. Things are going badly.'

'Bah...! A few bandits who pop up here and there; I'm telling you, insignificant bands on the loose.'

'Insignificant bands on the loose... Sure, you can tell me about it in a few months. The situation is looking uglier and uglier. Between those savages

entrar en burro en las iglesias y fusilan por chiste las imágenes, y los otros caribes que cortan el telégrafo y queman las estaciones..., verá usted, verá usted qué tortilla se nos prepara. Aquí nadie se entiende. ¡Mire usted que hasta Montpensier, que parecía formal, meterse en ese desafío estúpido! Él quería ser rey; pero el haber matado al perdis de su primo le cuesta la corona y a nosotros un ojo de la cara, porque como no venga Satanás en persona a arreglarnos, no sé lo que sucederá... Deme usted un cigarro ... si lo tiene usted ahí.

Borrén le alargó la petaca, y Baltasar encendió nerviosamente un pitillo.

–Vamos, ¿cuántos candidatos dirá usted que hay al trono? –prosiguió, echando leve bocanada de humo al techo–. Vaya usted contando por los dedos, si la paciencia le alcanza. Espartero..., uno. Dirá usted que es un estafermo; bien, pero los restos del partido progresista, todo cuanto gastó morrión, y algunos chiflados de buena fe, le aclaman. ¿No ha visto usted en las tiendas el retrato de Baldomero Primero con manto real? El hijo de Isabel Segunda, dos; su madre abdicó o abdicará. Éste, al menos, representa algo; pero es un rapaz: para jugar a la pelota serviría. El pretendiente, tres..., y mire usted, lo que es ése dará mucho juego; ya empieza todo el mundo a llamarle Carlos Séptimo. Reúne él solo más partidarios que todos los demás juntos, y gente cruda, de trabuco y pelo en pecho. El duque de Aosta, un italiano..., cuatro. Un alemán, que se llama Ho ... ho..., en fin, un nombre difícil; los periódicos satíricos lo convirtieron en *Ole, ole, si me eligen*..., cinco. La regencia trina..., seis o, por mejor decir, ocho. Y Ángel Primero..., nueve. ¡Ah! Se me olvidaba el de Portugal, que anda remiso ... y Montpensier. Once. ¿Qué tal?

–Pero..., así, candidatos formales... ¡Mozo, café y coñac!

–No, gracias, lo tomé en casa... Claro: candidatos serios, por hoy, don Carlos y la república. El caso es que entre todos no nos dejarán hueso sano... Por de pronto, yo me las guillo. ¿Quiere usted algo para aquellos vericuetos?

–Hombre..., ¡qué lástima! ¡Ahora que íbamos a emprenderla con la pitillera, que es de oro!

–¡Pchs!... Si algún trabucazo no lo impide..., a la vuelta.

who want to ride their donkeys into church and shoot at the holy images for fun, and those other barbarians who cut the telegraph lines and burn down the stations… You'll see what trouble they're cooking up for us. Nobody seems to agree with anyone else around here. Look, even Montpensier, who seemed a reliable person, gets involved in that stupid duel![15] He wanted to be king, but the fact that he killed that rake of a cousin of his cost him the crown and us a fortune, because unless Satan himself comes in person to sort us out, I don't know what will happen… Would you give me a cigarette … if you've got one.'

Borrén passed him his cigarette case, and Baltasar lit a cigarette nervously.

'Come on, how many candidates would you say there are for the throne?' he continued, blowing a small puff of smoke towards the ceiling. 'Get counting on your fingers, if you've got enough patience. Espartero … one. You might say he's a simpleton; fine, but the rest of the Progressive party, those who wore a morion helmet, and a few nutcases of good faith, all acclaim him. Haven't you seen in all the stores the portrait of Baldomero I with a royal mantle? Isabel II's son, number two; his mother has abdicated or is going to abdicate. He, at least, represents something, but he's a youngster, and all he'd be good for is playing ball. The pretender, number three … and look, that one is really going to make trouble; everyone's already starting to call him Charles VII. On his own he has more supporters than all the others put together, and they're crude people with blunderbusses and hairy chests. The Duke of Aosta, an Italian, number four. A German, whose name is Hu … hu … well, a difficult name.[16] The satirical newspapers have converted it into *Hurrah, hurrah if they elect me* … number five. The tripartite Regency … number six, or to put it better, number eight. And Angel I … number nine. Oh, I was forgetting the one from Portugal, who's going around doing nothing … and Montpensier.[xxxi] Eleven. What do you think?'

'But … how about serious candidates… Waiter, coffee and cognac!'

'No, thank you, I had some at home… Of course: serious candidates. For now, Don Carlos and the republic. The fact of the matter is that between them all, they won't leave us one sound bone… For the time being, I'm off. Do you want something for that rugged path ahead?'

'Really … what a pity! Just when we were going to start up something with the cigar maker, who really is a treasure.'

'Pshaw…! If some blunderbuss doesn't stop me … when I get back.'

---

15 See endnote xxiv.
16 The reference is to Leopold, Prince of Hohenzollern, one of the candidates for the Spanish throne.

XXIV

EL CONFLICTO RELIGIOSO

Desde que las Cortes Constituyentes votaron la monarquía, Amparo y sus correligionarias andaban furiosas. Corría el tiempo, y las esperanzas de la Unión del Norte no se realizaban, ni se cumplían los pronósticos de los diarios. ¡Que hoy!... ¡que mañana!... ¡que nunca, por lo visto! ¡En vez de la suspirada federal, un rey, un tirano de fijo, y tal vez un extranjero! Por estas razones en la fábrica se hacía política pesimista y se anunciaba y deseaba que al Gobierno «se lo llevase Judas». Dos cosas, sobre todo, alteraban la bilis de las cigarreras: el incremento del partido carlista y los ataques a la Virgen y a los santos. A despecho de la acusación de «echar contra Dios», lanzada por las campesinas a las ciudadanas, la verdad es que, con contadísimas excepciones, todas las cigarreras se manifestaban acordes y unánimes en achaques de devoción. Ellas serían más o menos ilustradas, pero allí había mucha y fervorosa piedad. Es cierto que sobre el altar de pésimo gusto dórico existente en cada taller depositaban las operarias sus mantones, sus paraguas, el hatillo de la comida; mas este género de familiaridad no indicaba falta de respeto, sino la misma costumbre de ver allí el ara santa, ante la cual nadie pasaba sin persignarse y hacer una genuflexión. Y es lo curioso que a medida que la revolución se desencadenaba y el republicanismo de la fábrica crecía, tomaban incremento las prácticas religiosas. El cepillo colocado al lado del altar, donde los días de cobranza cada operaria echaba alguna limosna, nunca se vio tan lleno de monedas de cobre; el cajón que contenía la cera de alumbrar estaba atestado de blandones y velas; más de sesenta cirios iluminaban los días de novena el retablo; primero les faltaría a las cigarreras agua para beber que aceite a la lámpara encendida diariamente ante sus imágenes predilectas, una Nuestra Señora de la Merced de doble tamaño con los cautivos arrodillados a sus plantas, un San Antón con el sayal muy adornado de esterilla de oro, un Niño-Dios con faldellines huecos y su mundito azul en las manos. Nunca se realizó con más lucimiento la novena de San José, que todas rezaron mientras trabajaban, volviéndose de cara al altar para decir los actos de fe y la letanía, y berreando el último día los gozos con mucha unción, aunque sin afinación bastante. Jamás

24

THE RELIGIOUS CONFLICT

From the moment that the constituent assembly voted for a monarchy, Amparo and her fellow party members went around in a rage. Time was flying by and the hopes of the Northern Union were not materialising, and nor were the predictions of the daily newspapers coming true. Maybe today…! Maybe tomorrow! Maybe never, apparently! Instead of the federal state they had longed for, a king, a tyrant for sure, and maybe a foreigner! For these reasons, the political atmosphere in the factory was turning pessimistic and they were announcing and wishing that the government 'go to hell'. Two things in particular galled the cigar makers: the growth of the Carlist party and the attacks on the Virgin and the saints. In spite of the accusation that 'they were going against God', hurled by women from the country at those from the city, the truth is that, with very rare exceptions, all the cigar makers revealed themselves to be in full and unanimous accord in matters of religious devotion. A woman might be more or less enlightened, but there was a lot of fervent piety there. It's true that the women workers deposited their shawls, umbrellas and little packs of food on the awful Doric altars found in each workshop; however, this kind of familiarity didn't indicate a lack of respect, but rather the same habit of seeing the sacred altar there which nobody would pass in front of without making the sign of the cross and genuflecting. And the curious thing is that as the revolution was breaking loose and republicanism growing in the factory, religious practices were increasing too. The alms box placed next to the altar, where each worker deposited a charitable offering on paydays, had never been so full of copper coins; the big box that contained the accoutrements for devotional lighting was crammed with wax tapers and candles; more than sixty long candles illuminated the altarpiece on novena days; the cigar makers would sooner go without water to drink than oil to light the lamp daily in front of their favourite images, a double size Our Lady of Mercy with captives kneeling at her feet, a Saint Anthony with a sackcloth heavily adorned with gold braid, and an Infant Jesus with a loose gown and a small blue globe of the world in his hands. Never was the novena of Saint Joseph celebrated with greater brilliance, as all the women prayed while they worked, turning their faces towards the altar to repeat the acts of faith and the litany, bellowing out on the final day the poem in honour of the Virgin with considerable

produjo tanto la colecta para la procesión del Santo Entierro y novena de los Dolores; y, por último, sin ocasión alguna tuvo el numen protector de la fábrica, la Virgen del Amparo, tantas ofertas, culto y limosnas, sin que por eso quedase olvidada su rival Nuestra Señora de la Guardia, estrella de los mares, patrona de los navegantes por la bravía costa.

Bien habría en la Granera media docena de espíritus fuertes, capaces de blasfemar y de hablar sin recato de cosas religiosas; pero dominados por la mayoría, no osaban soltar la lengua. A lo sumo se permitían maldecir de los curas, acusarlos de inmorales y codiciosos, o renegar de que se «metiesen en política» y tomasen las armas para traer el «escurantismo y la Inquisición»: cuestiones más trascendentales y profundas no se agitaban, y si a tanto se atreviese alguien, es seguro que le caería encima un diluvio de cuchufletas y de injurias.

–¡Está el mundo perdido! –decía la maestra del partido de Amparo, mujer de edad madura, de tristes ojos, vestida de luto siempre desde que había visto morir de viruelas a dos gallardos hijos que eran su orgullo–. ¡Está el mundo revuelto, muchachas! ¿No sabéis lo que pasa allá por las Cortes?

–¿Qué pasará?

–Que un diputado por Cataluña dice que dijo que ya no había Dios, y que la Virgen era esto y lo otro… Dios me perdone, Jesús mil veces.

–¿Y no le mataron allí mismo? ¡Pícaro, infame!

–¡Mal hablado, lengua de escorpión! ¡No habrá Dios para él, no; que él no lo tendrá!

–No, pues otro aún dijo otros horrores de barbaridá, que ya no me acuerdan.

–¡Empecatado! ¡Pimiento picante le debían echar en la boca!

–¡Ay! ¡Y una cosa que mete miedo! Dice que por esas capitales toda la gente anda asustadísima, porque se ha descubierto que hay una compañía que roba niños.

–¡Ángeles de mi alma! ¿Y para qué?, ¿para degollarlos?

–No, mujer; que son los protestantes, para llevarlos a educar allá a su modo en tierra de ingleses.

–¡Señor de la justicia! ¡Mucha maldad hay por el mundo adelante!

unction, though without much refinement. Never had the collection for the Holy Burial Procession and the novena of Our Lady of Sorrows produced so much money; and finally, without any special occasion, the Virgin of Shelter, the protective numen of the factory, had so many offerings and alms, so much homage paid to her, without her rival, Our Lady of the Guard, star of the seas, patron saint of mariners along the wild coast, being in any way forgotten.

There were of course half a dozen or so bold spirits in the Granary quite capable of blaspheming and speaking openly about religious questions, but they were outnumbered by the majority and didn't dare let their tongues loose. At the most, they allowed themselves to speak ill of priests, accusing them of being immoral and covetous, or denounce them for 'getting mixed up in politics' and for taking up arms to bring back 'obscurantism and the Inquisition'; more transcendental and profound questions were not initiated, and should anyone dare to do so, a deluge of jokes and insults would in all certainty rain down upon her.

'The world is doomed!' said the maestra of Amparo's group, a woman mature in years, with sad eyes, dressed constantly in mourning since she had seen her two handsome sons, who were her pride and joy, die of smallpox. 'The world is in turmoil, girls! Don't you know what's going on over there in parliament?'

'What can be going on?'

'They say a deputy from Catalonia said there's no more God, and that the Virgin was this and that… May God forgive me, sweet Jesus a thousand times over.'

'And they didn't kill him right there? The scoundrel, the villain!'

'That foul mouth, that evil tongue! There won't be any God for him. No, not for him!'

'No, but another one said even more barbaric horrors, which I can't remember now.'

'Damned wretch! Hot pepper is what they should put in his mouth!'

'Oh! And here's something to frighten you! They say that all the people in those capital cities run around horrified because it's been discovered there's a society that steals little children.'

'Those little angels! And for what purpose? To slit their throats?'

'No. It's the Protestants, to take them off and bring them up their way in the land of the English.'

'Almighty God of Justice! There's so much evil out there in the world!'

Conocido este estado de la opinión pública, puede comprenderse el efecto que produjo en la fábrica un rumor que comenzó a esparcirse quedito, muy quedo, y, como en el aria famosa de la «calumnia», fue convirtiéndose de cefirillo en huracán. Para comprender lo grave de la noticia, basta oír la conversación de *la Guardiana* con una vecina de mesa.

–¿Tú no sabes, Guardia? La *Píntiga* se metió protestanta.

–Y eso, ¿ qué es?

–Una religión de allá de los *inglis manglis*.

–No sé por qué se consienten por acá esas religiones. Maldito sea quien trae por acá semejantes demoniuras. ¡Y la bribona de la *Píntiga*, mire usted! ¡Nunca me gustó su cara de intiricia...

–Le dieron cuartos, mujer, le dieron cuartos...; ¡sí que tú piensas...!

–A mí... ¡más y que me diesen mil pesos duros en oro! Y soy una pobre, repobre, que sólo para tener bien vestiditos a mis pequeños me venían... ¡juy!

–¡Condenar el alma por mil pesos! Yo tampoco, chicas –intervenía la maestra.

–Saque allá, maestra, saque allá... Comerá uno borona toda la vida, gracias a Dios que la da, pero no andará en trapisondas.

–Y diga... ¿qué le hacen hacer los protestantes a la *Píntiga*? ¿Mil indecencias?

–Le mandan que vaya todas las tardes a una cuadra, que dice que pusieron allí la capilla de ellos..., y le hacen que cante unas cosas en una lengua, que ... no las entiende.

–Serán palabrotas y pecados. ¿Y ellos, quiénes son?

–Unos clérigos que se casan...

–¡En el nombre del Padre! ¿Pero se casan ... como nosotros?

–Como yo me casé..., vamos al caso, delante de la gente..., y llevan los chiquillos de la mano, con la desvergüenza del mundo.

–¡Anda, salero! ¿Y el arcebispo no los mete en la cárcel?

–¡Si ellos son contra el arcebispo, y contra los canónigos, y contra el Papa de Roma de acá! ¡Y contra Dios, y los santos, y la Virgen de la Guardia!

–Pero esa lavada de esa *Píntiga*..., ¡malos perros la coman! No, pues como se arrima de esa banda, ¡yo le diré cuántas son cinco!

–¡Y yo!

Once you grasp this state of public opinion, you can understand the effect produced in the factory by a rumour which started to spread about quietly, very quietly, and like in the famous aria about 'calumny', it began to turn from a gentle breeze into a hurricane. To understand the seriousness of the news, you only need to hear the conversation between *la Guardiana* and a neighbour at her table.

'Don't you know, Guardia? *La Píntiga* converted to Protestantism.'

'And what's that?'

'It's a religion over there where the *Inglander swindlers* live.'

'I don't understand why they tolerate those religions here. A curse on anyone who brings devil's work like that over here. And look at that dishonest *Píntiga*. I never liked that jaundiced face of hers…'

'They gave her money, they gave her money…; you must think…!'

'Me … not even if they gave me a thousand gold duros! And I'm poor, as poor as can be, that if they came to me with just enough to keep my little ones in clothes … phew!'

'To sell your soul for a thousand pieces of gold! Me neither, girls,' interrupted the maestra.

'You tell them, maestra, you tell them… You can go on eating maize all your life, thanks be to God, but not get mixed up in fiddles like that.'

'And tell me, what do the Protestants make *La Píntiga* do? Thousands of indecent things?

'They order her to go to a stable every day, which people say is where they set up one of their chapels … and they make her sing things in a language, which … she doesn't understand them.'

'They'll probably be obscene words and sinful things. And they, who are they?'

'They're the clergymen who get married…'

'In the name of the Father! Do they really get married … like us?'

'Just as I got married … let's say it as it is, right in front of people … and they take their little children by the hand, with all the impudence in the world.'

'Come on, you joker! And the archbishop doesn't put them in jail?'

'But they're against the archbishop and against the canons and against the Pope in Rome. And against God and the saints and the Virgin of the Guard!'

'But that hussy of a *Píntiga* … let wild hounds tear her to bits! No, if she's in with that gang, I'll tell her a thing or two!'

'And me!'

—¡Y yo!

Así crecía la hostilidad y se amontonaban densas nubes sobre la cabeza de la apóstata, a quien por el color de su tez biliosa y de su lacio pelo, por lo sombrío y zafio del mirar, llamaban *Píntiga*, nombre que dan en el país a cierta salamandra manchada de amarillo y negro. Era esta mujer capaz de comer suela de zapato a trueque de ahorrar un maravedí y no ajena a su conversión una libra esterlina, o doblón de a cinco, que para el caso es igual. Si lo cobró, y pudo coserlo en una media con otras economías anteriores, bien lo amargó aquellos días. Acercábase a una compañera, y ésta le volvía la espalda; su mesa quedó desierta, porque nadie quiso trabajar a su lado; ponía su mantón en el estante, y al punto se lo empujaban disimuladamente desde la otra parte de la sala, para que cayese y se manchase; dejaba su lío de comida en el altar, y lo veía retirado de allí con horror por diez manos a un tiempo; la maestra examinaba sus mazos de puros, antes de darlos por buenos y cabales, con ofensiva minuciosidad y ademán desconfiado. Un día de gran calor pidió a la operaria que halló más próxima que le prestase un poco de agua; y ésta, que acababa de destapar un colmado frasco de cristal para beber por él, le contestó secamente: «No tengo *meaja*». Señaló la *protestanta* el frasco, con ira silenciosa, y la operaria, levantándose, lo tomó y derramó por el suelo su contenido sin pronunciar una palabra. Púsose verde *la Píntiga*, y llevó la mano, sin saber lo que hacía, al cuchillo semicircular; pero de todos los rincones del taller se alzaron risas provocativas, y hubo de devorar el ultraje, so pena de ser despedazada por un millar de furiosas uñas. En mucho tiempo no se atrevió a volver a la fábrica, donde la corrían.

'And me!'

This is how the hostility grew and dense clouds gathered over the head of that apostate woman, who, because of the colour of her bilious complexion and lank hair, as well as her sombre, coarse expression, was called *Píntiga*, a name given in that region to a certain kind of black and yellow spotted salamander. This woman was capable of eating shoe leather if it meant saving a maravedi, or a pound sterling, which wasn't far removed from her conversion, or a five real doubloon, which is the same in this case. Even if she did collect it, and was able to sew it into one of her stockings with some other economies previously put away, it spoilt those days for her. She would go up to a work companion and the woman would turn her back on her. Her table was deserted because nobody wanted to work beside her; she would put her shawl on the shelf, and straight away someone from the other side of the room would furtively push it off, so it would fall and get soiled; she would leave her bundle of food on the altar and watch with horror as ten different hands removed it at the same time; the maestra would examine her bundles of cigars with an offensive meticulousness and a suspicious attitude before declaring them good and without defect. One very hot day she asked the woman working closest to her to lend her a little water; and the woman, who had just uncorked a full glass bottle to drink from, answered curtly: 'I don't have a *drop*.' The *Protestant woman* pointed at the bottle with silent anger, and her co-worker stood up, took it and emptied its contents on the floor without uttering a single word. *La Píntiga* turned green and, without knowing what she was doing, reached for the semi-circular cutting knife; but provocative laughter erupted from all corners of the workshop and she had to swallow the insult on penalty of being torn to shreds by a thousand frenzied fingernails. For a long time, she didn't dare to go back to the factory, because they would drive her away.

XXV
PRIMERA HAZAÑA DE *LA TRIBUNA*

Extramuros, al pie de las fortificaciones de Marineda, celébrase todos los años una fiesta conocida por «Las comiditas»; fiesta peculiar y característica de las cigarreras, que aquel día sacan el fondo del cofre a relucir y disponen una colación más o menos suculenta para despacharla en el campo; campo mezquino, árido, donde sólo vegetan cardos borriqueros y ortigas. Desde el lavadero público hasta el alto de Aguasanta, ameno y risueño, se había esparcido la gente, sentándose, si podía, a la sombra de un vallado o en la pendiente de un ribazo, y si no, donde Dios quería, al raso, sin paraguas ni quitasol. Y cuenta que ambos chismes podrían ser igualmente necesarios, porque el astro diurno, encapotado por nubarrones que amenazaban chubasquina, despedía claridad lívida y sorda, y a veces por la ahogada calma de la atmósfera atravesaban soplos de aire encendido, bocanadas de solano que amagaban tempestad.

No por eso había menos corros de baile y canto, menos puestos de rosquillas y *jinetes*, menos meriendas y comilonas. Aquí se escuchaba el rasgueo de guitarras y bandurrias; más allá retumbaba el bombo, y la gaita exhalaba su aguda y penetrante queja. Un ciego daba vueltas a una *zanfona*[29] que sonaba como el obstinado zumbido del moscardón, y al mismo tiempo vendía romances de guapezas y crímenes. A pocos pasos de la gente que comía, mendigos asquerosos imploraban la caridad: un elefantíaco enseñaba su rostro bulboso, un herpético descubría el cráneo pelado y lleno de pústulas, éste tendía una mano seca, aquel señalaba un muslo ulcerado, invocando a Santa Margarita para que nos libre de «males extraños». En un carretoncillo, un fenómeno sin piernas, sin brazos, con enorme cabezón envuelto en trapos viejos, y gafas verdes, exhalaba un grito ronco y suplicante, mientras una mocetona, de pie al lado del vehículo, recogía las limosnas. En el aire flotaban los efluvios de dos toneles de vino que ya iban quedando exangües, y el vaho del estofado, y el olor de las viandas frías. Oíanse canciones entonadas con voz vinosa y llantos de niños, de los cuales nadie se cuidaba.

Componíase el círculo en que figuraba Amparo de muchachas alegres, que habían esgrimido briosamente los dientes contra una razonable merienda. Allí estaba *la Comadreja*, a quien no era posible aguantar, de puro satisfecha

---

29   Instrumento popular de cuerda.

25

LA TRIBUNA'S FIRST EXPLOIT

Outside the city, at the foot of the fortifications of Marineda, a festival known as 'Las comiditas' is celebrated every year; a festival that is peculiar to and characteristic of the cigar makers who, on that day, dig deep into their coffers to make an impressive showing and they prepare a more or less succulent collation, which they dispose of in an open area, a sorry, arid field where only cotton thistle and nettles grow. The people had spread out from the public washing area to the Alto de Aguasanta, which was pleasant and cheerful, finding a place to sit whenever possible, in the shade of a protective wall or on the slope of an embankment, and if not, wherever God was willing, on the bare ground, with neither umbrella nor parasol. And you could count on both being equally necessary, because the diurnal star, covered by storm clouds threatening a downpour, was sending out a pale, dull light, and at times passsing through the stifling calm of the atmosphere would be puffs of fiery air, gusts of an east wind that threatened an impending storm.

This didn't mean there were fewer groups of dancers and singers, fewer stands selling ring-shaped pastries and *jinetes*, or fewer light snacks and lavish spreads. Over here you could listen to the strumming of guitars and bandurrias; over there, a bass drum was resounding and the bagpipes were breathing out their sharp, penetrating lament. A blind man was grinding a hurdy-gurdy, which sounded like the persistent buzzing of a bluebottle, and at the same time he was selling popular romances about derring-do and crimes. A few steps from the people eating were some repugnant beggars begging for charity: an elephantiac was pointing out his bilbous face, a man affected with herpes revealing his bald skull covered with pustules; this one held out a withered hand, that one pointed to an ulcerated thigh, invoking Saint Margaret to free us of 'alien ills'. In a small handcart, an armless and legless freak with an enormous head wrapped in old rags and wearing green glasses uttered a hoarse, plaintive shout, while a strapping girl standing next to the vehicle was collecting alms. The air was filled with the emanations floating up from two casks of wine, by now all but drained, and the aroma of the stew and the smell of the fried foods. You could hear songs intoned in wine-soaked voices and the crying of children over whom no one was watching.

The group that included Amparo consisted of cheerful girls who had vigorously wielded their teeth against a reasonable-sized luncheon. There as well was *the Weasel*, whom it was impossible to put up with, so self-satisfied

y vana, porque tenía en Marineda al capitán de la *Bella Luisa*, y si él no había querido convidarse a merendar por el *aquel del bien parecer*, contaba con que la acompañaría al final de la función. Allí también *la Guardiana*, penetrada de alegría por otra causa diversa: porque había traído consigo a dos de sus pequeños, el escrofuloso y la sordomudita; en cuanto al mayor, ni se podía soñar en llevarle a sitio alguno donde hubiese gente, porque le entraba enseguida la *aflición*. La niña sordomuda miraba alrededor, con ojos reflexivos, aquel mundo, del cual sólo le llegaban las imágenes visibles; por su parte el niño, que ya tendría sus trece años, y que hubiera sido gracioso a no desfigurarle los lamparones y la hipertrofia de los labios, gozaba mucho de la fiesta y se sonreía con la sonrisa inocente, semibestial, de los *bobos* de Velázquez. *La Guardiana* no se mostró muy comedora: los mejores bocados los reservó para sus hermanos.

–¿Qué tienes, Guardia? –le preguntó la radiante Ana.

–Mujer, algunos días parece que estoy así…, cansada. He de ir a que me levanten la paletilla, porque imposible que no se me cayese.[30]

–Aprensiones, aprensiones. Canta el *joven Telémaco*, Amparo.

Amparo y otras dos o tres del taller de cigarrillos, rendidas de calor y ahítas de comida, se habían tendido en una pequeña explanada, que formaba el glacis de la fortificación, adoptando diversas posturas, más o menos cómodas. Unas, desabrochándose el corpiño, se hacían aire con el pañuelo de seda doblado; otras, tumbadas boca abajo, sostenían el cuerpo en los codos y la barba en las palmas de las manos; otras sentadas a la turca, alzaban cuándo la pierna izquierda, cuándo la derecha, para evitar los calambres. Por la seca hierba andaban esparcidos tapones de botellas, papeles engrasados, espinas de merluza, cascos de vaso roto, un pañuelo de seda, una servilleta gorda.

Fuese efecto de la comida y del vinillo del país, ligero y alegre como unas Pascuas, o del aire solano, que tiene especial virtud excitante para los nervios, hallábanse las muchachas alborotadas, deseosas de meterse con alguien, de gritar, de hacer ruido. Estaban ebrias, no del escaso mosto, sino del vaivén y mareo de la romería, de los colores chillones, de los sonidos discordantes; sólo la sordomuda permanecía indiferente, con su límpida mirada infantil. La casualidad proporcionó a las briosas mozas un desahogo que tuvo mucho de cómico y pudo tener algo de dramático.

---

30   La paletilla caída aparece como una enfermedad relacionada con las clases populares y con Galicia. Se trata de una superstición según la cual se podía curar con el mero hecho de "levantar la paletilla", es decir un hombro, una tendencia a la depresión y una enfermedad caracterizada por falta de ánimo y de apetito.

and vain was she because the captain of the *Bella Luisa* was in Marineda, and if he hadn't wanted to treat himself to this picnic on account of 'proper appearances', she counted on his accompanying her when the festivities were over. *La Guardiana* was also there, full of joy for a different reason: because she had brought two of her little ones with her, the boy who was afflicted with scrofula and the deaf-mute girl; as for the older brother, you couldn't even dream of taking him to any place where there were people, because he would instantly be overcome by his *afflition*. The deaf-mute girl looked around with reflective eyes at that world from which only visual images reached her; for his part, the young boy, who would probably be thirteen now, and who would have been fine looking were he not disfigured by scrofula of the neck and hypertrophy of the lips, was really enjoying the festivities and he kept smiling with the innocent, almost bestial, smile of the fools in the paintings by Velázquez. *La Guardiana* wasn't eating very much: she reserved the best morsels for her brother and sister.

'What's wrong with you, Guardia?' the radiant Ana asked her.

'Some days it seems I'm like this ... tired out. I've got to go and have them sort out my shoulder, because there's no way it hasn't sunk down.'

'Apprehensions, apprehensions. Sing *The young Telemachus*, Amparo.'

Amparo and two or three other girls from the cigarette workshop, exhausted from the heat and gorged with food, had stretched out on a small esplanade formed by the glacis of the fortification, adopting various more or less comfortable positions. Some, unfastening their bodices, were fanning themselves with their folded silk scarves; others, lying face down on the ground, were supporting their bodies with their elbows and their chins in the palms of their hands; still others, sitting cross-legged, would first lift their left leg and then their right leg to prevent cramp. Spread out over the dry grass were bottle corks, greasy bits of paper, hake fishbones, shards of broken glass, a silk scarf and a thick napkin.

Whether it was the effect of the meal and the local plonk, as light and cheerful as a breath of fresh air, or perhaps the easterly breeze, which has an excitant effect on the nerves, the girls were agitated, anxious to pick on someone, or to shout and make noise. They were intoxicated, not from the paltry new wine imbibed, but rather from the bustle and dizziness of the festival, the strident colours, the discordant sounds; only the little deaf-mute remained indifferent, with her limpid, infantile expression. But chance provided the spirited girls with some relief, which had a very comic element and could be said to have some dramatic aspect too.

Es el caso que vieron adelantarse y dirigirse hacia ellas un individuo de extraña catadura, alto y delgado, vestido con larga hopalanda negra y acompañado de otro que formaba con él perfecto contraste, pues era rechoncho, pequeño y sanguíneo, y llevaba americana gris rabicorta. Al aspecto de la donosa pareja llovieron los comentarios.

–El del gabanón parece un cura –dijo *la Guardiana*.

–No es cura –afirmó *la Comadreja*–. ¿No le ves unas patillitas como las de un padronés?

–Pero, mujer, si lleva alzacuello.

–¡Qué alzacuello! Corbata negra.

–El gordo, es un *inguilis*.

–¡Ay Jesús! ¡Parece que le pintaron la barba con azafrán!

–¿Y aquello qué es? ¡Madre mía de la Guardia; un anteojo en un ojo sólo, y colgado en el aire! ¡Mira, mira!

–Callad, que vienen para acá.

–Vienen aquí en derechura.

–No, mujer.

–¡Dale! Viene y vienen. ¿Te convences, porfiosa?

–Es que les gustaste.

–No, tú. El del azafrán viene a casarse contigo.

–Pues a ti te mira mucho el clérigo mal comparado.

–¡Chis! Callad, que están cerca, alborotadoras de Judas.

–¡Callad! Que callen ellos si les da la gana.

Y Amparo y Ana cantaron a dúo:

Me gusta el gallo,
me gusta el gallo,
me gusta el gallo
con azafrán...

No obstante estos primeros indicios de hostilidad, los dos graves personajes se aproximaban al corro, con mucha prosopopeya. El de la hopalanda, no bien se acercó lo suficiente, pronunció un «a loz piez de uztedes, zeñoras», que hubiese provocado explosión de carcajadas, si al pronto no pudiese más la curiosidad que la risa. ¡Tenía el bueno del hombre una voz tan rara, ceceosa, a la andaluza, y una pronunciación tan recalcada!...

The fact is that they saw approaching and making his way towards them a strange-looking individual, tall and thin, dressed in a long, black houppelande, accompanied by another man, who was a perfect contrast to him, for he was plump, short and of sanguine complexion, and was wearing a short-tailed grey jacket. Comments on the appearance of this fine pair rained down.

'The one wearing the big coat looks like a priest,' said *la Guardiana*.

'He's not a priest,' *the Weasel* affirmed. 'Can't you see his sideburns like the ones men from Padrón wear?'

'But he's wearing a dog collar.'

'What do you mean a dog collar! It's a black tie.'

'The fat one, he's an *Engilish man*.'

'Oh my God! It looks like they painted his beard with saffron!'

'And what's that thing there? Holy Mother of God; an eyeglass for just one eye, hanging in the air! Look, look!'

'Be quiet, they're coming here.'

'They're coming straight here.'

'Please, no.'

'On and on! They really are coming. Do you believe me, you stubborn mule?'

'It's because they took a liking to you.'

'No, you. The one with the saffron beard is coming to marry you.'

'Well, the substandard clergyman keeps looking at you.'

'Shhh! Keep quiet, they're near to us, you double-crossing troublemakers.'

'Us keep quiet!' Let them keep quiet if they feel like it.'

And Ana and Amparo sang together:

I like the rooster,
I like the rooster,
I like the rooster
With saffron...

Notwithsatanding these early indications of hostility, the two grave personages approached the circle of women with a great deal of pomposity. No sooner did the one in the houppelande come close enough to them than he announced, 'I am your motht humble thervant,' which would have provoked explosive laughter if at that moment curiosity had not overcome laughter. The good man had such a strange voice, with an Andalusian lisp, and such an exaggerated pronunciation...!

–Tengo el honor –prosiguió, metiendo las manos en los bolsillos de su inmenso tabardo–de ofrecer a uztedes un librito de lectura muy provechosa para el ezpíritu, y ezpero me dispensarán el ozequio de repazarlo con atención. Yo les ruego reflexionen sobre el contenido impreso, zeñoras míaz. Diciendo y haciendo, les presentaba tres o cuatro volúmenes empastados y un haz de hojas volantes. Nadie estiró la mano para recoger los *imprezo*, y él fue depositando suavemente en los regazos de las muchachas el alijo. El inglés tripudo observaba el reparto con su fulgurante monóculo.

–¡Así Dios me salve –Ana fue la primera en hablar –; yo conozco a estos pajarracos! Oyes tú, Bárbara: ¿este no es el que puso la capilla en la cuadra?

–El mismo … es el que berrea allí por las tardes.

–¿El que le dio los cuartos a *la Píntiga*?

–Sí, mujer.

–Y éste, ¿no dice que fue cura?

–Dice que sí, allá en su país, y que ahora es cura de ellos y está casado.

–¡Casado!

–Bueno, está … con una viuda. Ya tienen… –y la muchacha remedó burlescamente el llanto de un recién nacido.

–¿Y el otro bazuncho?

–Es el que… –y frotó el índice con el pulgar, ademán expresivo que significa en todas partes soltar dinero.

Mientras duraban estas explicaciones en voz baja, Amparo había leído el título de algunos folletos: *La verdadera Iglesia de Jesús…, La redención del alma…, Cristo y Babilonia…, La fe del cristiano purificada de errores…, Roma, a la luz de la razón…* Entre los retazos de diálogo que llegaban a sus oídos y los fragmentos de hoja impresa en que fijaba la vista, penetró el misterio. Levantóse grave, determinada, como el día que peroró en el banquete del Círculo Rojo.

–Oiga usté –pronunció en tono despreciativo–, esto que nos ha dado usté no nos hace falta, ni para nada lo queremos. Vaya usté a engañar con ello a donde haya bobos.

–Zeñora, no ha zío mi ánimo…

–Pensará usté que somos como otras infelices, que las compran ustés por una triste peseta; pues sepa usté, ¡repelo!, que acá ni por las minas del Potosí renegamos como San Judas.

–Zeñora … hermanaz mía … tómense usté la molestia de reflexionar, y

'I have the honour,' he continued, putting his hands into the pockets of his immense tabard, 'to offer you a little book of readingth very beneficial to the thpirit, and I thintherely hope you will grant me the courtethy of peruthing it with care. I beg you to reflect on the printed contenth, my dear ladieth.'

No sooner said than done, he showed them three or four cloth-bound volumes and a bunch of leaflets. Nobody stretched out a hand to pick up the *printed content*, and he began gently depositing the contraband material in the girls' laps. The potbelllied Englishman observed the distribution through his shining monocle.

'Oh, God save me,' Ana was the first to speak, 'I know these great, ugly birds! Tell me, Barbara, isn't this the one who set up a chapel in the stable?'

'The very one ... he's the one who howls there every afternoon.'

'The one who gave the money to *La Píntiga*?'

'Yes, indeed.'

'And this one, doesn't he say he was a priest?'

'That's what he says, over there in his country, and that now he's one of their priests and he's married.'

'Married!'

'Well, he's ... with a widow. And they now have...' and the girl did a burlesque imitation of the crying of a newborn baby.

'And the chubby one?'

'He's the one who...' and she rubbed her index finger against her thumb, an expressive gesture signifying the dispensing of money.

While these explanations were going on in hushed tones, Amparo had read the titles of some of the pamphlets: *The True Church of Jesus ... The Redemption of the Soul ... Christ and Babylon ... Christian Faith Purified of Errors ... Rome, in the Light of Reason...* Between the snippets of dialogue that reached her ears and the fragments of printed material that caught her eye, she penetrated the mystery. She stood up, grave and determined, like the day she made a speech at the banquet at the Red Circle.

'Listen here,' she uttered in a contemptuous tone of voice, 'we don't need this stuff you've given us, and we certainly don't want it. Go to wherever you might find some fools and trick them with it.'

'Madame, it wathn't my intention...'

'You must think we're like those gullible fools you buy with a miserable pittance, but I'd like you to know, hang it, that here we wouldn't renounce our faith like Judas did for all the gold in the world.'

'Madame ... dear thithterth ... pleathe take the trouble to reflect, and

verán la pureza de mi intencionez, que zon darle a conocé la doctrina de Jezú nuetro Zalvaor...

Pronta como un rayo, y con fuerzas que duplicaba la cólera, Amparo desbarató la encuadernada Biblia, hizo añicos las hojas volantes, y lo disparó todo a la cara afilada del catequista y a la rubicunda del silencioso inglés, los cuales, habituados, sin duda, a tal género de escenas, volvieron grupas y trataron de escurrirse lo más pronto posible entre el concurso. Por su mal, era éste tan apretado y numeroso en aquel sitio, que o tenían que retroceder, dar un rodeo y volver a cruzar ante el grupo de muchachas, o aguardar una ocasión de filtrarse entre la gente. Optaron por lo primero, y avínoles mal, porque Amparo, como el coronel de batalla que ha olido la sangre, dilatadas las fosas nasales, brillantes los ojos, se preparaba a renovar la lid, animando a sus compañeras.

–Son los protestantes. A correrlos.

–A correrlos. ¡Viva!

–Van a pasar otra vez por aquí... Ánimo..., a ver quién les acierta mejor.

–¡Que vengan, que vengan! ¡Ahora entra lo bueno!

Recelosos, arrimados el uno al otro, probaron a deslizarse los dos apóstoles sin ser observados de las mozas, que ya los aguardaban haldas en cinta. Así que los vieron a tiro, enarbolaron cuál medio pan, cuál un trozo de empanada, cuál una pera, y Ana, rabiosa, no encontrando proyectil a mano, cogió a puñados la tierra para arrojársela. Cayó la granizada sobre los protestantes cuando menos se percataban de ello; un queso se aplanó sobre la faz del inglés, rompiéndole el monóculo; un gajo de cerezas desprendido por el hermano de *la Guardiana* se estrelló en la nuca del ministro, embadurnó lastimosamente. Al par que bombardeaban, denostaban las intrépidas muchachas al enemigo.

–Toma, a ver si reventáis –chillaba *la Comadreja*.

–De parte de Nuestra Señora –gritaba *la Guardiana*.

–Para que volváis a dar dinero por hacer maldades –vociferaba Amparo, lanzando con notable acierto un tenedor de palo al cura.

Cerrados los puños como para boxear, inyectado el rostro, fieros los azules ojos, vínose sobre el grupo el hijo de la Gran Bretaña, resuelto, sin duda, a hacer destrozos en las heroínas; amenazadora actitud que redobló el coraje de éstas.

you'll thee the pure nature of my intentions, which are for you to know the doctrine of Our Thaviour Jethuth…'

As quick as lightning, and with strength doubled by anger, Amparo tore apart the bound Bible, tore the pamphlets into tiny bits and threw the lot into the sharp-featured face of the catechist and the ruddy countenance of the silent Englishman, both of whom, undoubtedly used to scenes of this sort, turned back and tried to slip through the crowd as quickly as possible. Much to their ill fortune, the gathering was so tightly packed and numerous in that place, that they had either to retreat, make a detour and cross once more in front of the group of girls, or wait for an opportunity to disappear into the crowd. They chose the first option and it turned out badly for them, because Amparo, like a colonel in battle who has smelt blood, got ready to renew the fight, urging on her companions with flared nostrils and shining eyes.

'It's those Protestants. Let's run them off.'

'Let's run them off. Hurrah!'

'They're going to pass this way again… Come on … let's see who can best hit the target.'

'Let them come, let them come! Now the best bit's going to start!'

Apprehensive, staying close to each other, the two apostles tried to slip away without being observed by the girls, who were already waiting for them with their sleeves rolled up. As soon as the girls saw they were in range, one brandished half a loaf of bread, another a piece of meat pie, another a pear, and Ana, filled with fury, not finding a projectile to hand, grabbed handfuls of earth to throw at them. The hail of missiles fell on the Protestants when they least expected it; a piece of cheese hit the Englishman full in the face, breaking his monocle; a bunch of cherries let loose by *la Guardiana*'s brother, smashed against the back of the minister's neck and smeared it pitifully. At the same time they were bombarding them, the intrepid girls hurled insults at the enemy.

'Take that, and see if you burst,' screamed *the Weasel*.

'That one's for Our Lady,' shouted *la Guardiana*.

'So you won't pass around money again for doing wicked things,' Amparo shouted vociferously, hurling a wooden fork at the priest with considerable skill.

Clenching his fists as if to start boxing, his face flushed and his blue eyes wild, this son of Great Britain came towards the group, no doubt determined to wreak havoc on these heroines; a threatening posture that redoubled the women's mettle.

–Venga usted, venga usted, que aquí estamos –le decía Amparo con voz vibrante, bella en su indignación como irritada leona, asiendo con la diestra una botella; mientras Ana, pálida de ira, se apoderaba de la cazuela en que había venido el guisado, y las restantes amazonas buscaban armamento análogo.

Pero ya, al ruido de la escaramuza, se arremolinaba la gente, y gente adversa a los catequistas, a quienes conocían bastantes de los espectadores; y el ministro, verde de miedo, con turbada lengua aconsejaba a su acompañante una prudente retirada.

–Éjelas, miter Ezmite... (Smith). Éjelas, que no zaben lo que jazen... Éjelas, que aquí nadie noz ofenderá, de zeguro... Yo debo dar ejemplo de manzedumbre...

No hizo caso míster Ezmite, por demás mohíno y amostazado con el bombardeo de comestibles; pero antes de que llegase al grupo cumplióse la profecía del ministro, interponiéndose más de treinta personas, que rodearon a los malaventurados apóstoles apretándolos en términos que no les dejaban respirar. A poca distancia un agente de Policía presenciaba una rifa, y aunque harto veía con el rabo del ojo el motín, no dio el más leve indicio de querer intervenir en él, y hasta que vio a los dos catequistas abrirse paso trabajosamente y huir como perro con maza, perseguidos por la rechifla general, no volvió la cabeza ni se acercó, preguntando al descuido:

–¿Qué pasa aquí, señores?

'Come on, come on, we're here,' Amparo said to him in a vibrant voice, as beautiful in her indignation as a lioness that has been provoked, while grasping a bottle in her right hand; in the meantime, Ana, pale with anger, seized the casserole dish that had been used for the stew, and the remaining Amazons looked for similar armaments.

But by this time, with the noise of the skirmish, people began milling around, including people hostile to the catechists, whom many of the spectators knew; and the minister, green with fear, advised his companion in bewildered terms to beat a prudent retreat.

'Leave them, Mithtah Thmith. Leave them, for they know not what they do. …Leave them, becauth for thure nobody here will offend uth … I mutht thet an egthample of gentleneth…'

Mithter Thmith, who incidentally was annoyed and peeved by the bombardment of food, paid no attention; but before he reached the group, the minister's prophesy was fulfilled, and more than thirty persons stood in the way and surrounded the unfortunate apostles, pressing them in so they could hardly breathe. A short distance away, a policeman was witnessing a fight, and although he could plainly see the riot out of the corner of his eye, he didn't give the slightest indication of wanting to be involved in it, and not until he saw the two catechists laboriously break their way through and flee like a dog with its tail between its legs, pursued by widespread hissing and booing, did he turn his head and walk over, asking nonchalantly:

'What's going on here, then?'

XXVI

LADOS FLACOS

Para *la Comadreja* el desenlace de la romería fue delicioso: comenzaron a llover gotas anchas cuando ya se aproximaba la noche, y vino el capitán mercante a ofrecerle el brazo y un paraguas. A la luz de los faroles de la calle, que rielaba en el mojado pavimento, Amparo vio alejarse a la pareja y quedóse poseída de una especie de tristeza interior que rara vez domina a los temperamentos sanguíneos, alegres de suyo. Aquella melancolía atacaba a *la Tribuna* desde que no alimentaba su viva imaginación con espectáculos políticos y desde que al bullicio de la Unión del Norte sucedió la habitual y uniforme vida obrera de antes, sin asomo de conspiración ni de otros romancescos incidentes. Por distraerse, habló más con Ana de amoríos y menos de política. Ana se prestaba gustosa a semejantes coloquios. Llegó *la Tribuna* a saber de memoria al capitán de la *Bella Luisa*. Sus hábitos, sus viajes, sus caprichos, y el eterno proyecto de matrimonio, diferido siempre por altas razones de conveniencia, que explicaba Ana con sumo juicio y cordura. Si ella se quisiese casar con algún artista de esos ordinarios, un zapatero, verbigracia, cansada estaría de tener marido; pero ¿para qué? Para cargarse de familia, para vivir esclava, para sufrir a un hombre sin educación. No en sus días.

—¿Y si te deja plantada Raimundo? —preguntaba Amparo nombrando al galán de su amiga, como lo hacía ésta, por el nombre de pila.

—¡Qué ha de dejar, mujer…, qué ha de dejar! ¡Diez años de relaciones! Y luego, aquel señorío de estar tanto tiempo con un chico fino, eso no me lo quita nadie.

Amparo protestó: ella no entraba por cosas de ese jaez; quería poder enseñar la cara en cualquier parte; quería, como dijeron los señores de la Unión, moralidad y honradez ante todo.

—¿Si pensarás tú —replicó Ana viperinamente— que el de Sobrado venía a casarse contigo?

—¿El de Sobrado? ¿Y qué tengo yo que ver con el de Sobrado?

—Anduvo tras de ti, y si no estuviese fuera, sabe Dios… No digas, mujer, no digas, que bastantes veces le encontré yo por los alrededores de la fábrica.

—Bueno, bueno, ¿y qué? ¿Por qué, un suponer, no se había de casar

26

WEAK POINTS

The outcome of the picnic was delightful for *the Weasel*: heavy raindrops started to fall as night was approaching, and the merchant sea captain came to offer her his arm and an umbrella. By the light of the streetlamps shimmering on the wet pavement, Amparo saw the couple move away, and she was left there, possessed by a kind of inner sadness which rarely overpowers an intrinsically sanguine and cheerful temperament. That feeling of melancholy had been assailing *la Tribuna* ever since she had ceased fuelling her lively imagination with political spectacles, and ever since the activity of the Northern Union had been replaced by the habitual, uniform work life of before, without a trace of conspiracy or other novelesque incidents. For sheer distraction, she spoke to Ana more about love affairs and less about politics. Ana lent herself gladly to conversations of this sort. *La Tribuna* came to know by heart the captain of the *Bella Luisa*: his habits, his journeys, his whims, and the eternal prospect of marriage, always postponed for elevated reasons of convenience, which Ana explained with considerable judgement and good sense. If she wanted to marry some common or garden artisan, a shoe-maker for example, she would soon tire of having a husband; but why do that? To burden yourself with a family, to live like a slave, to put up with a man who had no manners. Never.

'What if Raimundo dumps you?' Amparo asked, calling her friend's beau, like Ana did, by his first name.

'How could he leave me ... how could he leave me! A ten-year relationship! And even then, no one could take away my distinction of being so long with a refined young man.'

Amparo protested: she didn't get involved in things of that sort; she wanted to be able to show her face anywhere; what she wanted, as the gentlemen from the Union said, was morality and integrity above all else.

'Maybe you think,' Ana replied venemously, 'that Sobrado fellow would consider marrying you.'

'That Sobrado fellow? What have I got to do with that Sobrado fellow?'

'He was after you, and if he weren't out of town, God knows ... There's nothing you can say, nothing at all, because many is the time I came across him near the factory.'

'All right, all right, what about it? Why, let's suppose, couldn't he marry

conmigo? Yo seré de igual madera que otras que pertenecían a mi clase, y ahora... Tú conoces a la de Negrero... aquella tan guapa que lleva abrigo de terciopelo y capota de tul blanco... Pues, hija mía, sardinera del muelle primero, cigarrera después, y luego la vino Dios a ver con ese marido tan rico... ¿Y la de Álvarez? A esa la acuerdan aquí liando puros, y en el día tiene una casa de tres pisos y un buen comercio en la calle de San Efrén... ¿Y la que casó con aquel coronel del regimiento de Zaragoza?... Una chiquilla, que también hacía pitillos... En la actualidad, para más, hay el aquel de que las clases son iguales; ese rey que trajeron dice que da la mano a todo el mundo, y la mujer abrazó en Madrid a una lavandera; y si viene la federal, entonces...

–Sí, sí, vele con eso a doña Dolores la de Sobrado.

–¡Pues... Jesús, Ave María! ¡No se allegue usted, que mancho! Me parece a mí que los de Sobrado no son de allá de la aristocracia, ni del barrio de Arriba. Aún hay quien los vio cargando fardos en el almacén de Freixé, el catalán; que por ahí empezaron, ¡repelo! Hijos del trabajo, como tú y como yo.

–Pero, mujer, si ya se sabe que son así; nada y nada, y vanidá que les parte el alma. Como el hijo es de tropa, piensa que sólo la princesa de Asturias sirve para él... Mira tú cómo ahora que las de García pierden el pleito están medio reñidas con ellas... Y eso que la mayor de Sobrado, la Lolita, no quiso apartarse de la amiga y sigue yendo allá...

–Corriente; ellos no nos querrán a los demás; pero los demás bien nos valemos sin ellos... Para comer yo no les he de pedir, y el hijo, si me quiere decir algo, ha de ser con el cura de la mano, que si no...

Echóse a reír *la Comadreja* y citó ejemplos dentro de la misma fábrica. ¿Qué les había sucedido a Antonia, a Pepita, a Leocadia? Y eran las que más hablaban y más se la echaban de plancheta. La que se conformaba con los de su clase, aún menos mal; pero la que andaba con señores...

–Esas cosas –añadió *la Comadreja*–no tienen remedio; nos hacen ver lo negro blanco...

–Si me quisiera perder –exclamó ofendida Amparo–no me faltaría por dónde, como a todas.

–¡Bueno! No cuadró, mujer, que lo demás... también no te gustarían los

me? I'm probably made of the same stuff as others who belonged to my class, and now... You know the Negrero girl ... that really attractive one who wears a velvet coat and a white tulle bonnet ... well, my girl, first of all a sardine seller on the wharf, next a cigar maker, and then she struck lucky with that very rich husband... And how about the Álvarez girl? They all remember her around here rolling cigars, and now she has a three-storey house and a thriving business on the Calle de San Efrén... And the one who married that colonel in the Saragossa regiment? A girl who also used to make cigarettes... And what's more, the fact is that nowadays all classes are equal; that king they brought in, they say he shakes hands with everybody, and his wife embraced a washerwoman in Madrid, and if ever a federal government comes about, then...'

'Yes, yes, go and tell that to Doña Dolores de Sobrado.'

'Well ... Jesus, Holy Mother! Don't come near me or I'll contaminate you! It seems to me that the Sobrados aren't the cream of the aristocracy, nor even from the Barrio de Arriba. There are still some who saw them loading bundles at the warehouse owned by Freixé, the Catalonian; that's where they started, hang it! Working people, like you and me.'

'But everybody knows that's what they're like; nothing, nothing at all, and bursting at the seams with vanity. Ever since the son has been in the army, she thinks only the Princess of Asturias is good enough for him... Just look at how they've kind of fallen out with the Garcías now that they're losing their lawsuit... In spite of which the oldest Sobrado girl, Lolita, wouldn't cut herself off from her friend and carries on going over there...'

'Of course, they probably don't like the rest of us, but we can manage perfectly well without them... I don't have to go begging them for something to eat, and the son, if he has anything to say to me, it will have to be with a priest at his side, and if not...'

The Weasel burst into laughter and cited a number of examples right inside the factory. What had happened to Antonia, to Pepita, to Leocadia? And they were the ones who talked and showed off the most. A girl who was satisfied with those of her own social class, thank heavens, but a girl who was running around with gentlemen...

'Those things,' *the Weasel* added, 'are beyond redemption; they make us see black as white...'

'If I wanted to lose my virtue,' Amparo explained in an offended manner, 'I'd have no trouble finding where to do so, like all the others.'

'All right! It wasn't appropriate, and as for all the rest ... you wouldn't

que no se te pusieron delante, porque hay hombres que se tiraría uno a la bahía por ellos, y otros que ni forrados de onzas... Y a veces los que le chistan a uno no se dan por entendidos... Y al fin y al cabo, hija, ¿qué se gana con vivir mártir? Nadie cree en la dinidá de una pobre.

–¿Y por qué ha de ser así? ¡Esa no es ley de Dios!

–No, pero... ¿qué quieres tú?

Quedábase Amparo pensativa. Cuantas sugestiones de inmoralidad trae consigo la vida fabril, el contacto forzoso de las miserias humanas; cuantas reflexiones de enervante fatalismo dicta el convencimiento de hallarse indefenso ante el mal, de verse empujado por circunstancias invencibles al precipicio, pesaban entonces sobre la cabeza gallarda de *la Tribuna*. Acaso, acaso tenía sobrada razón *la Comadreja*. ¿De qué sirve ser un santo si al fin la gente no lo cree ni lo estima; si, por más que uno se empeñe, no saldrá en toda la vida de ganar un jornal miserable; si no le ha de reportar el sacrificio honra ni provecho? ¿Qué han de hacer las pobres, despreciadas de todo el mundo, sin tener quien mire por ellas, más que perderse? ¡Cuántas chicas bonitas, y buenas al principio, había visto ella sucumbir en la batalla, desde que entró en su taller! «Pero... vamos a cuentas –añadía para su sayo la oradora–: diga lo que quiera Ana, ¿no conozco yo muchachas de bien aquí? ¡Está esa *Guardiana*, que es más pobre que las arañas y más limpia que el sol! Y de fea no tiene nada; es ... así..., delgadita... Ella se confiesa a menudo..., dice que el confesor le aconseja bien...»

Amparo se quedó cada vez más pensativa después de esta observación.

–Yo, confesar, me confesaría... Pero luego..., si el cura sabe que me meto en política... ¡Bah! Bien basta en Semana Santa... Tampoco yo, gracias a Dios, no soy ninguna perdida..., me parece.»

like those men who didn't show an interest in you, because there are men for whom you might throw yourself into the bay, and others, not even if they were rolling in it... And sometimes those men who say things to a girl pretend they didn't understand... After all, what do you gain by living like a martyr? Nobody believes in the dignity of a poor girl.'

'But why does it have to be that way? It's not God's law.'

'No, but ... what do you want?'

Amparo became thoughful. The many suggestions of immorality brought about by factory life and the forced contact with human misery; and the many reflections of an enervating fatalism dictated by the conviction of being unprotected in the face of evil, of being pushed by invincible circumstances from the beginning, were all weighing heavily on *la Tribuna*'s charming head at this moment. Maybe, maybe *the Weasel* was quite right. What good is it being a saint if in the end people neither believe it nor hold it in esteem; if, however much you persist, you won't rise above earning a pittance in your whole life, if your sacrifice brings you neither honour nor benefit? What can poor girls do, held in low esteem by everyone, with no one to look after their interests, other than become fallen women? How many pretty girls, and good at first, had she seen succumb in that battle since joining the workshop! 'But ... let's get down to facts,' our orator added to herself, 'whatever Ana may say, don't I know virtuous girls here? Just take *la Guardiana*, who is as poor as a church mouse and as pure as the driven snow! And not at all ugly; she's ... sort of ... slim... She goes to confession quite a lot ... she says her confessor gives her good advice...'

After this observation, Amparo became even more pensive.

'As for confessing, I would confess ... but, then ... if the priest finds out I'm involved in politics... Bah! It's plenty enough during Holy Week... And, thanks be to God, I'm not a fallen woman ... it seems to me.'

BODAS DE LOS PAJARITOS

Regresó Baltasar de Navarra y las Provincias firmemente resuelto a estrujar la vida, como si fuese un limón, para exprimirle bien el zumo. Habiendo visto de cerca la guerra civil, comprendió que no hacía sino empezar y que prometía ser encarnizada y duradera, a pesar de que la *Gaceta* anunciaba diariamente la dispersión de las últimas partidas y la presentación del postrer cabecilla. Desde luego, Baltasar traía un grado más, y ganas de precipitarse en algún abismo cubierto de flores, ya que las balas carlistas se lo toleraban. Vista de lejos, la opinión pública de su ciudad natal le pareció mucho menos temible, y resolvióse a arrostrarla, en caso de necesidad, si bien con maña y no provocándola de frente.

Más de una vez, bajo la ligera tienda de campaña o en algún caserío vascongado, se acordó de *la Tribuna* y creyó verla con el rojo mantón de Manila o con el traje blanco y azul de grumete. Las mujeres que encontraba por aquellos países no le distrajeron, porque eran generalmente toscas aldeanas curtidas del sol, y si tropezó con alguna beldad éuscara, ésta, en vez de sonreír al oficial amadeísta, le echó mil maldiciones. Además, Baltasar, frío y concentrado, no era de los que toman por asalto un corazón en un par de horas. De suerte que al volver a Marineda, en vez de rondar la fábrica, como antes, se resolvió, desde el primer día, a acompañar a Amparo cuando la viese salir; y ejecutó el propósito con su serenidad habitual. Mucho le favoreció para estos acompañamientos el cambio de domicilio de la muchacha, que vivía cerca del alto de la cuesta de San Hilario, en una casita que daba a la Olmeda, desde que faltando el señor Rosendo y Chinto, el bajo de la calle de los Castros se hizo muy caro y muy lujoso para dos mujeres solas. Como la Olmeda puede decirse que es un rincón campestre, prestóse al naciente idilio con el género de complacencia que hace de la Naturaleza amiga perenne de todos los enamorados, hasta de los menos poéticos y soñadores.

Febrero vio la aurora de aquel amor en un día clásico, el de la Candelaria, en que, según el dicho popular, celebran los pajaritos sus bodas sobre las ramas todavía desnudas de los árboles, para que con la llegada de la primavera coincida la fabricación del nido. Las vísperas de la fiesta eran muy señaladas en la fábrica: andaban esparcidos por las estanterías, sobre

NUPTIALS OF THE BIRDS

Baltasar returned fom Navarre and the Basque provinces firmly resolved to get the most out of life, as if it were a lemon, and he could squeeze out all its juice. Having seen the civil war from up close, he understood that it had only just begun and that it promised to be bloody and long-lived, in spite of the fact that every day the *Gazette* announced the dispersion of the last rebel groups and the appearance of the last ringleader. Of course, Baltasar was now a full rank higher and, spared by Carlist bullets, eager to throw himself into some abyss covered with flowers. Seen from afar, the public opinion of his native city seemed much less frightening to him, and he resolved to face it if necessary, albeit craftily and without openly provoking it.

More than once, under a light tent or in some Basque country house, he remembered *la Tribuna*, and he imagined her in her red shawl of embroidered silk or her white and blue ship's boy costume. The women he met in those parts of the country didn't amuse him, because they were generally ungainly country girls, tanned by the sun, and if he came across some Basque beauty, instead of smiling at the Amadeist officer, she would hurl endless curses at him. Besides, Baltasar, who was cold and intense, was not one of those to take a heart by assault in a couple of hours. So, when he returned to Marineda, instead of prowling around the factory as he had done before, he resolved from the very first day to accompany Amparo whenever he saw her come out, and he carried this resolution through with his customary serenity. Very much in his favour for escorting her was the girl's change of residence, for she was living very near the heights of the Cuesta de San Hilario, in a little house that faced La Olmeda, ever since the ground floor flat on the Calle de los Castros, with Señor Rosendo and Chinto no longer there, had proved too expensive and luxurious for two women living alone. Since it can be said of La Olmeda that it is a rural nook, it lent itself to the incipient idyll with the sort of satisfaction that makes Nature a perennial friend of all lovers, even the least poetic and idealistic of them.

February saw the dawn of that love on a classic day, on Candlemas Day,[xxxii] when, according to the popular saying, the birds celebrate their nuptials on the still naked branches of the trees, so the construction of the nest coincides with the arrival of spring. The day before the holiday was very special in the factory: bunches of rosemary sprays were spread out on the shelves, on

los altares, ocultos en los justillos de las mujeres, mezclados con la hoja, haces de rama de romero, y su perfume tónico y penetrante vencía al del tabaco mojado. En el centro de los haces se hincaban candelicas de blanca cera, y había otras candelas largas y amarillas, compradas por varas y que cortaban en trozos para hacer cuantas luces se quisiese; siendo el origen de traer estas candelas la creencia de que los niños muertos antes del bautismo y sepultados en las tinieblas del limbo, sólo el día de la Candelaria ven un rayo de claridad –la de la luz que encienden, pensando en ellos, sus madres–. Al día siguiente, en la iglesia, envueltas en el romero bendito, habían de arder todas las velitas microscópicas.

Ya se comprende que entre las cigarreras marinedinas –cuatro mil mujeres, al fin y al cabo– había muchas que querían enviar a sus hijos difuntos aquella caricia de ultratumba, fundir el hielo de la muerte al calor de la pobre candelilla; por otra parte, aun las que no tenían niños vivos ni difuntos, habían comprado romero, gustándoles su olor, y propuestas a llevarlo a la misa de la Candelaria, que al fin, como decía la señora Porcona con tono sentencioso, era «un día de los más grandes, hiiigas…, porque fue cuando la Virgen sintió el primer dolorito, por razón de que un cura que le llamaban Simeón le anunció lo que tenía que pasar Cristo en el mundo».

La tarde de la Candelaria, Amparo, llevando el romero bendito oculto en el pecho, despedía un aroma balsámico, que pudiera tomarse por suyo propio; tal era la lozanía y vigor de su organismo, cuya robustez, vencedora en la lucha con el medio ambiente, había crecido en razón directa de los mismos peligros y combates. Si la labor sedentaria, la viciada atmósfera, el alimento frío, pobre y escaso, eran parte a que en la fábrica hiciesen estragos la anemia y la clorosis, el individuo que lograba triunfar de estas malas condiciones ostentaba doble fuerza y salud. Así le acontecía a *la Tribuna*.

Como era día festivo, Baltasar no la esperó a la salida de la fábrica, sino en la Olmeda, a corta distancia de su casita. Había llegado Baltasar al mayor número de pulsaciones que determinaba en él la calentura amorosa. Su pasión, ni tierna, ni delicada, ni comedida, pero imperiosa y dominante, podía definirse gráfica y simbólicamente llamándola apetito de fumador que a toda costa aspira a consumir el más codiciadero cigarro que jamás produjo, no ya la fábrica de Marineda, sino todas las de la Península. Amparo, con

the altars, hidden in the women's bodices, mixed with the leaves, and their stimulating, penetrating perfume overcame the odour of the damp tobacco. In the centre of the bunches, small white wax candles were firmly set, and there were also longer yellow ones, bought by the yard and cut into sections to make as many lights as was wished; the origin of bringing these candles being the belief that children who die before they are baptised and are buried in the darkness of limbo can see a ray of light only on Candlemas Day – the flame their mothers light as they think of them. On the following day, in church, they were supposed to burn all the small microscopic candles wrapped in the blessed rosemary.

It is easy to understand that among the cigar makers in Marineda – four thousand women, after all – there were many who wished to send their dead children that caress from beyond the grave, to melt the chill of death with the warmth of the poor little candle; on the other hand, even those who had neither living nor dead children had bought some rosemary, because they liked its aroma, and were ready to bring it to mass on Candlemas Day, since, in the long run, as Señora Slattern said in a sententious tone, it was 'one of the greatest of days, ... because it was when the Virgin felt the first little pang, for the reason that a priest named Simeon had announced to her what Christ was going to have to undergo in this world.'

On the afternoon of Candlemas Day, Amparo, keeping the blessed rosemary hidden in her bosom, gave off a balmy fragrance which could well be taken as her own; so great was the vitality and vigour of her organism, the robustness of which, victorious in the struggle against her environment, had grown strong as a direct result of those very dangers and conflicts. If the sedentary labour, the foul atmosphere and the cold, inferior and insufficient nourishment played their part in the fact that anemia and chlorosis wreaked havoc in the factory; any individual who managed to triumph over these unhealthy conditions manifested extra strength and health. This is what happened to *la Tribuna*.

Because it was a holiday, Baltasar didn't wait for her at the factory exit, but rather in La Olmeda, a short distance from her small house. Baltasar had reached his maximum heart rate and this determined the extent of his love-sickness. His passion, neither tender, nor delicate, nor restrained, but rather imperious and dominating, could be defined graphically and symbolically by calling it the craving of a smoker who at all costs aspires to smoke the most sought-after cigar ever produced, not just in the factory in Marineda, but in every one of the whole Peninsula. Amparo, with her delicate throat

su garganta mórbida gallardamente puesta sobre los redondos hombros, con los tonos de ámbar de su satinada, morena y suave tez, parecíale a Baltasar un puro aromático y exquisito, elaborado con singular esmero, que estaba diciendo: «Fumadme.» Era imposible que desechase esta idea al contemplar de cerca el rostro lozano, los brillantes ojos, los mil encantos que acrecentaban el mérito de tan preciosa *regalía*. Y para que la similitud fuese más completa, el olor del cigarro había impregnado toda la ropa de *la Tribuna*, y exhalábase de ella un perfume fuerte, poderoso y embriagador, semejante al que se percibe al levantar el papel de seda que cubre los habanos en el cajón donde se guardan. Cuando por las tardes Baltasar lograba acercarse algún tanto a Amparo e inclinaba la cabeza para hablarle, sentíase envuelto en la penetrante ráfaga que se desprendía de ella, causándole en el paladar la grata titilación del humo de un rico veguero y el delicioso mareo de las primeras chupadas. Eran dos tentaciones que suelen andar separadas y que se habían unido; dos vicios que formaban alianza ofensiva: la mujer y el cigarro íntimamente enlazados y comunicándose encanto y prestigio para trastornar una cabeza masculina.

El día espiraba tranquilamente en aquella alameda, que en hora y estación semejante era casi un desierto. Sentáronse un rato Baltasar y *la Tribuna* en el parapeto del camino, protegidos por el silencio que reinaba en torno, y animados por la complicidad tácita del ocaso, del paisaje, de la serenidad universal de las cosas, que los sepultaba en profundo languidez y que relajaba sus fibras infundiéndoles blanda pereza muy semejante a la indiferencia moral. El sol languidecía como ellos; la Naturaleza meditaba. Hasta la bahía se hallaba aletargada; un gallardo queche blanco se mantenía inmóvil; dos paquebotes de vapor, con la negra y roja chimenea desprovista de su penacho de humo, dormitaban, y solamente un frágil bote, una cascarita de nuez, venía como una saeta desde la fronteriza playa de San Cosme, impulsado por dos remeros, y el brillo del agua, a cada palada, le formaba movible melena de chispas. Por donde no las alcanzaba el último resplandor solar, las olas estaban verdinegras y sombrías; al poniente, dorada red de movibles mallas parecía envolverlas.

A medida que avanzaba la sombra, levantábase del mar una brisa fresca, que agitaba por instantes los picos del pañuelo de Amparo y los cabellos rubios de Baltasar, en los cuales se detenían las postreras luces del sol, haciendo de su cabeza una testa de oro. Pronto la abandonaron, sin embargo, y también

gracefully placed on her rounded shoulders, with the amber tones of her dark, smooth, satin-like skin, seemed to Baltasar an exquisite, aromatic cigar, crafted with singular care that was saying to him: 'Smoke me.' It was impossible for him to cast aside this idea when he contemplated close up her fresh face, her shining eyes and the innumerable charms which enhanced the worth of so precious a large, fine cigar as a *regalia*. And in order to make the similarity even more complete, the smell of cigars had impregnated all of *la Tribuna*'s clothes, and she gave off a strong, powerful and intoxicating perfume, similar to what you notice when lifting the tissue paper that covers the Havana cigars in the box where they are kept. During afternoons when Baltasar managed to move somewhat closer to Amparo and leaned his head over to speak to her, he felt immersed in a penetrating waft that emanated from her, causing a pleasant titillation on his palate like the smoke of a fine cigar and the delightful dizziness of the first few puffs. They were two temptations that are usually kept separate, but which had joined together; two vices that formed an offensive alliance: the woman and the cigar, intimately linked together and communicating charm and prestige between one another in order to unhinge a masculine head.

The day was calmly coming to an end on that boulevard, which at that sort of hour and season was almost deserted. Baltasar and *la Tribuna* sat down for a while on the parapet along the road, protected by the silence that reigned around them and animated by the tacit complicity of the sunset, the landscape and the universal serenity of things, which buried them in a profound languor and relaxed the very fibres of their being, filling them with an exquisite indolence very similar to moral indifference. Like them the sun was languishing; Nature was meditating. Even the bay was lethargic; a graceful white ketch stayed motionless and two steam packet boats, their black and red funnels divested of their plumes of smoke, were snoozing; only one fragile boat, a little nutshell, was moving ahead like an arrow from the Playa de San Cosme opposite them, driven on by two rowers, and with each stroke of the oars, the brilliance of the water formed ever-changing tresses of sparkling drops. Wherever the last bit of sunlight didn't reach them, the waves were dark green and sombre; in the west, a golden net of variable mesh seemed to envelop them.

As the shadows kept advancing, a cool breeze rose up from the sea, and all the time it stirred the corners of Amparo's scarf and Baltasar's blond hair, where the last rays of the sun had come to rest, making his head like a gold crown. Soon, however, they abandoned it, and the mountains on the

las montañas del horizonte empezaron a confundirse con el agua, mientras la concha blanca del caserío marinedino se destacaba aún, pero perdiéndose más cada vez, como si al ausentarse la claridad se llevase consigo la piña de edificios y el encendido fulgor de los cristales en las galerías. Marineda, la *Nautilia* de los romanos, se envolvía en una clámide de tinieblas. En breve comenzaron a distinguirse algunas luces que oscilaban sobre la masa oscura de la población, y presto se cubrió toda ella de puntos lucientes como estrellas de oro en un celaje sombrío. La noche, que ya reinaba, era de esas entreclaras y lácteas, pero frías, en que el equinoccio de primavera se anuncia por no sé qué vaga trasparencia del cielo y del aire, y en modo alguno por la temperatura, que más bien parece recrudecerse. Baltasar y la muchacha, molestados quizá por el helado ambiente, se aproximaban el uno al otro, hablando no obstante de poca sustancia.

–No, Bilbao no es más bonito..., ni tampoco Santander, digan lo que quieran los santanderinos, que son muy patriotas. ¿Sabe usted lo que ha mejorado Marineda? ¿Y lo que está llamada a mejorar todavía? Esto crece a cada paso; vamos a tener barrios nuevos, magníficos, a la americana, ahí, donde usted ve aquella lucecita..., cabal: todo por ahí, a lo largo del baluarte.

–¿Y Madrí? ¿Es mucho mejor que Marineda? –interrogó Amparo, por decir algo, enrollando un cabo de su pañuelo.

–¡Ah! Madrid, ya ve usted..., al fin y al cabo, es la corte... Sólo la calle de Alcalá...

Este apacible diálogo encubría en Baltasar tempestuosos pensamientos; pero como no carecía de penetración y sabía que la muchacha era honrada, y orgullosa, y vivía de su trabajo, comprendió que no debía tratarla como a cualquier criatura abyecta, sino empezar mostrándole cierta deferencia y aun respeto, género de adulación a que es más sensible todavía la mujer del pueblo que la dama de alto copete, habituada ya a que todos le manifiesten miramientos y cortesía. Lisonjeó mucho a *la Tribuna* el ver que se habían con ella lo mismo que con las señoritas, y auguró bien del rendido galán. Mas al caer la noche, Baltasar creyó poder apoderarse a hurto de una mano morena, hoyosa y suave al tacto como la seda. Amparo pegó un respingo.

–Estése usted quieto... Y ya van dos veces que se lo digo, caramba.

–¿Por qué me trata usted así? –preguntó con pena fingida Baltasar, que en sus adentros renegaba de la virtud plebeya ¿Qué mal hay en...?

horizon also began to blend with the water, while the white horseshoe shape of Marineda's housing still stood out, but disappearing more and more, as if the diminishing brightness were taking the cluster of buildings away with it, along with the glowing brilliance of the window panes in the galleries. Marineda, the *Nautilia* of the Romans, was wrapping itself in a cloak of darkness. Before long, some lights that were oscillating over the dark mass of the town began to stand out, and quickly the whole place was covered with shining points of light, like golden stars in a sombre cloudscape. The night, which was now prevailing, was one of those which are fairly clear and lacteous, but cold, when the spring equinox is announced by a certain vague transparency of the sky and the air, and to some extent by the temperature, which somehow seems to worsen. Baltasar and the girl, perhaps troubled by the chilly temperature, drew closer to each other, talking nevertheless about matters of little substance.

'No, Bilbao isn't prettier … nor Santander, no matter what the residents there say, because they're very patriotic. Do you realise how much Marineda has improved? And how much it's still destined to improve? Everywhere you turn, it's developing; we're going to have some magnificent, new, American style districts, over there where you see that small light … exactly; all around there, along the length of the bastion.'

'And how about Madrid? Is it much better than Marineda?' Amparo asked, just to say something, rolling up one end of her scarf.

'Oh! Madrid, well, you see … after all, it's the capital… Just the Calle de Alcalá…'

This calm dialogue concealed Baltasar's tempestuous thoughts, but as he was not lacking in insight, and knew that the girl was honourable and proud and lived from her own work, he understood that he shouldn't treat her like some abject creature, but rather begin by showing her a certain deference, even respect, a kind of adulation to which a woman of the people is more sensitive than an aristocratic lady, one who is already accustomed to the fact that everyone shows her consideration and courtesy. *La Tribuna* was very flattered to see she was being treated the same as proper young ladies, and it all augured well for this devoted suitor. But as night fell, Baltasar thought he could slyly take hold of a dark, dimpled hand, smooth as silk to the touch. Amparo gave a start.

'Keep still… And that's twice I've told you, damn it.'

'Why do you treat me like this?' asked Baltasar with a feigned sorrow, for deep down he condemned plebeian virtue. 'What harm is there in…?'

–¿Por qué? –repitió Amparo con sumo brío–. Porque no me conviene a mí perderme por usted ni por nadie. ¡Sí que es uno tan bobo que no conozca cuándo quieren hacer burla de uno! Esas libertades se las toman ustedes con las chicas de la fábrica, que son tan buenas como cualquiera para conservar la conducta. ¿A que no hace usted esto con la de García, ni con las señoritas de la clase de usted?

«¡Diantre! –pensó Baltasar–, no es boba.»

Y al punto, mudando de táctica, habló con gran rapidez, diciendo que estaba enamorado, pero de veras; que para él no había categorías, distinciones ni vallas sociales, encontrándose el amor de por medio; que Amparo valía tanto como la más encopetada señorita, y que su desliz no provenía de falta de respeto, sino de sobra de cariño: todo lo cual esforzó con mil dulces e insinuantes inflexiones de voz. Amparo respondió *cantando* su credo y sus principios: ella no quería ser como otras chicas conocidas suyas, que por fiarse de un pícaro allí estaban perdidas; ella bien sabía lo que pasaba por el mundo, y cómo los hombres pensaban que las hijas del pueblo las daba Dios para servirles de juguete; lo que es ella, bien se había de librar de eso; bueno que se hablase un rato, en lo cual no hay malicia; pero ciertas libertades, no; ya podía saberlo el que se arrimase a ella. Baltasar juró y perjuró que su amor era de la más probada y acendrada pureza, y que sólo limpios e hidalgos propósitos cabían en él; y en el calor de la discusión, los dos interlocutores se volvieron a hallar sentados en el parapeto, y la mano antes esquiva se mostró más tratable, consintiendo que la prendiesen dos manos ajenas.

–Hoy se casan los pajaritos –murmuró Baltasar después de un breve instante de silencio.

–Día de la Candelaria… Hoy se casan –repitió ella con turbada voz, sintiendo en la palma de la mano el calor de la diestra de Baltasar, que amorosamente la oprimía.

Pero él fue discreto y no quiso abusar de la victoria, por temor de perder las ventajas adquiridas, y también porque empezaba a correr agudo frío en la solitaria alameda, y Amparo se levantó quejándose del relente y del aire, que cortaba como un cuchillo. Cruzáronse dos protestas de ternura, en voz baja, envueltas en el último apretón de manos, delante de la casa de la pitillera.

'Why?' Amparo repeated with extreme determination. 'Because it's not in my interest for you or anyone else to be my undoing. You'd have to be a real fool not to know when they're wanting to make fun of you! You and those like you take that kind of liberty with the girls from the factory, who are as good as anyone else at keeping up correct behaviour. Why don't you try that with the García girl, or with the young ladies of your own class?'

'By Jove!' Baltasar thought to himself. 'She's no fool.'

And instantly changing tactics, he began to speak very quickly, saying that he was in love, really and truly, that for him there were neither categories, nor distinctions, nor social barriers, where love finds itself involved; that Amparo was worth as much as the poshest lady, and that his indiscretion came not from any lack of respect, but rather from excessive affection; all this he reinforced with countlesss sweet, insinuating inflections of his voice. Amparo responded by *chanting* her credo and her principles: she had no wish to be like other girls of her acquaintance, who, because they trusted in a scoundrel, had become fallen women; she knew very well what was going on in the world, and how men thought that God granted them girls of the lower class to serve as their playthings; as for her, she would have no part in anything like that; it was fine to chat for a while, as there's no malice in that; but certain liberties, no; anyone who got closer to her should know that. Baltasar swore again and again that his love for her was truly proven and pure, and that only clean and noble intentions had a place in it; in the heat of the discussion, the two people speaking found themselves sitting on the parapet again, and the hand which had been elusive before turned out to be more amenable, and consented to have another person's two hands take hold of it.

'The birds are getting married today,' Baltasar murmured after a brief moment of silence.

'Candlemas Day ... they're get married today,' she repeated in a bewildered voice, feeling the warmth of Baltasar's right hand in the palm of her own hand, as he pressed it amorously.

But he was discreet and didn't try to abuse his victory, out of fear he might lose advantages already gained, and also because a sharp chill was beginning to run through the deserted lane; Amparo stood up, complaining about the evening dew and the air which cut like a knife. Two declarations of affection were exchanged in hushed tones, wrapped in a final pressing together of hands in front of the cigarette maker's house.

XXVIII

CONSEJERA Y AMIGA

Alguna que otra vez volvía Amparo a visitar su antigua calle, por ver a los amigos que allí había dejado. Pocos días después del de la Candelaria sintió deseos de realizar una expedición hacia aquella parte. Halló todo en el mismo estado; el barbero, muy ocupado en descañonar a un sargento, la saludó jovialmente; a la puerta de su casa divisó a la señora *Porreta* tomando el fresco, o el sol, que ambas cosas faltaban dentro del tugurio de la comadrona, la cual hacía extraña y risible figura sentada en una silleta baja, y muy esparrancada; sus pies, calzados con zapatillas de orillo, miraban uno a Poniente y otro a Levante; tenía caídas las medias, por deficiencia de ligas sin duda; en el formidable hueco del regazo descansaban sus manos, y mientras una chiquilla encanijada, nieta suya, le peinaba las canas greñas y le hacía dos *chicos* tamaños como bellotas, la insigne matrona no perdía el tiempo, y calcetaba con diligencia, manejando las metálicas agujas, que despedían vivos fulgores. Al ver a *la Tribuna*, se echó a reír con opaca risa.

–Hola, chica… salú y fraternidá… ¿Cómo está tu madre? ¿Y la revolución, cuándo la hasemos? ¿Cuándo me proclamas a mí reina de España?

Y como Amparo procurase escabullirse, la vieja subió el tono de sus carcajadas, semejantes al chirrido de una polea, y que hacían retemblar su vientre de ídolo chino.

–Sí, escápate, escápate… –murmuró–. Ahora bien te escapas… Ya bajarás la soberbia cuando yo te haga falta… ¿oyes, Amparo? Cuando necesitáis a la señora Pepa, venís como corderitos… ¡Quién te verá aquel día!, ¿Eh?…

–Dios delante, señora Pepa –contestó, altiva y picada Amparo–, otras la llamarán más pronto, señora. A no ser que me case…

–¡Sí, sí…, echar por la boca! El tiempo todo lo vense –afirmó con profético acento la comadre, cogiendo una hilera de puntos, que se le habían soltado al reír.

Siguió Amparo calle adelante, y llamó al tablero de Carmela, la encajera; pero con gran sorpresa suya, en vez de abrirse éste, se entreabrió la puerta

28

ADVISOR AND FRIEND

Now and again Amparo went back to visit her old street, to see the friends she she had left behind there. A few days after Candlemas Day she felt a sudden desire to undertake an expedition to that part of town. She found everything just the same; the barber, very busy giving a sergeant a close shave, greeted her cheerfully; she saw Señora *Starkers* at the door of her house, catching a breath of fresh air, or the sun, for both of these were lacking in the midwife's hovel. The latter made a strange, laughable figure, sitting there on a small, low chair, with her legs wide apart; she was wearing selvage slippers on her feet, one of which was facing west and the other east; her stockings had slipped down, undoubtedly because she wasn't wearing suspenders; her hands were resting in the formidable hollow of her lap, and while a sickly little girl, her grandchild, was combing out her grey mop of hair and making her two small chignons the size of acorns, the renowned midwife wasn't wasting any time, but was knitting diligently, operating the brightly glowing metallic needles. When she saw *la Tribuna*, she broke into a sort of gloomy laughter.

'Hello there … to health and fraternity… How's your mother? And the revolution, when are we going to start it? When are you going to proclaim me queen of Spain?'

And as Amparo tried to slip away, the old lady raised the tone of her guffaws, which were similar to the squeaking of a pulley and made her Buddha-like belly quiver.

'Yes, run away, run away…' she muttered. 'It's fine to run away now… But you'll soon get off your high horse when you need me … do you hear, Amparo? When you girls need Señora Pepa, you come like little lambs… Let's see what you're like on that day! Eh…?'

'As God is my witness, Señora Pepa,' Amparo answered haughtily and in a huff. 'Others will call on you more quickly than I do. Unless I get married…'

'Yes, yes … you're good at talking! But time conquers all,' the midwife affirmed in a prophetic tone, picking up a row of stitches she had dropped while laughing.

Amparo kept walking down the street and knocked at the door panel where Carmela the lacemaker lived; but to her great surprise, instead of it

interior que comunicaba con el portal, y se asomó Carmela animada, encendida la tez y con un júbilo nunca visto en ella.

–Entra, entra –dijo a la pitillera.

Ésta entró. El cuartito estaba en desorden; recogida la almohadilla de los encajes; había un baúl abierto y ya casi colmado, y los cuadros de lentejuela y estampas devotas, que solían adornar las paredes, faltaban de ellas.

–Hola… ¿Parece que vamos de viaje? –preguntó Amparo.

La respuesta de la encajera fue echarle al cuello los brazos, y pronunciar, con voz entrecortada de alegría:

–¿Luego tú no sabes, no sabes que Dios me dio la sorpresa? ¡Ya tengo el dote, chica…; me voy a Portomar a ver si me reciben allá en el convento!…

–¡Ahora que dicen que se acaban las monjas!

–Las de Portomar, no mujer…; ésas no… Hay un señorón liberal, allá en Madrí, que pidió por ellas…

–Pero… ¿y cómo, quién te dio el dote?

–Verás… Yo echaba todos los meses un décimo a la lotería…, todos los meses. Tú ya sabes que la tía me hacía trabajar los domingos por la mañana; pero por las tardes me decía: «Anda, distráete…, vete un poco a rezar a la iglesia.» Bien. Pues, señor, yo en vez de rezar, iba, ¿y qué hacía? Trabajaba unas puntillitas estrechas, sin que la tía lo supiese, y se las vendía a una mujer del mercado, diciéndole a Nuestra Señora: «No es pecado esto que hago, porque es para sacar a la lotería, y si saco es para entrar monja…» Pues etaquí que cada mes me tomaba mi décimo, y para que saliese bien, siempre echaba con algún santo. Unas veces llevaba de compañero a San Juan Bautista; otras, a San Antonio; otras, a Santa Bárbara…; y nada: ni tristes cinco duros. Entonces dije yo para mí: «Hay que ir a la fuente limpia; estos compañeros no valen.» ¿Y qué se me ocurrió? Tomé un decimito con un número muy lindo, mil ciento veintidós, y se lo fui a llevar al Niño Dios de las Madres Descalzas… y le dije: «Mira, Jesusito, si sale premiado, la metá para ti… Tenía una carita tan alegre cuando se lo dije, lo mismo que si me entendiese. Pues ¿quién te dice, mujer…?

Pausa de gran efecto.

opening, the inside door leading to the entryway half-opened and Carmela peered out, quite animated, her face somewhat flushed, with a joy never previously seen in her.

'Come in, come in,' she said to the cigarette maker.

She went inside. The small room was in a mess; the small cushion used for making lace had been cleared away; there was an open trunk almost stuffed to the brim, and the sequin pictures and religious prints which used to adorn the walls were no longer there.

'Hello ... it looks like we're going on a trip?' Amparo asked.

The lacemaker's answer was to throw her arms around her neck, and say the following in a voice choked with joy:

'So you don't know, you don't know that God gave me a real surprise? I've now got the dowry I need ... I'm off to Portomar to see if they'll accept me in the convent there!'

'Just now when they say they're putting an end to nuns!'

'Those in Portomar, no ... not those ones... There's a big shot over there in Madrid, a liberal who stepped in on their behalf...'

'But ... how, who gave you the dowry you needed?'

'You'll see... Every month I used to buy a tenth-part of a lottery ticket ... every month. You already know that my aunt made me work on Sunday mornings, but in the afternoon she would say to me: "Go on, enjoy yourself ... go to church and pray a little." All right. Well, now, I went and instead of praying what was I doing? I was making very narrow lace edging, without my aunt knowing, and selling it to a woman in the market, whilst saying to Our Lady: "It's not a sin what I'm doing, because it's to try to win the lottery, and if I do win, it's to become a nun..." Well, so it is that every month I'd take my tenth-part ticket, and in order to make it come out I always played with some saint. Sometimes I would have Saint John the Baptist as my companion, at other times Saint Anthony, other times Saint Barbara ... and it never worked, not even five measly duros. Then I said to myself: "You might just as well go to the very source; these companions are no good." And you know what occurred to me? I bought a little lottery ticket with a really nice number, one thousand one hundred and twenty-two, and I went and took it to the Infant Jesus of the Discalced Mothers ... and I said to him: "Look here, sweet Jesus, if it turns out that I win, half is for you..." He had such a happy, little face when I said it to him, just as if he understood me. Well, who would have guessed...?'

A pause for big effect.

–¿Quién te dice a ti … que al sorteo voy y miro la lista, y me veo un mil ciento veintidós como un sol? Me quedé aturdida, y mucho más porque el premio era de los grandes: cerca de mil pesos. Sólo que, como la metá es del Niño, a mí me queda el dote limpio y pelado…

–¿Y tu tía? –preguntó Amparo, como si censurase el regocijo de Carmela.

–¿Y sabes, mujer, que yo quise depositar el dote para cuando ella muriese y quedarme en su compañía, y no quiso? Dice que no, que bien claro está que Dios me llama para sí… Ella tiene buscada colocación en casa de un cura… Como está así, medio ciega, sólo en un sitio de poco trabajo puede servir. ¡Ay Niño Jesús de mi alma! ¡Cuántas lagrimitas tengo llorado aquí sin que nadie me viese! ¡Qué días! Es mejor hacer pitillos que encajes, chica. ¡Fumar, siempre fuma la gente; pero los encajes en invierno … es como vivir de coser telarañas!

Y levantándose, cogió un tiesto que estaba en la ventana y lo entregó a Amparo.

–Toma, me alegro de que hayas venido… Cuídame mucho la malva de olor, que por el camino tengo miedo de que se rompa el tarro.

Amparo cogió el tiesto y respiró el perfume de la planta, hundiendo la faz entre las aterciopeladas hojas. La encajera la miraba con sus pupilas siempre melancólicas y serenas.

–Amparo –dijo de pronto…

–¿Eh?… –respondió *la Tribuna*, sorprendida como si la despertasen de golpe.

–¿Te enfadas si te digo una cosa?

–No, mujer… ¿Y por qué me he de enfadar? –contestó fijando sus ojos gruesos y brillantes en la futura concepcionista.

–Pues quería decirte … que por ahí te pusieron un mote.

–¿Un mote?, ¿Y es cosa mala?

–Mala…, ¡qué sé yo! Te llaman *la Tribuna*.

–¿Y quién me lo llama?

–Los señoritos…, los hombres. Dicen que fue porque el día del convite…, no te parezca mal, que a mí me lo contaron así, inocentemente…, te dio un abrazo uno de aquellos señores de la *Samblea* … y que te dijo…

'Who could have guessed ... that I go to the draw and look at the list, and see there one thousand one hundred and twenty-two, just like a shining sun? I stood there dumbfounded, all the more because it was one of those big prizes: nearly one thousand pesos. It's just that, since half of it goes to the infant Jesus, the dowry needed for the convent is left to me clear and simple ...'

'And your aunt?' Amparo asked, as if she were censuring Carmela's rejoicing.

'And do you know that I wanted to deposit the money for the dowry for when she dies, and remain with her, but she didn't want to? She says no, that it's quite plain that God is calling me to Him... She's gone and found employment in a priest's house... Since she's like that, half blind, she can only be useful in a place where there's little to do. Oh, my sweet Infant Jesus! How many tears I've shed here without anybody seeing me! What days! It's better to make cigarettes than lace. As far as smoking goes, people will always smoke, but making lace in winter ... it's like making a living sewing cobwebs.'

And as she stood up, she grabbed a flower pot that was in the window and handed it to Amparo.

'Take it, I'm glad you've come... Take care of this mallow for me, because I'm afraid the pot will break on the trip.'

Amparo picked up the flower pot and breathed in the perfume of the plant, burying her face in the velvety leaves. The lacemaker looked at her with eyes that were perpetually melancholy and serene.

'Amparo,' she said all at once.

'What?' *la Tribuna* replied, as surprised as if she had been suddenly woken up.

'Will you be angry if I tell you something?'

'No... Why would I be angry?' she answered, fixing her big, shining eyes on the future Franciscan Sister of the Immaculate.

'I just wanted to tell you ... that they've given you a nickname round here.'

'A nickname? Is it something bad?'

'Bad ... what do I know! They call you *la Tribuna*.'

'And who calls me it?'

'The young gentlemen ... the men. They say it's because on the day of the big banquet ... don't take it badly, because they told it me like this, in all innocence ... one of those men of the *Sembly* embraced you ... and he said to you ...'

–¡Me llamó *Tribuna del pueblo*! –exclamó orgullosamente la muchacha–. ¡Ya se ve que me lo llamó!

–Y eso, ¿qué es, mujer?

–¿Lo qué?

–¿Eso de *Tribuna del pueblo*?

–Es…; ya se sabe, mujer, lo que es. Como tú no lees nunca un periódico…

–Ni falta que me hace…; pero dímelo tú, anda.

–Pues es … así a modo de una…, de una que habla con todos, supongamos.

–¿Que habla con todos?… ¿Y te lo dijo en tu cara?… ¡El Dulce nombre de María!

–Pero no hablar por mal, tonta; si no es por eso… Es hablar de los deberes del pueblo, de lo que ha de hacer; es istruir a las masas públicas…

–Vamos, como una maestra de escuela… Jesús, si pensé que…, ya decía yo; ¿había de ser tan descarado que se lo encajase allí, sin más ni más? Pero como por ahí se ríen cuando mentan eso…

–¡Bah!… No tienen qué hacer, y velay.

–Y … mira, ¿te digo otro cuento?

–Tú dirás…

–Me contaron … no tomes pesadumbre, que son dichos, que andaba tras de ti un señorito … de la oficialidá.

–¿Y si anda?

–Y si anda, haces muy mal en hacer caso de un oficial, mujer… A las chicas pobres no las buscan ellos para cosa buena, no y no… Y a las que son pobres y formales no se arriman, porque ven que no sacan raja…

–¡Eh! A modo…; no la armemos, Carmela. A mí nadie se arrima por la raja que saque, sino por el aquel de que le gustaré y vamos andando, que cada uno tiene sus gustos… Hoy en día, más que digan los reaccionarios, la istrucción iguala las clases, y no es como algún tiempo… No hay oficial ni señorito que valga…

–Mujer, yo no hablé por mal… Te quise avisar, porque siempre te tuve ley, que eres así … una infeliz, un pedazo de pan en tus interioridades… Déjate de políticas, no seas tonta, y de señoritos… Fuera de eso, ¿a mí qué se me importa? Es por tu bien…

'He called me *Tribune of the People!*' the girl exclaimed proudly. 'It's common knowledge that's what he called me!'

'But what is it?'

'What's what?'

'This business about *Tribune of the People!*'

'It's … well, everybody knows what it is. As you never read a newspaper…'

'Nor do I need to … but tell me, come on.'

'Well, it's … sort of like a … a woman who speaks to everyone, let's suppose.

'One who speaks to everyone … ? And he told you to your face…? Sweet Mary Mother of God!'

'But it wasn't to speak badly of me, you daft thing; that's not what it is… It means to speak about the duties of the people, of what has to be done; it means to instruck the public masses…'

'All right, like a schoolteacher … good heavens, and I thought … and I was about to say something; could he be so barefaced as to pass off an insult like that right there, without further ado? But as everyone around here laughs when they mention that…'

'Bah…! They've got nothing to do, and that's it.'

'But … look, can I tell you another story?'

'Go ahead…'

'They told me … don't feel bad, because it's just gossip, that a young gentleman was going after you … one of those army officers.'

'And what if he is?'

'Well, if he is after you, you're doing the wrong thing if you pay attention to an army officer… They don't go around looking for poor girls for something good, no, no… But if the girls are poor and responsible, they won't come close, because they can see that there'll be no pickings for them…'

'Eh! So … let's not make any more of it than it is, Carmela. Nobody's going to sidle up to me because of any pickings to be had, but only because he likes me and we get on, because everyone has their own tastes… Nowadays, no matter what the reactionaries may say, *educashun* makes all social classes equal, and it's not like in the old days… There's no officer or fancy gentlemen worth more…'

'Truly, I didn't say it out of spite … I just wanted to let you know, because I've always been devoted to you, because that's what you're like … you're good-natured, a really nice person at heart… Don't be foolish, forget politics and fancy gentlemen. Outside of that, what else could be in it for me? It's for your own good …'

Se dispuso Amparo a marcharse, cogiendo debajo del brazo su tarro; pero la afectuosa encajera la quiso abrazar antes.

–No quiero que quedemos reñidas... ¿Vas enfadada? Bien sabe Dios mi intención... Escríbeme a Portomar... Ya te contaré todo, todo.

Y se asomó a la puerta para ver alejarse a la garbosa muchacha, cuyo vestido de percal proyectó, por espacio de algunos segundos, una mancha clara sobre las oscuras paredes de las casas de enfrente.

Amparo prepared to leave, taking the pot under her arm; but the affectionate lacemaker wanted to embrace her first.

'I don't want us to be on bad terms... Are you angry? God knows my intentions are good... Write to me in Portomar ... I'll tell you everything, everything.'

And she looked out of the doorway to see going off into the distance the graceful girl whose percale dress, for the space of a few seconds, projected a bright stain against the dark walls of the houses opposite.

XXIX

UN DELITO

Desde la venida de Amadeo I tenían las cigarreras de Marineda a quién echar la culpa de cuantos males afligían a la fábrica. Cuando caminaba hacia España el nuevo rey, leíanse en los talleres, con pasión vehementísima, todos los periódicos que decían: «No vendrá.» Y el caso es que vino, con gran asombro de las operarias, a quienes la Prensa roja había vaticinado que la monarquía era «un yerto cadáver, sentenciado por la civilización a no abandonar su tumba». Alguna cigarrera abogó por el hijo de Víctor Manuel, rey liberal al cabo, que daba la mano a todos y no tenía maldita la soberbia; pero la inmensa mayoría convino en que, al fin, un rey era siempre un rey, y en que la monarquía no era la república federal, verdades tan palmarias que, por último, los disidentes hubieron de reconocerlas.

Otros motivos de irritación ayudaban a soliviantar los ánimos. Escaseaban las consignas y la hoja tan pronto era quebradiza y seca, como podrida y húmeda. No, trabajo habían de pasar los que fumasen semejante veneno; pero las que lo manejaban también estaban servidas. Al ir a estirar la hoja para hacer las capas, en vez de extenderse, se rompía, y en fabricar un cigarro se tardaba el tiempo que antes en concluir dos; y para mayor ignominia, había que echarle remiendos a la capa por el revés lo mismo que a una camisa vieja, lo cual era gran vergüenza para una cigarrera honrada y que sabe su obligación al dedillo. Las operarias alzaban los brazos ejecutando la desesperada pantomima popular, llevándose ambas manos a la cabeza, a la frente, al pecho, señalando con enérgicos ademanes el tabaco averiado e inútil, de imposible elaboración. Tan alteradas estaban, que al pasar las maestras les metían puñados de hoja en las narices, gritando que «olía a berzas»; y envalentonándose, lo hicieron también con los inspectores, y si el jefe se hubiera presentado en los talleres, apostaban que con el jefe repetirían la escena. En vano algunas maestras intentaron calmar el oleaje, prometiendo para el entrante mes, nuevas consignas: seguían las turbulencias, porque aquel Gobierno maldito, no contento con enviarles hoja de desperdicio, para más, daba en la flor de no pagarles. Pasaban días y días sin que la

29

A CRIME

Ever since the arrival on the scene of Amadeo 1, the cigar makers in Marineda had someone to blame for all the evils that afflicted the factory. When the new king was on his way to Spain, all the newspapers were being read in the workshops with the most vehement passion, announcing: 'He will not come.'[xxxiii] And the fact is that he did come, to the great astonishment of the workers, to whom the radical press had prophesied that the monarchy was 'a rigid corpse, sentenced by civilisation never to abandon its tomb'. An occasional cigar maker championed Victor Emmanuel's son, a liberal king after all, who shook hands with everyone, and had none of that accursed arrogance; but the vast majority agreed that, in the long run, a king was always a king, and that the monarchy was not the federal republic, truths so self-evident that the dissidents finally had to recognise them.

There were other reasons for the irritation that helped to rouse spirits. The consignments of tobacco were scarce and the leaves were either brittle and dry or rotten and damp. No, those who smoked poison like that would have a job of it, but those who handled it also had their share of troubles. When they went to stretch out the leaves in order to make the cigar wrappers, instead of spreading out, they broke, and it took them just as much time to make one cigar as it had previously taken them to finish two; what made it even more shameful was that they were compelled to put a patch on the inside part of the wrapper just as you would do for an old shirt, all of which was a great embarrassment for an honourable cigar maker, who had her sense of duty at her fingertips. The workers would raise their arms and perform the stock mime for desperation, lifting both hands to their heads, to their foreheads, to their bosoms, pointing out with energetic gestures how faulty, useless and impossible to work with the tobacco was. The workers were so upset that when the maestras passed by, they thrust fistfuls of tobacco leaves under their noses, shouting that 'it smelt of cabbage'; and plucking up their courage, they also did this with the inspectors, and if the manager had appeared in the workshops, they wagered that they would repeat the same scene with the manager. In vain did some of the maestras try to calm down the surge, promising new consignments for the coming month: the restlessness continued because that accursed government, not content with sending them worthless leaves, also had the bright idea of not paying them. Day after day passed by without the payroll office opening,

cobranza se abriese, y las pobres mujeres, tímidamente al principio, después en voz alta y angustiosa, preguntaban a las maestras: «Y luego, ¿cuándo nos darán los cuartos?» Fue en *crescendo* el runrún y se convirtió en formidable marejada. El instinto que impele a los amotinados a ponerse a las órdenes de alguien, aconsejó a las operarias del taller de cigarrillos arrimarse a Amparo buscando el calor de su tribunicia frase. Halláronse chasqueadas: Amparo no dio fuego. Oyó a todas y convino con ellas en que, efectivamente, era una picardía no pagarles lo suyo; y, ventilado este punto, siguió liando pitillos, sin añadir arenga, excitación, sermón político ni cosa que lo valiese. Admiradas se quedaron las turbas de semejante frialdad. ¡Si pudiesen penetrar en lo íntimo del alma de Amparo, en aquellos inexplorados rincones donde quizá ella misma no sabía con total exactitud lo que guardaba! ¡Si hubiesen visto brotar una figurita chica, chica, remotísima, como las que se ven con los anteojos de teatro cogidos a la inversa, pero que iba creciendo con rapidez asombrosa, y que en la nomenclatura interior de las ilusiones se llamaba *señora de Sobrado*! ¡Si advirtiesen cómo esa *señora*, microscópica, aún vestida del color del deseo, iba avanzando, avanzando, hasta colocarse en el eminente puesto que antes ocupaba *la Tribuna*, que se retiraba al fondo envuelta en su manto de un rojo más pálido cada vez!...

Atribuyóse a otras causas la indiferencia de la oradora. Amparo tenía los dedos listos y una boca no más que mantener; la crisis económica no podía importarle tanto como a las que reunían seis hijos, tres o cuatro hermanos, familia dilatada, sin más recursos que el trabajo de una mujer. El tiempo corría, y en la tienda se cansaban de fiarles; se veían perdidas; ¿cómo salir del apuro? ¡A los angelitos no era cosa de darles a comer las piedras de la calle! *La Guardiana*, hablando de su sordomuda, partía el corazón; ella primero consentía morir que privar a la niña de su cascarillita con azúcar y de su pan fresco de trigo; si era preciso, pediría una limosna: no sería la primera vez; y al oír esto todas sus amigas la atajaron: ¡Pedir limosna! ¡Qué humillación para la fábrica! No: se ayudarían mutuamente, como siempre; las que estaban mejor se rascarían el bolsillo para atender a las más necesitadas; y, en efecto, así se hizo, verificándose numerosas cuestaciones, siempre con fruto abundante.

Cierto día se difundió por la fábrica siniestro rumor: Rita de la Riberilla, una operaria, había sido cogida con tabaco. ¡Con tabaco! ¡Jesús, si parecía

and the poor women, timidly at first, then in loud distressed voices, would ask the maestras: 'So then, when will they give us our dough?' The murmur got louder and turned into a formidable wave. The instinct which impels mutineers to put themselves under someone's orders advised the women in the workshop making cigarettes to come to Amparo in search of the heat of her tribunicial oratory. They were disappointed: there was no burst of fire from Amparo. She listened to them all and agreed with them that it was indeed a despicable thing not to pay them what was theirs; and once this point had been aired, she carried on rolling cigarettes, without adding a harangue, passion, a political sermon or anything worthy of that. Such coolness astonished the throng of women. If only they could penetrate to the depths of Amparo's soul, into those unexplored corners where perhaps she herself did not know exactly what was hidden away! If only they had seen a little figure appear, very little and far away, like those you see with opera glasses when they are held the other way round, but one that was growing with astonishing rapidity, and which in the inner nomenclature of illusions was called *Señora de Sobrado*! If they could only see how that microscopic *señora*, still dressed in the colour of desire, kept advancing, advancing, until she was in the eminent position formerly occupied by *la Tribuna*, who was withdrawing into the background, wrapped in her cloak of red which kept getting paler and paler...!

The orator's indifference was attributed to other causes. Amparo had agile fingers and just one mouth to support; the economic crisis could not be as important for her as for those who were responsible for six children, three or four brothers and sisters, or an extended family, without any other resources than the work of one woman. Time was flying by and shops were getting tired of selling on credit; they looked lost; how could they get out of this predicament? You couldn't feed those little angels on stones from the street! It broke your heart when *la Guardiana* spoke of her little deaf-mute; she would rather consent to die than deprive the child of her precious cup of cocoa with sugar and her fresh wheat bread; she would go begging if it were necessary; it wouldn't be the first time; and when they heard this, all her friends cut her short: Go begging! What a humiliating thing for the factory! No: they would help one another, as always; those who were better off would dig deep in their pockets to take care of the neediest; and, in effect, this is how it was done, with numerous collections taking place, always with bountiful results.

On one certain day, a sinister rumour spread through the factory: Rita from La Riberilla, one of the workers, had been caught with tobacco. With

una santa aquella mujer chiquita, flaca, con los ojos ribeteados de llorar, que solía atarse a la cara un pañuelo negro a causa, quizá, del dolor de muelas! Pero algunas cigarreras, mejor informadas, se echaron a reír: ¿Dolor de muelas?, ¡Ya baja! Era que su marido la solfeaba todas las noches, y ella, por tapar los tolondrones y cardenales, se empañicaba así; también una vez se había presentado arrastrando la pierna derecha y diciendo que tenía reúma, y la reúma era un lapo atroz del esposo. Cuando llevaron a la culpable al despacho del jefe, lo primero que hizo fue llorar sin responder; y al cabo, hostigada ya, asaeteada a preguntas, se resolvía a confesar que «su hombre» la abría a golpes si no le llevaba todos los días tres cigarros de a cuarto... *La Comadreja*, con su carilla puntiaguda, cómicamente fruncida, remedaba a la perfección los entrecortados sollozos, el hipo y las súplicas de la delincuente.

–Tres cig...aaarros, señor menistrad...ooor, tres cig...aaarros sólo, que aun yo de aquí viva no saaal...ga si otra triste hilacha de taaab...aco apañé...; que yo no lo hiiice por cubicia,[31] tan cierto como que Dios bendito está en los diiiivinos sielos, sino que el hombre me da con el formón, que, perdonando la cara de usté, en una pierna me cortó la carne, que puedo enseñar la llaga, que aún no curó... Y él sólo quería el tabaco para fuuumar, que no es para vender ni haber negocio... Y ahora yo pierdo el pan, y mis hijos también... Porque, escuche y perdone; él me decía: ya que no traes cuartos hace un mes a la casa, tan siquiera trae cigarros, bribona...

El taller entero, a vueltas de la risa que le causaba la graciosa mímica de Ana, rompió en exclamaciones de lástima: robar no estaba bien hecho, claro que no; pero también hay que ponerse en la situación de cada uno; ¿Cómo se había de gobernar la infeliz, si su marido la tundía y hacía picadillo con ella? ¡Ay! ¡Dios nos libre de un mal hombre, de un vicioso! En fin, no era razón dejar morir de hambre a los chiquillos de la Rita; la fábrica daba limosnas a bastantes pobres de fuera: con más motivo a los de dentro; y la maestra recorrió el taller con el delantal hecho bolsa, y llovieron en él cuartos, perros y monedas de diferentes calibres en gran abundancia.[32] Al llegar frente a Amparo, ésta tuvo un rasgo que fue aplaudidísimo y le conquistó otra vez gran popularidad. Hacía ya una semana que la pitillera vivía del crédito, porque sus gastos de vestir la traían siempre atrasada; y cuando la cuestora se acercó a pedirle, no tenía la futura señora de Sobrado

31 Codicia. Las formas correctas en gallego son: *cobiza* y *cubiza*.
32 Véase *Apuntes autobiográficos*, *Obras completas*, *Tomo III*, pp. 725–6: ¡Pobres mujeres las de la Fábrica de la Coruña! Nunca se me olvida todo lo bueno instintivo que noté en ellas, su natural rectitud y su caridad espontánea. Capaces son de dar hasta la camisa, si ven *una lástima*, como ellas dicen.

tobacco! My God, but she looked like a saint, that skinny little woman with eyes red from crying, who used to tie a black scarf around her face, probably on account of toothache! But some of the better informed cigar makers burst into laughter. Toothache? That's a likely story! It was because her husband gave her a good thrashing every night, and she bundled her face up in this fashion to cover up the bumps and bruises; also, once she had turned up to work dragging her right leg and saying that she had a touch of rheumatism, and the rheumatism was in reality a dreadful blow from her husband. When they brought the guilty woman to the manager's office, the first thing she did was to cry without making any response; and in the end, after being harassed and pestered by questions, she decided to confess that 'her man' would rip her open if she didn't bring him three cheap cigars every day ... *The Weasel*, with her pointed little face and comical frown, mimicked to perfection the broken sobbing, the hiccups and the offender's pleading.

'Three cig…aaars, Señor ministrat…ooor, only three cig…aaars; may I never leea…ve here alive if I pinched any other measly shred of tooob… acco; because I didn't dooo it out of greed, as sure as blessed God is in hoooly heaven, but because my man lets me have it with a chisel, and forgive me for saying this, he cut the flesh open on one of my legs, and I can show the wound, because it still hasn't healed… And he only wanted the tobacco to smoooke, not to sell or do business with… And now I'm going to lose my job, and even my poor children too… Because, listen and forgive me; he said to me: since you haven't brought any money home for a month, at least bring some cigars, you layabout…'

The entire workshop, doubled up with the laughter brought on by Ana's delightful mimicry, burst into exclamations of pity: stealing wasn't the right thing to do, of course not, but you also have to put yourself in every other person's place; how was the wretched woman to be in control if her husband kept giving her a beating and made mincemeat out of her? Alas! May God protect us from a bad man, a vicious man! In short, it wasn't a reason to let Rita's little children die of hunger; the factory gave charity to quite a lot of poor people outside: all the more reason to help those inside; the maestra went all around the workshop with her apron made into a pouch, and pennies, coppers and coins of different sizes poured into it in great abundance. When she arrived in front of Amparo, the girl performed a widely applauded deed and won over great popularity once again. The cigar maker had been living on credit for a whole week now, because the money she spent on clothes kept her constantly short of funds; when the charity collector came up to her to ask for a donation, the future Señora de Sobrado didn't even have a brass

ni un ochavo roñoso en el bolsillo. Pero, cosa de un mes antes, había realizado uno de sus caprichos, comprando con las economías, en otro tiempo destinadas a salvar a la Asamblea, un par de pendientes largos de oro bajo, que eran su orgullo: quitóselos sin vacilar, y los echó en el delantal de la maestra. Alzóse un clamoreo, una aprobación ruidosa y vehemente, gritos agudos, voces humedecidas por el llanto, bendiciones casi inarticuladas, y al punto dos o tres objetos más de escaso valor, una sortija de plata, un dedal de lo mismo, vinieron despedidos desde las mesas próximas, cayeron en el delantal y se mezclaron con la calderilla.

Aquella tarde, al salir de los talleres, vieron las operarias, colgado cerca del quicio de la puerta, el cartel de rigor:

«Habiendo sido cogida con tabaco en el acto del registro la operaria del taller de cigarros comunes, Rita Méndez, del partido número 3, rancho 11, queda expulsada para siempre de la fábrica.

–*El administrador jefe*, FULANO DE TAL.»

Colocadas a ambos lados de la escalera, las cuadrilleras vigilaban para que el despejo se hiciese con orden; y sentadas en sus sillas, esperaban las maestras, más serias que de costumbre, a fin de proceder al registro. Acercábanse las operarias como abochornadas, y alzaban de prisa sus ropas, empeñándose en que se viese que no había gatuperio ni contrabando... Y las manos de las maestras palpaban y recorrían con inusitada severidad la cintura, el sobaco, el seno, y sus dedos rígidos, endurecidos por la sospecha, penetraban en las faltriqueras, separaban los pliegues de las sayas... Mientras, los bandos de mujeres iban saliendo con la cabeza caída –humilladas todas por el ajeno delito–; y el reloj antiguo de pesas, de tosca madera, pintado de color de ocre con churriguerescos adornos dorados, que grave y austero como un juez adornaba el zaguán, dio las seis.

farthing in her pocket. But, going back a month, she had satisfied one of her whims and bought with her savings, money which at another time would have been used to save the Assembly, a pair of long, low-carat gold earrings, which were her pride and joy: she removed them without hesitation and threw them into the maestra's apron. A clamorous uproar arose, a noisy, vehement approbation, high-pitched shouts, voices moistened with tears, almost inarticulate blessings, and immediately two or three other objects of limited value, a silver ring and a thimble of the same metal, flung from the nearby tables, fell into the apron and mixed in with the small change.

That afternoon, when they left the workshops, the workers saw hanging near the door frame the inevitable notice:

'Having been caught in possession of tobacco in the course of personal inspection, Rita Méndez, an employee in the workshop producing cigars, group number three, section eleven, is herewith permanently expelled from the factory.

Administrator-in-chief, Joe Bloggs.'

Standing on both sides of the stairway, the forewomen watched over the process of clearing up to see it was done in an orderly fashion; and sitting in their chairs, the maestras, more serious than usual, were waiting in order to go ahead with the inspection. The workers began approaching, somewhat embarrassed, and quickly raised their garments, determined to prove there was no dirty business or smuggled goods... And the maestras' hands felt and examined waists, armpits and breasts with unusual severity, and their rigid fingers, hardened by suspicion, entered the women's pockets and separated the folds of their skirts... In the meantime, the convoys of women were coming out with their heads down – all of them humiliated by someone else's crime – and the old weight driven clock, made of rough wood and painted ochre, with golden churriguerresque[17] ornamentations, which adorned the entrance hall as gravely and austerely as a judge, struck six o'clock.

---

17 Named after the architect and sculptor José Benito de Churriguera (1665–1752) and refering to the late Spanish baroque style, characterised by elaborate ornamentation and lavish decoration.

XXX
DÓNDE VIVÍA LA PROTAGONISTA

El barrio de Amparo era de gente pobre; abundaban en él las cigarreras, pescadores y *pescantinas*.[33] Las diligencias y los carruajes, al cruzar por la parte de la Olmeda, lo llenaban de polvo y ruido un instante, pero presto volvía a su mortecina paz aldeana. Sobre el parapeto del camino real que cae al mar, estaban siempre de codos algunos marineros, con gruesos zuecos de palo, faja de lana roja, gorro catalán; sus rostros curtidos, su sotabarba poblada y recia, su mirar franco, decían a las claras la libertad y rudeza de la vida marítima; a pocos pasos de este grupo, que rara vez faltaba de allí, se instalaba, en la confluencia de la alameda y la cuesta, el mercadillo: cestas de marchitas verduras, pescados, mariscos; pero nunca aves ni frutas de mérito.

Lo más característico del barrio eran los chiquillos. De cada casucha baja y roma, al salir el sol en el horizonte salía una tribu, una pollada, un hormiguero de ángeles, entre uno y doce años, que daba gloria. De ellos los había patizambos, que corrían como asustados palmípedos; de ellos, derechitos de piernas y ágiles como micos o ardillas; de ellos, bonitos como querubines, y de ellos, horribles y encogidos como los fetos que se conservan en aguardiente. Unos daban indicios de no sonarse los mocos en toda su vida, y otros se oreaban sin reparo, teniendo frescas aún las pústulas de la viruela o las ronchas del sarampión; a algunos, al través de la capa de suciedad y polvo que les afeaba el semblante, se les traslucía el carmín de la manzana y el brillo de la salud; otros ostentaban desgreñadas cabelleras, que si ahora eran zaleas o ruedos, hubieran sido suaves bucles cuando los peinaran las cariñosas manos de una madre. No era menos curiosa la indumentaria de esta pillería que sus figuras. Veíanse allí gabanes aprovechados de un hermano mayor, y tan desmesuradamente largos, que el talle besaba las corvas y los faldones barrían el piso, si ya un tijeretazo no los había suprimido; en cambio, no faltaba pantalón tan corto que, no logrando encubrir la rodilla, arregazaba impúdicamente descubriendo medio muslo. Zapatos, pocos, y esos muy estropeados y risueños, abiertos de boca y endeblillos de suela;

---

33 Vendedora a domicilio de pescado.

30

WHERE THE PROTAGONIST LIVED

Amparo's neighbourhood was one of poor people; there were plenty of cigar makers, fishermen and fish-sellers in it. When stagecoaches and carriages crossed through La Olmeda, they covered it with dust and filled it with noise for a moment, but it quickly returned to its moribund, rustic peace. Forever leaning their elbows on the parapet along the main road that drops down to the sea were various sailors wearing heavy wooden clogs, red woollen sashes and Catalan caps; their weather-beaten faces, their coarse, bushy jowls and their candid expressions spoke clearly of the freedom and roughness of life at sea; a few steps away from this group, which was rarely missing from here, a small marketplace was set up, at the very confluence of the boulevard and the Cuesta: baskets of wilting green vegetables, fish and shellfish, but never any fowl or fruit of decent quality.

The most characteristic thing about the neighbourhood was the little children. When the sun appeared on the horizon, a whole tribe of them came out of each of the dull, low hovels, a brood, a swarm of angels between the ages of one and twelve, a true delight; amongst them were knock-kneed ones who ran about like frightened web-footed animals; also, some with little, straight legs, as agile as monkeys or squirrels; plus, some as pretty as cherubim, and others as horrible and shrunken as foetuses preserved in liquor. Some gave every indication of having never blown the snot from their noses in all their lives, while others cleared their noses without qualms, revealing the still fresh smallpox pustules or measles rash; for some of them, a ruddy, apple-cheeked complexion and the splendour of good health showed through the layer of dirt and dust that made them look ugly; others paraded dishevelled heads of hair, which, if they now seemed like sheepskin or bristly round mats, would have become soft ringlets when combed by a mother's affectionate hands. The way this gang of rascals dressed was no less curious than their physical appearance. You could see overcoats there handed down from an older brother, so excessively long that the waist touched the backs of their knees and the coattails would have swept along the floor if a snip of the scissors hadn't already removed them; on the other hand, there were plenty of trousers so short that, not managing to cover the knees, were tucked up immodestly and revealed half the thighs. As for shoes, very few, and these were falling apart and smiling, the front gaping open and the soles thin and

ropa blanca, reducida a un jirón, porque, ¿quién les pone cosa sana para que luego se revuelquen en la carretera y se den de mojicones todo el santo día, y se cojan a la zaga de todos los carruajes, gritando: «¡Tralla, tralla!»?

De lo que ninguno carecía era de cobertera para el cráneo: cuál lucía hirsuta gorra de pelo, que le daba semejanza con un oso; cuál un agujereado fieltro sin forma ni color; cuál un canasto de paja tejido en el presidio, y cuál un enorme pañuelo de algodón, atado con tal arte, que las puntas simulaban orejas de liebre. ¡Oh, y qué cariño profesaban los benditos pilluelos a aquella parte de su vestimenta! Antes se dejarían cortar el dedo meñique que arrancar la gorra o el sombrero; nada les importaba volver a casa de noche sin una pierna del calzón o sin un brazo de la chaqueta; pero con la cabeza descubierta, sería para ellos el más grave disgusto.

Vivía el barrio entero en la calle, por poco que el tiempo estuviese apacible y la temperatura benigna. Ventanas y puertas se abrían de par en par, como diciendo que donde no hay no importa que entren ladrones; y en el marco de los agujeros por donde respiraban trabajosamente los ahogados edificios, se asomaba ya una mujer peinándose las guedejas, y de la cual sólo distinguía el transeúnte la rápida aparición del brazo blanco y la oscura aureola del cabello suelto; ya otra, remendando una saya vieja; ya lactando a un niño, cuyas carnes rollizas doraba el sol; ya mondando patatas y echándolas, una a una, en grosera cazuela... Esta vecina atravesaba con la *sella*[34] de relucientes aros camino de la fuente; aquélla se acomodaba a sacudir un refajo o a desocupar, mirando hacia todos lados con recelo, una jofaina; la de más acá salía con ímpetu a administrar una mano de azotes al chico que se tendía en el polvo; la de más allá volvía con una *pescada*,[35] cogida por las agallas, que se balanceaba y le flagelaba el vestido. Todas las excrecencias de la vida, los prosaicos menesteres que en los barrios opulentos se cumplen a sombra de tejado, salían allí a luz y a vista del público. Pañales pobres se secaban en las cancillas de las puertas; la cuna del recién nacido, colocada en el umbral, se exhibía tan sin reparo como las enaguas de la madre ... y, no obstante, el barrio no era triste; lejos de eso, los árboles próximos, el campo y mar colindantes, lo hacían por todo extremo saludable; el paso de los coches lo alborotaba; los chiquillos, piando como gorriones, le prestaban por momentos singular animación; apenas había casa sin jaula de codorniz o jilguero, sin alelíes o albahaca en el antepecho de las ventanas; y no

34 Herrada.
35 Merluza.

flimsy; for underwear, they were reduced to tattered bits of cloth, because who would put something whole on them so they could then roll around on the road and punch each other in the face the whole blessed day, and hang on to the rear of all the passing carriages, shouting: 'Giddy up, giddy up!'?

But none of them was without some covering for his skull: one showed off a bristly cap, which made him look like a bear; another wore a felt hat full of holes, of no real shape or colour; another had on a large straw basket woven in a prison; and another, an enormous cotton scarf, tied with such skill that the points were like a hare's ears. Oh, and what affection those blessed scamps had for that part of their clothing! They would sooner have their little fingers cut off than pull off their cap or hat; they didn't care one bit if they came home at night without a trouser leg or an arm of their jacket, but if their heads were uncovered it would be the most serious of blows for them.

The whole neighbourhood lived out on the street if the weather was pleasant and the temperature mild. Windows and doors opened wide, as if to say that where there is nothing, it doesn't matter if thieves come in; and in the frames of the holes through which the stuffy buildings laboriously breathed, a woman appeared combing her locks, and the only thing of her that a passerby could make out was the sudden appearance of a white arm and the dark halo of loose hair; then another woman, mending an old skirt; another, breast-feeding her child, its chubby body turned gold by the sun; yet another, peeling potatoes and throwing them, one by one, into a rough earthenware casserole ... This resident would walk by carrying a bucket with shiny hoops on her way to the fountain; that one was settling down to shake out an underskirt or, looking suspiciously in all directions, empty a washbasin; this one over here would rush out to administer a good spanking to a child lying down in the dust; the one over there was coming back with a hake, held by the gills, as it swung to and fro and flapped against her dress. All of life's excrescences, the prosaic functions which are carried out behind closed doors in opulent areas of the city, came out here, in full view of the public. Shoddy nappies were left to dry on the gates of the doorways; the cradle of a newborn baby, placed at the threshold, was exhibited with as little hesitation as for the mother's underskirts ... and nevertheless, the area wasn't sad; far from it; the nearby trees, the countryside and the adjacent sea made it all extremely wholesome; the passing of the coaches stirred it all up; the small children, chirping like sparrows, lent it exceptional animation at times; there was hardly a house without a caged quail or a goldfinch, without wallflowers or basil on the window sills; and no sooner was the sun shining

bien lucía el sol, las barricas de sardinas arenques, arrimadas a la pared y descubiertas, brillaban como gigantesca rueda de plata.

Tampoco faltaban allí comercios que, acatando la ley que obliga a los organismos a adaptarse al medio ambiente, se acomodaban a la pobreza de la barriada. Tiendecillas angostas, donde se vendían zarazas catalanas y pañuelos; abacerías de sucio escaparate, tras de cuyos vidrios un galán y una dama de pastaflora se miraban tristemente viéndose tan mosqueados y tan añejos, y las cajas tremendas de fósforos se mezclaban con garbanzos, fideos amarillos, aleluyas y naipes; figones que brindaban al apetito sardinas fritas y callos; almacenes en que se feriaban cucharas de palo, cestería, cribas y zuecos: tal era la industria de la cuesta de San Hilario. Allí se tuvo por notable caso el que un objeto adquirido se pagase de presente, y el crédito, palanca del moderno comercio, funcionaba con extraordinaria actividad.

Todo se compraba al fiado; cigarrera había que tardaba un año en saldar los chismes del oficio. Reinaba en el barrio cierta confianza, una especie de compadrazgo perpetuo, un comunismo amigable: de casa a casa se pedían prestados no solamente enseres y utensilios sino «una sed» de agua, «una nuez» de manteca, «un chiquito» de aceite, «una lágrima» de leche, «una nadita» de petróleo. Avisábanse mutuamente las madres cuando un niño se escapaba, se descalabraba o hacía cualquier diablura análoga; y como el derecho de azotar era recíproco, las infelices criaturas estaban en peligro de ser vapuleadas por el barrio entero.

Pronto se acostumbró la madre de Amparo a su nueva vecindad: tenía la cama próxima a la ventana, y nadie pasaba por allí sin detenerse a conversar un rato… Las pescaderas le referían sus *lances*, y la tullida compraba desde su lecho sardinas, pedía agua, oía chismes sin número, forjándose en cierto modo la ilusión de que tomaba el aire libre… Por lo que hace a Amparo, fue presto la reina del barrio: reíanse los marineros, abierta la boca de oreja a oreja, dilatando sus anchos semblantes de tritones, cuando la veían pasar; los carabineros del Resguardo le echaban flores… Casi todos manifestaron sentimiento al saber que «andaba» con un oficial, un señorito de allá del barrio de Abajo.

than barrels of herrings, close to the wall and opened up, glistened like a gigantic silver wheel.

Nor was there any lack of shops there which, complying with the law that obliges organisms to adapt to the environment, adjusted to the poverty of the district. Very small, narrow stores where they sold Catalan chintzes and headscarfs; grocery stores with filthy windows where, behind the glass, a handsome man and a lady, made of sponge cake, gazed sadly at each other, looking so spotty and so stale; and tremendous boxes of matches were mixed with chickpeas, yellow noodles, small religious prints and playing cards; cheap restaurants which offered fried sardines and tripe to whet the appetite; wholesale stores where they traded in wooden spoons, basketwork, sieves and clogs: such was the industry of the Cuesta de San Hilario. It was considered a significant thing there when an object was acquired and paid for on the spot, and credit, the driving force of modern commerce, functioned with extraordinary vitality.

Everything was bought on credit; there was one cigar maker who took a year to pay for the tools she used at work. A certain confidence reigned in the district, a kind of perpetual compaternity, an amicable communism: from one house to another they borrowed not only equipment and utensils, but also a 'splash' of water, a 'knob' of butter, a 'trickle' of oil, a 'teardrop of milk, a 'smidgen' of parrafin. The mothers always let each other know when a child ran off, hurt its head or got up to any similar prank, and, since the right to dish out a spanking was mutual, the unfortunate children were in danger of being thrashed by the entire neighbourhood.

Amparo's mother soon got used to her new neighbourhood: she had her bed next to the window and nobody could pass by there without stopping to chat for a while… The fishermen's wives told her about their *flings* and the crippled woman was able to buy sardines from her bed, ask for water, listen to the endless gossip, and to a certain extent build up the illusion of going out for fresh air… As for Amparo, she was soon queen of the neighbourhood: whenever they saw her pass by the sailors laughed, their mouths open from ear to ear and stretching their wide, newt-like faces; the customs offices from the customhouse paid her compliments… Almost everyone was sorry when they found out she 'was going around' with an army officer, a young gentleman from over there in the Barrio de Abajo.

XXXI
PALABRA DE CASAMIENTO

Desde que tuvo secretos que confiar, por natural instinto Amparo se arrimó a *la Comadreja* más que a *la Guardiana*. Ésta andaba no sé cómo, medio enferma, con la paletilla caída, según decía; y por más que se la levantó una saludadora[36] con los rezos y ensalmos de costumbre, la paletilla seguía en sus trece, y la muchacha tristona, pensando en cómo quedaban sus pequeños si se muriese ella. Hallaba Amparo en el semblante de *la Guardiana* no sé qué limpidez, qué tranquilidad honesta, que le helaban en los labios el cuento de amores cuando iba a empezarlo; al paso que Ana, con su nervioso buen humor, su cara puntiaguda rebosando curiosidad, convidaba a hablar. Amparo la tomó por confidente y hasta por compañera. Ana, viuda a la sazón de su capitán mercante, que andaba allá por Ribadeo, se prestó gustosa a ser, en cierto modo, la dueña guardadora de *la Tribuna*. Por su parte, Baltasar se apoderó de Borrén. Estaban aún los dos enamorados en el período comunicativo.

–¿Te dio palabra de casarse contigo? –preguntó a su amiga.

–No cuadró que yo se la pidiese… Una vez, con disimulo, le indiqué algo… ¡Si no fuese por la familia! ¡La madre, sobre todo, que es así!

Y Amparo cerraba el puño.

–¡Bah! Ve tomando paciencia once añitos, como yo… ¡Y si después lo consigues!…

–No, pues si no quiere casarse…, me parece que le doy despachaderas.

Ana notó, en estas bravatas, que se tambaleaba el alcázar de la firmeza tribunicia. Desde entonces su curiosidad perversa la espoleó, y en cierto modo le halagó la idea de que todas, por muy soberbias que fuesen, paraban en caer como ella había caído. Organizóse una especie de sociedad compuesta de cuatro personas: Amparo, Ana, Borrén y Baltasar; cada vez que celebraba sesión esta sociedad, ya se sabía que *la Comadreja* «cargaba» con el ronco y galanteador Borrén. Entreteníale con pesadas bromas, con todo género de indirectas y burletas, subrayadas por la risa de sus labios flacos, por el fruncimiento de su hocico de roedor. Ana sabía, como acostumbraba saberlo

---

36 Curandera que emplea oraciones y fórmulas mágicas para curar la rabia u otros males.

31

A PROMISE OF MARRIAGE

Since she had secrets to confide, Amparo's natural instinct was to be closer to *the Weasel* than *la Guardiana*. The latter was going around, God knows how, pretty much indisposed, with a strained upper back, according to what she said; and no matter how much a female quack straightened it up with her customary prayers and incantations, the pain in her back persisted, and the girl remained downhearted, pondering on how her little ones would be if she were to die. Amparo found a certain clearness in *la Guardiana*'s face, a certain modest tranquillity which made the story of her love affair freeze on her lips when she was going to begin it; while Ana, with her nervous good humour and her pointed face the picture of curiosity, invited you to speak. Amparo took her as a confidante and even as a companion. Ana, currently left on her own by her merchant captain, who was sailing out there around Ribadeo, gladly accepted being, to a certain extent, *la Tribuna*'s protecting duenna. Baltasar, for his part, took possession of Borrén. The two lovers were still in the communicative period.

'Did he give his word that he would marry you?' she asked her friend.

'It didn't look right for me to ask him for it … I did once furtively hint at something… If it weren't for his family! Especially his mother, and how she is!'

And Amparo clenched her fists.

'Bah! Try being patient for eleven whole years, like me… And if you get it then…!'

'No, if he doesn't want to get married … then I'll tell him a thing or two.'

Ana noticed that, for all this fighting talk, the fortress of her tribunicial resolution was shaking. From that time on, her perverse curiosity spurred her on, and to a certain extent she was flattered by the idea that all females, no matter how haughty they were, ended up as fallen women like her. A kind of fellowship was organised, consisting of four people – Amparo, Ana, Borrén and Baltasar – and every time this group had a meeting, it was common knowledge that *the Weasel* 'would take on' the raucous, flirtatious Borrén. She entertained him with tiresome jokes, with all kinds of innuendos and little tricks, accentuated by the laughter from her thin lips and the wrinkling up of her rodent-like nose. Ana knew, as she was used to knowing everything,

todo, la historia de Borrén, o, por mejor decir, su carencia de historia; y este carácter inofensivo del incansable faldero daba pie a *la Comadreja* para crucificarle a puras chanzas, para clavarle mil alfileres, para abrasarle. La travesura de pilluelo vicioso que distinguía a Ana le sirvió para olfatear la horrible timidez, el pánico extraño que afligía a aquel hombre tan pródigo en requiebros, tan aficionado al aroma del amor, y tan incapaz, por carácter, de gustarlo, como los soñadores que contemplan la luna de descolgarla del firmamento. ¡Pobre Borrén! Desde el sarcasmo hasta la mal rebozada injuria, todo lo devoró con resignación que podría llamarse angelical, si virtudes de este linaje negativo no fuesen más dignas del limbo que del cielo.

Vestía la primavera de verdor y hermosura cuanto tocaba, y convidados por la amable estación, los cuatro socios acostumbraban aprovechar las tardes de los días festivos, solazándose en los huertos que abundan en la vega marinedina, dominada por el camino real. Pese a su temperamento calculador y enemigo del escándalo, Baltasar cedía a la vehemente codicia del aromático veguero, hasta el punto de acompañar en público a la muchacha, si bien concretándose a aquel apartado rincón de la ciudad. Hacíalo, sin embargo, con tales restricciones, que Amparo se figuraba que lo comprometía dejándose ver a su lado.

En la vega se cultivaban legumbres y algún maíz; pero la prosa de este género de labranza la encubría la estación primaveral, adornándolos con una apretada red de floración; la col lucía un velo de oro pálido; la patata estaba salpicada de blancas estrellas; el cebollino parecía llovido de granizo copioso; las flores de coral del haba relucían como bocas incitantes, y en los linderos temblaban las sangrientas amapolas, y abría sus delicadas flores color lila el erizado cardo. Los sembrados de maíz, cuyos cotiledones comenzaban a salir de la tierra, hacían de trecho en trecho cuadrados de raso verdegay. Sobre todo un rincón había en la vega donde la Naturaleza, empeñada en vencer con su espontaneidad los artificios de la horticultura, lograba juntar, alrededor de un rústico pozo que suministraba muy fresca agua, dos o tres olmos más anchos que copudos, un grupo gracioso de mimbres, helechos y escolopendras, un rosal silvestre, algo, en fin, que rompía la uniformidad de la hortaliza. Aquel paraje era el favorito de Amparo y Baltasar, sobre todo desde que al lado, en los fresales, cuajados de flor blanca, empezaba a madurar el rojo fruto. El día de San José, Baltasar consiguió ya recoger para

Borrén's history, or more correctly, the lack of any history; this inoffensive character of his, of a tireless skirt-chaser, gave good cause to *the Weasel* to crucify him with endless jokes, to stick countless pins into him, to fill him with shame. The vicious, roguish waywardness which distinguished Ana served her well in sniffing out the dreadful timidity, the strange panic which afflicted that man, who was so generous in offering compliments, so fond of the aroma of love, but so inacapable, in his basic character, of enjoying it, like the dreamers who contemplate the moon, intent on taking it down from the firmament. Poor Borrén! From sarcasm to badly disguised insults, he swallowed everything with a resignation that could be called angelic, if virtues of this negative lineage were not more worthy of limbo than heaven.

Spring dressed everything it touched with greenness and beauty, and the four companions, encouraged by the agreeableness of the season, were wont to take advantage of the holiday afternoons, enjoying themselves in the vegetable gardens that are plentiful on the fertile lowland around Marineda, which the main road overlooks. In spite of his calculating nature and hostility towards scandal, Baltasar gave in to his vehement craving for this aromatic cigar, to the point where he accompanied the girl in public, although he did limit himself to that remote corner of the city. He did this, however, with such restrictions that Amparo imagined she was compromising him by letting herself be seen at his side.

Vegetables and some corn were grown on the fertile lowland, but the spring season hid the prosaic nature of this type of farming by decorating it with a thick net of flowering; the cabbages were sporting a veil of pale gold; the potatoes were sprinkled with white stars; the chives seemed like a shower of copious hail; the coral blossoms of the beans were glistening like provocative mouths, and, along the borders, the blood-red poppies were trembling and the prickly cardoon was opening its delicate, lilac-coloured petals. The fields sown with corn, with their cotyledons beginning to emerge from the earth, formed squares of light green satin every so often. There was especially one corner of the lowland where Nature, determined to overcome the artifices of horticulture with its own spontaneity, succeeded in bringing together, around a rustic well that provided very fresh water, two or three elm trees, wide rather than bushy, a delightful group of osiers, ferns and hart's tongue and a dog rose, something, in short, that broke the uniformity of the vegetable garden. That was Amparo and Baltasar's favourite spot, especially because to one side, in the strawberry beds crowded with white blossom, the red fruit was beginning to ripen. On the Feast Day of Saint Joseph, Baltasar already

la muchacha media docena de fresas en una hoja de col. Hasta mediados de abril aumentó la cosecha de fresilla; a principios de mayo comenzaba a disminuir, y escasearon los fresones de pulpa azucarosa, que tan suavemente humedecían la lengua. Un domingo del hermoso mes, hallándose reunida la *partie carrée* en la huerta a pretexto de fresas, ya a duras penas se rastreaba alguna escondida entre las hojas y gulusmeada[37] de babosas y caracoles.

–Don Enrique –exclamaba Ana dirigiéndose a Borrén–, ¿cuántas ha cogido usted ya? ¿Una y media? A ese paso, dentro de quince días las probaremos. No sirve usted ... ni para coger fresas.

–¿Cómo que no? Mire usted una preciosa que pillé ahora mismo... Le digo a usted, Anita, que sirvo para el caso.

–¿A ver? ¡Eso es lo que usted encuentra! Comida de bicharracos... ¡Huuuuy!

–¿Qué pasa? –exclamó, solícito, Borrén.

–¡Un babosón! –chilló ratonilmente Ana, sacudiendo los dedos y disparando el glutinoso animalucho al rostro de Borrén, que se pasó apaciblemente el pañuelo por las mejillas, amenazando a *la Comadreja* con la mano.

Amparo y Baltasar estaban un poco más desviados, y cerca del pozo que sombreaban los árboles. Picaban por turno las pocas fresas que tenía Amparo en el regazo sobre una hoja de berza. Las habían recogido juntos, y al hacerlo, sus manos trémulas y ávidas se encontraron entre el follaje.

–¡Eh..., dejad algunas! –les gritaba inútilmente Ana.

Amparo comía sin saber qué, por refrescarse la boca, donde notaba sequedad y amargor. Borrén miraba paternalmente el grupo, con ojos lánguidos de carnero a medio morir. *La Tribuna* pedía cuentas; Baltasar estaba por todo extremo obediente y cortés.

–¿Conque no fue usted a las *Flores de María*?

–No, mujer...; por quien soy que no fui. ¿No ves? Hoy es domingo; estarán llenas de gente las Flores, y el paseo brillante, con música y todo; y yo no pienso poner los pies en él.

–Los días de fiesta..., ¡vaya que! Sólo faltaba... ¡Es el único día que uno tiene libre; y se había usted de ir al paseo! ¿Pero ayer? ¿No entró usted ayer en San Efrén? ¿No cantaba la de García?

–¡Para lo bien que canta, hija! Parece un grillo.

–Pues ella dicen que se alaba de que va allí toda la oficialidad por oírla.

–Alabará..., ¿qué sé yo? Si no la veo hace mil años... Esa fresa es mía

---

37 Hollada, mordisqueada.

succeeded in picking half a dozen strawberries in a cabbage leaf for the girl. The harvest of sweet little strawberries increased up to the middle of April; it began to diminish at the beginning of May, and the big strawberries with a sugary pulp which moistened the tongue so gently, began to grow quite scarce. One Sunday in that lovely month, when the foursome, the *partie carrie*,[18] had gathered in the garden on the pretext of picking strawberries, it was only with great difficulty that you could track any down, hidden as they were among the leaves and nibbled away by slugs and snails.

'Don Enrique,' Ana exclaimed, addressing Borrén, 'how many have you picked already? One and a half? At that rate, we'll be tasting them in a fortnight. You're no use ... not even for picking strawberries.'

'What do you mean? Look at this lovely one I just got ... I'm telling you, Anita, that I'm good at this business.'

'Let's see. Is that what you found! Food for creepy-crawlies ... Yuck!'

'What's the matter?' Borrén exclaimed solicitously.

'A big, fat slug!' squeaked Ana like a mouse, shaking her fingers and hurling the revolting, glutinous creature at Borrén, who gently wiped his cheeks with a handkerchief and threatened *the Weasel* with his hand.

Amparo and Baltasar were a little off to one side, and near a well shaded by trees. They took it in turn to nibble at the few strawberries that Amparo had in her lap on a cabbage leaf. They had picked them together, and, whilst doing so, their trembling, eager hands had met amongst the foliage.

'Hey ... leave us a few!' Ana shouted at them to no avail.

Amparo was eating without knowing why, just to refresh her mouth, which she noticed was dry and bitter. Borrén was looking at the group in a paternal way, with the languid eyes of a half-dead sheep. *La Tribuna* was demanding a full account; Baltasar was extremely obedient and courteous.

'So you didn't go to the celebration of the *Flores de María*?'

'No ... it's not like me to go. Can't you see? Today is Sunday, and the Flores will be full of people; the procession will be resplendent, with music and everything, and I have no intention of setting foot there.'

'On feast days ... really! That's all I needed ... It's the only day one has free; you should have gone to the procession! But what about yesterday? Didn't you go into San Efrén yesterday? Wasn't the García girl singing?'

'Considering how she sings! She's like a cricket.'

'Well, everyone says she boasts that all the officers go there to hear her.'

'Does she boast ... how should I know? I haven't seen her for donkey's

---

18   A party of four persons (two men and two women).

—exclamó arrebatando una que Amparo llevaba a sus labios. Ella se la dejó robar, ruborizada y satisfecha.

—Y a su casa…, ¿tampoco va usted?

—Tampoco…, no seas celosa, chica. ¿Por qué hemos de hablar siempre de la de García y no de ti? ¡De nosotros! —añadió con expresión de contenida vehemencia.

Sintió la muchacha como una ola de fuego que la envolvía desde la planta de los pies hasta la raíz del cabello, y después un leve frío que le agolpó la sangre al corazón. Borrén se aproximó a la amante pareja, abriendo las manos llenas de tierra y de fresas despachurradas.

—Ya me duelen los riñones de andar a gatas —dijo—. Podíamos merendar, si a ustedes no les molesta, pollos.

—Por mí… —murmuró Amparo.

Ana se acercaba también, trayendo una servilleta anudada, que desató y tendió sobre el brocal del pozo. Reducíase la merienda a unos pastelillos de dulce y una botella de moscatel, regalo de Baltasar. Fueles preciso beber por el mismo vaso, único que había, y Ana, que era asquillosa y aprensiva, prefirió echar tragos por la botella, sin recelo de cortarse con los agudos cristales del roto gollete. Sus carrillos chupados se colorearon, su lengua se desató más que de costumbre; y por vía de diversión empezó a coger tierra a puñados y a esparcirla por la cabeza de Borrén. Después, levantándose, le propuso que «hiciese el remolino». Borrén no quería, ni a tres tirones; pero *la Comadreja* le asió de las manos, estribó en las puntas de los pies, muy juntas y arrimadas a las de su pareja, y echando el cuerpo atrás y dejando caer la cabeza hacia la espalda, empezó a girar, con gran lentitud al principio; poco a poco fue acelerando el volteo, hasta imprimirle vertiginosa rapidez. Cuando pasaba se veían un punto sus pómulos encendidos, sus ojos vagos y extraviados, su boca pálida, abierta para respirar mejor, su garganta espasmódica, rígida; mas no tardaba ni medio segundo en presentarse la asustada faz de Borrén, que se dejaba arrastrar sin que acertase a decir más palabra que «por Dios…, por Dios», con no fingida congoja. De repente se detuvo la peonza humana, con brusco movimiento, y se oyó un grito gutural. Ana se aplanó en el suelo.

Al ir a socorrerla, notó Amparo que ya no estaba sonrosada, sino del color de la cera, y que se le veía el blanco de los ojos. Baltasar subió precipitadamente el cubo del pozo, y casi colmado se lo volcó encima a la

years... That strawberry is mine,' he exclaimed as he snatched one away that Amparo was just putting to her lips. Blushing and self-satisfied, she let him steal it from her.'

'And her house ... don't you go there either?'

'No ... don't be jealous. Why must we always be talking about that García girl and not about you? About us!' he added with an expression of contained vehemence.

The girl felt like a wave of fire was enveloping her from the soles of her feet to the roots of her hair, followed by a slight chill which made the blood rush to her heart. Borrén approached the pair of lovers and opened his hands, which were covered in dirt and squashed strawberries.

'My back's already aching from crawling around,' he said. 'We could have our picnic now, if it doesn't bother you, my lovebirds.'

'As for me ...' Amparo murmured.

Ana came over too, bringing a napkin tied up in knots, which she undid and stretched out on the curb of the well. The snack amounted to nothing more than a few little cakes and a bottle of muscatel wine, a gift from Baltasar. They had to drink from the same glass, the only one they had, but Ana, who was qualmish and apprehensive, preferred to swig straight out of the bottle, without fear of cutting herself on the sharp glass edges of the broken neck. Her hollow cheeks turned red and her tongue grew looser than usual; and by way of diversion, she began to gather handfuls of earth and spread it over Borrén's head. Then she stood up and proposed that 'he swing her round and round'. Borrén didn't want to do it, never in a million years; but *the Weasel* grasped him by the hands, rested her weight on the tips of her toes, her feet together and very close to those of her partner, and letting her head fall towards her back, she began to whirl around, very slowly at first; little by little the whirling grew faster until it was marked by a vertiginous speed. When she passed by, for a moment you could see her flushed cheeks, her unfocused, vacant eyes, her pale mouth held open to breathe more easily, and her convulsive, rigid throat; but it only took a split second to catch sight of Borrén's frightened face, as he let himself be swept along, without managing to say a single word other than 'my God ... my God ...' with a distresss that wasn't feigned. Suddenly the human top stopped with a brusque movement and you could hear a guttural cry. Ana fell flat on the ground.

When she ran over to help her, Amparo noticed that her face was no longer pink but the colour of wax, and that you could see the whites of her eyes. Baltasar hastily brought up the bucket from the well and emptied

mareada *Comadreja*. Frotáronle mucho los pulsos y las sienes con el fresco líquido, y al fin la pupila fue bajando al globo de la córnea, mientras el pecho se dilataba con ruidoso suspiro. Dos minutos después estaba Ana en pie; pero quejándose de la cabeza, del corazón; declarando que tenía los huesos rotos, que se moría de frío; todo en voz baja y quejumbrosa, que nadie la tendría por la petulante moza de antes del desmayo.

–Mujer, vente a mi casa, te daré ropa seca –dijo Amparo.

–No, a la mía, a la mía... El cuerpo me pide cama.

–Duermes conmigo.

–No, a mi casita –insistió la abatida *Comadreja*–. Si va conmigo una fiebre, quiero estar en mis reales. ¡Ea!, adiós.

–Toma mi mantón siquiera –porfió *la Tribuna*.

–Bueno, venga... ¡Brr! Estoy hecha una sopa.

Y Ana, saludando con su esqueletada mano, ademán que indicaba un resto de intención festiva que aún retoñaba en ella, tomó el sendero que conducía al camino real. Entonces Baltasar miró a Borrén fijamente, con ojos expresivos más claros y categóricos que palabra alguna. Hay que decir –en abono del confidente universal– que titubeó. Sin alardear de moralista, bien puede un hombre blanco, que viste uniforme y peina barbas, encontrar que ciertos papeles son desairados y tontos. Una cosa es hablar, acompañar y animar, y otra... Por lo menos así pensaba Borrén, que más tenía de sandio rematado que de perverso. Y no obstante su repulsión, no supo resistir a la segunda ojeada, coercitiva al par que suplicante, del amigo. Bebió la hiel hasta las heces, y echó tras *la Comadreja*, pisando aturdidamente coles y maíz tierno.

–Espere usted, Anita, que la acompaño... –murmuraba–. Espere usted... Puede ocurrírsele a usted algo.

Encogióse de hombros Ana, y acortó el paso para dejar que se uniese Borrén. Emparejaron y caminaron en silencio por la carretera; Ana con los labios apretados y algo escalofriada y temblorosa, a pesar de ir muy arropada en el mantón. Al llegar a la entrada de la ciudad, la cigarrera se volvió y midió a Borrén con despreciativa ojeada de pies a cabeza.

–¿Se le ocurre a usted alguna cosa? –preguntó él, medio desvanecido aún, con ronquera que rayaba en afonía.

–Nada –respondió ella bruscamente. Y después, fijando en los de Borrén sus ojuelos verdes–: Don Enrique –añadió–, ¿sabe usted lo que venía pensando?

almost a full load on the dizzy *Weasel*. They rubbed her hands and temples with the cool liquid and finally her pupils started dropping down to the ball of the cornea, while her chest puffed out with a noisy sigh. Two minutes later Ana was on her feet, but complaining about her head and her heart, declaring that all her bones were broken, and that she was dying of cold; all this in a low, plaintive voice such that nobody would have taken her for the arrogant young woman from before the fainting fit.

'Come to my house, and I'll give you dry clothes,' said Amparo.

'No, mine, mine… My body's calling for a bed.'

'You can sleep with me.'

'No, to my little house,' the disheartened *Weasel* insisted. 'If I've got a fever, I want to be in my own place. So then! Good-bye.'

'At least take my shawl,' *la Tribuna* persisted.

'All right, let's have it… Brrr! I'm soaked to the skin!'

And Ana, waving at them with her skinny hand, a gesture that indicated a residue of festive intention that was maybe reappearing in her, took the path that led to the main road. It was then that Baltasar stared at Borrén with expressive eyes that were clearer and more explicit than any words. It has to be said – to the credit of this universal confidant – that he did hesitate. Without boasting of being a moralist, a white man wearing a uniform and sporting a beard might well find certain roles awkward and foolish. It is one thing talking, accompanying and encouraging, and another… At least that is how Borrén was thinking, for he was more of an utter fool than a wicked individual. And in spite of his repulsion, he couldn't resist his friend's second glance, which was as coercive as it was beseeching. He swallowed his bitterness to the very dregs and started after *the Weasel*, recklessly stepping on cabbages and young corn.

'Wait, Anita, let me accompany you…' he murmured. 'Wait… Something might happen to you.'

Ana shrugged her shoulders and slackened her pace to let Borrén catch up with her. They came together and walked along the road in silence, Ana with her lips shut tight and somewhat chilled and shivering, despite being all wrapped up in the shawl. When they reached the entrance to the city, the cigar maker turned and measured Borrén with a scornful glance from head to toe.

'Are you thinking about something?' he asked, still somewhat proud, with a hoarseness verging on loss of voice.

'Nothing,' she replied brusquely. And then, fixing her little green eyes on Borrén's, she added, 'Don Enrique, do you know what I've been thinking?'

–Diga usted…

–Que es usted una alhaja.

–¿Por qué me dice usted eso, bella Anita? –pronunció ya afablemente Borrén, que al verse entre gentes y en calles transitadas había recobrado su aplomo.

–Porque…, que uno se marche cuando enferma… ¡Pero usted! Pero ¡qué hombres! –articuló con ira–. ¡Si aunque se acabase la casta … no se perdía tanto así! Vaya, abur … que estoy medio trastornada y me da poco gusto ver gente.

–Iré con usted por si…

–¿Usted? –murmuró ella entre irónica y desdeñosa–. ¿Para qué? Abur, abur; ¡que si le ven con una muchacha de mi clase! Abur.

Y *la Comadreja* se escurrió por una callejuela, dejando a Borrén sin saber lo que le pasaba.

Cuando Baltasar y la oradora se quedaron solos, la tarde caía, no apacible y glacial como aquella de febrero, sino cálida, perezosa en despedirse del sol; nubes grises, pesados cirros se amontonaban en el cielo; el mar, picado y verdoso, mugía a lo lejos, y una franja de topacio orlaba el horizonte por la parte del poniente. Amparo tuvo un instante de temor.

–Me voy a mi casa –dijo levantándose.

–¡Amparo!… ¡Ahora, no! –pronunció con suplicantes inflexiones en la voz Baltasar–. No te marches, que estamos en el paraíso.

La Tribuna, paralizada, miró en derredor. Mezquino era el paraíso, en verdad. Un cuadro de coles, otro de cebollas, el fresal polvoroso, hollado por los pies de todo el mundo; los olmos bajos y achaparrados, los acirates llenos de blanquecinas ortigas, el pozo triste con su rechinante polea; mas estaban allí la juventud y el amor para hermosear tan pobre edén. Sonrió la muchacha posando blandamente en Baltasar sus abultados ojos negros.

–¿Por qué quieres escaparte, vamos? –interrogó él con dulce autoridad–. Si te escapas siempre de mí, si parece que te doy miedo, no tendrá nada de extraño que yo me vaya también al paseo, o a donde se me ocurra. Ya lo sabes –y acercándose más a ella, abrazándole el rostro con su anhelosa respiración–: ¿Me voy al paseo? –preguntó.

Amparo hizo un movimiento de cabeza que bien podía traducirse así: «No se vaya usted de ningún modo.»

'Tell me...'

'That you're a right one.'

'Why do you say that to me, my lovely Anita?' Borrén said, quite affably now, because he had recovered his aplomb on finding himself among other people and on busy streets.

'Because ... for one to go away when someone's ill ... but you! You men!' she articulated angrily. 'Even if your whole breed came to an end ... we wouldn't be losing that much! Go on, cheerio... I'm somewhat upset and I don't feel like seeing people.'

'I'll go with you in case...'

'You?' she muttered, somewhere between ironically and disdainfully. 'What for? Bye-bye, bye-bye; just imagine if they saw you with a girl of my class! Bye-bye.'

And *the Weasel* slipped away down a side street, leaving Borrén unaware of what was going on.

When Baltasar and the orator found themselves alone, the afternoon was coming to a close, not calm and icy like that afternoon in February, but warm and slow to bid farewell to the sun; grey and heavy cirrus clouds were piling up in the sky; the sea, choppy and greenish, was roaring in the distance, and a fringe of topaz bordered the horizon out towards the west. Amparo experienced a moment of fear.

'I'm going home,' she said, standing up.

'Amparo! Not now!' said Baltasar with imploring inflections in his voice. 'Don't go away, we're in paradise!'

Stupefied, *la Tribuna* looked all around her. Paradise was quite wretched, to tell the truth. A cabbage patch, another one with onions, the dust-covered strawberry bed, trampled by everyone's feet; the low, stunted elm trees, the ridges of earth between the patches, full of whitish nettles, the sad well with its squeaking pulley; but youth and love were there to beautify such an impoverished Eden. The girl smiled, her big dark eyes resting tenderly on Baltasar.

'Why do you want to run away, tell me?' he asked her with sweet authority. 'If you're always escaping from me, if it seems that I frighten you, then there'll be nothing strange about me also going to the procession, or wherever I choose to go. You know that very well,' and drawing closer to her, embracing her face with his anxious breath, he asked: 'Shall I go to the procession?'

Amparo made a movement with her head which might well be translated in this way: 'Don't go for any reason.'

–Me tratas tan mal…

–¿Usted qué quiere que haga?

–Que te portes mejor…

–Pues hablemos claros –exclamó ella, sacudiendo su marasmo y apoyándose en el brocal del pozo.

La roja luz del ocaso la envolvió entonces, su rostro se encendió como un ascua, y por segunda vez le pareció a Baltasar hecha de fuego.

–Di, hermosa…

–Usted … quiere comprometerme… ¡Quiere conducirse como se conducen los demás con las muchachas de mi esfera!

–No por cierto, hija; ¿de dónde lo sacas? No pienses tan mal de mí.

–Mire usted que yo bien sé lo que pasa por el mundo… Mucho de hablar, y de hablar, pero después…

Baltasar cogió una mano, que trascendía a fresas.

–Mi honor, don Baltasar, es como el de cualquiera, ¿sabe usted? Soy una hija del pueblo; pero tengo mi altivez … por lo mismo… Conque … ya puede usted comprenderme. La sociedá se opone a que usted me dé la mano de esposo.

–Y ¿por qué? –preguntó con soberano desparpajo el oficial.

–Y ¿por qué? –repitió la vanidad en el fondo del alma de *la Tribuna*.

–No sería yo el primero, ni el segundo, que se casase con… Hoy no hay clases…

–Y su familia…, su familia… ¿Piensa usted que no se desdeñarían de una hija del pueblo?

–¡Bah!… ¿Qué nos importa eso? Mi familia es una cosa, yo soy otra – repuso Baltasar, impaciente.

–¿Me promete usted casarse conmigo? –murmuró la inocentona de la oradora política.

–¡Sí, vida mía! –exclamó él, sin fijarse casi en lo que le preguntaban, pues estaba resuelto a decir amén a todo.

Pero Amparo retrocedió.

–¡No, no! –balbució trémula y espantada–. No basta el jarabe de pico… ¿Me lo jura usted…?

Baltasar era joven aún y no tenía temple de seductor de oficio. Vaciló, pero fue obra de un instante; carraspeó para afianzar la voz y exhaló:

–Lo juro.

'You treat me so badly...'

'What do you want me to do?'

'For you to behave better...'

'Well, let's speak frankly,' she exclaimed, shaking off her apathy and leaning on the curb of the well.

Then the red light from the sunset enveloped her completely, her face lit up like a glowing ember, and for the second time she seemed to Baltasar to be made of fire.

'Tell me, my lovely...'

'You ... want to compromise me... You want to behave like all the others behave with girls of my social class!'

'No, of course not. Where did you get that idea? Don't think so badly of me.'

'Look, I know very well what goes on in the world. ...A lot of talk, and more talk, but afterwards...'

Baltasar took hold of one of her hands, which smelled of strawberries.

'My honour, Don Baltasar, is like that of any other girl, do you know that? I'm a daughter of the people, but I have my pride ... for that very reason... So ... now you can understand me. Society is opposed to your offering me your hand as husband.'

'And why?' the officer asked with supreme self-confidence.

'Yes, why?' repeated the vanity at the depths of *la Tribuna*'s soul.

'I wouldn't be the first, nor the second to marry a... There are no social classes nowadays...'

'And your family ... your family... Do you think they wouldn't turn up their nose at a daughter of the people?'

'Bah...! What does that matter to us? My family is one thing and I'm another,' Baltasar retorted impatiently.

'Do you promise to marry me?' murmured the gullible political orator.

'Yes, my darling!' he exclaimed, hardly noting what he was being asked, since he was determined to agree to everything.

But Amparo moved backwards.

'No, no,' she stammered, trembling and frightened. 'Sweet words aren't enough... Do you swear to me...?'

Baltasar was still young and didn't have the disposition of a professional seducer. He hesitated, but only for an instant; he cleared his throat to strengthen his voice and exclaimed:

'I swear.'

Hubo un momento de silencio en que sólo se escuchó el delgado silbo del aire cruzando las copas de los olmos del camino y el lejano quejar del mar.

–¿Por el alma de su madre? ¿Por su condenación eterna?

Baltasar, con ahogada voz, articuló el perjurio.

–¿Delante de la Cara de Dios? –prosiguió Amparo, ansiosa.

De nuevo vaciló Baltasar un minuto. No era creyente macizo y fervoroso como Amparo, pero tampoco ateo persuadido; y sacudió sus labios ligero temblor al proferir la horrible blasfemia. Una cabeza pesada, cubierta de pelo copioso y rizo, descansaba ya sobre su pecho, y el balsámico olor de tabaco que impregnaba a *la Tribuna* le envolvía. Disipáronse sus escrúpulos y reiteró los juramentos y las promesas más solemnes.

Iba acabando de cerrar la noche, y un cuarto de amorosa luna hendía como un alfanje de plata los acumulados nubarrones. Por el camino real, mudo y sombrío, no pasaba nadie.

There was a moment of silence during which you could hear only the slight whistling of the air crossing through the tops of the elm trees and the distant moaning of the sea.

'On your mother's soul? At the price of your eternal damnation?'

In a choked voice Baltasar articulated the perjured response.

'As God is your witness?' Amparo continued anxiously.

Baltasar hesitated for a moment once again. He was not a staunch, fervent believer like Amparo, but neither was he a confirmed atheist; a slight trembling shook his lips as he uttered the horrible blasphemy. A drowsy head, covered with copious, curly hair, was resting on his chest, and the balsamic aroma of tobacco which impregnated *la Tribuna* enveloped him. His scruples were dispelled and he reiterated the most solemn oaths and promises.

Night was begining to fall and an amorous quarter-moon was splitting the gathering storm clouds like a silver cutlass. Nobody went by on the silent, sombre main road.

XXXII

LA TRIBUNA SE FORJA ILUSIONES

En los primeros tiempos, Baltasar, embriagado por el aroma del cigarro, se mostró más asiduo, olvidó su habitual reserva y obró como si no temiese la opinión del mundo ni de su familia. Es cierto que en el barrio apartado donde Amparo moraba no era fácil que le viesen las gentes de su trato; no obstante, alguna vez tropezó con conocidos, en ocasión de ir acompañando a la muchacha. Fuese por esta razón o por otras, no tardó en buscar lugares más recónditos para las entrevistas, a donde cada cual iba por su lado, no reuniéndose hasta estar al abrigo de ojos indiscretos. Uno de estos sitios era una especie de merendero unido a una fábrica de gaseosa, bebida muy favorita de las cigarreras. Ante la mesa de tosca piedra, roída por la intemperie, se sentaban Baltasar y Amparo, y allí les traían las botellas de cerveza, de gaseosa, cuyo alegre taponazo animaba de tiempo en tiempo el diálogo. Una parra tupida les prestaba sombra; algunas gallinas picoteaban los cuadros de un mezquino jardín; el lugar era silencioso, parecido a un gabinete muy soleado, pero oculto. Por entre las hojas de vid se filtraban los rayos del sol, y caían a veces, en movibles gotas de luz, sobre el rostro de Amparo, mientras Baltasar la contemplaba, admirando involuntariamente ciertas gracias y perfecciones de su rostro hechas para ser vistas de cerca, como la delicada red de venas que oscurecía sus párpados, las sinuosidades de su diminuta oreja, la nitidez del moreno cutis, donde la luz se perdía en medias tintas de miel; la caliente riqueza del color juvenil, la blancura de los dientes, la abundancia del cabello. Duró este inventario minucioso algún tiempo, al cabo del cual, Baltasar, habiendo aprendido de memoria estas y otras particularidades, y hablado con *la Tribuna* de todo lo que se podía hablar con ella, empezó a encontrar más largas las horas. Restringió las visitas al merendero, limitándolas a los días festivos; y mientras Amparo le preparaba *a mano* los cigarrillos que acostumbraba a consumir, él leía, arrancando al pitillo recién acabado nubes de humo. No sabiendo qué hacer, quiso enseñar a Amparo cómo se fumaba, a lo cual ella se prestó con repugnancia, alegando que las cigarreras no fuman, que casualmente están «hartas de ver tabaco», y que éste sólo era bueno para ponerse parches en las sienes cuando duele la cabeza. Discurriendo medios de entretenerse, Baltasar trajo a Amparo alguna novela para que se la leyese en voz alta; pero era tan fácil en llorar la pitillera así que los héroes se morían de amor o de

32
LA TRIBUNA BUILDS UP FALSE HOPES

Early on, Baltasar, intoxicated by the aroma of the cigar, was more assiduous; he forgot his customary reserve and acted as if he feared neither everyone else's nor his family's opinion. It's true that in the isolated neighbourhood where Amparo lived, it wasn't easy for him to be seen by people he knew; however, he did bump into some acquaintances on occasions while he was accompanying the girl. Whether it was for this reason or for others, he was quick to seek out more recondite places for their meetings, where they would both arrive on their own, not joining one another until they were away from prying eyes. One of these places was a kind of picnic area attached to a lemonade factory, a favourite drink of the cigar makers. Baltasar and Amparo would sit down in front of the rough stone table, worn away by the elements, and there they were brought bottles of beer and lemonade, and the cheerful popping of corks would animate their dialogue from time to time. A thickly grown grapevine provided them with shade; some hens would peck at the flower beds of a miserable garden; the place was silent, like a study that was very sunny but hidden away. The sun's rays filtered through the vine leaves, and at times they fell as moving drops of light on Amparo's face, while Baltasar contemplated her, involuntarily admiring certain charms and perfections in her features, best seen from close up, like the delicate mesh of veins that darkened her eyelids, the sinuosities of her tiny ear, the purity of her dark skin where the light was lost in honeyed half-tones, the warm richness of her youthful colour, the whiteness of her teeth and the abundance of her hair. This meticulous inventory lasted some time, and when it was over, Baltasar, having learned these and other characteristics by memory, and talked with *la Tribuna* about everything one could talk with her about, began to find the hours longer and longer. He restricted the number of visits to the picnic area, limiting them to feast days, and while Amparo made *with her own hands* the cigarettes he was in the habit of smoking, he would read, puffing clouds of smoke from the newly-made cigarette. Not knowing what else to do, he tried to teach Amparo how to smoke, which she agreed to with repugnance, contending that cigar makers don't smoke, that they happen to be 'sick of seeing tobacco', and that it was only good for putting poultices on your temples when you have a headache. Thinking up ways to amuse himself, Baltasar brought Amparo a novel so that he could read it out loud

otra enfermedad por el estilo, que convencido el mancebo de que se ponía tonta, suprimió los libros. En suma, Baltasar y Amparo se hallaron como dos cuerpos unidos un instante por la afinidad amorosa, separados después por repulsiones invencibles, y que tendían incesantemente a irse cada cual por su lado.

Para colmo de aburrimiento, reparó Baltasar que, al paso que él aspiraba a ocultar diestramente su aventura, Amparo, que ya tenía puesta toda su esperanza en las falaces palabras y en el compromiso creado por el seductor, se perdía porque los viesen juntos, porque la publicidad remachase el clavo con que imaginaba haberle fijado para siempre. Quería ostentarle, como Ana ostentaba su capitán mercante; quería que la familia de Sobrado supiese lo que sucedía y rabiase, y que la de García, la orgullosa damisela, se enterase también de que Baltasar la dejaba por *la Tribuna*; ¡por *la Tribuna*! Quemadas ya las naves, a Amparo le convenía hacer ruido, tanto como a Baltasar guardar silencio. De esta diversa disposición de ánimo nacieron las primeras disputas, leves y cortas aún, de los dos amantes, reyertas que al principio sirvieron de diversión a Baltasar, porque, a veces, hasta la contrariedad distrae. Al menos, mientras duraban, no venía el importuno bostezo a descoyuntar las mandíbulas. Peor sería hablar de política, conversación que Baltasar había prohibido y a la cual *la Tribuna* se manifestaba más aficionada de algún tiempo a esta parte.

No era del todo sistemática la conducta de Amparo al buscar publicidad en sus amoríos; su carácter la impulsaba a ello. Superficial y vehemente, gustábanle las apariencias y exterioridades; la lisonjeaba andar en lenguas y ser envidiada, nunca compadecida. El día que dio sus pendientes de oro para la Rita, no le quedaba en casa un ochavo, y por pueril orgullo dijo a todas que tenía dinero, amenguando así el valor de su noble rasgo. Ahora, durante sus relaciones con Baltasar, trabajaba más que nunca y se vestía lo mejor posible, para hacer creer que el señorito de Sobrado era con ella dadivoso. Se regocijaba interiormente de que la sostuviesen sus ágiles dedos, mientras el barrio le envidiaba larguezas que no recibía: es más, que rechazaría con desdén si se las ofrecieran. Su vanidad era doble: quería que el público tuviese a Baltasar por liberal, y que Baltasar no la tuviese a ella por mercenaria. Y Baltasar, si pagaba la gaseosa, los pastelillos, alguna vez las entradas del teatro, en lo demás se mostraba digno heredero y sucesor

to her; but the cigar maker cried so easily as soon as the heroes died of love or some other such illness that the officer, convinced she was just being silly, put an end to the books. In short, Baltasar and Amparo were like two bodies joined together for an instant by some amorous affinity, separated afterwards by invincible repulsions, and who tended incessantly to go off each in their own direction.

To top off his sense of boredom, Baltasar noticed that while he tried to hide his adventure skilfully, Amparo, who already had all her hopes placed in the deceitful words and commitment invented by the seducer, was dying for them to be seen together, for the attention to hammer down the nail with which she imagined she had secured him for all time. She wanted to show him off, as Ana showed off her merchant captain; she wanted the Sobrado family to know what was going on and to be furious, and for the García girl, that proud and young unmarried lady, also to find out that Baltasar was abandoning her for *la Tribuna*; for *la Tribuna*! Now that all the boats had been burned, it suited Amparo to make some noise, as much as it did Baltasar to maintain silence. The first arguments between the two lovers, still minor and short-lived, arose from this difference in their frames of mind, quarrels which in the beginning served Baltasar as a kind of diversion, because sometimes even contrariness is a distraction. At least, as long as they lasted, there was no inconvenient yawn to make his jaw almost dislocate. It would be worse to talk of politics, a topic of conversation Baltasar had prohibited, and for which *la Tribuna* showed herself to be even more enthusiastic for some time.

Amparo's conduct was not at all systematic in her search to make her love affair public knowledge; her character pushed her in that direction. Superficial and vehement, she liked outward appearances and show; it flattered her being the talk of the town and envied, but never pitied. The day she gave her golden earrings for Rita, she didn't have a cent left in the house, but told everyone, out of childish pride, that she had some money, thus diminishing the value of her noble gesture. Now, during her relationship with Baltasar, she worked harder than ever and dressed as best she could to make everyone believe that the young master Sobrado was generous with her. She was inwardly glad that her agile fingers supported her, while the neighbourhood envied her for the largesse she didn't receive; what's more, she would have disdainfully refused it if she had been offered it. Her vanity was two-fold: she wanted the public to consider Baltasar liberal, and Baltasar not to consider her mercenary. And Baltasar, if he paid for the lemonade, the tarts and occasionally the tickets for the theatre, showed himself to be the true heir and successor of Doña Dolores

de doña Dolores Andeza de Sobrado. Nunca pensó o nunca quiso pensar (que hasta a esto del pensar sobre una cosa suele determinarse la voluntad libremente) en lo que comería aquella buena moza, si sería caldo o borona, si bebería agua clara, y cómo se las compondría para presentársele siempre con enagua almidonada y crujiente, bata de percal saltando de limpia, botitas finas de rusel, pañuelo nuevo de seda. El cigarro era aromático y selecto: ¿qué le importaba al fumador el modo de elaborarlo?

Entre tanto, Amparo disfrutaba viendo la rabia de sus rivales en la fábrica, la sonrisilla de Ana, las indirectas, los codazos, la atmósfera de curiosidad que se condensaba en torno de su persona, llegando a tanto su desvanecimiento, que se hacía a sí propia regalos misteriosos para que creyese la gente que procedían de Sobrado; se prendía en el pecho ramilletes de flores, y hasta llegó a adquirir una sortija de plata con un corazón de esmalte azul, por el retegustazo de que pensasen ser fineza de Baltasar. Cuando le preguntaban si era cierto que se casaba con un señorito, sonreía, se hacía la enojada como de chanza, y fingía mirar disimuladamente la sortija... ¡Casarse! Y ¿por qué no? ¿No éramos todos iguales desde la revolución acá? ¿No era soberano el pueblo? Y las ideas igualitarias volvían en tropel a dominarla y a lisonjear sus deseos. Pues si se había hecho la revolución y la Unión del Norte, y todo, sería para que tuviésemos igualdad, que si no, bien pudieron las cosas quedarse como estaban... Lo malo era que nos mandase ese rey italiano, ese Macarroni, que daba al traste con la libertad... Pero iba a caer, y ya no cabía duda, llegaba la república.

Con estos pensamientos entretenía las horas de trabajo en la fábrica. A cada pitillo que enrollaba, al suave crujido del papel, una cándida esperanza surgía en su corazón. Cuando ella fuese señora, no había de portarse como otras altaneras, que estuvieron allí liando cigarros lo mismo que ella, y ahora, porque arrastraban seda, miraban por cima del hombro a sus amigas de ayer. ¡Quia! Ella las saludaría en la calle, cuando las viese, con afabilidad suma. Por lo que hace a recibirlas de visita..., eso, según y conforme dispusiese su marido; pero, ¿qué trabajo cuesta un saludo? A Ana pensaba enseñarle su casa. ¡Su casa! ¡Una casa como la de Sobrado, con sillería de damasco carmesí, consola de caoba, espejo de marco dorado, piano, reloj de sobremesa y tantas bujías encendidas! Y Amparo, cerrando los ojos, creía sentir en el

Andeza de Sobrado in everything else. Never did he think or never did he want to think (for even in this matter of thinking about something, the will usually makes up its mind freely) about what that fine young woman would have eaten, if it would have been broth or corn bread, whether she would have drunk clear water, and how she always managed to appear with a starched, crisp petticoat, an immaculately clean percale gown, fine little woollen serge boots and a new silk scarf. The cigar was aromatic and select; what did it matter to the smoker how it was made?

In the meantime, Amparo enjoyed seeing her rivals' anger at the factory: Ana's little smile, the innuendos and nudging of elbows, the atmosphere of curiosity that condensed around her person, her vanity reaching such a degree as to make mysterious gifts to herself so people would believe they had come from Sobrado; she fastened bunches of flowers to her bosom and even ended up acquiring a silver ring with a heart of blue enamel, just for the immense pleasure of others thinking it was a gift from Baltasar. When they asked her if it was true that she was going to marry a young gentleman, she would smile, become angry as a joke, and pretend to look furtively at her ring … Get married! Well, why not? Weren't we all equal since that revolution here? Weren't the people sovereign now? And all the egalitarian ideas rushed back to dominate her and flatter her desires. And if they had made a revolution and formed the Northern Union, and all that, it would be so we all had equality, and if not, things might just as well have stayed as they were … The bad thing was that they sent us that Italian king, that Macaroni,[19] who was putting an end to freedom … But he was going to fall, and there was no longer any doubt, the republic was coming.

She whiled away the hours at work in the factory with these thoughts. For every cigarette that she rolled, with the soft rustling of its paper, a candid hope surged up in her heart. When she was a lady, she wasn't going to behave like other haughty girls, who had worked there rolling cigarettes like she was doing, and who now, just because they wore long silk dresses, looked down on their friends from yesterday. Not on your life! She would greet them in the street with the utmost affability whenever she saw them. As for having them come to visit … that would be as her husband wished; but how much trouble is it to greet someone? She intended to show Ana her house. Her house! A house like the one the Sobrado family had, with crimson damask chairs, a mahogany console table, a mirror with a gold frame, a piano, a mantel clock and so many lighted candles. And Amparo,

---

19   Amadeo I, the first and only prince of the House of Savoy to sit on the throne of Spain.

rostro el frío cierzo de la noche de Reyes... Cuando entraba descalza en el portal de Sobrado a cantar villancicos, ¿imaginó que se enamorase de ella Baltasar? Pues así como había sucedido esto, *lo otro*...

No obstante, dentro de la fábrica misma hubo escépticas que auguraron mal de los enredos en que se metía Amparo. ¡Casarse, casarse! Pronto se dice; pero del dicho al hecho... ¿Regalos? ¡Vaya unos regalos para un hijo de Sobrado! ¡Sortijas de plata, ramos de a dos cuartos! ¡Bah, bah! Ya se sabía en lo que paraban ciertas cosas. Aunque sordos, estos rumores no fueron tan disimulados que no llegasen a la interesada, y unidos a otras pequeñeces que ella observaba también, empezaron a clavarle en el alma el dardo de los más crueles recelos. Baltasar enfriaba a ojos vistas: a cada paso mostraba más cautela, adoptaba mayores precauciones, descubría más su carácter previsor y el interés de esconder su trato con la muchacha, como se oculta una enfermedad humillante. Mostrábase aún tierno y apasionado en las entrevistas; pero se negaba obstinadamente a acompañar a Amparo dos pasos más allá de la puerta.

Todo lo referido, notó desde su cama la paralítica, y hallábase sumamente inquieta y quejosa, por varias razones: entre otras, porque desde que Amparo gastaba cuanto ganaba en botas nuevas y enaguas bordadas, ella se veía privada de algunas comodidades y golosinas que no le escatimaban antes. Malo era que su hija se perdiese y malo también que, tratando con señores, en vez de traer dinero a casa, se empeñase, y tuviese que pasarse las noches haciendo pitillos de encargo para poder comer. ¡Y mucho de flores! ¡Y mucho de chambras con puntillas! ¡Qué necesidad!

Confidente de estas lamentaciones era Chinto, que solía venir a pasarse con la tullida largas horas al salir del trabajo, desde que supo cuán propicia se había mostrado a su pretensión matrimonial. Aún volvía la vieja a la carga de tiempo en tiempo, y hablaba de Chinto a su hija; él no sería fino ni buen mozo, pero era un burro de carga, un lobo para el trabajo y un infeliz. Autorizada, sin duda, por tan buenas intenciones, la paralítica disponía de Chinto como de un yerno. Una vez, cuando empezó a escasear el dinero, rogóle que «fuese por seis cuartos de azúcar para la cascarilla a la tienda de la esquina, que ya serían abonados». El mozo salió y volvió con un cucurucho de papel de estraza henchido de azúcar moreno; del pago no se habló más.

closing her eyes, could almost feel the cold north wind on her face of that Twelfth Night ... When she had come barefoot into the entryway of the Sobrado house to sing Christmas carols, did she imagine that Baltasar would fall in love with her? Well, just as this had happened, *so all the rest ...*

Nevertheless, there were sceptics inside the factory itself who foresaw difficulties in the intrigues in which Amparo was getting involved. Get married, get married! It's easy to say, but there's many a slip ... Gifts? Some gifts for a son of the Sobrado family! Silver rings, two a penny bouquets! Bah, bah! Everyone knew how certain things ended. These rumours, although suppressed, were not so concealed that they didn't reach the interested party, and in conjunction with other petty things she noticed, began to stick into her soul the dart of the cruellest misgivings. Baltasar was visibly growing colder: he was becoming more wary at every step and adopted greater precautions, revealing ever more his foresight and his desire to hide his relationship with the girl, as one might conceal a humiliating disease. He still came across as tender and passionate during their meetings, but he obstinately refused to accompany Amparo even two steps beyond the doorway.

The paralysed woman noticed all of this from her bed, and was extremely anxious and annoyed for various reasons: among others, because ever since Amparo had started spending everything she earned on new boots and embroidered underskirts, she found herself deprived of a number of comforts and treats which hadn't been skimped on before. It was bad enough that her daughter should become a fallen woman, and equally bad that, having a relationship with fancy gentlemen instead of bringing home money, she should get into debt and have to spend her nights making cigarettes on special order so that she could eat. And all the flowers! And the lace-edged camisoles! A lot of use they were!

Her confidant in all these lamentations was Chinto, who used to come and spend long hours with the crippled woman after work, ever since he found out how well-disposed she had shown herself to his marital aspirations. The old lady still renewed the attack from time to time and talked to her daughter about Chinto; he might not be a refined or good-looking fellow, but he was a hard worker, a real pack horse and a good-natured person. Such good intentions undoubtedly gave the paralysed lady the authority to use Chinto as if he were her son-in-law. Once, when money began to grow scarce, she begged him 'to go to the corner shop for six *cuartos* worth of sugar for her cocoa, that they would be paid back'. The young fellow went

Otro día le encargó de tomar un décimo para el próximo sorteo; la vieja, por tranquilizar su conciencia de empedernida jugadora, dijo que si «le caía» partirían como buenos amigos. Poco a poco, y ayudando a ello lo muy distraída que Amparo andaba, volvió Chinto a amarrarse al antiguo yugo, a obedecer ciegamente a la despótica voz de la tullida; hízole los recados, le arregló el cuarto, le trajo remedios, le dio unturas. Y no quiere decir esto que la pobre mujer se propusiese deliberadamente explotar al mozo, sino que, a su edad y en su estado, ciertos cuidados y mimos son tan necesarios como el aire respirable.

Curioso espectáculo en verdad el que ofrecía Chinto, descolorido, flaco, casi harapiento, cuidando de aquella mujer que no era su madre, que siempre le había tratado con dureza; y mientras él mondaba las patatas para el caldo del día siguiente, o mullía el jergón de la impedida, Amparo regresaba, a la plateada luz de la luna de verano, que prolongaba sobre la carretera de la Olmeda la sombra de los majestuosos árboles, de alguna cita en lugares escondidos, en los solitarios huertos, o en el desierto camino del cerro de Aguasanta.

out and returned with a brown paper cone filled with brown sugar; about the payment, not a word more was said. On another day she gave him the job of getting a lottery ticket for the next draw; the old lady, to appease her conscience as an inveterate gambler, said that 'if her number came up' they would share it out like good friends. Little by little, and helped by Amparo having her mind on other things, Chinto fastened the old yoke again, blindly obeying the despotic voice of the crippled woman; he ran errands for her, tidied up her room, brought her remedies, put ointment on her. And this does not mean that the poor woman deliberately intended to exploit the lad, but that at her age and with her state of health, a little care and pampering is as necessary as the air we breathe.

It was in truth a curious spectacle that Chinto offered, pale, skinny, almost in rags, caring for that woman who wasn't his mother, who had always treated him harshly; while he peeled the potatoes for the next day's broth, or fluffed up the disabled woman's mattress, Amparo would return, by the silvery light of the summer moon, which prolonged the shadows of the majestic trees on the Carretera de la Olmeda, from some tryst in secluded places, in the solitary vegetable gardens or on the deserted road to the Cerro de Aguasanta.

XXXIII

LAS HOJAS CAEN

Aconteció que, cuando ya se aproximaba el otoño, la paralítica llamó a Amparo a la cabecera de su lecho, con tono y ademanes singulares, murmurando sordamente:

–Acércate aquí, anda.

Amparo se acercó con la cabeza baja. La madre extendió la mano, le cogió violentamente la barbilla para que alzase el rostro, y con voz aguda y terrible gritó:

–¿Y ahora?

Calló la hija. Constábale que la persona que la interrogaba así había vivido largos años orgullosa de su matrimonio legítimo, de su honestidad plebeya, de su marido trabajador, de que en la Fábrica los citasen a entrambos por modelo de familia unida, de que en cierta ocasión el jefe hubiese proferido palabras honrosas para ella, llamándole mujer «formal y de bien». Sí, Amparo lo sabía, y por eso callaba. Repetidas veces la paralítica le diera consejos, haciendo funestos vaticinios, que se cumplían al fin. Incorporada a medias sobre la cama, concentrando en los ojos la vida furiosa de su cuerpo, repitió la madre, con desprecio y con ira:

–¿Y ahora?

Amparo permaneció pálida e inmóvil. La tullida sintió un hormigueo en la palma de la mano, y la estampó ruidosamente en la mejilla de su hija, que se tambaleó, retrocedió escondiendo el rostro, y se fue a sentar en la silla más próxima.

–¡Sinvergüenza, raída, eso de mí no lo aprendiste! –vociferó la enferma, algo desahogada ya después del bofetón.

No respondió nada la oradora, que diera entonces de buen grado su popularidad, y hasta el advenimiento de la ideal república, por hallarse siete estados debajo de tierra. No obstante, se sorbió estoicamente las lágrimas abrasadoras que asomaban a sus ojos, y abatida, reconociendo y acatando la autoridad maternal, balbució:

–Me ha dado palabra de casamiento.

–¡Y te lo creíste!

–No sé por qué no… –exclamó la muchacha con acento más firme ya–. Yo soy como otras, tan buena como la que más… Hoy en día no estamos en

33

THE FALLING LEAVES

As Autumn was approaching it happened that the paralysed woman called Amparo over to the head of her bed, murmuring in a muffled voice with extraordinary tone and gestures:

'Come over here, come on.'

Amparo moved closer with her head bowed. Her mother extended her hand, seized her violently by the chin so that she would raise her face, and shouted in a shrill, frightening voice:

'And now what?'

The daughter kept quiet. She felt certain that the person interrogating her in this manner had lived many years proud of her legitimate marriage, her plebeian decency, her hard-working husband, the fact that they were both cited in the factory as a model of a united family, and that on a certain occasion the manager had expressed words honouring her, calling her a 'responsible and upright' woman. This Amparo knew only too well and that's why she said nothing. The paralysed woman would repeatedly give her advice, making ill-fated predictions which would finally come true. Half sitting up in bed, concentrating all the furious life of her body in her eyes, her mother repeated with scorn and anger:

'And now what?'

Amparo remained pale and motionless. The bedridden woman felt a tingling in the palm of her hand, and gave a loud slap on the cheek to her daughter, who staggered, moved back with her face hidden, and went to sit down in the nearest chair.

'You brazen, shameless fool, you didn't learn that from me!' yelled the invalid, already feeling somewhat appeased after the slap.

The orator didn't reply, and she would willingly have given up her popularity and even the advent of the ideal republic if she could only find herself six furlongs under the ground. Nevertheless, she stoically soaked up the searing tears that were coming to her eyes, and thoroughly disheartened, recognising and respecting maternal authority, stammered:

'He gave me his word he'd marry me.'

'And you believed him!'

'I don't know why not...' exclaimed the girl in a tone that was firmer now. 'I'm like other girls, as good as anyone who is more... Nowadays, we

tiempos de ser los hombres desiguales... Hoy todos somos unos, señora...,
se acabaron esas tiranías.

Meneó la cabeza la paralítica, con la tenaz desconfianza de los viejos
indigentes que nunca han visto llover del cielo torreznos asados.

–El pobre, pobre es –pronunció melancólicamente...–. Tú te quedarás
pobre, y el señorito se irá riendo... –Y a esta idea, sintiendo renacer su furor
chilló–: Sácateme de delante, indina,[38] que te mato; si te dieron palabras, que
te las cumplan.

Amparo se agachó, y salió temblando. A solas, recobró energía, y calculó
que tal vez hacía mal en desesperarse; acaso su mala ventura sería un lazo
más que acabase de unir a Baltasar con ella para siempre. Sí, no podía
suceder de otro modo, a menos que tuviese entrañas de tigre.

Esperó con afán el domingo, día de cita en el merendero de la gaseosa.
Madrugó; llegó mucho antes que Baltasar. El otoño iba despojando a la parra
de su pomposo follaje recortado, y los nudosos sarmientos parecían brazos
de esqueleto mal envueltos en los jirones de púrpura de las pocas hojas
restantes. Algún racimo negreaba en lo alto. En unas tinas viejas arrimadas
al banco de piedra, había botellas vacías que semejaban embarcaciones
náufragas varadas en un arenal. Amparo sentía mucho frío cuando Baltasar
llegó.

Sentóse éste al lado de la muchacha, que le presentó un paquete de sus
cigarrillos predilectos, emboquillados, bastante largos, liados con gran
esmero. Baltasar tomó uno y lo encendió, chupándolo nerviosamente con
rápidas aspiraciones. Toda mujer prendada de un hombre llega a conocer por
sus movimientos más leves, por los actos que distraída y casi mecánicamente
ejecuta, el talante de que está. Amparo sabía que cuando Baltasar fumaba
así, no se distinguía por lo jocoso y afable. Como la luz del sol no hallaba
obstáculos para filtrarse al través de la deshojada parra, el rostro del
mancebo, bañado de claridad, parecía duro y anguloso; su bigote, blondo
a la sombra, tenía ahora un dorado metálico; sus ojos zarcos miraban con
glacial limpidez. La pobre *Tribuna*, tan intrépida cuando peroraba, se halló
del todo cortada y recelosa, y creyó sentir que le anudaban la garganta con
un dogal. Esperó en vano una expansión, una caricia dulce y apasionada,
que no vino. Baltasar se callaba cosas muy buenas, y seguía taciturno. De
cuando en cuando el soplo de las ráfagas otoñales desprendía una de las
postreras hojas de vid, que caía arrugada y amarillenta sobre la mesa de

---

38 Forma gallega del adjetivo 'indigna'.

don't live in a time when people aren't equal… Today we are all as one …
that old tyranny is over.'

The paralysed woman shook her head, with that tenacious distrust of the
old and needy who have never seen food rain down from heaven.

'The poor are poor,' she declared in a melancholy way. 'You'll remain poor
and the rich young gentleman will go off laughing…,' and feeling her fury
rise up again at this idea, she screamed: 'Get out of my sight, you unworthy
child, or I'll kill you; if he gave you his word, then let him stick to it.'

Amparo cowered and went out trembling. When she was alone, she
recovered her energy and calculated that maybe she was wrong to despair;
perhaps her bad luck would be a knot that would end up joining her to
Baltasar forever. Yes, it couldn't happen any other way, unless he had the
heart of a tiger.

She waited for Sunday eagerly, the day of their meeting at the picnic
area that served lemonade. She got up early; she arrived a long time before
Baltasar. Autumn was beginning to strip the grapevine of its splendid, pared
down foliage, and the knotty vine shoots looked like the arms of a skeleton
poorly wrapped in the purple tatters of the few remaining leaves. Some bunch
or other was turning black at the top. In some old tubs, pushed up against
the stone bench, there were empty bottles that resembled shipwrecked boats
run aground on a sandy shore. Amparo was feeling very cold by the time
Baltasar arrived.

He sat down beside the girl and she handed him a packet of his favourite
cigarettes, tipped, quite long and rolled with painstaking care. Baltasar took
one and lit it, sucking at it nervously and inhaling rapidly. Any woman
captivated by a man comes to know what mood he is in by his slightest
movements, by the actions he performs in a distracted, almost mechanical
way. Amparo knew that when Baltasar smoked like that, jocularity and
affability would not be to the fore. Since the sunlight encountered no
obstacles as it filtered through the leafless grapevine, the young man's face,
bathed in bright light, looked hard and angular; his moustache, which was
blond even in the shade, now had a metallic gilt to it; his light blue eyes
looked out with icy limpidity. Poor *la Tribuna*, so intrepid when making
speeches, found herself totally tongue-tied and apprehensive, and felt as if a
noose were knotted around her throat. She waited in vain for a development,
a sweet, impassioned caress, but it didn't come. Baltasar kept quiet for good
reason and remained taciturn. From time to time, a gust of autumn wind
detached one of the last remaining leaves from the grapevine, and it would

granito, entre los dos amantes, produciendo un ruidito seco. ¡Pin! En los oídos de Baltasar resonaba la voz de doña Dolores, exclamando: «Chico, ¿no sabes que las de García…, ¡pásmate!, ganan el pleito en el Supremo? Lo sé de fijo por el mismo abogado de aquí.» ¡Pin, pin! Y Amparo, a su vez, escuchaba frases coléricas: «Si te dieron palabras, que te las cumplan». ¡Pinnn!… Una hoja purpúrea descendía con lentitud… «Baltasarito, hijo, van a calzarse ciento y no sé cuántos miles de duros, si ganan».

Al fin, Baltasar fue el primero que rompió el silencio… Habló del trabajo que le costaba venir, de lo necesario que era el recato, de que tendrían que verse menos… Decía todo esto con acento duro, como si Amparo fuese culpable respecto de él en algo. La cigarrera le escuchaba muda, con los labios blancos, mirando fijamente al rostro de Baltasar, que tenía la expresión distraída del mal pagador que no quiere recordar su deuda. Y era lo peor del caso que, por más que *la Tribuna* pretendía echar mano de su oratoria, que le hubiese venido de perlas entonces, no encontraba frases con que empezar a tratar el asunto más importante. Al fin, como viese con asombro levantarse a Baltasar diciendo que le esperaba el coronel para asuntos del servicio, ella también se alzó resuelta, y le dio la noticia clara y brutalmente, sin ambages ni rodeos, sintiendo hervir dentro del pecho una cólera que centuplicaba su natural valor.

Un relámpago de sorpresa cruzó por las pupilas trasparentes y yertas de Sobrado; mas al punto se plegó su delgada boca, y diríase que le habían cerrado el semblante con llave doble y selládolo con siete sellos. Era otro Baltasar distinto del mancebo gracioso, halagüeño y felino de las horas veraniegas. Amparo notó que representaba diez años más.

−Ahora −dijo, plantándose delante de él− es justo que me cumplas la palabra.

−Ahora… −repitió él con voz lenta−. La palabra…

−¡De casarte conmigo! Me parece que me sobra derecho para pedir…

−Mujer… −contestó Baltasar reposadamente, sacudiendo la ceniza del pitillo−, no todas las cosas salen a medida del deseo. Las circunstancias le obligan a uno a mil transacciones, que… Yo quisiera, lo mismo que tú, que fuese mañana, pero ponte en mi caso… Mi madre … mi padre … mi familia…

fall, wrinkled and yellowish onto the granite table, between the two lovers, producing a faint, sharp sound. Ping! Doña Dolores's voice resounded in Baltasar's ears as she exclaimed: 'My boy, don't you know that the Garcías … you'll be amazed! … have won their case in the Supreme Court? I know it for sure from the lawyer himself here.' Ping, ping! And Amparo, for her part, heard the irascible words: 'If he gave you his word, let him stick to it.' Ping! …A purple leaf was falling slowly… 'Baltasar, my dear son, if they win, they're going to get a hundred and who knows how many thousands of duros.'

Finally, Baltasar was the first to break the silence… He spoke of how much trouble it was for him to come, how necessary it was to be cautious, and how they would have to see each other less often… He said all this in a harsh tone, as if in some way Amparo were guilty in her relationship with him. The cigar maker listened to him in silence, with pale lips, looking intently at Baltasar's face, which had the casual expression of a bad payer who doesn't want to remember his debt. And the worst of it was that, no matter how much *la Tribuna* intended to make use of her oratorical ability, which would have come at the right moment just then, she couldn't find the words to begin to deal with so important a matter. Finally, when she saw to her surprise Baltasar stand up, saying that the colonel was waiting for him to discuss some military matters, she rose too, full of resolve, and gave him the news clearly and abruptly, straight to the point and without beating around the bush, feeling a fury boil up inside her breast which increased her natural courage a hundredfold.

A lightning bolt of surprise crossed over Sobrado's clear, frozen eyes, but straight away his thin mouth puckered, and one might say his expression had been doublelocked and sealed with seven seals. It was a different Baltasar now from the charming, flattering, feline young man of those summer days. Amparo noticed that he looked ten years older.

'Now,' she said, planting herself in front of him, 'it's only right that you keep your word.'

'Now…' he repeated slowly. 'My word.'

'To marry me! It seems to me that I have more than every right to ask…'

'My dear…' Baltasar answered quietly, shaking the ash from his cigarette, 'not all things turn out as we would wish. Circumstances necessitate thousands of compromises, which … I would like, just as you would, for it to be tomorrow, but put yourself in my situation… My mother … my father … my family…'

–¡Tu familia, tu familia! ¿Pues no dijiste que ella era una cosa y tú otra? ¿Le echo yo alguna mancha a tu familia, por si acaso? ¿Soy hija de algún ajusticiado, o de algún capitán de gavilla? ¿No estamos en tiempos de igualdad? ¿No es mi madre tan honrada como la tuya, repelo?

–No es eso … yo no te digo que…

–¿Pues qué dices entonces, que te quedas ahí callado? ¿Tienes algo que echarme en cara? ¿No me gano yo la vida trabajando honradamente, sin pedírtelo a ti ni a nadie? ¿Te he pedido algo, te he pedido algo? ¿Ando yo con otros?

–¿Quién te dice semejante cosa? Pero sucede que hoy por hoy lo que tú deseas, es decir, lo que deseamos, es imposible.

–¡Imposible!

–Por algún tiempo no más… No me hallo todavía en situación de prescindir de mi familia…; cuando alcance una graduación superior y pueda vivir con el sueldo…

–¿No eres ya capitán?

–Graduado; pero la efectividad… En fin, te lo repito, hazte cargo; en las circunstancias por que atravieso no cabe una determinación semejante. Sería menester estar loco. Y digo más; créeme, hija; tenemos que ser muy prudentes para no comprometernos.

–¡No comprometernos! –gimió con amargura la muchacha–. ¡No comprometernos! ¿Pero tú te has figurado –pronunció, reponiéndose y recobrando su impetuoso carácter– que yo soy tonta? ¿Piensas que me puedes meter el dedo en la boca? ¿Qué compromiso ni qué… ¡repelo! te viene a ti de todo esto? ¡La comprometida, la engañada y la perdida soy yo!

Dejóse caer en el banco de piedra, y apoyando la sien en la fría mesa de granito, rompió en convulsivos sollozos.

–No grites, hija –murmuró Baltasar, aproximándose–. No llores … que pueden oírte y es un escándalo. Amparo, mujer, vamos, no hay motivo para esos gritos.

La crisis fue corta. Levantóse la oradora con los ojos encendidos, pero sin que una lágrima escaldase su mejilla morena. Indignada, miró a Baltasar y lo encontró sereno, inconmovible, con su fina y sonrosada tez y sus ojos garzos y trasparentes, en los cuales se reflejaba la luz del cielo sin comunicarles calor. Él quiso hacer dos o tres zalamerías a la muchacha para conjurar la tormenta; pero su ademán era violento, sus movimientos automáticos.

'Your family, your family! But didn't you say that they were one thing and you another? Do I cast any blemish on your family, by any chance? Am I the daughter of an executed criminal, or of the leader of a gang of thieves? Aren't we living in a time of equality? Isn't my mother as honourable as yours, hang it?'

'It's not that ... I'm not saying that...'

'Well, what are you saying then, that you sit there so quiet? Have you got something to throw in my face? Don't I earn my living honestly, without asking you or anyone else for anything? Have I asked you for anything, have I asked you for anything? Do I go with other men?'

'Who's saying any such thing to you? But it happens that right now, what you desire, that is to say, what we both desire, is impossible.'

'Impossible!'

'But only for a short time ... I'm still not in a position to do without my family... When I reach a higher rank and can live on my salary...'

'Aren't you already a captain?'

'Commissioned, but the actual appointment... In short, I repeat what I said to you, realise the situation; in the circumstances I'm going through, a decision like that isn't possible. You'd have to be crazy. And I'll say one thing more: believe me, we have to be very prudent so that we don't compromise ourselves.'

'Don't compromise ourselves!' the girl wailed bitterly. 'Don't compromise ourselves! But do you think,' she declared, regaining her composure and recovering her impetuous character, 'I'm stupid? Do you imagine you can string me along? What compromising situation or other, hang it, has anything to do with you in all of this? The one who's compromised, the one who's deceived, the one who's lost her honour is me!'

She let herself fall back on the stone bench, and, leaning her temple against the cold granite tabletop, began to sob convulsively.

'Don't shout, my dear,' Baltasar murmured as he drew closer to her. 'Don't cry ... people can hear you and it will cause a scandal. Amparo, come on now, there's no reason for all this shouting.'

The crisis was short-lived. The orator stood up, her eyes blazing, without a single tear scalding her dark cheek. She looked at Baltasar indignantly and found him to be serene and unmoved, with his fine, pink skin and his clear, blue eyes, where the light from the sky was reflected without giving any warmth to them. He tried to make two or three flattering remarks to the girl to ward off the storm, but his gesture was violent and his movements

Amparo le rechazó, y se colocó por segunda vez delante de él en actitud agresiva.

–Habla claro… ¿nos casamos o no?

–Ahora no puede ser, ya te lo he dicho –contestó él sin perder su continente flemático.

–¿Y cuándo?

–¡Qué sé yo! El tiempo, el tiempo dirá. Pero has de tener calma, hija … un poco de calma.

–Pues abur, hasta que me pagues lo que me debes –exclamó ella en voz vibrante, sin cuidarse de que la oyesen desde la casa o desde el camino los transeúntes–. Yo no soy más tu juguete, para que lo sepas: no me da la gana de andarme escondiendo, de ir con estas noches de frío a Aguasanta y a mil sitios así por darte gusto.

Avanzó tres pasos más, y poniendo la mano en el hombro del oficial:

–El día menos pensado… –pronunció–, cuando te vea en las Filas o en la calle Mayor…, me cojo de tu brazo delante de las señoritas, ¿oyes?, y canto allí mismo, allí…, todo lo que pasa. Y cuando venga la nuestra…, o te hacemos pedazos, o cumples con Dios y conmigo. ¿Entiendes, falsario?

Y en voz queda, con acento de religioso terror:

–¿Tú no tienes miedo a condenarte? Pues si mueres así … más fijo que la luz, te condenas. Y si viene la federal … que Dios la traiga y la Virgen Santísima … te mato, ¿oyes?, para que vayas más pronto al infierno.

Diciendo así, diole un empujón, y le volvió la espalda, saliendo con paso rápido, la frente alta, la mirada llameante, a pesar del peregrino desfallecimiento, de la desusada conmoción interior que le avisaba de que ahorrase tales escenas. Al salir *la Tribuna*, una ráfaga más fuerte desparramó por la mesa muchas hojas de vid, que danzaron un instante sobre la superficie de granito, y cayeron al húmedo suelo.

«¿Lo hará? –meditó Baltasar a sus solas–. ¿Me vendrá a abochornar en público? Tengo para mí que no… Estos genios vivos y prontos son del primer momento; pasado éste, quedan como malvas. Quiá…, no lo hace. Sin embargo, me convendría salir de Marineda una temporadita…»

Al pensar esto, miraba maquinalmente a las hojas secas, que valsaban con lánguido y desmayado ritmo.

«Pero ¿y Josefina? Si las noticias de mamá son ciertas, no va a ser posible

perfunctory. Amparo pushed him away and stood for a second time in front of him in an aggressive posture.

'Speak clearly... Are we getting married or not?'

'It can't be now; I've already told you,' he replied without losing his phlegmatic bearing.

'When then?'

'How do I know! Time, time will tell. But you must be calm, dear ... a bit of calm.'

'Well, goodbye then, until you pay me what you owe me,' she exclaimed in a vibrant voice, without caring if passers-by could hear her from inside the place or from the road. 'I'm not going to be your plaything any more, just so you know it. I don't like going around hiding, going to Aguasanta on these cold nights, or any other places like that to please you.'

She advanced a few steps more and put her hand on the officer's shoulder:

'One day when you least expect it...' she said, 'when I see you on Las Filas or on the Calle Mayor ... I'll take hold of your arm in front of all those fine young ladies, do you hear me? There, right there, I'll sing out everything that's going on. And when our turn comes ... we'll either tear you to pieces or you'll keep your promise to God and to me. Do you understand, you liar?'

And in a soft voice, in a tone of religious terror:

'Aren't you afraid you'll be damned? Because if you die like this ... one thing is sure, you'll be damned. And if we have a federal government ... may God and the holy Virgin bring it us ... I'm going to kill you – do you hear me? – so that you go to hell more quickly.'

As she said this, she gave him a push and turned her back on him, leaving with a quick pace, her head high, her eyes flaming, in spite of the peculiar weakness, the unaccustomed inner upheaval that warned her to avoid such scenes. When *la Tribuna* left, a stronger gust of wind scattered lots of grapevine leaves onto the table, and they danced for a moment on the granite surface and then fell to the damp ground.

'Will she do it?' Baltasar meditated when he was alone. 'Will she come and shame me in public? My feeling is she won't... These fiery, quick tempers last only a moment; when this is over, they're meek and mild. Nonsense ... she won't do it. Nevertheless, it would be best for me to leave Marineda for a brief spell...'

As he was thinking this, he looked inadvertently at the dry leaves waltzing about with a languid, exhausted rhythm.

'But what about Josefina? If mama's news is correct, it won't be possible

abandonar una proporción que tal vez no vuelva a encontrar en mi vida. ¡Qué mil diablos! Y esa chica era guapa... ¡Lo que es guapa! ¡Qué tonterías! ¿Por qué se buscará uno estos conflictos? ¡Yo que tengo juicio para diez!»

Impaciente, tiró el cigarro que estaba concluyendo. Un átomo de fuego brilló entre las hojas, que crujieron encogiéndose, y a poco la colilla se apagó.

to abandon an opportunity that maybe I'll never find again in my life. What the devil! And that girl was pretty ... She's really pretty! What foolishness! Why would one seek out these kinds of conflicts? I've got more than my fair share of common-sense!'

He impatiently threw away the cigarette he was finishing. An atom of flame shone among the leaves, which crackled as they shrivelled up, and the cigarette butt soon went out.

SEGUNDA HAZAÑA DE *LA TRIBUNA*

Frío es el invierno que llega; pero las noticias de Madrid vienen calentitas, abrasando. La cosa está abocada, el italiano va a abdicar porque ya no es posible que resista más la atmósfera de hostilidad, de inquina, que le rodea. Él mismo se declara aburrido y harto de tanto contratiempo, de la grosería de sus áulicos, de la guerra carlista, del vocerío cantonal, del universal desbarajuste. No hay remedio, las distancias se estrechan, el horizonte se tiñe de rojo, la federal avanza.

La fábrica ha recobrado su *Tribuna*. Es verdad que ésta vuelve herida y maltrecha de su primer salida en busca de aventuras; mas no por eso se ha desprestigiado. Sin embargo, los momentos en que empezó a conocerse su desdicha fueron para Amparo de una vergüenza quemante. Sus pocos años, su falta de experiencia, su vanidad fogosa, contribuyeron a hacer la prueba más terrible. Pero en tan crítica ocasión no se desmintió la solidaridad de la fábrica. Si alguna envidia excitaba antaño la hermosura, garbo y labia irrestañable de la chica, ahora se volvió lástima, y las imprecaciones fueron contra el eterno enemigo: el hombre. ¡Estos malditos de Dios, recondenados, que sólo están para echar a perder a las muchachas buenas! ¡Estos señores, que se divierten en hacer daño! ¡Ay, si alguien se portase así con sus hermanas, con sus hijitas, quién los oiría y quién los vería abalanzarse como perros! ¿Por qué no se establecía una ley para eso, caramba? ¡Si al que debe una peseta se la hacen pagar más que de prisa, me parece a mí que estas deudas aún son más sagradas, demontre! ¡Sólo que ya se ve; la justicia la hay de dos maneras: una a rajatabla para los pobres, y otra de manga ancha, muy complaciente, para los ricos!

Algunas cigarreras optimistas se atrevieron a indicar que acaso Sobrado se casaría, o por lo menos reconocería lo que viniese.

–Sí, sí... ¡esperar por eso, papanatas! ¡Ahora se estará sacudiendo la levita y burlándose bien!

–No sabes ... yo no quiero que ella lo oiga, ni lo entienda –decía *la Comadreja* a *la Guardiana*–, pero ese descarado ya vuelve a andar tras de la de García.

–¡Bribón! –exclama *la Guardiana*–. Y ¿quién le ve tan juicioso como parece?

LA TRIBUNA'S SECOND EXPLOIT

Cold is the winter that is on its way, but the news that comes from Madrid is warm, burning like fire. Things are quite imminent; the Italian is going to abdicate because it's no longer possible for him to withstand the atmosphere of hostility and ill will that surrounds him. He himself has asserted that he is bored and fed up with so many setbacks, with the vulgarity of his courtiers, with the Carlist War, with the regional uproar and with the universal chaos. There is no solution: the distances are getting narrower, the horizon is tinged with red, the federal republic is advancing.[xxxiv]

The factory has recovered its *Tribuna*. It's true that she is returning wounded and battered from her first sally in search of adventures, but she has not lost her prestige as a result. Nevertheless, the moments when her misfortune began to be known about were a cause of burning shame for Amparo. Her tender years, her lack of experience, and her spirited vanity helped to make her ordeal even more terrible. But the solidarity at the factory did not prove false on so critical an occasion. If the girl's beauty, grace and unstoppable gift of the gab had aroused some envy in days gone by, it had now turned into pity, and all imprecations were against the eternal enemy: men. Those godforsaken, damned wretches who were only good at ruining decent girls! Those fancy young gentlemen who enjoy doing harm! Oh, but if anyone behaved like that with their sisters and their precious young daughters, you'd hear and you'd see them pounce like dogs! Why wasn't a law laid down for that, damn it? If someone who owes a peseta is made to pay it in more than a hurry, it seems to me that these debts are even more sacred, what the devil! Except that it's plain to see there are two kinds of justice: one to the letter for the poor, and the other lenient and accommodating for the rich!

A few optimistic cigar makers dared to suggest that perhaps Sobrado would marry her, or at least properly recognise the outcome.

'Sure, sure … You'll wait a long time for that, you simpletons! Right now he'll be laughing up his sleeve at us, and having a good joke!'

'You may not know this … and I don't want her to hear it or find out about it,' *the Weasel* said to *la Guardiana*, 'but that scoundrel is already running after the García girl again!'

'The rogue!' *la Guardiana* exclaimed. 'And who would think it of him, as upstanding as he appears?'

–Pues conforme te lo digo.

–Amparo tampoco debió hacerle caso.

–Mujer, uno es de carne, que no es de piedra.

–¿Se te figura a ti que a cada uno le faltan ocasiones? –replicó la muchacha–. Pues si no hubiese más que... ¡Madre querida de la Guardia! No, Ana; la mujer se ha de defender ella. Civiles y carabineros a la puerta, no se los pone nadie. Y las chicas pobres, que no heredamos más mayorazgo que la honradez... Hasta te digo que la culpa mayor la tiene quien se deja embobar.

–Pues a mí me da lástima ella, que es la que pierde.

–A mí también. Lástima, sí.

Y a todo el mundo se la daba. ¡Quién hubiera reconocido a la brillante oradora del banquete del Círculo Rojo en aquella mujer que pasaba con el mantón cruzado, vestida de oscuro, ojerosa, deshecha! Sin embargo, sus facultades oratorias no habían disminuido; sólo sí cambiado algún tanto de estilo y carácter. Tenían ahora sus palabras, en vez del impetuoso brío de antes, un dejo amargo, una sombría y patética elocuencia. No era su tono el enfático de la Prensa, sino otro más sincero, que brotaba del corazón ulcerado y del alma dolorida. En sus labios, la república federal no fue tan sólo la mejor forma de gobierno, época ideal de libertad, paz y fraternidad humana, sino período de vindicta, plazo señalado por la justicia del cielo, reivindicación largo tiempo esperada por el pueblo oprimido, vejado, trasquilado como mansa oveja. Un aura socialista palpitó en sus palabras, que estremecieron la fábrica toda, máxime cuando el desconcierto de la Hacienda dio lugar a que se retrasase nuevamente la paga en aquella dependencia del Estado. Entonces pudo hablar a su sabor *la Tribuna*, despacharse a su gusto. ¡Ay de Dios! ¿Qué les importaba a los señorones de Madrid..., a los pícaros de los ministros, de los empleados, que ellas falleciesen de hambre? ¡Los sueldos de ellos estarían bien pagados, de fijo! No, no se descuidarían en cobrar, y en comer, y en llenar la bolsa. ¡Y si fuesen los ministros los únicos a reírse del que está debajo! ¡Pero a todos los ricos del mundo se les daba una higa de que cuatro mil mujeres careciesen de pan que llevar a la boca!

Y al decir esto, Amparo se incorporaba, casi se ponía de pie en la silla, a pesar de los enérgicos y apremiantes chis de la maestra, a pesar del inspector de labores que desde hacía un momento estaba asomado a la entrada del taller, silencioso y grave.

'Well, I'm telling it you as it is.'

'Amparo should never have paid him any attention either.'

'Truly, one is made of flesh, not of stone.'

'Do you imagine that each one of us doesn't have opportunities like that?' the girl replied. 'Because if it were nothing more than … Sweet Mother of God! No, Ana; a woman has to protect herself. Nobody puts policemen or guards at our doors. And we poor girls, the only estate we inherit is our honour… I'll even say that any girl who allows herself to be beguiled has only herself to blame.'

'Well, as for me, I feel sorry for her, because she's the one who's lost everything.'

'The same for me. Pity, yes.'

And everybody felt it for her. Who would have recognised the brilliant orator from the banquet at the Red Circle in that woman who passed by in her twill cloth shawl, dressed in dark colours, with rings under her eyes, worn out! Nevertheless, her oratorical powers hadn't diminished, but they had somewhat changed in style and character. Instead of the impetuous spirit from before, her words now had a bitter touch, a sombre, pathetic eloquence. Hers was not the emphatic tone of the press, but rather another more sincere one, which sprouted from a wounded heart and a soul in pain. On her lips, a federal republic was not only the best form of government, an ideal time of liberty, peace and human brotherhood, but also a period of vengeance, a time marked by heavenly justice, a long awaited demand by an oppressed, harrassed people that had been shorn like tame sheep. A socialist aura palpitated in her words as they shook the entire factory, particularly when the disorder in the Ministry of Finance led to wages in that department being postponed again. Then *la Tribuna* could speak as she wished, she could really lay into them. Good Lord! What did it matter to those big shots in Madrid … those rogues of ministers, those clerks, if the women died of hunger? Their own salaries would be paid on time, for sure! No, they wouldn't neglect to get their wages, to eat and to fill their pockets. And you needn't think that the ministers were the only ones to laugh at those beneath them! But all the rich people in the whole world couldn't care a fig if four thousand women were short of bread to feed their mouths!

And as she said this, Amparo would sit up, almost standing on her chair, in spite of the maestra's emphatic and urgent shushes, and in spite of the production inspector, who for the last few moments had been peering in at the entrance to the workshop, looking silent and grave.

–¡Qué cuenta tan larga... –proseguía la oradora, animándose al ver el mágico y terrible efecto de sus palabras...–, qué cuenta tan larga darán a Dios algún día esas sanguijuelas, que nos chupan la sangre toda! Digo yo, y quiero que me digan, por qué nadie me contesta a esto, ni puede contestarme: ¿Hizo Dios dos castas de hombres, por si acaso, una de pobres y otra de ricos? ¿Hizo a unos para que se paseasen, durmiesen, anduviesen majos, y hartos, y contentos, y a otros para sudar siempre y arrimar el hombro a todas las labores, y morir como perros sin que nadie se acuerde de que vinieron al mundo? ¿Qué justicia es ésta, retepelo? Unos trabajan la tierra, otros comen el trigo: unos siembran y otros recogen; tú, un suponer, plantaste la viña, pues yo vengo con mis manos lavadas y me bebo el vino.

–Pero el que lo tiene, lo tiene –interrumpía la conservadora *Comadreja*.

–Ya se sabe que el que lo tiene, lo tiene; pero ahora vamos al caso de que es preciso que a todos les llegue su día, y que cuantos nacemos iguales gocemos de lo mismo, ¡tan siquiera un par de horas! ¡Siempre unos holgando y otros reventando! Pues no ha de durar hasta el fin de los siglos, que alguna vez se ha de volver la tortilla.

–El que está debajo, mujer, debajito se queda.

–¡Conversación! Mira tú: en París, de Francia, el cuento ese de la *Comun*... ¡Anda si pusieron lo de arriba abajo! ¡Anda si se sacudieron! No quedó cosa con cosa...; así, así debemos hacer aquí, si no nos pagan.

–Y allá, ¿qué hicieron?

Amparo bajó la voz.

–Prender fuego ... a todos los edificios públicos.

Un murmullo de indignación y horror salió de la mayor parte de las bocas.

–Y a las casas de los ricos..., y...

–¡Asús! ¡Fuego, mujer!

–Y afusil..., y afusil..., ar...

–Afusilar..., ¿a quién, mujer, a quién?

–A..., a los prisioneros, y al arzobispo, y a los cur...

–¡Infames!

–¡Tigres!

–¡Calla, calla, que parece que la sangre se me cuajó toda!... ¿Y quién hizo eso? ¡Pues vaya unas barbaridás que cuentas!

'What a long account…' continued the orator, animated by the sight of the magical and terrible effect of her words, 'what a long account they'll have to give to God one day, those leeches who suck out all our blood! I say this, and I want them to tell me, because nobody is going to answer this, nor can they even reply to me: did God create two castes of people, by chance, one poor and the other rich? Did He make some so they could go out for a stroll, sleep, walk around all dressed up, satiated and contented, and others to sweat all the time and put their shoulders to the wheel for all manner of hard work, and to die like dogs without anyone remembering that they had come into the world? What kind of justice is this, hang it and hang it twice over? Some work the land and others eat the grain; some sow and others reap; you, let us suppose, planted the vines and I come along with my clean hands and drink up the wine.'

'But those who have, have it all,' interrupted the conservative *Weasel*.

'We know very well that those who have, have it all; but let's now get down to the business of it being necessary for everyone to have his day, and that all of us who are born equal will have the same, if only for a couple of hours! Always some taking it easy and others dropping dead! Well, it doesn't have to go on till the end of time, because sooner or later we have to turn the tables.'

'The ones who are at the bottom will stay right there at the bottom.'

'Idle conversation! Look here: in Paris, France, that business of the *Commune*[xxxv]… Just see how they put everything that was on top onto the bottom! Just see how they shook things up! They didn't leave one thing untouched … that's what, that's what we ought to do here, if they don't pay us.'

'And what did they do there?'

Amparo lowered her voice.

'Set fire … to all the public buildings.'

A murmur of indignation and horror came from most of the mouths.

'And to the rich people's houses … and…'

'My God! Set on fire!'

'And shoo … and shoo…ting.'

'Shooting … who, who?'

'The … the prisoners, and the archbishop and the prie…'

'Those wicked people!'

'Wild tigers!'

'Be quiet, be quiet, because I feel as if all my blood has curdled…! And who did all that? I can't believe the atrocities you're telling us!'

–Si yo no las cuento para decir que … que esté bien hecho eso de… de prender fuego y afusilar… ¡No, caramba! ¡No me entendéis, no os da la gana de entenderme! Lo que digo es que … hay que tener hígados, y no dejarse sobar ni que le echen a uno el yugo al cuello sin defenderse… Lo que digo es que, cuando no le dan a uno por bien lo suyo, lo muy suyo…, lo que tiene ganado y reganado… Cuando no se lo dan, si uno no es tonto…, lo pide…, y si se lo niegan…, lo coge.

–Eso, clarito.

–Tienes razón. Nosotras hacemos cigarros, ¿eh?, pues bien regular es que nos abonen lo nuestro.

–No, y apuradamente no es ley de Dios esa desigualdad y esa diferencia de unos zampar y ayunar otros.

–Lo que es yo, mañana, o me pagan o no entro al trabajo.

–Ni yo.

–Ni yo.

–Si todas hiciésemos otro tanto…, y si además, nos viesen bien determinadas a armar el gran cristo…

–¡Mañana…, lo que es mañana! ¿Habéis de hacer lo que yo os diga?

–Bueno.

–Pues venid temprano…, tempranito.

A la madrugada siguiente los alrededores de la fábrica, la calle del Sol, la calzada que conduce al mar, se fueron llenando de mujeres que, más silenciosas de lo que suelen mostrarse las hembras reunidas, tenían vuelto el rostro hacia la puerta de entrada del patio principal. Cuando ésta se abrió, por unánime impulso se precipitaron dentro, e invadieron el zaguán en tropel, sin hacer caso de los esfuerzos del portero para conservar el orden; pero en vez de subir a los talleres, se estacionaron allí, apretadas, amenazadoras, cerrando el paso a las que, llegando tarde, o ajenas a la conjuración, intentaban atravesar más allá de la portería. Sordos rumores, voces ahogadas, imprecaciones que presto hallaban eco, corrían por el concurso, que se iba animando, y comunicándose ardimiento y firmeza. En primera fila, al extremo del zaguán, estaba Amparo, pálida y con los ojos encendidos, la voz ya algo tomada de perorar, y, sin embargo, llena de energía, incitando y conteniendo a la vez la humana marea.

–Calma –decíales con hondo acento–, calma y serenidá… Tiempo habrá para todo: aguardar.

'But I'm not telling them as a way of saying ... it was a good thing this business of ... setting fire and shooting... Goodness, no! You don't understand me, you don't want to understand me! What I'm saying is that ... you have to have guts, and not let them beat you down, or put a yoke around your neck without defending yourself... What I'm saying is that when they don't willingly give you what's yours, what is truly yours ... what you've earned and more than earned... When they don't give it to you, if you're not stupid ... you ask for it ... and if they still refuse it you ... you take it.'

'That's it, exactly.'

'You're right. We make cigars, don't we? Well, it's only right that they pay us what's ours.'

'No, that inequality and that difference of some gorging themselves and others going hungry is not exactly God's law.'

'As for me, tomorrow either they pay me or I don't come to work.'

'Nor I.'

'Nor I.'

'If we all did the same thing ... and if, in addition, they saw that we were really determined to raise hell...'

'Tomorrow ... just wait till tomorrow! Are you willing to do as I tell you?'

'All right.'

'Well, come early ... really early.'

On the following morning, at the crack of dawn, the areas surrounding the factory, the Calle del Sol and the road leading to the sea, were filling up with women who, more silent than females gathered together usually are, had their faces turned towards the entrance doorway of the main courtyard. When this was opened, they rushed inside with a unanimous impulse and invaded the hallway en masse, paying no attention to the caretaker's efforts to maintain order; but instead of going upstairs to the workshops, they stationed themselves right there, squashed together and menacing, blocking the way to those who, arriving later or unconnected with the conspiracy, tried to cross beyond the caretaker's office. Hushed murmurs, muffled voices and imprecations that were immediately echoed, ran through the gathering, which was getting more animated as courage and steadfastness spread. In the first row, at one end of the hallway, stood Amparo, pale and with passionate eyes, her voice already somewhat hoarse from all the speechmaking, and yet full of energy, inciting and restraining that human tide at the same time.

'Keep calm,' she said to them in a deep tone of voice, 'calm and serenity... There'll be time for everything: just wait.'

Pero algunos gritos, los empellones, y dos o tres disputas que se promovieron entre el gentío, iban empujando, mal de su grado, a *la Tribuna* hacia la vetusta escalera del taller, cuando en éste se sintieron pasos que conmovían el piso, y un inspector de labores, con la fisonomía inquieta del que olfatea graves trastornos, apareció en el descanso. Empezaba a preguntar, más bien con el ademán que con la boca: «¿Qué es esto?», a tiempo que Amparo, sacando del bolsillo un pito de barro, arrimólo a los labios y arrancó de él agudo silbido. Diez o doce silbidos más, partiendo de diferentes puntos, corearon aquella romanza de pito, y el inspector se detuvo, sin atreverse a bajar los escalones que faltaban. Dos o tres viejas desvenadoras se adelantaron hacia él, profiriendo chillidos temerosos, y tocándole casi, y se oyó un sordo «¡muera!». Sin embargo, el funcionario se rehízo, y cruzándose de brazos se adelantó algo mudada la color, pero resuelto.

–¿Qué sucede? ¿Qué significa este escándalo? –preguntó a Amparo, a quien halló más próxima–. ¿Qué modo es éste de entrar en los talleres?

–Es que no entramos hoy –respondió *la Tribuna*.

Y cien voces confirmaron la frase.

–No se entra, no se entra.

–¿No entran ustedes? Pues ¿qué pasa?

–Que se hacen con nosotras iniquidás, y no aguantamos.

–No, no aguantamos. ¡Mueran las iniquidás! ¡Viva la libertá! ¡Justicia seca! –clamaron desde todas partes. Y dos o tres maestras, cogidas en el remolino, alzaban las manos desesperadamente, haciendo señas al inspector.

–¿Pero qué piden ustedes?

–¿No oyes, hijo? Jos–ti–cia –berreó una desvenadora al oído mismo del empleado.

–Que nos paguen, que nos paguen, y que nos paguen –exclamó enérgicamente Amparo, mientras el rumor de la muchedumbre se hacía tempestuoso.

–Vuelvan ustedes, por de pronto, al orden y a la compostura que...

–No nos da la gana.

–¡Que baile el cancán!

–¡Muera!

Y otra vez la sinfonía de pitos rasgó el aire.

–No pedimos nada que no sea nuestro –explicó Amparo con gran

But several shouts, all the shoving and two or three disputes that erupted among the crowd, were pushing *la Tribuna*, much against her will, towards the very old stairway that led to the workshops, when footsteps which shook the floor could be felt on it, and a production inspector, with the uneasy expression of one who can sniff out serious trouble, appeared on the landing. He was beginning to ask, more with a gesture than with his mouth: 'What's all this?' at the very moment when Amparo, taking a clay whistle out of her pocket, brought it up to her lips and let out a shrill blast from it. Ten or twelve more blasts, coming from different places, played a whistle romance in chorus, and the inspector stopped, not daring to go down the remaining steps. Two or three old women who deveined the tobacco leaves moved towards him, uttering frightening shrieks, all but touching him, and a muffled 'Die!' could be heard. Nevertheless, the official pulled himself together and, crossing his arms, moved forward, his colour somewhat changed, but resolute.

'What's going on? What's meant by this scandalous behaviour?' he asked Amparo, who was the closest to him. 'What kind of manner is this to come into the workshops?'

'The thing is we're not coming in today,' *la Tribuna* replied.

And a hundred voices confirmed her statement.

'We're not coming in, we're not coming in.'

'You're not coming in? Well, what's the matter?'

'They're doing us an injustice and we won't put up with it.'

'No, we won't put up with it. An end to injustice! Long live freedom! Plain and simple justice!' came shouts from every side. And two or three of the maestras, caught up in the throng, raised their hands in desperation, making signs to the inspector.

'But what are you asking for?'

'Can't you hear? Joo—sti—sah,' bellowed one of the women who deveined tobacco leaves, right in the functionary's ear.

'Let them pay us, let them pay us, let them pay us once and for all,' Amparo exclaimed vigorously, as the rumble from the crowd became turbulent.

'For the time being, let's have some law and order...'

'We don't want to.'

'Why don't you dance the cancan!'

'Why don't you go and die!'

And once again the symphony of whistles rent the air.

'We're not asking for anything that isn't ours,' Amparo explained very

sosiego–. Es imposible que por más tiempo la fábrica se esté así, sin cobrar un cuarto… Nuestro dinero, y abur.

–Voy a consultar con mis superiores –respondió el inspector, retirándose entre vociferaciones y risotadas.

Apenas le vieron desaparecer, se calmó la efervescencia un tanto. «Va a consultar» se decían las unas a las otras… «¿Nos pagarán?»

–Si nos pagan –declaró *la Tribuna*, belicosa y resuelta como nunca–, es que nos tienen miedo. ¡Adelante! Lo que es hoy, la hacemos, y buena.

–Debimos cogerlo y rustrirlo en aceite –gruñó la voz oscura de la vieja–. ¡Fretirlo[39] como si fuera un pancho … que vea lo que es la necesidá y los trabajitos que uno pasa!

–Orden y unión, ciudadanas… –repetía Amparo, con los brazos extendidos.

Trascurridos diez minutos volvió el inspector acompañado de un viejecillo enjuto y seco como un pedazo de yesca, que era el mismo contador en persona. El jefe no juzgaba oportuno por entonces comprometer su dignidad presentándose ante las amotinadas, y por medida de precaución había reunido en la oficina a los empleados y consultaba con ellos, conviniendo en que la sublevación no era tan temible en la Granera como lo sería en otras Fábricas de España, atendido el pacífico carácter del país. No quisiera él estar ahora en Sevilla.

–¿Qué recado nos trae? –gritaron al inspector las sublevadas.

–Óiganme ustedes.

–Cuartos, cuartos, y no tanta parolería.

–Tengo chiquillos que aguardan que les compre mollete… ¿oyúste?, y no puedo perder el tiempo.

–Se pagará… hoy mismo … un mes de los que se adeudan.

Hondo murmullo atravesó por la multitud, llegando a las últimas filas el «¿Pagan, sí o no? Pagan… ¡Un mes…! ¡Un mes…! Para poca salú…, no consentir…; todo junto!» Amparo tomó la palabra.

–Como usted conoce, ciudadano inspector…, un mes no es lo que se nos debe, y lo que nos corresponde, y a lo que tenemos derechos inalienables e individuales… Estamos resueltas, pero resueltas de verdá, a conseguir que nos abonen nuestro jornal; ganado honrosamente con el sudor de nuestras frentes, y del que sólo la injusticia y la opresión más impía se nos pueden incautar…

---

39 Freírlo.

calmly. 'It just isn't possible for the factory to stay like this, without us getting a penny... Our money, and so long.'

'I'm going to consult with my superiors,' the inspector responded, withdrawing amidst the shouting and loud laughter.

Hardly had they seen him disappear than the agitation died down a bit. 'He's going to consult,' some women said to others...'Will they pay us?'

'If they pay us,' *la Tribuna* declared, as bellicose and resolute as ever, 'it's because they're afraid of us. Carry on! As for today, we're going to do it and do it right.'

'We should have grabbed him and roasted him in oil,' grunted the old woman in a gloomy voice. 'Fry him as if he were a young sea bream ... let him see what poverty is really like and the drudgery we endure!'

'Order and union, fellow citizens,' Amparo repeated with her arms held out.

After ten minutes had passed, the inspector returned, accompanied by a little old man, as skinny and dried up as a piece of tinder, who was none other than the bookkeeper himself in person. The manager didn't consider it opportune at that moment to compromise his dignity by presenting himself before the the mutineers, and by way of precaution had gathered his staff together in the office and was consulting with them; they all agreed that the uprising wasn't as fearsome in the Granary as it would be in other factories in Spain, considering the peaceful character of the region. He wouldn't like to be in Seville right now.

'What message do you bring us?' the rebellious women shouted at the inspector.

'Listen to me, all of you.'

'Our money, our money, and less hot air.'

'I have little children who are waiting for me to buy them muffins ... d'ya hear? I can't waste my time.'

'You'll be paid ... this very day ... for one month of the money they owe you.'

A low murmur ran through the multitude and reached the very last rows, and it said, 'Are they paying us, yes or no? They are paying... One month...! One month...! For that little reco ... not agree to it ... all in one go!' Amparo took the floor.

'As you know, citizen inspector ... one month is not what we are owed, and what we have coming to us, and what we have an inalienable and individual right to... We are resolved, and I mean really resolved, to get them to pay us our daily wages, which we have earned honestly by the sweat of our brows, and which only the most ungodly justice and oppression can take from us ...'

–Todo eso es muy cierto, pero ¿qué quieren ustedes que hagamos? Si la Dirección nos hubiese remitido fondos, ya estarían satisfechos los dos meses... Por de pronto se les ofrece a ustedes uno, y se les ruega que despejen el local en buen orden y sin ocasionar disturbios... De lo contrario, la guardia va a proceder al despejo...

–¡La guardia! ¡Que nos la echen! ¡Que venga! ¡Acá la guardia!

Cuatro soldados al mando de un cabo, total cinco hombres, bregaban ya en la puerta de entrada con las más reacias y temibles. No tenían, dijeron ellos después, corazón para hacer uso de sus armas; aparte de que no se les había mandado tampoco semejante cosa. Limitábanse a coger del brazo a las mujeres y a irlas sacando al patio; era una lucha parcial, en que había de todo: chillidos, pellizcos, risas, palabras indecorosas, amenazas sordas y feroces.

Pero sucedió que un soldado, al cual una cigarrera clavó las uñas en la nuca, echó a correr, trajo de la garita el fusil y apuntó al grupo: al instante mismo un pánico indecible se apoderó de las más cercanas, y se oyeron gritos convulsivos, imprecaciones, súplicas desgarradoras, ayes de dolor que partían el alma, y las mujeres, en revuelto tropel, se precipitaron fuera del zaguán, y corrieron buscando la salida del patio, empujándose, cayendo, pisoteándose en su ciego terror, arracimadas como locas en la puerta, impidiéndose mutuamente salir, y chillando lo mismo que si todas las ametralladoras del mundo estuviesen apuntadas y prontas a disparar contra ellas.

Quedóse en medio del zaguán la insigne *Tribuna*, sola, rezagada, vencida, llena de cólera ante tan vergonzosa dispersión de sus ejércitos. Para mostrar que ella no temía ni se fugaba, fue saliendo a pasos lentos y llegó al patio en ocasión que la guardia, aprovechándose de la ventaja fácilmente adquirida, expulsaba a las últimas revolucionarias, sin mostrar gran enojo. Por galantería, el soldado del fusil administró a Amparo un blando culatazo, diciéndole: «Ea..., afuera...» *La Tribuna* se volvió, mirólo con regia dignidad ofendida, y sacando el pito, silbó al soldado. Después cruzó la puerta que se le cerró en las mismas espaldas, con gran estrépito de goznes y cerrojos.

Al verse fuera ya, miró asombrada en torno suyo y halló que una gran multitud rodeaba el edificio por todos lados. No sólo las que estaban

'All that is very true, but what do you want us to do? If the managing directors had sent us the funds, the two months owed to you would have already been paid... For the time being, we're offering you one month, and we beg you to clear these premises in an orderly fashion, without creating any disturbance... Otherwise, the Civil Guard will proceed with clearing everyone out...'

'The Civil Guard! Send them in! Let them come! Here they are!'

Four soldiers under the command of a sergeant, a total of five men, were already struggling at the entrance doorway with the most stubborn and fearsome of the women. They said later on that they didn't have the heart to make use of their weapons; besides which, they hadn't been told to do any such thing. All they did was grab the women by the arms and remove them into the courtyard; it was a partial struggle, in which there was a bit of everything: screams, pinches, laughter, improper words and fierce, muted threats.

But it so happened that a soldier, in whose nape a cigar maker dug her fingernails, started to run, brought back a rifle from the sentry box and pointed it at the group: at that very moment, an indescribable panic took hold of the women nearest him, and you could hear convulsive shouts, cursing, heart-breaking pleas and cries of pain that rent your very soul, and the women, in a mad, disorderly rush, dashed out of the hallway and ran looking for the exit to the courtyard, pushing one another, falling down, trampling on each other in blind terror, all bunched together in the doorway like mad women, preventing each other from getting out, and screaming as if all the machine guns in the world were pointed and ready to fire at them.

The distinguished *Tribuna* stayed in the middle of the hallway, alone, left behind, defeated, filled with anger at so shameful a dispersion of her armies. To show that she was neither afraid nor was running away, she started to leave with slow steps and reached the courtyard at the very same time that the Guard, making the most of an easily acquired advantage, was expelling the last remaining revolutionaries, without showing any great anger. Out of sheer gallantry, the soldier with the rifle gently prodded Amparo with the butt of his weapon, saying, 'Come on ... outside...' *La Tribuna* turned around, looked at him with regal, offended dignity, and pulling out her whistle blew it right at the soldier. Then she went through the door, which closed behind her with a resounding clatter of hinges and bolts.

When she saw she was now outside, she looked around in astonishment and found that a great multitude was surrounding the building on all sides.

dentro, sino otras muchas que habían ido llegando, formaban un cordón amenazador en torno de los viejos muros de la Granera. *La Tribuna*, viendo y oyendo que sus dispersas huestes se rehacían, comenzó a animarlas y a exhortarlas, a fin de que no sufriesen otra vez tan humillante derrota. Ya las que habían sido arrojadas por los soldados, al contacto de la resuelta muchedumbre, recobraron los ánimos decaídos, y enseñaban el puño a la muralla profiriendo invectivas.

Hicieron ruidosa ovación a su capitana que empezó a recorrer las filas calentando a las que aún tenían recelo o no estaban dispuestas a gritar. Y eligiendo dos o tres de las más animosas, mandóles que arrancasen una de las desiguales y vacilantes piedras de la calzada, que se movían como dientes de viejo en sus alveolos, y, alzándola lo mejor posible, la condujeron ante la puerta que les acababan de cerrar en sus mismas narices.

Brotó de entre los espectadores un clamoreo al ver ejecutar esta operación con tino y rapidez y oír retemblar las hojas de la puerta cuando la lápida cayó contra el quicio.

–Hacen barricadas –exclamó una cigarrera que recordaba los tiempos de la Milicia Nacional.

–¡Borricadas, borricadas –exclamaba una maestra– nos va a dar por cara todo este barullo!

El propósito de las desempedradoras no era ciertamente hacer barricadas, sino otra cosa más sencilla: o bien echar abajo la puerta a puros cantazos, o bien elevar delante un montón de piedras por el cual se pudiese practicar el escalamiento. En su imprevisión estratégica olvidaban que del otro lado, al extremo del callejón del Sol, existía un portillo, un lado débil, sobre el cual debería cargar el empuje del ataque. No estaba la generala en jefe para tales cálculos: cegada por la rabia, Amparo no pensaba sino en atravesar otra vez la misma puerta por donde la habían expulsado –¡oh rubor!– cuatro soldados y un cabo. Así es que arrancada ya, casi con las uñas, la primer baldosa, se procedió a desencajar la segunda.

Apoyadas en el muro de una casita de pescadores, donde había redes colgadas a secar, *la Guardiana* y *la Comadreja* miraban el motín sin tomar parte en él. Ana era remilgada, endeble como un junco, y jamás podrían sus descarnadas manos, forzudas sólo en los momentos de excitación nerviosa, levantar ni una peladilla de arroyo algo grande; en cuanto a *la Guardiana*,

Not only those who had been inside, but also many others who had kept arriving, were forming a threatening cordon around the old walls of the Granary. *La Tribuna*, seeing and hearing that her dispersed followers were regrouping, began to encourage and exhort them, so that they wouldn't suffer so humiliating a defeat again. Even those who had been thrown out by the soldiers, on making contact with this resolute crowd, recovered their dampened spirits and showed their fists to the wall, hurling invectives at it.

They gave their captain a noisy ovation as she began to make her way through the ranks, encouraging those who still had misgivings or weren't prepared to shout. And choosing two or three of the bravest, she ordered them to tear up one of the uneven, wobbly stones from the roadway, which moved back and forth like an old man's teeth in their sockets; lifting it as best as they could, they brought it over in front of the door which had just been closed right in their faces.

A clamour erupted from among the spectators on seeing this operation carried out so skilfully and quickly, and hearing the leaves of the door tremble when the stone fell against the frame.

'They're setting up blockades,' exclaimed one of the cigar makers who remembered the days of the National Guard.

'Block'eads, block'eads,' exclaimed one of the maestras, 'that's what all this racket will make us look like!'

The intention of the women who had moved the paving stone was certainly not to set up barricades, but something far simpler: either to knock down the door by pounding the stone against it, or else to raise a pile of stones in front of it, over which they could climb. In their lack of strategic foresight, they forgot that there was a wicket gate on the other side, at the far end of the Callejón del Sol, a weak spot where they should have unleashed the thrust of their attack. The commanding general wasn't in the mood for such calculations: blinded with rage, Amparo was thinking only of going back through the same door from which she had been thrown out – oh, the shame! – by four soldiers and a sergeant. So it was that with the first flagstone already uprooted, almost with their fingernails, they proceeded to dislodge the second.

Leaning against the wall of a fisherman's cottage where there were nets hanging out to dry, *la Guardiana* and *the Weasel* watched the mutiny without participating in it. Ana was prim and finicky, as feeble as a reed, and her scrawny hands, strong only during moments of nervous excitement, would never have been able to lift even a rather large pebble from a brook; as for

se creía obligada a permanecer allí, puesto que al fin el tumulto era «cosa de la fábrica»; pero desaprobándolo, porque indudablemente, de todo aquello iban a resultar «desgracias».

–¡Mira Amparo, tan adelantada en meses, y cómo ella trajina!

–Es el demonche. Ella sola levanta la piedra –contestó Ana, con la reverencia de los débiles hacia la fuerza física.

Mas la primera piedra era enorme: una losa de un metro de longitud y gruesa y ancha a proporción, y constituía un problema de dinámica al trasportarla sin auxilio de máquina alguna. Para echada a hombros de una sola persona era enorme y la aplastaría; para llevada en vilo entre varias, no se sabía cómo subirla.

Amparo discurrió irla enderezando y rodando hasta la puerta, y en efecto, el sistema dio buen resultado y la piedra llegó a su sitio. Al punto que la vio colocada, tornó con infatigable ardor a intentar descuajar un nuevo proyectil. En esta faena y brega estaban entretenidas las pronunciadas, sin reparar que el sol calentaba más de lo justo y que ya eran casi las once de la mañana, cuando un rumor contenido, temeroso, leve al principio, se propagó entre el concurso cayendo como lluvia helada sobre el entusiasmo general, y causando notable descenso en los gritos y vociferaciones que coreaban el arranque de las piedras.

¿Quién dio la noticia? Un pilluelo, que, con los calzones remangados, venía al trote largo desde la plaza de la Fruta, allá en el barrio de Arriba. Oídos sus informes, las miradas se volvieron ansiosamente hacia los cuatro puntos cardinales, y cada boca murmuró pegándose a cada oído ajeno dos palabras preñadas de espanto: «Viene tropa.»

Al notar la oleada del creciente rumor, abandonó *la Tribuna* la piedra que traía entre manos, y volvióse iracunda, con la mirada rechispeante, a la inerme multitud. Su rostro, su ademán, decían claramente: «Ahora vuelven estas cobardonas a dejarme aquí plantada». En efecto, el nombrar tropa bastó para que tomasen el portante algunas de las más animosas barricaderas. ¡Pero qué fue cuando, en el punto más lejano del horizonte, se vio aparecer una nube de polvo, y cuando se oyó como el trote de muchos caballos reunidos!

Amparo anima a sus huestes. Con la nariz dilatada, los brazos extendidos, diríase que la aparición de las brigadas de caballería y fuerzas de la Guardia Civil que desembocan, unas por el camino real, otras por San Hilario,

la Guardiana, she felt obliged to remain there, since the whole tumult was a 'factory affair', after all; but disapproving of it, because, beyond any doubt, only 'terrible things' would result from all that.

'Look at Amparo, so far advanced in months, and how she keeps toiling away!'

'She's got the devil in her. She's lifting the stone by herself,' Ana replied with the reverence the weak have for physical strength.

But the first stone was enormous: a slab a metre in length and of equal proportion in thickness and width, and transporting it without the aid of some machine constituted a problem of dynamics. If one person placed it on his shoulders, it was enormous and it would crush him; if several persons carried it unsupported in the air between them, they wouldn't know how to lift it up.

Amparo considered standing it upright and rolling it to the door, and, in fact, the system proved effective, and the stone reached its place. As soon as she saw it in place, she tried again with indefatigable fervour to uproot a new projectile. The insurrectionists were busy with this task and struggle, without noticing that the sun was getting hotter than usual and that it was almost eleven o'clock in the morning, when a restrained murmur, timorous and slight at first, spread among the gathering, falling like freezing rain on the general enthusiasm, and causing a notable decline in the screaming and shouting that accompanied the tearing up of the stones.

Who gave the news? An urchin who, with his trousers rolled up, came at full pelt from La Plaza de la Fruta, up there in the Barrio de Arriba. When the information had been heard, all eyes turned anxiously towards the four cardinal points, and each mouth moved right up to each neighbour's ear and murmured a few words full of terror: 'The troops are coming.'

When she noted the surge of this growing murmur, *la Tribuna* abandoned the stone she was carrying in her hands and, with a sparkle in her eyes, turned around irately to the defenceless crowd. Her face and her gesture said quite clearly: 'Now these great cowards will leave me here in the lurch again.' Indeed, the very mention of the troops was enough for some of the most courageous barricade builders to clear off. But imagine what happened when they saw a cloud of dust appear on the most distant point of the horizon, and when they heard a sound like that of many horses trotting together!

Amparo encourages her followers. With her nostrils flaring and her arms stretched out, you could say the appearance of the cavalry brigades and the forces of the Civil Guard as they flow out, some along the main road and

redobla su guerrero ardor, acrecienta su cólera. «No nos comerán– grita–. Vamos a tirarles piedras, a lo menos tengamos ese gusto...» Nadie quiere tenerlo. La losa enorme es abandonada; las que más gritaban se escurren por donde pueden; cuando las brigadas llegan a las puertas de la Granera, el motín se ha disuelto, sin dejar más señales de su existencia que dos medianas baldosas, arrimadas al portón, y algunas mujeres dispersas, inofensivas, en medrosa actitud.

others by way of San Hilario, redouble her warlike courage and increase her anger. 'They won't eat us up,' she shouts. 'Let's throw stones at them; at least we'll have that pleasure…' Nobody wants to have it. The enormous slab is abandoned; those who were shouting the most slip away in whatever direction they can; when the brigades arrive at the entry to the Granary, the mutiny has disbanded, leaving no signs of it having existed other than two middle-sized flagstones pressed up against the large door and a few inoffensive women scattered around, looking frightened.

XXXV

LA TRIBUNA SE PORTA COMO QUIEN ES

Cada vez más fría la estación invernal y más calientes las noticias que de allá fuera vienen a conmover la Fábrica. Por de pronto, no quedaron estériles las disposiciones marciales demostradas el día del motín, y al siguiente cobraron las operarias sus haberes integros. No era cosa de provocar el enojo del pueblo en el estado actual de España, que parecía ya la casa de Tócame Roque. Nadie se entendía; al ejército se le conocía por la «tropa amadeísta»; la artillería presentaba dimisión en masa; el Maestrazgo ardía, Saballs llamaba «cabecilla» a Gaminde y Gaminde le devolvía el calificativo; los Hierros ordenaban a una compañía entera de ferrocarriles suspender la circulación de trenes; corría en Cataluña moneda con el busto de Carlos VII, y la reina de más tristes destinos, la mujer de Amadeo I, a la cual tirios y troyanos nombraban desdeñosamente *la Cisterna*, daba al mundo con terror y lágrimas un mísero infante, y ningún obispo se prestaba a bautizar el vástago regio. Así andaba la patria. Más adelante se ha visto que podía encontrarse mucho peor.

Amparo se encontraba abatida desde el memorable día del pronunciamiento. Había hecho tal gasto de energía y de fuerza muscular removiendo los pedruscos de la calzada, y tal derroche de laringe excitando a las remisas y miedosas, que por algún tiempo no quedó de provecho para cosa alguna. Entre el frío, la lluvia que, al ir a la fábrica la acribillaba a alfilerazos en la piel o la bañaba con gruesos y anchos goterones que se deshacían aplastándose en su mantón y la fatiga inherente a su estado, viose sumida en marasmo constante, que a veces iluminaba, a manera de relámpago que divide un cielo oscuro, aquella última y robusta esperanza en el advenimiento de la federal. ¡Cuán triste veía el cielo, y el aire, y todo en derredor! Parecíale a Amparo que los lugares testigos de sus dichas y sus yerros habían sido devastados, arrasados por mano aleve. La tierra del huerto que Baltasar había llamado *paraíso*, desnuda, en barbecho, aguardaba la vegetación. De los verdes y gayos maizales sólo quedaban rastrojos. Los árboles de la carretera alzaban sus ramas peladas y escuetas al brumoso cielo. El piso, lleno de charcos formados por la lluvia, se hallaba intransitable, y delante de la misma casa de *la Tribuna* una gran poza obstruía el paso;

35

LA TRIBUNA BEHAVES AS BEFITS HER

Ever colder is the winter season and hotter the news that comes from beyond it to shake the factory. For the time being, the military formations on show on the day of the mutiny were not unproductive, and on the following day the workers collected their full wages. There was no need to provoke the anger of the people in the present state of Spain, which now seemed like the house of Tócame Roque.[xxxvi] Nobody got on with anybody else; the army came to be known as the 'Amadeist troops'; the artillery was submitting its resignation en masse; the region of Maestrazgo was in flames; Saballs was calling Gaminde a 'ringleader', and Gaminde returned the compliment;[xxxvii] the Hierros ordered an entire railroad company to suspend operation of the trains; a coin with the bust of Carlos VII was circulating in Catalonia, and the ill-starred queen, the wife of Amadeo I, whom Tyrians and Trojans had disdainfully named *la Cisterna*, brought a wretched infante into the world, amidst terror and tears, and no bishop was prepared to baptise the royal scion.[xxxviii] That was the state of the nation. Later on it became apparent that things could get much worse.

Amparo was somewhat disheartened since the memorable day of the uprising. She had expended so much of her energy and muscular strength removing the rough stones from the roadway, and taken so much out of her larynx inciting the reluctant, frightened women, that for some time afterwards she was good for nothing. Between the cold and the rain that stung her skin like pinpricks as she went to the factory, or bathed her with big, heavy drops that exploded as they smashed against her shawl, and the fatigue that was inherent in her condition, she was plunged in a constant apathy which at times, like a flash of lightning cutting through a darkened sky, was illuminated by that final, robust hope for the coming of a federal state. How sad the sky, the air and everything all around looked! It seemed to Amparo that the places that had been witness to her happiness and her errors had been devastated, ravaged by a treacherous hand. The ground in the vegetable gardens which Baltasar had called *paradise* was now barren, lying fallow, awaiting new vegetation. Only the stubble remained from the green and bright maize fields. The trees along the road raised their bare, unadorned branches to the misty sky. The ground, covered with puddles of rain, was impassable, and a huge pool of water in front of *la Tribuna*'s house obstructed the way; in order to enter,

para entrar, Amparo tenía que saltarla, y como no calculase bien el brinco, sucedíale meter el pie en el agua helada y cenagosa, y haber de mudarse después las medias y el calzado. Algunas veces encontraba a Chinto, que se ofrecía a darle la mano para pasar el mal paso, y su ademán compasivo la encendía en ira. ¡Ser compadecida por semejante bestia! ¡A esto llegábamos después de tanto sueño, de tanta aspiración hacia la vida fácil y brillante, hacia la dicha!

Así iba desgranándose el racimo de los días de invierno, lentos, aunque cortos, sin que Amparo distinguiese un rayo de claridad en el firmamento ni en su destino. Aplanóse su espíritu, y cometió un acto de flaqueza. No veía a Baltasar desde la disputa en el merendero, y sintió, de pronto, deseo invencible de hablar con él, para suplicar o para increpar –ella misma no sabía para qué–; pero, en suma, para desfogar, para romper aquella horrible monotonía del tiempo que pasaba inalterable. Envióle el mensaje por Ana. Pero Baltasar respondió: «Ya iré.»

–¿Piensa usted ir? –le preguntaba Borrén aquella tarde.

–¿A qué? ¿A oír lástimas que no puedo remediar? ¡Algo bueno daría por estar ahora en Guipúzcoa!

–¡Hombre!… ¡Pobre chica!

Baltasar tomó su café a sorbos, muy pensativo. Calculaba que la avaricia de su madre le exponía, tal vez, a un compromiso grave. Era falta de habilidad no remitir a Amparo siquiera mil reales para tenerla contenta mientras él no aseguraba a Josefina, que, engreída ahora con la perspectiva del caudal, lo había acogido con hartos remilgos y escrúpulos, dificultando reanudar sus antiguos amorcillos. ¡Bah! El caso era ganar tiempo, porque apenas pusiese tierra en medio, el peligro cesaba… No obstante, el prudente Baltasar temía, temía una campanada inoportuna, que diese al traste con sus nuevos planes.

–¿Qué te dijo? –interrogó ansiosamente Amparo.

–Que vendría –repuso *la Comadreja*.

–Pero… ¿cuándo?

–No quiso explicar cuándo.

–¿Piensa él que estoy yo para esas calmas?

–Lo que él no tiene es gana de verte el pelo.

Amparo dejó caer la cabeza sobre el pecho, y su rostro se nubló con expresión tal de desconsuelo y enojo, que Ana la miró compadecida.

–Si algún día…, si pronto… viene la República…, la santa federal, ¡así Dios me salve!, Ana, lo arrastro!

Amparo had to leap over it, and if she didn't estimate the jump correctly, her foot would land in the icy, muddy water, and she would have to change her stockings and shoes afterwards. She sometimes ran into Chinto, who would offer to give her his hand to cross over this bad spot, and his compassionate gesture made her burn with rage. Being pitied by a brute like that! That's what we've come to after so many dreams, so many aspirations towards an easy, brilliant life and towards happiness.

In this way the cluster of winter days were picked off, slow-moving but short, without Amparo being able to distinguish a single ray of brightness, either in the firmament or her own destiny. She became discouraged and committed an act of weakness. She hadn't seen Baltasar since the argument with him at the picnic area, and she suddenly felt an insurmountable desire to talk to him in order to implore him or rebuke him – she herself didn't really know why – but, in short, in order to vent her anger, to break that horrible monotony of time that passed by inalterably. She sent him a message through Ana. But Baltasar replied: 'I'll come.'

'Do you intend to go?' Borrén asked him that afternoon.

'What for? To hear tales of woe I can't resolve? I'd give a lot to be in Guipúzcoa right now!'

'Really …! That poor girl!'

Baltasar sipped his coffee very pensively. He calculated that his mother's greed was perhaps exposing him to a serious commitment. It was lack of tact not to send Amparo at least a thousand reales to keep her satisfied, while he didn't reassure Josefina who, now puffed up at the prospect of wealth, had welcomed him with more than enough finickiness and scruples, making it difficult for him to resume his old flirtatious ways. Bah! It was a question of gaining time, because as soon as he made himself scarce, the danger would cease… Nevertheless, the prudent Baltasar was afraid, afraid of an untimely scandal that might mess up his new plans.

'What did he say to you?' Amparo asked anxiously.

'That he would come,' replied *the Weasel*.

'But … when?'

'He wouldn't say when.'

'Does he think I've got time for that?'

'What he wants is not to see hide nor hair of you.'

Amparo let her head drop to her breast, and her face clouded over with an expression of such dispair and anger that Ana looked at her with pity.

'If some day … if soon … the Republic comes … that holy federal state, so help me God! Ana, I'll finish with him.'

Ana se echó a reír con su delgada risa estridente.

–No seas tonta, mujer…, no seas tonta… ¡Para divertirlo y darle un mal rato, no tienes que aguardar por República ni repúblico!

–¿Que no?

–¿Sabes lo que yo había de hacer? Pues esto mismo. Coger pluma y papel… ¿Conoce tu letra?

–Nunca le escribí.

–Mejor. Pues escribirle a la de García una carta bien explicada, para que no se deje engañar por él.

–¿Un anónimo? ¡Quita allá!

–Un avisito … contándole lo que hizo contigo. No seas boba; anda, más merece.

Pasaba esta conversación a la salida de la fábrica; Ana llevó a Amparo a su casa, en la calle de la Sastrería. Subieron a un cuartuco; *la Comadreja* dio a su amiga recado de escribir, y entre las dos compusieron la siguiente epístola, que fielmente se traslada a la estampa:

> «Estimada señorita: halguien que la estima le abisa que quien se quiere casar con Usté tiene compormetida huna Chica onrada, y lea dado palbra de casarse con ella. Es el de Sobrado, parque Usté no dude, y Usté se informará y veráque es verdá. Q. b. s. m.
>
> *Un afetísimo amigo.*»

La Comadreja cerró, dictó sobre y señas, puso lacre fino del que ella usaba para escribir a su capitán, pegó un sello, y dijo a *la Tribuna*:

–Ahora, de paso que vuelves a tu casa, la echas en el correo con disimulo.

Al bajar la escalera, estrecha y oscura como boca de lobo, zumbábanle a Amparo los oídos y apretaba convulsivamente la carta, llevándola oculta bajo el mantón. La oprimía como oprimiría un puñal, con vengativo empeño y no sin cierto interior escalofrío. Se representaba a la orgullosa señorita de García rompiendo el sobre, leyendo, palideciendo, llorando… «¡Que pene! –decíase a sí propia la oradora–. ¡Que sufra como yo!…» ¿Y qué tiene que ver? Si ella pierde un pretendiente, yo he perdido la conducta y cuanto perder cabe… Después pensaba en Baltasar… y en los Sobrados todos… ¡Ah! ¡Buen chasco esperaba a la avarienta de la madre, que contaba

Ana burst into laughter with her sharp, strident laugh.

'Don't be silly … don't be silly… To distract him and give him a hard time, you don't have to wait for the Republic or anything else!'

'No?'

'Do you know what I'd do? Well, just this. Pick up pen and paper… Does he know your handwriting?'

'I never wrote to him.'

'All the better. Well, write a letter to the García girl, explaining everything, so she won't let herself be deceived by him.'

'An anymous letter? Get away with you!'

'A little warning … telling her what he did to you. Don't be silly; go on, he deserves far worse.'

This conversation occurred as they were leaving the factory. Ana took Amparo to her house on the Calle de la Sastrería. They went up to her dingy little room; *the Weasel* gave her friend some writing materials and between the two they composed the following epistle, which is faithfully transcribed here in print:

> 'My dear young lady: someone who holds you in esteem advices you that the one who wonts to marry you has compormised a nonourable Girl, and as given her is word heel marry her. It is Sobrado, so you should not doubt it, and so you will fined out and see its true.
>
> Yr obt svt
> A very dear friend.'

The Weasel closed the letter, dictated the name and address on the envelope and put on the fine sealing wax she used when she wrote to her captain, stuck on a stamp and said to *la Tribuna*:

'Now, on the way back home, you can secretly drop it in the mail.'

As she went down the stairs, which were narrow and dark like a wolf's mouth, Amparo's ears were buzzing and she grasped the letter convulsively, concealing it under her shawl. She was squeezing it, as one would squeeze a dagger, with a vindictive tenacity and not without a certain shudder inside. She could easily imagine the proud Señorita de García tearing open the envelope, reading, turning pale and weeping… 'Let her feel wretched!' the orator said to herself. 'Let her suffer as I do…!' And what does that have to do with it? If she loses a suitor, I've lost my good name and whatever else there is to lose … Then she thought about Baltasar … and the whole Sobrado family … Oh! A real disappointment was awaiting that greedy mother, who

con establecer brillantemente a su hijo! No la habían querido a ella..., pues ahora iban a verse desairados a su turno... ¡Ya probarían lo bien que sabe!

Rumiaba estas ideas a medida que adelantaba por la calle de la Sastrería, calle torcida, mal empedrada, en cuyos adoquines tropezaba de vez en cuando, mientras la luz vaga de los faroles del alumbrado público, proyectándose un momento, arrojaba a las paredes blanqueadas de las casas su silueta furtiva, de líneas desfiguradas, fantasmagóricas, prolongadas por la funda del pañolón. En la oscura noche invernal, caminando con paso atentado para salvar los charcos que dejara la lluvia de la tarde, parecíale a Amparo ir a cometer un delito, y, herida, sintiendo el dolor de su agravio, este pensamiento la embriagaba. Maquinalmente, al llegar a la entrada de la calle estrecha de San Efrén bajó una mano para recoger el vestido, que se iba manchando de barro, y al hacerlo aflojáronse sus dedos y dejó de apretar la carta, cuyo satinado papel le acariciaba la epidermis... Al cruzar la travesía del Puerto, su cabeza pareció despejarse, y vio el escaparate de la tercena y el buzón, con las fauces abiertas, como gritando «aquí estoy yo». Amparo soltó el vestido y sacó de debajo del mantón la mano derecha y la misiva... Detúvose antes de alzar el brazo.

«¡Un anónimo!», pensaba.

Su indómita generosidad popular se despertó. La pequeñez de la villana acción se hacía muy patente al ir a perpetrarla.

«Debí decirle a Ana que la echase ella... Yo no tengo cara a esto –murmuró entre sí–. Y si no la echo, me llamará boba... Pues mejor... ¡Esto es indecente! –balbució, adelantando la carta hasta tocar el buzón–. No, repelo –exclamó casi en voz alta, bajando la mano–. Esto es una cochinada... ¡Más vale ahogarlos donde los encuentre!»

Dio precipitadamente la vuelta y se metió por un callejón que lindaba con la travesía del Puerto, desembocando en el muelle. Ofrecióse de pronto a sus ojos el agua negra de la bahía, que no alumbraban la luna ni las estrellas, y donde los barcos inmóviles parecían más negros aún. Arrimóse al parapeto. Una brisa salitrosa, picante, le envolvió la faz. Despejósele completamente el cerebro, y con viveza suma hizo pedazos la epístola anónima. Los blancos fragmentos revolotearon un instante, como voladoras falenas,[40] y cayeron sordamente en el agua que chapoteaba contra el muro del embarcadero.

---

40   Mariposas nocturnas.

was counting on setting up a brilliant future for her son! They hadn't wanted her ... well now it was their turn to find themselves spurned ... Now they would find out what that tastes like!

She was ruminating on these ideas as she walked along the Calle de la Sastrería, a winding and badly paved street, on the flagstones of which she stumbled from time to time, while the dim light momentarily projected from the streetlamps of the public lighting system, cast against the whitewashed walls of the houses, her furtive silhouette with misshapen, phantasmagoric lines, prolonged by the outline of her shawl. In the dark winter night, as she walked with cautious steps to avoid the puddles left over from the afternoon rain, it seemed to Amparo that she was going to commit a crime, and injured, feeling the pain of the affront to her, this thought intoxicated her. As she reached the entry to the narrow Calle de San Efrén, she instinctively lowered her hand to gather up her dress, which was getting stained with mud, and on doing so her fingers loosened their hold and she stopped squeezing the letter with its glossy paper caressing her skin ... As she crossed the Travesía del Puerto, her head seemed to clear and she saw the window of the state wholesale tobacco warehouse and the mailbox with its jaws opened wide, as if shouting, 'Here I am.' Amparo let go of her dress and took her right hand and the missive from under her shawl ... She stopped before raising her arm.

'An anonymous letter,' she thought.

Her indomitable, working-class generosity was awakened. The small-mindedness of this base action became patently clear as she was about to perpetrate it.

'I should have told Ana to post it ... I haven't got the heart for this,' she murmured to herself. 'And if I don't post it, she'll call me a fool ... Well, all the better ... this is indecent!' she stammered, moving the letter forward until it touched the letter-box. 'No, hang it,' she exclaimed almost out loud as she lowered her hand. 'This is a dirty trick ...! It would be better to silence them wherever I run into them!'

She hastily turned around and took an alley that was adjacent to the Travesía del Puerto, and led into the wharf. Suddenly appearing before her eyes was the black water of the bay, with neither moon nor stars to light it up, and where motionless ships seemed even blacker. She moved closer to the parapet. A nitrous, biting breeze enveloped her. Her brain was completely clear now and she tore the anonymous letter into pieces with great spirit. The white fragments fluttered about for an instant, like flying moths, and fell silently into the water that splashed against the wall of the quay.

XXXVI

ENSAYO SOBRE LA LITERATURA
DRAMÁTICA REVOLUCIONARIA

No hay remedio, esto se va y lo otro avanza a galope. ¿Cuándo se retira Amadeo? ¿Hoy? ¿Mañana? Y si el italiano no perdió de vista todavía la tierra española, ya es como si viviésemos en plena República; no estará proclamada, pero ¿qué más da? Todo el mundo cuenta con ella de un instante a otro.

Sólo bajo la monarquía de merengue, que se va derritiendo y consumiendo al calor de la revolución, podía ser representable el drama que anunciaban los carteles del coliseo marinedino: *Valencianos con honra*. Aunque Amparo no iba a parte alguna, tanto oyó hablar de lo intencionado y subversivo que era el drama famoso, y de cómo pintaba a los republicanos cual son y no cual los retrata el pincel reaccionario, que resolvió asistir. Instalóse con Ana en el paraíso, donde se amontonaba inmensa concurrencia, que les metía los pies por la cintura, los codos por las ingles: a duras penas lograron las dos muchachas apoderarse de su sitio; al fin consiguieron embutirse de medio lado en delanteras, y allí se mantuvieron prensadas, comprimidas, sin poder ni enjugarse el sudor de la frente. El calor era espeso, asfixiante. Al alzarse el telón vino una bocanada de aire más respirable a aquel horno; poco duró, pero al menos dio ánimos para atender a las primeras escenas del drama.

El cual merecía bien que se sufriese la asfixia y otros géneros de tortura, a trueque de verlo representar. Desde la exposición tuvo conmovidos y suspensos a los espectadores. No podía ser de más actualidad el argumento, basado en los sucesos políticos de Valencia de 1869. Jugaba en el enredo un espía, un vil espía, perseguidor y delator de una familia republicana a machamartillo. Perdonado este pícaro en el primer acto por los magnánimos conspiradores a quienes vendió, claro está que no había de enmendarse, y que en los actos siguientes volvería a hacer de las suyas; no lo creyeron así los protagonistas del drama, pero en cambio la concurrencia de la cazuela lo

36

AN ESSAY ON REVOLUTIONARY
DRAMATIC LITERATURE

There's nothing for it; this is departing and the other is galloping forward. When is Amadeo withdrawing? Today? Tomorrow? And even if the Italian hasn't yet lost sight of Spanish soil, it's as if we were already living in the midst of the Republic; it's probably not proclaimed yet, but what difference does that make? Everyone is counting on it from one moment to the next.

Only under a monarchy that's like a meringue, which keeps melting and wasting away with the heat of the revolution, would it be possible to perform the drama which the posters in front of the theatre in Marineda were announcing: *Valencians With Honour*. Although Amparo hadn't been going anywhere, she heard so much talk about how this famous drama was well-intentioned and subversive, and how it depicted the republicans as they were and not as they are portayed by the reactionary paintbrush, that she made up her mind to attend. She settled down with Ana in the gods, where crowded together was a huge audience, sticking legs in their backs and elbows in their groins: the two girls only managed to take possession of their seats with great difficulty; they finally succeeded in squeezing themselves into some front row seats sitting half sideways, and there they remained, pressed together and squashed without even being able to wipe the sweat from their brows. The heat was oppressive and asphyxiating. When the curtain went up, a blast of more breathable air entered that oven; it didn't last long, but at least it gave them the necessary encouragement to pay attention to the first scenes of the drama.

It turned out to be well worth suffering the suffocation and the other forms of torture in exchange for seeing the performance. From the opening exposition it kept the spectators moved and filled with suspense. The storyline, based on the political events in Valencia in 1869, couldn't have been more topical. Playing a part in the plot was a spy, a vile spy, a persecutor of and informer against a staunch republican family. After this rogue was pardoned in the first act by the magnanimous conspirators he had betrayed, it is patently clear that he had no intention of mending his ways and that in the following acts he would get up to his old tricks again; the protagonists of the drama didn't believe so, but the audience in the gods, on the other hand, had a

presintió, y en medio del calor sofocante se oían voces ahogadas de emoción exclamando: «¡Ay! ¿Para qué perdonarán a ese tunante?... » «¡Ya verás cómo los ha de vender otra vez!... » «¡Como yo le atrapase no le soltaba, no!». Verdad es que si el bellaco del espía era tan malo que no tenía el diablo por dónde cogerlo, en cambio los personajes republicanos ofrecían modelos de lealtad y dechados de virtudes. Cuando en el mismo acto primero una esposa se abraza a su marido, que parte al combate, declarando con noble resolución que quiere seguirle y compartir los riesgos de la lid, Amparo sintió como un nudo, como una bola que se le formaba en la garganta, y haciendo un supremo esfuerzo, se agarró a la barandilla de la cazuela y gritó: «¡Bien!..., ¡muy bien!», dos o tres veces, luciendo su voz de contralto. Era aquel drama el mismo que ella había soñado en otro tiempo, cuando llegaron a Marineda los delegados de Cantabria, de cuyos riesgos y aventuras tanto deseara ser partícipe. La escena final del acto, donde todos los voluntarios republicanos, entre el fragor de la lid empeñada, doblan la rodilla al aparecer el Señor acompañado de las monjas de San Gregorio, aflojó suavemente los tirantes nervios de la concurrencia. Una especie de rocío refrigerante de honradez, dulzura y religiosidad se derramó sobre el público; las gentes experimentaban impulsos de abrazarse, de rezar y de charlar. ¡Después dirán que los oscurantistas se levantan por la religión! ¡Sí, sí! ¡Por cobrar las contribuciones y destruir *ferrocarriles*! ¡Que vengan a oír esto! ¿Quién duda que los mejores cristianos son los federales?

Pasóse el entreacto en vivos comentarios acerca del drama, que causaba favorabilísima impresión. Personas grandes se limpiaban los ojos con el dorso de la mano, haciendo tiernos momos de llanto. ¡Cuidado que se necesitaba talento y sabiduría para escribir piezas así! Sólo era irritante lo de dejar al espía con vida, porque de fijo, en el acto próximo, iba a salir con alguna barrabasada gorda. De tal suerte imperaba el entusiasmo, que nadie se ocupaba en mirar a la gente de abajo, a pesar de hallarse de bote en bote el coliseo; y como tardase en subir el telón, hubo pateos y aplausos impacientes y furiosos. Al fin dio principio el ansiado acto segundo.

Graduaba el autor hábilmente los efectos dramáticos, manejando con destreza los resortes del terror y la piedad. Ahora presentaba un mancebito que volvía de la lucha callejera a su casa, herido mortalmente, y consternando a su familia del modo que cualquiera puede figurarse. La actriz encargada de este interesante papel se había puesto sobre su cabello natural una peluca de ricitos cortos que la hacía semejante a un perro de aguas; circundaban sus

feeling, and you could hear voices choked with emotion in the suffocating heat, exclaiming: 'Oh! Why will they pardon that villain ...?' 'You'll see how he's going to sell them out again ...!' 'If I got my hands on him, I wouldn't let him go, no!' It's true that if that villain of a spy was so evil that even the devil was no match for him, the republican characters, on the other hand, represented models of loyalty and paragons of virtue. When, in the very first act, a wife embraces her husband who is setting off for combat, declaring with noble resolution that she wants to follow him and share the risks of the struggle, Amparo felt something like a knot, like a ball forming in her throat, and with a supreme effort she held on to the upper gallery railing and shouted: 'Well said ... very well said!' two or three times, showing off her contralto voice. That drama was the same one she had dreamed of at another time when the delegates from Cantabria, in whose risks and adventures she had wanted so much to take part, arrived in Marineda. The final scene of the act, where all the republican volunteers, amidst the din of the heated battle, bend their knees when the Lord appears accompanied by the nuns of Saint Gregory, gently loosened the taut nerves of the audience. A sort of cooling dew of honour, sweetness and religiosity spread out over the public; people felt a desire to embrace each other, to pray and to chat. And then they'll say that the obscurants are the ones who stand up for religion! Yes, yes! For collecting taxes and destroying *railroads*! Let them come and listen to this! Who can doubt that the best Christians are the federalists?

The interval was spent making lively comments about the drama, which left everyone with a very favourable impression. Grown people wiped their eyes with the backs of their hands, pulling funny, tender faces as they wept. Remember, you needed talent and wisdom to write plays like that! The only irritating thing was letting the spy live, because he was definitely going to come out with some really big dirty trick in the next act. Such enthusiasm prevailed that nobody spent time looking down at the people below, in spite of the fact that the colosseum was jam-packed; and if the curtain took too long to rise, there was a stamping of feet and impatient and angry applause. Finally the long-awaited second act began.

The author skilfully gauged the dramatic effects, deftly handling the devices of terror and compassion. Now he introduced a tender young lad who was returning home from the street fighting, mortally wounded and filling his family with dismay, as anyone can imagine. The actress entrusted with this interesting role had put a wig with short little curls over her natural hair, which made her look like a water spaniel; her eyes were encircled by dark,

ojos románticas ojeras marcadas al difumino; espesa capa de polvos de arroz imitaba la palidez de la agonía; llevaba americana muy floja para disimular la amplitud de las caderas, y entró tambaleándose y dando traspiés, con la mano apoyada en la región del pecho donde se suponía estar la herida. Por el paraíso circuló un rumor misterioso y profundo, el rugido opaco de la emoción que se comprime y refrena para mejor estallar después. Comenzó la escena de la despedida del moribundo y su familia. Cuando el padre, comandante de los voluntarios republicanos, dijo adiós al hijo confiándole la bandera, en unos versos que terminan así:

> Lleva la palma en la mano,
> mientras la patria en ofrenda
> te da este sudario en prenda…

y corriendo hacia la concha del apuntador y mudando la voz llorona en un vocejón estentóreo, gritó cerrando de puños:

> ¡Viva el pueblo soberano!

los llantos histéricos de las mujeres fueron cubiertos, devorados por el clamor que se alzó compacto y fortísimo, repitiendo frenéticamente el «¡viva!», a la vez que un huracán de palmadas asordó el coliseo. Contagiados, electrizados por la exaltación del público, los actores se esmeraban, bordaban su papel, y, fuera de sí, se abrazaban realmente, y se daban verdaderas puñadas en el tórax. Amparo, con medio cuerpo fuera de la barandilla, palmoteaba a más y mejor.

Durante el segundo entreacto, las gentes prensadas en la cazuela se hallaron unas miajas más anchas y cómodas, ya sea porque su volumen se había ido sentando y acomodándose al espacio, ya porque algunas, indispuestas con tan alta temperatura, mal de su grado hubieron de retirarse. Ana logró, pues, revolverse y escudriñar con sus perspicaces ojos de gato los ámbitos del teatro todo. Dio un expresivo codazo a *la Tribuna*, que miró hacia donde le señalaba su amiga, y divisó a las de García en un palco platea.

Fijóse especialmente en Josefina, que estaba elegante y sencilla, con traje de alpaca blanca adornado de terciopelo negro. A toda su familia, desde la madre hasta Nisita, les rebosaba el contento visiblemente; pero Josefina, en particular, no parece sino que se había esponjado con las buenas nuevas del pleito. La proximidad de la fortuna animaba, como un reflejo dorado, su tez, y hacía fulgecer en sus ojos chispas áureas. Recostada en la silla, gozaba

romantic rings applied with a stump pencil; a heavy layer of rice powder was used to imitate the pallor of death throes; she wore a loose-fitting jacket to hide the width of her hips, and she came on stage staggering and stumbling, her hand resting on the part of her breast where the wound was supposed to be. A mysterious, profound murmur circulated through the upper gallery, the dull roar of an emotion that is repressed and constrained, so that it might better explode later. The farewell scene between the dying boy and his family began. When the father, the commander of the republican volunteers, bade his son farewell, entrusting the flag to him, in verses that ended as follows:

Carry the palm leaf in your hand,
while the fatherland, as an offering,
gives you this shroud as a pledge …

and running towards the prompt box and changing his weeping voice to a powerful, stentorian roar, he shouted as he clenched his fists:

Long live the sovereign people!

The hysterical crying of the women was covered over and absorbed by the clamour that rose up densely and loudly, with the frenzied repetition of 'Long may it live!' at the same time that a hurricane of deafening applause filled the theatre. The actors, infected and electrified by this public exaltation, did their best, embroidered their roles, and, beside themselves, embraced each other for real and gave one another proper punches in the chest. Amparo, with half her body over the railing, really clapped her hands.

During the second interval, the people pressed together in the upper gallery found they had a bit more room and comfort, either because the bulk of their bodies had settled and become accustomed to the space available, or because some people, feeling unwell due to the high temperature, had unwillingly had to depart. Ana was then able to turn around and scrutinise the whole range of the theatre with her keen, catlike eyes. She gave an expressive nudge with her elbow to *la Tribuna*, who looked in the direction indicated by her friend and made out the García women in a ground-floor box.

She especially noticed Josefina, who looked elegant and simple in a white alpaca dress trimmed with black velvet. Her whole family, from the mother to Nisita, was visibly bubbling with happiness, but Josefina in particular seemed to have completely blossomed with the good news of the lawsuit. The proximity of a fortune in the offing livened up her complexion, like a shining reflection, and made golden sparks flash in her eyes. Reclining in her chair,

beatíficamente del triunfo, exponiendo a la admiración de los inquilinos de las *lunetas* el cuerpecillo ajustado, púdico, la línea fugitiva que se elevaba desde la cintura al hombro, el gracioso manejo de abanico, el movimiento delicado con que subía los gemelos a la altura de las cejas. No acertaba Amparo a apartar los ojos de su vencedora rival, y a duras penas la distrajo de aquella contemplación acerba el principio del tercer acto.

Salía en éste un oficial del Ejército, que, agradecido a la hospitalidad que le habían otorgado en la casa republicana, salvaba a su vez a los dueños de ella; patético rasgo, corona de todos los excelentes sentimientos que abundaban en el drama. Cuando más moqueaba la gente y se oían más hipidos y sollozos, Amparo sintió que su mirada, atraída por irresistible imán, se clavaba otra vez en el palco de García. Abrióse la puerta, y entró Baltasar, ceñido el fino talle por un uniforme intachable; y después de saludar cortésmente a la madre y a las niñas, se sentó al lado de la mayor, arreglándose el pelo con la enguantada mano, y estirando levemente, con notable desembarazo, la tirilla. Dirigió a Josefina en voz baja dos o tres palabras que, según el movimiento con que las acompañó, debían ser: «¿Qué tal esto?». Y la de García alzó los hombros de un modo imperceptible, que claramente significaba: «Pcsh… Un dramón muy populachero y muy cursi.» Definida así la función, Baltasar tomó familiarmente el abanico de la joven, y mientras lo cerraba y abría y lo daba vueltas como para informarse bien del paisaje, se entabló una de esas conversaciones íntimas, salpicadas de coqueterías, de reticencias, de miradas intensas y cortas, de ahogadas risas, diálogos en que reina dulce abandono, que no serían posibles mano a mano y en la soledad, y nunca se producen mejor que entre el tumulto de un sitio público, ante miles de testigos, en el desierto de las multitudes.

–Pero no ves, mujer… ¡qué poca vergüenza! –exclamaba Ana, señalando al grupo, del cual no se apartaban las pupilas de Amparo. Después del…, del aviso, ¿no sabes? –añadió al oído.

La Tribuna no contestó. Ana ignoraba la destrucción del anónimo. Amparo, avergonzándose de su noble impulso, no quería confesarlo, temerosa de que *la Comadreja* la tratase de *babiona* y de *pápara*, y aun de que repitiese la carta por cuenta propia. Ahora … ahora, clavando las uñas en la franela roja del barandal, sentía que el corazón se le inundaba de hiel

she blissfully enjoyed her triumph, exposing, much to the admiration of the occupants of the stalls, her tightly fitted, chaste young body, the fleeting line that rose up from her waist to her shoulders, the graceful manipulation of her fan and the delicate movement with which she raised her opera glasses to the height of her brows. Amparo couldn't avert her eyes from her victorious rival, and it was only with considerable difficulty that the beginning of the third act took her mind off that bitter contemplation.

In this act an army officer came on, thankful for the hospitality he had been granted in the republican house, and he in turn saved its owners; it was a touching gesture, the pinnacle of all the noble sentiments that abounded in the drama. Just when people were snivelling the most and you could hear the most whimpering and sobbing, Amparo felt that her gaze, drawn by some irresistible magnet, was fixed once again on the García's theatre box. The door opened and Baltasar came in, a spotless uniform tightly fitting his fine physique; and after courteously greeting the mother and the young girls, he sat down beside the eldest, rearranging his hair with his gloved hand, and gently stretching his neckband with noticeable self-confidence. In a hushed voice he directed two or three words to Josefina, which, from the movement that accompanied them, must have been: 'What do you think of this?' And the García girl shrugged her shoulders almost imperceptibly, which clearly signified: 'Pfff … a melodrama, very common and in very poor taste.' Once the performance had been so defined, Baltasar took the young woman's fan familiarly, and whilst he closed, opened and turned it around as if to find out more about the landscape on it, one of those intimate conversations was struck up, sprinkled with flirtatious remarks, innuendos, intense, brief glances, stifled laughter and dialogues dominated by sweet abandonment, none of which would have been possible had they been together by themselves, and which never develop better than within the tumult of a public place, before thousands of witnesses, in the desert of crowds of people.

'But can't you see … he has no shame!' Ana exclaimed, pointing at the group from which Amparo couldn't look away. 'After your … your warning, isn't that so?' she added, whispering in her ear.

La Tribuna didn't reply. Ana didn't know about the destruction of the anonymous letter. Amparo, ashamed of her noble impulse, didn't want to confess to it, fearing that *the Weasel* would call her a *muggins* and a *bumpkin*, and even that she should try to do the letter again on her own. Now … now … digging her fingernails into the red flannel of the railing, she felt that her heart was overflowing with bile and poison; there was nothing

y veneno; nada, estaba visto que era tonta; ¿por qué no echó la carta en el correo? Pero no; esa miserable y artera venganza no la satisfacía; cara a cara, sin miedo ni engaño, con la misma generosidad de los personajes del drama, debía ella pedir cuenta de sus agravios. Y mientras se le hinchaba el pecho, hirviendo en colérica indignación, el grupo de abajo era cada vez más íntimo, y Baltasar y Josefina conversaban con mayor confianza, aprovechándose de que el público, impresionado por la muerte del espía infame que, al fin, hallaba condigno castigo a sus fechorías, no curaba de lo que pudiese suceder por los palcos. De Josefina, que tenía la cabeza vuelta, sólo se alcanzaban a ver los bucles del artístico peinado, la mancha roja de una camelia prendida entre la oreja y el arranque del blanco cuello, y la bola de coral del pendiente, que oscilaba a cada movimiento de su dueña.

Bien quisiera *la Tribuna* salir, librarse de la sensación lancinante[41] que le producía tal vista; pero la gente que la rodeaba por todas partes, como las sardinas a las sardinas en la banasta, no le consentía moverse mientras el telón no se bajase. Un poco antes de terminarse el drama, vio a las de García que se levantaban, y a Baltasar que les ponía los abrigos a todas con suma deferencia, empezando por la madre; después se cerró la puerta del palco, y quedóse Amparo con las pupilas fijas maquinalmente en aquel espacio vacío. Aún tardó algunos minutos en comenzar el desagüe de la cazuela, y el estrepitoso descenso por las escaleras abajo. Cogiéronse Amparo y Ana de bracero, y empujadas por todos lados arribaron al vestíbulo y de allí salieron a la calle, donde el frío cortante de la noche liquidó al punto el sudor en que estaban ensopadas sus frentes. Sintió *la Comadreja* que el brazo de Amparo temblaba, y la miró, y le halló desencajada la faz.

–Tú no estás bien, chica... ¿qué tienes? ¿Te da algo por la cabeza?

–Suéltame –contestó con voz opaca *la Tribuna*–. A donde voy no me hace falta compañía.

–¡María Santísima!, ¿adónde vas, mujer?, ¿Qué es eso?

–¡Que adónde voy! Pues a apedrearles la casa, para que lo sepas.

Y recogió el mantón, como para quedarse con los brazos libres.

–Tú loqueas ... Anda a dormir.

–O me dejas o me tiro al mar –respondió con tal acento de desesperación la muchacha, que Ana la soltó, y echó a andar a su lado, midiendo el paso por el de la terrible y colérica *Tribuna*.

---

41 Dolor intenso.

for it, it was apparent that she was a fool; why did she not post the letter? But no; such despicable, crafty vengeance couldn't satisfy her. She should ask for her grievances to be settled face to face, without fear or deception, with the same generosity as those characters in the drama. And while her breast was surging, seething with angry indignation, the group down below was becoming more and more intimate, and Baltasar and Josefina were conversing more openly, taking advantage of the fact that the public, affected by the death of the infamous spy who had finally met a fitting punishment for his misdemeanours, was unmindful of what might be going on in the theatre boxes. All that could be seen of Josefina, whose head was turned away, were the ringlets of her artistic coiffure, the red patch of a camellia fastened between her ear and the top of her white neck, and the coral ball of her earring, which swung back and forth with her every movement.

La Tribuna would gladly have left and freed herself of the piercing sensation this sight produced in her; but the people surrounding her on all sides, packed like sardines, made it impossible for her to move until the curtain came down. Just before the drama finished, she saw the García women stand up and Baltasar help them all on with their coats with the greatest of deference, beginning with the mother; then the theatre box door closed and Amparo was left there with her eyes mechanically fixed on that empty space. It still took a few minutes before they began pouring out of the gods and noisily going down the staircase. Amparo and Ana took each other's arm, and after being pushed from all sides, they reached the foyer, and from there they went out into the street where the bitterly cold night immediately evaporated the sweat drenching their foreheads. *The Weasel* felt that Amparo's arm was trembling, and she looked at her and found her face contorted.

'You're not looking well … What's wrong? Is it something with your head?'

'Let go of me,' *la Tribuna* replied in a lifeless voice. 'Where I'm going, I don't need company.'

'Holy Mother of God! Where are you going? What's this about?'

'You ask where I'm going? Well, to throw stones at their house, for your information.'

And she gathered up her shawl as if to leave her arms free.

'You're talking nonsense … Go and have a sleep.'

'Either you leave me alone or I'll throw myself into the sea,' the girl replied with such a tone of desperation that Ana let go of her and started to walk by her side, measuring her pace by that of the ill-tempered and angry *Tribuna*.

–Te digo que se la apedreo, mujer; tan cierto como que ahora es de noche y Dios nos ve. ¡Repelo! ¡No hay sino hacer irrisión de las gentes ... de las infelices mujeres ... de los pobres! ¿Pero tú has visto qué descaro, qué descaro tan atroz? En mi cara..., en mi cara misma..., ¡Me valga San Dios, que esto no pasa entre los negros de allá de Guinea!

–Bueno... Y ahora, ¿qué se hace con perderse..., con ir a la cárcel mujer?

–Desahogarme, Ana..., porque me ahogo, que toda la noche pensé que con un cordel me estaban apretando la nuez... ¡Romperles los vidrios, retepelo! ¡Armar un belén, avergonzarlos, canario! ¡Y que no me piquen las manos y que duerma yo a gusto hoy! ¡Que tengo las asaduras aquí –señaló a la garganta– y el corazón apretao, apretao!

–Pero mujer..., mira, considera...

–No considero, no miro nada...

Este diálogo duraba mientras cruzaron las dos amigas el páramo de Solares en dirección al barrio de Arriba, por donde suponía Amparo que iba Baltasar acompañando a las de García hasta su casa. El aire frío y el silencio de las calles del barrio templaron, no obstante, la sangre enardecida de *la Tribuna*. Parecióle entrar en algún claustro donde todo fuese quietud y melancolía. No hollaba un transeúnte el pavimento, que resonaba con solemnidad; y cuando menos lo pensaban las dos expedicionarias, les cerró el paso una iglesia, la de Santa María Magdalena, alta, muda, con pórtico de ojiva, donde la luz de los faroles dibujaba los vagos contornos de dos santos de piedra que se miraban inmóviles. Involuntariamente *la Tribuna* bajó la voz, y al cruzar por delante del pórtico se santiguó, sin darse cuenta de lo que hacía, y recortó y contuvo el paso. Ana iba a aprovechar la coyuntura para hacer a la determinada *Tribuna* mil reflexiones, a tiempo que un oficial, que volvía de la plaza de la Fruta, cruzó casi rozándose con ellas y sin verlas, cantando entre dientes no sé qué polca o pasodoble. Reconoció Amparo a Baltasar, y echó tras él como el lebrel tras la res que persigue. ¿Oyó Baltasar las pisadas de *la Tribuna* y pudo reconocerlas? Lo cierto es que se perdió de vista al revolver de la esquina, y que, por muy diligentes que anduvieron las que le seguían, no lograron darlo alcance.

'I'm telling you that I'm going to throw stones at it; that's as certain as it's now night and God is watching us. Hang it! All they can do is make a laughing-stock out of people ... of unfortunate women ... of the poor! Have you ever seen such cheek, such outrageous cheek? In my face ... in my very face ... May Holy God help me, but things like this don't happen even among the blacks over there in Guinea!'

'All right ... And now, what do you gain by ruining yourself ... by going to prison?'

'Just to get it out of my system, Ana ... because I'm choking, because all night I felt as if they were squeezing my neck with a rope ... Smash their windows, a plague on them! Kick up a rumpus, put them all to shame, hang it and hang it twice over! Only then will my hands not be stinging and will I be able to sleep in peace today! My guts are right here,' she pointed to her throat, 'and my heart is all tightened up, all tightened up!'

'But ... take a good look, consider ...'

'I won't consider, I won't look at anything...'

This dialogue lasted all the time the two friends crossed the Páramo de Solares, in the direction of the Barrio de Arriba, where Amparo supposed that Baltasar was accompanying the García women to their house. However, the cold air and the silence of the streets in this district cooled down *la Tribuna*'s boiling blood. It seemed to her that she had entered some cloister where everything was stillness and melancholy. Not a single passerby was treading on the pavement, which resounded solemnly; and when the two explorers least expected it, a church blocked their way, that of Santa María Magdalena, tall and silent, with an ogival portico, where the light from the street lamps traced the vague contours of two motionless stone saints who were staring at each other. *La Tribuna* involuntarily lowered her voice, and as she passed in front of the portico she made the sign of the cross, without realising what she was doing, and then she slowed down her pace and stopped. Ana was about to take advantage of this juncture to offer the determined *Tribuna* her many thoughts, when at that moment an officer, returning from the Plaza de la Fruta, almost brushed into them as he passed by without seeing them, humming some polka or *paso doble*. Amparo recognised Baltasar and started after him, like a greyhound chasing after wild game. Did Baltasar hear *la Tribuna*'s footsteps and did he recognise them? What is certain is that he was lost from sight when he turned the corner, and that no matter how quickly the women following him walked they didn't manage to catch up with him.

–Voy a llamarlo a la puerta –exclamó Amparo.

–Mujer, ¿estás loca?… ¡Una casa de la calle Mayor! –murmuró Ana, con respetuoso miedo–. ¿Tú sabes la que se armaría?

En horas semejantes la calle Mayor ofrecía imponente aspecto. Las altas casas, defendidas por la brillante coraza de sus galerías refulgentes, en cuyos vidrios centelleaba la luz de los faroles, estaban cerradas, silenciosas y serias. Algún lejano aldabonazo retumbaba allá…, en lo más remoto, y sobre las losas, el golpe del chuzo del sereno repercutía con majestad. Amparo se detuvo ante la casa de los Sobrados. Era ésta de tres pisos, con dos galerías blancas muy encristaladas y puerta barnizada, en la cual se destacaba la mano de bronce del aldabón. Y entre el silencio y la calma nocturna se alzaba tan severa, tan penetrada de su importante papel comercial, tan cerrada a los extraños, tan protectora del sueño de sus respetables inquilinos, que *la Tribuna* sintió repentino hervor en la sangre, y tembló nuevamente de estéril rabia, viendo que por más que se deshiciese allí, al pie del impasible edificio, no sería escuchada ni atendida. Accesos de furor sacudieron un instante sus miembros al hallarse impotente contra los muros blancos, que parecían mirarla con apacible indiferencia; y de pronto, bajándose, recogió un trozo de ladrillo que la casualidad le mostró, a la luz de un farol, caído en el suelo, y con airada mano trazó una cruz roja sobre la oscura puerta reluciente de barniz, cruz roja que dio mucho que pensar los días siguientes a doña Dolores y al tío Isidoro que recelaban un saqueo a mano armada.

'I'm going to call him to the door,' Amparo exclaimed.

'Are you mad ...? A house on the Calle Mayor!' Ana murmured with respectful fear. 'Do you realise what a commotion you'd cause?'

At that particular hour, the Calle Mayor made an imposing impression. The tall houses, protected by the shining armour of their gleaming galleries, in whose windows the lights of the streetlamps were flickering, were closed up, silent and grave. A distant knock on a door resounded over there ... so very far away, and the blows of the night watchman's metal-tipped stick on the flagstones echoed majestically. Amparo stopped in front of the Sobrado house. It was three storeys high, with two white galleries full of glass windows, and a varnished door on which the bronze hand of the door knocker was prominenet. And in the midst of the silence and nocturnal calm, it rose up so severe, so permeated with its important commercial role, so closed off to outsiders and so protective of the sleep of its respectable tenants, that *la Tribuna* felt her blood suddenly boil, and she trembled once again with sterile rage as she realised that no matter how much she exploded there, at the foot of that impassive building, no one would hear her or pay her any attention. Fits of anger shook her limbs for an instant as she found herself impotent against those white walls, which seemed to look at her with mild indifference; and suddenly bending down, she picked up from the ground a piece of brick she happened to see in the light of a street lamp, and angrily traced a red cross with it on the dark, shining, varnished door, a red cross that gave Doña Dolores and Uncle Isidoro a lot to think about on the days that followed, because they feared an armed robbery.

XXXVII

LUCINA PLEBEYA

Vestíase Amparo, antes de salir a la fábrica, reflexionando que diluviaba, que de noche se habían oído varios truenos, que se quedaría gustosa en casa, y aun entre cobertores, si no necesitase saber noticias, excitarse, oír voces anhelosas que decían: «Ahora sí que llegó la nuestra… Macarroni se va de esta vez … hay un parte de Madrí, que viene la República … mañana se proclama.»

Al salir de su fementido lecho, la transición del calor al frío la hizo sentir en las entrañas dolorcillos como si se las royese poquito a poco un ratón. Púsose pálida, y le ocurrió la terrible idea de que llegaba la hora. Volvióse al lecho, creyendo que allí se calentaría; cerró los ojos y no quiso pensar. Un deseo profundo de anonadamiento y de quietud se unía en ella a tal vergüenza y aflicción, que se tapó la cara con la sábana, prometiéndose no pedir socorro, no llamar a nadie. Mas comoquiera que el tiempo pasaba y los dolorcillos no volvían se resolvió a levantarse, y al atar la enagua, de nuevo le pareció que le mordían los intestinos agudos dientes. Vistióse no obstante, y se dio a pasear por la estancia, a tiempo que una mano llamó a la puerta del cuartuco, y antes que Amparo se resolviese a decir «adelante», Ana entró.

–¿Vienes?

–No puedo.

–¿Pasa algo, hay novedá?

–Creo … que sí.

–¿Qué sientes, mujer?

–Frío, mucho frío…, y sueño, un sueño que me dormiría en pie…; pero al mismo tiempo rabio por andar… ¡Qué rareza!

–¿Aviso a la señora Pepa?

–¡No!… ¡Qué vergüenza! Jesús, mi Dios… Ana querida, no la avises.

–¡Qué remedio, mujer! ¿Sigue eso?

–Sigue…, ¡infeliz de mí, que nunca yo naciese!

–Acuéstate sobre la cama.

37
A PLEBEIAN LUCINA[20]

Before setting out for the factory, Amparo was getting dressed, thinking about the fact that it was pouring with rain, that several thunderclaps had been heard during the night, and that she would gladly stop at home, and even under the blankets, were it not for her need to know the news, to be excited, to hear eager voices saying: 'Our turn has come... Macaroni is leaving once and for all ... there's a report from Madrid that the Republic is on its way... It will be proclaimed tomorrow.'

When she left her deceptive bed, the transition from the warmth to the cold made her feel little pains in her innards, as if a mouse were gnawing at them bit by bit. She turned pale, and the terrible idea occurred to her that the time had come. She went back to bed, thinking that she would get warmer there; she closed her eyes and tried not to think. A profound desire for annihilation and quietude combined in her with such shame and affliction that she covered her face with the sheet, promising herself not to seek help or call for anyone. But in view of the fact that time was passing and the slight pains hadn't come back, she resolved to get up, and as she tied her underskirt, once again it seemed to her that sharp teeth were biting into her intestines. Nevertheless, she dressed and began to pace around the room, just as a hand knocked at the door of her poky little room and, before Amparo resolved to say, 'Come in,' Ana entered.

'Are you coming?'

'I can't.'

'Is something wrong? Anything new?'

'I think ... there is.'

'What can you feel, tell me?'

'Cold, very cold ... and sleepy. I could sleep standing up ... but at the same time I'm dying to walk around... It's so strange!'

'Shall I let Señora Pepa know?'

'No ... I'd be so ashamed! Jesus, God ... dearest Ana, don't tell her.'

'I've got no choice! Can you still feel it?'

'I keep feeling it ... poor wretched me! I wish I'd never been born!'

'Just lie down on the bed.'

20　Lucina was the goddess of childbirth who safeguarded the lives of women in labour. Her name was generally taken to mean 'she who brings children into the light'.

Con su viveza ratonil, Ana arropó a la paciente, y ya se dirigía a la puerta, cuando una quebrantada voz la llamó:

–Llévale la cascarilla a mi madre…, dile que me duele la cabeza…, no le digas la verdá, por el alma de quien más quieras…

–Sí que no se hará ella de cargo…

Amparo se quedó algo tranquila; sólo a veces, un dolor lento y sordo la obligaba a incorporarse apoyándose sobre el codo, exhalando reprimidos ayes. Ana corría, corría, sin cuidarse de la lluvia, hacia la ciudad. Cerca de dos horas tardó, a pesar de su ligereza, en volver acompañada de un bulto enorme, del cual sólo se veían desde lejos dos magnos chanclos que embarcaban el agua llovediza, y un paraguazo de algodón azul con cuento y varillas de latón dorado. Bufaba la insigne comadrona y resoplaba, ahogándose, a pesar del ningún calor y de la mucha y glacial humedad de la atmósfera; cuando penetró en la casucha, revolvióse en ella como un monstruo marino en la angosta tinaja en que lo enseñaba el domador. Fuese derecha a la cama de la paralítica, y le dijo dos o tres frases, entre lástima y chunga, que a ésta le supieron a acíbar; cabalmente estaba deshaciéndose de ver que ni podía ayudar a su hija en el trance, ni acompañarla siquiera; aquella habitación era tan próxima a la calle, que ni soñaba en traer allí a la paciente.

Consumíase la pobre mujer presa en su jergón, penetrada súbitamente de la ternura que sienten las madres por sus hijas mientras éstas sufren la terrible crisis que ellas ya atravesaron… Chinto se encontraba allí semejante a un palomino atontado… Entró la comadrona donde la llamaba su deber, y el mozo y la vieja se quedaron tabique por medio, ayudándose a sobrellevar la angustia de la tragedia que para ellos se representaba a telón corrido… La tullida maldecía de su hija, que en tal ocasión se había puesto, y al mismo tiempo lloriqueaba por no poder asistirla. Y a cada cinco minutos la señora Pepa entraba en el cuartuco, llenándolo con su corpulencia descomunal, y ordenando militarmente a Chinto que corriese a desempeñar algún recado indispensable.

–Aceite, rapaz… ¡un poco de aceite!

–¿Qué tal? –interrogaba la madre.

–Bien, mujer, bien… ¡Aceite, porreta!

Lo que no se encontraba en la casa Chinto salía disparado a pedirlo fuera, prestado en la de un vecino, o fiado en las tiendas. Generalmente, al recoger una cosa, la comadrona exigía ya otra.

With her mouse-like quickness, Ana tucked the patient up and was heading towards the door when a weak voice called out to her.

'Take the cocoa to my mother … tell her I've got a headache … don't tell her the truth, by all that you hold dear…'

'She won't realise what's…'

Amparo remained somewhat relieved; only occasionally did a slow, dull pain oblige her to sit up, leaning on her elbow, heaving repressed moans. Ana kept running, running towards the city, without worrying about the rain. In spite of her agility, she took almost two hours to return, accompanied by an enormous bulky shape, of which all that could be seen from a distance were two great big galoshes filling up with rainwater, and a large umbrella made of blue cotton, with the tip and ribs made of gilt brass. The renowned midwife was huffing and puffing, gasping for breath, in spite of the lack of heat and the fact that the air was so icy and damp; when she went into the shabby little house, she moved around it like a sea monster in a large earthenware vat where the trainer displayed it. She went straight to the paralysed woman's bed and said a few words to her, in a mixture of pity and jest, which tasted as bitter as gall to the mother; she was going completely to pieces as she saw that she could neither help her daughter at this critical moment, nor even be by her side; that room was so close to the street that she wouldn't even dream of bringing the patient there.

The poor woman, consumed with anguish, was captive on her straw mattress, suddenly overcome by the tenderness mothers feel for their daughters whilst they endure the terrible crisis which they themselves have already gone through … Chinto was there like a silly fool… The midwife went in where duty called her, and the young man and the old lady remained behind the partition wall between the rooms, helping one another to endure the anguish of the tragedy that was being performed for them behind a drawn curtain … The crippled old woman cursed her daughter for having put herself in such a situation, while simultaneously whining about not being able to help her out. And every five minutes Señora Pepa would come into her small dingy room, filling it with her enormous corpulence, and ordering Chinto in miltary fashion to run and carry out some indispensable errand.

'Oil, boy … a little oil!'

'How are things?' the mother asked.

'Fine, just fine… Oil, starkers!'

What wasn't in the house, Chinto shot out to get elsewhere, either borrowed from a neighbour or on credit in the shops. Generally, whenever she took one thing, the midwife would ask him for another.

–Un gotito de anís…

–¿Anís? ¿Para qué? –preguntaba la tullida.

–Para mí, porreta, que soy de Dios y tengo cuerpo y también se me abre como si me lo cortasen con un cuchillo.

Y Chinto se echaba dócilmente a la calle en busca de anís.

Volvía a presentarse la terrible comadre, toda fatigosa y sofocada.

–Vino… ¿Hay vino?

–¿Para ti? –murmuraba, sin poder contenerse, la impedida.

–Para ti, para ti… ¡Para ella, demonche, que bien necesita ánimos la pobre!… ¿Piensas tú que yo le doy desas jaropías[42] de los médicos, desos calmantes y durmientes? ¡Calmantes! Fuersa, fuersa es lo que hace falta y vino, que alegra al hombre las pajarillas, ¡porreta!

Quince minutos después:

–Tres onsas de chocolate, del mejor… Y mira, de camino a ver si encuentras una gallinita bien gorda, y le vas retorciendo el pescuezo… Pide también un cabito de cera…, las planchadoras que haya por aquí han de tener…

–¿De cera?

–De cera, ¡porreta! ¿Si sabré yo lo que me pido? Y pon agua a la lumbre. Y Chinto entraba, salía, dando zancadas a través del lodo, trayendo a la exigente facultativa cera, espliego, romero, vino blanco y tinto, anís, aceite, ruda, todas las drogas y comestibles que reclamaba… En los breves intervalos que tenía de descanso el solícito mozo, se sentaba en una silla baja, al lado del lecho de la tullida, quejándose de que le faltaban las piernas de algún tiempo acá, él mismo no sabía cómo, y parece que la respiración se le acababa enteramente; el médico le afirmaba que se le había metido polvillo de tabaco en los *broncos* y en los *pulmones*… Boh, boh…, ¿qué saben los médicos lo que no tiene dentro del cuerpo? Hablaba así en voz baja, para no dejar de prestar oídos a los lamentos de la paciente, que recorrían variada escala de tonos; primero habían sido gemidos sofocados; luego, quejidos hondos y rápidos, como los que arranca el reiterado golpe de un instrumento cortante; en pos vinieron ayes articulados, violentos, anhelosos, cual si la laringe quisiese beberse todo el aire ambiente para enviarlo a las conturbadas entrañas; y trascurrido algún tiempo, la voz se alteró, se hizo ronca, oscura, como si naciese más abajo del pulmón, en las

---

42 Jarabes.

'Just a drop of anisette...'

'Anisette? What for?' asked the paralysed woman.

'For me, starkers, because I'm human, and I have a body and also I'm being opened up as if I were being cut with a knife.'

And Chinto would meekly dash out into the street in search of anisette.

The imposing midwife would turn up again, completely out of breath and panting heavily.

'Wine ... is there any wine?'

'For you?' the disabled woman muttered, unable to contain herself.

'For you, for you! ...For her, what the devil, because the poor thing is really in need of courage...! Do you think I'm going to give her some of them medicinal syrups the doctors use, them sedatives and sleeping potions? Sedatives! Strenth, strenth, that's what she needs, and wine, which really lightens the spirit, starkers!'

Fifteen minutes later:

'Three ounces of chocolate, the best quality ... and look, see on the way if you find a fat young hen, and you can wring its neck... Ask for a small stub of beeswax as well ... the women who do the ironing around here must have some...'

'Beeswax?'

'Beeswax, starkers! I should know what I'm asking for? And put some water on the fire.'

And Chinto came in and went out, taking great strides through the mud, bringing this demanding physician beeswax, lavender, rosemary, white and red wine, anisette, oil, rue and all the drugs and provisions she demanded... During the brief intervals of rest which the solicitous young fellow had, he would sit down on a low chair beside the crippled woman's bed, complaining that he'd been weak in the legs for some time now, he himself didn't know why, and that he seemed to be completely out of breath; the doctor had assured him that the fine tobacco dust had got into his *bronchial tubes* and his *lungs*... Pooh, pooh ... what do doctors know about what's going on inside your body? He spoke this way in a low voice so as not to stop lending an ear to the patient's laments, which covered a varied scale of musical tones; at first, there had been stifled groans; then deep, rapid moans, like those caused by repeated blows from a sharp instrument; after this came articulated, violent, panting screams, as if her larynx were trying to swallow all the air around her and send it down to her troubled innards; after some time had elapsed, her voice changed, became hoarse and muffled, as if it

profundidades, en lo íntimo del organismo. A todo esto llovía, y la tarde de invierno caía prontamente, y el celaje gris ceniza parecía muy bajo, muy próximo a la tierra. Chinto encendió el candil de petróleo, y trajo caldo a la paralítica, y permaneció sentado, sin chistar, con las rodillas altas, los pies apoyados en el travesaño de la silla, la barba entre las palmas de las manos. Hacía un rato que el tabique no transmitía queja alguna. Dos o tres amigas de la fábrica, entre ellas *la Guardiana*, que ya no se quejaba de la paletilla, entraban un momento, se ofrecían, se retiraban con ademanes compasivos, con resignados movimientos de hombros, con reflexiones pesimistas acerca de la fatalidad y de la ingratitud de los hombres. De improviso se renovaron los gritos, que en el nocturno abandono parecían más lúgubres; durante aquella hora de angustia suprema, la mujer moribunda retrocedía al lenguaje inarticulado de la infancia, a la emisión prolongada, plañidera, terrible, de una sola vocal. Y cada vez era más frecuente, más desesperada la queja.

Serían las once cuando la señora Pepa se presentó en el cuarto de la tullida, enjugándose el rostro con el reverso de la mano. Sobre su frente baja y achatada y en su grosera faz de Cibeles de granito se advertía una preocupación, una sombra.

–¿Cómo va?

–Tarda, ¡porreta! Estas primerizas, como no saben bien el camino… –y la comadre, hizo que se reía para manifestar tranquilidad; pero un segundo después, añadió–: Puede ser que … porque uno no quiere embrollos ni dolores de cabeza, ¿oyes? Yo soy clara como el agua, vamos…, y no se me murieron en las manos, ¡porreta!, sino dos, en la edá que tengo… Después, los médicos hablan… Y yo cuanto puedo hago y unturas y friegas de Dios llevo dado en ella…

Al afirmar esto, la comadre se limpiaba a las caderas sus gigantescas manos pringosas.

–¿Habrá que avisar al médico? –gimoteó la tullida.

–¡Porreta!, a mi edá no gusta verse envuelta en cuentos… Luego, después, que si hiso así, que si pudo haser asá…, que si la señora Pepa sabe o no sabe el oficio… Menéate ya, dormilón –añadió despóticamente, volviéndose a Chinto–. Ya estás corriendo por el médico, ¡ganso!

Chinto salió sin cuidarse del agua que continuaba cayendo tercamente del

were originating below the lungs, in the very depths, the intimate parts of her organism. And all the time it kept raining, and the winter evening fell quickly, and the ashen grey cloud formations seemed very low, very close to the ground. Chinto lit the oil lamp and brought the paralysed woman her broth, and remained there seated, without opening his mouth, his knees drawn up, his feet resting on the rung of the chair, his chin between the palms of his hands. Not a single groan had come from the other side of the partition for a while now. Two or three friends from the factory, including *la Guardiana*, who was no longer complaining about the pain in her back, came in for a moment, offered to help, then departed with expressions of compassion on their faces, with resigned movements of their shoulders, and with pessimistic reflections concerning fate and the ingratitude of men. All of a sudden, the cries started up again, and in the midst of that nocturnal desolation they seemed more lugubrious; during that hour of supreme anguish, the moribund woman regressed to the inarticulate language of infancy, to the prolonged, plaintive, terrifying emission of a single vowel. And her groans grew more and more frequent, more and more desperate.

It must have been eleven o'clock when Señora Pepa appeared again in the crippled woman's room, wiping her face with the back of her hand. A preoccupation, a shadow was noticeable over her low, flat forehead and on her coarse face which was like a granite Cybele.

'How's it going?'

'It's taking time, starkers! These first-time mothers, as they don't really know the way...' the midwife tried to laugh to show how calm she was; but a second later, she added, 'It may be that ... because one doesn't want confusion or headaches, do you hear? I'm crystal clear ... and only two, starkers, have ever died in my hands, and that at my age ... And afterwards, the doctors started talking ... And I've done everything I can, and God knows, the number of ointments and massages I've used on her ...'

As she affirmed this, the midwife wiped her gigantic greasy hands on her hips.

'Should we send for the doctor?' the crippled woman wailed.

'Starkers, at my age you don't like to be tangled up in these troubles ... When it's all done, afterwards, they wonder if you did it this way or if you might have done it that way ... or if Señora Pepa really knows or doesn't know her job ... Get a move on, sleepyhead,' she added despotically as she turned to Chinto. 'Get running for the doctor now, you dimwit!'

Chinto went out, paying no heed to the water that continued falling

negro cielo, y corrió, perseguido por aquella voz cada vez más dolorida, más agonizante, que atravesaba el tabique, mientras la impedida se lamentaba de que, además de morírsele la hija, iba a tener que abonar –¿y con qué, Jesús del alma?– los honorarios de un facultativo. El silencio era tétrico, el tiempo pasaba con lentitud, medido por el chisporroteo del candil y por un clamor ya exhausto, que más se parecía al aullido del animal espirante que a la queja humana. Media noche era por filo cuando Chinto entró acompañado del médico. Acostumbrado debía de estar éste a tan críticas situaciones, porque lo primero que hizo fue dejar el chorreante impermeable en una silla, arremangarse tranquilamente las mangas del gabán y los puños de la camisa, y tomar de manos de Chinto una caja cuadrilonga que arrimó a un rincón. Después entró en el cuarto de la paciente, y se oyó la voz gruñosa de la comadre, empeñada en darle explicaciones…

A eso de un cuarto de hora más tarde volvió el soldado de la ciencia a presentarse y pidió agua para lavarse las manos… Mientras Chinto buscaba torpemente una jofaina, la madre, llorosa, temblando, preguntaba nuevas.

–¡Bah!…, no tenga usted cuidado… Ese chico me dijo que se trataba de un lance muy peligroso, y me traje los chismes…, no sé para qué: una muchacha como un castillo, con formación admirable, una versión que se hizo en un decir Jesús… Estamos concluyendo. Ahora, la comadre basta, pero yo seré testigo.

Lavóse las manos mientras esto decía, y tornó a su puesto. La mecha de petróleo, consumida, carbonizada, atufaba la habitación, dejándola casi en tinieblas, cuando dos o tres gritos, no ya desfallecidos, sino, al contrario, grandes, potentes, victoriosos, conmovieron la habitación, y tras de ellos se oyó, perceptible y claro, un vagido.

stubbornly from the black sky, and he ran, pursued by that ever more pained, more agonising voice that came through the partition, while the disabled woman was lamenting the fact that, in addition to her daughter dying she was going to have to pay – and with what, sweet Jesus? – the doctor's fees. The silence was gloomy, time passed slowly, measured by the spluttering of the oil lamp and by a noise, now completely exhausted, which resembled the howling of a dying animal more than a human lament. It was midnight exactly when Chinto came in accompanied by the doctor. The latter must have been accustomed to such critical situations, because the first thing he did was to leave his dripping raincoat on a chair, calmly roll up his coat sleeves and shirt cuffs, and take a rectangular case from Chinto's hands which he pushed in a corner. Then he went into the patient's room and the midwife's grumbling voice could be heard, determined to give him explanations…

About a quarter of an hour later, this soldier of science appeared again and asked for some water to wash his hands… While Chinto looked clumsily for a washbasin, the mother was weeping and trembling as she asked for some news.

'Bah…! There's nothing to worry about… That young fellow told me it was a very dangerous situation, so I brought along my instruments… I don't know why: a girl that's a tower of strength, just the right build, a baby turned into the head-down position in the twinkling of an eye… We're coming to the end. The midwife can manage now, but I'll watch.'

He washed his hands as he said this, and went back to his post. The wick in the oil lamp, used up and burnt to a cinder, filled the room with fumes, leaving it in virtual darkness, when two or three screams, not feeble now, but on the contrary strong, powerful and victorious, shook the room, and after these, you could hear, perceptibly and clearly, the wail of a newborn baby.

XXXVIII
¡POR FIN LLEGÓ!

Amparo descansa abismada en el reposo inefable de las primeras horas. Sin embargo, a medida que la luz de la pálida mañana entra por el ventanillo, vuelve la memoria y la conciencia de sí misma. Llama a Chinto ceceándolo.

–¿Qué quieres, mujer?

–Vas a ir corriendo al cuartel de Infantería… Parece que ahora no sale la tropa de los cuarteles.

–Bueno.

–Si no está allí don Baltasar, a su casa… ¿La sabes?

–La sé. ¿Qué le digo?

–Le dirás… ¡Veremos cómo sabes dar el recado! Le dirás que tengo un niño… ¿oyes? No vayas a equivocarte…

–Bueno, un niño…

–Un niño…, no sea que digas una niña, tonto; un niño, un niño.

–¿No le digo más?

–Y que ya sabe lo que me ofreció…, y que si quiere ponerse por padre de la criatura… y que mañana se bautiza.

–¿Nada más?

–Nada más… Esto…, bien clarito.

Chinto salía cuando entraba Ana, que se había ido a su casa a dormir. Venía muy misteriosa, como el que trae nuevas estupendas.

–¿Y ese valor, y el pequeño? –preguntó alzando la sábana y la manta y sacando del tibio rincón donde yacía, un bulto, un paquete, un pañuelo de lana, entre cuyos dobletes se columbraba una carita microscópica, amoratada; unos ojuelos cerrados, unas faccioncillas peregrinamente serias, con la seriedad cómica de los recién nacidos. Ana empezó a hablarle, a decirle mil zalamerías a aquel bollo que del mundo exterior sólo conocía las sensaciones de calor y frío; buscó una cucharilla y le paladeó con agua azucarada; arregló la gorra protectora del cráneo, blando y colorado como una berenjena, y después se sentó a la cabecera del lecho, depositando en el regazo el fajado muñeco.

–¿No sabes? –exclamó, abriendo por fin la esclusa de sus noticias–. Encontré a la que les cose a las de García… No te alteres, mujer, alégrate; se

38
IT FINALLY ARRIVED

Amparo is resting, plunged in the ineffable repose of the early hours of the morning. However, as the pale morning light enters through the small window, memory and self-consciousness return. She calls Chinto over.

'What do you want, tell me?'

'Go and run over to the infantry barracks… It seems that the garrison no longer leaves its quarters.'

'All right.'

'If Don Baltasar isn't there, go to his house… Do you know where it is?'

'Yes. What shall I tell him?'

'You'll tell him… Let's see how well you can give this message! You'll tell him that I've had a boy … do you hear? Don't go and make a mistake…'

'All right, a boy.'

'A boy … and don't go and say a girl, you fool. A boy, a boy.'

'Don't I say anything else?'

'And that he already knows what he offered me … and if he wants to accept responsibility as the child's father … and it will be baptised tomorrow.'

'Nothing more?'

'Nothing more… Just that … nice and clear.'

Chinto was leaving just as Ana, who had gone home to sleep, was coming in. She seemed very mysterious, like one who is bringing stupendous news.

'And how are things, and the little one?' she asked as she raised the sheet and blanket and picked up a bundle from the warm corner where it was lying, a package, a woollen shawl, between the folds of which a microscopic, purplish little face could be glimpsed; a pair of small, closed eyes, tiny features which were strangely serious, with the comic gravity of the newly-born. Ana began to speak to him, to say countless flattering words to that bun, whose awareness of the outside world was only the sensations of hot and cold; she found a teaspoon and gave him a taste of sugar-flavoured water; she adjusted the protective bonnet on his skull, which was soft and the colour of an aubergine, and then sat down at the head of the bed, depositing the swaddled doll in her lap.

'Do you know something?' she exclaimed, finally opening up the floodgates of her news. 'I ran into the girl who sews for the García family…

largan esta tarde para Madrí, porque tuvieron parte de que ganaron el pleito y van a arreglarlo allá todo.

Volvió Amparo el rostro con lánguido movimiento, murmurando:

–Dios vaya con ellas.

–No sé que no les pase algo en el camino, porque anda todo revuelto... Me dijo esa misma chica que hoy, sin falta, venía la República...

–Hace ... ocho días que la están anunciando...

–Calla, no hables, que te puede venir el delirio...

Y *la Comadreja* se dedicó a arrullar al infante, mientras Amparo se sepultaba otra vez en un sopor que le dejaba el cerebro hueco, la cabeza vacía, anonadando su pensamiento y haciéndola insensible a lo que pasaba en torno suyo. Los pasos de Chinto la llamaron a la vida otra vez. Abrió los ojos, que, en la palidez amarillosa de su morena cara, parecían mayores y azulados. Chinto se acercó andando de puntillas, torpón y zambo como siempre. Además, parecía hallarse muy turbado.

–Caro me costó que me dejasen pasar al cuartel –murmuró con su estropajosa habla de paisano, que salía a relucir de nuevo en los lances difíciles–. No se puede andar... Todo está revuelto... La gente corre como loca por las calles... Allí ... dice que se marchó el rey... Que en Madrí hay República.

Medio se incorporó Amparo, apartando de la frente los negros cabellos, lacios con el sudor que los empapaba...

–¿Qué me dices? –balbució.

–Lo que te digo, mujer... El alcalde y el gobernador ya echaron muchos bandos, que los vi en las esquinas... Y están poniendo trapos de color en los balcones.

–¿Será la cierta? –clamó, alzando las manos–. Sigue, sigue.

–Pues fui al cuartel..., y allí no estaba...

–¿Irías a su casa volando? –interrogó Amparo, temblona.

–Fui ... y dice que...

–Acaba, maldito.

–Y dice que... –Chinto se devanó los sesos buscando una fórmula diplomática–. Dice que no está en el pueblo, porque..., porque ayer se marchó a Madrí.

Don't be upset, please, try to be happy; they're all leaving for Madrid this afternoon, because they've received a message saying they'd won their lawsuit, and they're going there to sort it all out.'

Amparo turned her head with a languid movement and murmured:

'May God go with them.'

'I'm not sure that something won't happen to them on the way, because everything is in disorder. That same girl told me that today, without fail, the Republic was coming...'

'They've been announcing that for ... eight days.'

'Be quiet, don't talk, or you might get delirious...'

And *the Weasel* spent her time lulling the infant to sleep, while Amparo buried herself again in a drowsiness which, leaving her brain empty and her head vacant, completely overwhelmed all thoughts and made her unaffected by what was going on around her. Chinto's footsteps brought her back to life again. She opened her eyes, which seemed even larger and bluer against the yellowish pallor of her swarthy complexion. Chinto walked over on tip-toe, as clumsy and knock-kneed as ever. Besides, he seemed to be very upset.

'It was very hard to get them to let me into the barracks,' he murmured with the stammering speech of a country boy, which always came to light in difficult moments. 'You can't walk around... Everything's in turmoil... People are running around like crazy in the streets... Over there ... they say the king has gone... That there's a republic in Madrid.'[21]

Amparo sat up halfway, pushing her black hair away from her forehead, which was lank from being drenched in sweat...

'What are you telling me?' she stammered.

'Just what I'm telling you... The mayor and the governor have already issued lots of edicts, and I saw them on the street corners... And they're putting out red flags on the balconies.'

'Can it really be true?' she exclaimed, raising her hands. 'Go on, go on.'

'Well, I went to the barracks ... and he wasn't there...'

'Then you must have gone flying to his house?' Amparo inquired, trembling.

'I went ... and they say that...'

'Finish what you're saying, damn you.'

'And they say that...' Chinto racked his brains to find a diplomatic way of putting it. 'They say he's no longer here in town, because ... because he went off to Madrid yesterday.'

---

21 The First Spanish Republic was declared by a parliamentary majority on February 11, 1873.

Quiso abrir la boca Amparo y articular algo, pero su dolorida laringe no alcanzó a emitir un sonido. Echóse ambos puños a los cabellos y se los mesó con tan repentina furia, que algunos, arrancados, cayeron retorciéndose como negros viborĕznos sobre el embozo de la cama... Las uñas, desatentadas, recorrieron el contraído semblante y lo arañaron y ofendieron...

–Lárgate, que me voy a levantar –dijo por fin a Chinto–, a ver si reúno gente y quemo aquella maldita madriguera de los de Sobrado.

–Sí, lárgate –añadió Ana–. ¡Para las buenas noticias que traes!

En vez de obedecer, acercóse Chinto a la cama, donde jadeaba Amparo, partida, hecha pedazos, por el horrible esfuerzo de su cólera.

–Mujer, oyes, mujer... –pronunció con voz que quería suavizar y que sólo lograba ensordecer–, no te aflijas, no te mates... Allí..., yo..., yo me pondré por padre, y nos casaremos, si quieres..., y si no, no..., lo que digas.

Como generosa yegua de pura sangre a la cual pretendiesen enganchar haciendo tronco con un individuo de la raza asinina, *la Tribuna* se irguió, y saltándosele los ojos de las órbitas, los carrillos inflamados por la fiebre, gritó:

–Sal, sal de ahí, bruto... ¡Quieres condenarme!

Fuese el emisario de malas nuevas con la música a otra parte, cabizbajo, convencido de que era un criminal, y la oradora permaneció sentada en la cama, arrugando las ropas en la contorsión desesperada de sus miembros y cuerpo.

–¡Justicia! –clamaba–. ¡Justicia! ¡Justicia al pueblo!... ¡Favor, Madre mía del Amparo! ¡Virgen de la Guardia! Pero ¿cómo consientes esto? ¡La palabra, la palabra, la palaaaabra...; los derechos que ... matar a los oficiales, a los oficia...!

Un principio de fiebre y delirio se traslucía en la incoherencia de sus palabras. Su cabeza se trastornaba y aguda jaqueca le atarazaba las sienes. Dejóse caer aletargada sobre las fundas, respirando trabajosamente, casi convulsa. Ana se sintió iluminada por una idea feliz. Tomó el muñeco vivo, y sin decir una palabra, lo acostó con su madre, arrimándolo al seno, que el angelito buscó a tientas, a hocicadas, con su boca de seda, desdentada, húmeda y suave. Dos lágrimas refrigerantes asomaron a los párpados de *la Tribuna*, rezumaron al través de las pestañas espesas, humedecieron la escaldada mejilla, y en pos vinieron otras, que se apresuraban, desahogando el corazón y aliviando la calentura que empezaba...

Amparo tried to open her mouth and say something, but her sore larynx didn't manage to utter a sound. She raised both her fists to her hair and began tearing it out with such sudden rage that some was torn out and fell in a tangle on the upper fold of the bedsheet like little black vipers... Her fingernails went thoughtlessly up and down her contorted face, scratching and wounding it...

'Clear off, because I'm going to get up,' she finally said to Chinto, 'and see if I can get some people together and burn down that accursed den of the Sobrado family.'

'Yes, clear off,' Ana added. 'For all the good news you've brought.'

Instead of obeying, Chinto moved closer to the bed where Amparo was gasping for breath, crushed and worn out by the appalling strain of her anger.

'Listen,' he announced in a voice he wanted to soften, but which he only succeeded in making more deafening. 'Don't get upset, don't destroy yourself... So ... I ... I'll take over as the baby's father, and we'll get married, if you want ... and if not, we won't ... whatever you say...'

La Tribuna sat up straight, like a noble, thoroughbred mare, which they try to harness to a member of the donkey tribe in order to make a team; and with her eyes leaping out of their sockets and her cheeks flushed with fever, she shouted:

'Get out, get out of here, you lout... You must want to damn me altogether.'

The emissary of bad news cleared off, his head bowed low, convinced that he was a criminal, and the orator remained sitting in her bed, crumpling up the bed linen with the desperate twisting of her limbs and her body.

'Justice,' she implored. 'Justice! Justice for the people...! Help, my sweet Madre del Amparo! Blessed Virgin of the Guard! But, how can you allow this to happen? His word, his word, his woord ... the rights that ... to kill the officers, the offi...!'

The onset of fever and delirium were plain to see in the incoherence of her words. Her head felt dizzy and a sharp pain began biting into her temples. She fell back drowsily onto the pillows, breathing laboriously, almost convulsively. Ana felt enlightened by an inspired idea. She picked up the living doll and, without saying a word, lay him down with his mother, pressing him up close to her breast, which the little angel groped around for, rooting around with his silken, toothless, moist and soft little mouth. Two cooling tears appeared on *la Tribuna*'s eyelids, seeped through her thick eyelashes, dampened her burning cheek, and then others followed, hurrying along, comforting her heart and soothing the temperature that was beginning...

Al exterior, las ráfagas de la triste brisa de febrero silbaban en los deshojados árboles del camino y se estrellaban en las paredes de la casita. Oíase el paso de las cigarreras que regresaban de la fábrica; no pisadas iguales, elásticas y cadenciosas como las que solían dar al retirarse a sus hogares diariamente, sino un andar caprichoso, apresurado, turbulento. Del grupo más compacto, del pelotón más resuelto y numeroso, que tal vez se componía de veinte o treinta mujeres juntas, salieron algunas voces gritando:

—¡Viva la República federal!

Outside, the gusts of the sad February breeze were whistling through the leafless trees along the road and crashing against the walls of the little house. The cigar makers' steps returning from the factory could be heard; not steady, flexible and cadenced footsteps like the usual ones when they went home each day, but a capricious, hurried and turbulent step. From among the most compact group, the most resolved and numerous throng, which consisted of perhaps twenty or thirty women walking together, some voices burst out shouting:

'Long live the federal republic!'

NOTES

i. A collection of realistic sketches of local life and manners written by José María de Pereda and published in 1864.

ii. Bazán uses her native city of La Coruña as a basis for the fictional city of Marineda. All of the places referred to in *La Tribuna* are fictional creations based on specific locations in La Coruña. It is also the setting for *Doña Milagros*, *Memorias de un solterón* and *La piedra angular*.

iii. Orbajosa was created by Benito Pérez Galdós in *Doña Perfecta*, Villabermeja is a creation of Juan Valera in his novel *El comendor Mendoza* and Coteruco de la Rinconada is a town in José María de Pereda's *Don Gonzalo González de la Gonzalera*.

iv. Antonio de Trueba (1819–89) was a Spanish regionalist poet and short-story writer. He is best known for his collections of stories on Basque life, the most popular of which is *Cuentos populares de color de rosa*.

   Fernán is Fernán Caballero, the pseudonym of Cecilia Böhl de Faber (1796–1877). Poverty induced her to publish her writings and her best-known work is *La gaviota* from 1849. The novel, considered a precursor of the 19th-century Spanish realistic novel, is influenced by costumbrismo, the literary movement that depicted in short prose sketches the rapidly changing customs of rural Spain.

v. Zola's *L'assommoir* and the Goncourt brothers' *Germinie Lacerteux* are amongst the most frequently mentioned examples of Naturalism (see section 5 of the introduction to this edition). *L'assommoir*, the seventh novel in Zola's twenty-volume series *Les Rougon-Macquart*, is a study of alcoholism and poverty in working-class Paris. *Germinie Lacerteux*, which the authors describe in the preface as 'la clinique de l'Amour' (a clinic of Love), is based on actual observation by the authors of their own maidservant, Rose Malingre, whose double life of vice and debauchery they had never suspected.

vi. Joseph-Marie Eugène Sue (1804–57) was a French writer who established the genre of roman-feuilleton (newspaper serial). His best-known works are *Les mystères de Paris* (1842–43), featuring 'Rodolphe', the mysterious prince who haunts the Parisian underworld in disguise, and *Le Juif errant* (1845–47). He was strongly affected by the socialist ideas of the day and his works deal with many of the social problems caused by the Industrial Revolution.

vii. Benito Pérez Galdós (1843–1920) is the most important Spanish novelist of the nineteenth century. His works include *Doña Perfecta*, *Fortunata y Jacinta*, *La de Bringas* and *Misericordia*.

   José María de Pereda (1833–1905) was a Spanish regionalist novelist who wrote mainly about the northern area around Santander. Born into a strict Catholic family, a brother 29 years his senior who succeeded in making a

fortune in Cuba provided him with an income that allowed him to become an independent writer. His political adherence was to Carlism and his works include *De tal palo, tal astilla* (1880), *Peñas arriba* (1893) and *Sotileza* (1884).

viii. The Spanish real, introduced by King Pedro 1 of Castile, was the Spanish currency from the mid-14th century until 1864, when the escudo replaced it. The value of the coins mentioned in *La Tribuna* are, in ascending order, *real*, *peseta*, *duro*, *doblón*.

ix. *San Severín* is a girls' game in which lots are drawn to see who is *madre* or *directora*. The other girls join hands and form a circle around her. When the *madre* gives the order, they start turning around her in a wheel, all singing a rhyme about how, for example, a shoemaker works ('San Severín, de la buena vida; así, así trabajan los zapateros, así, así, así'). The *madre* or *directora* imitates the actions of the named tradesperson and the other girls have to follow what she does. Instead of shoemaker, the *madre* or *directora* can name any other job, always imitating the appropriate actions along with 'así, así, así'. Any girl who fails to follow the actions loses and becomes the new *madre or directora*.

　　La viudita requires an odd number of girls. One stands in the middle and the others wheel round slowly to the rhythm of the singing, which the girl in the centre begins on her own ('Yo soy viudita del conde de Oré; quería casarme, y no hallo con quien'). The circle of girls answer with the same tune ('Tan linda como eres, y no hallas con quien? Escoge a tu gusto que aquí tienes diez'). The girl in the centre then looks at all the others whilst singing ('Contigo sí, contigo no, contigo sí me casaré yo'). When she sings the last word she hugs one of the girls in the ring. The other girls follow suit and, as there is an odd number, one will be left without a partner … the next widow.

x. The Barrio de Arriba corresponds to the Ciudad Vieja (a Cidade Vella in gallego) and the Barrio de Abajo to La Pescadería (a Peixería in gallego) in La Coruña.

xi. As well as celebrating their birthdays, many Spaniards celebrate their *santo* or *onomástica*. This is the day when the saint whose name they have is honoured in the Christian calendar. It used to be quite common for babies to be named after the saint whose day they were born on. So a boy born in Spain on January 6 (Saint Balthasar's day) stood a good chance of being christened Baltasar.

xii. Xosé Ramón Barreiro Fernández and Patricia Carballal Miñán, 'El vino en la obra de Emilia Pardo Bazán', La Tribuna. *Cadernos de estudios da Casa museo Emilia Pardo Bazán* (A Couruña: RAG, 2004), p. 93:
　　'Matizaba Doña Emilia que se trata de vino de Castilla, porque el del país o del Ribeiro, por ser el habitual ya no significaba el vino de celebración' (Doña Emilia pointed out that it is Castilian wine, because wine that was local or from the Ribeiro region, as it was usual, no longer signified wine for celebrations.

xiii. Pardo Bazán nearly always refers to *gallego* as a dialect. See Marisa Sotela Vázquez, 'Emilia Pardo Bazán y la lengua catalana', *Cuadernos Hispanoamericanos*, 595 (January 200), p. 53:

'...la lengua nacional es, a su juicio, «la que logra prevalecer e imponerse en una nación; y las demás que en ella se hablen, dialectos». (...the national language is, in her opinion, 'the one which manages to win through and impose itself on a nation; and the others that are spoken there are dialects'). However, Pardo Bazán does refer to Galician as a language on at least one occasion, as shown in Yago Rodríguez Yáñez's article 'La preocupación lingüística de Emilia Pardo Bazán: El hallazgo de un texto en gallego' in *La Tribuna. Cadernos de estudios da Casa museo Emilia Pardo Bazán* (A Coruña: RAG, 2010/11, no. 8), p. 218: «Tout le monde, en Galice, connait la paisible et sympathique individualité de l'auteur de la poésie la plus célébrée qui ait été écrite en langue galicienne» (Everyone in Galicia is familiar with the peaceful and nice individuality of the author of the most famous poetry that has been written in the the Galician language). This is what Emilia Pardo Bazán wrote referring to the poet Eduardo Pondal.

xiv. The 'entierro de la sardina' (burial of the sardine) is a Spanish custom celebrating the end of carnival season on Ash Wednesday. It parodies a funeral and culminates with the solemn procession of a sardine around the streets in a coffin. The ceremony is a symbolical burial of the past in the hope of creating a better future. The first image of this 'burial' was Goya's oil painting *El Entierro de la Sardina*, dated between 1812 and 1819.

A piñata is a container, usually made of papier-mâché pottery. It is decorated, filled with small toys and/or sweets, and then broken as part of a ceremony or celebration.

xv. An 1866 rebellion led by General Juan Prim, an admirer of Abraham Lincoln, and a revolt of the sergeants at San Gil barracks in Madrid, sent a signal to Spanish liberals and republicans that there was serious unrest with the state of affairs in Spain. Liberals and republican exiles abroad laid the framework for a major uprising to overthrow Isabel, the Bourbon monarch who was increasingly seen by Spanish liberals and republicans as the source of Spain's decline. The Glorious Revolution that took place in Spain in 1868 resulted in her deposition. Admiral Juan Topete issued a revolutionary proclamation at Cadiz on September 18, 1868. Quickly uprisings occurred throughout Spain. At the Battle of Alcolea, near Cordoba, rebel forces led by General Francisco Serrano decisively defeated the royal army under General Manuel Pavia y Lacy on September 28, 1868. The queen fled to France on the following day. While Spain was in turmoil, a provisional government was established that annulled reactionary laws, abolished the Jesuits and other religious orders, and ensured universal male suffrage and freedom of the press. Serrano and

Prim, the government leaders, summoned a constituent Cortes that voted by a considerable margin to have a monarchical form of government. Serrano was named regent and Prim headed the ministry. The regime, threatened by Carlist and republican uprisings, now faced the unenviable task of choosing a new monarch.

xvi. Pierre Joseph Proudhon (1809–65) was an influential French socialist reformer who wrote on liberty, justice and equality.

Francisco Pi y Margell (1823–1901) was a leading liberal intellectual and served in a number of roles during the time of the republic.

xvii. Salustiano Olózaga (1805–73) was a Spanish politician, diplomat and writer. He was one of the main opposition leaders after the death of Fernando VII.

xviii. Francisco Serrano Domínguez, 1st Duke of la Torre, Count of San Antonio (1810–85) was one of the chief military politicians of nineteenth-century Spain. After the Revolution of 1868 which dethroned Isabel II, Serrano became chief of the executive power, but political preeminence rested with Juan Prim y Prats, the prime minister. Serrano served as regent until January 1871, when Amadeus of Savoy became king. On Amadeus's abdication (February 1873) and the formation of the First Republic, Serrano went into exile in France. But, after the coup d'état of January 1874, Serrano again headed the government until he was once more driven into exile upon the accession of Alfonso XII in December 1874. Serrano decided to recognise Alfonso in 1881, and he resumed his political career.

xix. Emilio Castelar was known as the greatest and most flowery orator of his generation and Emilia Pardo Bazán, having heard his speeches in Spanish parliament, dedicated many articles to him.

xx. In Greek mythology Sisyphus, the king of Ephyra, was a cunning rogue who cheated death twice. He was punished in Tartarus for his craftiness by being forced to roll an immense boulder up a hill, only to watch it roll back down, repeating this action for eternity.

xxi. In Greek mythology Dido and her followers fled from Tyre, landing on the shores of North Africa. There Iarbas agreed to sell Dido as much land as the hide of a bull could cover. Dido cut a bull's hide into thin strips and used it to outline a large area of land. On that site, Dido built Carthage, which one day would be Rome's great enemy, and became its queen. In Virgil's epic poem Aeneas and his men were shipwrecked near Carthage at the time when Dido was building the new city. She welcomed them and even spoke of a union between Aeneas' Trojans and her people: 'Tros Tyriusque mihi nullo discrimine agetur' (Trojan and Tyrian will be treated without distinction as far as I'm concerned).

xxii. Cuba's fight for independence was a huge problem for Spain, and the Ten Years' War that began in October 1868 made considerable demands both in terms of manpower and money. This resulted in the abandonment of two

commitments that had given the Glorious Revolution popular backing: the ending of conscription and food taxes.

xxiii. Carlism was a significant ideological force in Spanish politics from 1833 until the end of the Francoist regime in 1975. It was a right-wing political movement opposed to liberal secularism and economic and political modernism, receiving considerable support from the Spanish Catholic Church and strong in the rural Basque provinces, Navarre, Valencia, Aragon and parts of Catalonia. A dynastic conflict between supporters of Fernando VII's brother Carlos and the backers of the king's infant daughter Isabel, the three Carlist Wars (1833–39, 1846–49, 1872–76) epitomised the struggle between liberal and reactionary Spain.

xxiv. Antonio Felipe de Orleans, duke of Montpensier, was one of the leading claimants to the throne after Isabel II was deposed. He was sentenced to a month in prison when he killed the infante Don Enrique Borbón in a duel.

xxv. Rafael Riego y Núñez (1784–1823) was a Spanish general and liberal politician. One of the members of parliament who voted for a reduction in the king's powers, he was found guilty of treason and hanged in La Plaza de la Cebada in Madrid. The song carrying his name, composed by José Melchor Gomis, became the national anthem during the Second Spanish Republic.

Guiseppe Garibaldi (1807–67) was an Italian general and patriot who made a large and important contribution to the unification of Italy. The anthem carrying his name, the 'Inno di Garibaldi', was popular with revolutionaries everywhere.

xxvi. El Terso was a name given to the Carlist pretender, Carlos María de Borbón y Austria-Este.

xxvii. Joaquín Elío y Ezpeleta (1803–76) was a Carlist general who was involved in all three Carlist wars. Although sentenced to death for his participation in the conspiracy that led to the abortive uprising at San Carlos de la Rápita, he was pardoned by Queen Isabel.

xxviii. Mariana Pineda (1804–31), a Spanish political heroine found in possession of a flag embroidered with the motto 'Ley, Libertad, Igualdad', was executed by garrotte in her native Granada. She was the inspiration for Federico Lorca's first successful play.

xxix. Cesare Cantù (1804–95) was an Italian historian and political leader who wrote *Storia universale* (*Universal History*), a huge work of 72 volumes.

xxx. An *indiano* is an emigrant or descendant of an emigrant who returned to Spain after having made a fortune in the Americas, especially Cuba, Argentina, Uruguay, Venezuela and Mexico. The word is particularly associated with lower-class Spaniards, particularly from the north of Spain, who emigrated throughout the nineteenth century. Many returned years later, having made a fortune, and built a colonial-style house in their home village.

xxxi. Isabel II was deposed in the Glorious Revolution of 1868 and sent into exile.

The *Cortes*, eager to establish a new Royal family before the Carlists rose up again or the revolutionaries swayed public opinion, opted for a monarchy. However, the search for a suitable king proved extremely problematic. General Prim, a perennial rebel during Isabel's reign, remarked that 'encontrar a un rey democrático en Europa es tan difícil como encontrar un ateo en el cielo (finding a democratic king in Europe is as hard as finding an atheist in Heaven). In addition, few potential candidates would relish the prospect of succeeding a monarch who had just been driven out, or of attempting to govern a nation as divided and war-torn as Spain. The main nominees were:

- the aged Baldomero Espartero. He was brought up as an option and, even after he rejected the notion of being named king, he still gained eight votes in the final tally.
- Isabel's young son Alfonso (the future Alfonso XII of Spain), who only gained two votes.
- the Carlist pretender, Carlos María de Borbón y Austria-Este.
- the Duke of Aosta, the second son of Vittorio Emanuele II who in 1861 had become the first king of a newly unified Italy. His liberal credentials were strong and he was less controversial and divisive than a German or French monarch would be. He was eventually proclaimed king of Spain, with the name of Amadeo I in November 1870, having received 191 votes.
- Prince Leopold of Hohenzollern-Sigmaringen. His nomination triggered off the Franco-Prussian War, as Napoleon III could not accept the prospect of a relative of the King of Prussia ascending to the Spanish throne.
- Fernando II, the former regent of neighbouring Portugal. He rejected an offer to assume the throne of Spain.
- Antonio Felipe de Orleans, duke of Montpensier. Although he ruined his chances when he killed the infante Don Enrique Borbón in a duel, he still received 27 votes.

xxxii. Candlemas, known as *Candelaria* in Spanish speaking countries, is a Christian holiday commemorating the ritual purification of Mary, 40 days after the birth of Jesus. It also marks the ritual presentation of the baby Jesus to God in the Temple at Jerusalem. It falls on February 2, which is the 40th day of the Christmas/Epiphany period. The Gospel of Luke says that Simeon held the baby Jesus and called him a Light to the World. The festival is called Candlemas because this was the day that all the Church's candles for the year were blessed.

xxxiii. The Duke of Aosta was proclaimed king of Spain on November 16, 1870. He arrived in Madrid on January 2, 1871.

xxxiv. Amadeo I didn't abdicate until February 11, 1873. On this same day the First Spanish Republic was declared.

xxxv. The Paris Commune, described by Karl Marx as an example of the 'dictatorship

of the proletariat', was a radical socialist and revolutionary government that ruled the French capital from 18 March to 28 May 1871. It was a consequence of the Franco-Prussian war which broke out in 1870 when Prince Leopold of Hohenzollern-Sigmarin, a relative of the King of Prussia, was offered the throne of Spain. The French troops who were mobilised were thought to be among the best in the world. They had effective weapons, two very experienced generals (Bazaine and Macmahon), and their Emperor, Napoléon III, was blessed with an iconic name guaranteed to inspire French soldiers. This, along with the popular stereotype of the German as a dreamy, philosophical being, perpetrated by Madame de Staël's *De l'Allemagne*, made the French totally unprepared for the efficient Prussian fighting machine that confronted them. The most notable defeats were at Metz, where 180,000 soldiers under Marshal Bazaine were forced to surrender, and Sedan, when Napoléon III – the 'Napoléon le Petit' ridiculed by Victor Hugo in *Les Châtiments* – was captured along with 100,000 troops. News reached Paris and the Second Empire was overthrown and replaced by a provisional government calling itself the 'Government of National Defence'. Parisians were defiant and refused to accept defeat. The Prussians arrived at the gates of Paris in September 1870 and surrounded the city. Léon Gambetta, the leading figure in the provisional government, organised new French armies in the countryside after escaping from the besieged capital in a balloon. However, they were no match for the German forces and the Government of National Defence, feeling that Paris would accept an end to the war, signed a peace treaty with Prussia in January 1871 which ratified the loss of Alsace-Lorraine and imposed a war indemnity of 5 billion francs. With Prussian troops occupying northern France until the sum was forthcoming, Paris reacted to the humiliation by electing a municipal goverment which took on the title of 'the Commune' with its seat in the Hôtel de Ville and its symbol the red flag. Adolphe Thiers, executive head of the provisional national government, attempted to remove the cannons of the Parisian National Guard. Resistance broke out and Thiers fled to Versailles. While the victorious Prussians affected neutrality outside the city, the Versailles troops began a siege of Paris (April 11) to regain national control. A civil war was fought between the Commune and the troops of the Versailles government. The fighting, which intensified over five weeks, culminated in 'la semaine sanglante' (Bloody Week) of 21–28 May, during which the Versailles troops entered the city despite the desperate but ineffective defense of the communards, who threw up barricades, shot hostages (including the archbishop of Paris), and burned the Tuileries palace, the city hall, and the palace of justice. On May 28 the commune was finally defeated. Severe reprisals followed, resulting in more than 18,000 Parisians dead, 38,000 arrested and almost 7,000 deported.

xxxvi. This refers to an apartment building in Madrid demolished in 1850.

Notorious for unruly behaviour, fighting and general disorder, Tócame Roque was immortalised by Ramón de la Cruz in *La Petra y la Juana*.

xxxvii. General Francisco Savalls was a Carlist commander, and General Eugenio Gaminde y Lafont a general of the Amadeist forces during the First Carlist War.

xxxviii. *La Cisterna* (the Cistern) refers to Amadeo's queen, Maria Vittoria dal Pozzo della Cisterna (1847–76), the Duchess of Aosta.